GREAT ILLUSTRATED CLASSICS

IVANHOE

Sir Walter Scott

**adapted by
Malvina G. Vogel**

**Illustrations by
Pablo Marcos Studios**

**BARONET
BOOKS**

BARONET BOOKS, New York, New York

BRIGHTON

GREAT ILLUSTRATED CLASSICS

edited by
Joshua E. Hanft

Contents

About the Author

On August 15, 1771, Walter Scott was born in Edinburgh, Scotland. When he was still a baby, Walter contracted a form of polio that left him lame for life. While his brothers and sisters ran about playing, Walter became an avid reader. Although he studied law to please his father, he began writing in his free time and found success with his poems, ballads, and essays.

Years afterward, Walter became intrigued with the idea of writing historical novels. He placed his fictional characters in actual historical events (the Crusades and tournaments at Ashby), alongside actual people in history (King Richard the Lion-Hearted, Prince John, and Robin Hood). While his novels were all very successful, *Ivanhoe* became his most popular.

Strangely enough, no one knew that it was Walter Scott who wrote these novels, for he published them anonymously. Novels were considered a trivial form of literature at that time, and Scott feared risking his reputation as a fine poet and his standing as a court magistrate by putting his name to such works, even though they made him a very rich man. He couldn't know then that he would later be renowned as the originator of the historical novel, a writer who would influence other writers all over the world.

Agonizing stomach problems plagued Scott throughout his life. They created such pain that many of his novels, including *Ivanhoe*, were dictated by him to a servant while he lay in bed, getting up only to act out a scene or some dialogue as he wrote it.

For his great contributions to English literature, he was made a baronet by King George IV and addressed by the title *Sir*.

Sir Walter Scott lived his life by the very same code of chivalry his knights lived by, with truth and honor and courage, until his death in 1832.

Was He Dead or Was He a Prisoner?

CHAPTER 1

Saxon and Norman Enemies

In the year 1192, the people of England
feared for the life of their beloved king,
Richard I, also called Richard the Lion-Hearted. Was he dead or was he a prisoner somewhere? He had been returning home from his
Crusade in the Holy Land when he disappeared. The Crusades were religious wars
being fought in Jerusalem by Christians from
all over Europe against Turkish invaders.

Rumors reached England accusing Richard's brother, Prince John, of plotting the
king's imprisonment in some foreign country

so he could rule in his place, which he had been doing during Richard's absence.

Both Richard and John were Plantagenets, the French royal family that was descended from William of Normandy, the king who had conquered England over a hundred years earlier. Even now, many Englishmen, or Saxons as they called themselves, had a fierce hatred for the nobles they called Normans.

On their part, the Normans considered the Saxons beneath them, and they haughtily demanded obedience and respect from them at all times.

In spite of these feelings, many nobles and knights, both Saxon and Norman, had followed Richard on his Crusade. Some had gone because of their Christian beliefs, while others sought military glory or simply had the spirit of adventure.

Two of these knights, both Normans, had recently returned from the Holy Land and were now riding at the head of their party of squires

Two Knights Had Recently Returned.

and guards through Sherwood Forest, near the village of Sheffield. The knights, Brian de Bois-Guilbert and Maurice de Bracy, were on their way to the town of Ashby, where a tournament to show off their knightly skills was to be held in a few days.

This was not the safest of roads for the horsemen, even with their guards, since a gallant band of outlaws, led by the notorious Robin of Locksley and his Merry Men, roamed this forest, robbing even the bravest travelers. Now, with Ashby still a day's ride away and a storm approaching quickly, the travelers needed to find a place to spend the night.

Nearing a fork in the road, the riders overtook a lone man dressed in a long, black hooded cloak and carrying a tall staff. The cross of palm leaves attached to the staff identified him as a Palmer, a religious pilgrim recently returned from the Holy Land.

Bois-Guilbert called out, "You there, do you know a nobleman's castle nearby where we can

A Lone Man in a Long, Black-hooded Cloak

be fed and lodged overnight with proper hospitality due our positions and titles?"

"Certainly, my Lord," replied the Palmer. "The castle of Rotherwood, home of Cedric the Saxon, is near. I'm headed there myself and will gladly show you the way."

"Cedric?" mumbled De Bracy. "That wealthy Saxon nobleman hates all of us. He surely won't welcome Normans at his castle."

"We're not *asking* for his hospitality," sneered Bois-Guilbert arrogantly. "Normans have a right to *demand* it of any Saxon."

"But we wouldn't want to arouse Cedric's anger, especially in front of his beautiful daughter, Lady Rowena," cautioned De Bracy.

"My Lords," interrupted the Palmer, "Lady Rowena is not Cedric's daughter. She's a princess, a distant relative whom he raised. But she's as dear to him as if she *were* his daughter. If she were offended in any way, Cedric wouldn't think twice about sending you or any knight from his house."

"We're Not *Asking* for His Hospitality."

"So I've heard," added De Bracy. "People say he is so fierce and so protective of her that he even banished his own son, Ivanhoe, from his home because the young man fell in love with her. Cedric insists on someone of royal blood— a prince, at least—as her husband. I also heard that he disinherited his son for going on the Crusade with the king."

"This is certainly one man whose anger we don't want to provoke," said Bois-Guilbert. "We must be certain to show him the utmost respect and politeness at Rotherwood."

As the Palmer led the travelers deep into the woods, he seemed to know every twist and turn of the path that led to Rotherwood. And well he should, for he had lived there all his life.

But as familiar as the Palmer was with these woods, even he couldn't detect the band of Merry Men hiding on either side of the path, waiting for the signal from their leader, Robin of Locksley, to attack and rob the travelers.

The Band of Merry Men

But that signal never came. The only sound was a gasp, as Robin whispered to his friend and advisor, Friar Tuck, "Good Lord! That's Ivanhoe at the front of that group of travelers! He must have just returned from the Crusades. At least *he* hasn't met the dreadful fate that our beloved King Richard did!"

"That's true," said the Friar. "But why is he dressed as a Palmer? Why is he leading those Norman knights to his father's castle? To a man who considers him dead? Has he now turned traitor and sided with the Normans?"

"I think not, good Tuck," said Robin. "Ivanhoe is too loyal a Saxon and too brave a knight to ever turn against his people. I'm certain he's planning something, and I'm just as certain that we'll find out what it is before many days pass!"

"Good Lord! That's Ivanhoe!"

The Home of Cedric the Saxon

CHAPTER 2

Visitors to Rotherwood

When Ivanhoe led the Normans out of the woods, he pointed ahead to a cluster of low stone buildings surrounded by a moat and a tall stockade fence. "That is Rotherwood," he said, "the home of Cedric the Saxon."

Once the travelers identified themselves, the drawbridge was lowered and the Normans and their party entered the courtyard.

A servant showed them into a huge hall, where a long table in the shape of a "T" was set for the evening meal. Across the top, the table was raised on a carpeted dais a step above the long, lower end.

Cedric the Saxon sat in a large, carved chair at the center of the dais table, with the Lady Rowena seated on his right. He was anxious to start his evening meal when a servant appeared at the door and announced, "My Lord, the good knights Brian de Bois-Guilbert and Maurice de Bracy, with their squires and guards, request your hospitality and lodging for the night."

"Normans!" Cedric muttered to Rowena in disgust. "Even though Bois-Guilbert has proven himself a brave and fearless knight in the Holy Land and he *is* a Knight Templar who has taken all the vows of chivalry plus those that prohibit him from marrying, I know him to be a cruel, arrogant man. And as for that De Bracy, why he's only a puppet doing Prince John's bidding. Still, it is only for one night and I cannot deny my hospitality to anyone, Saxon or Norman." Then aloud, he replied to his servant, "Invite them to enter and join us

"Normans!" Cedric Muttered in Disgust.

at dinner. They are welcome at Rotherwood."

The two knights entered the hall and approached the dais, while their attendants and the Palmer seated themselves at the foot of the long, lower table with the servants.

Cedric rose to greet his guests and, with a wave of his hand, motioned them to the two carved dais seats at his left.

As he took his seat, Maurice de Bracy was so captivated by the beautiful princess Rowena that he couldn't tear his eyes away from her face. But Rowena didn't care for such admiring looks from a Norman and she glared at De Bracy until he lowered his eyes.

Cedric caught these looks and reminded De Bracy, "Sir Knight, a Saxon princess does not welcome the attentions of Norman knights and Templars whose ancestors took away her lands and murdered her sub—"

Bois-Guilbert angrily interrupted his host. "We have been fighting and dying in the Holy Land in England's name. Surely we can pay a

Captivated by the Beautiful Princess Rowena

compliment to an English lady."

De Bracy tried to soften the Templar's angry words. "Sir Cedric, I meant no offense to the Lady Rowena, and I ask her pardon for staring at her, but never have I seen such beauty anywhere! May I apologize by offering to escort you both along these dangerous roads to the tournament at Ashby?"

"I have no need for an escort to travel in my own land!" snapped Cedric indignantly. "And I don't know if we're even going to the tournament. To me, it's nothing more than a Norman game of showing off and practicing for war."

"I accept your apology, Sir Knight," Rowena told De Bracy. "But rather than give me compliments, give me news of the war in the Holy Land." What she wanted to hear most was news of Ivanhoe, but she couldn't come right out and ask for such news because no one at Rotherwood was allowed to mention his name.

But before either knight could give Rowena any news, a servant entered the hall to an-

"I Have No Need for an Escort!"

nounce that a stranger was at the gate begging for hospitality for the night.

"Bring him in, whoever he is," ordered Cedric. "With this storm raging, no one deserves to spend the night outdoors."

A few minutes later, a tall, thin old man appeared at the door to the hall. "I am Isaac of York," he stated, bowing to Cedric and removing his high, square cap.

The master of Rotherwood invited Isaac to join them at dinner by waving him to a place at the lower end of the table. But none of the servants or guests made room for the old man because he was a Jew.

Only the Palmer rose from his place. "Sit here by the fire, old man," he said. "My clothes have dried and I have eaten. Yours are still soaked and you need food as well."

With that, the Palmer walked towards the dais. Bois-Guilbert was busy praising the superior fighting abilities of his Templars when Rowena interrupted him.

"I am Isaac of York."

"But your knights weren't able to win back Jerusalem, were they?" she taunted. "And the Templars weren't there alone. Weren't King Richard's gallant knights with him as well?"

"They were only second best," sneered the Templar scornfully.

"They were second to NONE!" mocked a voice nearby.

Everyone turned to where the Palmer was standing, his face still hidden by the hood of his cloak. "I repeat, Richard's men were second to none! Think back, Bois-Guilbert, to a tournament held at Acre during a break in the war. King Richard and five of his Saxon knights competed against six of your Norman knights, including De Bracy and yourself. Do you remember how that turned out?"

While De Bracy hung his head in embarrassment, Bois-Guilbert scowled with rage. He reached for his sword, then realized that this was not the place to start a fight.

Cedric, however, was delighted to learn of a

"Richard's Men Were Second to None!"

IVANHOE

Saxon victory, and he said, "Tell me, good Palmer, who were those noble Saxon knights?"

"Gladly, my Lord." And the Palmer named five of the combatants.

"Yes, yes, and who was the sixth?" shouted Cedric eagerly.

"A young knight who's not very well known. I don't remember his name."

"I doubt that your memory has suddenly failed you, Sir Palmer," said the Templar. "I'll tell you who that knight was, Lord Cedric, for in spite of his youth, he was renowned for his ability in battle, and he defeated me only because my horse fell. If he were in England at this moment, in fact at the tournament at Ashby this week, I'd gladly challenge Ivanhoe to a combat again."

Cedric gasped, but didn't utter a word.

"Yes, I do recall now," said the Palmer softly. "His name *was* Ivanhoe. The young knight was wounded in battle and stayed behind to convalesce when Richard left. But he fell into

"I'd Gladly Challenge Ivanhoe Again!"

the hands of some of your Norman friends, Sir Templar, and they didn't treat him too well. I imagine he's recovered by now and on the way home. When he arrives, I'm certain he'll accept your challenge."

"And if he refuses," warned Bois-Guilbert, "I'll proclaim him a coward throughout all of Europe!"

"That will never be necessary!" shouted Rowena, jumping up angrily. "I've known Ivanhoe since we were children, and I add my own guarantee to that of this holy Palmer. If Ivanhoe hadn't been wounded and were here now, he'd be the first to defend the honor of Saxon England at Ashby."

Cedric now broke his silence. "Sir Templar, if you need further assurance of the honor of a true Saxon, I give you mine. The honor of Cedric stands behind the honor of his son, Ivanhoe!"

"That Will Never Be Necessary!"

"Seize Him and Hold Him for Ransom."

CHAPTER 3

Rescuing Isaac from Danger

After dinner, Cedric ordered his servants to lead his guests to their chambers for the night. As the travelers were leaving the dining hall, the Palmer overheard Brian de Bois-Guilbert whispering orders to his men.

"When Isaac of York leaves in the morning, follow him. As soon as he is out of sight of Rotherwood, seize him and take him to the castle of Reginald Front-de-Boeuf. We'll rob Isaac of the money he carries and hold him for ransom as well. His friends will pay well for his release."

IVANHOE

The Palmer pretended not to have heard anything as he was escorted by Cedric's long-time family servant, Gurth, along a dark stone passageway in the servants' part of the castle. Ahead of them, they saw Isaac being led into one room, and beyond that was the door which Gurth opened for the Palmer. The Palmer lay down fully dressed on a crude straw bed. When he was certain that Gurth and the other servants had all retired to their own rooms, he tiptoed out of his and silently entered Isaac's.

The old man was moaning and tossing uneasily in his sleep when the Palmer nudged him with his staff. Isaac's eyes flew open in a panic.

"Don't be afraid of me, Isaac. I'm your friend," whispered the Palmer. "I've come to warn you that Bois-Guilbert's men will seize you when you leave in the morning. You must leave tonight if you want to avoid danger."

The old man tried to rise up from his bed, but he fell to his knees in terror and began to weep.

"Don't Be Afraid! I'm Your Friend."

"There's no time for weeping. We must leave Rotherwood immediately while everyone is asleep. I know every path in this forest and I'll lead you to safety."

Isaac, however, was suspicious. "Don't betray me, Palmer. I'm only a poor merchant."

"Why would I do such a thing? Even if you were rich, I have no need of money. I'm a Palmer who has taken the vows of poverty."

"Then I thank you, good Palmer," said Isaac with a sigh of relief. "But so many of your English nobles persecute my people when we lend them money, which they use only to support their extravagant lifestyles. Then they refuse to pay it back and threaten us. We're always in danger. Why, even Prince John himself, does this. And almost every nobleman follows his lead. So please try to understand why I was suspicious. But I do believe you. Let us hurry and leave."

"I must first find someone I can trust to unlock the gate for us." And the Palmer hurried

"We Must Leave Rotherwood Immediately."

out the door and crossed the hallway into Gurth's room.

"Wake up, Gurth," he ordered. "I need you to unlock the rear gate and let down the drawbridge. Isaac and I wish to leave."

"No one leaves until the gate is opened in the morning," mumbled Gurth, turning over to go back to sleep.

The Palmer then leaned over the bed and whispered something in the servant's ear. Gurth immediately jumped up and nervously pulled on his shirt and pants. He bowed to the Palmer, then rushed out the door.

Isaac, who had been watching at the door, was puzzled at the sudden change in Gurth's behavior. But he followed the Palmer as he hurried behind Gurth into the passageway.

As the three headed out of the building, the Palmer ordered Gurth, "Bring Isaac's mule to the other side of the moat and borrow one from Cedric's stables for me."

Gurth ran to the stables and several min-

The Palmer Hurried Behind Gurth.

utes later met the two men with the mules outside the castle walls. After Isaac and the Palmer had mounted their mules, the Palmer reached down to shake Gurth's hand. But the servant drew the hand up to his lips and kissed it respectfully.

"God be with you," he whispered. "I promise to join you at Ashby as soon as I can, my Lord. And I thank you for naming me your squire. I pledge my loyalty in serving you."

Isaac and the Palmer rode in silence for many hours until they reached the edge of the town of Sheffield. As the road forked, they drew their mules to a halt.

"Please come with me to my friend Zareth," said Isaac. "He's a wealthy man and will most certainly help me repay your kindness."

"I don't need any payment or any reward," insisted the Palmer.

"But I know there *is* something you do need. A horse and armor, perhaps?"

The Palmer jerked up his head, startled.

They Rode in Silence.

"How did you guess that? After all, you see me dressed as a holy man and holy men don't have a need for armor."

"Forgive me," said Isaac, smiling. "But your words of warning last night were not those of a holy man, and when you bent over my bed, I saw a knight's chain under your robe. But that's not important now. I have a friend in Sheffield who sells the finest horses and weapons in England. You will pick out what you need, and when the tournament is over, you can return them or pay him."

"But surely you know that if I lose in the tournament, my horse and armor and weapons will be forfeited to the winning knight."

"In my heart I know you will *not* lose, my son. Besides, I don't care about forfeiting a horse or armor or some weapons. But I *do* care about you losing a limb or your life."

"Thank you, Isaac. Let us be off."

"I Know You Will *Not* Lose"

The Tournament at Ashby

CHAPTER 4

The Tournament at Ashby

Even though the lower classes of Englishmen lived under the poorest conditions and suffered from a lack of food, neither poverty nor work nor illness stopped the masses from attending a tournament. Great distances didn't keep nobles or knights away either.

The tournament at Ashby was certain to be even more spectacular than others because the most famous knights in the land were facing each other and because Prince John was to be there to crown the Champion.

The field on which the tournament was to

take place was a beautiful grassy meadow, a quarter-mile long and surrounded by wooded slopes on all sides. A palisade—a fence of pointed wooden stakes—enclosed the field of combat, with openings at the northern and southern ends through which the combatants would enter and face each other.

Outside the openings at the southern end, five magnificent pavilions, or tents, had been set up, each in colors matching those of the knight occupying it. In front of each pavilion hung the knight's shield, guarded diligently by his loyal squire. The center pavilion, the pavilion of honor, had been assigned to Brian de Bois-Guilbert, who was considered the Champion of all the knights.

At the northern end, pavilions had been set up for the challengers, along with those for servants and refreshment sellers.

On the eastern and western sides, galleries had been erected and covered with carpets. Here, knights, nobles, town officials, all with

Pavilions for the Challengers

their ladies, would be seated from the center
to the end, according to their rank and wealth.
The poor masses, however, used the slopes of
the surrounding hills and branches of the trees
from which to view the tournament.

One gallery at the center of the eastern side
stood higher than those alongside it. A richly
decorated canopy with the royal coat of arms
covered a raised throne on which Prince John
was seated. Perched on his hand was his pet
falcon. John's handsome but haughty face
turned from side to side as he boldly eyed the
ladies in the galleries, knowing that the one
selected as Queen of Beauty and Love would
soon be seated on the flowered throne beside
him.

John's eyes stopped on a beautiful, dark-
haired young woman clinging to the arm of
Isaac of York as they made their way to their
seats a distance away from the prince. The
woman's diamond necklace and rich silk gown
had already attracted the attention and envy

He Boldly Eyed the Ladies in the Gallery.

of many ladies in the gallery.

"Isaac of York, my friend and banker!" called Prince John, mocking the old man from whom he often borrowed money. "Who is that lovely lady on your arm?"

"This is my daughter Rebecca, Your Grace," answered Isaac with a low bow.

"Her beauty requires that she sit closer to the royal gallery. Bring her here." And John turned to the noble family in the gallery beside his and ordered, "Cedric, my Saxon lord, move over and make room for Isaac and his daughter."

When Cedric chose to ignore the prince's order, Maurice de Bracy, seated beside John, jumped up and reached his lance out toward Cedric. But the Lord of Rotherwood was even quicker with his sword and, with a single blow, cut off the knight's lance at its tip.

"Good shot!" called a distant voice from a nearby tree branch.

"Good shot! Good shot!" repeated a chorus of

"Good Shot!"

voices from tree branches around him.

Prince John looked in the direction of the voices, his face red with rage. The yeoman, or commoner, who had first called out, was dressed in Lincoln-green and carried a six-foot-long bow in his hand. The men in trees around him were dressed in the same green, except for a rather stout friar in a brown robe. All were cheering the yeoman on.

"That's tellin' 'em, Robin!"

"We'll take Cedric's sword over De Bracy's lance anytime, won't we, Robin?"

At that moment, Waldemar Fitzurse, the prince's chief advisor, whispered in John's ear, "Stay calm, Your Highness. If you answer these yeomen in anger, their cheering will spread to the rest of the crowd and make you look ridiculous. I know these yeomen. They're a band from Sherwood Forest who are loyal to your brother Richard. They'd like nothing better than to embarrass you in front of this huge crowd and ruin this day."

"That's Tellin' 'em, Robin!"

Sulking as he nodded in agreement, Prince John then gave the order for the herald to announce the rules of the tournament.

The trumpets sounded and the crowd became silent. The herald rode to the center of the lists, the field of combat, and began to read from a scroll.

"First, the five knights in this tournament agree to accept all challengers.

"Second, a challenger shall choose any knight as his opponent by touching that knight's shield with his lance. A touch with the *blunt end* of the lance means a courtesy match in which the winner only needs to break his opponent's lance. A touch with the *point* of the lance is the challenge for a fight to the death.

"Third, the knight who breaks five lances today will be named Champion for the day and will crown his choice for Queen of Beauty and Love for the rest of the tournament."

The tournament began, and for the first four sets, Bois-Guilbert, De Bracy, Front-de-Boeuf,

The Trumpets Sounded.

and two other Norman knights easily defeated their Saxon challengers in courtesy matches. The spectators, most of whom were Saxons, were disappointed, but no Saxon felt this disappointment as strongly as Cedric.

"This day is going badly for England," he said to Lady Rowena. "Isn't there anyone to defend the honor of our country? Isn't there anyone to defeat those Normans, especially that arrogant Templar, Bois-Guilbert, and keep him from being crowned champion?"

As if in answer to his question, a single trumpet blare sounded from the northern end of the lists to announce a new challenger. All eyes turned north. A knight, in a suit of steel armor inlaid with gold, rode in through the gate astride a fine-looking white horse. His shield's symbol pictured a young oak tree pulled out of the ground by its roots. Across the shield was etched the word "Disinherited."

As the knight rode through the lists, he saluted Prince John by lowering his lance.

On the Shield Was Etched "Disinherited."

Something about the way he carried himself seemed to please the crowd, and they soon began calling out the names of the knights each wanted him to challenge.

But the Disinherited Knight had obviously made up his mind in advance, for he rode directly to the pavilions of four knights and touched each one's shield with the blunt end of his sword. Then he rode to the center pavilion and reined his horse to a halt. He raised his lance and struck the shield of Brian de Bois-Guilbert with its point.

The crowd gasped in disbelief! Brian de Bois-Guilbert, himself, gasped in disbelief! The Disinherited Knight was challenging him to a fight to the death!

But the Templar immediately regained his composure and haughtily demanded, "You had better have gone to church this morning to confess your sins, Sir Knight, for you are about to die, if not at the hands of my fellow Normans, then surely at mine!"

The Crowd Gasped in Disbelief!

"I think not, Bois-Guilbert, and I would suggest that you take a fresh horse and lance for yourself, for you will need both when you face me!" With that, the Disinherited Knight dug his spurs into his horse's sides and galloped to the northern end of the lists to await the call to combat.

Bois-Guilbert returned to the southern end, where he took the advice of his challenger. He ordered a rested, vigorous horse, a stronger lance, and a thicker shield. Then he stood in front of his pavilion to watch the Disinherited Knight take on De Bracy, Front-de-Boeuf, and two other Normans, one after the other. On his first pass against them, he easily unseated each knight.

As the defeated De Bracy returned to his pavilion, Bois-Guilbert came up to him and said, "I've been watching that knight very closely, and there's something strangely familiar about his style. I almost get the feeling I've seen him fight before. Maybe I've even fought

He Easily Unseated Each Knight.

him myself."

"We'll know soon enough," said De Bracy. "He'll have to remove his visor and helmet at the end of the tournament."

It was now Bois-Guilbert's turn to face his challenger. As he took his position at the southern end of the lists, a hush fell over the spectators. Most were on the side of the courageous Disinherited Knight, but feared he was now doomed to death.

At Prince John's signal, the trumpets blared and the knights sped towards each other. Lances were thrust at shields, sending shocks through both men. Their horses recoiled backwards, but recovered their balance. The knights turned and rode away, each to his own end of the lists, amid shouts and applause from the spectators.

Once the two were in position, the crowd became silent again. The trumpets blared to signal the second charge, and the knights galloped towards each other.

The Knights Sped Toward Each Other.

The Templar struck first, his lance crashing into the Disinherited Knight's shield with such force that the wooden pole shattered to pieces. But at that exact moment, the Disinherited Knight thrust his lance into the Templar's visor, where its point stuck in the bars.

As Bois-Guilbert tried to keep his balance, the strap on his saddle broke, throwing him to the ground. In a rage because of his disgrace and the jeers of the crowd, he got to his feet and drew his sword.

The Disinherited Knight jumped down from his horse with his own sword drawn. The rules of the tournament, however, did not permit the two to continue their combat on foot, and the officials separated them before their swords could strike a blow.

"You may be Champion today, Sir Knight, but we'll meet again," swore Brian de Bois-Guilbert. "And then no one will separate us."

"I'll be ready to meet you any time and with

"We'll Meet Again!"

any weapon. And it will be a fight to the death!"

The officials then asked the new Champion to raise his visor when he faced the prince, but he refused very courteously. Since the laws of chivalry permitted any knight to enter a tournament disguised, Prince John could not insist that the Champion unmask.

John was angry that his favorite Norman knights had been defeated, and he stormed at Fitzurse, "I cannot believe that there's a knight in England capable of defeating five of my finest knights and we haven't heard of him. Do you have any idea who he is?"

"None at all, Your Highness, unless he's a knight who went with King Richard to the Holy Land and has now returned home. Perhaps it's even the king himself!"

Prince John turned pale as death. "Heaven forbid!" he gasped and he shrank down on his throne. "Fitzurse, stand by me and protect me. See to it that my knights do the same."

Prince John Turned Pale as Death.

"Your Highness, you are in no danger. This Champion before you is not as tall or as broad as your brother. Look at him and see."

John nodded nervously, then made a speech praising the Champion, as was the custom. He waited for a reply from the Knight, but all he received as his thanks was a deep bow.

Continuing on with the ceremonies, Prince John announced, "Sir Disinherited Knight, it is now your duty to name the fair lady of your choice to be Queen of Beauty and Love." And he placed a crown of gold hearts on the tip of the Knight's lance.

The Disinherited Knight rode along the galleries and didn't stop until he was in front of Lady Rowena. Cedric's smile, which had been on his face since the mysterious stranger defeated the five Normans, now widened as he realized that a Saxon lady was to be crowned Queen.

A cheer went up from the crowd as the Champion tilted his lance towards Rowena, so

A Cheer Went Up from the Crowd.

that the crown could slide into her hands.

"Long live Lady Rowena! Long live the Saxon princess!" chanted the crowd.

Although these cheers infuriated Prince John and his advisors, they knew that the rules of chivalry—rules the Normans, themselves, had made years ago—required them to accept the choice made by the Champion. So, John left his throne and made his way to the gallery where Rowena and Cedric were seated.

He took the golden crown from her hands and placed it on her head. "Let this crown be the symbol of your choice as Queen at this tournament. I invite you and your noble father to be my guests tonight at a banquet at Ashby Castle."

Cedric would never consider dining with the king he hated, but for Rowena's sake he declined the invitation with politeness.

John then turned to the Disinherited Knight and said, "Surely *you* will celebrate your victory at the banquet with me?"

"Long Live Lady Rowena!"

"I regret, My Prince, that I cannot. I'm very tired from today's tournament and I must rest for tomorrow's combat."

Prince John was not accustomed to having his invitations refused, and as he turned to leave, his voice dripped with sarcasm. "Then we will just have to force ourselves to dine without our Queen or Champion!"

Waldemar Fitzurse turned away, muttering to himself, "This foolish behavior will turn the people against the prince. But I can't control every word he speaks, and I dare not criticize him if I want to protect my position at court and my head as well."

So Fitzurse shrugged his shoulders and followed Prince John out of the gallery.

The first tournament day was ended.

"Without Our Queen or Champion!"

He Found Gurth Waiting.

CHAPTER 5

A Debt Is Repaid

When the Disinherited Knight returned to his pavilion, he found Gurth waiting. After serving dinner to his master, the young squire announced, "My Lord, the five squires belonging to the knights you defeated today are outside, each with his master's horse and weapons and armor."

"Yes, Gurth. According to the laws of chivalry, I have the right to keep their battle gear or demand payment if I return them. I'll see these squires in a moment, as soon as I cover my face with the hood on my robe. I don't want to be recognized."

Once that was done, the Disinherited Knight stepped outside. To four of the squires, he explained, "Sirs, please tell your masters that I commend them on their bravery in the tournament. I don't want their horses or weapons or armor, but I do want payment, since I must pay for all the equipment I used in the tournament."

"Each of our masters offers you fifty gold coins," said Front-de-Boeuf's squire, speaking for all five.

"I thank you and accept it from four of your masters," said the Disinherited Knight. Then turning to the fifth man, Bois-Guilbert's squire, he said, "Tell your master that I refuse any payment from him. My fight with him is not over. When we next meet in the lists, I will fight him to the death!"

When the Disinherited Knight went back into his pavilion, he handed Gurth ten gold coins. "I know the risk you took leaving my

"I Refuse Any Payment."

father and coming to serve me, loyal Gurth, so we must both keep our identities secret. Now I need you to ride into Ashby and find Isaac. Give him this bag of gold to pay his friend for my horse and armor and weapons."

Within the hour, Gurth had found Isaac and Rebecca staying at the home of their friend. The squire was admitted into the house and shown into Isaac and Rebecca's apartment. After explaining why he had come, he counted out the eighty coins the old man asked for.

"Your master is a fine young man," Isaac told Gurth. "I was just telling my daughter that very thing, wasn't I, Rebec— Now, where has my daughter gone?" Then turning back to Gurth, Isaac continued, "Tell your master that Rebecca and I wish him well in the tournament tomorrow."

As Gurth was about to leave the darkened house, Rebecca came out of a room near the front door. "Good squire," she whispered, "please come in here for a moment."

"Come Here for a Moment!"

Gurth followed Rebecca into the room. The young woman whispered, "How much money did my father ask your master to pay?"

"Eighty gold coins, my lady."

"My father was jesting with you, good man. He owes your master much more than these pieces of gold could ever repay." Then she handed Gurth a purse and continued. "You will find one hundred gold coins here. Return eighty to your master and keep the other twenty for yourself. Oh, and don't waste time thanking me. Just hurry back to your master and be careful traveling through this crowded town at this late hour."

Gurth thanked Rebecca and hurriedly left the house. Once he was out on the dark street, he whispered to himself, "She's an angel from heaven! Twenty pieces of gold from her, added to the ten from my brave master! Soon I'll be able to buy my freedom and truly be a squire to my young lord without hiding my face or my name from anyone."

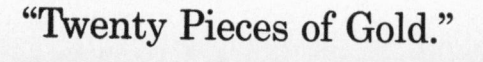

"Twenty Pieces of Gold."

Each Would Choose a Side.

CHAPTER 6

The Mysterious Black Knight

The crowd began to gather in the galleries early the next morning, eager to get a good seat for the second day of the tournament. Today would have one hundred knights, all fighting at the same time. Each would choose a side, either the side of the Disinherited Knight—the Champion of the previous day, or the side of Bois-Guilbert—the Champion supported by Prince John.

Once all the spectators were seated, the trumpets announced the arrival of Prince John, escorting Lady Rowena to her Queen's throne beside him.

The knights lined up facing each other at opposite ends of the lists as the herald announced the weapons and rules of that day's combat. He finished by stating, "The battle will come to an end when Prince John decides that too much blood has been spilled and he throws down his staff."

The trumpets sounded once again, and the knights galloped towards each other, meeting in the middle with a deafening crash.

The dust raised by a hundred horses made it impossible for the crowd to view the battle. But when the dust cleared, half the knights could be seen off their horses, fighting hand to hand, while many others lay wounded or dead in the dirt.

Of those still astride their horses, many had tossed away their broken lances and were now fighting with swords and battle-axes. From one moment to the next, one side or the other seemed to be winning. Blows and shouts

Dust Raised by a Hundred Horses!

almost drowned out the moans of the wounded as they were trampled under the feet of maddened horses. This was no longer a courteous display of chivalry among knights; this was only blood and terror and death!

The crowd cheered loudly with each blow, and even the ladies clapped their hands and waved their veils to encourage the knights.

"Fight on, brave knights!" urged Prince John. "Death is better than defeat!"

As the battle continued, the Disinherited Knight and Bois-Guilbert tried to find each other in the crush and confusion of men and horses. But lesser opponents, eager to face a Champion, kept them apart until only a few knights were left.

The two Champions were striking at each other with their swords, much to the delight and admiration of the crowd. Then Maurice de Bracy and Reginald Front-de-Boeuf defeated their opponents at the same moment and immediately charged in from opposite sides to

"Fight on, Brave Knights!"

join the attack on the Disinherited Knight.

Seeing this unfair and unexpected behavior, the crowd let out a warning cry. "Take care, Sir Disinherited! Look to the side!"

Suddenly aware of this new danger, the Disinherited Knight struck a full blow at Bois-Guilbert, then reined back his horse to escape the two knights bearing down on him. They were galloping at such speed that they almost smashed into each other. But at the last minute, they wheeled around and, along with Bois-Guilbert, lunged at the Disinherited Knight with their weapons.

The bravery and skill of the Disinherited Knight in turning and wheeling and striking at one, then the other, permitted him to hold off his opponents. While the crowd continued to applaud his skill, they feared he was doomed to defeat and death unless Prince John stopped this unfair battle.

The crowd started protesting. Even his advisors appealed to him. But John refused to

"Look to the Side!"

throw down his staff. "I will not stop the combat!" he snapped. "This arrogant fellow has chosen to hide his name and his face, in addition to insulting me by refusing my hospitality. He may have won the prize in the name of the Saxons yesterday; however, today it's the Normans' turn to—"

But Prince John was suddenly interrupted by a gasp from the crowd. All eyes turned to a tall, powerfully built knight speeding into the lists on a huge black horse. He was covered from head to toe with black armor, and his hand held a large black shield.

At that moment, the Disinherited Knight was fighting off blows from Bois-Guilbert's sword, with Front de Boeuf's battle-axe ready to come down on his head. But the Black Knight reached them in time to swing his sword at Front-de-Boeuf and fling him off his horse. He then turned to De Bracy and wrenched the Norman's mace from his hand. He swung it over his head and brought it down

From Head to Toe with Black Armor

on De Bracy, knocking him into the dirt, stunned.

With the fight even once again, the Black Knight galloped off the field as the crowd cheered. Then they turned their attention back to the two remaining combatants.

Bois-Guilbert's horse had been wounded and now fell to the ground. With his foot tangled in the stirrup, the Templar lay on the field, helpless, as the Disinherited Knight stood over him.

"Give up and admit defeat!" he cried, waving his sword at the Templar.

Seeing his Champion knight about to be disgraced, Prince John threw down his staff to save Bois-Guilbert and himself that embarrassment. The combat was over.

Chivalry then required Prince John to name the outstanding fighter of the day. "I name the Black Knight," he announced.

"But Your Highness," said Fitzurse, "the victory today was won by the Disinherited

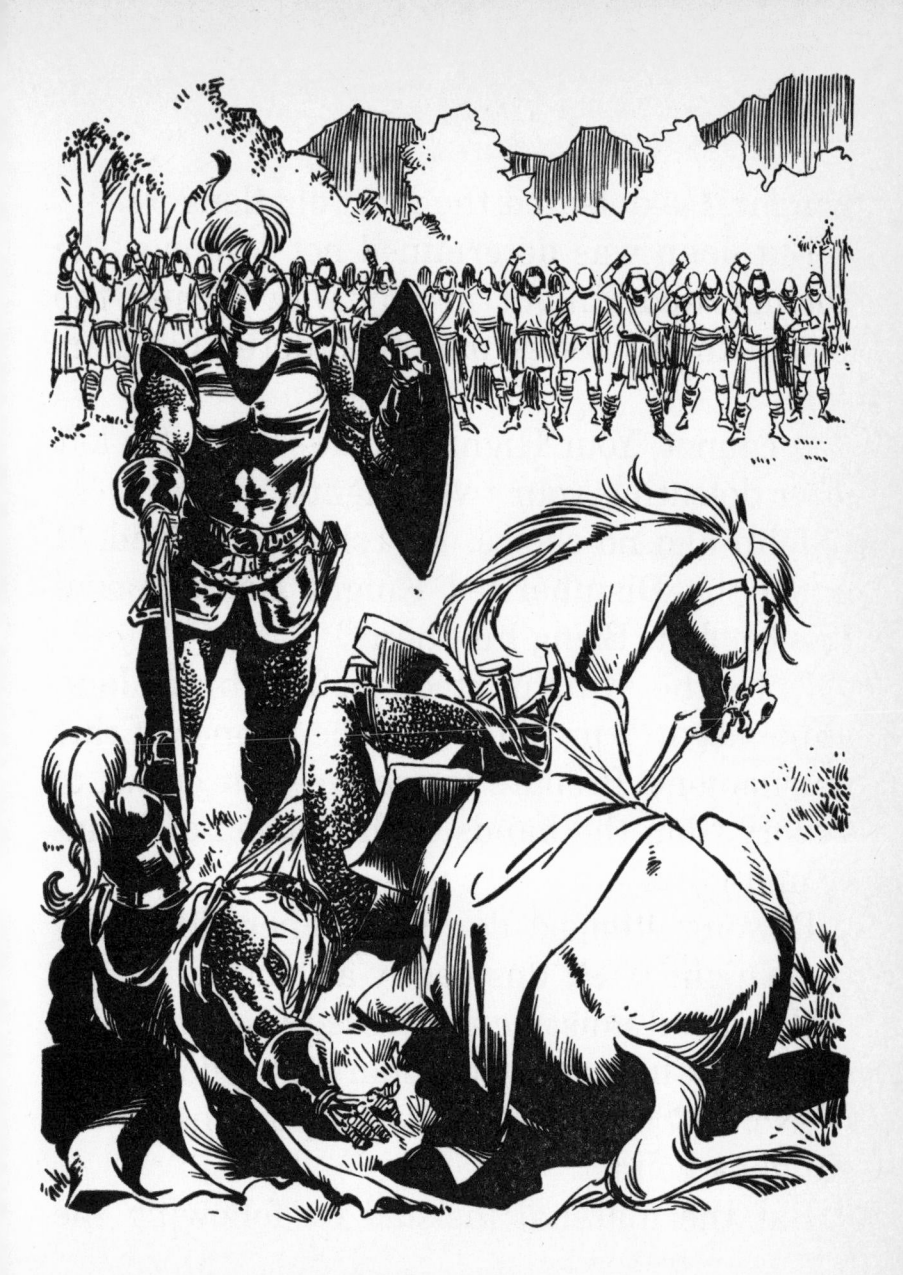

"Give Up and Admit Defeat!"

Knight. He defeated the most challengers."

But John was determined not to honor the Disinherited Knight in any way. "Bring the Black Knight before me," he ordered his marshal.

"I cannot, Your Highness. He's gone. He left after defeating your two knights."

John had no choice. He reluctantly said, "I name the Disinherited Knight Champion of this combat. Bring him here."

Once the Knight stood before him, John announced, "I proclaim you the winner of this tournament. Prepare to receive your crown of victory from the hands of the Queen of Beauty and Love."

Rowena stepped down from her throne as the Knight knelt unsteadily at her feet.

"His head must be uncovered in order to be crowned Champion," the marshal ordered.

"No, no," came a weak voice from inside the Knight's helmet.

But the marshal insisted on following the

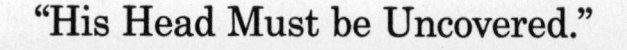

"His Head Must be Uncovered."

proper rules, and he slowly and carefully removed the Champion's helmet. A head of short, blond hair framed the pale, bloody face of a handsome young man of twenty-five.

Rowena gasped as she recognized the face of the man she loved. But she quickly forced herself to continue the ceremonies so as not to reveal his identity to the prince.

Placing the crown on the wounded man's drooping head, she proclaimed, "I name you Champion of this tournament, and never was a man more worthy of it than you, Sir Knight."

The Knight pressed her hand to his lips, then he fell, unconscious, at her feet.

Confusion spread among the spectators. But for Cedric, the sudden appearance of his disinherited son came as a complete shock. He rushed to Rowena's side in time to see the marshal removing his son's armor.

"Good grief!" he cried as he held Rowena. "The tip of a lance has broken off and is embedded in Ivanhoe's side!"

"I Name You Champion of this Tournament."

Carrying Him off the Field.

CHAPTER 7

A Warning for Prince John

"Ivanhoe!" Prince John cried to Fitzurse. "He's my brother's loyal Saxon follower. This can only mean trouble for me."

"I don't think so, Your Highness. See how seriously wounded he is. His friends are already carrying him off the field."

"And the Lady Rowena, where has she gone?" demanded Prince John, seeing the empty chair beside him.

"I suppose she's gone to grieve for the wounded knight she loves," sneered De Bracy.

"I have other plans for that wealthy Saxon

beauty," said the prince with a cruel laugh. "I'll make her the bride of a loyal Norman, like you, De Bracy. What do you think about having such a rich and beautiful wife?"

"I'd be grateful till my dying day, Your Highness." And De Bracy bowed deeply.

Any further conversation about Rowena was interrupted at that moment by a guard who approached Prince John and handed him a letter. "This was delivered by a messenger from France, Your Highness."

"F-France?" the prince gasped to Fitzurse. "The country where Richard is imprisoned!" His hands trembled as he unfolded the paper, and his face turned deathly pale at the words: BE WARNED! THE KING HAS ESCAPED!

"We must end the tournament immediately!" John shrieked. "I must flee for my life!"

"Stay calm," said Fitzurse. "Your people mustn't suspect that anything is wrong. We'll say that you've been called away on urgent matters of state and must cancel the events

"I Must Flee for My Life."

scheduled for tomorrow."

"That won't do any good!" cried Prince John, pacing in the gallery. "My people have heard the roar of the lion, the roar of Richard the Lion-Hearted, shaking the woods. Nothing will give my nobles the courage to stand by me."

"If only he had a little courage himself," Fitzurse whispered to De Bracy. "But the moment he hears his brother's name, he changes from a strong, insolent tyrant to a shameless, pitiful weakling."

"Then it's up to us to keep his subjects loyal," replied De Bracy. "Promises of favors and gifts of gold should do that. And we must see to it that John is crowned king as soon as possible. This must be done if we are to further our own ambitions and add to our own fortunes."

"And what of your plans for Lady Rowena?" asked Fitzurse. "She seems to care only for her Saxon knight."

The Roar of Richard the Lion-Hearted

"I've been planning to make her my bride since I first saw her at Rotherwood. Having John in favor of this marriage only adds to my determination."

"How will you get Rowena to agree to it?"

"With an ingenious plan. I'll follow Cedric's party when they leave Ashby tonight. Then, disguised as an outlaw of the forest, I'll kidnap Rowena. Later, a brave knight will rescue her from the outlaws and carry her off to Front-de-Boeuf's castle. *I* will be that knight. It's such a romantic plan, Rowena can't possibly resist it. She'll be eager to marry me. In any event, I'll keep her at the castle until she agrees to it."

"But you can't do this alone."

"Bois-Guilbert's men will help. And now, like a true knight, I'm off to win the hand and heart of the beautiful Rowena."

As De Bracy turned to go, he didn't hear Fitzurse mutter after him, "Like a true knight? Ha! Like an utter fool!"

Only the Bloody Dirt Remained.

CHAPTER 8

Kidnapped!

When Ivanhoe lost consciousness on the field, many people rushed to help him. By the time Gurth reached the spot where his master had fallen, Ivanhoe was gone, and only the bloody dirt remained.

Cedric was distressed at seeing Ivanhoe wounded, but he couldn't bring himself to go to his disinherited son in front of such a large crowd. So he sent his servant, Oswald, ordering him, "Take Ivanhoe to Ashby and find the best doctor there for him."

But Oswald didn't find Ivanhoe either;

instead, he found Gurth, who had been in such a rush to come to his master's aid, he had forgotten to hide his face with his hood. As soon as Oswald recognized him as the servant who had escaped from Rotherwood, he overpowered him and tied his hands.

"I'm taking you back to Cedric," he told Gurth as he led him off the field.

As to where Ivanhoe was, all they could learn was that the Disinherited Knight had been lifted onto a litter carried by four well-dressed servants and taken away.

Oswald caught up with Cedric's party when they stopped to rest several hours after leaving Ashby. Although Gurth pleaded to be allowed to search for Ivanhoe, Cedric said no. As long as he was certain that his son was alive and probably being cared for by friends, he planned to return home and continue his life as usual . . . *without his disinherited son!*

The group started up again once Oswald and Gurth had taken their places at the rear.

He Tied His Hands.

The road ahead would take them through a large forest where many bands of outlaws roamed. Cedric was certain that his ten servants, plus Oswald and Gurth, would be enough protection for Lady Rowena, her attendants, and himself.

They hadn't gone far into the forest when cries for help reached them. Riding toward the place where the cries were coming from, they saw an old man pacing back and forth, ringing his hands and moaning in terror. A young woman was on her knees reaching into a curtained litter on the ground.

"Thank heaven, it's you, Sir Cedric!" wept the old man. "It is I, Isaac, with my daughter Rebecca. We left Ashby with six body-guards and mules to carry our sick friend in the litter. Everything was fine until we were warned by a woodcutter of a band of outlaws up ahead. Our bodyguards ran off, taking our money and our mules. I fear we'll be attacked and murdered unless you protect us and let us travel

"Thank Heaven, it's You."

with you."

"We must give them servants and horses to take them to the next village," Rowena told Cedric.

But Rebecca jumped up from the litter and hurried to Rowena. "Please, my lady, I beg you to take us with you. I'm not asking for myself or for my aged father, but for the man who is near death inside this litter."

Rowena was touched by Rebecca's pleas, and she turned to Cedric. "These people need our help. We must take them with us."

Cedric couldn't deny Rowena anything, so he ordered the litter placed on two of his mules and gave Rebecca and Isaac two horses. Gurth had been left unguarded during this time, and he managed to slip away without being missed. Still, he stayed a short distance away in the forest, keeping the group in sight, hoping to learn where Ivanhoe was.

The very moment that Oswald discovered Gurth's disappearance was the moment that

Touched by Rebecca's Pleas

an attack came. Outlaws dressed in Lincoln-green tunics, with black helmets covering their faces, surrounded them.

"For merry England!" shouted the outlaws, hoping that their words and clothes would convince their victims that they were Saxon bandits who lived in this forest.

In spite of Cedric's brave defense, his party couldn't fight against so many bandits with so many weapons. In moments, they were surrounded and taken prisoner.

Gurth watched as Cedric and his party were led away. "I must go for help," he said as he turned his mule. But his way was blocked by another outlaw dressed in Lincoln-green. This outlaw, however, did not have his face hidden by a helmet.

"Who has the nerve to take prisoners here in my forest?" the outlaw demanded.

"*Your* forest? Since when does an outlaw own a forest? And who are you?" Gurth asked.

"I'm Robin of Locksley, but my men call me

"I'm Robin of Locksley."

Robin Hood. Now tell me what happened."

"You should know, Robin. It was your men who took the prisoners. They were dressed just like you."

"*My men?* I'll see about that right now. Wait here and don't move."

Gurth waited only a few minutes for Robin to return with news.

"Good squire, I crept up behind those outlaws. They're not my men, but I learned who they are and where they're heading. They don't plan to harm any of their prisoners. But since they do outnumber us, it would be foolish to try a rescue now. Come with me. I'll gather my band and we'll make our rescue plans together."

Gurth turned his mule and followed Robin through the forest for the next three hours. When they reached a huge oak tree, five men in Lincoln-green tunics jumped up and came running to welcome their leader.

Robin told them what happened. "There's a

Running to Welcome Their Leader

group of bandits impersonating us in the forest. They've kidnapped Lord Cedric's party and are heading towards the castle of Baron Front-de-Boeuf at Torquilstone. We must gather all our men and leave by morning if we hope to rescue the prisoners."

"I offer you my help, too," came a voice from the bushes. And out stepped the Black Knight who had come to Ivanhoe's aid in the tournament.

"Brave knight, we welcome all good Saxons who are loyal to King Richard," said Robin. "But how did you come to our oak tree?"

"Through the kindness of Friar Tuck, who gave me food and lodging at his chapel on my way out of Ashby. When he told me who his friends were, I asked him to present me to the brave Robin of Locksley. There's not a man in all of England who hasn't heard of your daring deeds. We arrived just moments ago, in time to join in the rescue."

Out Stepped the Black Knight.

With Their Faces Hidden

CHAPTER 9

Prisoners at Torquilstone

While Robin waited overnight for the arrival of his men, the mysterious outlaws were hurrying their prisoners along the road. The two leaders, still with their faces hidden, rode at the front, talking quietly.

"Isn't it time to put the second half of your plan into action, De Bracy?" asked Bois-Guilbert.

"I've changed my mind. I'm not going to put on my knight's clothes and rescue Rowena here on the road. Instead, when we get to Torquilstone, I'll confess everything to her.

She'll surely understand that my love for her drove me to take these desperate actions."

"I myself am greatly intrigued by the beautiful Rebecca," said Bois-Guilbert.

"Rebecca? I would think you'd be more interested in the beauty of her father's money bag than in the beauty of the maiden."

"I want both," sneered Bois-Guilbert. "And I'll get both. Remember, we must pay that greedy Front-de-Boeuf for using his castle."

When the party left the woods and saw the walls of Torquilstone in the distance, Cedric gasped in recognition. "We are at the very castle that King Richard gave to Ivanhoe years ago, the very same castle that Prince John gave to that brute, Front-de-Boeuf, while Ivanhoe was in the Holy Land. Now I understand. These outlaws are not English, as they pretend. They're Normans in disguise, taking us to a Norman castle!"

When the party reached the castle gate, the drawbridge was lowered to let them enter.

"They're Normans in Disguise."

Once inside the courtyard, Cedric was separated from Rowena, and Isaac was dragged from Rebecca, even though both fathers tearfully pleaded to stay with their daughters. All were separated from their servants too.

Cedric was taken to a large room, where he was treated politely by his Norman guards and served an elaborate meal.

Isaac, however, was thrown into a dungeon far below ground. As he huddled on the damp ground in one corner, he looked around him. Fastened to the walls were shackles and chains from earlier tortures and even some bones from earlier prisoners. In the middle of the floor was a large fire-pit covered with a rusty iron grate.

After several hours of sitting quietly with his hands folded in prayer, Isaac heard hinges creaking as the door was opened. The huge form of Front-de-Boeuf entered, followed by a guard carrying two large baskets.

The savage baron's cruel smile struck terror

His Hands Folded in Prayer

in the heart of the old man as he signaled the guard to open one basket. The man did so, taking out a scale and some weights, and placing them in front of Isaac.

"Isaac of York," cried Front-de-Boeuf menacingly, "on this scale you are to weigh out a thousand pounds of gold . . . or face the most terrible punishment any man could imagine!"

"T-There is not that much gold in all of York or among all of my people," gasped Isaac. "Please, noble knight, have pity on me. I am old and poor and helpless."

"Old and helpless, yes. But poor? No! I warn you I will torture you long and painfully until you die. Prisoners richer and more important than you have died in this dungeon over the years and no one ever knew what became of them."

Front-de-Boeuf then gave orders to his guard. "Empty the coals from the other basket into the fire-pit and strike the flint and steel together to get the sparks to light them. Then

"I Will Torture You Long and Painfully!"

fan the fire with the bellows until the coals are red-hot."

Once the coals were glowing and the guard had replaced the grate on top of the pit, Front-de-Boeuf turned back to Isaac. "See that grate, old man? It's becoming red-hot, a red-hot bed for you to lie on until you slowly burn to death. That is your choice—a fiery death or the gold I demand!"

"I don't have that much gold!"

With a cruel smile, the baron ordered, "Seize him and toss him on the grate!"

"No, wait! I'll pay," screamed Isaac. "But I'll have to go to my countrymen and beg and borrow that huge amount."

"I won't allow you to leave here. The gold must be delivered to this dungeon before you can be set free."

"And when it's delivered, will my daughter and our sick friend and everyone in Cedric's party be freed too?"

"Their ransom isn't up to me. It's being

"Toss Him on the Grate!"

decided upon by others in the castle."

"If you won't let me leave, you must permit my daughter Rebecca to go to York to borrow the gold for me."

"Rebecca is your daughter? . . . But I can't let her go. She is Brian de Bois-Guilbert's prisoner. She belongs to him just as if he won her from a challenger in a tournament."

"No! No! No!" shrieked Isaac as if his whole body were being burnt over the fire at that very moment. "Torture me, burn me, but spare my daughter. The Templar is evil. He's a cruel knight who will dishonor her!"

"Dog! How dare you insult as fine a knight as Bois-Guilbert!"

"Do what you will with me, robber and villain! I will pay you nothing unless Rebecca is returned to me safely. She is a thousand times dearer to me than my own body!"

"Then your cursed old body shall be thrown on the bed of fire, Isaac of York!"

"A Thousand Times Dearer to Me!"

"A Prisoner of Your Beauty"

CHAPTER 10

Surprise Visitors

The Lady Rowena had been taken to the only chamber decent enough for a Saxon princess.

She remained alone there for several hours until Maurice De Bracy entered, now dressed in knightly finery. He bowed, then reached out his arm to lead Rowena to a seat.

"I prefer to stand in the company of my jailer, Sir Knight," snapped Rowena.

"I'm not your jailer, fair lady, but a prisoner of your beauty."

"I do not know you, sir, and you have no

right to speak to a lady in such a familiar way, especially one you have kidnapped while you were disguised. Your courteous tongue does not forgive your evil deed. I want nothing to do with a man such as you."

De Bracy was confused that Rowena was offended by his gallant compliment, so he resumed his arrogant Norman ways. "Since you don't welcome my polite language, I shall be forced to speak more boldly. You shall *never* leave this castle, Lady Rowena, unless it is as the bride of Maurice de Bracy!"

"Never!"

"Don't be so quick to reject me, my lady. And don't hold out hopes that you'll be the bride of your beloved Ivanhoe, for at this very minute he's a prisoner in this castle too."

"Ivanhoe here? You're lying!"

"No, my lady. I recognized him as he was carried in on his litter. But only *I* know his true identity. One word to Front-de-Boeuf, however, and Ivanhoe is a dead man. The

"I Want Nothing To Do with You."

baron will stop at nothing, even murder, to keep this castle as his own. Now shall I go to Front-de-Boeuf to prove it to you?"

"No, no, please don't do that! I believe you. Save Ivanhoe, I beg you!"

"Only by agreeing to marry me can you save his life and free yourself from this castle. If you refuse, you'll remain a prisoner and both Ivanhoe *and* Cedric will die."

At the added threat against her beloved guardian's life, Rowena's courage left her, and she burst into hysterical weeping.

De Bracy began to pace back and forth helplessly. "'I can't bear the pain I've caused this beautiful woman," he said to himself. "How I wish I was as hard-hearted as Front-de-Boeuf! What am I do without losing face among my friends?"

Meanwhile, Rebecca had been taken to a small room high in a turret. Her first act had been to inspect the room, searching for a way to escape, but the window led only to a

High in a Turret

parapet, or balcony, outside the turret.

Rebecca was a strong-willed, courageous young woman, but she began to tremble when the door opened and one of the kidnappers entered. His cap was pulled down over the upper half of his face, and he held his cloak over the lower half.

When the outlaw just stood there, without saying a word, Rebecca guessed at what he wanted. She hurriedly took two bracelets off her arm and unclasped her necklace. "Take these," she said, reaching them out to the man, "and be merciful to my father and me."

"Beautiful lady, these diamonds cannot sparkle as magnificently as your eyes do. It is not diamonds or gold that I seek, for your father will provide all the gold we need. No, you must pay your ransom with your beauty and your love."

"You're no outlaw!" cried Rebecca, "No outlaw would refuse such jewels. You're a Norman. Uncover yourself if you dare!"

"You're No Outlaw!"

"You have guessed," said Brian de Bois-Guilbert, dropping his cloak from his face. "And truly, I have no need for your jewels. Rather, I would be pleased to add many more to your beautiful neck and arms."

"What can you want of me? We have nothing in common. You are a Christian and I am a Jewess. We could never marry."

Bois-Guilbert laughed mockingly. "Marry a Jewess? Never! Besides, my vows as a Templar prevent me from marrying anyone. But those vows do not prevent me from loving you as a man loves a woman."

"How dare you offend me! May God forgive you for suggesting such a vile thing!"

"I don't need you to scold me," snapped Bois-Guilbert, his eyes flashing. "You forget that you are my prisoner and I have the right to take from you anything I wish."

"Stand back, Sir Knight!" cried Rebecca. "If you overpower me, I will renounce you all over Europe. I will shame you among your Christ-

"Stand Back, Sir Knight!"

ian friends for having sinned with a Jewess."

"What you say is true, but who will hear your voice outside the walls of this castle? No, Rebecca, only three things can save you. Give up your religion, become a Christian, and accept my love."

"I spit at you, vile knight! Give up my religion? Never! My God has given me a way to escape from you." And Rebecca threw open the window and ran to the edge of the parapet, where she stood ready to jump off.

Taken by surprise, Bois-Guilbert followed after to stop her. "Wait!" he shouted.

"Stop where you are, cruel knight. If you come one step closer, I'll throw myself off this parapet. I'd rather be crushed in the courtyard below than be the victim of your brutality." As she said this, Rebecca threw her hands up towards heaven as if asking for God's mercy before she jumped.

Bois-Guilbert admired Rebecca's strength and courage. "Come down, reckless girl," he

Ready to Jump Off

said gently. "I promise I will not offend you ever again."

"I don't trust you."

"I swear I will not harm you. If you won't come off that ledge for *your* sake, then do it for your father's. Please don't be afraid of me. Let me be your friend. And perhaps one day, when you know me better, you might learn to love me."

Rebecca sensed an honesty in the Templar's words. "I'll trust you for now," she said as she got down off the ledge.

Just then, a bugle call sounded outside the castle. "I must go now and see what news that messenger brings." And Bois-Guilbert hurried from the parapet.

Shaken at having come so close to death, Rebecca stumbled back inside and dropped to her knees in prayer. "Thank You, God, for protecting me. And please give Your protection to my father and Ivanhoe as well."

Dropped to Her Knees in Prayer

A Challenge from the Black Knight

CHAPTER 11

Switched Identities

The bugle call that brought Bois-Guilbert in from the parapet also gave De Bracy an excuse to leave his embarrassing situation in Rowena's room. It also interrupted Front-de-Boeuf's cruel plans for torturing Isaac.

The three Normans met in the great hall, where a guard brought in the letter delivered by the messenger.

Bois-Guilbert grabbed the letter and read aloud, *"I, the Black Knight who challenged you at Ashby, demand that you release the prisoners you kidnapped. If you do not release them within one hour, Robin of Locksley and I have hundreds of men ready to attack Torquilstone and destroy you."*

The three men stared at each other in disbelief. Front-de-Boeuf was the first to speak. "These outlaws not only outnumber us, but they hate me as well. I've been punishing them all these years when I catch them in my forest where they hunt for food."

"Then let's not wait till they come at us," suggested De Bracy. "Let's attack them first."

"We don't have enough men to do that and also guard the castle," said Front-de-Boeuf. "Can't we get any help from your friends in nearby castles?" asked Bois-Guilbert.

"They're all in York for John's coronation where we should be too. But perhaps we can send a messenger to the prince or to them."

"And have him captured by those outlaws when he enters the forest?" argued De Bracy.

"I have a plan that will get our message through safely," said Front-de-Boeuf. Then he

"They Hate Me."

quickly wrote a return message: *The prisoners are ours and we will not release them. We plan to execute Cedric at dawn, so send in a priest to hear his final confession.*

"Take this letter to the messenger outside," Front-de-Boeuf told his guard.

Within the hour, that letter was delivered to Robin, Gurth, and the Black Knight at the big oak tree. By now, hundreds of Robin's men had gathered, along with many neighboring towns-people and all the servants from Rotherwood.

The Black Knight read the message, then offered his plan. "I don't think they'll execute Cedric immediately. But since they want a priest, we can have one of our men enter the castle in that disguise. He can bring word back to us as to their defenses."

Gurth had an even better plan. "Let *me* go in as a priest. I'll look over their defenses and also try to rescue Cedric. I owe it to him and to my young master Ivanhoe, wherever he might be."

"Let *Me* Go in as a Priest"

Robin agreed to let Gurth try. He called to Tuck, "Give Gurth your robe, good friar."

Tuck removed his robe and pulled it over Gurth's head. As he tied a rope belt around the squire's waist and hung a heavy cross around his neck, he gave him a few words of advice. "No matter what any of those Normans ask you, just answer with two words in a deep, serious voice, *'Pax vobiscum.'* That's Latin for 'Peace be with you.'"

"Pax vobiscum," practiced Gurth as he got on his mule and set off for Torquilstone.

Gurth next repeated his *Pax vobiscum* to cover his trembling knees as he stood before Front-de-Boeuf, explaining, "I'm a poor monk who was attacked by a band of thieves in the forest. They forced me to come here to hear a dying man's final confession."

"And how many thieves were in this band, holy father?" asked Front-de-Boeuf.

"Hundreds, even thousands! *I* even feared for my life," lied the pretended friar.

"I'm a Poor Monk."

"What!" cried Bois-Guilbert, entering the room. "We must send for help immediately. I'll write the message and have this holy man deliver it when he leaves here."

A servant led the friar to Cedric's room. At a nod from the friar, he left them alone.

"Pax vobiscum," said Gurth in a deep, serious voice as he pulled his hood over his face. "I have come to prepare you for death, noble Cedric."

"What! Wicked as these Normans are, they wouldn't dare put me to death!"

"I fear they have no conscience, my son."

"Then I shall die like a man," declared Cedric, and he knelt down to pray.

"Look and listen first, noble master," said Gurth, resuming his normal voice and pushing back the hood of his robe.

"Gurth!" gasped Cedric. "What are you doing here, and in the robe of a holy man?"

"Don't ask me anything. Just put on my robe and leave this castle immediately. I'll put on

"Gurth! What Are You Doing Here?"

your cloak and cap, and stay here in your place."

"I can't leave you here. They'd hang you! And I can't leave without Rowena and the rest of my party. Isn't there a chance of rescue for all of us?"

"Yes. Five hundred men are waiting to attack this castle, but they need your help."

"But how can I get out?" argued Cedric. "How will I answer a Norman who might stop me? I don't know any priestly language."

"Two words will get you past any Norman. *Pax vobiscum.* Just say it in a deep, serious voice. And if someone tries any more Latin on you, just pretend you're deaf."

Cedric finally nodded tearfully and let Gurth put the robe on him. He hugged the brave young man, then rushed from the room. When he reached the hallway, Cedric found Front-de-Boeuf waiting, a paper in his hand.

"Sir Friar, those thieves outside the castle must be prevented from attacking us. Carry

Cedric Nodded Tearfully.

this letter to the prince at York."

The friar nodded, then mumbled his *Pax vobiscum* and hurried to join Robin and the Black Knight in the woods. On the way, he tore up the letter and threw it in the moat.

Inside the castle, Front-de-Boeuf ordered Cedric brought before him. The man who was led in had his cap pulled down over his face and stood in a shadowy part of the room to avoid being recognized.

"Well, gallant Saxon, how are you enjoying our hospitality at Torquilstone?" sneered Front-de-Boeuf. "Are you interested in paying a ransom to save your worthless life or shall I hang you upside down from the iron bars of the castle window?"

"I don't have one cent for ransom, Baron. And since my memory hasn't been too good lately, perhaps hanging me upside down will improve my brain."

"What kind of nonsense is that?" cried Front-de-Boeuf, pushing the cap off Gurth's

"What Kind of Nonsense is That?"

head. "Who are you?"

"I can answer that," said De Bracy, entering the room. "He's Cedric's servant, the one who ran off to become Ivanhoe's squire."

The baron then turned to his guard. "You fool! Go and bring me the real Cedric!"

""But, Sir, no one else was in the room."

"Good Lord!" cried De Bracy. "Cedric must have escaped in the friar's robe!"

"And you," screamed Front-de-Boeuf, lunging at Gurth, "I'll tear your head from your body and throw you off the castle walls!"

"Calm yourself," said De Bracy. "He's only a simple peasant and not worth killing."

"You seem to forget, De Bracy, that because of him, our message will never reach York. We'll never get help from anyone."

"Then it's time for us to prepare for an attack and not stand here talking. Summon Bois-Guilbert and let's position our men."

From their place on the wall, the three Norman knights looked out over the forest

"Go and Bring Me the Real Cedric."

surrounding the castle.

Bois-Guilbert pointed into the distance and said, "Those men are very well organized. They've taken cover behind every tree and bush, and never once have they exposed themselves within the shooting range of our bows. I'm certain they're being led by some noble knight or gentleman highly skilled in the art of war."

"I think I see such a leader," said De Bracy. "Look, in the distance, at the tall man in black armor. It's the Black Knight who came to Ivanhoe's aid at Ashby and who defeated Front-de-Boeuf and me."

"And since he disappeared right after his victory before I could challenge him again, I shall have my revenge on him now!" swore the baron.

So, as the Saxons approached Torquilstone, the Normans got ready for their attack.

"It's the Black Knight."

"Brave Knight!"

CHAPTER 12

The Attack on Torquilstone

When the prisoners first arrived at Torquilstone, the litter carrying Isaac's "sick friend" was taken to a turret room just beyond Rebecca's. Once Bois-Guilbert had left her room, the young woman hurried to the wounded knight and bent over the unconscious form of Ivanhoe.

"How pale and weak you are from losing so much blood, brave knight!" she whispered as she began changing his bloody bandages.

Ivanhoe's eyes fluttered for a moment, then focused on the beautiful young woman.

"W-Where am I?" he muttered in confusion. "And w-who are you?"

"I am Rebecca, daughter of Isaac of York, the man you saved from cruel robbers. My father's servants carried you off the field at Ashby after you fainted, and we brought you to the inn where we were staying. It was there that I began treating your wounds."

"You? A woman?" Ivanhoe was amazed.

"Don't doubt my ability, Sir Knight. I learned the art of healing from Miriam, the most respected woman in our tribe. I've spent my life using that knowledge to heal my people as well as yours."

"Then I thank you, my dear Rebecca. But tell me, are we still at the inn at Ashby?"

"No, while you were unconscious, but with your bleeding slowed down, we decided to set out for our home in York, where I had all my medicines and salves with which to properly treat you. We made you comfortable in my litter, and you were making the journey very well

"I am Rebecca."

until the men we hired to carry the litter took our mules and ran off."

"Then w-what—? H-How—? W-Where?"

"Cedric's party found us and permitted us to travel with them. But not long after, we were attacked by a band of outlaws, who turned out to be hateful Norman knights in disguise. They brought us here to Torquilstone, then separated us—Cedric, his servants, your squire Gurth, my father, and—"

"Good Lord! Rowena too?" cried Ivanhoe, pushing himself up and groaning in pain.

Rebecca nodded. "Yes, the Lady Rowena too. She is in another part of the castle."

"Then I must—I must—" But the effort to rise was too much for Ivanhoe, and he fell back, exhausted, and was soon asleep again.

"Rest well, brave knight." And Rebecca bent down to kiss Ivanhoe's pale cheek.

Rebecca never moved from Ivanhoe's side during the hours that the Black Knight and his men were preparing for the attack, the same

"Rest Well!"

hours that the Norman commanders spent on the walls watching those preparations.

When Ivanhoe finally stirred again, his strength seemed to be returning. "Thank you, dear Rebecca, my gentle doctor," he said. "Has our situation changed at all?"

"Our Norman captors have spent many hours making preparations to defend the castle. When I stepped out on the parapet and looked towards the woods, I saw hundreds of armed Saxons. They seemed to be taking their orders from the same Black Knight who came to your aid at Ashby."

"If only I could be there with them," Ivanhoe muttered impatiently. "The bugle signals the beginning of the attack. Listen! Hear the shouts, the whiz of arrows flying through the air, the crashing of rocks being hurled down from the battlements. I must—"

"You mustn't even *think* of getting up, Ivanhoe. You've lost too much blood; you're too weak. I'll stand at the window and tell you

"Hear the Shouts, the Whiz of Arrows."

everything that's happening."

"No! You mustn't!" cried Ivanhoe. "An arrow could hit you at any moment. Please, Rebecca, you mustn't risk injury or death."

But Rebecca knew how important the battle was to Ivanhoe, so she ignored his warnings and ran up the two steps leading to the latticed window. "They're advancing now. I see hundreds of them, the first line with huge shields and wooden battering rams, and behind them, archers loading their long-bows, shooting, and reloading. Arrows are flying in such a heavy attack that I can barely see the bowmen who shot them."

"The attack can't go on this way," said Ivanhoe in frustration. "Saxon arrows won't pierce and collapse stone walls. The castle must be stormed by pure force."

"Wait! I think the Black Knight is doing just that. His men are smashing the gate with their battle-axes and a battering ram.... The barricade's down! They're rushing in.... Oh,

no! The Normans are running out, pushing them back.... Now the Black Knight and Front-de-Boeuf are facing each other, swinging, lunging, slashing. Front-de-Boeuf is down. He's not moving.... Bois-Guilbert is dragging his body inside the walls."

"And our forces?"

"They have ladders up against the outer walls, but the Normans are hurling rocks and tree trunks down on them. Still the Black Knight fights, harder than any man there. Rocks and tree trunks can't stop him!"

"There is only one man in all of England who can fight like that!" cried Ivanhoe, as he joyfully raised his weak body to a sitting position. "Only one man whose heart and arm fight with that kind of strength for the love of England and his people!"

"Wait! They're dropping a long raft across the moat to make a floating bridge.... Now they're crossing it.... They're inside the gates and up on the battlements.... Wait! The

"Only One Man in All of England."

Normans are fleeing back into the castle."

When the two Norman leaders met inside the hall, De Bracy reported, "On my side of the wall, Robin Hood led his archers in a heavy attack, but we held our position."

Bois-Guilbert shook his head. "I couldn't hold mine. The baron is dead. Do you think we can still defend Torquilstone?"

"Hardly. We're greatly outnumbered, and I fear we'll have to give up our prisoners if we hope to escape with our lives."

"Shame on you, De Bracy! We'd be ridiculed till our dying day. I'd rather die here than be dishonored. To the walls! Let us fight!"

But as they ran from the hall, their way was blocked by a wall of smoke and flames.

"The fire is coming up from the dungeon!" cried Bois-Guilbert. "The entire western side of the castle is in flames."

"The stupidity of Front-de-Boeuf! The fire must have spread from the dungeon pit where he was planning to torture Isaac."

"The Castle is in Flames."

And so it had, with a little help from the shrewd old man. For when his guards heard the Saxons attacking the western side of the castle, they ran off. Left alone, Isaac saw his chance to divert the Normans' attention from fighting Saxons to fighting fires. So he began tossing into the pit anything he could find that would burn—chairs, tables, planks, rags, straw—before he made his own escape from the dungeon.

When De Bracy realized that the fire was out of control and blocking most of the exits, he shouted, "What are we to do?"

"We must get our men out the rear gate," cried Bois-Guilbert. "It's the only entrance where there's been no fighting. Hurry!"

Minutes later, De Bracy and Bois-Guilbert flung open the gate, only to crash into the Black Knight. The Norman soldiers behind them drew back in fear.

De Bracy screamed at them, "Dogs! Are you such cowards that you let one man frighten

Tossing Things into the Pit

you and block your only escape?"

"That man is the devil!" cried one guard.

"Get out of my way then!" raged De Bracy. "I'll face him myself."

Maurice De Bracy and the Black Knight fought hand to hand, each dealing furious blows with his sword on the other. Finally, one blow from the Black Knight landed with such force that De Bracy fell to the ground.

Bending over him, his dagger against the Norman's throat, the Black Knight demanded, "Give up, De Bracy, or you're a dead man!"

"Give up to an unknown victor? Ha! I won't be dishonored by admitting I was defeated by a nameless peasant! So, either tell me who you are or go ahead and kill me!"

The Black Knight knelt closer to De Bracy whispered something in his ear.

Maurice De Bracy's defiance disappeared and he meekly admitted, "I give up."

"Then turn yourself over to my men at the drawbridge. I'll deal with you later."

"I Give Up."

"Before I go, I think you'd like to know that Ivanhoe is a prisoner here. He's badly wounded and as soon as the fire spreads, he'll be trapped in the burning castle."

"Ivanhoe a prisoner? In danger of dying? Quickly, tell me where he is."

The instant De Bracy pointed to a winding stairway, the Black Knight was gone. De Bracy then headed to the drawbridge, where many of his men were surrendering to Cedric and Robin Hood.

Meanwhile, the fire was spreading and smoke was beginning to seep into Ivanhoe's room. Rebecca was still at the window when she heard shouts of "Water! Water!"

She ran to the door, but faced a wall of flames. "The castle's on fire!" she cried.

"You must save yourself, Rebecca," begged Ivanhoe. "You can't worry about me."

"I refuse to leave you. If we're both not rescued, I'll die with you. . . . And yet, oh God, my father! What will happen to him?"

"You Must Save Yourself."

At that moment, the door was flung open and Bois-Guilbert crashed into the room. His broken and bloody armor was charred from the flames. "I'm here to save you, Rebecca. Follow me quickly. I'll lead you to safety."

"I'll go only if you save my father and this wounded knight as well."

"A knight must be prepared to meet death no matter how, and I don't much care how an old man dies either. Now come!"

"Beast! I would rather die in this fire than be rescued by a savage like you!"

"You have no choice, Rebecca." And Bois-Guilbert picked up the terrified young woman, who shrieked and clawed at his face as he carried her out of the room.

"Dog!" cried Ivanhoe. "Put her down! I'll kill you for this."

Moments later, the Black Knight burst into the room. "Thank God you're safe, Ivanhoe." And he picked up the young knight as easily as Bois-Guilbert had lifted Rebecca and

"You Have No Choice, Rebecca."

carried him to the rear gate and to safety.

Leaving Ivanhoe in the care of two of his men, the Black Knight went back into the castle to rescue the other prisoners.

Saxons ran from room to room, searching out the Norman defenders. Many had already fled. Those who resisted felt the blade of Saxon swords, and only those who surrendered left the castle alive.

Amid all this confusion, Cedric rushed about in search of Rowena. He found her in her room, kneeling in prayer, preparing to meet her death. He hurried her out of the smoke-filled room and down to safety.

The Norman who had been ordered to guard Gurth discovered the smoke as it crept into the room. Afraid of being trapped, the man rushed for the nearest stairway, leaving the room unlocked. Gurth then had no trouble escaping down into the courtyard.

In the middle of the courtyard, Brian de Bois-Guilbert was mounting his horse and

Preparing To Meet Her Death

placing Rebecca in front of him. He was surrounded by several of his men who were protecting their leader as he made his escape.

Saxons were coming at him from all sides, their bows ready to shoot. Bois-Guilbert spurred his horse into a gallop across the drawbridge, calling back, "Your bows are useless, Saxon archers! You dare not shoot for fear of hitting Rebecca!"

At that moment, Friar Tuck and several of Robin's band stepped out into the courtyard. "We went down to the cellar to rescue some good food and wine from the fire, and look who we found wandering through the hallway, looking for the way out." And he gripped the arm of Isaac of York, who was gasping for air as he stumbled across the stone floor.

The old man lifted his eyes in time to see two riders crossing the drawbridge on one horse. He clutched at his breast as tears filled his eyes and rolled down his cheeks. "My child! My Rebecca!"

"My Child! My Rebecca!"

A Pile of Burnt Wood and Stone.

CHAPTER 13

De Bracy Brings News
to Prince John

From the edge of the forest, the victorious Saxons and their Norman prisoners gazed in wonder as the towering flames lit up the evening sky. Before the fire burned itself out, Torquilstone Castle had collapsed to the ground, a pile of burnt wood and stone.

After several minutes, Robin spoke to the Black Knight and Cedric. "My men gathered many treasures from the castle before the fire got out of control. I want to divide them evenly and reward our men as well."

"I have no need of any further treasures," replied Cedric, "and I am able to reward my men from my own wealth."

"And I," added the Black Knight, "ask only that Maurice de Bracy be given to me as my prisoner, to do with as I wish."

Robin nodded. "I'll do as you ask, but I'd prefer to hang the Norman dog!"

"Thank you, Robin," said the Black Knight as he wheeled his horse around and made his way towards De Bracy.

"You are free," he told the Norman. "I'll take no revenge against you if you leave England at once. But if you ever return to this land, you will pay for your crimes with your life."

De Bracy bowed to the Black Knight, then leaped onto the back of a horse rescued from Front-de-Boeuf's stables and set off for York. He was loyal enough to Prince John to want to warn him not to proceed with the ceremonies crowning himself king.

De Bracy rode all night and reached York

"You Are Free."

the following morning. By then, reports had reached Prince John that his three trusted Norman knights had been killed or taken prisoner at Torquilstone as the result of De Bracy's foolish kidnapping scheme.

"If those three knights are still alive, I'll hang them!" John raged to Fitzurse. "They were to be here to support me at my coronation, not disrupt it by some ridiculous kidnapping to impress a Saxon woman!"

"Just remember, Your Highness, that if they *are* alive, they'll be important friends and could be dangerous enemies."

"Yes, yes, yes," replied John impatiently. "But we'll find out soon enough. There's De Bracy entering the hall now."

"Good God!" cried Fitzurse. "He's covered with blood and dirt. The battle must have been terrible. Try to hide your anger."

Prince John stood to welcome De Bracy. "What news do you bring, my loyal knight?"

"Bad news, I fear. Front-de-Boeuf is dead

"He's Covered with Blood and Dirt."

and Bois-Guilbert has fled with Rebecca of York. But I have worse news, Your Highness. Your brother Richard is in England, alive."

Prince John's knees buckled under him, and he clutched a chair for support. "You're mad, De Bracy! What you say is impossible!"

"No, Your Highness. I spoke with him myself. He's been disguised so no one knew who he was. But he revealed his identity to me."

"Where is he now?"

"With the outlaw band that attacked and destroyed Torquilstone."

"Then you must capture him before he returns to claim the throne!"

"I? No, Your Highness. I've been warned to leave England under penalty of death, and I'll flee to France now that I've done my duty to you. I'd advise you to escape as well, rather than suffer the shame or even death that Richard would inflict on you."

"Leave at once, coward! I have no need for knights who refuse to do my bidding!"

"You're Mad, De Bracy!"

Once De Bracy had bowed and gone, Prince John turned to Fitzurse. "And now, my good Waldemar, will you, too, fail me or do you have the loyalty and courage to find Richard the Lion-Hearted and see to it that he never reaches York alive?"

Waldemar Fitzurse saw an opportunity to further ensure his rise to power as Chancellor once John was crowned king. So he bowed low and replied, "While I am not a violent man, Your Highness, my loyalty to you and my promise to help you gain the throne require me to do what you ask. I will summon my most trusted men and carry out your orders."

Even though Fitzurse had been his trusted advisor, by now Prince John was so crazed, he was doubting everyone's loyalty. As the man turned his back and left the hall, John muttered to himself, "If you betray me, Waldemar Fitzurse, I'll have your head, even if Richard were breaking down the doors of my castle while I was doing it!"

He Was Doubting Everyone's Loyalty.

"It's Bois-Gilbert and Rebecca."

CHAPTER 14

Accused of Sorcery!

Prince John spent the entire day pacing nervously in his private apartment and the entire night tossing and turning in his bed. The following morning, Fitzurse entered the hall with more surprising news. "Your Highness, you have more visitors today."

"I don't care to see anyone!"

"I think you'll want to see these two. It's Bois-Guilbert and Rebecca."

"Bring them both in. Now maybe we'll find out what really happened at Torquilstone."

Prince John hid his anger as he welcomed

the Templar. "Sir Brian, how glad I am to see that you escaped unharmed from the fires at Torquilstone. But why did you take the daughter of Isaac with you?"

"I love this woman and didn't want any harm to come to her."

"Harm!" cried Rebecca angrily. "You kidnapped me and are holding me prisoner."

At that moment, Fitzurse whispered something to the prince, and John turned to Rebecca. "I am told that you are a sorceress, a witch with great powers. Why couldn't you use those powers to escape from this knight?"

"I am *not* a sorceress, Your Highness. I use my healing powers only to ease the pain of the sick and wounded. My medicines and ointments are made with ingredients that respected Jewish physicians have been using for centuries to cure your people and mine. I was taught to use them by Miriam, who—"

"—Who was accused of witchcraft and burned at the stake!" shouted Fitzurse.

"I Am *Not* a Sorceress."

"She was *not* a witch! Nor am I."

"But surely you must be," said John, smiling cruelly. "Look at how you have enchanted one of the bravest and most loyal knights in all of England. Why, he risked his life rescuing you from the fire and now he risks his reputation by bringing you here."

"That is true, Your Highness," admitted Bois-Guilbert. "I *did* risk my life and my honor. I confessed my love to Rebecca and she rejected me. Even now she continues to reject me. What am I to do?"

"The matter is not for you to decide, Sir Brian," Prince John said firmly. "I decree that this woman is to be brought to trial tomorrow morning on charges of witchcraft."

Even Fitzurse was shocked at the speed with which the prince was scheduling the trial. Then he thought to himself, "I guess a trial can proceed rapidly when the judge has already decided on the verdict and the sentence in advance." But he leaned over to the

Charges of Witchcraft.

prince and whispered, "Do we have enough evidence against this woman to convict her?"

"Find witnesses who will testify to her sorcery, even if you have to pay them to lie about it," John whispered back. Then aloud, he ordered, "Guards, lock this woman in a room and see to it that no one, not even Sir Brian de Bois-Guilbert, talks to her."

"But Your Highness," protested the Templar, "I love this woman. If it please—"

"Say no more, Sir Brian. I am doing what is best for your honor and for England. Be here for the sorceress's trial tomorrow. . . . And you, Fitzurse, see to it that all of York is notified of this trial, all the nobles and peasants. I'll show them just how brilliant and powerful a king I can be!"

"Actually stupid and weak," thought Fitzurse. "But with a brilliant and powerful chancellor like me at his side, no one need ever know!"

"Actually Stupid and Weak."

Crowding To See the Witch

CHAPTER 15

Demand a Trial by Combat

The castle bell tolled eight when the guards unlocked Rebecca's door and led the young woman to the great hall. Seated on a raised throne was Prince John, with Fitzurse at his side. Below him were seats for the Norman knights already in York for his coronation. Those seats were all filled, except the one reserved for Brian de Bois-Guilbert.

Along both sides of the long hall were wooden benches for the peasants. But as Rebecca was being led in, they were on their feet, crowding to see the witch. As she passed through them, her head down and her arms at her sides, Rebecca felt a piece of paper being pushed into her hand. She didn't look to see who had passed it to her or what was written on it. She was just grateful at the thought that somewhere in this crowd, she had a friend.

At the same moment that Rebecca was seated on a small wooden bench in the center of the hall, Bois-Guilbert slid into his seat in the row of knights.

At a signal from Prince John, Waldemar Fitzurse unrolled a scroll and began to read. "By order of John, Prince of England, we have summoned before us Rebecca of York on charges of witchcraft and sorcery, and of using those powers to put under her spell a true and honest knight of the finest order, Sir Brian de Bois-Guilbert."

The first witness, a castle guard, told such an exaggerated story of Bois-Guilbert's bravery during the fire that he swore, "The knight must have been under the spell of some

Unrolling a Scroll

supernatural power, like a witch's."

The next witness, a poor peasant, was dragged in on crutches. He tearfully testified that years ago an illness had left him bedridden, but after Rebecca treated him, he was able to walk again, even though it was on crutches. "She meant me no harm. She treated me no differently because I am a Christian than she treated her own people, and she even gave me a supply of that ointment to use on my weak legs." And the man reached into his tunic and took out a tin.

Fitzurse grabbed the tin and passed it to two of the king's medical advisors—one, a monk and the other, a barber. The men examined the ointment, which was nothing more than a mixture of some herbs, but they were unable to identify it. Not wanting to admit their ignorance, they reported to Fitzurse, "It is no ointment known to man. It must have been given to that woman by the devil!"

Gasps of horror passed among the crowd.

Ointments from the Devil!

Heads nodded and fingers pointed at the accused woman.

The next witness was a soldier who testified, "I saw her bending over a wounded man at Torquilstone. She made some magical signs over his wounds and chanted some mysterious words. Suddenly, the iron tip of an arrow popped out of his wound without a drop of blood showing. Moments later, the wound was healed as if it had never been there. The dying man then stood up and stepped out onto the parapet to help us defend the castle."

"And were there any other incidents of this woman's sorcery?" asked Fitzurse.

"Yes, I saw another. The witch was standing on the edge of the parapet outside her window. I thought she was going to jump, even though Sir Brian de Bois-Guilbert was with her. Then suddenly, she changed herself into a black swan and flew around the castle three times. When she landed once more on the parapet, she changed back into a woman."

Fingers Pointed at the Accused Woman!

This time, the crowd was stunned into silence, afraid that if they whispered even one word, the witch would enchant them.

Fitzurse broke the silence. "You have heard the evidence against you, Rebecca of York. Before Prince John pronounces your sentence, do you have anything to say?"

Rebecca stood proudly and spoke with dignity. "I have committed no crime by relieving the suffering of the sick or wounded, whether they be Christians or Jews. And certainly you, Sir Brian, know that these monstrous accusations are lies. On your honor as a knight, will you not speak up for me?"

Bois-Guilbert's face twisted in pain as he looked from Rebecca to Prince John. What was more important—his love for this fearless young woman or his loyalty to Prince John and his honor among his fellow knights? He knew he couldn't change the verdict, but there was a chance of changing Rebecca's death sentence—the cruel, slow torture of being burned

"Will You Not Speak Up for Me?"

at the stake!

In a voice barely above a whisper, Bois-Guilbert said, "The paper! The paper!"

"Aha!" cried Fitzurse. "That's more proof. The knight is so bewitched by this woman, he can only babble about some paper. She must have a magic spell written on some paper."

But Rebecca understood what Bois-Guilbert meant. She looked down at the piece of paper hidden in her hand and silently read the words on it: *Demand a trial by combat.* She quickly crumpled it without being seen and tucked it into the sleeve of her dress. Then lifting her head high, she spoke in a proud, clear voice. "I still swear that I am innocent, that the accusations against me are all lies. I have only one chance left to save my life according to your laws of chivalry, and that chance is by demanding a trial by combat. If someone will come forth and fight on my behalf and win, I shall be set free. If not, I am prepared to die."

As she said that, Rebecca tore off her glove

"The Paper! The Paper!"

and threw it at Prince John's feet—a challenge that couldn't be refused.

Prince John picked up the glove with an evil laugh. "I accept this challenge. The prisoner has three days in which to find someone to defend her against my own Champion. To defend the honor of the crown, I now name the noble knight, Sir Brian de Bois-Guilbert!"

The Templar shuddered and thought, "How cruel of him to choose me! How can I live with myself, knowing I'll be the one who'll send the woman I love to her death?"

The crippled peasant, who had been forced to testify, offered to carry Rebecca's plea to Isaac. "Tell my father that the one man who would surely face Bois-Guilbert as my Champion is Ivanhoe. But I fear he is still too weak to fight. So, if my father can't find anyone else, I shall die with courage."

A Challenge that Couldn't Be Refused.

"I know I Must Leave."

CHAPTER 16

The Final Battle

After the Black Knight rescued Ivanhoe from the burning castle, Gurth took him to a convent to rest while his wounds healed. Rebecca's ointments had been so effective that after only a few days, Ivanhoe was on his feet and anxious to leave. He explained to Gurth, "I have a strange feeling that something evil is about to happen. I can't explain it, but I know I must leave."

Gurth had almost convinced Ivanhoe to rest for one more day when a messenger rode in with an urgent letter from Isaac for him.

"My premonition of evil has come to pass," said Ivanhoe after reading the letter. "I must leave immediately and ride hard if I am to reach York in time to to help Rebecca."

So Ivanhoe set off for York, where a field of combat and death was already set up outside the castle walls. Galleries and benches had been built for the spectators. Piles of dried sticks had been heaped around a stake where a witch would be burned.

At dawn, church bells summoned everyone. Peasants and lesser nobles crowded into their seats. A trumpet announced the entry of the royal procession. Prince John rode in first, followed by Bois-Guilbert and high-ranking nobles and knights.

Behind the riders walked the prisoner, in a plain white dress. All of her jewelry had been taken from her for fear that some of it contained charms with which she could summon powers from the devil. She held her head high and her face showed dignity and courage.

A Royal Procession

She was led to a black chair placed in front of the funeral pyre. Before she sat down, she glanced at the stake, then shut her eyes and shuddered.

After a flourish of the trumpets, a herald stepped forward and announced, "Hear ye! Hear ye! Here stands Sir Brian de Bois-Guilbert ready to do battle with any challenger who comes forth to defend Rebecca of York."

The trumpets sounded again. Then silence. And more silence. No challenger appeared.

"We've waited three days for a challenger. We'll wait one more hour," said Prince John, "to show that I *am* a fair and just ruler."

During that hour, Rebecca's eyes were fixed on the ground. She didn't raise them until Bois-Guilbert rode towards her.

"Don't come near me, you hard-hearted man!" she whispered. "It's your fault that I'm to go to my death at the stake."

"I can't let that happen. I was given permission to speak to you by telling the prince that

No Challenger Appeared.

you might confess to me. But that's not what I want. Please, Rebecca, climb up on my horse with me. We will flee this combat and flee England together. I no longer care that the name of Bois-Guilbert will be shamed and dishonored. I care only that you live."

"Leave me! You are my enemy. You are evil! I'd rather die than run away with you."

Fitzurse came out onto the field and asked the Templar, "Well, has she confessed?"

"No. Take your hands off my reins or —"

But at that moment, a knight sped onto the field and stopped the Templar's protest. In spite of the crowd's desire to see a witch burned, a cry went up. "A challenger is here! Rebecca's challenger has arrived!"

But as horse and rider came closer, the exhausted appearance of the animal and the unsteady posture of the rider dismayed the crowd. However, when the knight was asked to identify himself, he spoke in a firm voice.

"I am a noble knight ready to defend Rebec-

A Knight Sped onto the Field.

ca with my sword and lance, to prove that the accusations against her are false, and to defy Brian de Bois-Guilbert, who is a traitor, a liar, and a murderer!"

"Who dares make those accusations? Your name, Sir Knight?" demanded the Templar.

Raising his helmet, the knight replied, "A name and lance you know well, Bois-Guilbert, for they defeated you in tournaments in the Holy Land and at Ashby. My name is Ivanhoe!"

With that, he closed his visor and rode toward his starting post, his lance upright. The Templar did the same, but as his squire assisted him in his final preparations, he noticed that his master's face was strangely pale and he was almost gasping for breath.

Once the two knights were in place, the trumpets blared and the charge began. Ivanhoe's weary horse went down at the first thrust of Bois-Guilbert's lance. Even though Ivanhoe's lance barely touched the Templar's

"My name is Ivanhoe!"

shield, Bois-Guilbert reeled in the saddle and fell from his horse.

Ivanhoe pulled himself free from under his fallen horse and got to his feet. Placing his sword at the bars of the Templar's visor, Ivanhoe commanded, "Give up or die!" But Bois-Guilbert didn't move.

"Wait! Don't slay him!" cried Prince John. "We acknowledge you, Ivanhoe, the winner."

John's guards rushed onto the field to aid the Templar, but when they removed his helmet, they found his eyes closed and his face ashen. Brian de Bois-Guilbert was dead.

"He didn't die from my lance," said Ivanhoe, "and I don't claim his horse or armor or weapons as my reward. His heart failed him as a punishment for his crimes."

At that moment, hundreds of horses rode onto the field, shaking the ground before them. Leading the group of knights and soldiers and yeomen was the Black Knight.

Stopping before Ivanhoe, the Black Knight

Brian de Bois-Gilbert was Dead.

cried, "Foolish lad! You shouldn't have attempted this combat while you were still so weak. But it turned out well, and you saved the maiden's life."

Then, turning to the royal gallery, the Black Knight called, "Waldemar Fitzurse, I arrest you on charges of treason."

"Who dares arrest my advisor?" demanded Prince John.

"I do," replied the Black Knight, as he removed his helmet. "I, King Richard of England, the brother you hoped was dead."

Prince John fell back into his chair. "But-but I didn't—"

"Silence, brother! In spite of your treachery, I cannot condemn you, my own flesh and blood, to death. You will stay at our mother's castle until all is quiet and there is peace between Saxons and Normans."

"Long live King Richard! Long live the Lion-Hearted!" cheered the spectators.

Isaac had arrived with King Richard and

"The Brother You Hoped Was Dead."

now rushed to his daughter's side. "Let us hurry and thank Ivanhoe this very moment."

"No, I cannot. I fear that I will show my true feelings for him, and that can never be. Ivanhoe loves Rowena and it is she who will become his wife, just as they have planned for so many years. I have no place in his life."

"As you wish, my child," said Isaac as he took his daughter in his arms and led her off the field.

Rebecca and Isaac traveled to Spain, where they lived peacefully and where Rebecca continued caring for the sick and wounded.

Cedric welcomed Ivanhoe back into his home, proud of his son's bravery and happy to approve of his marriage to Rowena.

King Richard's hopes for peace finally did come to pass, and Saxons and Normans learned to live together. As for Ivanhoe, he went on to distinguish himself in the service of King Richard for many years to come.

Happy To Approve His Marriage

MICROLITHOGRAPHY

Science and Technology

MICROLITHOGRAPHY
Science and Technology

edited by

James R. Sheats
Hewlett-Packard Laboratories
Palo Alto, California

Bruce W. Smith
Rochester Institute of Technology
Rochester, New York

MARCEL DEKKER, INC.   NEW YORK · BASEL

Library of Congress Cataloging-in-Publication Data

Sheats, James R.
  Microlithography: science and technology / James R. Sheats, Bruce W. Smith.
    p. cm.
  Includes bibliographical references and index.
  ISBN 0-8247-9953-4 (alk. paper)
    1. Microlithography. 2. Integrated circuits—Masks. 3. Metal oxide semiconductors,
Complementary—Design and construction. 4. Manufacturing processes. I. Smith,
Bruce W. II. Title.
TK7836.S46   1998
621.3815'31--dc21   98-16713
                                                                                CIP

The publisher offers discounts on this book when ordered in bulk quantities. For more information, write to Special Sales/Professional Marketing at the address below.

This book is printed on acid-free paper.

MARCEL DEKKER, INC.
270 Madison Avenue, New York, New York 10016
http://www.dekker.com

Current printing (last digit):
10 9 8 7 6 5

PRINTED IN THE UNITED STATES OF AMERICA

Preface

The science and practice of microlithography have grown over the last twenty years or so into one of the most sophisticated aspects of the entire integrated circuit (IC) fabrication process. The successful execution of patterning techniques is of the utmost importance to the final product: the cost of a modern complementary metal oxide semiconductor (CMOS) IC process can be closely estimated simply from the number of masking levels. Thus this is an appropriate time for a text that simultaneously provides an introduction for the novice and a useful reference for the experienced worker. We have conceived this volume with such a diverse audience in mind. It is sufficiently self-contained to serve as a complete text in microlithography, requiring only an undergraduate background in physical science or engineering. At the same time, enough detail has been included to provide useful guidance and reference information for active participants in the field.

Part I begins by providing a general overview of microlithography, first from the perspective of the imaging machine (Chapter 1), and then by an exposition of quantitative principles with which the entire process can be modeled on a computer (Chapter 2). The next five chapters are devoted to the machinery of imaging. Chapter 3 provides a thorough treatment of both theoretical and practical optics, including discussion of aberrations, material properties, and optical image enhancement techniques. Chapter 4 introduces the excimer laser, which is a necessary component of the imaging system for modern high-resolution lithography. Chapter 5 develops the theory according to which alignment systems are constructed, and Chapters 6 and 7 complete the coverage of instrumentation with an overview of the fundamentals of electron beam and x-ray lithography, respectively. These two chapters have a different character from the rest of the book, since such systems are not used to a significant extent in high-volume IC production (although optical masks are made exclusively with e-beam lithography). These techniques may play a role in manufacturing as feature sizes approach the limits of conventional device physics, at around 0.07–0.1 µm, and the reader is given a sufficient acquaintance with the surrounding issues to evaluate the trends as they develop.

The next part deals with resists (Chapter 8), including both industry-standard diazonaphthoquinone systems and chemical amplification systems and their processing. Single-layer resist processing—the approach still used almost exclusively in manufacturing today—is covered in Chapter 9, and Chapter 10 describes the multilayer techniques that are likely to be needed as exposure wavelengths move further into the far ultraviolet. The interplay of resist design with plasma etching, which is the dominant etch technique for high-resolution lithography, is addressed in Chapter 11.

Chapter 12 describes the important subject of how to measure the results of a lithographic process and provides extensive accuracy and precision analysis for a variety of tools (including electron beam, optical, and atomic force microscopes). Finally, Chapter 13 takes a tentative peek at the future of nanolithography," in which critical feature widths may be less than 100 nm, and patterning based on conventional optics will be impossible. One possibility is to simply continue the trend of reducing wavelength, which takes one into x-rays. Unfortunately, this "simple" continuation leads into an entirely different and formidable set of material, instrumental, and process issues, and as discussed in Chapter 7, may or may not be economically feasible. The alternatives, also in the research stage, are direct writing with high-energy electron beams (using multiple emitting tips to get sufficient speed) or proximal probe techniques (based on the fundamental concept of the scanning tunneling microscope). From this discussion one can see that despite the immense power of present-day microlithography, there is plenty of room for innovation in the decade to come.

James R. Sheats
Bruce W. Smith

Contents

Part II. Resists and Processing

Part III. Metrology and Nanolithography

Contributors

Palash Das   Cymer, Inc., San Diego, California

Elizabeth A. Dobisz   Naval Research Laboratory, Washington, D.C.

Gregg M. Gallatin   SVG Lithography, Wilton, Connecticut

Maureen Hanratty   Texas Instruments, Dallas, Texas

Michael S. Hibbs   IBM Microelectronic Division, Essex Junction, Vermont

Roderick R. Kunz   Massachusetts Institute of Technology, Lexington, Massachusetts

Chris A. Mack   FINLE Technologies, Austin, Texas

Herschel M. Marchman*   AT&T Bell Laboratories, Murray Hill, New Jersey

Geraint Owen   Hewlett-Packard Laboratories, Palo Alto, California

Martin C. Peckerar   Naval Research Laboratory, Washington, D.C.

Current affiliation: Texas Instruments SPDC, Dallas Texas

F. Keith Perkins   Naval Research Laboratory, Washington, D.C.

Uday Sengupta   ASIA QUEST Inc., San Diego, California

James R. Sheats   Hewlett-Packard Laboratories, Palo Alto, California

Bruce W. Smith   Rochester Institute of Technology, Rochester, New York

Takumi Ueno   Hitachi Ltd., Ibaraki-ken, Japan

MICROLITHOGRAPHY

Science and Technology

1

System Overview of Optical Steppers and Scanners

Michael S. Hibbs

IBM Microelectronic Division
Essex Junction, Vermont

1 INTRODUCTION

Microlithography is a manufacturing process for producing highly accurate, microscopic, two-dimensional patterns in a photosensitive resist material. These patterns are replicas of a master pattern on a durable photomask, typically made of a thin patterned layer of chromium on a transparent glass plate. At the end of the lithographic process, the photoresist is used to create a useful structure in the device that is being built. For example, trenches can be etched into an insulator, or a uniform coating of metal can be etched to leave a network of electrical wiring on the surface of a semiconductor chip. Microlithography is used at every stage of the semiconductor manufacturing process. An advanced memory chip can have 20 or more masking levels, and approximately one third of the total cost of semiconductor manufacture can be attributed to microlithographic processing.

The progress of microlithography has been measured by the ever-smaller sizes of the images that can be printed. There is a strong economic incentive for improving lens resolution. A decrease in minimum image size by a factor of 2 leads to a factor of 4 increase in the number of circuits that can be built on a given area of the semiconductor chip, as well as significant increases in switching speeds. It has been traditional to define a decrease in minimum image size by a factor of $1/\sqrt{2}$ as a new lithographic generation. These lithographic generations are roughly coincident with generations of dynamic random-access memory (DRAM) chips, which are defined by an increase in memory storage by a factor of 4. Table 1

1

Table 1 Seven Lithographic and DRAM Generations

DRAM storage (megabits)	1	4	16	64	256	1024	4096
Minimum image size (μm)	1.00	0.70	0.50	0.35	0.25	0.18	0.13

shows the correspondence of lithographic and DRAM generations. About half of the 4× increase per generation in DRAM capacity is due to the reduced lithographic image size, and the remaining increase is accomplished by advances in design techniques and by increasing the physical dimensions of the DRAM. Historically, there have been about 3 years between lithographic generations, with leading-edge manufacturing at 0.35 μm starting in 1995.

2 THE LITHOGRAPHIC EXPOSURE SYSTEM

At the heart of the microlithographic process is the exposure system. This complex piece of machinery projects the image of a desired photomask pattern onto the surface of the semiconductor device being fabricated on a silicon wafer. The image is captured in a thin layer of a resist material and transformed into a permanent part of the device by a series of chemical etch or deposition processes. The accuracy with which the pattern must be formed is astonishing: lines smaller than a micron must be produced with dimensional tolerances of a few tens of nanometers, and the pattern must be aligned with underlying layers of patterns to better than one fourth of the minimum line width. All of these tolerances must be met throughout an exposure field of several square centimeters. A lithographic exposure system filling an enclosure the size of a small office and costing several million dollars is used to meet these severe requirements.

An exposure system for optical microlithography consists of three parts: a lithographic lens, an illumination system, and a wafer positioning system. A typical exposure system will be described in detail, followed by an expanded description of the many possible variations on the typical design.

2.1 The Lithographic Projection Lens

The lithographic lens is a physically large, compound lens. It is made up of 10 to 20 simple lens elements, mounted in a massive, rigid barrel. The total assembly can weigh more than 100 pounds. The large number of elements is needed to correct optical aberrations to a very high degree over a 30-mm circular field of exposure. The lens is designed to produce an optical image of a photomask, reduced by a demagnification of 5×. A silicon wafer, containing hundreds of partially fabricated integrated circuits, is exposed to this image. The image is captured by a layer of photosensitive resist, and this latent image

Figure 1 Optical layout of a small-field, experimental lithographic lens. This lens was designed in 1985. More recent lenses used in commercial microlithography are even more complex.

will eventually be chemically developed to leave the desired resist pattern. Every aspect of the lens design has extremely tight tolerances. In order to produce the smallest possible images, the resolution of the lens must be limited only by fundamental diffraction effects. In practice, this means that the total wavefront aberration at every point in the exposure field must be less than 1/10 of the optical wavelength. The focal plane of the lens must not deviate from planarity by more than about 0.1 μm over the entire usable exposure field, and the maximum transverse geometrical distortion must be less than about 0.05 μm. The lens is corrected for chromatic aberration over a narrow range of wavelengths centered on the illumination wavelength of 365 nm.

2.2   The Illumination Subsystem

The illumination source for the exposure system is a 1000-W, high-pressure mercury arc lamp. An elliptical mirror is used to collect this light, and the undesired wavelengths are removed with multilayer dielectric filters. The remaining 365-nm light is sent through a series of relay optics and uniformizing optics and is then projected through the photomask. Nonuniformity of the illumination

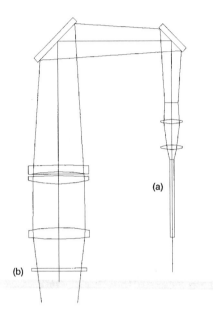

Figure 2   A rather simple, experimental illuminator. Laser light is randomized in a light tunnel (a), then projected through a series of five lenses and two folding mirrors onto a photomask (b). This illuminator was designed to be used with the lithographic lens in Fig. 1.

intensity at the photomask must be less than about 1%. The light continues through the photomask to form an image of the effective illumination source in the entrance pupil of the lithographic lens. The fraction of the pupil filled by the illumination source's image determines the degree of coherence in the lithographic lens's image formation. The light traversing the entire chain of illuminator and lithographic lens optics forms an image with an intensity of a few hundred mW/cm^2. A fast shutter within the illuminator assembly exposes the photoresist to the image for a few tenths of a second. The integrated energy of each exposure must be repeatable to within 1%. Although the tolerances of the illuminator are not as tight as those of the lithographic lens, its optical quality must be surprisingly high. Severe aberrations in the illumination optics will produce a variety of problems in the final image, even if there are no aberrations in the lithographic lens.

2.3   The Wafer Positioning Subsystem

The wafer positioning system is one of the most precise mechanical systems used in any technology today. A silicon wafer, typically 150 to 200 mm in diameter, may contain 100 or more semiconductor devices, called "chips." Each chip in its turn must be physically aligned to the image being projected by the lithographic lens and held in alignment with a tolerance of about 100 nm during the exposure. To expose all the chips on a wafer sequentially, the wafer is held by a vacuum chuck on an ultraprecision x-y stage. The stage position is determined by laser interferometry to an accuracy of better than 20 nm. The stage has less than 1 second to move between successive exposure sites and settle to within the alignment tolerance before the next exposure begins. This sequence of stepping from one exposure to the next has led this type of system to be called a step-and-repeat lithographic system, or more informally a "stepper." Prior to exposure, the position of the wafer must be determined as accurately as possible with an automatic alignment system. This system looks for standardized alignment marks that were printed on the wafer during previous levels of lithography. The position of these marks is determined by one of a variety of optical detection techniques. A number of different alignment strategies can be used, but at minimum the within-plane rotation error of the wafer and its x- and y-translation errors must be determined relative to the projected image. The positioning system must reduce these errors to within the alignment tolerance before each exposure begins.

The stepper must also automatically detect the surface of the resist and position this surface at the correct height to match the exact focal plane of the stepper lens within a tolerance of about 200 nm. In order to meet this tolerance over a large exposure field, it is also necessary to detect and correct tilt errors along two orthogonal axes. The wafer surface is not flat enough to guarantee that the focus tolerance will be satisfied everywhere on the wafer simultaneously, so the automated focus procedure is repeated at every exposure site on the wafer.

During the entire process of loading a wafer, aligning, stepping, focusing, exposing, and unloading, speed of the process is of utmost importance. A stepper that can expose 60 wafers in an hour can pay back its huge capital cost twice as fast as a stepper than can manage only 30 wafers per hour.

3 VARIATIONS ON A THEME

The typical stepper outlined in the previous section has been the standard equipment for semiconductor microlithography for the past 10 years. But a number of other styles of equipment have been used as well. Some of these other variations were the historical predecessors of today's steppers. Many of them are still in use today, earning their keep by providing low-cost lithography for low-density semiconductor designs. Other variations on the basic design fill specialized niches in the lithography market or represent new designs that may someday become the new standard.

3.1 Optical Contact Printing and Proximity Printing

The earliest exposure systems were contact printers and proximity printers. In these systems, a chrome-on-glass mask is held in close proximity or in actual contact with a photoresist-covered wafer. The resist is exposed through the back side of the mask by a flood exposure source. The mask pattern covers the entire wafer and is necessarily designed with a magnification of 1×. Alignment is accomplished by an operator manipulating a mechanical stage to superimpose two previously printed alignment marks on the wafer with corresponding alignment marks on the mask. Alignment of the two pairs of marks is verified by the operator through a split-field microscope that can view opposite sides of the wafer simultaneously. The wafer and mask can be aligned with respect to rotation and displacement on two orthogonal axes.

Contact printing provides higher resolution than proximity printing but at the cost of enormous wear and tear on the masks. No matter how scrupulous the attention to cleanliness, particles of dirt eventually are ground into the surfaces of the wafer and the mask during the exposure. A frequent source of contamination is fragments of photoresist that adhere to the surface of the mask when it makes contact with the wafer. Masks have to be cleaned frequently and finally replaced as they wear out. This technology is not used in mainstream semiconductor manufacture today.

Proximity printing is much more kind to the masks but in many ways is a more demanding technology [1]. The proximity gap has to be as small as possible to avoid loss of resolution from optical diffraction. The resolution limit for a proximity printer is proportional to $\sqrt{\lambda d}$, where λ is the exposure wavelength and d is the proximity gap. When optical or near-ultraviolet exposure wavelengths are used, the minimum image sizes that can be practically achieved are around 2 or 3 μm. This limits optical proximity printing to the most undemanding applications of semiconductor lithography.

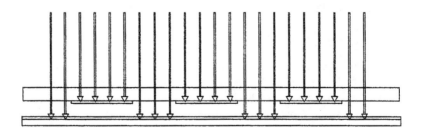

Figure 3   In optical proximity printing light is blocked from the photosensitive resist layer by chromium patterns on a photomask. The gap between the mask and the resist must be as small as possible to minimize diffractive blurring at the edges of the patterns.

3.2 X-ray Proximity Lithography

A more modern variation of optical proximity printing is x-ray proximity lithography. The diffractive effects that limit resolution are greatly reduced by the very short wavelengths of the x-rays used, typically around 1.0 to 1.5 nm, corresponding to a 1-keV x-ray energy. This represents a wavelength decrease of a factor of 300 relative to optical proximity lithography, or an improvement in resolution by a factor of about 15. X-ray proximity lithography is capable of the best resolution of any lithographic technology today, but it has been held back from large-scale manufacturing by a variety of technical and financial hurdles [2]. The electron synchrotron used as the x-ray source is very expensive and must support a very high volume of wafer production to make it affordable. Since a single electron synchrotron will act as the illumination source for a dozen wafer aligners or more, a failure of the synchrotron could halt production on an entire manufacturing line.

Each x-ray mask alignment system requires a helium atmosphere to prevent absorption and scattering of the x-rays. This complicates the transfer of wafers and masks to and from the exposure system.

The most challenging feature of x-ray proximity lithography is the difficulty of producing the 1× membrane mask to the required tolerances. Since the mask-making infrastructure in the semiconductor industry is largely geared to 4× and 5× reduction masks, considerable improvements in mask-making technology are needed to produce the much smaller features on a 1× mask. Proportional reductions in line width tolerance and placement tolerance are also needed. X-ray proximity lithography has been under development for many years with the support of national governments and large semiconductor corporations. The continued progress of optical reduction lithography has always kept x-ray proximity lithography in the role of a "next-generation" technology. This will probably continue to be the case until optical lithography runs into serious difficulties at image dimensions between 0.15 and 0.10 μm. At that time, x-rays may become the dominant microlithographic technology, or they may be overtaken by one of the other experimental lithographic techniques that are now at the stage of laboratory research projects.

3.3 1× Scanners

In the 1970s, optical proximity printing was replaced by the newly developed scanning lithography [3]. Optical scanners are able to project the image of a mask through a lens system onto the surface of a wafer. The mask is the same as that used by a proximity printer: a 1× chrome-on-glass pattern that is large enough to cover the entire wafer. But the use of a projection system means that masks are no longer damaged by accidental or deliberate contact with the wafer surface. It would be difficult to design a lens capable of projecting micron-scale images onto an entire 4- to 6-inch wafer in a single field of view. But a clever design by the Perkin-Elmer Corporation allows wafers of this size to be printed by simultaneously scanning the mask and wafer through a lens field shaped like a narrow arc. The lens design takes advantage of the fact that most lens aberrations are functions of the radial position within the field of view. A lens with an extremely large circular field can be designed, with aberrations corrected only at a single radius within this field. An aperture limits the exposure field to a narrow arc centered on this radius. Because the projector operates at 1× magnification, a rather simple mechanical system can scan the wafer and mask simultaneously through the object and image fields of the lens.

Resolution of the projection optics is determined by the wavelength and numerical aperture using Rayleigh's formula,

$$D = k_1 \frac{\lambda}{\text{NA}}$$

where D is the minimum dimension that can be printed, λ is the exposure wavelength, and NA is the numerical aperture of the projection lens. The proportionality constant k_1 is a dimensionless number in an approximate range from 0.6 to 0.8. The numerical aperture of the Perkin-Elmer scanner is about 0.17,

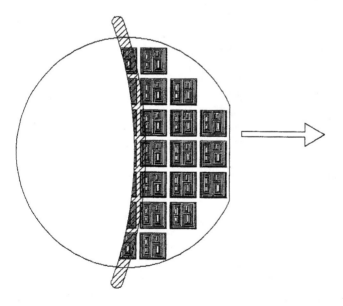

Figure 4   A scanning exposure system projects the image of a 1× mask into an arc-shaped slit. The wafer and mask are simultaneously scanned across the field aperture (shaded area) until the entire wafer is exposed.

and its illumination source contains a broad band of wavelengths centered around 400 nm. The Rayleigh formula predicts a minimum image size somewhat smaller than 2 μm for this system.

The 1× scanners are still in common use for semiconductor lithography throughout the world. Resolution of these systems can be pushed to nearly 1 μm by using a deep-ultraviolet light source at 250-nm wavelength. But the most advanced lithography is being done by reduction projectors, similar to the one described in the example at the beginning of this chapter. The one advantage still retained by a 1× scanner is the immense size of the scanned field. Some semiconductor devices, such as two-dimensional video detector arrays, require this large field size, but in most cases the need for smaller images has driven lithography toward steppers or the newer step-and-scan technology.

3.4 Reduction Steppers

Steppers were first commercialized in the early 1980s [4]. A projection lens is used with a field size just large enough to expose one or two semiconductor chips. The fields are exposed sequentially, with the wafer being repositioned by an accurate *x-y* stage between exposures. The time to expose a wafer is considerably greater than with a scanner, but there are some great advantages to

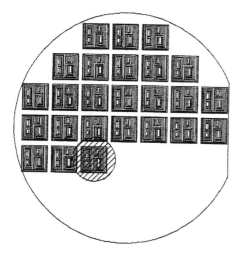

Figure 5   A stepper employs reduction optics and exposes only one chip at a time. The 4× or 5× mask remains stationary with respect to the lens, whose maximum exposure field is shown as the shaded area. After each chip is exposed, a high-precision stage moves the wafer to the position where the next exposure will occur. If the chip pattern is small enough, two or more chips may be printed in each exposure.

stepper lithography. The stepper lens can be made with a considerably higher numerical aperture than is practical for the full-wafer scanner lenses. The earliest steppers had numerical apertures of 0.28, yielding a resolution of about 1.25 μm at an exposure wavelength of 436 nm (the mercury g line). Another key advantage of steppers is their ability to use a reduction lens. The demagnification factor of 4× to 10× provides considerable relief in the minimum feature size and dimensional tolerances that are required on the mask.

The resolution of steppers has improved considerably since their first introduction. The numerical aperture of lithographic lens designs has gradually increased, so that today values above 0.50 are commonly available. At the same time, there have been incremental changes in the exposure wavelength. In the mid-1980s there was a shift from the g-line (436 nm) to i-line (365 nm) wavelength for leading-edge lithography. More recently steppers are being designed to use deep-ultraviolet wavelengths around 248 nm. This combination of higher numerical aperture and shorter wavelength allows a resolution of 0.5 μm to be routinely achieved and 0.35-μm resolution to be produced in the most advanced production lines of 1995. Future extensions to numerical apertures greater than 0.60, coupled with recent advances in lithographic enhancement techniques such as phase-shifting masks and off-axis illumination, give lithographers great confidence that 0.25-μm resolution will be a practical reality in the very near future. Even the 0.18-μm lithographic generation is being targeted in semiconductor development laboratories around the world, with the expectation that a combination of enhancement techniques and even shorter wavelengths (around 193 nm) will achieve this target before the year 2000.

3.5   1× Steppers

Although the main development of lithography over the past decade has been with the use of reduction steppers, a few other notable lithographic techniques have been used. The Ultratech Stepper Corporation developed a stepper with 1× magnification, using a particularly simple and elegant lens design. This lens design has been adapted to numerical apertures from 0.35 to 0.70 and wavelengths from 436 nm to 193 nm. The requirement for a 1× mask has prevented the general acceptance of this technology for the most critical levels of lithography, but it is an economical alternative for the less demanding masking levels [5].

3.6   Step-and-Scan

As lithographic image sizes evolve to smaller and smaller dimensions, the size of the semiconductor chip has been gradually increasing. DRAM chips are usually designed as rectangles, with a 2:1 length-to-width ratio. A typical 16-megabit DRAM has dimensions slightly less than 10 × 20 mm, and the linear dimensions tend to increase by 15 to 20% each generation. Two adjacent

DRAM chips form a square that fits into a circular lens field that must be 28 to 30 mm in diameter. Logic circuits, such as microprocessor chips, usually have a square aspect ratio and put similar demands on the field size. The combined requirements of higher numerical aperture and larger field size have been an enormous challenge for lithographic lens design and fabrication. One way to ease the demands on field size is to return to scanning technology. Recently developed lithographic exposure equipment employs a technique called "step-and-scan," in which a reduction lens is used to scan the image of a large exposure field onto a portion of a wafer [6]. The wafer is then moved to a new position where the scanning process is repeated. The lens field is required only to be a narrow slit, as in the older full-wafer scanners. This allows a scanned exposure whose height is the diameter of the static lens field and whose length is limited only by the size of the mask and the travel of the mask-positioning stage.

Step-and-scan technology puts great demands on the mechanical tolerances of the stage motion. Whereas a traditional step-and-repeat system has only to move the wafer rapidly to a new position and hold it accurately in one position during exposure, the step-and-scan mechanism has to move both the mask and wafer simultaneously, holding the positional tolerances within a few tens of nanometers continuously during the scan. Since the step-and-scan technique is

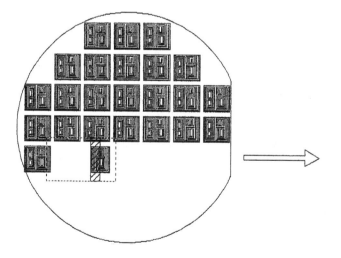

Figure 6 A step-and-scan system combines the operations of a stepper and a scanner. The dashed outline represents the maximum scanned region. The shaded area is the slit-shaped exposure field aperture. The wafer and mask are simultaneously scanned across the field aperture. At the end of the scan, the wafer is stepped to a new position, where the scanning process is repeated. In this example, the 4× mask contains two chip patterns.

used for reduction lithography, the mask must scan at a much different speed than the wafer and possibly in the opposite direction. All of the step-and-scan equipment designed so far has used a 4× reduction ratio. This allows the very large scanned field to be accommodated on a smaller mask than a 5× reduction ratio would permit. It also allows a very accurate digital comparison of the positional data from the wafer stage and mask stage interferometers.

The first step-and-scan exposure system was developed by the Perkin-Elmer Corporation, using an arc-shaped exposure slit. The projection lens had a numerical aperture of 0.35 and was designed to use a broadband light source centered at a wavelength of 248 nm. The advantage of the fixed-radius arc field was not as great for a high-numerical-aperture reduction lens as it had been for the 1× scanners, and all recent step-and-scan systems have been designed with a rectangular slit aperture along a diameter of a conventional circular lens field. Step-and-scan lithographic equipment is now manufactured by Silicon Valley Group Lithography Systems (SVGL), the industrial successor to the Perkin-Elmer lithographic division. Nearly all manufacturers of lithographic equipment have started development work on step-and-scan systems.

Although the difficulties of step-and-scan technology are obvious, the benefit of a large scanned field is great. There are also a few more subtle advantages of step-and-scan technology. Because the exposure field is scanned, a single feature on the mask is imaged through a number of different parts of the lens. Any localized aberrations or distortions in the lens will be somewhat reduced by averaging along the scan direction. Also, any local nonuniformity of illumination intensity is unimportant, as long as the intensity integrated along the scan direction is constant.

3.7 Direct Writing

All of these microlithographic technologies have one thing in common. They are able to print massive amounts of information in parallel. Other technologies have been developed for writing lithographic patterns in a serial fashion. For example, several varieties of electron beam lithographic systems exist. Other systems use scanned, focused laser beams to write patterns in photoresist. The great failure of all of these serial technologies has been their speed of operation. A semiconductor circuit pattern may consist of a 21×21 mm square filled with patterns having a minimum resolvable image size of 0.35 μm. If a pixel is defined as a square one minimum image on a side, then the circuit in this example will be made up of 3.6×10^9 pixels. A serial pattern writer scanning in a raster fashion must sequentially address every one of these pixels. At a data rate of 40 MHz, it will take 90 seconds to write each circuit pattern. If there are 60 such patterns on a wafer, the the wafer writing time will be 1.5 hours. This is nearly two orders of magnitude slower than a parallel exposure system.

Various tricks have been used to increase writing speeds of serial exposure systems (often called direct-write systems). For example, a vector scan strategy may improve the speed of writing by eliminating the need to raster over un-patterned areas of the circuit. A certain amount of parallelism in pattern writing has been introduced with shaped-beam systems, which can project a variable-sized rectangular electron beam [7]. An even greater amount of parallelism is achieved with electron beam cell projectors [8]. These systems use a stencil mask with a small repeating section of a larger circuit pattern. (A stencil mask consists of a thin, strong membrane with holes pierced through the material where the mask pattern is to be printed. These types of mask must be used whenever there is no suitable transparent material to act as the substrate for the absorbing pattern, as with electron beams, soft x-rays, or ion beams. Stencil masks have difficulty with long transparent lines and closed transparent rings, which break the continuity of the membrane. Because of this, stencil masks are usually designed as two complementary patterns, which are exposed sequentially to produce the desired pattern of exposure.) A large circuit can be stitched together from a library of these repeating patterns, using a rectangular shaped-beam strategy to fill in parts of the circuit that are not in the cell library.

But even the fastest direct-write systems are far slower than parallel-exposure systems. Very rarely, direct-write systems have been used for commercial lithography on low-volume, high-value semiconductor circuits. They have also been used occasionally for early development of advanced semiconductor designs, when the parallel-exposure equipment capable of the required resolution has not been developed yet. But the most common use of serial-exposure equipment has been for mask making. In this application, the slow writing time is not as serious an issue. It can make economic sense to spend hours writing a valuable mask. In any case, there is no way to create a pattern from computer data without using a serial-writing system. All of the parallel-printing systems are based on the prior existence of a mask.

3.8 Soft X-Ray Projection Lithography/Extreme Ultraviolet Lithography

The prospect of exploiting the soft x-ray spectrum for projection lithography has recently stirred excitement among researchers. This region of the spectrum, with photon energies around 100 eV and wavelengths around 10 to 15 nm, can be considered either the low-energy end of the x-ray spectrum or the short-wavelength limit of the extreme ultraviolet. Multilayer interference coatings with good x-ray reflectivity at normal incidence have been developed for the x-ray astronomy community. The thought of using these x-ray mirrors as components of an all-reflective lithographic lens has provoked a flurry of research activity. A diffraction-limited lens designed for a 13-nm exposure wavelength can achieve a resolution of 0.1 µm with a numerical aperture of only 0.10. This very modest numerical aperture could allow a fairly simple optical design. Such a projection lens can also be designed with an image size reduction, which eases the tolerances on the mask [9].

The practical difficulties associated with this experimental technology are great. The stepper and x-ray beam delivery line must be in a vacuum or helium atmosphere to prevent absorption and scattering of the x-rays. The multilayer interference mirrors require deposition of tens to hundreds of very accurate films only a few nanometers thick. These mirrors reflect a rather narrow band of x-ray wavelengths and have a reflectivity that varies strongly with angle of incidence. The actual reflectivity achieved by this technology is roughly 50%, which is extremely high for a normal-incidence x-ray mirror but dismally low by the standards of visible-light optics. This reduces the total transmission of an x-ray lithographic lens to a very low value if more than two or three mirrors are used in the entire assembly. The most severe problem with soft x-ray projection lithography is the extremely tight tolerance on the surface accuracy of the lenses. Since wavefront aberrations must be a small fraction of the exposure wavelength and the exposure wavelength is about 13 nm, the surface of each mirror must be finished to tolerances approximating 1 nm or less. Even if this accuracy can be achieved, it will be a difficult task to maintain the surface tolerances in the presence of thermal and mechanical stresses from the environment and the x-ray beam. Lithographic masks for the soft x-ray region of the spectrum must be either stencil masks or reflective masks, both of which have several practical difficulties. From today's perspective, soft x-ray or extreme ultraviolet reduction lithography appears to be destined to remain in the laboratory for many years to come.

3.9 Particle Beam Lithography

Electron beam lithography has already been mentioned as one of the direct-writing lithographic techniques. Charged particle beams have also been explored as exposure sources for masked pattern lithography. Development work has been done on electron beam proximity printing, as well as cell projection using electron beams as the illumination source. Electrons accelerated to several tens of keV can efficiently expose many kinds of optical photoresists, as well as specialized electron beam resists. In some respects, electrons have an advantage over light. They do not suffer from optical thin-film interference, which can cause difficulty with controlling the processes of optical lithography (see Section 6.2). Their wavelengths are vanishingly short compared to the wavelengths of optical or x-ray radiation used for lithography. A 10-keV electron has a wavelength of 0.012 nm, and more energetic electrons have correspondingly shorter wavelengths. The shortness of the wavelength, relative to the feature sizes being printed, means that any diffractive spreading of the electron beam image can be ignored. This also means that diffraction does not impose any significant limit on the depth of focus for an electron beam image. As an added benefit, most electron beam exposure systems can be operated as scanning electron microscopes for very accurate acquisition of wafer alignment marks.

There are some serious problems with electron beam lithography, as well. The electrons tend to scatter within the photoresist and also within the wafer substrate beneath the resist layer. These scattered electrons slightly expose the resist in a halo around each of the exposed features. A dense array of features may contain enough scattered electrons to seriously overexpose the resist and drive the critical line width measurements out of their specified tolerances. To counteract this, complex computer algorithms have been designed to anticipate the problem and adjust the dose of each feature to compensate for scattered electrons from neighboring features [10]. In direct-write electron beam systems, this proximity correction is applied directly to the pattern-writing software. Masked electron beam lithography must have its proximity corrections applied to the mask design.

Electron beam lithography on highly insulating substrates can be very difficult because electrostatic charges induced by the exposure beam can force the beam out of its intended path, distorting the printed pattern. In addition, electrical forces between electrons in the beam can cause the beam to lose its collimation, the problem becoming worse with increasing current density.

Because of the electron scattering problem, it has been proposed to use heavier charged particles, such as protons or heavier ions, for masked lithographic exposures [11]. Heavy ions have very little tendency to scatter but are still susceptible to beam deflections from electrostatic charges on the substrate. Ion beams are more sensitive than electron beams to interactions between ions within the beam, due to the slower ion velocity and resulting higher charge per unit volume.

Except for electron beam cell projection, which has been used in semiconductor development, masked particle beam lithography has remained at the early stages of research. The difficulty of using stencil masks, which are required for this technology, and the necessity of exposing the wafers in a vacuum chamber have considerably dampened enthusiasm for this lithographic technique.

4 LITHOGRAPHIC LIGHT SOURCES

4.1 Requirements

Light sources of fairly high power and radiance are required to meet the demands of a modern, high-speed lithographic exposure system. The optical power required at the wafer is easily calculated from the sensitivity of the photoresist and the time allowed for the exposure. A typical resist used at midultraviolet wavelengths (365 to 436 nm) may require an optical energy density of 100 mJ/cm^2 for its exposure. If the exposure is to take 0.5 second or less, a minimum optical power density of 200 mW/cm^2 is required. Often power densities of 500 to 1000 mW/cm^2 are provided, in order to allow for lower resist sensitivities or shorter exposure times. The total illuminated areas that a stepper projects onto a wafer may be a circle 30 mm in diameter, which has an area of about 7 cm^2. If the power density for this example is taken to be 500 mW/cm^2, then a total power of 3.5 W is required. This is a substantial amount of optical power.

4.2 Radiance

Radiance (also known as luminance or brightness) is a concept that may be somewhat less familiar than power density. It is defined as the power density per steradian (the unit of solid angle) and has units of W/cm^2·sr. This quantity is important because fundamental thermodynamic laws prevent the radiance at any point in an optical imaging system from being greater than the radiance of the light source. If light is lost due to absorption or inefficient mirrors in the optical system, the radiance will decrease. Likewise, an aperture that removes a portion of the light will reduce the radiance.

The concept of radiance is important because it may limit the amount of optical power than can be captured from the light source and delivered to the wafer. The power from a diffuse light source cannot be concentrated to make an intense one. If the stepper designer wants to shorten the exposure time per field, he must get a light source with more power, and the power must be concentrated within a region of surface area similar to that of the light source being replaced. If the additional power is emitted from a larger area within the light source, it probably cannot be focused within the exposure field.

4.3 Mercury-Xenon Arc Lamps

The requirements for high power and high radiance have led to the choice of high-pressure mercury-xenon arc lamps as light sources for lithography. These lamps emit their light from a compact region a few millimeters in diameter, and have total power emissions from about 100 to over 2000 W. A large fraction of the total power emerges as infrared and visible light energy, which must be removed from the optical path with multilayer dielectric filters and directed to a liquid-cooled optical trap that can remove the large heat load from the system. The useful portion of the spectrum consists of several bright emission lines in the near ultraviolet and a continuous emission spectrum in the deep ultraviolet. Because of their optical dispersion, refractive lithographic lenses can use only a single emission line, either the g line at 435.83 nm, the h line at 404.65 nm,

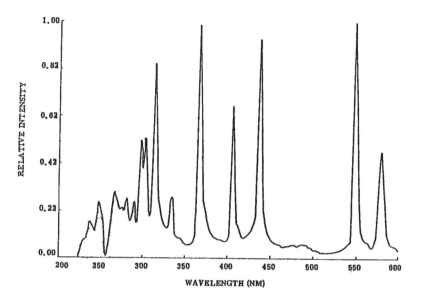

Figure 7   The mercury arc spectrum. The g line at 436 nm, the h line at 405 nm, the i line at 365 nm, and the emission region centered at 248 nm have all been used for microlithography.

or the i line at 365.48 nm. Each of these lines contains less than 2% of the total power of the arc lamp. The broad emission region between about 235 and 260 nm has also been used as a light source for deep-UV lithography, but the power available in this region is less than that of the line emissions.

4.4   The Arc-Lamp Illumination System

A rather complex illumination system or condenser collects the light from the arc lamp, projecting it through the mask into the entrance pupil of the lithographic projection optics. The illumination system first collects light from a large angular region surrounding the arc, using a paraboloidal or ellipsoidal mirror. The light is sent through one or more multilayer dielectric filters to remove all except the emission line that will be used by the projections optics. The light emitted from the arc lamp is not uniform enough to be used without further modification. In order to meet the ±1% uniformity requirement for mask illumination, a uniformizing or beam-randomizing technique is used. Two common optical uniformizing devices are light tunnels and fly's-eye lenses. Both of these devices create multiple images of the arc lamp. Light from the multiple images is recombined to yield an averaged intensity that is much more uniform than the raw output of the lamp. The illumination system projects this combined, uniform beam of light through the mask. The illuminator optics direct the light in such a way that it passes through the mask plane and comes to a focus in the entrance pupil of the lithographic projection optics. The technique of focusing the illumination source in the entrance pupil of the image-forming optics is called Köhler illumination. If a fly's eye or light tunnel is used in the system, the resulting multiple images of the arc lamp will be found focused in a neat array in the entrance pupil of the lithographic lens.

A number of problems can occur if the illumination system does not accurately focus an image of the light source in the center of the entrance pupil of the lithographic lens [12]. The entrance and exit pupils of a lens are optically conjugate planes. This means that an object in the plane of the entrance pupil will have an image in the plane of the exit pupil. The exit pupil in a telecentric lithographic lens is located at infinity. But if the illumination source is focused above or below the plane of the entrance pupil, then its image will not be in the proper location at infinity. This leads to the classic telecentricity error, a change of magnification with shifts in focus.

An error in centering the image of the illumination source in the entrance pupil will cause an error known as focus walk. This means that the lithographic image will move from side to side as the focus shifts up and down. Focus walk will make the alignment baseline change with changes of focus and can affect the alignment accuracy.

Spherical aberration in the illuminator optics causes light passing through the edge of the mask to focus at a different position than light passing through the center. This means that the image of the illumination source will be at different positions for each location in the image field and that the third-order distortion characteristics of the image will change with a shift in focus.

4.5 Excimer Lasers

Laser light sources have been developed to provide higher power at deep-UV wavelengths [13]. The only laser light source that has been successfully introduced for commercial wafer steppers, so far, is the excimer laser. An excimer is an exotic molecule formed by one atom each of a noble gas and halogen. This dimeric molecule is bound only in a quasi-stable excited state. The word excimer was coined from the phrase "excited dimer." When the excited state decays, the molecule falls apart into its two constituent atoms. A variety of noble gas chloride and fluoride excimers can be used as laser gain media.

The krypton fluoride excimer laser, operating at a wavelength of 248 nm, is coming into increasing use for commercial lithography. It has many features that make it attractive as a lithographic light source and a few undesirable features as well. The laser has considerably more usable power at 248 nm than the mercury arc lamp emission spectrum between 235 and 260 nm. The radiance

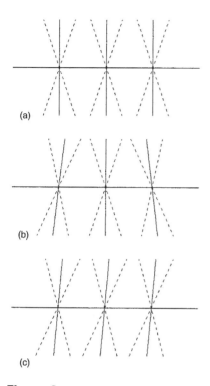

(a)

(b)

(c)

Figure 8 (a) A telecentric pupil illuminates each point on the wafer's surface with a cone of light whose axis is perpendicular to the surface. (b) The effects of a telecentricity error, in which the illumination does not appear to come from infinity. If the wafer surface is not perfectly located at the position of best focus, the separation between the three images will change, leading to a magnification error. (c) The effects of a decentration of the illumination within the pupil. In this situation, a change in focus induces a side-to-side shift in the image position.

of a laser is many orders of magnitude larger than that of a mercury arc lamp, because the laser emits a highly collimated beam of light, whereas the arc lamp emits light isotropically. The excimer laser's spectral line width is about 0.5 nm. Although this is somewhat narrower than the line width of a high-pressure mercury arc lamp, it is extremely wide compared to most lasers. The reason for this is the lack of a well-defined ground state for the energy level transition that defines the laser wavelength, the ground state in this case being two dissociated atoms.

Excimer lasers have a very low degree of coherence compared to most other kinds of lasers. The laser cavity operates with a very large number of spatial modes, giving it low spatial coherence, and the relatively broad line width results in low temporal coherence. Low coherence is very desirable for a lithographic light source. If the degree of coherence is too high, undesirable interference patterns can be formed within the aerial image. These effects of interference may appear as a grainy pattern of bright and dark modulation or as linear or circular fringe patterns in the illuminated parts of the image. The term speckle is often applied to this sort of coherent interference effect. Although speckle is relatively slight with excimer laser illumination, it is still a factor to consider in the design of the illumination system.

The 0.5-nm natural spectral width of the 248-nm excimer laser is not narrow enough to meet the bandwidth requirements of refractive lithographic lenses. These lenses are made of a single material—fused silica—and have essentially no chromatic correction. The high level of chromatic aberration associated with these lenses forces the illumination source to have a spectral line width of less than 0.003 nm (3 pm). Krypton fluoride excimer lasers have been modified to produce this spectral line width or less. A variety of techniques have been used, mostly involving dispersive elements such as prisms, diffraction gratings, and/or etalons within the optical cavity of the excimer laser. Addition of these elements reduces the total power of the laser somewhat and tends to decrease the stability of the power level. A rather complex feedback system is required to hold the center wavelength of the line-narrowed laser constant to about the same picometer level of accuracy. If the laser wavelength drifts by a few picometers, the focus of the lithographic lens may shift by several hundred nanometers.

There are several difficulties associated with using an excimer laser as a lithographic light source. The most significant problem is the pulsed nature of the excimer laser light. Excimer lasers in the power range useful for lithography (between 2 and 20 W) typically produce pulses of laser energy at a rate of 200 to 1000 Hz. Each pulse is between 5 and 20 nsec in length. Because of the extremely short pulses and the relatively long time between pulses, the peak power within each pulse is extremely high even when the time-averaged power is relatively modest. For example, an excimer laser running at 400 Hz with an average power of 10 W and a 10-nsec pulse length will have a peak power of 2.5 MW for the duration of each pulse. Peak powers in this range can cause damage to optical materials and coatings if the laser beam is concentrated in a small area. Although optical materials vary over a large range in their susceptibility to laser damage, peak power in the range of 5 MW/cm^2 can produce some degradation to a lithographic lens after prolonged exposure. Many of the damage mechanisms are functions of the square of the power density, so design features that keep the power density low are very desirable. The lithographic lens can be designed to avoid high concentrations of light within the lens material. Increases in the repetition rate of the laser are also beneficial, since this produces the same average power with a lower energy per pulse. It is also possible to modify the laser optics and electronics to produce somewhat longer pulses, which proportionately decreases the peak power within each pulse.

Pulsed lasers also present a problem in exposure control. A typical control scheme for a static-field stepper is to integrate the pulse energy until the required exposure has been accumulated, at which point a signal is sent to stop the laser from pulsing. This requires a minimum of 100 pulses in order to achieve a dose control accuracy of 1%. With the low repetition rates of early models of excimer lasers, the requirement of 100 pulses for each exposure slowed the rate of wafer exposures considerably. More sophisticated exposure control schemes have been developed, using several high-energy pulses to build up the exposure rapidly, then reducing the laser power to a low value to trim the exposure to its final value. Laser repetition rates have been steadily increasing as excimer laser lithography has developed. Between better control schemes and higher laser repetition rates, exposure speeds of excimer laser steppers are at least the equal of those of arc lamp systems.

Early models of excimer lasers used in prototype lithographic systems had pulse-to-pulse energy variations of up to 30%. This does not seriously affect the exposure control system, which can integrate pulses over a broad range of energies. It does cause the exposure time for each field to vary with the statistical fluctuations of the pulse energies. This is not a concern for a static-field stepper, but it is a serious problem when excimer lasers are used as light sources for scanning or step-and-scan systems. Scanners require a light source that does not fluctuate in time, because they must scan at a constant velocity. A pulsed light source is not impossible to use with a scanning system, as long as a sufficiently large number of pulses are accumulated during the time the exposure slit sweeps across a point on the wafer. The number of pulses required is determined by the pulse-to-pulse stability of the laser and the uniformity requirements of the final exposure on the wafer's surface. The distribution of the laser's pulse energy is reduced by approximately the square root of the number of pulses that are accumulated. To reduce a 30% pulse energy distribution to 1% would require accumulating about 900 pulses, which would make any scanned exposure system impracticably slow. Fortunately, excimer lasers used in lithography have a pulse stability much better than that of the earliest systems and it is continuing to improve. With pulse-to-pulse variations of 7.5%, only 56 pulses are required to bring the uniformity of the accumulated dose to 1%. A laser with a repetition rate of 400 Hz, illuminating a scanned exposure slit 5 mm wide, can produce the needed 56 pulses with a scanning speed of about 36 mm/sec. This scanning speed is lower than is desirable for full productivity of a step-and-scan system. Improvements to bring the pulse-to-pulse stability of the laser below 4.5% would allow the desired 1% exposure stability to be achieved with only 20 pulses, allowing the scanning speed for this example to rise to 100 mm/sec. Increase of the laser repetition rate to 1000 Hz would allow the scanning speed to rise to 89 mm/sec, even with no improvement in pulse-to-pulse stability. Another improvement in allowable scan speeds can be made by increasing the width of the scanning slit. Scan rates in the 90 to 100 mm/sec range are competitive with scan rates achieved with arc lamp sources. There is every reason to believe that incremental improvements in the laser will allow the first step-and-scan systems using excimer laser light sources to be competitive in scanning speed with the systems using arc lamp illumination.

Aside from the pulsed light output, there are a few other undesirable features of excimer laser light sources. The laser is physically large, occupying roughly 2 × 5 ft in the crowded and expensive floor space around the stepper. The laser itself is expensive, adding 5% to 10% to the cost of the stepper. Its plasma cavity is filled with a rather costly mixture of high-purity gases, including toxic and corrosive fluorine. The plasma cavity is not permanently sealed and needs to be refilled with new gas on a fairly regular basis. This requires a gas-handling system that meets rigorous industrial safety requirements for toxic gases. The electrical efficiency of an excimer laser is rather low, and the total electrical power consumption can be greater than 10 kW while the laser is operating. The pulsed power generation tends to produce a large amount of radiofrequency noise, which must be carefully shielded within the laser enclosure to prevent damage to sensitive computer equipment in the area where the laser is installed. The ultraviolet light output of the laser is very dangerous to human eyes and skin, and fairly elaborate safety precautions are required when maintenance work is done on the laser. Lithographic excimer lasers are classified as class IV lasers by federal laser standards and require an interlocked enclosure and beam line to prevent anyone operating the system from being exposed to the laser light.

Improvements in lithographic excimer lasers are continually being made. Not only are the pulse stability, repetition rate, and spectral line width constantly being improved, but factors affecting convenience of operation are also being actively developed. The interval between laser gas exchanges has increased by more than a factor of 10 since the earliest excimer lasers were used for lithography, and this improvement is continuing. A new technique for generating fluorine from a chemical source within the laser shows promise of eliminating much of the toxic gas delivery system associated with excimer lasers. As the technology of lithographic excimer lasers becomes more mature, the reliability of the lasers has improved and frequency-of-repair rates have decreased.

Excimer lasers will very likely be used as light sources for another generation of lithography at an exposure wavelength of 193 nm [14]. This is the wavelength of the argon fluoride excimer laser. No fundamental changes have to be made to allow a krypton fluoride laser to operate as an argon fluoride laser. In fact, most excimer lasers sold for scientific research can be operated at a variety of excimer wavelengths by merely changing the composition of gas in the laser's plasma tube and the mirrors that make up the optical cavity. Argon fluoride excimer lasers are somewhat more temperamental than krypton fluoride lasers. The shorter wavelength leads to faster degradation of optics that are exposed to the high optical power densities inside the laser cavity. The gain characteristics of the argon fluoride gas make it somewhat difficult to design a 193-nm excimer laser with a narrow spectral line width. The features that are desirable in the 248-nm krypton fluoride excimer laser, such as long pulse length and high repetition rate, are even more desirable in the 193-nm argon fluoride excimer laser, due to the greater ability of the 193-nm wavelength to damage optical materials. None of these difficulties seems to be insurmountable, and development of 193-nm lithographic systems is proceeding at several locations around the world.

Although not technically an excimer laser, the pulsed fluorine laser with an emission line at 157 nm is very similar to the excimers in its operating characteristics. This laser has attracted some interest as a possible lithographic light source extending even further into the short-wavelength region of the ultraviolet spectrum. Difficulties at this wavelength are significantly greater than those of the 248-nm and 193-nm excimers. The fluorine laser emission is considerably less efficient than that of either the krypton fluoride or argon fluoride excimer laser, but fluorine lasers have been manufactured that are capable of a few watts of 157-nm output. At this wavelength, fused silica is no longer transparent enough to be used as a refractive lens material. This leaves only crystalline materials like calcium fluoride to be used for 157-nm lenses. So far, the technology for making lenses of lithographic quality from fluorine salts is not as advanced as that for fused silica, although development work is continuing on these materials. A more serious difficulty with a 157-nm exposure wavelength is the loss of optical transmission of oxygen below about 180 nm. A stepper operating at 157 nm would require an atmosphere of nitrogen or helium around the stepper and laser beam transport. There is some possibility that an all-reflective lens design, similar to those under development for soft x-ray projection lithography, could be designed for the 157-nm wavelength. Although 157-nm lithography shares many of the difficulties of other developmental lithographies, such as all-reflective lenses and a special atmosphere in the optical path, the reward for this inconvenience is only a 23% improvement in resolution beyond the 193-nm exposure wavelength. This makes it likely that experimental technologies with higher potential payoffs will receive greater attention.

4.6 Other Laser Light Sources

Other light sources have been investigated for possible use in microlithography. The neodymium yttrium-aluminum-garnet (YAG) laser has a large number of applications in the laser industry, and its technology is very mature. The neodymium YAG laser's fundamental wavelength of 1064 nm can be readily converted to wavelengths useful for lithographic light sources by harmonic frequency multiplication techniques. The two wavelengths with the greatest potential application to lithography are the 266-nm fourth harmonic and the 213-nm fifth harmonic [15]. The successful development of 248-nm excimer laser lithography has diverted interest from the 266-nm wavelength, and the work now in progress to develop the 193-nm excimer wavelength may similarly suppress the development of the 213-nm neodymium YAG harmonic.

A YAG laser produces its light in pulses, like an excimer. Unlike the gaseous excimer gain medium, the laser gain medium is a solid crystalline rod. For applications requiring several watts of power, the rod is pumped by a lamp emitting a broad band of visible wavelengths. This light is not used very efficiently to pump the gain medium, and considerable amounts of heat are generated in the YAG rod. This limits the repetition rate of the laser to roughly 50 Hz. As discussed before, it is desirable to have a repetition rate much higher than this. If the neodymium YAG laser is pumped by an 800 to 900-nm infrared laser diode, the efficiency is much higher than with optical lamp pumping. The reduction in heat generation allows the repetition rate to be increased to the kilohertz range. A solid-state laser operating at 1000 Hz should be an attractive alternative to a complex, toxic gas–filled excimer laser. But, not surprisingly, there are some difficulties with using diode-pumped YAG lasers for lithography. When the technique of diode pumping was first developed, the laser diodes required to produce several watts of 266- or 213-nm laser power were prohibitively expensive. The price of laser diodes has been dropping steadily and does not present the insurmountable obstacle that it once did, but high-powered diode-pumped YAG lasers are still very expensive. A fairly severe problem is caused by the extremely high coherence of this type of laser. Elaborate measures must be taken to prevent or reduce the effects of coherent interference (speckle) in the image. The frequency-multiplied, diode-pumped YAG laser is potentially a very reliable and trouble-free laser. But it has not yet been developed to the level of the lithographic excimer laser, which has a demonstrated record of practical use, including data on such important industrial parameters as maintenance intervals, mean time between failures (MTBF), and mean time to repair (MTTR).

Copper vapor lasers have also been proposed as lithographic light sources, but no serious development work has been done for this application. The 510-nm fundamental wavelength can be frequency doubled to produce a 255-nm ultraviolet beam. The copper vapor laser, like the excimer and neodymium YAG lasers, is a pulsed light source, but the repetition rates are typically over 10 kHz. Coherence of the 510-nm direct output of the laser can be very low, but the frequency-doubling process requires that the laser be operated with an extremely coherent output. The benefits and problems associated with a frequency-doubled copper vapor laser are very similar to those of the frequency-quadrupled neodymium YAG laser. Considering the early lead that excimer lasers have taken in the market for deep-UV lithographic light sources, it is unlikely that either of these alternative lasers will be seen in commercial lithographic equipment.

4.7 Nonoptical Illumination Sources

Electron synchrotrons have already been mentioned as sources of 1-keV x-rays for x-ray proximity lithography [16]. These use technology developed for elementary particle research in the 1960s and 1970s to accelerate electrons to approximately 1 GeV and to maintain them at that energy, circulating in an evacuated ring of pipe surrounded by a strong magnetic field. The stored beam of electrons radiates x-rays, generated by a process called synchrotron radiation. The x-rays produced by an electron synchrotron storage ring have a suitable wavelength, intensity, and collimation to be used for x-ray proximity lithography. The magnets used to generate the synchrotron radiation can also be retuned to generate x-rays in the soft x-ray or extreme ultraviolet range. A synchrotron x-ray source can supply beams of x-rays to about 10 to 20 wafer aligners. If the cost of the synchrotron is divided among all of the wafer aligners, then it does not grossly inflate the normally expensive cost of each lithographic exposure system. But if the lithographic exposure demands of the manufacturing facility are not sufficient to load the synchrotron fully, then the cost of each exposure system will rise. Likewise, if the demand for exposures exceeds the capacity of one synchrotron, an additional synchrotron will need to be installed. This makes the cost of a small additional amount of lithographic capacity become extremely large. Often this is referred to as the problem of granularity.

Other sources of x-rays have been developed to avoid the expense of an electron synchrotron. Ideally, each x-ray stepper should have its own illumination source, just as optical steppers do. Extremely hot, high-density plasmas are efficient sources of x-rays. Dense plasma sources are often called point sources, to differentiate them from the collimated x-ray beams emitted by synchrotron storage rings. A point source of x-rays can be generated by a magnetically confined electrical discharge or a very energetic pulsed laser beam focused to a small point on a solid target. These x-ray point sources are not as ideal for lithography as a collimated source. Because the radiation is emitted isotropically from a small region, there is a trade-off between angular divergence of the beam and the energy density available to expose the resist. If the mask and wafer are placed close to the source of x-ray emission, the maximum energy will be intercepted, but the beam will diverge widely. A diverging x-ray beam used for proximity printing will make the magnification of the image printed on the wafer become sensitive to the gap between the mask and the wafer. This is analogous to a telecentricity error in a projection lens (see Section 5.1). In addition, there is a possibility of contaminating the mask with debris from the plasma, especially in the case of laser-generated point sources.

In contrast to x-ray sources, electron sources are simple and compact. A hot filament provides a copious source of electrons, which can be accelerated to any desired energy with electrostatic fields. Higher intensity and radiance can be achieved with the use of materials like lanthanum and zirconium in the electron source or the use of field emission sources.

Ion sources are also compact but somewhat more complex than electron sources. They use radiofrequency power to create an ionized plasma. The ions are extracted by electric fields and accelerated similarly to electrons.

5   OPTICAL CONSIDERATIONS

5.1   Requirements

Above all else, a lithographic exposure system is defined by the properties of its projection lens. Lithographic lenses are unique in their simultaneous requirements for diffraction-limited image formation, large field size, extremely low field curvature, a magnification accurate to six decimal places, and near-zero distortion. (In the technical jargon of lithography, distortion refers to errors in image placement. The lowest orders of placement error, namely x and y offset, magnification, and rotation, are not included in the lens distortion specification.) Whereas a good-quality camera lens may have distortion that allows an image placement error of 1 or 2% of the field of view, the permissible distortion of a modern lithographic lens is only 1 or 2 parts per million. Fortunately, a high degree of chromatic correction is not required, since an extremely monochromatic light source can be selected. In fact, lenses designed for ultraviolet excimer laser light sources may have no chromatic correction whatever. The lithographic lens needs to achieve its designed level of performance for only one well-defined object plane and one image plane, and so the design is totally optimized for these two conjugate planes.

A lens with high numerical aperture can give diffraction-limited performance only within a narrow focal range. A second Rayleigh formula gives an expression for depth of focus:

$$\Delta Z = k_2 \frac{\lambda}{NA^2}$$

where ΔZ is the depth of focus, λ is the exposure wavelength, and NA is the numerical aperture of the lens. The value of the proportionality constant k_2 depends on the criteria used to define acceptable imaging and on the type of feature being imaged. A convenient rule of thumb is to use $k_2 = 0.8$ as the total depth of focus for a mix of different feature types. Some particular feature types, such as equal line and space gratings, may have a much greater value of k_2.

There is another somewhat unobvious requirement for a lithographic lens called telecentricity. This term means that the effective exit pupil of the lens is located at infinity. Under this condition, the light forming the images converges symmetrically around the normal to the wafer surface at every point in the exposure field. If the wafer is exposed slightly out of focus, the images will blur slightly, but the exposure field as a whole will not exhibit any change in magnification. If the lens pupil were not at infinity, a rather insignificant focus error could cause a severe change in magnification. Some lenses are deliberately designed to be telecentric on the wafer side but nontelecentric on the mask side. This allows the lens magnification to be fine-tuned by changing the separation between the mask and the lithographic lens. Other lenses are telecentric on both the wafer side and the mask side (called a double-telecentric design). With double-telecentric lenses, magnification adjustments must be made by other means.

5.2 Lens Control

The ability to adjust magnification through a range of ±50 ppm or so is needed to compensate for slight changes in lens or wafer temperature or for differences in calibration between different steppers. Changing the mask-to-lens separation in a nontelecentric lithographic lens is only one common technique. Often lithographic lenses are made with a movable element that induces magnification changes when it is displaced along the lens axis by a calibrated amount. In some designs, the internal gas pressure in the lithographic lens can be accurately adjusted to induce a known magnification shift. The magnification of a lens designed to use a line-narrowed excimer laser light source can be changed by deliberate shifts in the laser wavelength. Most of these methods for magnification adjustment also induce shifts in the focal position of the lens. The focus shift that results from a magnification correction can be calculated and fed back to the software of the focus control system.

5.3 Lens Defects

Stray light scattered from imperfections in the lens material, coatings, or lens-mounting hardware can cause an undesirable haze of light in regions of the image that are intended to be dark. This imperfection, sometimes called flare, reduces the image contrast and generally degrades the quality of the lithography. A surprisingly large amount of flare sometimes occurs in lithographic lenses. More than 5% of the illumination intensity is sometimes scattered into the nominally dark areas of the image. Although this level of flare can be tolerated by a high-contrast resist, it would be preferable to reduce the flare to less than 2%.

Optical aberrations in either the lithographic projection lens or the illuminator can lead to a variety of problems in the image. Simple tests can sometimes be used to identify a particular aberration in a lithographic lens, but often a high-order aberration will have no particular signature other than a general loss of contrast or a reduced depth of focus. Many manufacturers of advanced lithographic systems have turned to sophisticated interferometric techniques to characterize the aberrations of their lenses. A phase-measuring interferometer can detect errors approaching 1/1000 of a wavelength in the optical wave front.

5.4   Coherence

Even a lens that is totally free of aberrations may not give perfect images from the perspective of the lithographer. The degree of coherence of the illumination has a strong effect on the image formation. Too high a degree of coherence can cause "ringing," in which the image profile tends to oscillate near a sharp corner, and faint ghost images may appear in areas adjacent to the features being printed. On the other hand, a low degree of coherence can cause excessive rounding of corners in the printed images, as well as loss of contrast at the image boundaries. The degree of coherence is determined by the pupil filling ratio of the illuminator, called σ. This number is the fraction of the projection lens's entrance pupil diameter that is filled by light from the illuminator. Highly coherent illumination corresponds to small values of sigma, and relatively incoherent illumination results from large values of sigma. A coherence of $\sigma = 0.7$ gives nearly the best shape fidelity for a two-dimensional feature. But there has been a tendency for lithographers to use a greater degree of coherence, $\sigma = 0.6$ or even $\sigma = 0.5$, because of the greater image contrast that results. This sort of image formation, neither totally coherent nor totally incoherent, is often called partially coherent imaging [17].

5.5   Proximity Effects

Some problems in lithography are caused by the fundamental physics of image formation. Even in the absence of any optical aberrations, the widths of lines in the lithographic image are influenced by other nearby features. This is often called the optical proximity effect. The systematic biases caused by this effect, although small, are quite undesirable. For example, the maximum speed of a logic circuit is greatly influenced by the uniformity of the transistor gate dimensions across the total area of the circuit. But optical proximity effects give an isolated line a width somewhat greater than that of an identical line in a cluster of equal lines and spaces. This so-called isolated-to-grouped bias is a serious concern. It is actually possible to introduce deliberate lens aberrations that reduce the isolated-to-grouped bias, but there is always a fear that any aberrations will reduce image contrast and degrade the quality of the lithography. It

MASK OBJECT   0.1

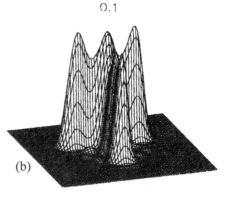

(a)   (b)

        0.3   0.5

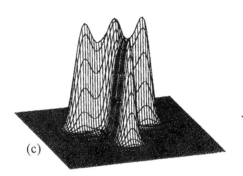   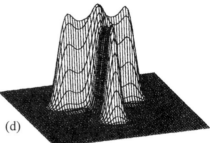

(c)   (d)

        0.7   0.9

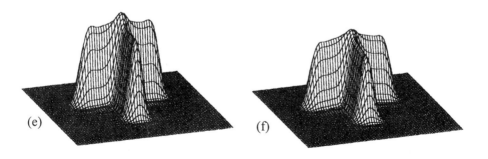

(e)   (f)

Figure 9 The computer-modeled aerial image of a T-shaped mask object (a) is shown, projected with five different pupil-filling ratios (σ = 0.1 to 0.9). Vertical height in each figure (b–f) represents the light intensity at the wafer surface. Note the high contrast but excessive amounts of ringing in the images with the greatest coherence or lowest values of σ. The bars in the mask object have dimensions of 0.7 λ/NA.

is also possible to introduce selective image size biases into the photomask to compensate for optical proximity effects. But the bookkeeping required to keep track of the density-related biases necessary in a complex mask pattern is daunting. No totally satisfactory solution exists for this general problem, but computer algorithms for generating optical proximity corrections on the mask are under development in several universities and industrial research laboratories today and may be put into use within a few years.

The final output of the lithographic illuminator, photomask, and lithographic lens is an aerial image, or image in space. This image is as perfect as the mask maker's and lens maker's art can make it. But the image must interact with a complex stack of thin films and patterns on the surface of the wafer to form a latent image within the bulk of the photoresist.

6   LATENT IMAGE FORMATION

6.1   Photoresist

Photoresists are typically mixtures of an organic polymer and a photosensitive compound. A variety of other chemicals may be included to modify the optical or physical properties of the resist or to participate in the reactions between the photosensitive materials and the polymer. Resist is applied to the surface of a wafer in an organic solvent using a process called spin casting.

When the aerial image interacts with photoresist, chemical changes are induced in its photosensitive components. When the exposure is over, the image is captured as a pattern of altered chemicals in the resist. This chemical pattern is called the latent image. When the resist-coated wafer is exposed to a developer, the developer chemistry selectively dissolves either the exposed or the unexposed parts of the resist. Positive-tone resists are defined as resists whose exposed areas are removed by the developer. Negative-tone resists are removed by the developer only in the unexposed areas. Choice of a positive- or negative-tone resist is dictated by a number of considerations, including the relative defect levels of positive and negative photomasks, the performance of the available positive and negative resists, and the differences in the fundamental optics of positive and negative image formation. (Perhaps surprisingly, complementary photomasks, with clear and opaque areas exactly reversed, do not produce aerial image intensity profiles that are exact inverses of each other.)

Photoresist, unlike typical photographic emulsion, is designed to have an extremely high contrast. This means that its response to the aerial image is quite nonlinear and tends to exhibit a sort of threshold response. The aerial image of a tightly spaced grating may have an intensity profile that resembles a sine curve, with very shallow slopes at the transitions between bright and dark areas. If this intensity profile were translated directly into a resist thickness profile, the resulting resist patterns would be unacceptable for semiconductor manufacturing. But the nonlinear resist response can provide a very steep sidewall in a printed feature, even when the contrast of the aerial image is low.

The width of a feature printed in photoresist is a fairly sensitive function of the exposure energy. To minimize line width variation, stringent requirements must be placed on the exposure uniformity and repeatability. Typically the allowable line width tolerance is ±10% (or less) of the minimum feature size. For a 0.35-µm feature, this implies line width control of ±35 nm or better. Because there are several factors contributing to line width variation, the portion due to exposure variations must be quite small. Exposure equipment is typically designed to limit intrafield exposure variation and field-to-field variation to ±1%. Over a moderate range of values, deliberate changes in exposure energy can be used to fine-tune the dimensions of the printed features. In positive-tone photoresist, a 10% increase in exposure energy can give a 5 to 10% reduction in the size of a minimum-sized feature.

6.2 Thin-Film Interference and the Swing Curve

The optical interaction of the aerial image with the wafer can be very complicated. In the later stages of semiconductor manufacture, many thin layers of semitransparent films will have been deposited on the surface of the wafer, topped by approximately a micron of photoresist. Every surface in this film stack will reflect some fraction of the light and transmit the rest. The reflected light interferes with the transmitted light to form standing waves in the resist. Standing waves have two undesirable effects. First, they create a series of un-

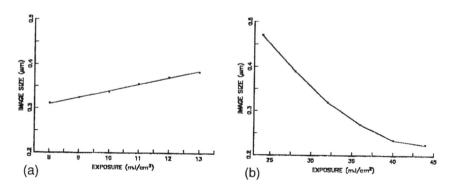

Figure 10 Two plots of line width versus exposure energy. (a) A rather sensitive negative-toned resist, with good exposure latitude. The curve in (b) has a much steeper slope, indicating a much narrower exposure window for good line width control. The second resist is positive toned and is less sensitive than the resist in (a).

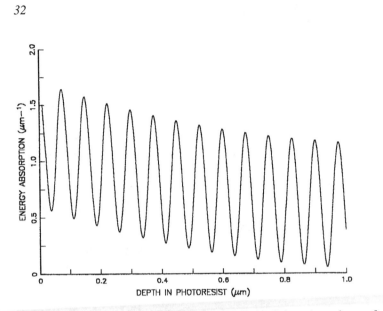

Figure 11 Optical energy absorption versus depth in a 1-μm layer of photoresist. The effect of standing waves is very prominent, with the regions of maximum absorption separated by a spacing of λ/2n. This resist is rather opaque, and the loss of energy is evident from the top to the bottom surface of the resist.

desirable horizontal ridges in the resist sidewalls, corresponding to the peaks and troughs in the standing wave intensity. But more seriously, the standing waves affect the total amount of light captured by the layer of resist. A slight change in thickness of the resist can dramatically change the amount of light absorbed by the resist, effectively changing its sensitivity to the exposure. A graph of resist sensitivity versus thickness will show a regular pattern of oscillations, often referred to as the swing curve. The swing between maximum and minimum sensitivity occurs with a thickness change of λ/4n, where λ is the exposure wavelength and *n* is the resist's index of refraction. Because of the direct relationship between resist sensitivity and line width, the swing curve can

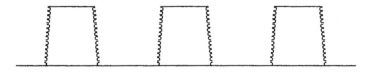

Figure 12 Standing waves set up by optical interference within the layer of photoresist can lead to undesirable ridges in the sidewalls of the developed resist pattern.

make slight variations in resist thickness show up as serious variations in line width. The greatest line width stability is achieved when the resist thickness is tuned to an extremum in the swing curve. For best control, resist thickness must be held within about ±10 nm of the optimum thickness. Variations in chip surface topography may make it impossible to achieve this level of control everywhere on the wafer.

A swing curve can also be generated by variations in the thickness of a transparent film that lies somewhere in the stack of films underneath the resist [18]. This allows a change in an earlier deposition process to unexpectedly affect the behavior of a previously stable lithographic process. Ideally, all films on the wafer surface should be designed for thicknesses to minimize the swing curve in the resist. But because of the many other process and design requirements on these films, it is rare that their thicknesses can be controlled solely for the benefit of the lithography.

The swing curve has the greatest amplitude when the exposure illumination is monochromatic. If a broad band of exposure wavelengths is used, the amplitude of the swing curve can be greatly suppressed. The band of wavelengths used in refractive lithographic lenses is not sufficiently broad to have much effect on the swing curve. But reflective lens designs allow optical bandwidths of 10 to 20 nm or more. This can significantly reduce the swing curve, to the point that careful optimization of the resist thickness may no longer be necessary.

6.3 Mask Reflectivity

Light that is specularly reflected from the wafer surface will be transmitted backward through the projection lens and eventually strike the front surface of the mask. If the mask has a high degree of reflectivity, as uncoated chromium does, this light will be once again reflected back to the wafer surface. Since this light has made three trips through the projection optics the images will be substantially broadened by diffraction. This can result in a faint halo of light around each bright area in the image, causing some loss in contrast. The effect is substantially the same as the flare caused by random light scattering in the lens. The almost universally adopted solution to this problem is an antireflective coating on the chromium surface of the mask. This can easily reduce the mask reflectivity from more than 50% to around 10% and considerably suppresses the problem of reflected light.

6.4 Wafer Topography

In addition to the problems caused by planar reflective films on the wafer, there is a set of problems that result from the three-dimensional circuit structures etched into the wafer surface. Photoresist tends to bridge across micron-scale pits and bumps in the wafer, leaving a planar surface. But longer scale varia-

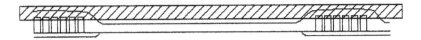

Figure 13   In the presence of severe topographical variations across the chip surface, it may be impossible to project a focused image into all parts of the resist at the same time. The shaded area represents the stepper's depth of focus. It has been centered on the higher regions of topography, leaving the lower regions badly out of focus.

tions in the wafer surface are conformally coated by resist, producing a non-planar resist surface to interact with the planar aerial image. This vertical wafer topography directly reduces the usable depth of focus. Vertical surfaces on the sides of etched structures can also reflect light into regions that were intended to receive no exposure. This effect is often called reflective notching, and in severe cases, circuit layouts may have to be completely redesigned before a working device can be manufactured.

6.5 Control of Standing-Wave Effects

A number of solutions to all of these problems have been worked out over the years. Horizontal ridges in resist sidewalls, induced by standing waves, can usually be reduced or eliminated by baking the resist after exposure. This postexposure bake allows the chemicals forming the latent image to diffuse far enough to eliminate the ridges—about 50 nm—without significantly degrading the contrast at the edge of the image. The postexposure bake does nothing to reduce the swing curve, which is the other main effect of standing waves.

Reflective notching and the swing curve can be reduced to some extent by using dyed photoresist. The optical density of the photoresist can be increased enough to suppress the light reflected from the bottom surface of the resist. This is a fairly delicate balancing act, since too much opacity will reduce the exposure at the bottom surface of the resist and seriously degrade the sidewall profiles. An antireflective coating (often referred to by the acronym ARC) provides a much better optical solution to the problems of reflective notching and the swing curve. In this technique, a thin layer of a heavily dyed polymer or an opaque inorganic material is applied to the wafer underneath the photoresist layer. The optical absorption of this ARC layer is high enough to decouple the resist from the complex optical behavior of any underlying film stacks. Ideally, the index of refraction of the ARC should be matched to that of the photoresist, so that there are no reflections from the resist-ARC interface. If this index matching is done perfectly, the swing curve will be totally suppressed. Although this is an elegant technique on paper, there are many practical difficulties with ARC layers. The ARC material must not be attacked by the casting solvent of the resist, nor may it interact chemically with the resist during exposure and development. The ARC adds substantially to the cost, time, and complexity of the photoresist application process. After the resist is developed, the ARC layer must be removed from the open areas by an etch process. There is typically very little etch selectivity between organic ARCs and photoresist, so the ARC removal step often removes a substantial amount of resist and may degrade the resist's sidewall profile. This means that the ARC layer must be as thin as possible, preferably less than 10% of the resist thickness. If the ARC must be this thin, its optical absorbance must be very high. Aside from the difficulty of finding dyes with high enough levels of absorbance, a large discrepancy between the absorbance of the resist and that of the ARC makes it impossible to get an accurate match of the index of refraction. So a fairly substantial swing curve usually remains a part of the lithographic process, even when an ARC is used. This remaining swing curve can be controlled by holding the resist thickness within tight tolerance limits.

The swing curve can also be controlled with an antireflective layer on the top surface of the resist [19]. This is because the light-trapping effect that induces the swing curve is caused by optical interference between light waves reflected from the top and bottom surfaces of the resist layer. If there is no reflection from the top surface, this interference effect will not occur. A simple interference coating can be used, consisting of a quarter-wavelength thickness of a material whose index of refraction is the square root of the photoresist's index. Since photoresists typically have refractive indices that lie between 1.5 and 1.8, a top ARC should have a refractive index between 1.2 and 1.35. There are rather few materials of any kind with indices in this range, but some have been found and used for this application. The optical benefits of a top ARC are not as great as those of a conventional bottom-surface ARC, since reflective notching, thin-film interference from substrate films, and sidewall ridges are not suppressed. But top ARC has some substantial process advantages over the conventional ARC. If a water soluble material is used for the top ARC, it does not have much tendency to interact with the resist during spin casting of the top-ARC layer. The top ARC can actually protect the underlying resist from airborne chemical contamination, which is a well-known problem for some types of modern photoresists. After the exposure is completed, the top ARC can be stripped without affecting the resist thickness or sidewall profiles. In fact, top ARC can be designed to dissolve in the aqueous base solutions that are typically used as developers for photoresist, eliminating the need for a separate stripping step. (It should be noted that this clever use of a water-soluble film cannot be used for bottom-surface ARC. If a bottom ARC washes away in the developer, the resist features sitting on top of it will wash away as well!) Using a moderately effective bottom-surface ARC along with a combined top ARC and chemical barrier should provide the maximum benefits. But the expense and complexity of this belt-and-suspenders approach usually make it unrealis-

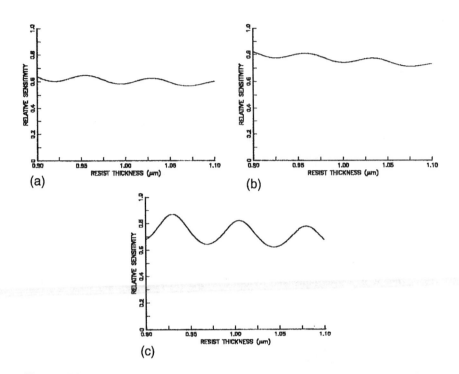

Figure 14   A series of swing curves, showing the improvements that can be achieved with antireflective coatings (ARCs). (a) The suppression in swing curve when a bottom-surface ARC is used. (b) A similar suppression of swing curve by a top-surface ARC. Note that more light is coupled into the resist with the top ARC, increasing the resist's effective sensitivity. (c) The much larger swing curve when no ARC is used. In these computer-modeled curves, resist sensitivity is taken as the optical absorption per unit volume of resist.

tic in practice. Because of the cost, ARCs of both kinds are usually avoided unless a particular lithographic level cannot be made to work without them.

6.6   Control of Topographic Effects

Chip surface topography presents a challenge for lithography, even when reflective notching and the swing curve are suppressed by ARCs. When the wafer surface within the exposure field is not completely flat, it may be impossible to get both high and low areas into focus at the same time. If the topographical variations occur over a short distance, then the resist may planarize the irregularities. But it will still be difficult to create images on the thick and thin parts of the resist with the same exposure. A variety of optical tricks and wafer planarization techniques have been developed to cope with this problem. The most successful planarizing technique has been chemical-mechanical polish, in which the surface of the wafer is planarized by polishing it with a slurry of chemical and physical abrasives, much as one might polish an optical surface. This technique can leave a nearly ideal planar surface for the next layer of lithographic image formation.

6.7 Latent Image Stability

The stability of the latent image varies greatly from one type of resist to another. Some resists allow exposed wafers to be stored for several days between exposure and development. But there are also many resists that must be developed within minutes of exposure. If these resists are used, an automated wafer developer must be integrated with the exposure system, so that each wafer can be developed immediately after exposure. This combination of exposure system and wafer processing equipment is referred to as an integrated photosector or photocluster.

7 THE RESIST IMAGE

7.1 Resist Development

After the latent image is created in resist, a development process is used to produce the final resist image. The first step in this process is a postexposure bake. Some types of resist (especially the so-called chemically amplified resists) require this bake to complete the formation of the latent image by accelerating reactions between the exposed photosensitizer and the other components of the resist. Other types of resist are also baked to reduce the sidewall ridges resulting from standing waves. The baked resist is then developed in an aqueous base solution. In many cases, this just involves immersing an open-sided container of wafers in a solution of potassium hydroxide (KOH). This simple process has become more complicated in recent years as attempts are made to improve uniformity of the development, to reduce contamination of the wafer surface by metallic ions from the developer, and to reduce costs. Today a more typical development would be done on a specialized single-wafer developer, which would mechanically transport each wafer in its turn to a turntable, flood the surface of the wafer with a shallow puddle of metal ion–free developer (such as tetramethylammonium hydroxide, TMAH), then rinse the wafer and spin it dry.

7.2 Etch Masking

The developed resist image can be used as a template or mask for a variety of processes. Most commonly, an etch is performed after the image formation. The wafer can be immersed in a tank of liquid etchant. The resist image is not affected by the etchant, but the unprotected areas of the wafer surface are etched away. For a wet etch, the important properties of the resist are its adhesion and the dimension at the base of the resist images. Details of the resist sidewall profile are relatively unimportant. However, wet etches are seldom used in critical levels of advanced semiconductor manufacturing. This is because wet chemical etches of amorphous films are isotropic. As well as etching vertically through the film, the etch proceeds horizontally at an equal rate, undercutting the resist image and making it hard to control the final etched pattern size.

Much better pattern size control is achieved with reactive ion etching (RIE). In this process, the wafer surface is exposed to the bombardment of chemically reactive ions in a vacuum chamber. Electric and/or magnetic fields direct the ions against the wafer surface at normal incidence, and the resulting etch can be extremely anisotropic. This prevents the undercut usually seen with wet etches and allows a much greater degree of dimensional control.

Reactive ion etching places a much different set of requirements on the resist profile than does a wet etch process. Because the RIE process removes ma-

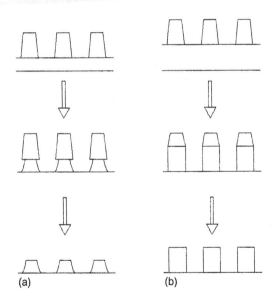

(a)   (b)

Figure 15 A comparison of wet and dry etch processes. The wet etch process shown in (a) is isotropic and tends to undercut the resist pattern. The etch does not attack the resist, and the final etch profiles are sloped. In contrast, the reactive-ion etch (RIE) process shown in (b) can be used to etch a much thicker film while retaining nearly vertical sidewall slopes. The resist is partially eroded during the RIE process. The bottom illustration in each series shows the etched pattern after the resist is stripped.

terial by both chemical reaction and mechanical bombardment, it tends to erode the resist much more than a wet etch. This makes the profile of the resist sidewall very important. Any shape other than a straight, vertical sidewall with square corners at the top and foot of the resist image is undesirable, because it allows the transfer of a sloped profile into the final etched structure. A variety of profile defects, such as sidewall slopes, T-tops, and image feet, can be induced by deficiencies in the photoresist process.

Another set of profile defects can result from the properties of the aerial image. With today's high-NA lithographic lenses, the aerial image can change substantially over the thickness of the resist. This leads to different resist profiles, depending on whether the best focus of the aerial image is at the top, bottom, or middle of the resist film. Although the best resist image profiles can be formed in thin resist, aggressive RIE processes may force the use of a thick resist layer. Trade-offs between the needs of the etch process and the lithographic process commonly result in a resist thickness between 0.5 and 1.5 μm. As lateral image dimensions shrink below 0.5 μm, the height-to-width ratio (or aspect ratio) of the resist images can become very large. Resist adhesion failure can become a problem for aspect ratios greater than about 3:1. Surface tension in the liquid developer has a tendency to make clusters of tall, thin resist structures topple together.

Although resist patterns most frequently are used as etch masks, there are other important uses as well. The resist pattern can be used to block ion implantation or to block deposition of metal films. Ion implants require square resist profiles, similar to the profiles required for RIE. But the thickness requirements are dictated by the stopping range of the energetic ions in the resist material. For ion implants in the MeV range, a resist thickness considerably greater than 1 μm may be required. Fortunately, implant masks do not usually put great demands on the lithographic resolution or overlay tolerance.

Both etch and implant processes put fairly strong demands on the physical and thermal durability of the resist material. The etch resistance and thermal stability of the developed resist image may be enhanced by a variety of resist-hardening treatments. These may involve diffusion of etch-resistant additives (such as silicon compounds) into the already patterned resist. But more frequently the hardening treatment consists of a high-temperature bake and/or ultraviolet flood exposure of the wafer. These processes tend to cross-link the resist polymers and greatly toughen the material. A large number of g-line, i-line, and 248-nm (deep-UV) resists can be successfully UV or bake hardened, but there are some resists that do not cross-link under these treatments. The choice of whether or not to use resist-hardening treatments is dictated by details of the etch process and the etch resistance of the untreated resist.

As the image size shrinks from one lithographic generation to the next, there has been no corresponding reduction of the resist thickness required by the etch or implant processes. If anything, there is tendency to more aggressive etches and higher energy ion implants. This is pushing resist images to ever-higher aspect ratios. Already 0.35-μm features in 1.0-μm-thick resist have an aspect ratio of 3:1. This is likely to grow to around 4:1 in the following generation. If resist processes start to fail at these high aspect ratios, there will have to be a migration to more complex resist processes. High aspect ratios can be readily (if expensively) achieved with multilayer resist (MLR) processes or top-surface-imaging (TSI) resists.

7.3 Multilayer Resist Process

A multilayer resist consists of one or two nonphotosensitive films, covered with a thin top layer of photoresist. The resist is exposed and developed normally; then the image is transferred into the bottom layers by one or more RIE processes. The patterned bottom layer then acts as a mask for a different RIE process to etch the substrate. For example, the top layer may be a resist with a high silicon content. This will block an oxygen etch, which can be used to pat-

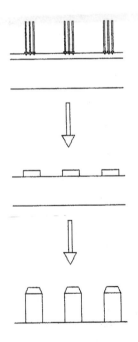

Figure 16   In a multilayer resist (MLR) process, a thin photosensitive layer is exposed and developed. The pattern is then transferred into an inert layer of polymer by a dry etch process. The imaging layer must have a higher resistance to the pattern transfer etch. Very small features can be created in thick layers of polymer, with nearly vertical sidewall profiles.

tern an underlying polymer layer. The patterned polymer acts as the mask for the substrate etch. Another MLR process uses a sandwich of three layers: a bottom polymer and a top resist layer separated by a thin layer of silicon dioxide. After the resist layer is exposed and developed, the thin oxide layer is etched with a fluorine RIE. Then the oxide acts as a mask to etch the underlying polymer with an oxygen etch. Finally, the patterned polymer layer is used to mask a substrate etch. A multilayer resist process allows the customization of each layer to its function. The bottom polymer layer can be engineered for maximum etch resistance, while the top resist layer is specialized for good image formation. The sidewall profiles are generated by reactive ion etching and tend to be extremely straight and vertical. It is relatively easy to create features with very high aspect ratios in multilayer resists. The cost of MLR is apt to be very high, due to the multiple layers of materials that have to be deposited and the corresponding multiple RIE steps.

7.4   Top-Surface Imaging

Top-surface-imaging resists are deposited in a single layer, like conventional resists. These resists are deliberately made extremely opaque, and the aerial image does not penetrate very deeply into the surface. The latent image formed in the surface is "developed" by treating it with a liquid or gaseous silicon-bearing material. Depending on the chemistry of the process, the exposed surface areas of the resist will either exclude or preferentially absorb the silylating agent. The silicon incorporated in the surface acts as an etch barrier for an oxygen RIE, which creates the final resist profile. Top-surface imaging shares most of the advantages of MLR but at somewhat reduced cost. It is still a more expensive process than standard single-layer resist. TSI resist images often suffer from vertical striations in the sidewalls and from unwanted spikes of resist in areas that are intended to be clear. The presence or absence of these types of defects is quite sensitive to the etch conditions.

7.5   Deposition Masking and the Liftoff Process

Use of resist as a mask for material deposition is less common but is still an important application of lithography. Rarely, a selective deposition process is used to grow a crystalline or polycrystalline material on exposed areas of the wafer surface. Because of the selectivity of the chemical deposition process, no material is deposited on the resist surface. The resist sidewalls act as templates for the deposited material, and the resist must be thick enough to prevent overgrowth of the deposition past its top surface. Other than this, there are no special demands on the resist used as a mask for selective deposition.

Another masked deposition process involves nonselective deposition of a film over the top of the resist image. The undesired material deposited on top

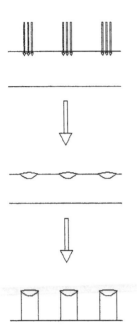

Figure 17 Top-surface imaging (TSI) uses a very opaque resist, whose surface is activated by exposure to light. The photoactivated areas selectively absorb organic silicon-bearing compounds during a silylation step. These silylated areas act as an etch barrier and the pattern can be transferred into the bulk of the resist with a dry etch process.

of the resist is removed when the resist is stripped. This is known as the liftoff process. A very specialized resist profile is required for the liftoff process to be successful. A vertical or positively sloped profile can allow the deposited material to form bridges between the material on the resist and that on the wafer surface. These bridges anchor down the material that is intended to be removed. There are various resist processes, some of them quite complex, for producing the needed negatively sloped or undercut resist profile.

7.6   Directly Patterned Insulators

There is one final application of lithography that should be mentioned. It is possible to incorporate the patterned resist directly into the final semiconductor device, usually as an insulating layer. This is difficult to do near the beginning of the chip fabrication process because high-temperature steps that are encountered later in the process would destroy the organic resist polymers. But photosensitive polyimide materials have been used as photodefinable insulators in some of the later stages of semiconductor fabrication.

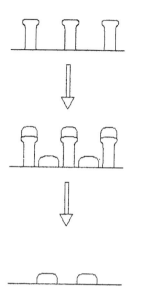

Figure 18 The liftoff process requires a specialized undercut photoresist profile. A thin layer of metal is deposited on the wafer surface. The metal that lies on top of the photoresist is washed away when the resist is stripped, leaving only the metal that was directly deposited on the wafer surface.

7.7 Resist Stripping

The final step in the lithographic process is stripping the resist that remains on the wafer after the etch, deposition, or ion implant process is complete. If the resist has not been chemically altered by the processing, it can often be removed with an organic solvent. But resists that have been heavily cross-linked during processing, or by a deliberate resist-hardening step, are much harder to remove. This problem, well known to anyone who has tried to clean the neglected top of his kitchen stove, is usually solved with powerful chemical oxidants or an oxygen plasma asher, which oxidizes the organic resist polymers with practically no residue.

8 ALIGNMENT AND OVERLAY

Image formation and alignment of the image to previous levels of patterns are equally critical parts of the lithographic process. Alignment techniques have evolved over many years from simple two-point alignments to very sophisticated multiterm models. This has brought overlay tolerances over a 10-year period from 0.5 μm to below 0.1 μm today. Over the years that semiconductor microlithography has been evolving, overlay requirements have generally scaled linearly with the minimum feature size. Different technologies have different proportionality factors, but in general the overlay tolerance requirement has been between 25 and 40% of the minimum feature size. If anything, there has been a tendency for overlay tolerance to become an even smaller fraction of the minimum feature size.

8.1 Definitions

Most technically educated people have a general idea of what alignment and overlay mean, but there are enough subtleties in the jargon of semiconductor manufacturing that a few definitions should be given. Both alignment accuracy and overlay accuracy are the positional errors resulting when a second-level lithographic image is superimposed on a first-level pattern on a wafer. Alignment accuracy is measured only at the location of the alignment marks. This measurement serves to demonstrate the accuracy of the stepper's alignment system. The total overlay accuracy is measured everywhere on the wafer, not just in the places where the alignment marks are located. It includes a number of error terms beyond those included in the alignment error. In particular, lens distortion, chuck-induced wafer distortion, and image placement errors on the mask can give significant overlay errors, even if the alignment at the position of the alignment marks is perfect. Of course, it is the total overlay error that determines the production yield and quality of the semiconductor circuits being manufactured.

Alignment and overlay could have been defined in terms of the mean length of the placement error vectors across the wafer. But it has been more productive in semiconductor technology to resolve placement error into x and y components and to analyze each component separately as a scalar error. This is because integrated circuits are designed on a rectangular grid, with dimensions and tolerances specified in Cartesian coordinates. If a histogram is made of the x-axis overlay error at many points across a wafer, the result will be a more or less Gaussian distribution of scalar errors. The number quoted as the x-axis overlay or alignment error is the absolute value of the mean error plus three times the standard deviation of the distribution about the mean:

$$\text{Overlay}_x = |\overline{X}| + 3\sigma_x$$

The y-axis overlay and alignment errors will have an analogous form.

The evolutionary improvement of overlay tolerance has paralleled the improvements in optical resolution for many years, but the technologies involved in overlay are nearly independent of those involved in image formation. Resolution improvements are largely driven by increases in numerical aperture and reduction of optical aberrations in the lithographic lens. Although lens distortion is a significant component of the overlay budget, most of the overlay accuracy depends on the technologies of alignment mark detection, stage accuracy, photomask tolerance, thermal control, and wafer chucking.

8.2 Alignment Methodology

Overlay errors consist of a mixture of random and systematic placement errors. The random component is usually small, and the best alignment strategy is usually to measure and correct as many of the systematic terms as possible.

Before the wafer is placed on the vacuum chuck, it is mechanically prealigned to a tolerance of a few tens of microns. This prealignment is good enough to bring alignment marks on the wafer within range of the alignment mark detection system, but the rotation and x- and y-translation errors must be measured and corrected before the wafer is exposed. A minimum of two alignment marks must be measured to correct rotation and x and y translation. Use of two alignment marks also gives information about the wafer scale. If the previous level of lithography was exposed on a poorly calibrated stepper, or if the wafer dimensions have changed because of thermal effects, then the information on wafer scale can be used to adjust the stepping size to improve the overlay. Use of a third alignment mark adds information about wafer scale along a second axis and about orthogonality of the stepping axes. These terms usually need to be corrected to bring overlay into the 0.1-μm regime.

Each alignment mark that is measured provides two pieces of information—its x and y coordinates. This means that $2n$ alignment terms can be derived from n alignment mark measurements. It is usually not productive to correct stepping errors higher than the six terms just described: x and y translation, wafer rotation, x and y wafer scale, and stepping orthogonality. However, a large number of alignment mark positions can be measured on the wafer and used to calculate an overspecified or constrained fit to these six terms. The additional measurements provide redundant information that reduces the error on each term.

An additional set of systematic alignment terms results from errors within a single exposure field. The dominant terms are intrafield magnification error and field rotation relative to the stepping axes. In a static-field stepper, the lens symmetry prevents any differences between magnification in the x and y direction (known as anamorphism). But there are higher order terms which are important. Third-order distortion (barrel or pincushion distortion) is a variation of magnification along a radius of the circular exposure field. X- and y-trapezoid errors result from a tilted mask in an optical system that is not telecentric on the mask side. As the name implies, trapezoid errors distort a square coordinate grid into a trapezoidal grid.

In previous generations of steppers, these intrafield errors (except for third-order distortion, which is a property of the lens design) were removed during the initial installation of the system and readjusted at periodic maintenance in-

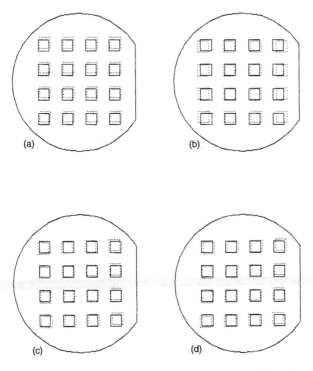

Figure 19 Common wafer-scale overlay errors. The solid chip outlines represent the prior exposure level and the dotted outlines are the newly aligned exposures. (a) A simple *x* and *y* translation error. (b) A positive wafer scale error in *x* and a negative wafer scale error in *y*. (c) An illustration of wafer rotation. (d) An illustration of stepping orthogonality error.

tervals. Today, most advanced steppers have the ability to adjust magnification and field rotation on each wafer to minimize overlay error. Alignment marks in at least two different locations within the exposure field are needed to measure these two intrafield terms.

Step-and-scan exposure systems can have additional intrafield error terms. Because the total exposure field is built up by a scanning slit, an error in the scanning speed of either the mask or wafer can produce a difference between the *x* and *y* field magnifications. If the mask and the wafer scans are not exactly parallel, then an intrafield orthogonality error (often called skew) is generated. Of course, the lens magnification and field rotation errors seen in static exposure steppers are also present in step-and-scan systems. A minimum of three intrafield alignment marks is necessary to characterize *x* and *y* translation, *x* and *y* field magnification, field rotation, and skew in such a system.

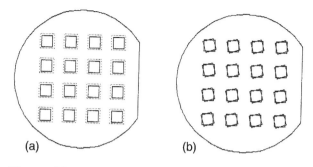

Figure 20 Correctable intrafield overlay errors. (a) A field magnification error; (b) field rotation. Contrast these with the corresponding wafer magnification and rotation errors in Fig. 19b and c. There are many higher orders of intrafield distortion errors, but in general they cannot be corrected except by modifications to the lens assembly.

8.3 Global Mapping Alignment

Intrafield and stepping error terms can be simultaneously derived in a constrained fit to a large number of measured alignment mark positions across the wafer. This alignment strategy is called global mapping. It requires that the wafer be stepped past the alignment mark detector while position information on several alignment marks is collected. After a quick computer analysis of the data, corrections to the intrafield and stepping parameters of the system are made, and the wafer exposure begins. The corrections made after the mapping are assumed to be stable during the 1 or 2 minutes required to expose the wafer.

Global mapping has been a very successful alignment strategy. Its main drawback is the length of time required for the mapping pass, which degrades the productivity of the system. Two-point global alignment and site-by-site alignment are the main strategies competing with global mapping. Because two-point global alignment is able to correct for only x and y translation, wafer rotation, and isotropic wafer scale errors, it can succeed only if the stage orthogonality is very good and the intrafield error terms are very small and stable over time. It also requires that all previous levels of lithography have very low values of these terms. Although most stepper manufacturers have adopted global mapping alignment, ASM Lithography has been very successful with a highly accurate two-point alignment strategy.

8.4 Site-by-Site Alignment

Site-by-site alignment can be performed by most steppers with global mapping capability. In this alignment strategy, alignment marks at each exposure site are measured and corrections specific to that site are calculated. The site is exposed after the alignment measurement is done, and the process is repeated at the next exposure site. The time required for this process is usually greater than that required for global mapping, due to the need for alignment mark measurements at each exposure site on the wafer. The accuracy of site-by-site alignment can be better than that of global mapping, but this is not always the case. As long as the alignment is done to a lithographic level in which the systematic component of placement error is greater than the random component, the data-averaging ability of global mapping can yield a better final overlay.

In general, global mapping reduces random measurement errors that occur during detection of the alignment mark positions, while site-by-site alignment does a better job of matching random placement errors of the previous level of lithography. As long as the random placement errors are small, global mapping can be expected to give better results than site-by-site alignment.

8.5   Alignment Sequence

Global mapping, two-point global alignment, and site-by-site alignment are all used to align the current exposure to a previous level of lithographic patterns. Another important part of the alignment strategy is to determine the alignment sequence. This is the choice of the previous level to which the current level should align. One common choice is level-to-level alignment. With this strategy, each level of lithographic exposure is aligned to the most recent previous critical level. (Levels (sometimes called layers) of lithographic exposures are classified as critical or noncritical depending on the image sizes and overlay tolerances. Critical levels have image sizes at or near the lithographic resolution limits and the tightest overlay tolerances. Noncritical levels have image sizes and overlay tolerances that are relaxed by 1.5× to 2× or more from those of the critical levels.) This provides the most accurate possible alignment between adjacent critical levels. But critical levels that are separated by another intervening critical level are related only by a second-order alignment. This will be less accurate than a first-order alignment by a factor of $\sqrt{2}$. More distantly separated levels will have even less accurate alignments to each other. In general, a high-order alignment will have an alignment error which is the root sum square of the individual alignment errors in the sequence. If all of the alignments in the sequence have the same magnitude of error, than an nth-order alignment error will be greater than a first-order alignment error by a factor of $\sqrt{n}$.

Another common alignment strategy is called zero-level alignment. In this strategy, every level of lithographic exposure is aligned to the first level that was printed on the wafer. This first level may be the first processing level or a specialized alignment level (called the zero level) containing nothing but alignment marks. With this strategy, every level has an accurate first-order alignment to the first level and a less accurate second-order alignment to every other level.

The choice of whether to use zero-level or level-to-level alignment depends on the needs of the semiconductor circuits being fabricated. In many cases, the most stringent requirement is for alignment of adjacent critical levels, and alignment to more remote levels is not as important. In this case, level-to-level alignment is clearly called for. But after a chain of six or eight level-to-level alignments, the first and last levels printed will have a 2.5× to 3× degradation in the accuracy of their alignment relative to a first-order alignment. Zero-level alignments suffer from another problem. Many semiconductor processing steps are designed to leave extremely planar surfaces on the wafer. For example, chemical-mechanical polishing leaves a nearly optical finish on the water surface. If an opaque film is deposited on top of such a planarized surface, any underlying alignment marks will be completely hidden. Even in less severe cases, the accumulation of many levels of processing may seriously degrade the visibility of a zero-level alignment mark.

Often a mixed strategy is adopted. If zero-level alignment marks become unusable after a particular level of processing, then a new set of marks can be printed and used for successive levels of alignment. If a level-to-level alignment strategy fails because of the inaccuracy of a third- or fourth-order alignment, then the alignment of that level may be changed to an earlier level in the alignment sequence. Generally speaking, the impact of any particular alignment sequence on the overlay accuracy between any two exposure levels should be well known to the circuit designer, and the design tolerances must take these figures into account from the start of any new circuit design.

8.6 Distortion Matching

After all of the correctable alignment terms have been measured and corrected, there are still some systematic but uncorrectable overlay errors. One important term is lens distortion. Although lens distortion has dramatically improved over the years (to values below 50 nm today), it is still an important term in the overlay budget. The distortion characteristics of a lens tend to be stable over time, so if both levels in a particular alignment are exposed on the same stepper, the relative distortion error between the two levels will be close to zero. This strategy is called dedication. It is a remarkably unpopular strategy in large-scale semiconductor manufacture. A large amount of bookkeeping is required to ensure that each wafer lot is returned to its dedicated stepper for every level of lithography. Scheduling problems are apt to occur, in which some steppers are forced to stand idle while others have a large backlog of work. Worst of all, the failure of a single stepper can completely halt production on a large number of wafer lots.

Lithographic lenses made by a single manufacturer to the same design tend to have similar distortion characteristics. This means that two masking levels exposed on steppers with the same lens design will usually have lower overlay errors than the absolute lens distortion values would predict. It is quite likely that a semiconductor fabricator will dedicate production of a particular product to a set of steppers of one model. As well as providing the best overlay (short of single-stepper lot dedication), a set of identical steppers provides benefits for operating training, maintenance, and spare parts inventory. For an additional cost, stepper manufacturers will often guarantee distortion matching within a set of steppers to much tighter tolerances than the absolute distortion tolerance of that model.

Overlay between steppers of different models or from different manufacturers is likely to give the worst distortion matching. This strategy is often called mix-and-match. There may be several reasons for adopting a mix-and-match strategy. A small number of very expensive steppers may be purchased to run a level with particularly tight dimensional tolerances, but a cheaper stepper model may be used for all the other levels. Often a semiconductor fabricator will have a number of older steppers that are adequate for the less critical levels of lithography. These will have to achieve a reasonable overlay tolerance with newer steppers that expose the more difficult levels. In recent years, improvements in lens design and fabrication have greatly reduced the total distortion levels in lithographic lenses. As this improvement continues, the characteristic distortion signatures of different lens designs have become less pronounced. Today there are several examples of successful mix-and-match alignment strategies in commercial semiconductor manufacturing.

The distortion characteristics of step-and-scan systems are different from those of static exposure lenses. Because the exposure field is scanned across the wafer, every point in the printed image represents the average of the distortion along the direction of the scan. This averaging effect somewhat reduces the distortion of the scanned exposure. (Scanning an exposure field with a small amount of distortion also makes the images move slightly during the scan. This induces a slight blurring of the image. If the magnitude of the distortion vectors is small compared to the minimum image size, then the blurring effect is negligible.) The distortion plot of a scanned exposure may have a variety of different displacement vectors across the long axis of the scanning slit. But in the scanned direction, the displacement vectors in every row will be nearly identical. In contrast, the distortion plot of a conventional static stepper field typically has displacement vectors that are oriented along radii of the field, and the distortion plot tends to have a rotational symmetry about its center.

There is a potential solution to the problem of distortion matching among a set of steppers. If the masks used on these steppers are made with their patterns appropriately placed to cancel the measured distortion signature of each stepper, then nearly perfect distortion matching can be achieved. As with most utopian ideas, this one has many practical difficulties. There are costs and logistical difficulties in dedicating masks to a particular stepper, just as there are in dedicating wafer lots to a particular stepper. The software infrastructure required to merge stepper distortion data with mask design data has not been developed. Masks are designed on a discrete grid, and distortion corrections can be made only when they exceed the grid spacing. The discontinuity that occurs where the pattern is displaced by one grid space can cause problems in the mask inspection and even in the circuit performance at that location. The possibility remains that mask corrections for lithographic lens distortion may be used in the future, but it will probably not happen as long as lens distortion continues to improve at the present rate.

8.7 Off-Axis Alignment

The sensors used to detect alignment mark positions have always used some form of optical position detection. The simplest technique is to have one or more microscope objectives mounted close to the lithographic projection lens and focused on the wafer's surface when it is mounted on the vacuum chuck. The image of the alignment mark is captured by a television camera or some other form of image scanner, and the position of the mark is determined by either a human operator or an automated image detection mechanism. Operator-assisted alignments are almost totally obsolete in modern lithographic exposure equipment, and automated alignment systems have become very sophisticated. Alignment by use of external microscope objectives is called off-axis alignment. The alternative to off-axis alignment is called through-the-lens (TTL) alignment. As the name implies, this technique captures the image of a wafer alignment mark directly through the lithographic projection lens.

With off-axis alignment, every wafer alignment mark is stepped to the position of the detection microscope. Its x and y positions are recorded in absolute stage coordinates. After the mapping pass is complete, a calculation is done to derive the systematic alignment error terms. The position of the wafer relative to the alignment microscope is now known extremely accurately. An x and y offset must be added to the position of the wafer in order to translate the data from the alignment microscope's location to that of the center of the mask's projected image. This offset vector is usually called the baseline. Any error in the value of the baseline will lead directly to an overlay error in the wafer exposure. A number of factors can affect stability of the baseline. Temperature changes in the stepper environment can cause serious baseline drifts because of thermal expansion of the stepper body. Every time a mask is removed and replaced, the accuracy with which the mask is returned to its original position directly affects the baseline. The mask is aligned to its amounting fixture in the stepper by use of specialized mask alignment marks, which are part of the chromium pattern generated by the original mask data. Any pattern placement error affecting these marks during the mask-making process also adds a term to the baseline error.

In older generations of steppers, baseline drift was a significant source of overlay error. Baseline was corrected at frequent service intervals by a painstaking process of exposing lithographic test wafers and analyzing their overlay errors. In between corrections, the baseline—and the overlay on all the wafers exposed on the system—drifted. Baseline stability in modern steppers has improved greatly, due to improved temperature control, better mounting technology for the alignment microscopes, and relocating the microscopes closer to the projection lens, which physically shortens the baseline. Another key improvement has been a technology for rapid, automated measurement of the baseline. A specialized, miniature alignment mark detector can be built into the stepper's wafer stage. (In some steppers, the arrangement described here is reversed. Instead of using a detector on the stage, an illuminated alignment mark is mounted on the stage. The image of this mark is projected backward through the lithographic projection lens onto the surface of the mask. The alignment between the mask and the projected alignment mark is measured by a detector above the mask.) This detector is designed to measure the position of the projected image of an alignment mark built into the mask pattern on every mask used on that stepper. Permanently etched into the faceplate of the detector on the stage is a normal wafer alignment mark. After the image of the mask alignment mark has been measured, the stage moves the detector to the off-axis alignment position. There the etched wafer alignment mark on the detector faceplate is measured by the normal alignment microscope. The difference between these two measured positions, plus the small separation between the detector and the etched alignment mark, equals the baseline. The accuracy of the baseline is now determined by the accuracy of the stage-positioning interferometers and the stability of the few-millimeter spacing between the detector and the etched alignment mark. The detector faceplate can be made of a material with a low thermal expansion coefficient, like fused silica, to further reduce any remaining baseline drift. This automated baseline measurement can be made as often as necessary to keep the baseline drift within the desired tolerances.

In high-volume manufacturing, baseline drift can be kept to a minimum by the techniques of statistical process control. By feeding back corrections from the constant stream of overlay measurements on product wafers, the need for periodic recalibration of baseline can be completely eliminated.

8.8   Through-the-Lens Alignment

Through-the-lens alignment avoids the problem of baseline stability by directly comparing an alignment mark on the mask to the image of a wafer alignment mark projected through the lithographic projection lens. There are a number of techniques for doing this. One typical method is to illuminate the wafer alignment mark through a matching transparent window in the mask. The projected image is reflected back through the window in the mask and its intensity is measured by a simple light detector. The wafer is scanned so that the image of the wafer alignment mark passes across the window in the mask, and the position of maximum signal strength is recorded. The wafer scan is done in both the x and y directions to determine both coordinates of the wafer alignment mark.

Although TTL alignment is a very direct and accurate technique, it also suffers from a few problems. The numerical aperture of the detection optics is limited to that of the lithographic projection lens, even though a higher NA might be desirable to increase the resolution of the alignment mark's image. Because the wafer alignment mark must be projected through the lithographic lens, it should be illuminated with the lens's designed wavelength. But this wavelength will expose the photoresist over each alignment mark that is measured. This is often quite undesirable, because it precludes the mask designer from making a choice about whether or not to expose the alignment mark in order to protect it from the next level of processing. The alignment wavelength can be shifted to a longer wavelength to protect the resist from exposure, but the projection lens will have to be modified in order to accept the different wavelength. This is often done by inserting very small auxiliary lenses in the light path that is used for the TTL alignment. These lenses correct the focal length of the lens for the alignment wavelength but interfere with only a small region at the edge of the lens field that is reserved for use by the mask alignment mark.

Whether the exposure wavelength or a longer wavelength is used, the chromatic aberration of the lithographic lens forces the use of monochromatic light for the TTL alignment. Helium-neon or argon-ion lasers are often used as light sources for TTL alignment. Monochromatic light is not ideal for detecting wafer alignment marks. Because these marks are usually made of one or more layers of thin films, they exhibit a strong swing curve when illuminated by monochromatic light. For some particular film stacks, the optical contrast of the alignment mark may almost vanish at the alignment wavelength. This problem is not as likely to occur with broadband (white light) illumination, which is usually used in off-axis alignment systems.

In general, off-axis alignment offers more flexibility in the design of the detector. Because it is decoupled from the projection optics, there is a free choice of numerical apertures and alignment wavelengths. There is no interference with the optical or mechanical design of the projection lens, as there usually is with TTL alignment detectors. Off-axis alignment may require an additional amount of travel in the wafer stage, in order that all parts of the wafer can be viewed by the alignment mark detector. But the most serious difficulty with off-axis alignment is the baseline stability. If the baseline requires frequent recalibration, then the availability and productivity of the stepper will suffer.

8.9   Alignment Mark Design

The alignment mark design is usually specified by the stepper manufacturer, rather than being left up to the imagination of the mask designer. The alignment mark detector is optimized for best performance with one particular mark design. At minimum, the mark must have structures in two orthogonal directions, so that its x and y position can be measured. A simple cross-shaped mark has been used successfully in the past. But there are benefits gained by measuring multiple structures within the alignment mark. Today many alignment marks are shaped like gratings, with several horizontal and vertical bars. This allows the measurement error to be reduced by averaging the position error from the measurement of each bar. It also reduces the effect of tiny edge placement errors that may have occurred in the manufacture of the mask that was used to print the mark on the wafer and effects of edge roughness in the etched image of the mark. The size of the alignment mark involves a trade-off between signal strength and the availability of space in the chip design. Alignment marks have been used with a variety of sizes, from less than 50 μm to more than 150 μm on a side. The space allowed for an alignment mark also depends on the prealignment accuracy of the wafer and the capture area of the alignment mark detector. If the alignment marks are placed too close to other structures on the mask, the detector may not be able to find the alignment mark reliably. In order to reduce the requirement for a dead band around the alignment mark, some stepper manufacturers use a two-step alignment procedure. A crude two-point global alignment is made using large marks that are printed in only two places on the wafer. This brings the wafer position well within the capture range of the small fine-alignment targets within each exposure field.

8.10   Alignment Mark Detection

The technology for alignment mark detection has advanced steadily since the beginning of microlithography. Normal microscope objectives with bright-field illumination were used originally. Dark-field illumination has the advantage that only the edges of the alignment marks are detected. This often provides a cleaner signal that can be more easily analyzed. In standard dark-field illumination, light is projected onto the wafer surface at grazing incidence, and the scattered light is captured by a normal microscope objective. A technique sometimes called reverse dark-field detection is often used. In this arrangement, light is projected through the central portion of the microscope objective onto the wafer surface. The directly reflected light is blocked by the illuminator assembly, but light scattered from the edges of the alignment mark are captured by the outer portions of the microscope objective. This provides a compact dark-field microscope. Because of the blocked central region, the microscope uses an annular pupil, which forms an image with good contrast in the edges of features. Some types of process films, especially grainy metal films, do not give good alignment signals with dark-field imaging. Because of this, many steppers provide both bright-field and dark-field alignment capability. Bright-field, standard dark-field, and reverse dark-field detection can be used for either off-axis or TTL alignment.

A great amount of sophisticated signal analysis is often used to reduce the raw output of the alignment microscope to an accurate alignment mark position. All of the available information in the signal is used to reduce susceptibility to detection noise and process-induced variability in the appearance of the mark on the wafer.

9 MECHANICAL CONSIDERATIONS

9.1 The Laser Heterodyne Interferometer

In addition to the wonderful optical perfection of a lithographic exposure system, there is an almost miraculous mechanical accuracy. The overlay tolerance needed to produce a modern integrated circuit can be less than 100 nm. This requirement must be met by mechanically holding a wafer at the correct position, within the overlay tolerances, during the lithographic exposure. There are no clever optical or electronic ways of steering the aerial image the last few microns into its final alignment. The entire 200-mm wafer must physically be in the right place. This is the equivalent of bringing a 32-mile iceberg to dock with an accuracy of 1 inch.

The technology that enables this remarkable accuracy is the laser heterodyne interferometer. An extremely stable helium-neon laser is operated in a carefully controlled magnetic field. Under these conditions, the spectrum of the laser beam is split into two components with slightly different wavelengths. This effect is called Zeeman splitting. Each of the two Zeeman components has a different polarization. This allows them to be separated and sent along different optical paths. One beam is reflected from a mirror mounted on the wafer stage. The other beam is reflected from a stationary reference surface near the moving stage. Preferably, this reference surface should be rigidly attached to the lithographic lens. After the two beams are reflected, their planes of polarization are rotated to coincide with each other, and the two beams are allowed to interfere with each other on the surface of a simple power sensor. Because the two beams have different wavelengths and therefore different optical frequencies, a beat frequency will be generated. This beat frequency is just the difference between the optical frequencies of the two Zeeman components of the laser beam. It is on the order of a few MHz. When the stage begins moving, the frequency of the signal changes by $2v/\lambda$, where v is the stage velocity and λ is 632.8 nm, the helium-neon laser wavelength. This change in frequency is caused by the Doppler shift in the beam reflected from the moving stage. A stage velocity of 1 m/sec will cause a frequency shift of 3.16 MHz, and a velocity of 1 mm/sec will cause a frequency shift of 3.16 kHz. We now have an accurate relationship between stage velocity and frequency. But what we want is a measurement of stage position. This is accomplished by comparing the frequency of the stage interferometer signal with the beat frequency of a pair of beams directly out of the laser. The two beat frequencies are monitored by a sensitive phase comparator. If the stage is stationary, the phase of the two signals will remain locked together. If the stage begins to move, the phase of the stage interferometer signal will begin to drift relative to the signal directly from the laser. When the phase has drifted one full cycle (2π), the stage will have moved a distance of $\lambda/2$ (316.4 nm). The phase comparator can keep track of phase differences from a fraction of a cycle to several million cycles, corresponding to distance scales from a few nanometers to several meters.

One helium-neon interferometer laser supplies all the metrology needs of the wafer stage. After the beam is split into the two Zeeman components, each com-

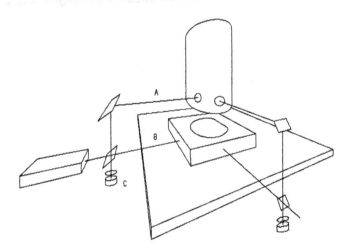

Figure 21 A simplified drawing of a stepper's stage interferometer. A polarizing beam splitter sends one component of the laser beam to the stage along path B, while a second component at slightly different wavelength travels along a reference path A to the lens mounting assembly. The retroreflected beams from the stage and the lens assembly are recombined in the beamsplitter and collected by a detector C. Analysis of the beat frequency in the combined beam allows the stage position to be tracked to high accuracy. The second axis of stage motion is tracked by another interferometer assembly. Some components that control the beam polarization within the interferometer have been omitted for simplicity.

ponent is further split into as many beams as are needed to monitor the stage properly. Each of the final pairs of beams forms its own independent interferometer. The minimum stage control requires one interferometer on both the x and y axes. The laser beams are aimed so that they would intersect at the center of the lithographic projection lens's exposure field. Linearity of the stage travel and orthogonality of the axes are guaranteed by the flatness and orthogonality of two mirrors mounted on the stage. To ensure that the axis orthogonality cannot be lost because of one of the mirrors slipping in its mount, the two mirrors are usually ground from a single piece of glass. With two-interferometer control, the yaw, pitch, and roll accuracies of the stage are guaranteed only by the mechanical tolerances of the ways. Pitch and roll errors are relatively insignificant because they result in overlay errors proportional to the cosine of the angular errors. But yaw (rotation in the plane of the wafer surface) can be a serious problem because it has the same effect on overlay as a field rotation error. Three-interferometer stage control is very common today. With this strategy, an additional interferometer monitors the mirror on one axis to eliminate yaw errors.

9.2 Atmospheric Effects

Although interferometer control is extremely accurate, there are some factors that affect its accuracy and must be carefully regulated. Since the length scale of interferometry is the laser wavelength, anything that affects the laser wave-

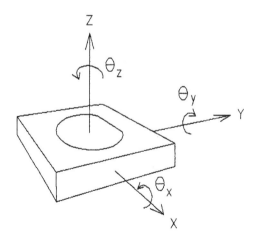

Figure 22 Three axes of translational motion and three axes of rotation on a wafer stage. X, Y, and θ_Z must be controlled to high precision to ensure the accuracy of overlay. The Z, θ_X, and θ_Y axes affect focus and field tilt and can be controlled to somewhat lower precision.

length will cause a corresponding change in the length scale of the stage positioning. The laser's optical frequency is extremely well controlled, but changes in the wavelength can be induced by any changes in the index of refraction of the air. Barometric pressure and air temperature affect the refractive index of air, but slow changes in these variables can be monitored and corrected. In fact, slow drifts in the interferometry are not very important because the stage interferometers are used both for measuring the position of the wafer alignment marks and for determining the position of the exposure. Errors in the length scale tend to cancel (except where they affect the baseline). But rapid changes in the air index can cause serious problems for the stage accuracy. Air turbulence in the interferometer paths can cause just this sort of problem. A fairly large effort has been made by stepper manufacturers to enclose or otherwise shield the light paths of the stage interferometers from stray air flows. Heat sources near the interferometers, such as stage drive motors, have been relocated or water cooled. More work remains to be done in this area, especially considering the inexorable tightening of overlay tolerances and future plans to convert wafer sizes from 200 to 300 mm, which will increase the optical path length of the interferometers.

9.3 Wafer Stage Design

Wafer stage design varies considerably from manufacturer to manufacturer. All the designs have laser interferometers tied into a feedback loop to ensure the accurate position of the stage during exposure. Many designs use a low-mass, high-precision stage with a travel of only a few millimeters. This stage carries the wafer chuck and the interferometer mirrors. It sits on top of a coarse positioning stage with long travel. The coarse stage may be driven by fairly conventional stepper motors and lead screws. The high-precision stage is usually driven directly by magnetic fields. When the high-precision stage is driven to a target position, the coarse stage acts as a slave, following the motion of the fine stage to keep it within its allowable range of travel. The control system must be carefully tuned to allow both stages to move rapidly to a new position and settle within the alignment tolerances, without overshoot or oscillation, and within a time of less than 1 second. Coarse stages have been designed with roller bearings, air bearings, and sliding plastic bearings. High-precision stages have used flexure suspension or magnetic field suspension.

Not all advanced wafer stage designs follow the coarse stage and fine stage design. Some of the most accurate steppers use a single massive stage, driven directly by magnetic fields.

Requirements on the stages of step-and-scan exposure equipment are even more severe. When the stage on a static exposure stepper gets slightly out of adjustment, the only effect may be a slight increase in settling time before the stepper is ready to make an exposure. But the stage on a step-and-scan system must be within its position tolerance continuously throughout the scan. It must also run synchronously with a moving mask stage. But these systems have been successfully built, and generally with the same stage design principles as conventional steppers.

Mounted on the stage are the interferometer mirrors and the wafer chuck. The chuck is supported by a mechanism that can rotate the chuck to correct wafer rotation error from the prealigner. There may also be a vertical axis motion for wafer focus adjustment and even tilt adjustments along two axes to perform wafer leveling. All of these motions must be made without introducing any transverse displacements in the wafer position, because the interferometer mirrors do not follow these fine adjustments. Often, flexure suspension is used for the tilt and rotation adjustments. Because of the difficulty of performing this many motions without introducing any translation errors, there is a tendency to move these functions to a position between the coarse and fine stages, so that the interferometer mirrors will pick up any translations that occur. At the extreme, monolithic structures have been designed consisting of the interferometer mirrors and a wafer chuck all ground from a single piece of low-thermal-expansion ceramic. This structure can be moved through six axes of motion (three translation and three rotation). It is monitored by five interferometers, which track all of the motions except the z axis (or axis of focus).

9.4 The Wafer Chuck

The wafer chuck has a difficult job to perform. It must hold a wafer flat to extremely tight tolerances (on the order of 100 to 200 nm) all the way across the wafer's surface. At this scale of tolerances, micron-sized particles of dirt or thin residues of resist on the back side of the wafer will result in a completely unacceptable wafer surface flatness. Particle contamination and wafer back-side residues are minimized by strict control of the resist application process and by particle filtration of the air supply in the stepper enclosure. The chuck is made as resistant as possible to any remaining particle contamination by using a low-contact-area design. This design, sometimes called a bed of nails, consists of a regular array of rather small studs whose tips are ground and polished so that they are coplanar with the other studs in the array to the accuracy of an optical flat. The space between the studs is used as a vacuum channel to pull the wafer against the chuck's surface. The space also provides a region where a stray particle on the back side of the wafer may exist without lifting the wafer surface. The actual fraction of the wafer area in contact with the chuck may be as low as 5%, providing considerable immunity to back-side particle contamination. The symmetry of the stud array must be broken at the edge of the wafer, where a thin solid rim forms a vacuum seal. This region of discontinuity frequently causes problems in maintaining flatness all the way to the edge of the wafer.

At the end of the lithographic exposure, the chuck must release the wafer and allow a wafer handler to remove it. This causes another set of problems. It is almost impossible for a vacuum handler to pick up a wafer by the front surface without leaving an unacceptable level of particle contamination behind. Although front-surface handler were once in common use, it is rare to find them today. The only other alternative is to somehow get a vacuum handler onto the back surface of the wafer. Sometimes a section of the chuck is cut away near the edge to give the handler access to the wafer back side. But the quality of lithography over the cutout section invariably suffers. The unsupported part of the wafer curls and ripples unpredictably, depending on the stresses in that part of the wafer. Another solution has been to lift the wafer away from the chuck with pins inserted through the back of the chuck. This allows good access for a back-side wafer handler and is generally a good solution. But the necessity for a vacuum seal around the lifter pin locations and the disruption of the chuck pattern there may cause local problems in wafer flatness.

9.5 Automatic Focus Systems

Silicon wafers, especially after deposition of a few process films or subjection to hot processing, tend to become somewhat curled or bowed (on the scale of several microns) when they are not held on a vacuum chuck. The vacuum chuck does a good job of flattening the wafer, but there are still some surface irregularities at the micron scale. The wafer may also have some degree of wedge between the front and back surfaces. Because of these irregularities, a surface-referencing sensor is used to detect the position and levelness of the top wafer surface, so that it can be brought into the proper focal plane for exposure.

A variety of surface sensors have been used in the focus mechanisms of steppers. One common type is a grazing-incidence optical sensor. With this technique, a beam of light is focused onto the surface of the wafer at a shallow, grazing angle (less than $5°$ from the plane of the surface). The reflected light is collected by a lens system and focused onto a position detector. The wavelength chosen for this surface measurement must be much longer than the lithographic exposure wavelength, so that the focus mechanism does not expose the photoresist. Frequently, near-infrared laser diodes are used for this application. The shallow angle of reflection is intended give the maximum geometrical sensitivity to the wafer's surface position and also to enhance the signal from the top of the resist. If a more vertical angle of incidence were used, there would be a danger that the sensor might look through the resist and any transparent films beneath the resist, finally detecting a reflective metal or silicon layer deep below the surface. The great advantage of the grazing-angle optical sensor is its ability to de-

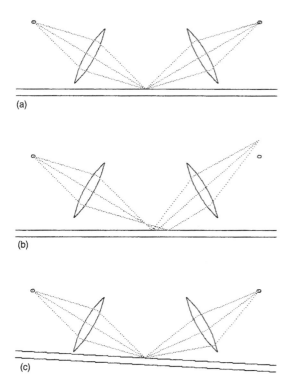

(a)

(b)

(c)

Figure 23 A grazing-incidence optical sensor used as a stepper autofocus mechanism. Light from a source on the left is focused at a point where the wafer surface must be located for best performance of the lithographic projection lens (not shown). If the wafer surface is in the correct position, as in (a), the spot of light is reflected and refocused on a detector on the right. If the wafer surface is too high or low, as in (b), the reflected light is not centered on the detector and an error signal is generated. (c) The optics do not generate an error if the wafer surface is tilted.

tect the wafer surface at the actual location where the exposure is going to take place, without blocking or otherwise interfering with the exposure light path.

A second surface-sensing technique that has been used successfully is the air gauge. A small-diameter air tube is placed in close proximity to the wafer surface, so that the wafer surface blocks the end of the tube. The rate at which air escapes from the tube is strongly dependent on the gap between the wafer and the end of the tube. By monitoring this flow rate, the position of the wafer surface can be very accurately determined. Air gauges are compact, simple, and reliable. They are sensitive only to the physical surface of the resist and are never fooled by multiple reflections in a complex film stack. But they are not completely ideal. They can be placed close to the exposure field, but they cannot intrude into it without blocking some of the image. This leaves two choices. The exposure field can be surrounded with several air gauges and their average can be taken as the best guess of the surface position within the exposure field. Or the air gauge can take a measurement at the actual exposure site on the wafer before it is moved into the exposure position. This second option is not desirable because it adds a time-consuming extra stage movement to every exposure. Because the air gauges are outside the exposure field, they may fall of the edge of the wafer if a site near the edge of the wafer is exposed. This may require some complexity in the sensing and positioning software to ignore the signals from air gauges that are off the wafer. A surprisingly large amount of air is emitted by air gauges. This can cause turbulence in the critical area where the lithographic image is formed, unless the air gauges are shut off during every exposure. Another problem that has been seen is particle contamination of the wafer surface, carried in by air flow from the gauges.

The third commonly used form of surface detector is the capacitance gauge. A small, flat electrode is mounted near the lithographic exposure lens close to the wafer surface. This electrode and the conductive silicon wafer form a capacitor. The capacitance is a function of the electrode geometry and of the gap between the electrode and the wafer. When the wafer is in position under the capacitance gauge, the capacitance is measured electronically and the gap spacing is accurately determined. A capacitance gauge is somewhat larger than an air gauge, the electrode typically being a few millimeters in diameter. It has similar problems to the air gauge in its inability to intrude into the exposure field and its likelihood to fall of the edge of the wafer for some exposure sites. But capacitance gauges do not induce any air turbulence or particle contamination. The capacitance gauge actually measures the distance to the uppermost conductive film on the wafer, not to the physical surface of the resist. At first glance, this would seem like a serious deficiency. But the insulating films (including the photoresist) on the surface of the wafer have very high dielectric constants relative to air. This means that the air gap between the capacitance gauge and the wafer is weighted much more heavily than the dielectric layers in the capacitance measurement. Although there is still a theoretical concern about the meaning of capacitance gauge measurements when thick insulating films are present, in practice capacitance gauges have given very stable focus settings over a large range of different film stacks.

9.6 Automatic Leveling Systems

Because of the large size of the exposure field in modern steppers (up to 30-mm field diameter) and the very shallow depth of focus for high-resolution imaging, it is usually not sufficient to determine the focus position at only one point in the exposure field. Many years ago, when depths of focus were large and exposure fields were small, the mechanical levelness of the chuck was the only guarantee that the wafer surface was not tilted relative to the lithographic image. In more recent years, leveling of the wafer has been corrected by a global leveling technique: The wafer surface detector is stepped to three locations across the wafer and the surface heights are recorded. Corrections to two axes of tilt are made to bring the three measured points to the same height. Any surface irregularities of the wafer are ignored. This low level of correction is not always sufficient today. Site-by-site leveling is becoming increasingly desirable.

With detectors outside the exposure field (i.e., air gauges or capacitance gauges), three or four detectors can be placed around the periphery of the field. The field tilt can be calculated for these external positions and assumed with a good degree of confidence to be the same as the tilt within the field. Optical sensors can be designed to measure several discrete points within the exposure field and calculate tilt in the same way. A different optical technique has also been used. If a collimated beam of infrared light is reflected from the wafer surface within the exposure field, it can be collected by a lens and focused to a point. The position of this point is not sensitive to the vertical displacement of the wafer surface, but it is sensitive to tip and tilt of the surface [20]. If a quadrant detector monitors the position of the spot of light, its output can be used to level the wafer within the exposure field. This measurement automatically averages the tilt over all of the field that is illuminated by the collimated beam, rather than sampling the tilt at three or four discrete points. If desired, the entire exposure field can be illuminated and used for the tilt measurement.

With global wafer leveling, the leveling could be done before the alignment mapping, and any translations introduced by the leveling mechanism would not matter. But with site-by-site leveling, any translation arising from the leveling process will show up in overlay error. The leveling mechanism has to be designed with this in mind. Fortunately, leveling usually involves very small angular corrections in the wafer tilt. The ultimate answer to the problem of leveling without inducing translation errors is five-axis interferometry, which can cleanly separate the pitch and roll motions used to level the stage from x and y translational motions.

Step-and-scan systems face a slightly different local leveling issue. Because the scanning field moves continuously during exposure, it has the capability of following the irregularities of the wafer surface. This capability is often called terrain following. The scanning field does not actually tilt to match the surface in the direction of scanning, but the field is so short in that direction (about 5 mm) that the amount of defocus at the leading and trailing edges is small. If two focus sensors are used, one at each end of the long axis of the scanning field, then there is potential to adjust the roll axis continually during scanning

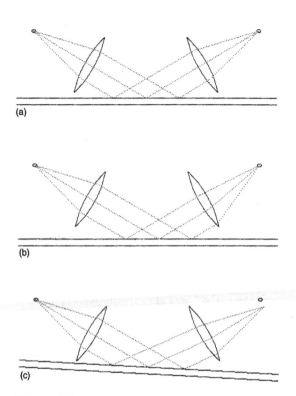

Figure 24   An optical sensor used for wafer leveling. This mechanism is very analogous to the focus sensor in Fig. 23. A collimated beam of light from the source on the left is accurately refocused on a detector on the right if the wafer is level, as in (a). Vertical displacements of the wafer surface, as in (b), do not affect the detector. But tilts of the wafer surface generate an error signal, as shown in (c).

to keep both ends of the scanning field in focus. This results in a very accurate two-axis terrain-following capability. The terrain following ability of step-and-scan systems allows them to match focus to an irregular wafer surface in much more detail than can be done with the large, planar exposure field of a traditional stepper.

9.7   Wafer Prealignment

A rather mundane but very important piece of the lithographic exposure system is the wafer prealigner. This mechanism mechanically positions the wafer and orients its rotation to the proper angle before it is placed on the wafer chuck for exposure. The prealignment is done without reference to any lithographic patterns printed on the wafer. The process uses only the physical outline of the wafer to determine its position. Early prealignment systems were fairly crude affairs, with electromechanical or pneumatic solenoids tapping the edges of the wafer into centration on a prealignment chuck. When the wafer was centered, the prealignment chuck rotated it while a photodiode searched its edge for an alignment structure, typically a flattened section of the edge, but occasionally a small V-shaped notch. Today's prealigners still use a rotating prealignment chuck, but the mechanical positioners are no longer used (banging on the edge of a wafer generates too much particle contamination). Instead, optical sensors map the edge of the wafer while it is rotating, and the centration of the wafer and rotation of the alignment flat (or notch) are calculated from the information collected by the sensor. After the wafer is rotated and translated into its final position, it must be transferred onto the wafer chuck that will hold it during exposure. The transfer arm used for this purpose must maintain the accuracy of the prealignment and is a fairly high-precision piece of equipment. Of course, there is no problem with positioning the wafer chuck accurately to receive the wafer from the transfer arm, since it is mounted on an interferometer stage. The handoffs from prealignment chuck to the transfer arm and from transfer arm to the wafer chuck must be timed properly so that the vacuum clamp of the receiving mechanism is activated before the vacuum clamp of the sending mechanism is turned off. The entire transfer must be as rapid as possible, because the stepper is doing no exposures during the transfer, and it is expensive to let it sit idle. The same transfer arm can also be used to unload the wafer at the end of its exposure, but the operation is simpler and faster if a second transfer arm is used for this purpose.

After the prealignment is complete, the wafer will be positioned on the wafer chuck to an accuracy of better than 50 μm. The alignment flat (or notch) will be accurately oriented to some direction relative to the top of the mask image. Perhaps surprisingly, there is no standard convention among stepper makers for the orientation of the alignment flat relative to the mask image. The flat has been variously oriented at the top, bottom, or right side of the wafer by different manufacturers at different times. For a stepper with a symmetrical exposure field, this problem is only a matter of orienting the pattern properly on the mask, regardless of where the nominal top side of the mask is located. But for exposure equipment with rectangular exposure fields, such as step-and-scan systems and some steppers, there is the possibility of serious incompatibility if one manufacturer orients the long axis of the exposure field parallel to the flat and another chooses a perpendicular orientation. Greater flexibility would result if the wafer flat orientation could be specified to the prealigner by software commands, but many steppers allow only a single flat orientation.

9.8   The Wafer Transport System

A lithographic exposure system is a large piece of equipment, and within it wafers must follow a winding path from an input station to a prealigner, transfer mechanism, wafer chuck, unload mechanism, and finally to an output station. The mechanisms that move the wafers along this path must be fast, clean, and (above all) reliable. A wafer-handling system that occasionally drops wafers is disastrous. Aside from the enormous cost of a 200-mm wafer populated by microprocessor chips, the fragments from a broken wafer will contaminate the stepper enclosure with particles of silicon dust and take the stepper out of production until the mess can be cleaned up. Most steppers use at least a few vacuum handlers. These devices hold the wafer by a vacuum channel in a flat piece of metal in contact with the back surface of the wafer. A vacuum sensor is used to ensure that the wafer is clamped before it is moved to its new location. The mechanism that rotates the vacuum handler from one position to another must be designed to avoid particle generation. Some steppers use nothing but vacuum handlers to maneuver the wafer from place to place. Other steppers have used conveyor belts or air tracks to move the wafers. The conveyor belts, consisting of parallel pairs of elastic bands running on rotating guides, are quite clean and reliable. Air tracks, which use jets of air to float wafers down flat track surfaces, tend to release too much compressed air into the stepper environment, with a corresponding risk of carrying particle contamination into the stepper. Air tracks were commonly used in steppers several years ago but are rare today.

The general issue of particle contamination has received great attention from stepper manufacturers for several years. Stepper components with a tendency to generate particle contamination have been redesigned. The environmental air circulation within the stepper chamber uses particle filters that are extremely efficient at cleaning the air surrounding the stepper. In normal use, a stepper will add fewer than five particles greater than 0.25 µm in diameter to a 200-mm wafer in a complete pass through the system. If particles are released into the stepper environment (for example, by maintenance or repair activities), the air circulation system will return the air to its normal cleanliness within about 10 minutes.

9.9   Vibration

Steppers are notoriously sensitive to vibration. This is not surprising, considering the 100-nm tolerances with which the image must be aligned. The mask and wafer in a stepper are typically separated by 500 to 800 mm, and it is difficult to hold them in good relative alignment in the presence of vibration. Vibration generated by the stepper itself has been minimized by engineering design of the components. There was a time when several components generated enough vibration to cause serious problems. The first solution was to prevent the operation of these components (typically wafer handlers and other moving equipment) during the exposure and stepping procedure. But to achieve good productivity, many of the stepper components must work in parallel. For example, the total rate of production would suffer greatly if the prealigner could not begin aligning a new wafer until the previous wafer had been exposed. But stepper components in use today have been redesigned so that they do not interfere with the exposure process. Externally generated vibrations are a more serious problem. Floors in a large factory tend to vibrate fairly actively. Even a semiconductor fabricator, which doesn't have much heavy moving equipment, can suffer from this problem. Large air-handling systems generate large amounts of vibration, which can easily be transmitted along the floor. Large vacuum pumps are also common in many wafer fabricating processes and are serious sources of vibration. Steppers are isolated from floor vibrations as much as possible by air isolation pedestals. These passively isolate the stepper from the floor by suspending it on relatively weak springs made of compressed air. Some lithographic exposure systems have an active feedback vibration suppression system built into their supporting frames. Even with these measures, lithographic equipment requires a quiet floor.

Semiconductor manufacturers are acutely aware of the vibration requirements of their lithographic equipment. Buildings that are designed to house semiconductor fabricators have many expensive features to ensure that vibration on the manufacturing floor is minimized. Air-handling equipment is usually suspended in a "penthouse" above the manufacturing area and anchored to an independent foundation. Heavy vacuum pumps are often placed in a basement area beneath the manufacturing floor. The manufacturing floor itself is frequently mounted on heavy pillars anchored to bed rock. The floor is vibrationally isolated from surrounding office and service areas of the building. Even with these precautions, there is usually an effort to find an especially quiet part of the floor to locate the lithographic exposure equipment.

Manufacturers of exposure equipment often supply facility specifications that include detailed requirements on floor vibration. This is usually in the form of a vibration spectrum, showing the maximum accelerometer readings allowed at the installation site from a few Hz to a few kHz. Horizontal and vertical components of floor vibration are both important and may have different specifications.

Vibration causes problems when it induces relative motion between the aerial image and the surface of the wafer. If the vibration is parallel to the plane of the image and the period of oscillation is short relative to the exposure time, the image will be smeared across the surface, degrading the contrast of the latent image captured by the resist. The allowable transverse vibration should be considerably less than the minimum image size in order not to degrade the printed image resolution. There is remarkably less sensitivity to vibration in the

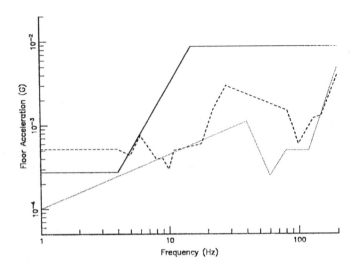

Figure 25   Maximum floor vibration specifications for a random selection of three optical exposure and measurement systems. The sensitivity to vibration depends on the optical resolution for which the equipment is designed, as well as the efficiency of its vibration isolation system.

direction perpendicular to the image plane (i.e., along the axis of focus or z axis). Aerial image modeling shows that there is very little degradation of the image contrast for z-axis vibration amplitudes up to the full depth of focus.

Only differential motion between the wafer and aerial image causes problems. Very low vibration frequencies tend to move the image and the wafer simultaneously, as a solid body. Without a great deal of structural modeling, it is very difficult to predict how an accelerometer reading on the floor of the factory will translate into the amplitude of image vibration across the surface of a wafer.

9.10   Mask Handlers

In addition to the mechanisms that the stepper uses for wafer handling, there is likely to be another entire set of mechanisms for automatically loading, aligning, and unloading masks. Previous generations of steppers required that masks by manually loaded and aligned. A hand-held mask was placed on a mask platen and aligned with a mechanical manipulation system while mask-to-platen alignment marks were inspected through a microscope. The procedure required good eyesight, considerably dexterity, and great care to avoid dropping the valuable mask. Today's automatic mask loaders represent a great improvement over the manual system. A mask library holds from 6 to 12 masks in protective cassettes. Any of these masks can be specified for an exposure by the stepper's control software. The selected mask is removed from its cassette by a vacuum arm or a mechanically clamped carrier. It is moved past a laser bar code reader, which reads a bar code on the mask and verifies that it is indeed the mask that was requested. (In the days of manual mask loading, a surprising number of wafer exposures were ruined because the wrong mask was selected from the storage rack.) The mask is loaded onto the mask platen and the alignment of the mask to the platen is done by an automatic manipulator. The entire procedure can be nearly as quick as loading a wafer to be exposed (although there is a great deal of variation in loading speed from one stepper manufacturer to another). With a fast automatic mask loader, it is possible to expose more than one mask pattern on each wafer by changing masks while the wafer is still on the exposure chuck.

9.11 Integrated Photo Cluster

The traditional way to load wafers into an exposure system is to mount a wafer cassette carrying 25 wafers onto a loading station. Wafers are removed from the cassette by a vacuum handler, one at a time as they are needed. At the end of the exposure, each wafer is loaded into an empty output cassette. Sometimes an additional rejected wafer cassette is provided for wafers that fail the automatic alignment procedure. When all the exposures are over, an operator unloads the filled output cassette and puts it into a protective wafer carrying box to be carried to the photoresist development station.

There is a tendency today to integrate an exposure system with a system that applies photoresist and another system that develops the exposed wafers. The combination of these three systems is called an integrated photosector or photocluster. With such an arrangement, clean wafers can be loaded into the input station of the cluster and half an hour later patterned, developed wafers can be unloaded and carried away. This has great benefits for reducing the total processing time of a lot of wafers through the manufacturing line. When the three functions of resist application, exposure, and development are separated, the wafers have a tendency to sit on a shelf for several hours between being unloaded from one system and started on the next. In the case of resists with low chemical stability of the latent image, there is also a benefit for developing each wafer immediately after it is exposed. The main drawback of such a system is the increased complexity of the system and the corresponding decrease in the mean time between failures.

An exposure system that is part of a photocluster may be built with no loading station or output station for wafer cassettes. Every wafer that comes into the system is handed from the resist application system directly to a vacuum handler arm in the stepper, and every wafer that comes out is handed directly to the resist developer. A robotic wafer handler is used to manage the transfers between the exposure system and the wafer processing systems. The software that controls the whole cluster is apt to be quite complex, interfacing with three different types of systems, often made by different manufacturers.

9.12 Cost of Ownership and Throughput Modeling

The economics of semiconductor manufacturing depend heavily on the productivity of the very expensive equipment used. Complex cost-of-ownership models are used to quantify the effects of all the factors involved in the final cost of wafer processing. Many of these factors, such as the cost of photoresist and developer and the amount of idle time on the equipment, are not under the control of the equipment manufacturer. The principal factors that depend on the manufacturer of the exposure system are the system's capital cost, mean time between failures, mean time to repair, and throughput. These numbers have all steadily increased over the years. Today, a single advanced lithographic stepper or step-and-scan exposure system may cost from $4 million to $7 million. Mean time between failures has been approaching 1000 hours for several models. Throughput is generally above 50 wafers per hour (wph) for 200-mm wafers.

The number quoted as the throughput for an exposure system is the maximum number of wafers per hour for a wafer layout completely populated with the system's maximum field size. Actual throughput for semiconductor products made on the system will vary considerably depending on the size of the exposed field area for that particular product and the number of fields on the wafer. For purposes of establishing the timing of bakes, resist development cycles, and other processes in the photocluster, it is important to know the actual throughput for each product. A simple model can be used to estimate throughput. The exposure time for each field is calculated by dividing the exposure requirement for the photoresist (in mJ/cm^2) by the power density of the illumination in the exposure field (in mW/cm^2). In a step-and-scan system the calculation is somewhat different. Because the power density within the illuminated slit does not need to be uniform along the direction of scan, the relevant variable is the integral of the power density along the scan direction. This quantity might be called the linear power density and has units of mW/cm. The linear power density divided by the exposure requirement of the resist (in mJ/cm^2) is the scan speed in cm/sec. The illuminated slit must overscan the mask image by one slit width in order to complete the exposure. The total length of scan divided by the scan speed is the exposure time. Typical exposure times for both steppers and step-and-scan systems are about 0.5 second.

After each exposure is completed, the stage moves to the next exposure site. For short steps between adjacent exposure sites, this stepping time can be approximated by a constant value. If a more accurate number is needed it can be calculated from a detailed analysis of the stage acceleration, maximum velocity, and settling time. The number of exposure sites, times the sum of the stepping time and the exposure time, is the total exposure time of the wafer. At the end of the exposure, there is a delay while one wafer is unloaded and the next is loaded. The sum of this wafer exchange time and the wafer exposure time is the inverse of the steady-state throughput. A 60-wafer-per-hour throughput rate allows 1 minute for each wafer, which may be broken down into 15 seconds for wafer exchange, 0.5 second for each exposure, and 0.5 second to step between exposures for 45 image fields on the wafer.

The actual throughput achieved by an exposure system is less than the steady-state throughput because of a factor called lot overhead. Lot overhead is the time required for the first wafer in a lot to arrive at the exposure chuck, plus the time required for the last wafer in the lot to be moved from the chuck to the output station. Its effect is distributed across the total number of wafers in the lot. For a 25-wafer lot running at a steady-state throughput of 60 wafers per hour, each minute of lot overhead reduces the net throughput by about 4%.

The trend toward linking wafer processing equipment and exposure systems into an integrated photocluster can have serious effects on lot overhead. Although the addition of a resist application track and a wafer development track

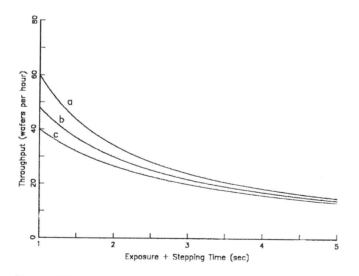

Figure 26 The relationship between stepper throughput and exposure time. Curves a, b, and c correspond to wafer overhead times of 15, 30, and 45 seconds, respectively. It is assumed that 45 exposure fields are required to populate the wafer fully.

does not change the steady-state throughput of the exposure system, there is a great increase in the processing time before the first exposure begins and after the last exposure ends. If a new lot cannot be started until the previous lot has completely finished all the processing steps and been removed from the system, the actual throughput of the total photocluster will be considerably less than the steady-state throughput. To remedy this situation, complex software controls on the photocluster are needed to allow lots to be cascaded. That is, a new lot must be started as soon as the input station is empty, while the previous lot is still being processed. The software must recognize the boundary between the two lots and change the processing recipe when the first wafer of the new lot arrives at each processing station.

10   TEMPERATURE AND ENVIRONMENTAL CONTROL

Lithographic exposure equipment is quite sensitive to temperature variations. The baseline offset between the lithographic lens and the off-axis alignment microscope will vary with thermal expansion of the structural materials. The index of refraction of glass and fused silica changes with temperature, altering the optical behavior of the lithographic projection lens. The index of refraction of air is also a function of temperature. This can affect the lithographic lens and the performance of the stage interferometers. In most cases, a rapid change in temperature causes more serious effects than a slow drift. For most lens designs, a change from one stable temperature to another primarily causes changes in focus and magnification, which can be measured and corrected. But some lens designs react to temperature changes by developing aberrations that are not so easily corrected. The calibration of the stage interferometers is also sensitive to temperature. If the temperature changes during the course of a wafer alignment and exposure, there may be serious errors in the stepping-scale term of the overlay.

10.1   The Environmental Chamber

This thermal sensitivity requires that the stepper be housed in an enclosed environmental chamber, with the ability to control temperature to $\pm 0.1°C$ or better. Some manufacturers supplement the thermal control of the environmental chamber with water coils on particularly sensitive elements of the system or on heat-generating items like motors or arc lamps. As long as the environmental chamber remains closed, it can maintain very accurate temperature control. But if it is frequently necessary to open the chamber (to manually free a stuck wafer, for example), the chamber may suffer a large temperature fluctuation that takes a long time to stabilize. Fortunately, steppers today very rarely need any sort of manual intervention in their operations. In many cases, the most frequent reason for opening the environmental chamber is to replace masks in the mask library. The consequences of opening the chamber can be reduced if the manufacturing area around the environmental chamber is maintained at the same mean temperature as the inside (although with a looser tolerance for fluctuations). Because of the desirability of keeping the stepper temperature close to that of the surrounding factory, it is usually designed to operate at a fixed temperature between 20°C and 22°C, which is a fairly standard range of environmental temperatures in a semiconductor clean room.

The environmental chamber maintains a constant flow of air past the stepper to keep the temperature uniform and within its specifications. The air is passed through high-efficiency particle filters before flowing through the chamber. As long as care has been taken that the stepper's moving parts do not generate additional particle contamination, the environment in the environmental enclosure is very clean. Wafers are exposed to this environment for several minutes during transport, prealignment, and exposure, with fewer than five additional particles added per pass through the system.

10.2 Chemical Filtration

In some circumstances, especially when acid-catalyzed deep-UV resists are used in the stepper, chemical air filters are used in series with the particle filters. These types of resists are extremely sensitive to airborne vapors of volatile base compounds, such as amines. Some resists show degradation of the printed image profile with exposure to as little as a few parts per billion of particular chemical vapors. Several types of chemical filters, relying on either absorption or chemical reaction with the atmospheric contaminants, have been developed for use in the air circulation units of environmental chambers. These chemical filters are frequently used in the air supply of wafer processing equipment as well.

Another type of chemical contamination has also been seen in deep-UV steppers. Lens surfaces that are exposed to high fluxes of ultraviolet light will occasionally become coated with a film of some sort of contaminant. Sometimes the film will be nearly invisible to visual inspection but will show up strongly in transmission tests at deep-UV wavelengths. In other cases, the contamination can be seen as a thick film of material. The problem is usually seen in regions where light intensity is the greatest, as in the illuminator optics of a stepper with an excimer laser light source. But lens surface contamination has been seen in lithographic projection lenses as well. The occurrence of this problem seems somewhat random, and the different occurrences that have been seen here have varied enough in detail that they may have been caused by several different mechanisms. As more anecdotal reports of lens contamination emerge, more understanding of this problem will develop.

10.3 Effects of Temperature, Pressure, and Humidity

Although the environmental chamber does an excellent job of protecting the exposure system and the wafers from thermal drift, particle contamination, and chemical contamination, it can do nothing to control variations of atmospheric pressure. It is not practical to make a chamber strong enough to hold a constant pressure as the barometer fluctuates through a ±50 millitorr range. (Fifty millitorr is about 1 pound per square inch. On a 4 × 8 foot construction panel, this gives a load of slightly more than 2 tons.) A constant-pressure environmental chamber would pose other difficulties, such as slow and complex air-lock mechanisms to load and unload wafers. Although atmospheric pressure cannot be readily controlled, it has a stronger effect on the index of refraction of air than do temperature variations. At room temperature and atmospheric pressure, a 1°C temperature change will change the index of refraction of air by roughly -10^{-6} (−1 ppm). But in an environmental chamber where the temperature variation is ±0.1°C, the thermally induced index change will be ±0.1 ppm, corresponding to an interferometer error of ±20 nm over a 200-mm stage travel. An atmospheric pressure change of 1 millitorr will produce an index change of about 0.36 ppm. With a change of 50 millitorr in barometric pressure, an index change of 18 ppm will occur, shifting the stage interferometer calibration by 3.6 μm across 200 mm of stage travel. Although this comparison makes the effect of temperature appear insignificant relative to that of barometric pressure, it should be kept in mind that temperature changes also induce thermal expansion of critical structures and cause changes in the index of refraction of optical glasses. Fused silica, by far the most common refractive material used in deep-UV lithographic lenses, has an index of refraction with an unusually high thermal sensitivity. Its index changes approximately +15 ppm per °C, when the index is measured in the deep UV. Note that this change of index has the opposite sign of the value for air. Other glasses vary greatly in their sensitivity to temperature, with index changes from −10 to +20 ppm per °C, but most commonly used optical glasses have thermal index changes between 0 and +5 ppm per °C.

The index of refraction of air has a relatively low sensitivity to humidity, changing by approximately 1 ppm for a change between 0% and 100% relative humidity for air at 21°C. Humidity is usually controlled to ±10% within a wafer fabrication facility anyway, in order to avoid problems with sensitive processes like resist application. This keeps the humidity component of the air index variation to ±0.1 ppm. Sometimes an additional level of humidity control is provided by the stepper environmental chamber, but often it is not.

10.4 Compensation for Barometric and Thermal Effects

The effects of uncontrolled barometric pressure variations and the residual effects of temperature and humidity variation are often compensated by an additional control loop in the stage interferometers and the lens control system. A small weather station is installed inside the stepper environmental enclosure. Its output is used to calculate corrections to the index of refraction of the air in the stepper enclosure. This can be used directly to apply corrections to the distance scale of the stage interferometers. Corrections to the lithographic projection lens are more complex. Information from the weather station is combined with additional temperature measurements on the lens housing. The amount of field magnification and focus shift are calculated from a model based on the lens design or empirical data and automatically corrected.

These corrections are made to compensate for slow drifts in external environmental conditions. Internally generated heating effects must also be taken into account. It has been found that some lithographic lenses are heated enough by light absorbed during the lithographic exposure that their focal positions can shift significantly. This heating cannot be reliably detected by temperature sensors on the outside of the lens housing, because the heat is generated deep inside the lens and takes a long time to get to the surface. However, the focus drift can be experimentally measured as a function of exposure time and mask transmission. The time dependence is approximated by a negative exponential curve $(1 - e^{-t/\tau})$, which asymptotically approaches the focus value for a "hot" lens. When an exposure is complete, the lens begins to cool. The focus follows the inverse of the heating curve, but usually with a different (and longer) time constant τ'. If these lens heating effects are well characterized, the stepper's computer controller can predict the focus drift with its knowledge of how long the shutter has been open and closed over its recent history of operation. The stepper can adjust the focus to follow this prediction as it goes through its normal business of exposing wafers. Although this is an open-loop control process, with no feedback mechanism, it is also an extremely well-behaved control process. The focus predictions of the equations are limited to the range between the hot-lens and the cold-lens focus values. There is no tendency for error to accumulate, because contributions of the exposure history further in the past then three or four times τ' fall rapidly to zero. If the stepper sits idle, the focus remains stable at the cold-lens value.

It should be noted that the average optical transmission of each mask determines the difference between the cold-lens focus, and the hot-lens focus, as well as the time constant for heating, τ. A mask that is mostly opaque will not generate much lens heating, whereas one that has mostly transparent areas will allow the maximum heating effect. The average transmission of each mask used in a stepper with lens-heating corrections will need to be known in order to generate the correct value for the hot-lens focus and the time constant for heating. Depending on details of the lithographic lens design and the optical materials used in its construction, lens heating effects may or may not be significant enough to require this sort of correction procedure. A number of lithographic lenses use no lens-heating corrections at all.

11 MASK ISSUES

11.1 Mask Fabrication

Optical masks are made on a substrate of glass or fused silica. Typical masks for a 4× or 5× reduction stepper are 5×5 or 6×6 inches square, and between 0.090 and 0.250 inch thick. Although much more massive and expensive than the thinner substrates, 0.250-inch masks are considerably more resistant to deformation by clamping forces on the mask platen. As larger exposure fields become more common, 6-inch masks are coming into more frequent use. With further increases in field sizes, it is likely that a larger mask format will be required. In fact, the first step-and-scan exposure system that was developed, the Perkin-Elmer Micrascan (now manufactured by SVG Lithography), had the capability of scanning a 20×50 mm field. With a 4× reduction, this would have required an 80×200 mm mask pattern. Allowing an additional space for clamping the mask on the platen, a 9-inch mask dimension would have been required in the scan direction. At the time of the Micrascan's debut, there was no mask-making equipment available that could pattern a 9-inch mask, and so the scanned field had to be limited to 20×32.5 mm. This was the maximum field size that could be accommodated on a 6-inch mask.

This points out a distressing fact of life. Mask-making equipment is expensive and specialized, and the market for new equipment of this type is very small. It is not easy for manufacturers of mask-making systems to justify economically the large development effort needed to make significant changes in their technology. Today, many years after the ability to use a 9-inch mask was first developed, there is still no equipment capable of making such a mask.

Fused silica is usually used in preference to borosilicate glass for mask making, due to its low coefficient of thermal expansion. It is always used for masks in the deep-UV portion of the spectrum from 248 to 193 nm, because other types of glass are not sufficiently transparent at these wavelengths. Chromium has for many years been the material of choice for the patterned layer on the masks' surface. A layer of chromium less than 0.1 μm thick will block 99.9% of the incident light. The technology for etching chromium is well developed, and the material is extremely durable. The recent development of phase-shifting mask technology has led to the use of some materials other than chromium for the patterned mask layer, but these materials are not yet in general use.

Masks must be generated from an electronically stored original pattern. Some sort of direct-writing lithographic technique is required to create the pattern on a mask blank coated with photoresist. Both electron beam and laser beam mask writers are in common use. The amount of data that must be transferred onto the mask surface may be in the gigabyte range, and the time to write a complex mask is often several hours.

After the resist is developed, the pattern is transferred to the film of chromium absorber, usually with a wet etch process. Although the mask features are typically four or five times larger than the images created on the wafer (due to the reduction of the lithographic lens), the tolerances on the mask dimensions are a much smaller percentage of the feature size. Because of these tight tolerances and the continuing reduction of feature dimensions on the mask, there will probably be a shift to an anisotropic reactive-ion etch for transferring the pattern to the chromium mask layer in the future.

11.2 Feature Size Tolerances

The dimensional tolerance of critical resist patterns on a wafers's surface may be ±10% of the minimum feature size. Many factors can induce variations in line width, including nonuniformity of resist thickness, variations in bake temperatures or developer concentration, changes of the exposure energy, aberrations in the projection lens, and variations in the size of the features on the photomask. Because the mask represents only one of many contributions to variations in the size of the resist feature, it must have a tighter fractional dimensional tolerance than the resist image. It is not completely obvious how to apportion the allowable dimensional variation among the various sources of error. If the errors are independent and normally distributed, then there is a temptation to add them in quadrature (i.e., take the square root of the sum of squares, or RSS). This gives the dominant weight in the error budget to the largest source of error and allows smaller errors to be ignored. Unfortunately, this sort of analysis ignores an important feature of the problem, namely the differences in the spatial distribution of the different sources of error.

As an example of this, let us examine just two important contributions to line width error: exposure repeatability and mask dimensional error. The distribution of exposure energies may be completely random in time and may be characterized by a Gaussian distribution about some mean value. Because of the relationship between exposure and resist image size, the errors in exposure will create a Gaussian distribution in image sizes across a large number of exposures. Likewise, the distribution of feature sizes on a photomask (for a set of features with the same nominal dimension) may randomly vary across the mask's surface, with a Gaussian distribution of errors about the mean dimension. Yet these two sources of dimensional error in the resist image cannot be added in quadrature. Combining errors with an RSS, instead of a straight addition, accounts for the fact that random, uncorrelated errors will only rarely experience a maximum positive excursion on the same experimental measurement. Statistically, it is much more likely that a maximum error of one term will occur with an average error of the other term. But when combining errors of exposure energy with errors of mask feature sizes, there is no possibility of such a cancellation. When the exposure energy fluctuates to a higher value, the entire exposure field is overexposed, and the transparent mask feature that has the highest positive departure from nominal image size will determine whether the chip fails its dimensional tolerances. Conversely, if the energy fluctuates low, the most undersized transparent feature will determine whether the chip fails. The key thing to notice is that the oversized and undersized mask features are distributed across the mask surface, but the errors in exposure energy affect the entire mask simultaneously. Thus a difference in spatial distribution of errors prevents them from being added in quadrature, even though the errors are uncorrelated and normally distributed.

An analysis of other sources of dimensional error in the resist image shows few that have the same spatial distribution as mask errors. This forces the mask dimensional tolerance to be added linearly in the error budget for image size control on the wafer and makes the control of feature sizes on the mask correspondingly more critical. A typical minimum feature size on a mask may be 1.4 μm, with a tolerance of 3.5%, or 50 nm (3σ). When printed with 4× reduction on a wafer, the resist image size will be 0.35 μm with a required accuracy of ±10%. In this example, the mask error has consumed fully one third of the total error budget.

11.3   Feature Placement Tolerance

The control of image placement on the wafer surface is subject to tolerances that are nearly as tight as those for image size control. Once again, the mask contribution to image placement error is only one component of many. Thermal wafer distortions, chucking errors, lens distortion, errors in wafer stage motion, and errors in acquisition of wafer alignment marks also make significant contributions to the total image placement or overlay budget. The spatial distribution of errors in mask feature placement also determines whether the mask contribution can be added in quadrature or must be added linearly. Some components of mask error can be corrected by the lithographic optics. For example, a small magnification error in the mask can be corrected by the magnification adjustment in the lithographic projection lens. For this reason, correctable errors are usually removed mathematically when the mask feature placement tolerance is calculated. But the higher order, uncorrectable terms usually must be added linearly in the image overlay budget.

The total overlay tolerance for the resist image on an underlying level is quite dependent on the details of the semiconductor product's design but is often around 20 to 30% of the minimum image size. The corresponding feature placement tolerance on the mask is about 5% of the minimum mask dimension, or 70 nm (3σ) on a mask with 1.4-μm minimum feature sizes.

11.4 Inspection and Repair

When a mask is made, it must be perfect. Any defects in the pattern will destroy the functionality of the semiconductor circuit that is printed with that mask. Before a mask is delivered to the semiconductor manufacturing line, it is passed through an automated mask inspection system that searches for any defects in the pattern. There are two possible strategies in mask inspection, known as die-to-database and die-to-die inspection. The first method involves an automated scanning microscope that compares the mask pattern directly with the computer data used to generate the mask. This requires a very large data handling capability, similar to that needed by the mask writer itself. Any discrepancy between the inspected mask pattern and the data set used to create it is flagged as an error. The inspection criteria cannot be set so restrictively that random variations in line width or image placement are reported as defects. A typical minimum defect size that can be reliably detected without producing too many false-positive error detections is currently about 0.25 μm. This number is steadily decreasing as the mask feature sizes and tolerances become smaller from year to year. A mask defect may be either an undesired transparent spot in the chromium absorber or a piece of absorber (either chromium or a dirt particle) where a clear area is supposed to be. These types of defects are called clear defects and opaque defects, respectively. As mask requirements become more and more stringent, new categories of defects, such as phase errors in transparent regions of the mask, have been discovered. There is as yet no satisfactory method of detecting these types of phase defects with a fast mask inspection system.

Die-to-die inspection can be used only on a mask with two or more identical chip patterns. It is fairly common for two, three, or even four chips to be exposed in a single large stepper field, in order to improve the stepper throughput. The die-to-die inspection system scans both chip patterns and compares them, point by point. Any difference between the two patterns is recorded as a defect in the mask. This does not require the massive data handling capacity of die-to-datebase inspection. In general, die-to-die inspection is rather insensitive to process deficiencies like rounded corners on mask features, which may be common to all the features on the mask.

The cost and time involved in making a mask are too great to allow the mask to be discarded for small defects. If defects are found, attempts are made to repair the mask. Opaque defects can be blasted away by a focused pulse of laser light, or eroded by ion milling, using a focused beam of gallium ions. Clear defects that must be made opaque can be covered with patches using laser-assisted or ion beam–assisted chemical deposition processes. Successful repairs have been made with good regularity using these techniques, but considerable improvements in the equipment used for mask repair are needed in the next few years. As image tolerances continually shrink and new types of masks involving phase-shifting materials are developed, some fundamental improvements in mask repair technology will be required.

As noted above, the inspection criteria cannot be set tight enough to detect small errors in feature size or placement. These important parameters are determined in a separate measurement step, using specialized image placement measurement equipment and image size measuring microscopes. Image sizes and placement errors are statistically sampled over dozens to hundreds of sites across the mask. If the mean or standard deviation of the measured feature sizes is not within the specifications, there is no choice but to rebuild the mask. The same is true when the image placement tolerances are exceeded. There is no mask repair process capable of correcting these properties.

11.5   Particulate Contamination and Pellicles

When a mask has been written, inspected, repaired, and delivered to the semiconductor manufacturing line, it might be assumed that it can be used to produce perfect images without any further concerns until it is made obsolete by a new mask design. But the mask faces a life of hazards. There is an obvious possibility of dropping and breaking the valuable object during manual or automatic handling. Electrostatic discharge has recently been recognized as another hazard. If a small discharge of static electricity occurs when the mask is picked up, a surge of current through micron-sized chromium lines on the mask can actually melt the lines and destroy parts of the pattern. But the most serious threat to a mask is a simple particle of dirt. If an airborne dirt speck lands in a critical transparent area of the mask, the circuits printed with that mask may no longer be functional. Wafer fabrication facilities are probably the cleanest working environments in the world, but a mask will inevitably pick up dust particles after several months of handling and use for wafer exposures. The mask can be cleaned using a variety of washing techniques, often involving ultrasonic agitation, high-pressure jets of water, or automated scrubbing of the surface with brushes. Often, powerful oxidizing chemicals are used to consume any organic particles on the mask's surface. These procedures cannot be repeated very frequently without posing their own threat to the mask pattern.

A better solution to the problem of dirt on the mask is to protect the surface with a thin transparent membrane called a pellicle. A pellicle is suspended on a frame 5 to 10 mm above the mask surface. The frame seals the edges of the pellicle so that there is no route for dust particles to reach the mask's surface.

When a dust particle lands on the pellicle, it is so far out of the focal plane that it is essentially invisible to the projection optics. If a pellicle height of 10 mm is used, particles up to 150 μm in diameter will cause less than a 1% obscuration of the projection lens pupil area for a point on the mask directly beneath the particle. Thin (0.090 inch) masks are sometimes given a pellicle on the back, as well as the front surface. Back-side pellicles are often not used on thick (0.250 inch) masks, because the back surface of the mask is already reasonably far from the focal plane of the projection optics. The effectiveness of a pellicle increases with higher numerical aperture of the projection lens, smaller lens reduction factor, and increased height of the pellicle.

A mask-protecting pellicle is directly in the optical path of the lithographic projection lens, so its optical effects must be carefully considered. The pellicle acts as a freestanding interference film, and its transmission is sensitive to the exact thickness relative to the exposure wavelength. Pellicles are typically designed for a thickness that maximizes the transmission. A transparent film with parallel surfaces a few millimeters from the focal plane will produce a certain amount of spherical aberration, but this is minimized if the pellicle is thin. Typical pellicles are only 1 to 2 μm thick and produce less than 0.1 wave of spherical aberration. Any variations of the pellicle's thickness across a transverse distance of 1 or 2 mm will show up directly as wavefront aberrations in the aerial image. Small tilts in the pellicle's orientation relative to the mask surface have little significant effect. A wedge angle between the front and rear pellicle

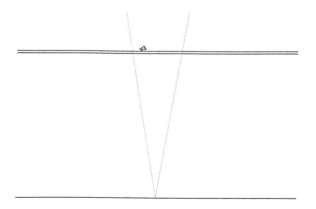

Figure 27   The function of a mask pellicle is to keep dirt particles from falling onto the surface of a mask. This figure illustrates a large particle of dirt on the top surface of a pellicle. The dotted lines represent the cone of illumination angles that pass through the mask surface. At 10 mm separation from the mask surface, the dirt particle interrupts an insignificant amount of energy from any one point on the mask's surface.

surfaces will induce a transverse shift in the image that is projected by the lithographic lens. If the amount of wedge varies over the surface of the pellicle, surprisingly large image distortions can be produced. The amount of transverse image displacement is equal to $h(n-1)\theta_w/M$, where h is the pellicle height, n is the index of refraction of the pellicle material, θ_w is the wedge angle, and M is the reduction factor of the lithographic lens. For a 10-mm pellicle height, a refractive index of 1.6, and a lens reduction of 4×, θ_w must be less than 30 μr if the image displacement is to be kept below 45 nm.

Several materials have been used for pellicles, such as nitrocellulose acetate and various Teflon-like fluorocarbons. When a pellicle is used with deep-UV exposure wavelengths, transparency of the pellicle and its resistance to photo-erosion at those wavelengths must be carefully evaluated.

Although pellicles do a very good job of protecting the wafer's surface, a large enough dust particle on the pellicle can still cause a dark spot in the aerial image. Some steppers provide a pellicle inspection system that can detect large dust particles using scattered light. The pellicle can be inspected very time the mask is loaded or unloaded to provide an extra measure of protection.

11.6   Field-Defining Blades

The patterned area of the mask rarely fills the stepper field to its extremes. When the mask is made, there must be an opaque chromium border to define the limits of the exposed area. This allows each field to be butted against the adjacent fields without stray light from one field double-exposing its neighbor. The chromium that defines the border must be free of pinhole defects, which would print as spots of light in a neighboring chip. It is expensive to inspect and repair all the pinholes in a large expanse of chromium. For this reason, almost all steppers have field-defining blades that block all of the light that would hit the mask, except in a rectangular area where the desired pattern exists. The blades then take over the job of blocking light leaks, except in a small region surrounding the patterned area, which must be free of pinholes. It is desirable that the field-defining blades be as sharply focused as possible, to avoid a wide blurred area or penumbra at their edges. Some amount of penumbra—on the order of 100 μm—is unavoidable, so the limits of the exposed field must always be defined by a chromium border.

The field-defining blades are also useful in a few special circumstances. For diagnostic and engineering purposes, the blades may be used to define a small subregion of the mask pattern that can be used to expose a compact matrix of exposure and focus values. In this case, the fuzzy edges of the field can be ignored. The blades can also be used to select among several different patterns printed on the same mask. For example, a global wafer alignment mark or a specialized test structure could be defined on the same mask as a normal exposure pattern. The specialized pattern could be rapidly selected by moving the blades, avoiding the slow procedure of changing a realigning the mask. This would allow two or more different patterns to be printed on each wafer without the necessity of changing masks.

12 CONTROL OF THE LITHOGRAPHIC EXPOSURE SYSTEM

12.1 Microprocessor Control of Subsystems

Lithographic exposure systems have to perform several complex functions in the course of their operations. Some of these functions are performed by specialized analog or digital electronics designed by the system's manufacturer. Other functions are complex enough to require a small computer or microprocessor to control their execution. For example, magnification and focus control of the lithographic projection lens requires a stream of calculations, using inputs from temperature sensors, atmospheric data from the internal weather station, and often a running history of exposure times for calculating lens-heating effects. This task cannot easily be performed by analog circuitry, so a dedicated microprocessor controller is often used. Other functions have also been turned over to microprocessors in systems made by various manufacturers. Excimer lasers, used as light sources for the lithographic exposure in some steppers, usually have an internal microprocessor control system. The environmental enclosure often has its own microprocessor control. Wafer transport and prealignment functions are sometimes managed by a dedicated microprocessor. A similar control system can be used for the automatic transportation of masks between the mask library and mask platen and for alignment of the mask. Some manufacturers have used an independent computer controller for the acquisition of wafer alignment marks and the analysis of alignment corrections.

The exposure system also has a process control computer that controls the operation of the system, as well as coordinating the activities of the microprocessor-controlled subsystems. Often the controlling computer is also used to create, edit, and store the data files that specify the details of the operations that are to be performed on each incoming lot of wafers. These data files, called job control files or product files, include information on the mask or masks to be used, the alignment strategy to be used, location of the alignment marks to be measured on the wafer, and the exact placement and exposure energy for each field that is to be printed on the wafer. In some systems these bookkeeping functions are delegated to an auxiliary computer, which also acts as an interface to the operator.

Control of the stepper's various subsystems with microprocessor controllers has been a fairly successful strategy. The modularity that results from this approach has simplified the design of the control system. There have occasionally been problems with communication and data transfer links between the microprocessors and the central computer. Recently, some manufacturers have started integrating the microprocessor functions into a single, powerful controlling computer or workstation.

12.2 Photocluster Control

There has also been an increase in the complexity of the control system caused by linking wafer processing equipment and the exposure system into an integrated photocluster. The simplest photocluster arrangements simply provide a robotic mechanism to transfer the wafer between the wafer processing tracks and the exposure system, with a few data lines to exchange information when a wafer is waiting to be transferred. But the increasing need to cascade wafer lots through the photocluster without breaks between lots has forced the development of a much more complex level of control.

12.3 Communication Links

Frequently a data link is provided for communications between the exposure system and a central computer that monitors the entire manufacturing operation. The Semiconductor Equipment Communications Standard (SECS II) protocols are often used. This link allows the central computer to collect diagnostic data generated by the exposure system and track the performance of the system. It also allows the detailed job control files to be stored on the central computer and transferred to the exposure system at the time of use. This ensures that every exposure system on the factory floor is using the same version of every job control file and makes it possible to revise or update the job control files in one central location.

A central computer system linked to each exposure system on the factory floor can automatically collect data on the operating conditions of each system and detect changes that may signal the need for maintenance. The same central computer can track the progress of each lot of wafers throughout its many processing steps, accumulating a valuable record for analysis of process variables that affect yield. There has been an emphasis on automated data collection, often using computer-readable bar codes on masks and wafer boxes to avoid the errors inherent in manual data entry. The possibility of tracking individual wafers via a miniature computer-readable code near the wafer's edge has been considered.

12.4 Stepper Self-Metrology

Every year shows an increased level of sophistication in stepper design. As stepper control systems are improved, there has been a trend toward including a greater level of self-metrology and self-calibration functions. Automatic baseline measurement systems (discussed in Section 8.7) are often provided on exposure systems with off-axis alignment. The same type of image detection optics that are used for the baseline measurement can often be used to analyze the aerial image projected by a lithographic lens [21]. If a detector on the wafer stage is scanned through the aerial image, the steepness of the transition between the bright and dark areas of the image can be used as an indication of the image quality. It is difficult to make a practical detector that can sample on a fine enough scale to discriminate details of a high-resolution stepper image. But another trick is possible. The aerial image of a small feature can be scanned across the sharply defined edge of a rather large light detector. The detected signal represents the spatial integral of the aerial image in the direction of the scan. It can be mathematically differentiated to reconstruct the shape of the aerial image.

Best focus can be defined as the position where the aerial image achieves the highest contrast. By repeatedly measuring the contrast of the aerial image through a range of focus settings, the location of the best focus can be found. Using an aerial image measurement system in this way allows the stepper to calibrate its automatic focus mechanism to the actual position of the aerial image and correct for any drifts in the projection optics.

Besides simple determination of best focus, aerial image measurements can be used to diagnose some forms of projection lens problems. Field tilts and field curvature can be readily measured by determining the best focus at many points in the exposure field and analyzing the deviation from flatness. Astigmatism can be determined by comparing positions of best focus for two perpendicular orientations of lines. The field tilt measurements can be used to calibrate the automatic leveling system. But there are no automated adjustments for field curvature or astigmatism. Instead, these measurements are useful for monitoring the health of the lithographic lens so that any degradation of the imaging can be detected early.

Most of the aerial image measurements described here can be done with an equivalent analysis of the developed image in resist. For example, a sequence of exposures through focus can be analyzed for the best focus at several points across the image field, providing the same information on tilt and field curvature as an aerial image measurement. But measurements in resist are extremely time consuming, compared to automated aerial image measurements. A complete analysis of field curvature and astigmatism using developed photoresist images could easily require several hours of painstaking data collection with a microscope. Such a procedure may be practical to perform only as an initial test of a stepper at installation. An automated measurement, on the other hand, can be performed as part of a daily or weekly monitoring program.

The automatic focus mechanism can be used to perform another test of the stepper's health. With the availability of the appropriate software, the stepper can analyze the surface flatness of a wafer on the exposure chuck. The automatic focus mechanism, whether it is an optical mechanism, capacitance gauge, or air gauge, can sample the wafer's surface at dozens or hundreds of positions and create a map of the surface figure. This analysis provides important information, not so much about the wafer, but rather about the flatness of the chuck. Wafer chucks are subject to contamination by specks of debris carried in on the back sides of wafers. A single large particle transferred onto the chuck can create a high spot on the surface of every wafer that passes through the exposure system, until the contamination is discovered and removed. Occasional automated wafer surface measurements can greatly reduce the risk of yield loss from this source. To reduce the effect of random nonflatness of the wafers used in this measurement, a set of selected ultraflat wafers can be reserved for this purpose. Recently, ion-polished silicon wafers with a surface flatness of better than ±50 nm (total range) have become available from Hughes Danbury Optical Systems. (The term "surface flatness" is used loosely here. Because the wafer is vacuum clamped to the chuck, the relevant parameter is actually wafer parallelism, which is equivalent to surface flatness if the chuck is ideally flat.) These wafers should be nearly ideal to use when mapping chuck flatness.

12.5   Stepper Operating Procedures

The ultimate cost-effectiveness of the lithographic operations performed in a semiconductor fabrication plant depends on a number of factors. The raw throughput of the stepper, in wafers per hour, is important. But other factors can have a significant effect on the cost of operations. Strategies such as dedication of lots to particular steppers (in order to achieve the best possible overlay) can result in scheduling problems and high amounts of idle time. One of the most significant impacts on stepper productivity is from the use of "send-ahead" wafers. This manufacturing technique requires one or more wafers from each lot to be exposed, developed, and measured for line width and/or overlay before the rest of the lot is exposed. The measurements on the send-ahead wafer are used to correct the exposure energy or adjust the alignment by small amounts. If the stepper is allowed to sit idle while the send-ahead wafer is developed and measured, there will be a tremendous loss of productivity. A more effective strategy is to interleave wafer lots and send-ahead wafers so that a lot can be exposed while the send-ahead wafer for the next lot is being developed and analyzed. This requires a sort of logistical juggling act, with some risk of confusing the correction data of one lot for that of another. Even with this strategy, there is substantial waste of time. The send-ahead wafer is subject to the full lot overhead, including the time to load the lot control software and the mask, plus the time to load and unload the wafer.

A manufacturing facility that produces large quantities of a single semiconductor product can attempt a different send-ahead strategy. A large batch of several lots that require the same masking level can be accumulated and run as a superlot with a single send-ahead wafer. This may introduce serious logistical problems as lots are delayed to accumulate a large batch.

The most successful strategy can be adopted when such a large volume of a single semiconductor product is being manufactured that a stepper can be completely dedicated to a single mask level of that product. When every wafer is exposed with the same mask, the concept of send-ahead wafers is no longer needed. Instead, statistical process control can be introduced. Sample wafers can be pulled at intervals from the product stream, and measurements from these samples can be fed back to control the stepper exposure and alignment.

Of course, the most desirable situation would be one in which the stepper is so stable and insensitive to variations in alignment marks that send-ahead wafers are not needed. This goal has been pursued by all stepper manufacturers with some degree of success. Nearly all semiconductor manufacturers have found some way of operating without send-ahead wafers, due to the serious loss in productivity that they cause. When the stability of the stepper is great enough, lots can be exposed with a so-called risk strategy. The entire lot is exposed without a send-ahead wafer, and then sample wafers are measured for line width and overlay. If the lot fails one of these measurements, it is reworked. The resist is stripped and reapplied, then the lot is exposed again with corrected values of alignment or exposure. As long as only a small fraction of lots require rework, the risk strategy can be much more effective than a strategy requiring a send-ahead for each lot. The risk strategy is most successful when the steppers and processes are so stable that the line width and overlay are rarely outside the tolerance specifications and when the flow of wafers through each stepper is continuous enough that statistical feedback from the lot measurements can be used to fine-tune the stepper settings.

13 OPTICAL ENHANCEMENT TECHNIQUES

An optical lithographic projection system is usually designed for perfection in each component of the system. The mask is designed to represent the ideal pattern that the circuit designer intends to see on the surface of the wafer. The projection lens is designed to form the most accurate image of the mask that is possible. The photoresist and etch processes are designed to capture faithfully the image of the mask and transfer its pattern into the surface of the wafer. Any lack of fidelity in the image transfer, whether caused by mechanical imperfections or by fundamental limitations in the physics and chemistry, tends to be cumulative. The errors in the mask are faithfully transmitted by the optics, and the optical diffractive limitations of the projection lens are just as faithfully recorded by the photoresist.

Instead of striving for perfect masks, perfect optics, and perfect resist and etch processes, it may be more practical for some of these elements of the lithographic process to be designed to compensate for the deficiencies of the others. For example, masks can be designed to correct some undesirable effects of optical diffraction. The nonlinear nature of photoresist has been exploited since the earliest days of microlithography to compensate for the shallow slope of the aerial image's intensity profile. Etch biases can sometimes compensate for biases of the aerial image and the photoresist process.

It is sometimes possible to use a trick of optics to enhance some aspect of the image forming process. Usually this exacts a cost of some sort. For example, the multiple-exposure process known as FLEX (described below) can greatly enhance the depth of focus of small contact holes in a positive-toned resist. This comes at the cost of reduced image contrast for all the features on the mask. But for some applications this trade-off can be very advantageous.

13.1 Optical Proximity Corrections

The physical nature of optical image formation leads to interference between closely spaced features within the aerial image. This can lead to a variety of undesirable effects. As discussed in Section 5.5, a prominent proximity effect is the relative image size bias between isolated and tightly grouped lines in the aerial image. This effect can be disastrous if the circuit design demands that isolated and grouped lines print at the same dimension, as when the lines form gates of transistors that must all switch at the same speed. In simple cases, the circuit designer can manually introduce a dimensional bias into his design, which will correct for the optical proximity effect. To extend this to a general optical proximity correction algorithm will require a fairly massive computer program, with the ability to model the aerial image of millions of individual features in the mask pattern and add a correcting bias to each. The more sophisticated of these programs attempt to correct the two-dimensional shape of the aerial image in detail, instead of just adding a one-dimensional bias to the line width. This can result in a mask design so complicated, and with such a large number of tiny pattern corrections, that the mask generation equipment and the automated die-to-database inspection systems used to inspect the mask for defects cannot handle the massive quantity of data.

Pattern-dependent biases are only one form of optical proximity effect. Corner rounding and general loss of shape fidelity in small features are caused by the inability of the lithographic projection lens to resolve details below the optical diffraction limit of that lens. These effects are often classified as another form of optical proximity effect. Sophisticated circuit designers have learned to accept corner rounding as a fact of life and to design circuit patterns with the knowledge that a square corner will inevitably become rounded when the pattern is projected onto the wafer. Rules of thumb are often employed, such as applying a radius to each corner equal to one half of the minimum resolvable feature size, when determining how the designed pattern will be realized as a physical pattern on the wafer. Today, image-modeling software is becoming available that allows the designer to get a rapid preview of the aerial images that will result when his patterns are printed on the wafer. This has the potential to improve the reliability of the mask design process.

Even though corner rounding has been accommodated in circuit designs, there are instances in which sharper corners on circuit features could lead to improvements in the circuit's performance. For example, contact holes often benefit by having the largest surface area possible, within the constraints of limited x and y dimensions. A contact hole printed as a square may give substantially better performance than one printed as a circle. Trench capacitors gain improved capacitance if their perimeter lengths are maximized. Corner rounding tends to reduce the perimeter of a feature and is undesirable in this application. Electrically isolated regions of the wafer surface are sometimes defined by the intersection of insulating structures printed at two or more levels. Corner rounding may reduce the overlap between two insulating regions, increasing the risk of a short circuit.

Corner rounding can be reduced by the addition of pattern structures that enhance the amount of light transmitted through the corners of transparent mask features or by increasing the amount of chromium absorber at the corners of opaque mask features. These additional structures are often called serifs, in analogy to the tiny decorations at the ends of lines in printed letters and numerals. The serifs effectively increase the modulation at high spatial frequencies, in order to compensate for the diffractive loss of high spatial frequencies in the transmission of the lithographic lens [22].

As with most things in life, the benefits of serifs do not come without a price. Serifs add a huge number of features to the data volume of the mask, potentially overloading the data-handling capability of the mask generation and inspection equipment. The size of the serif is typically much smaller than the minimum feature size on the mask, causing difficulty in the mask manufacturing process. The aerial image in the region of the serif typically has a low contrast relative to conventional mask features. This can cause an undesirable amount of feature size variation with changes in exposure and focus. If the difficulties with mask generation and inspection can be overcome, it is likely that serifs will find several applications in lithography. But for now, this technology is at a fairly early stage of development.

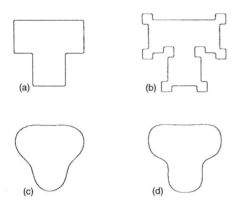

Figure 28 A T-shaped feature (a), with dimensions near the resolution limit of the projection lens, is printed as a rather featureless blob (c) on the wafer. Addition of decorative serifs (b) brings the printed image (d) much closer to the shape originally designed. The multitude of tiny features in b pose immense difficulties for the mask maker.

13.2 Mask Transmission Modification

Optical proximity correction by image size biasing or the addition of serifs uses fairly standard mask-making technology. The proximity corrections are simply modifications of the original design patterns. There are more radical ways to modify the mask to print images beyond the normal capability of the lithographic lens. Corner rounding and the general issue of shape fidelity could be remedied if there were a way to increase the mask transmission above 100% in the corners of transparent mask features. This is not physically possible, but there is an equivalent technique. If the transparent parts of the mask are covered with a partially absorbing film and the illumination intensity is increased to compensate for this, there will be no difference in the image formation compared to a standard mask image. If the partially absorbing film is now removed in selected regions of the mask, the desired effect of >100% mask transmission will be effectively achieved [23].

Bright spots in the corners of transparent mask features would have effects similar to those of serifs, increasing the modulation in these regions. The presence or absence of the partially absorbing film around opaque features could selectively bias the printed image sizes. It should be noted that this technique is asymmetrical with respect to bright and dark features. It is possible to put a superbright spot into the corner of a transparent feature, but there are no superdark spots available to enhance the corners of opaque features.

The symmetry could be restored by creating a mask with four levels of transmission: 0, 20, 80, and 100%, for example. The 20% level would be used for opaque features and the 80% level for transparent features. The 0 and 100% levels would be used only where enhanced image modulation was needed. It should be obvious that the image contrast of such a mask will be considerably less than that of a conventional mask. But if the resist process can cope with the lower image contrast, the reward will be an increased fidelity of image shapes.

If free rein is given to the imagination, masks can be designed with multiple levels of transmission, approaching a continuous gray scale in the limit. If such a mask could be built, it could provide a high level of correction for optical proximity effects. But the practical difficulties of such a task are disheartening. There are no technologies for patterning, inspecting, or repairing masks with multiple levels of transmission. Although such technologies could be developed, the enormous cost would probably not be worth the modest benefits of gray-scale masks.

A marginally more practical method exists for achieving the same results as a gray-scale mask. Newspaper and book publishers have long used a technology called half-toning to print photographs containing many shades of gray on a medium that can support only black and white images. By subdividing a gray-scale mask pattern into many subresolution patterns of clear and opaque spots, the gray-scale mask could be printed using only binary mask technology. Unfortunately, the data volume for such a mask would be impossibly large for today's mask-generating and -inspecting equipment.

Mask transmission modifications may remain a subject of academic study, but there is little likelihood that they will ever be seen in semiconductor manufacturing. The difficulties simply outweigh the benefits.

13.3 Phase-Shifting Masks

The concept of increasing the resolution of a lithographic image by modifying the optical phase of the mask transmission was proposed by Levenson et al. in 1982 [24]. This proposal was very slow to catch the interest of the lithographic community, due to the difficulties of creating a defect-free phase-shifting mask and the continual improvement in the resolution achievable by conventional technologies. As the level of difficulty in conventional lithography has increased, there has been a corresponding surge of interest in phase-shifting masks. By now, phase-shifting masks are being seriously developed at several industrial and government development laboratories around the world.

Several distinct types of phase masks have been invented. All share the common feature that some transparent areas of the mask are given a 180° shift in optical phase relative to nearby transparent areas. The interaction between the aerial images of two features with a relative phase difference of 180° generates an interference node or dark band between the two features. This allows two adjacent bright features to be printed much closer together than would be the case on a conventional mask. Except for the obvious difficulties in fabricating such masks, the drawbacks to their use are surprisingly small.

The first type of optical phase-shifting mask to be developed was the so-called alternating-phase mask. In this type of mask, closely spaced transparent features are given alternate phases of 0° and 180°. The interference between the alternating phases allows the features to be spaced very closely together. Under ideal circumstances, the maximum resolution of an alternating-phase mask may be 50% better than that of a conventional mask. A mask consisting of closely spaced transparent lines in an opaque background gains the maximum benefit from this phase-shifting technique. Some feature geometries may make it difficult or impossible to use the alternating-phase approach. For example, tightly packed features that are laid out in a brick pattern, with alternating rows offset from each other, cannot be given phase assignments that allow every feature to have a phase opposite to that of its neighbors. Nonrepetitive patterns can rarely

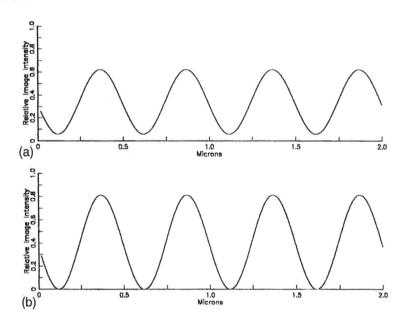

Figure 29   The benefits of an alternating-phase mask. (a) Aerial image of a line-space grating near the resolution limit of a stepper using a conventional mask. The line width of the image is 0.5 λ/NA. When alternating clear areas are given a 180° phase shift on the mask, as in (b), the contrast of the aerial image is markedly improved.

be given phase assignments that meet the alternating-phase requirement. Another type of problem occurs in a mask with opaque features in a transparent background. Although there may be a way to create an alternating-phase pattern within a block of opaque features, there will be a problem at the edges of the array, where the two opposite phases must meet at a boundary. Interference between the two phases will make this boundary print as a dark line. Cures for these problems have been proposed, involving the use of additional phase values between 0° and 180°, but few of these cures have been totally satisfactory.

Phase-shifted regions on an alternating-phase mask can be created either by etching the proper distance into the fused silica mask substrate or by adding a calibrated thickness of a transparent material to the surface of the mask. The re-

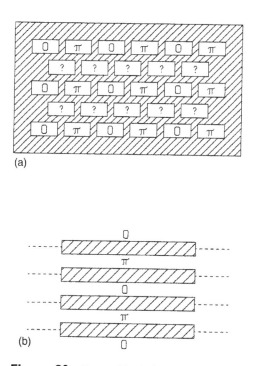

(a)

(b)

Figure 30 Intractable design problems for alternating-phase masks. In (a) there is no way to assign phases so that a 180° phase difference occurs between adjacent transparent features. In this example, the phases have been assigned to the odd-numbered rows, but there is no way to assign phases consistently to the even rows. (b) A problem that occurs when a mask consists of isolated opaque features in a clear background. Although the alternating-phase condition is met within the array of lines and spaces, the opposite phases will collide at the end of each line. At the boundaries, marked by a dashed line, an unwanted, thin dark line will print.

gions that receive the phase shift must be defined in a second mask-writing process, aligned accurately to the previously created chromium mask pattern. No good techniques for inspecting or repairing alternating-phase masks are available today, and the ultimate acceptance of this type of mask will depend heavily on the eventual development of these two technologies.

Because alternating-phase masks are not universally applicable to all types of mask patterns, other types of phase-shifting techniques have been devised. With one method, a narrow, 180° phase-shifted rim is added to every transparent feature on the mask. The optical interference from this rim steepens the slope of the aerial image at the transition between transparent and opaque regions of the mask. A variety of procedures have been invented for creating this phase rim during the mask-making process, without requiring a second, aligned, mask-writing step. Masks using this rim-shifting technique do not provide as much lithographic benefit as do alternating-phase masks, but they do not suffer from the pattern restrictions that afflict the alternating-phase masks. The lack of inspection and repair technology for phase-shifted regions of the mask is holding back development of rim-shifting masks, as it is with alternating-phase masks.

Another pattern-independent phase-shifting technique is the use of a partially transmitting, 180° phase-shifting film to replace the chromium absorbing layer on the mask. Interference between light from the transparent regions of the mask and phase-shifted light passing through the partially transmitting absorber gives a steep slope to the aerial image of feature edges. Transmission of the phase-shifting absorber in the range from 5 to 10% seems to give the best results. Away from the interference region at the edges of the mask features, the partially transmitting absorber allows a fairly undesirable amount of light to fall on the photoresist. But a high-contrast photoresist is not seriously affected by this light, which falls below the resist's exposure threshold. The contrast enhancement from partially transmitting phase shifters is rather mild compared to alternating-phase masks. However, the technology for making these masks is much easier than for other styles of phase masks. The phase-shifting absorber can usually be patterned just as though it were a layer of chromium. With appropriate adjustments in detection thresholds, mask defects can be detected with normal inspection equipment. Although the inspection does not reveal any errors in phase, it does detect the presence or absence of the absorbing film. Isolated defects, either clear or opaque, can be repaired with conventional mask repair techniques. Defects in the critical region at the edge of an opaque feature cannot be repaired today, but there is considerable confidence that an acceptable repair process can be developed. Because of the relative simplicity of making a partially transmitting phase mask, this will probably be the first style of phase mask to be used in commercial semiconductor manufacturing.

The most radical application of phase-shifting technology is in the phase edge mask. This type of mask consists only of transparent fused silica, with a

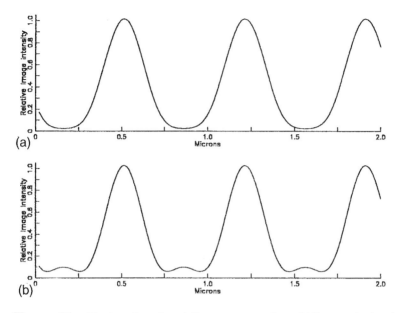

Figure 31 The benefits of partially transparent phase-shifting mask absorbers. (a) Aerial image of a line-space grating using a conventional mask. The line width of the image is 0.7 λ/NA. (b) Aerial image that results when the opaque absorber is replaced with a material that transmits 6% of the incident light with a 180° phase shift. The slope of the aerial image is steepened, but a certain amount of light leaks into the dark spaces between the bright lines.

pattern etched into the surface to a depth yielding a 180° phase shift. Only the edges of the etched regions project images onto the wafer, but these images are the smallest features that can be transmitted through the lithographic lens. The resolution of a phase edge mask can be twice as good as that of a conventional chromium mask. There are serious limitations to the types of features that can be printed with a phase edge mask. All of the lines in the printed pattern represent the perimeter of etched regions on the mask, so they must always form closed loops.

It is rare that a semiconductor circuit requires a closed loop. The loops may be opened by exposing the pattern with a second "trimming" mask, but this adds a great deal of complexity to the process. All of the lines printed by a phase edge mask are the same width. This puts a serious constraint on the circuit designer, who is used to considerably greater latitude in the types of features he can specify. There is a possibility that hybrid masks containing some conventional chromium features and some phase edge structures may provide the ultimate form of phase mask, but the challenges to mask fabrication, inspection, and repair technologies are severe.

13.4   Off-Axis Illumination

Until recently, the standard form of illumination for lithographic lenses was a circular pupil fill, centered in the entrance pupil of the projection optics. The only variable that lithographers occasionally played with was the pupil filling ratio, which determines the degree of partial coherence in the image formation. In 1992, researchers at Canon, Inc. [25] and the Nikon Corporation [26] introduced quadrupole illumination, which has significant benefits for imaging small features. Today several different pupil illumination patterns are available on steppers, often as software-selectable options. These can be selected as appropriate for each mask pattern that is exposed on the stepper.

The process of image formation can most easily be understood for a simple structure such as a grating of equal lines and spaces. Also for simplicity, it is best to consider the contribution to the image formation from a single point of illumination. The actual image formed by an extended source of illumination is just the sum of the images formed by the individual points sources within the extended source.

A grating mask, illuminated by a single point of illumination, will create a series of diffracted images of the illumination source in the pupil of the lithographic lens. The lens aperture acts as a filter, excluding the higher diffracted orders. When the lens recombines the diffracted orders that fall within its aperture, it forms an image with the higher spatial frequency content removed. A grating with the minimum resolvable pitch will cast its ±1st-order diffraction just inside the lens aperture, along with the undiffracted illumination point at the center of the pupil (the 0th diffraction order). The diffraction from gratings with smaller pitches will fall completely outside the pupil aperture, and the gratings will not be resolved.

If the point of illumination is moved away from the center of the pupil, closer to the edge of the aperture, then it is possible to resolve a grating with a smaller pitch than can be resolved with on-axis illumination. The −1st diffracted order will now fall completely out of the pupil aperture, but the 0th and +1st orders will be transmitted to form an image. The asymmetry between the 0th and +1st orders leads to severe telecentricity errors. However, the symmetry can be restored by illuminating with two point sources, placed on opposite sides of the pupil. The final image will be composed of the 0th and +1st diffracted orders from one source and the 0th and −1st diffracted orders from the other. This type of illumination is called dipole illumination, and it provides the best possible resolution for conventional masks with features oriented perpendicular to a line passing through the two illuminated spots in the pupil. On the

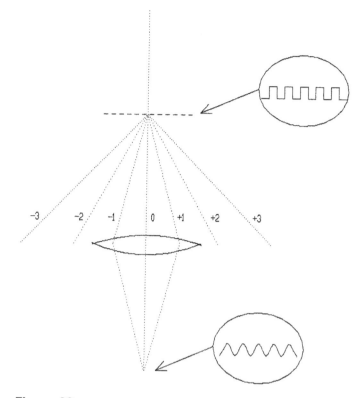

Figure 32 With conventional illumination, the incident light is directed at the center of the lens pupil. A mask consisting of a line-space grating near the resolution limit of the lens diffracts light into a multitude of symmetrical diffracted orders. The lens accepts only the 0th and ±1st orders. When these orders are recombined into an image, the high spatial frequencies contained in the 2nd and higher orders are lost, leading to marked rounding of the aerial image. When the mask pitch becomes so small that the ±1st diffracted orders fall outside the lens aperture, the image contrast falls to zero.

other hand, features oriented parallel to this line will not see the dipole illumination and will have a much larger resolution limit. Differences in imaging properties for two different orientations of lines are usually not desirable, although it is possible to imagine a mask design with all of the critical dimensions aligned along one axis.

In order to improve the symmetry between the x and y axes, it seems fairly obvious to add another pair of illuminated spots at the top and bottom of the pupil. A more careful analysis of this situation shows that it has an undesirable characteristic. The light sources at 6 o'clock and 12 o'clock spoil the dipole il-

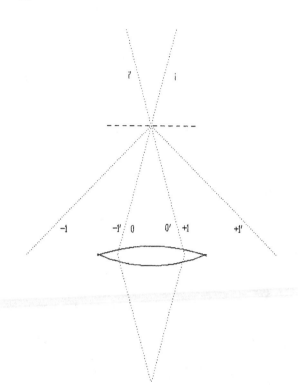

Figure 33 With off-axis illumination, the incident light i is directed toward the edge of the lens pupil. The 0th and +1st diffracted orders are captured to form an image. Because the 0th and 1st orders can be separated by the full width of the pupil, an image can be formed with a much tighter pitch than would be possible with conventional illumination. To create symmetrical pupil illumination, a second off-axis beam i′ is used as well. The 0th and −1st orders of this beam form another image, identical to that formed by the illumination from i. The intensities from these two identical images are added together in the final image.

lumination for vertically oriented lines, and the light sources at 3 o'clock and 9 o'clock have the same effect on horizontally oriented lines. The quadrupole illumination introduced by Nikon and Canon is a more clever way of achieving dipole illumination along two axes. The four illuminated spots are placed at the ends of two diagonal lines passing through the center of the pupil. This provides two dipole illumination patterns for features oriented along either the x or y axis. The separation of the two dipoles can be at most 70% of the separation of a single dipole, so the enhancement in resolution is not nearly as great. But the ability to print both x- and y-oriented features with the same resolution is fairly important. It should be noted that features oriented along the ±45° diagonals of the field will not see the dipole illumination and will suffer considerably worse resolution than features oriented along the x and y axes. Although this is somewhat undesirable, it can usually be tolerated because critical features are rarely oriented at odd angles to the sides of the chip.

Some of the benefits of dipole or quadrupole illumination can be achieved with an annular ring of illumination. Annular illumination does not give as

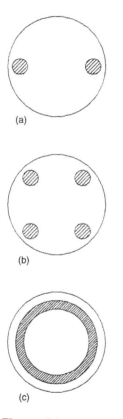

(a)

(b)

(c)

Figure 34 Three unconventional forms of pupil illumination. The shaded areas represent the illuminated portions of the circular pupil. (a) Dipole illumination, which provides a benefit only for lines oriented along the y axis. Quadrupole illumination, illustrated in (b), provides benefits for lines oriented along the x and y axes but gives much poorer results for 45° angled lines. Annular illumination (c) provides milder benefits than dipole or quadrupole illumination, but the benefits are independent of feature orientation.

strong a resolution enhancement as the other two forms of off-axis illumination, but it does have completely symmetrical imaging behavior.

One of the most attractive features of off-axis illumination is its relative ease of use. The stepper manufacturer can usually provide any of the illumination patterns described above by simply inserting an aperture at the appropriate location in the stepper's illuminator. Often a series of apertures can be provided on a turret, and the particular aperture desired for any mask can be automatically supplied by the stepper control program. The most difficult design issues for these forms of illumination are the loss of illumination intensity when an off-axis aperture is used and maintenance of good field illumination uniformity when changing from one aperture to another.

13.5 Pupil Plane Filtration

Modifications to masks and the illumination system have been intensively studied for their benefits to the practice of lithography. The projection lens is the last remaining optical component that could be modified to provide some sort of lithographic enhancement. Any modification to the lens behavior can be defined in terms of a transmission or phase filter in the pupil plane.

Apodization filters are a well-known example of pupil modification sometimes used in astronomical telescopes. By gradually reducing the transmission toward the outer parts of the pupil, an apodization filter reduces optical oscillations or "ringing" at the edges of an image. (The word "apodize" was coined from the Greek words meaning "no foot." The foot on the image is caused by the abrupt discontinuity in transmission of high spatial frequencies at the limits of the pupil.) These oscillations are very small at the coherence values used in lithography and generally of no concern. But filters with different patterns of transmission may have some advantages. Reducing the transmission at the center of the pupil can enhance the contrast of small features, at the cost of reducing the contrast of large features. Phase modifications in the lens pupil can affect the relative biases between isolated and grouped features. (It should be noted that a phase variation in the pupil plane is just another name for an optical aberration. A phase filter in the pupil plane simply introduces a controlled aberration into the projection optics.) Combinations of phase and transmission filtration can sometimes be found that enhance the depth of focus or contrast of some types of image features.

Pupil plane filters cannot be introduced into a stepper as easily as illumination filters can. Most frequently, the pupil plane of the projection lens is not physically accessible. The optical tolerances and alignment tolerances of a pupil plane filter are apt to be extremely tight, since the filter will actually become a part of the projection optics. It is likely that such a filter would have to be permanently built into the stepper lens, instead of being quickly changed to suit the needs of a particular mask level. For now, pupil plane filtration remains the subject of study but will probably not be seen in commercial lithographic equipment for many years.

14 LITHOGRAPHIC TRICKS

A wonderful variety of ingenious techniques have been used in the practice of lithography. Some of these tricks are used in the day-to-day business of exposing wafers, and others are useful only for unusual requirements of an experiment or early development project. What follows is only a partial list of the most interesting tricks available.

14.1 Multiple Exposures Through Focus (FLEX)

In 1987 researchers at the Hitachi corporation came up with an ingenious method for increasing the depth of focus which they called FLEX, for Focus Latitude Enhancement Exposure [27]. This technique works especially well for contact holes. These minimum-sized transparent features in an opaque background typically have the shallowest depth of focus of anything that the lithographer tries to print. If the etched pattern on the wafer's surface has a large amount of vertical height variation, it may be impossible to print contact holes on the high and low parts of the pattern at the same focus setting. Fukuda et al. [27] realized that the exposure field can be exposed twice, once with low regions of the surface in focus and once focusing on the high regions. Each contact hole image will consist of two superimposed images, one in focus and one out of focus. The out-of-focus image spreads over a broad region and contributes only a small background haze to the in-focus image.

This technique can be also be used on wafer surfaces with more than two planes of topography or with random surface variations caused by wafer non-flatness. The two exposures are made with only a slight change in focus, so that their in-focus ranges overlap. This effectively stretches the depth of focus without seriously degrading the image contrast by the presence of the out-of-focus image. The technique can be further extended by exposing at three or more different focal positions or even continuously exposing through a range of focus. If an attempt is made to extend the focal range too much, the process will eventually fail because the many out-of-focus images will degrade the contrast of the in-focus image until it is unusable.

Isolated bright lines and line-space gratings receive much less benefit from FLEX than do contact holes. The out-of-focus image of a line or grating does not subside into a negligible background as fast as that of a contact hole and induces a much greater degradation in the in-focus image. If the reduced contrast can be compensated by a high-contrast resist process, some increased

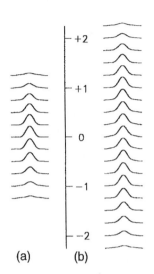

(a)   (b)

Figure 35 The FLEX technique allows a great increase in depth of focus for small, isolated, bright features. (a) Aerial image of a 0.35-µm contact hole through ±1 µm of focus. (b) Aerial image of the same feature, double exposed with a 1.75-µm focus shift between exposures. The depth of focus is nearly double that of the conventional exposure technique. With close inspection, it can be seen that the contrast of the aerial image at best focus is slightly worse for the FLEX exposures.

depth of focus may be achieved for line-space gratings. But the greatest benefit of FLEX is seen in extending the depth of focus of contact holes.

Use of FLEX tends to increase exposure time somewhat, due to the stepper's need to shift focus one or more times during the exposure of each field. The technique also requires modification to the stepper software to accommodate the double exposure. Otherwise, it is one of the easiest lithographic tricks to implement and seems to be used fairly frequently.

14.2 Lateral Image Displacement

Another trick involving double-exposed images can be used to print lines that are smaller than the normal resolution of the lithographic optics. If the aerial image is shifted laterally between two exposures of a dark line, then the resulting latent image in resist will be the sum of the two exposures. The left side of the image will be formed by one of the two exposures and the right side by the other. By varying the amount of lateral shift between the two exposures, the size of the resulting image can be varied and very small lines may be produced. Horizontal and vertical lines can be produced at the same time with this technique by shifting the image along a 45° diagonal.

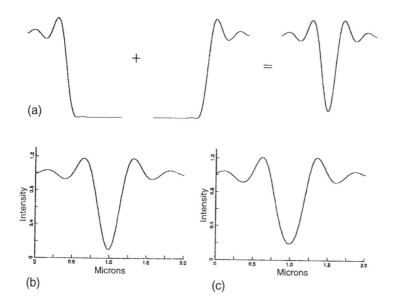

Figure 36 Use of lateral image displacement to produce very small dark features. Two large dark features are superimposed, using a double exposure, to create a very narrow dark feature in the region of overlap. (a) The result of adding the aerial images of two edges to produce a single dark feature. (b) The same double-exposed composite feature on graphical axes, for comparison with the aerial image of a conventionally exposed dark feature in (c). Benefits of the technique are real, but the practical difficulties are severe. The technique works only with extremely coherent illumination ($\sigma = 0.2$ in this example).

The benefits of this trick are rather mild, and the drawbacks are rather severe. The only difference between the aerial image of a single small line and that of a line built up from two exposures of image edges is the difference in coherence between the two cases. In the lateral image displacement technique, the light forming one edge of the image is incoherent with the light forming the other edge. In a single small feature, the light forming the two edges has a considerable amount of relative coherence. This difference gives a modest benefit in contrast to the image formed with lateral image displacement. Images formed with this technique cannot be printed on a tight pitch. A grating with equal lines and spaces is impossible because of the constraints of geometry. Only lines with horizontal or vertical orientation can be used.

Lateral image displacement has been used in a small number of experimental studies, but there do not seem to be any cases of its use in semiconductor manufacturing. Other techniques for producing subresolution features on large pitches are more easily used.

14.3   Resist Image Modifications

The most common way to produce images below the resolution limit of the lithographic optics is to use some chemical or etch technique to reduce the size of the developed image in resist. The resist may be partially eroded in an oxygen plasma to reduce the image size in a controlled way. This reduces the image size but cannot reduce the pitch. It also reduces the resist thickness, which is quite undesirable.

Another trick, with nearly the opposite effect, is to diffuse a material into the exposed and developed resist to induce swelling of the resist patterns. In this case, the spaces between the resist images can be reduced to dimensions below the resolution limits of the optics.

Both of these tricks have seen limited use in semiconductor development laboratories and occasionally in semiconductor manufacturing as well. Often they serve as stopgap measures to produce very small features on relatively large pitches before the lenses becomes available to produce the needed image sizes with conventional lithographic techniques.

Simple changes of exposure can also be used to bias the size of a resist image. Overexposing a positive resist will make the resist lines become smaller, and underexposing will make the spaces smaller. This works very well for small changes in image size and is the usual method of controlling image size in a manufacturing line. However, large over- or underexposures to achieve subresolution lines or spaces usually result in a drastic loss of depth of focus and are not as controllable as the postdevelopment resist image modifications.

14.4   Side-wall Image Transfer

Another technique with the ability to produce subresolution features is a processing trick called side-wall image transfer. A conformal coating of a material like silicon dioxide is deposited over the developed resist image. Then the oxide is etched with a very directional etch until the planar areas of oxide are removed. This leaves the resist features surrounded by collars of silicon dioxide. If the resist is then removed with an oxygen etch, only the oxide collars will remain. These collars form a durable etch mask, shaped like the outline of the original photoresist pattern. The effect is almost identical to that of a chromeless, phase edge mask. Only feature edges are printed, and all of the lines have a fixed, narrow width. All of the features form closed loops, and a second, trim mask is required to cut the loops open. In the case of sidewall image transfer, the line width is determined by the thickness of the original conformal oxide coating.

Very narrow lines with well-controlled widths can be formed with this process. The line width control is limited by the verticality of the original resist

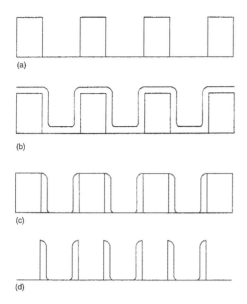

Figure 37 Sidewall image transfer. This nonoptical lithographic trick uses wafer processing techniques to produce extremely small patterns on a very tight pitch. The photoresist pattern produced in (a) has a conformal coating of a material such as silicon dioxide applied in (b). The oxide is etched away with a directional etch, leaving the wafer surface and the top of the resist pattern exposed but the sidewalls of the resist images still coated with oxide. After the resist is stripped, the freestanding oxide sidewalls form a series of very narrow features on a pitch equal to twice that of the original photoresist features.

image sidewalls, the accuracy of the conformal coating, and the directionality of the etch and is practically independent of optical diffraction effects. The pitch of the sidewall pattern can be one half that of the original pattern in resist.

This trick does not seem to have been used in semiconductor manufacturing, mostly due to the serious design limitations and the relative complexity of the processing required. It does provide a way of generating very small lines for early semiconductor device studies, long before the standard techniques of lithography can create the same image sizes.

14.5 Field Stitching

Most of the tricks described in this section were developed to surpass the resolution limits of the lithographic lens or to extend the depth of focus. Field stitching is a multiple exposure technique intended to increase the field size. Very large chips can be built up by accurately abutting two or more subchips, each of which can fit into a single exposure field of a stepper. For the most accurate stitching boundary, the wafer must be exposed with each of the subchips before the wafer is removed from the exposure chuck. This requires that one or more mask changing operations must be performed for each wafer exposure, which greatly reduces the system throughput.

Because of the high accuracy of automatic mask loading systems and wafer stages, the alignment at the field-stitching boundaries can be remarkably good. The chip must be designed with no features having critical tolerances right at the stitching boundary, and it may not be possible to traverse the stitching boundary with lines on the minimum pitch. But otherwise, there are few impediments to the use of field stitching.

Field-stitching strategies have not found their way into commercial manufacturing, partly because of the low throughput inherent in the scheme, but also because there is rarely a need for a chip that is too large to fit into a single stepper field. Field stitching is sometimes contemplated in the earliest stages of a development program, when the only steppers that can support the small lithographic dimensions are experimental prototypes with small field sizes. But commercial steppers with suitable field sizes have always been available by the time the chip reaches the manufacturing stage.

Future development of field stitching has been largely preempted by the step-and-scan technology, which in some ways can be considered a sort of continuous field-stitching technique.

REFERENCES

1. Lin, B. J., *J. Vac Sci. Technol.*, *12*, 1317 (1975).
2. DellaGuardia, R., Wasik, C., Puisto, D., Fair, R., Liebman, L., Rocque, J., Nash, S., Lamberti, A., Collini, G., French, R., Vampatella, B., Gifford, G., Nastasi, V., Sa, P., Volkringer, F., Zell, T., Seeger, D., and Warlaumont, J., Fabrication of 64 megabit DRAM using X-ray lithography. *Proc. SPIE*, *2437*, 112–125 (1995).
3. Markle, D. A., *Solid State Technol.*, *50*(6), 68 (1974).
4. Bruning, J. H., *J. Vac. Sci. Technol.*, *17*, 1147 (1980).
5. Urbano, J. T., Anberg, D. E., Flores, G. E., and Litt, L., Performance results of large field mix-match lithography. *Proc. IEEE/SEMI Adv. Semicond. Manf. Conf.*, 1994, p. 38.
6. Buckley, J. D., and Karatzas, C., Step-and-scan: a system overview of a new lithography tool. *Proc. SPIE*, *1088*, 424–433 (1989).
7. Pfeiffer, H. C., Davis, D. E., Enichen, W. A., Gordon, M. S., Groves, T. R., Hartley, J. G., Quickle, R. J., Rockrohr, J. D., Stickel, W., and Weber, E. V., EL-4, a new generation electron-beam lithography system, *J. Vac. Sci. Technol. B*, *11*(6) 2332–2341 (1993).
8. Okamoto, Y., Saitou, N., Haruo, Y., and Sakitani, Y., High speed electron beam cell projection exposure system, *IEICE Trans. Elect.*, *E77-C*(3), 445–452 (1994).

9. Jewell, T. E., Optical system design issues in development of projection camera for EUV lithography, *Proc. SPIE, 2437*, 340–346 (1995).

10. Zhu, J., Cui, Z., and Prewett, P. D., Experimental study of proximity effect corrections in electron beam lithography, *Proc. SPIE, 2437*, 375–382 (1995).

11. Bruenger, W. H., Loeschner, H., Fallman, W., Finkelstein, W., and Melngailis, J., Evaluation of critical design parameters of an ion projector for 1 Gbit DRAM production, *Microelectron. Eng.*, 27(1–4), 323–326 (1995).

12. Goodman, D. S., and Rosenbluth, A. E., Condenser aberrations in Koehler illumination, *Proc. SPIE, 922*, 108–134 (1988).

13. Pol, V., Bennewitz, J. H., Escher, G. C., Feldman, M., Firtion, V. A., Jewell, T. E., Wilcomb, B. E., and Clemens, J. T., *Proc. SPIE, 633*, 6–16 (1986).

14. Hibbs, M., and Kunz, R., The 193-nm full-field step-and-scan prototype at MIT Lincoln Laboratory, *Proc. SPIE, 2440*, 40–48 (1995).

15. Hutchinson, J. M., Partlo, W. N., Hsu, R., and Oldham, W. G., 213 nm lithography, *Microelectron. Eng.*, 21(1–4), 15–18 (1993).

16. Wilson, M. N., Smith, A. I. C., Kempson, V. C., Townsend, M. C., Schouten, J. C., Anderson, R. J., Jorden, A. R., Suller, V. P., and Poole, M. W., Helios 1 compact superconducting storage ring X-ray source, *IBM J. Res. Dev.*, 37(3), 351–371 (1993).

17. Hopkins, H. H., On the diffraction theory of optical images, *Proc. R. Soc. Lond.*, A-217, 408–432 (1953).

18. Dunn, D. D., Bruce, J. A., and Hibbs, M. S., DUV photolithography linewidth variations from reflective substrates, *Proc. SPIE, 1463*, 8–15 (1991).

19. Brunner, T. A., Optimization of optical properties of resist processes, *Proc. SPIE, 1466* (1991).

20. Suwa, K., and Ushida, K., The optical stepper with a high numerical aperture i-line lens and a field-by-field leveling system, *Proc. SPIE, 922*, 270–276 (1988).

21. Unger, R., and DiSessa, P., New i-line and deep-UV optical wafer steppers, *Proc. SPIE, 1463*, 725–742 (1991).

22. Starikov, A., Use of a single size square serif for variable print bias compensation in microlithography: method, design, and practice, *Proc. SPIE, 1088*, 34–46 (1989).

23. Han, W.-S., Sohn, C.-J., Kang, H.-Y., Koh, Y.-B., and Lee, M.-Y., Overcoming of a global topography and improvement of lithographic performance using a transmittance controlled mask (TCM), *Proc. SPIE, 2197*, 140–149 (1994).

24. Levenson, M. D., Viswanathan, N. S., and Simpson, R. A., Improving resolution in photolithography with a phase-shifting mask, *IEEE Trans. Electron Devices*, ED-29(12), 1812–1846 (1982).

25. Noguchi, M., Muraki, M., Iwasaki, Y., and Suzuki, A., Subhalf micron lithography system with phase-shifting effect, *Proc. SPIE, 1674*, 92–104 (1992).

26. Shiraishi, N., Hirukawa, S., Takeuchi, Y., and Magome, N., New imaging technique for 64M-DRAM, *Proc. SPIE, 1674*, 741–752 (1992).

27. Fukuda, H., Hasegawa, N., and Okazaki, S., Improvement of defocus tolerance in a half-micron optical lithography by the focus latitude enhancement exposure method: simulation and experiment, *J. Vac. Sci. Technol. B*, 7(4), (1989).

2

Optical Lithography Modeling

Chris A. Mack

FINLE Technologies
Austin, Texas

1 INTRODUCTION

Optical lithography modeling began in the early 1970s, when Rick Dill started an effort at IBM Yorktown Heights Research Center to describe the basic steps of the lithography process with mathematical equations. At a time when lithography was considered a true art, such an approach was met with much skepticism. The results of their pioneering work were published in a landmark series of papers in 1975 [1–4], now referred to as the "Dill papers." These papers not only gave birth to the field of lithography modeling, they represented the first serious attempt to describe lithography not as an art but as a science. These papers presented a simple model for image formation with incoherent illumination, the first-order kinetic "Dill model" of exposure, and an empirical model for development coupled with a cell algorithm for photoresist profile calculations. The Dill papers are still the most referenced works in the body of lithography literature.

While Dill's group worked on the beginnings of lithography simulation, a professor from the University of California at Berkeley, Andy Neureuther, spent a year on sabbatical working with Dill. Upon returning to Berkeley, Neureuther and another professor, Bill Oldham, started their own modeling effort. In 1979 they presented the first result of their effort, the lithography modeling program SAMPLE [5]. SAMPLE improved the start of the art in lithography modeling by adding partial coherence to the image calculations and by replacing the cell algorithm for dissolution calculations with a string algorithm. But more important, SAMPLE was made available to the lithography community. For the first time, researchers in the field could use modeling as a tool to help understand and improve their lithography processes.

The author began working in the area of lithographic simulation in 1983 and in 1985 introduced the model PROLITH (the positive resist optical lithography model) [6]. This model added an analytical expression for the standing wave intensity in the resist, a prebake model, a kinetic model for resist development (now known as the Mack model), and the first model for contact and proximity printing. PROLITH was also the first lithography model to run on a personal computer (the IBM PC), making lithography modeling accessible to all lithographers, from advanced researchers to process development engineers to manufacturing engineers. Over the years, PROLITH advanced to include a model for contrast enhancement materials, the extended source method for partially coherent image calculations, and an advanced focus model for high numerical aperture imaging.

Since the late 1980s, commercial lithography simulation software has been available to the semiconductor community, providing dramatic improvements in the usability and graphics capabilities of the models. Lithography modeling has now become an accepted tool for use in a wide variety of lithography applications.

2   STRUCTURE OF A LITHOGRAPHY MODEL

Any lithography model must simulate the basic lithographic steps of image formation, resist exposure, postexposure bake diffusion, and development to obtain a final resist profile. Figure 1 shows a basic schematic of the calculation steps required for lithography modeling. Following is a brief overview of the physical models found in a typical lithography simulator. More details of these models can be found in subsequent sections.

Aerial image: The extended source method or Hopkin's method can be used to predict the aerial image of a partially coherent diffraction-limited or aberrated projection system based on scalar diffraction theory. Single-wavelength and broadband illuminations are possible. The image model must account for the important effect of image defocus through the resist film at a minimum. Mask patterns can be one-dimensional lines and spaces or two-dimensional contacts and islands, as well as arbitrarily complex two-dimensional mask features. The masks often vary in the magnitude and phase of their transmission in what are called phase-shifting masks. The illumination source may be of a conventional disk shape or other more complicated shapes as in off-axis illumination. For very high numerical apertures (NA), vector calculations should be used.

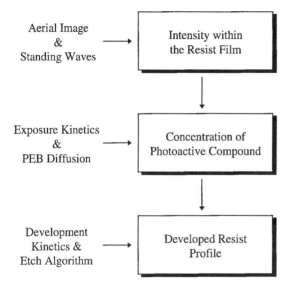

Figure 1   Flow diagram of a lithography model.

Standing waves: An analytical expression is used to calculate the standing wave intensity as a function of depth into the resist, including the effects of resist bleaching, on planar substrates. Film stacks can be defined below the resist with up to many layers between the resist and substrate. Contrast enhancement layers or top-layer antireflection coatings can also be included. The high-NA models should include the effects of nonvertical light propagation.

Prebake: Thermal decomposition of the photoresist photoactive compound during prebake is modeled using first-order kinetics resulting in a change in the resist's optical properties (the Dill parameters *A* and *B*). Other important effects of baking have not yet been modeled.

Exposure: First-order kinetics are used to model the chemistry of exposure using the standard Dill *ABC* parameters. Both positive and negative resists can be used.

Postexposure bake: A diffusion calculation allows the postexposure bake to reduce the effects of standing waves. For chemically amplified resists, this diffusion includes an amplification reaction that accounts for crosslinking, blocking, or deblocking in an acid-catalyzed reaction. Acid loss mechanisms and nonconstant diffusivity could also be needed.

Development: A model relating resist dissolution rate to the chemical composition of the film is used in conjunction with an etching algorithm to determine the resist profile. Surface inhibition or enhancement can also be present. Alternatively, a data file of development rate information could be used in lieu of a model.

CD measurement: The measurement of the photoresist line width should give accuracy and flexibility to match the model to an actual critical dimension (CD) measurement tool.

The combination of the models described above provides a complete mathematical description of the optical lithography process. Use of the models incorporated in a simulation software package allows the user to investigate many interesting and important aspects of optical lithography. The following sections describe each of the models in detail, including derivations of most of the mathematical models as well as physical descriptions of their basis.

Of course, there is more work that has been done in the field of lithography simulation than is possible to report in one chapter. Typically there are several approaches, sometimes equivalent, sometimes not, that can be applied to each problem. Although the models presented here are representative of the possible solutions, they are not necessarily comprehensive reviews of all possible models.

3 AERIAL IMAGE FORMATION

3.1 Basic Imaging Theory

Consider the generic projection system shown in Fig. 2. It consists of a light source, a condenser lens, the mask, the objective lens, and finally the resist-coated wafer. The combination of the light source and the condenser lens is called the illumination system. In optical design terms a lens is a system of (possibly many) lens elements. Each lens element is an individual piece of glass (refractive element) or a mirror (reflective element). The purpose of the illumination system is to deliver light to the mask (and eventually into the objective lens) with sufficient intensity, the proper directionality and spectral characteristics, and adequate uniformity across the field. The light then passes through the clear areas of the mask and diffracts on its way to the objective lens. The purpose of the objective lens is to pick up a portion of the diffraction pattern and project an image onto the wafer which, one hopes, will resemble the mask pattern.

The first and most basic phenomenon occurring here is the diffraction of light. Diffraction is usually thought of as the bending of light as it passes through an aperture, which is certainly an appropriate description for diffraction by a lithographic mask. More correctly, diffraction theory simply describes how light propagates. This propagation includes the effects of the surroundings (boundaries). Maxwell's equations describe how electromagnetic waves propagate, but with partial differential equations of vector quantities that, for general boundary conditions, are extremely difficult to solve without the aid of a pow-

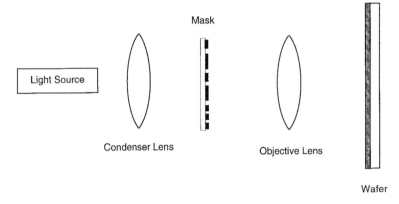

Figure 2 Block diagram of a generic projection system.

erful computer. A simpler approach is to decouple artificially the electric and magnetic field vectors and describe light as a scalar quantity. Under most conditions scalar diffraction theory is surprisingly accurate. Scalar diffraction theory was first rigorously used by Kirchhoff in 1882 and involves performing one numerical integration (much simpler than solving partial differential equations!). Kirchhoff diffraction was further simplified by Fresnel for the case in which the distance away from the diffracting plane (that is, the distance from the mask to the objective lens) is much greater than the wavelength of light. Finally, if the mask is illuminated by a spherical wave that converges to a point at the entrance to the objective lens, Fresnel diffraction simplifies to Fraunhofer diffraction.

Let us describe the electric field transmittance of a mask pattern as $m(x,y)$, where the mask is in the x,y-plane and $m(x,y)$ has in general both magnitude and phase. For a simple chrome-glass mask, the mask pattern becomes binary: $m(x,y)$ is 1 under the glass and 0 under the chrome. Let the x',y' plane be the diffraction plane, that is, the entrance to the objective lens, and let z be the distance from the mask to the objective lens. Finally, we will assume monochromatic light of wavelength λ and that the entire system is in air (so that its index of refraction can be dropped). Then, the electric field of our diffraction pattern, $E(x',y')$, is given by the Fraunhofer diffraction integral:

$$E(x',y') = \int\limits_{-\infty}^{\infty} \int\limits_{-\infty}^{\infty} m(x,y)e^{-2\pi i(f_x x + f_y y)} \, dx \, dy \qquad (1)$$

where $f_x = x'/(z\lambda)$ and $f_y = y'/(z\lambda)$ and they are called the spatial frequencies of the diffraction pattern.

For many scientists and engineers (and especially electrical engineers), this equation should be quite familiar: it is simply a Fourier transform. Thus, the diffraction pattern (i.e., the electric field distribution as it enters the objective lens) is just the Fourier transform of the mask pattern. This is the principle behind an entire field of science called Fourier optics (for more information, consult Goodman's classic textbook [7]). Figure 3 shows two mask patterns, one an isolated space, the other a series of equal lines and spaces, both infinitely long in the y direction. The resulting mask pattern functions, $m(x)$, look like a square pulse and a square wave, respectively. The Fourier transforms are easily found in tables or textbooks and are also shown in Fig. 3. The isolated space gives rise to a sinc function diffraction pattern, and the equal lines and spaces yield discrete diffraction orders.

Let's take a closer look at the diffraction pattern for equal lines and spaces. Notice that the graphs of the diffraction patterns in Fig. 3 use spatial frequency as the x axis. Since z and λ are fixed for a given stepper, the spatial frequency is simply a scaled x' coordinate. At the center of the objective lens entrance ($f_x = 0$) the diffraction pattern has a bright spot called the zero order. The zero order is the light that passes through the mask and is not diffracted. The zero order can be thought of as "DC" light, providing power but no information as to the size of the features on the mask. To either side of the zero order are two peaks called the first diffraction orders. These peaks occur at spatial frequencies of $\pm 1/p$ where p is the pitch of the mask pattern (line width plus space width). Since the position of these diffraction orders depends on the mask pitch, their position contains information about the pitch. It is this information that the objective lens will use to reproduce the image of the mask. In fact, for the objective lens to form a true image of the mask it must have the zero order and at least one higher order. In addition to the first order,

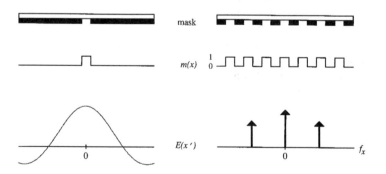

Figure 3 Two typical mask patterns, an isolated space and an array of equal lines and spaces, and the resulting Fraunhofer diffraction patterns.

there can be many higher orders, with the nth order occurring at a spatial frequency of n/p.

Summarizing, given a mask in the x-y plane described by its electric field transmission $m(x,y)$, the electric field M as it enters the objective lens (the x'-y' plane) is given by

$$M(f_x, f_y) = \mathcal{F}\{m(x,y)\} \tag{2}$$

where the symbol $\mathcal{F}$ represents the Fourier transform and f_x and f_y are the spatial frequencies and are simply scaled coordinates in the x'-y' plane.

We are now ready to describe what happens next and follow the diffracted light as it enters the objective lens. In general, the diffraction pattern extends throughout the x'-y' plane. However, the objective lens, being only of finite size, cannot collect all of the light in the diffraction pattern. Typically, lenses used in microlithography are circularly symmetric and the entrance to the objective lens can be thought of as a circular aperture. Only the portions of the mask diffraction pattern that fall inside the aperture of the objective lens go on to form the image. Of course, we can describe the size of the lens aperture by its radius, but a more common and useful description is to define the maximum angle of diffracted light that can enter the lens. Consider the geometry shown in Fig. 4. Light passing through the mask is diffracted at various angles. Given a lens of a certain size placed a certain distance from the mask, there is some maximum angle of diffraction α, for which diffracted light just makes it into the lens. Light emerging from the mask at larger angles misses the lens and is not used in forming the image. The most convenient way to describe the size of the lens aperture is by its numerical aperture, defined as the sine of the maximum half-angle of diffracted light that can enter the lens times the index of refraction of the surrounding medium. In the case of lithography, all of the lenses are in air and the numerical aperture is given by $NA = \sin \alpha$. (Note that the spatial frequency is the sine of the diffracted angle divided by the wavelength of light. Thus, the maximum spatial frequency that can enter the objective lens is given by NA/λ.) Obviously, the numerical aperture is going to be quite important. A large numerical aperture means that a larger portion of the diffraction pattern is captured by the objective lens. For a small numerical aperture, much more of the diffracted light is lost.

To proceed further, we must now describe how the lens affects the light entering it. Obviously, we would like the image to resemble the mask pattern. Since diffraction gives the Fourier transform of the mask, if the lens could give the inverse Fourier transform of the diffraction pattern, the resulting image would resemble the mask pattern. In fact, spherical lenses do behave in this way. We can define an ideal imaging lens as one that produces an image that is identically equal to the Fourier transform of the light distribution entering the lens. It is the goal of lens designers and manufacturers to create lenses as close

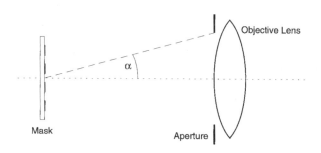

Figure 4   The numerical aperture is defined as NA = sin α where α is the maximum half-angle of the diffracted light that can enter the objective lens.

as possible to this ideal. Does an ideal lens produce a perfect image? No. Because of the finite size of the numerical aperture, only a portion of the diffraction pattern enters the lens. Thus, even an ideal lens cannot produce a perfect image unless the lens is infinitely big. Since in the case of an ideal lens the image is limited only by the diffracted light that does not make it through the lens, we call such an ideal system diffraction limited.

In order to write our final equation for the formation of an image, let us define the objective lens pupil function P (a pupil is just another name for an aperture). The pupil function of an ideal lens simply describes what portion of light enters the lens: it is one inside the aperture and zero outside:

$$P(f_x, f_y) = \begin{cases} 1, & \sqrt{f_x^2 + f_y^2} < NA/\lambda \\ 0, & \sqrt{f_x^2 + f_y^2} > NA/\lambda \end{cases} \tag{3}$$

Thus, the product of the pupil function and the diffraction pattern describes the light entering the objective lens. Combining this with our description of how a lens behaves gives us our final expression for the electric field at the image plane (that is, at the wafer):

$$E(x, y) = \mathcal{F}^{-1} \{ M(f_x, f_y) P(f_x, f_y) \} \tag{4}$$

The aerial image is defined as the intensity distribution at the wafer and is simply the square of the magnitude of the electric field.

Consider the full imaging process. First, light passing through the mask is diffracted. The diffraction pattern can be described as the Fourier transform of the mask pattern. Since the objective lens is of finite size, only a portion of the diffraction pattern actually enters the lens. The numerical aperture describes the maximum angle of diffracted light that enters the lens and the pupil function is used to describe this behavior mathematically. Finally, the effect of the lens is to take the inverse Fourier transform of the light entering the lens to give an image that resembles the mask pattern. If the lens is ideal, the quality of the resulting image is limited only by how much of the diffraction pattern is collected. This type of imaging system is called diffraction limited.

Although we have completely described the behavior of a simple ideal imaging system, we must add one more complication before we have described the operation of a projection system for lithography. So far, we have assumed that the mask is illuminated by spatially coherent light. Coherent illumination means simply that the light striking the mask arrives from only one direction. We have further assumed that the coherent illumination on the mask is normally incident. The result was a diffraction pattern that was centered in the entrance to the objective lens. What would happen if we changed the direction of the illumination so that the light struck the mask at some angle θ'? The effect is simply to shift the diffraction pattern with respect to the lens aperture (in terms of spatial frequency, the amount shifted is $\sin \theta'/\lambda$). Recalling that only the portion of the diffraction pattern passing through the lens aperture is used to form the image, it is quite apparent that this shift in the position of the diffraction pattern can have a profound effect on the resulting image. Letting f_x' and f_y' be the shift in the spatial frequency due to the tilted illumination, Eq. 4 becomes

$$E(x, y, f_x', f_y') = \mathcal{F}^{-1} \{M(f_x - f_x', f_y - f_y')P(f_x, f_y)\} \qquad (5)$$

If the illumination of the mask is composed of light coming from a range of angles rather than just one angle, the illumination is called *partially coherent*. If one angle of illumination causes a shift in the diffraction pattern, a range of angles will cause a range of shifts, resulting in broadened diffraction orders. One can characterize the range of angles used for the illumination in several ways, but the most common is the partial coherence factor, σ (also called the degree of partial coherence, or the pupil filling function, or just the partial coherence). The partial coherence is defined as the sine of the half-angle of the illumination cone divided by the objective lens numerical aperture. It is thus a measure of the angular range of the illumination relative to the angular acceptance of the lens. Finally, if the range of angles striking the mask extends from $-90°$ to $90°$ (that is, all possible angles), the illumination is said to be incoherent.

The extended source method for partially coherent image calculations is based on dividing the full source into individual point sources. Each point source is coherent and results in an aerial image given by Eq. 5. Two point sources from the extended source, however, do not interact coherently with each other. Thus, the contributions of these two sources must be added to each other incoherently (that is, the intensities are added together). The full aerial image is determined by calculating the coherent aerial image from each point on the source and then integrating the intensity over the source.

3.2 Aberrations

Aberrations can be defined as the deviation of the real behavior of an imaging system from its ideal behavior (the ideal behavior was described above using Fourier optics as diffraction-limited imaging). Aberrations are inherent in the behavior of all lens systems and come from three basic sources: defects of construction, defects of use, and defects of design. Defects of construction include rough or inaccurate lens surfaces, inhomogeneous glass, incorrect lens thicknesses or spacings, and tilted or decentered lens elements. Defects of use include use of the wrong illumination or tilt of the lens system with respect to the optical axis of the imaging system. Also, changes in the environmental conditions during use, such as the temperature of the lens or the barometric pressure of the air, result in defects of use. Defects of design may be a bit of a misnomer, since the aberrations of a lens design are not mistakenly designed into the lens, but rather were not designed out of the lens. All lenses have aberrated behavior because the Fourier optics behavior of a lens is only approximately true and is based on a linearized Snell's law for small angles. It is the job of a lens designer to combine elements of different shapes and properties so that the aberrations of each individual lens element tend to cancel in the sum of all of the elements, giving a lens system with only a small residual amount of aberrations. It is impossible to design a lens system with absolutely no aberrations.

Mathematically, aberrations are described as a wavefront deviation, the difference in phase (or path difference) of the actual wavefront emerging from the lens compared to the ideal wavefront as predicted from Fourier optics. This phase difference is a function of the position within the lens pupil, most conveniently described in polar coordinates. This wavefront deviation is in general quite complicated, so the mathematical form used to describe it is also quite complicated. The most common model for describing the phase error across the pupil is the Zernike polynomial, a 36-term polynomial of powers of the radial position R and trigonometric functions of the polar angle θ. The Zernike polynomial can be arranged in many ways, but most lens design software and lens measuring equipment in use today can employ the fringe or circle Zernike polynomial, defined below:

$$
\begin{aligned}
W(R,\theta) =\ & Z1*R*\cos\theta \\
& + Z2*R*\sin\theta \\
& + Z3*(2*R*R - 1) \\
& + Z4*R*R*\cos 2\theta \\
& + Z5*R*R*\sin 2\theta \\
& + Z6*(3*R*R - 2)*R*\cos\theta \\
& + Z7*(3*R*R - 2)*R*\sin\theta
\end{aligned}
$$

$$+ Z8*(6*R**4 - 6*R*R + 1)$$
$$+ Z9*R**3*\cos 3\theta$$
$$+ Z10*R**3*\sin 3\theta$$
$$+ Z11*(4*R*R - 3)*R*R*\cos 2\theta$$
$$+ Z12*(4*R*R - 3)*R*R*\sin 2\theta$$
$$+ Z13*(10*R**4 - 12*R*R + 3)*R*\cos \theta$$
$$+ Z14*(10*R**4 - 12*R*R + 3)*R*\sin \theta$$
$$+ Z15*(20*R**6 - 30*R**4 + 12*R*R - 1)$$
$$+ Z16*R**4*\cos 4\theta$$
$$+ Z17*R**4*\sin 4\theta$$
$$+ Z18*(5*R*R - 4)*R**3*\cos 3\theta$$
$$+ Z19*(5*R*R - 4)*R**3*\sin 3\theta$$
$$+ Z20*(15*R**4 - 20*R*R + 6)*R*R*\cos 2\theta$$
$$+ Z21*(15*R**4 - 20*R*R + 6)*R*R*\sin 2\theta$$
$$+ Z22*(35*R**6 - 60*R**4 + 30*R*R - 4)*R*\cos \theta$$
$$+ Z23*(35*R**6 - 60*R**4 + 30*R*R - 4)*R*\sin \theta$$
$$+ Z24*(70*R**8 - 140*R**6 + 90*R**4 - 20*R*R+1)$$
$$+ Z25*R**5*\cos 5\theta$$
$$+ Z26*R**5*\sin 5\theta$$
$$+ Z27*(6*R*R - 5)*R**4*\cos 4\theta$$
$$+ Z28*(6*R*R - 5)*R**4*\sin 4\theta$$
$$+ Z29*(21*R**4 - 30*R*R + 10)*R**3*\cos 3\theta$$
$$+ Z30*(21*R**4 - 30*R*R + 10)*R**3*\sin 3\theta$$
$$+ Z31*(56*R**6 - 105*R**4 + 60*R**2 - 10)*R*R*\cos 2\theta$$
$$+ Z32*(56*R**6 - 105*R**4 + 60*R**2 - 10)*R*R*\sin 2\theta$$
$$+ Z33*(126*R**8 - 280*R**6 + 210*R**4 - 60*R*R + 5)*R*\cos \theta$$
$$+ Z34*(126*R**8 - 280*R**6 + 210*R**4 - 60*R*R + 5)*R*\sin \theta$$
$$+ Z35*(252*R**10 - 630*R**8 + 560*R**6 - 210*R**4 + 30*R*R - 1)$$
$$+ Z36*(924*R**12 - 2772*R**10 + 3150*R**8 - 1680*R**6 + 420*R**4 - 42*R*R + 1) \tag{6}$$

where $W(R,\theta)$ is the optical path difference relative to the wavelength and Zi is called the ith Zernike coefficient. It is the magnitude of the Zernike coefficients that determines the aberration behavior of a lens. They have units of optical path length relative to the wavelength.

The impact of aberrations on the aerial image can be calculated by modifying the pupil function of the lens with the aberration phase error given by Eq. 6.

$$P(f_x, f_y) = P_{\text{ideal}}(f_x, f_y)e^{i2\pi W(R,\theta)} \tag{7}$$

3.3 Zero-Order Scalar Model

Calculation of an aerial image means, quite literally, determining the image in air. Of course, in lithography one projects this image into photoresist. The propagation of the image into resist can be quite complicated, so models usually make one or more approximations. This section and the sections that follow describe approximations made in determining the intensity of light within the photoresist.

The lithography simulator SAMPLE [8] and the 1985 version of PROLITH [9] used the simple imaging approximation first proposed by Dill et al. [10] to calculate the propagation of an aerial image in photoresist. First, an aerial image $I_i(x)$ is calculated as if projected into air (x being along the surface of the wafer and perpendicular to the propagation direction of the image). Second, a standing wave intensity $I_s(z)$ is calculated assuming a plane wave of light is normally incident on the photoresist-coated substrate (where z is defined as zero at the top of the resist and is positive going into the resist). Then, it is assumed that the actual intensity within the resist film $I(x,z)$ can be approximated by

$$I(x,z) \approx I_i(x)I_s(z) \tag{8}$$

For very low numerical apertures and reasonably thin photoresists, these approximations are valid. They begin to fail when the aerial image changes as it propagates through the resist (i.e., it defocuses) or when the light entering the resist is appreciably nonnormal. Note that if the photoresist bleaches (changes its optical properties during exposure), only $I_s(z)$ changes in this approximation.

3.4 First-Order Scalar Model

The first attempt to correct one of the deficiencies of the zero-order model was made by the author [11] and, independently, by Bernard [12]. The aerial image, while propagating through the resist, is continuously changing focus. Thus, even in air, the aerial image is a function of both x and z. An aerial image simulator calculates images as a function of x and the distance from the plane of best focus, δ. Letting δ_0 be the defocus distance of the image at the top of the photoresist, the defocus within the photoresist at any position z is given by

$$\delta(z) = \delta_o + \frac{z}{n} \tag{9}$$

where n is the real part of the index of refraction of the photoresist. The intensity within the resist is then given by

$$I(x,z) = I_i(x,\delta(z))I_s(z) \tag{10}$$

Here the assumption of normally incident plane waves is still used when calculating the standing wave intensity.

3.5 High-NA Scalar Model

The light propagating through the resist can be thought of as various plane waves traveling through the resist in different directions. Consider first the propagation of the light in the absence of diffraction by a mask pattern (that is, exposure of the resist by a large open area). The spatial dimensions of the light source determine the characteristics of the light entering the photoresist. For the simple case of a coherent point source of illumination centered on the optical axis, the light traveling into the photoresist would be the normally incident plane wave used in the calculations presented above. The standing wave intensity within the resist can be determined analytically [13] as the square of the magnitude of the electric field given by

$$E(z) = \frac{\tau_{12}E_I\left(e^{-i2\pi n_2 z/\lambda} + \rho_{23}\tau_D^2 e^{i2\pi n_2 z/\lambda}\right)}{1 + \rho_{12}\rho_{23}\tau_D^2} \tag{11}$$

where the subscripts 1, 2, and 3 refer to air, the photoresist, and the substrate, respectively, D is the resist thickness, E_I is the incident electrical field, λ is the wavelength and where

complex index of refraction of film j: $\mathbf{n}_j = n_j - i\kappa_j$

transmission coefficient from i to j: $\tau_{ij} = \dfrac{2\mathbf{n}_i}{\mathbf{n}_i + \mathbf{n}_j}$

reflection coefficient from i to j: $\rho_{ij} = \dfrac{\mathbf{n}_i - \mathbf{n}_j}{\mathbf{n}_i + \mathbf{n}_j}$

internal transmittance of the resist: $\tau_D = e^{-i2\pi n_2 D/\lambda}$

A more complete description of the standing wave equation (11) is given in Section 4.

The above expression can be easily modified for the case of nonnormally incident plane waves. Suppose a plane wave is incident on the resist film at some angle θ_1. The angle of the plane wave inside the resist will be θ_2 as determined from Snell's law. An analysis of the propagation of this plane wave within the resist will give an expression similar to Eq. 11 but with the position z replaced with $z \cos \theta_2$.

$$E(z,\theta_2) = \frac{\tau_{12}(\theta_2)E_I\left(e^{-i2\pi n_2 z \cos\theta_2/\lambda} + \rho_{23}(\theta_2)\tau_D^2(\theta_2)e^{i2\pi n_2 z \cos\theta_2/\lambda}\right)}{1 + \rho_{12}(\theta_2)\rho_{23}(\theta_2)\tau_D^2(\theta_2)} \tag{12}$$

The transmission and reflection coefficients are now functions of the angle of incidence and are given by the Fresnel formulas (see Section 4). A similar approach was taken by Bernard and Urbach [14].

By calculating the standing wave intensity at one incident angle θ_1 to give $I_s(z,\theta_1)$, the full standing wave intensity can be determined by integrating over all angles. Each incident angle comes from a given point in the illumination source, so that integration over angles is the same as integration over the source. Thus, the effect of partial coherence on the standing waves is accounted for. Note that for the model described here the effect of the nonnormal incidence is included only with respect to the zero-order light (the light that is not diffracted by the mask).

Besides the basic modeling approaches described above, there are two issues that apply to any model. First, the effects of defocus are taken into account by describing defocus as a phase error at the pupil plane. Essentially, if the curvature of the wavefront exiting the objective lens pupil is such that it focuses in the wrong place (i.e., not where you want it), one can consider the wavefront curvature to be wrong. Simple geometry then relates the optical path difference (OPD) of the actual wavefront from the desired wavefront as function of the angle of the light exiting the lens, θ.

$$OPD(\theta) = \delta(1 - \cos \theta) \tag{13}$$

Computation of the imaging usually involves a change in variables where the main variable used is $\sin \theta$. Thus, the cosine adds some algebraic complexity to the calculations. For this reason, it is common in optics texts to simplify the OPD function for small angles (i.e., low numerical apertures).

$$OPD(\theta) = \delta(1 - \cos \theta) \approx \frac{\delta}{2}\sin^2 \theta \tag{14}$$

Again, the approximation is not necessary and is made only to simplify the resulting equations. In this work, the approximate defocus expression is used in the first-order scalar model. The high-NA model uses the exact defocus expression.

Reduction in the imaging system adds an interesting complication. Light entering the objective lens will leave the lens with no loss in energy (the lossless lens assumption). However, if there is reduction in the lens, the intensity distribution of the light entering will be different from that leaving since the intensity is the energy spread over a changing area. The result is a radiometric correction well known in optics [15] and first applied to lithography by Cole et al. [16].

3.6 Full Scalar and Vector Models

The above method for calculating the image intensity within the resist still makes the assumption of separability, that an aerial image and a standing wave intensity can be calculated independently and then multiplied together to give the total intensity. This assumption is not required. Instead, one could calculate the full $I(x,z)$ at once making only the standard scalar approximation. The formation of the image can be described as the summation of plane waves. For coherent illumination, each diffraction order gives one plane wave propagating into the resist. Interference between the zero order and the higher orders produces the desired image. Each point in the illumination source will produce another image that will add incoherently (i.e., intensities will add) to give the total image. Equation 12 describes the propagation of a plane wave in a stratified medium at any arbitrary angle. By applying this equation to each diffraction order (not just the zero order as in the high-NA scalar model), an exact scalar representation of the full intensity within the resist is obtained.

Light is an electromagnetic wave that can be described by time-varying electric and magnetic field vectors. In lithography, the materials used are generally nonmagnetic so that only the electric field is of interest. The electric field vector is described by its three vector components. Maxwell's equations, sometimes put into the form of the wave equation, govern the propagation of the electric field vector. The scalar approximation assumes that the three components of the electric field vector can be treated separately as scalar quantities and each scalar electric field component must individually satisfy the wave equation. Furthermore, when two fields of light (say, two plane waves) are added together, the scalar approximation means that the sum of the fields would simply be the sum of the scalar amplitudes of the two fields.

The scalar approximation is commonly used throughout optics and is known to be accurate under many conditions. There is one simple situation, however, in which the scalar approximation is not adequate. Consider the interference of two plane waves traveling past each other. If each plane wave is treated as a vector, they will interfere only if there is some overlap in their electric field vectors. If the vectors are parallel, there will be complete interference. If, however, their electric fields are at right angles to each other there will be no interference. The scalar approximation essentially assumes that the electric field vectors are always parallel and will always give complete interference. These differences come into play in lithography when considering the propagation of plane waves traveling through the resist at large angles. For large angles, the scalar approximation may fail to account for these vectors effects. Thus, a vector model would keep track of the vector direction of the electric field and use this information when adding two plane waves together [17,18].

4 STANDING WAVES

When a thin dielectric film placed between two semi-infinite media (e.g., a thin coating on a reflecting substrate) is exposed to monochromatic light, standing waves are produced in the film. This effect has been well documented for such cases as antireflection coatings and photoresist exposure [19–23]. In the former, the standing wave effect is used to reduce reflections from the substrate. In the latter, standing waves are an undesirable side effect of the exposure process. Unlike the antireflection application, photolithography applications require a knowledge of the intensity of the light within the thin film itself. Previous work [22,23] on determining the intensity within a thin photoresist film has been limited to numerical solutions based on Berning's matrix method [24]. This section presents an analytical expression for the standing wave intensity within a thin film [25]. This film may be homogeneous or of a known inhomogeneity. The film may be on a substrate or between one or more other thin films. The incident light can be normally incident or incident at some angle.

Consider a thin film of thickness D and complex index of refraction n_2 deposited on a thick substrate with complex index of refraction n_3 in an ambient environment of index n_1. An electromagnetic plane wave is normally incident on this film. Let E_1, E_2, and E_3 be the electric fields in the ambient, thin film, and substrate, respectively (see Fig. 5). Assuming monochromatic illumination, the electric field in each region is a plane wave or the sum of two plane waves traveling in opposite directions (i.e., a standing wave). Maxwell's equations require certain boundary conditions to be met at each interface: specifically, E_j and the magnetic field H_j are continuous across the

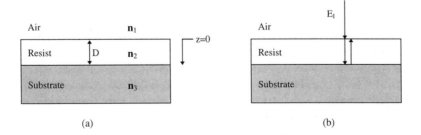

(a)   (b)

Figure 5   Film stack showing geometry for standing wave derivation.

boundaries $z = 0$ and $z = D$. Solving the resulting equations simultaneously, the electric field in region 2 can be shown to be [25]

$$E_2(x,\ y,\ z) = E_1(x,\ y) \frac{\tau_{12}\left(e^{-i2\pi n_2 z/\lambda} + \rho_{23}\tau_D^2 e^{i2\pi n_2 z/\lambda}\right)}{1 + \rho_{12}\rho_{23}\tau_D^2} \qquad (15)$$

where $E_1(x,y)$ = the incident wave at $z = 0$, which is a plane wave
$\rho_{ij} = (\mathbf{n}_i - \mathbf{n}_j)/(\mathbf{n}_i + \mathbf{n}_j)$, the reflection coefficient
$\tau_{ij} = 2\mathbf{n}_i/(\mathbf{n}_i + \mathbf{n}_j)$, the transmission coefficient
$\tau_D = \exp(-ik_2 D)$, the internal transmittance of the film
$k_j = 2\pi \mathbf{n}_j/\lambda$, the propagation constant
$\mathbf{n}_j = \mathbf{n}_j - i\kappa_j$, the complex index of refraction
λ = vacuum wavelength of the incident light.

Equation 15 is the basic standing wave expression where film 2 represents the photoresist. Squaring the magnitude of the electric field gives the standing wave intensity. Note that absorption is taken into account in this expression through the imaginary part of the index of refraction. The common absorption coefficient α is related to the imaginary part of the index by

$$\alpha = \frac{4\pi\kappa}{\lambda} \qquad (16)$$

It is very common to have more than one film coated on a substrate. The problem then becomes that of two or more absorbing thin films on a substrate. An analysis similar to that for one film yields the following result for the electric field in the top layer of an m-1 layer system:

$$E_2(x,\ y,\ z) = E_1(x,\ y) \frac{\tau_{12}\left(e^{-i2\pi n_2 z/\lambda} + \rho_{23}'\tau_D^2 e^{i2\pi n_2 z/\lambda}\right)}{1 + \rho_{12}\rho_{23}'\tau_D^2} \qquad (17)$$

where

$$\rho_{23}' = \frac{\mathbf{n}_2 - \mathbf{n}_3 X_3}{\mathbf{n}_2 + \mathbf{n}_3 X_3}$$

$$X_3 = \frac{1 - \rho_{34}'\tau_{D3}^2}{1 + \rho_{34}'\tau_{D3}^2}$$

$$\rho_{34}' = \frac{\mathbf{n}_3 - \mathbf{n}_4 X_4}{\mathbf{n}_3 + \mathbf{n}_4 X_4}$$

.
.
.

$$X_m = \frac{1 - \rho_{m,m+1}\tau_{Dm}^2}{1 + \rho_{m,m+1}\tau_{Dm}^2}$$

$$\rho_{m,m+1} = \frac{\mathbf{n}_m - \mathbf{n}_{m+1}}{\mathbf{n}_m + \mathbf{n}_{m+1}}$$

$$\tau_{Dj} = e^{-ik_j D_j}$$

and all other parameters are defined previously. The parameter ρ_{23}' is the effective reflection coefficient between the thin film and what lies beneath it.

If the thin film in question is not the top film (layer 2), the intensity can be calculated in layer j from

$$E_j(x, y, z) = E_{\text{Ieff}}(x, y)\tau_{j-1,j}^* \frac{\left(e^{-ik_j z_j} + \rho_{j,j+1}'\tau_{Dj}^2 e^{ik_j z_j}\right)}{1 + \rho_{j-1,j}^* \rho_{j,j+1}' \tau_{Dj}^2} \tag{18}$$

where $\tau_{j-1,j}^* = 1 + \rho_{j-1,j}^*$. The effective reflection coefficient ρ^* is analogous to the coefficient ρ', looking in the opposite direction. E_{Ieff} is the effective intensity incident on layer j. Both E_{Ieff} and ρ^* are defined in detail in Ref. 25.

If the film in question is not homogeneous, the equations above are, in general, not valid. Let us, however, examine one special case in which the inhomogeneity takes the form of small variations in the imaginary part of the index of refraction of the film in the z direction, leaving the real part constant. In this case, the absorbance *Abs* is no longer simply αz but becomes

$$\text{Abs}(z) = \int_0^z \alpha(z')dz' \tag{19}$$

It can be shown that Eqs. 15–18 are still valid if the anisotropic expression for absorbance (19) is used. Thus, $I(z)$ can be found if the absorption coefficient is known as a function of z. Figure 6 shows a typical result of the standing wave intensity within a photoresist film coated on an oxide on silicon film stack.

Equation 15 can be easily modified for the case of nonnormally incident plane waves. Suppose a plane wave is incident on the resist film at some angle θ_1. The angle of the plane wave inside the resist will be θ_2 as determined from Snell's law. An analysis of the propagation of this plane wave within the resist will give an expression similar to Eq. 15 but with the position z replaced with $z \cos \theta_2$.

$$E(z, \theta_2) = \frac{\tau_{12}(\theta_2)E_1\left(e^{-i2\pi n_2 z \cos\theta_2/\lambda} + \rho_{23}(\theta_2)\tau_D^2(\theta_2)e^{i2\pi n_2 z \cos\theta_2/\lambda}\right)}{1 + \rho_{12}(\theta_2)\rho_{23}(\theta_2)\tau_D^2(\theta_2)} \tag{20}$$

The transmission and reflection coefficients are now functions of the angle of incidence (as well as the polarization of the incident light) and are given by the Fresnel formulas.

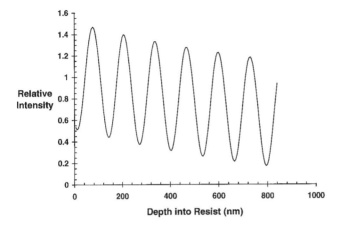

Figure 6 Standing wave intensity within a photoresist film at the start of exposure (850 nm of resist on 100 nm of SiO$_2$ on silicon, λ = 436 nm). The intensity shown is relative to the incident intensity.

$$\rho_{ij\perp}(\theta) = \frac{\mathbf{n}_i \cos(\theta_i) - \mathbf{n}_j \cos(\theta_j)}{\mathbf{n}_i \cos(\theta_i) + \mathbf{n}_j \cos(\theta_j)}$$

$$\tau_{ij\perp}(\theta) = \frac{2\mathbf{n}_i \cos(\theta_i)}{\mathbf{n}_i \cos(\theta_i) + \mathbf{n}_j \cos(\theta_j)}$$

$$\rho_{ij\parallel}(\theta) = \frac{\mathbf{n}_i \cos(\theta_j) - \mathbf{n}_j \cos(\theta_i)}{\mathbf{n}_i \cos(\theta_j) + \mathbf{n}_j \cos(\theta_i)}$$

$$\tau_{ij\parallel}(\theta) = \frac{2\mathbf{n}_i \cos(\theta_i)}{\mathbf{n}_i \cos(\theta_j) + \mathbf{n}_j \cos(\theta_i)} \qquad (21)$$

For the typical unpolarized case, the light entering the resist will become polarized (but only slightly). Thus, a separate standing wave can be calculated for each polarization and the resulting intensities summed to give the total intensity.

5 PHOTORESIST EXPOSURE KINETICS

The kinetics of photoresist exposure are intimately tied to the phenomenon of absorption. The discussion below begins with a description of absorption, followed by the chemical kinetics of exposure. Finally, the chemistry of chemically amplified resists will be reviewed.

5.1 Absorption

The phenomenon of absorption can be viewed on a macroscopic or a microscopic scale. On the macro level, absorption is described by the familiar Lambert and Beer laws, which give a linear relationship between absorbance and path length times the concentration of the absorbing species. On the micro level, a photon is absorbed by an atom or molecule, promoting an electron to a higher energy state. Both methods of analysis yield useful information needed in describing the effects of light on a photoresist.

The basic law of absorption is an empirical one with no known exceptions. It was first expressed by Lambert in differential form as

$$\frac{dI}{dz} = -\alpha I \tag{22}$$

where I is the intensity of light traveling in the z direction through a medium, and α is the absorption coefficient of the medium and has units of inverse length. In a homogeneous medium (i.e., α is not a function of z), Eq. 22 may be integrated to yield

$$I(z) = I_0 \exp(-\alpha z) \tag{23}$$

where z is the distance the light has traveled through the medium and I_0 is the intensity at $z = 0$. If the medium is inhomogeneous, Eq. 23 becomes

$$I(z) = I_0 \exp(-Abs(z)) \tag{24}$$

where

$$Abs(z) = \int_0^z \alpha(z')dz' = \textit{the absorbance}$$

When working with electromagnetic radiation, it is often convenient to describe the radiation by its complex electric field vector. The electric field can implicitly account for absorption by using a complex index of refraction $\mathbf{n}$ such that

$$\mathbf{n} = n - i\kappa \tag{25}$$

The imaginary part of the index of refraction, sometimes called the extinction coefficient, is related to the absorption coefficient by

$$\alpha = 4\pi\kappa / \lambda \tag{26}$$

In 1852 Beer showed that for dilute solutions the absorption coefficient is proportional to the concentration of the absorbing species in the solution.

$$\alpha_{solution} = ac \tag{27}$$

where a is the molar absorption coefficient, given by $a = \alpha MW/\rho$, MW is the molecular weight, ρ is the density, and c is the concentration. The stipulation that the solution be dilute expresses a fundamental limitation of Beer's law. At high concentrations, where absorbing molecules are close together, the absorption of a photon by one molecule may be affected by a nearby molecule [26]. Since this interaction is concentration dependent, it causes deviation from the linear relation (27). Also, an apparent deviation from Beer's law occurs if the real part of the index of refraction changes appreciably with concentration. Thus, the validity of Beer's law should always be verified over the concentration range of interest.

For an N-component homogeneous solid, the overall absorption coefficient becomes

$$\alpha_T = \sum_{j=1}^{N} a_j c_j \tag{28}$$

Of the total amount of light absorbed, the fraction of light that is absorbed by component i is given by

$$\frac{I_{Ai}}{I_{AT}} = \left(\frac{a_i c_i}{\alpha_T} \right) \tag{29}$$

where I_{AT} is the total light absorbed by the film and I_{Ai} is the light absorbed by component i.

We will now apply the concepts of macroscopic absorption to a typical positive photoresist. A diazonaphthoquinone positive photoresist (such as AZ1350J) is made up of four major components: a base resin R which gives the resist its structural properties, a photoactive compound M (abbreviated PAC), exposure products P generated by the reaction of M with ultraviolet light, and a solvent S. Although photoresist drying during prebake is intended to drive off solvents, thermal studies have shown that a resist may contain 10% solvent after a 30-minute 100°C prebake [27,28]. The absorption coefficient α is then

$$\alpha = a_M M + a_P P + a_R R + a_S S \tag{30}$$

If M_0 is the initial PAC concentration (i.e., with no ultraviolet exposure), the stoichiometry of the exposure reaction gives

$$P = M_0 - M \tag{31}$$

Equation 30 may be rewritten as [29]

$$\alpha = Am + B \tag{32}$$

where $\quad A = (a_M - a_P)M_0$
$\qquad B = a_P M_0 + a_R R + a_S S$
$\qquad m = M/M_0$

A and B are called the bleachable and nonbleachable absorption coefficients, respectively, and make up the first two Dill photoresist parameters [29].

The quantities A and B are experimentally measurable [29] and can be easily related to typical resist absorbance curves, measured using an ultraviolet (UV) spectrophotometer. When the resist is fully exposed, $M = 0$ and

$$\alpha_{exposed} = B \tag{33}$$

Similarly, when the resist is unexposed, $m = 1$ ($M = M_0$) and

$$\alpha_{unexposed} = A + B \tag{34}$$

From this A may be found by

$$A = \alpha_{unexposed} - \alpha_{exposed} \tag{35}$$

Thus, $A(\lambda)$ and $B(\lambda)$ may be determined from the UV absorbance curves of unexposed and completely exposed resist (Fig. 7).

As mentioned previously, Beer's law is empirical in nature and, thus, should be verified experimentally. In the case of positive photoresists, this means formulating resist mixtures with different ratios of photoactive compound to resin and measuring the resulting A parameters. Previous work has shown that Beer's law is valid for conventional photoresists over the full practical range of PAC concentrations [30].

5.2 Exposure Kinetics

On a microscopic level, the absorption process can be thought of as photons being absorbed by an atom or molecule causing an outer electron to be pro-

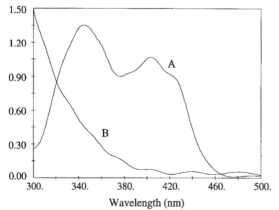

Figure 7 Resist parameters A and B as a function of wavelength measured using a UV spectrophotometer.

moted to a higher energy state. This phenomenon is especially important for the photoactive compound, since it is the absorption of UV light that leads to the chemical conversion of *M* to *P*.

$$M \xrightarrow{UV} P \qquad (36)$$

This concept is stated in the first law of photochemistry: only the light that is absorbed by a molecule can be effective in producing photochemical change in the molecule. The actual chemistry of diazonaphthoquinone exposure is given below.

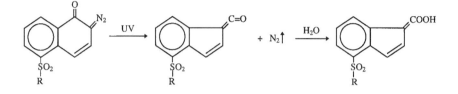

The chemical reaction (36) can be rewritten in general form as

$$M \underset{k_2}{\overset{k_1}{\rightleftharpoons}} M* \xrightarrow{k_3} P \qquad (37)$$

where *M* is the photoactive compound (PAC); $M*$ is the molecule in an excited state: *P* is the carboxylic acid (product); and k_1, k_2, k_3 are the rate constants for the reactions. Simple kinetics can now be applied. The proposed mechanism (37) assumes that all reactions are first order. Thus, the rate equation for each species can be written.

$$\frac{dM}{dt} = k_2 M* - k_1 M$$

$$\frac{dM*}{dt} = k_1 M - (k_2 + k_3) M*$$

$$\frac{dP}{dt} = k_3 M* \qquad (38)$$

A system of three coupled linear first-order differential equations can be solved exactly using Laplace transforms and the initial conditions

$$M(t = 0) = M_0$$

$$M*(t = 0) = P(t = 0) = 0 \qquad (39)$$

However, if one uses the steady-state approximation the solution becomes much simpler. This approximation assumes that in a very short time the excited molecule $M*$ comes to a steady state, i.e., $M*$ is formed as quickly as it disappears. In mathematical form,

$$\frac{dM^*}{dt} = 0 \tag{40}$$

A previous study has shown that M^* does indeed come to a steady state quickly, on the order of 10^{-8} seconds or faster [31]. Thus,

$$\frac{dM}{dt} = -KM \tag{41}$$

where

$$K = \frac{k_1 k_3}{k_2 + k_3}$$

Assuming K remains constant with time,

$$M = M_0 \exp(-Kt) \tag{42}$$

The overall rate constant K is a function of the intensity of the exposure radiation. An analysis of the microscopic absorption of a photon predicts that K is directly proportional to the intensity of the exposing radiation [30]. Thus, a more useful form of Eq. 41 is

$$\frac{dm}{dt} = -CIm \tag{43}$$

where the relative PAC concentration ($m = M/M_0$) has been used and C is the standard exposure rate constant and the third Dill photoresist parameter.

A solution to the exposure rate equation (43) is simple if the intensity within the resist is constant throughout the exposure. However, this is generally not the case. In fact, many resists bleach upon exposure; that is, they become more transparent as the photoactive compound M is converted to product P. This corresponds to a positive value of A, as seen, for example, in Fig. 7. Since the intensity varies as a function of exposure time, this variation must be known in order to solve the exposure rate equation. In the simplest possible case, a resist film coated on a substrate of the same index of refraction, only absorption affects the intensity within the resist. Thus, Lambert's law of absorption, coupled with Beer's law, couple be applied.

$$\frac{dI}{dz} = -(Am + B)I \tag{44}$$

where Eq. 32 was used to relate the absorption coefficient to the relative PAC concentration. Equations 43 and 44 are coupled and thus become first-order nonlinear partial differential equations that must be solved simultaneous. The solution to Eqs. 43 and 44 was first carried out numerically for the case of lithography simulation [29] but in fact was solved analytically by Herrick [32] many years earlier. The same solution was also presented more recently by Diamond and Sheats [33] and by Babu and Barouch [34]. These solutions take the form of a single numerical integration, which is much simpler than solving two differential equations!

Although an analytical solution exists for the simple problem of exposure with absorption only, in more realistic problems the variation of intensity with depth in the film is more complicated than Eq. 44. In fact, the general exposure situation results in the formation of standing waves, as discussed previously. In such a case, Eqs. 15–18 can give the intensity within the resist as a function of the PAC distribution $m(x,y,z,t)$. Initially, this distribution is simply $m(x,y,z,0) = 1$. Thus, equation 15 for example would give $I(x,y,z,0)$. The exposure equation 43 can then be integrated over a small increment of exposure time Δt to produce the PAC distribution $m(x,y,z,\Delta t)$. The assumption is that over this small increment in exposure time the intensity remains relatively constant, leading to the exponential solution. This new PAC distribution is then used to calculate the new intensity distribution $I(x,y,z,\Delta t)$, which in turn is used to generate the PAC distribution at the next increment of exposure time $m(x,y,z,2\Delta t)$. This process continues until the final exposure time is reached.

5.3 Chemically Amplified Resists

Chemically amplified photoresists are composed of a polymer resin (possibly "blocked" to inhibit dissolution), a photoacid generator (PAG), and possibly a crosslinking agent, dye, or other additive. As the name implies, the photoacid generator forms a strong acid when exposed to deep-UV light. Ito and Willson [35] first proposed the use of an aryl onium salt, and triphenylsulfonium salts have been studied extensively as PAGs. The reaction of a common PAG is shown below:

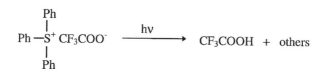

The acid generated in this case (trifluoroacetic acid) is a derivative of acetic acid where the electron-drawing properties of the fluorines are used to increase greatly the acidity of the molecule. The PAG is mixed with the polymer resin at a concentration of typically 5–15% by weight, with 10% as a typical formulation.

The kinetics of the exposure reaction are standard first order:

$$\frac{\partial G}{\partial t} = -CIG \tag{45}$$

where G is the concentration of PAG at time t (the initial PAG concentration is

G_0), I is the exposure intensity, and C is the exposure rate constant. For constant intensity, the rate equation can be solved for G:

$$G = G_0 e^{-CIt} \tag{46}$$

The acid concentration H is given by

$$H = G_0 - G = G_0(1 - e^{-CIt}) \tag{47}$$

Exposure of the resist with an aerial image $I(x)$ results in an acid latent image $H(x)$. A postexposure bake (PEB) is then used to thermally induce a chemical reaction. This may be the activation of a crosslinking agent for a negative resist or the deblocking of the polymer resin for a positive resist. The reaction is catalyzed by the acid, so the acid is not consumed by the reaction and H remains constant. Ito and Willson [35] first proposed the concept of deblocking a polymer to change its solubility. A base polymer such as poly(p-hydroxystyrene), PHS, is used which is very soluble in an aqueous base developer. It is the hydroxyl groups that give the PHS its high solubility, so by "blocking" these sites (by reacting the hydroxyl group with some longer chain molecule) the solubility can be reduced. Ito and Willson employed a t-butoxycarbonyl group (tBOC), resulting in a very slowly dissolving polymer. In the presence of acid and heat, the tBOC-blocked polymer will undergo acidolysis to generate the soluble hydroxyl group, as shown below.

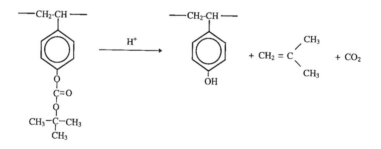

One drawback of this scheme is that the cleaved tBOC is volatile and will evaporate, causing film shrinkage in the exposed areas. Larger molecular weight blocking groups can be used to reduce this film shrinkage to acceptable levels (below 10%). Also, the blocking group is such an effective inhibitor of dissolution that nearly every blocked site on the polymer must be deblocked in order to obtain significant dissolution. Thus, the photoresist can be made more "sensitive" by only partially blocking the PHS. Typical photoresists use 10–30% of the hydroxyl groups blocked, with 20% a typical value. Molecular weights for the PHS run in the range of 3000 to 5000, giving about 20 to 35 hydroxyl groups per molecule.

Using M as the concentration of some reactive site, these sites are consumed (i.e., are reacted) according to kinetics of some unknown order in H and first order in M [36]:

$$\frac{\partial M}{\partial t'} = -K_{amp} M H^n \qquad (48)$$

where K_{amp} is the rate constant of the amplification reaction (crosslinking, deblocking, etc.) and t' is the bake time. Simple theory would indicate that $n = 1$ but the general form will be used here. Assuming H is constant, Eq. 48 can be solved for the concentration of reacted sites X:

$$X = M_0 - M = M_0 \left(1 - e^{-K_{amp} H^n t'} \right) \qquad (49)$$

(Note: Although H+ is not consumed by the reaction, the value of H is not locally constant. Diffusion during the PEB and acid loss mechanisms cause local changes in the acid concentration, thus requiring the use of a reaction-diffusion system of equations. The approximation that H is constant is a useful one, however, which gives insight into the reaction as well as accurate results under some conditions.)

It is useful here to normalize the concentrations to some initial values. This results in a normalized acid concentration h and normalized reacted and unreacted sites x and m:

$$h = \frac{H}{G_0}, \quad x = \frac{X}{M_0}, \quad m = \frac{M}{M_0} \qquad (50)$$

Equations 47 and 49 become

$$h = 1 - e^{-CIt}$$
$$m = 1 - x = e^{-\alpha h^n} \qquad (51)$$

where α is a lumped "amplification" constant equal to $G_0^n K_{amp} t'$. The result of the PEB is an amplified latent image $m(x)$, corresponding to an exposed latent image $h(x)$, resulting from the aerial image $I(x)$.

The foregoing analysis of the kinetics of the amplification reaction assumed a locally constant concentration of acid H. Although this could be exactly true in some circumstances, it is typically only an approximation and is often a poor approximation. In reality, the acid diffuses during the bake. In one dimension, the standard diffusion equation takes the form

$$\frac{\partial H}{\partial t'} = \frac{\partial}{\partial x} \left(D_H \frac{\partial H}{\partial x} \right) \qquad (52)$$

where D_H is the diffusivity of acid in the photoresist. Solving this equation requires a number of things: two boundary conditions, one initial condition, and a knowledge of the diffusivity as a function of position and time.

The initial condition is the initial acid distribution within the film, $H(x,0)$, resulting from the exposure of the PAG. The two boundary conditions are at the top and bottom surfaces of the photoresist film. The boundary at the wafer surface is assumed to be impermeable, giving a boundary condition of no diffusion into the wafer. The boundary condition at the top of the wafer will depend on the diffusion of acid into the atmosphere above the wafer. Although such acid loss is a distinct possibility, it will not be treated here. Instead, the top surface of the resist will also be assumed to be impermeable.

The solution of Eq. 52 can now be performed if the diffusivity of the acid in the photoresist is known. Unfortunately, this solution is complicated by two very important factors: the diffusivity is a strong function of temperature and, most probably, the extent of amplification. Since the temperature is changing with time during the bake, the diffusivity will be time dependent. The concentration dependence of diffusivity results from an increase in free volume for typical positive resists: as the amplification reaction proceeds, the polymer blocking group evaporates, resulting in a decrease in film thickness but also an increase in free volume. Since the acid concentration is time and position dependent, the diffusivity in Eq. 52 must be determined as a part of the solution of Eq. 52 by an iterative method. The resulting simultaneous solution of Eqs. 48 and 52 is called a reaction-diffusion system.

The temperature dependence of the diffusivity can be expressed in a standard Arrhenius form:

$$D_0(T) = A_R \exp(-E_a / RT) \tag{53}$$

where D_0 is a general diffusivity, A_r is the Arrhenius coefficient, and E_a is the activation energy. A full treatment of the amplification reaction would include a thermal model of the hotplate in order to determine the actual time-temperature history of the wafer [37]. To simplify the problem, an ideal temperature distribution will be assumed: the temperature of the resist is zero (low enough for no diffusion or reaction) until the start of the bake, at which time it immediately rises to the final bake temperature, stays constant for the duration of the bake, then instantly falls back to zero.

The concentration dependence of the diffusivity is less obvious. Several authors have proposed and verified the use of different models for the concentration dependence of diffusion within a polymer. Of course, the simplest form (besides a constant diffusivity) would be a linear model. Letting D_0 be the diffusivity of acid in completely unreacted resist and D_f the diffusivity of acid in resist which has been completely reacted,

$$D_H = D_0 + x(D_f - D_0) \tag{54}$$

Here, diffusivity is expressed as a function of the extent of the amplification reaction. Another common form is the Fujita-Doolittle equation [38], which can be predicted theoretically using free-volume arguments. A form of that equation that is convenient for calculations is shown here:

$$D_H = D_0 \exp\left(\frac{\alpha x}{1 + \beta x}\right) \tag{55}$$

where α and β are experimentally determined constants and are, in general, temperature dependent. Other concentration relations are also possible [39], but the Fujita-Doolittle expression will be used in this work.

Through a variety of mechanisms, acid formed by exposure of the resist film can be lost and thus not contribute to the catalyzed reaction to change the resist solubility. There are two basic types of acid loss: loss that occurs between exposure and postexposure bake and loss that occurs during the postexposure bake.

The first type of loss leads to delay time effects—the resulting lithography is affected by the delay time between exposure and postexposure bake. Delay time effects can be very severe and, of course, are very detrimental to the use of such a resist in a manufacturing environment [40,41]. The typical mechanism for delay time acid loss is the diffusion of atmospheric base contaminants into the top surface of the resist. The result is a neutralization of the acid near the top of the resist and a corresponding reduced amplification. For a negative resist, the top portion of a line is not insolubilized and resist is lost from the top of the line. For a positive resist, the effects are more devastating. Sufficient base contamination can make the top of the resist insoluble, blocking dissolution into the bulk of the resist. In extreme cases, no patterns can be observed after development. Another possible delay time acid loss mechanism is base contamination from the substrate, as has been observed on TiN substrates [41].

The effects of acid loss due to atmospheric base contaminants can be accounted for in a straightforward manner [42]. The base diffuses slowly from the top surface of the resist into the bulk. Assuming that the concentration of base contaminant in contact with the top of the resist remains constant, the diffusion equation can be solved for the concentration of base, B, as function of depth into the resist film:

$$B = B_0 \exp\left(-(z/\sigma)^2\right) \tag{56}$$

where B_0 is the base concentration at the top of the resist film, z is the depth into the resist ($z = 0$ at the top of the film), and σ is the diffusion length of the base in resist. The standard assumption of constant diffusivity has been made here, so the diffusion length goes as the square root of the delay time.

Since the acid generated by exposure for most resist systems of interest is fairly strong, it is a good approximation to assume that all of the base contaminant will react with acid if there is sufficient acid present. Thus, the acid concentration at the beginning of the PEB, H^*, is related to the acid concentration after exposure, H, by

$$H^* = H - B \quad \text{or} \quad h^* = h - b \tag{57}$$

where the lowercase symbols again represent the concentration relative to G_0, the initial photoacid generator concentration.

Acid loss during the PEB could occur by other mechanisms. For example, as the acid diffuses through the polymer, it may encounter sites that "trap" the acid, rendering it unusable for further amplification. If these traps were in much greater abundance than the acid itself (for example, sites on the polymer), the resulting acid loss rate would be first order.

$$\frac{\partial h}{\partial t'} = -K_{loss} h \tag{58}$$

where K_{loss} is the acid loss reaction rate constant. Of course, other more complicated acid loss mechanisms can be proposed, but in the absence of data supporting them, the simple first-order loss mechanism will be used here.

Acid can also be lost at the two interfaces of the resist. At the top of the resist, acid can evaporate. The amount of evaporation is a function of the size of the acid and the degree of its interaction with the resist polymer. A small acid (such as the trifluoroacetic acid discussed above) may have very significant evaporation. A separate rate equation can be written for the rate of evaporation of acid:

$$\left.\frac{\partial h}{\partial t'}\right|_{z=0} = -K_{evap}\left(h(0,t) - h_{air}(0,t)\right) \tag{59}$$

where $z = 0$ is the top of the resist and h_{air} is the acid concentration in the atmosphere just above the photoresist surface. Typically, the PEB takes place in a reasonably open environment with enough airflow to eliminate any buildup of evaporated acid above the resist, making $h_{air} = 0$. If K_{evap} is very small, then virtually no evaporation takes place and we say that the top boundary of the resist is impenetrable. If K_{evap} is very large (resulting in evaporation that is much faster than the rate of diffusion), the effect is to bring the surface concentration of acid in the resist to zero.

At the substrate there is also a possible mechanism for acid loss. Substrates containing nitrogen (such as titanium nitride and silicon nitride) often exhibit a foot at the bottom of the resist profile [41]. Most likely, the nitrogen acts as a site for trapping acid molecules, which gives a locally diminished acid concentration at the bottom of the resist. This, of course, leads to reduced amplification and a slower development rate, resulting in the resist foot. The kinetics of this substrate acid loss will depend on the concentration of acid trap sites at the substrate, S. It will be more useful to express this concentration relative to the initial concentration of PAG.

$$s = \frac{S}{G_0} \tag{60}$$

A simple trapping mechanism would have one substrate trap site react with one acid molecule.

$$\left.\frac{\partial h}{\partial t'}\right|_{z=D} = -K_{trap}h(D,t)s \tag{61}$$

Of course, the trap sites would be consumed at the same rate as the acid. Thus, knowing the rate constant K_{trap} and the initial relative concentration of substrate trapping sites s_0, one can include Eq. 61 in the overall mechanism of acid loss.

The combination of a reacting system and a diffusing system where the diffusivity is dependent on the extent of reaction is called a reaction-diffusion system. The solution of such a system is the simultaneous solution of Eqs. 48 and 52 using Eq. 47 as an initial condition and Eq. 54 or 55 to describe the reaction-dependent diffusivity. Of course, any or all of the acid loss mechanisms can also be included. A convenient and straightforward method for solving such equations is the finite difference method (see, for example, [43]). The equations are solved by approximating the differential equations by difference equations. By marching through time and solving for all space at each time step, the final solution is the result after the final time step. A key part of an accurate solution is the choice of a sufficiently small time step. If the spatial dimension of interest is Δx (or Δy or Δz), the time step should be chosen such that the diffusion length is less than Δx (using a diffusion length of about one third of Δx is common).

6 PHOTORESIST BAKE EFFECTS

6.1 Prebake

The purpose of a positive photoresist prebake is to dry the resist by removing solvent from the film. However, as with most thermal processing steps, the bake has other effects on the photoresist. When heated to temperatures above about 70°C, the photoactive compound (PAC) of a diazo-type positive photoresist begins to decompose to nonphotosensitive products. The reaction mechanism is thought to be identical to that of the PAC reaction during ultraviolet exposure [44–47].

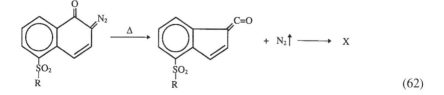

$$\tag{62}$$

The identify of the product X will be discussed in a following section.

To determine the concentration of PAC as a function of prebake time and temperature, consider the first-order decomposition reaction,

$$M \xrightarrow{\Delta} X \tag{63}$$

where M is the photoactive compound. If we let M_0' be the concentration of PAC before prebake and M_0 the concentration of PAC after prebake, simple kinetics tell us that

$$\frac{dM_0}{dt} = -K_T M_0$$
$$M_0 = M_0' \exp(-K_T t_b)$$
$$m' = \exp(-K_T t_b) \tag{64}$$

where t_b = bake time
K_T = decomposition rate constant at temperature T
$m' = M_0/M_0'$

The dependence of K_T upon temperature may be described by the Arrhenius equation,

$$K_T = A_r \exp(-E_a / RT) \tag{65}$$

where A_r = Arrhenius coefficient
E_a = activation energy
R = universal gas constant.

Thus, the two parameters E_a and A_r allow us to know m' as a function of the pre-bake conditions, provided Arrhenius behavior is followed. In polymer systems, caution must be exercised since bake temperatures near the glass transition temperature sometimes lead to non-Arrhenius behavior. For normal prebakes of typical photoresists, the Arrhenius model appears well founded.

The effect of this decomposition is a change in the chemical makeup of the photoresist. Thus, any parameters that are dependent on the quantitative composition of the resist are also dependent on prebake. The most important of these parameters fall into two categories: (1) optical (exposure) parameters such as the resist absorption coefficient and (2) development parameters such as the development rates of unexposed and completely exposed resist. A technique will be described to measure E_a and A_r and thus quantify these effects of prebake.

In the model proposed by Dill et al. [48], the exposure of a positive photoresist can be characterized by the three parameters A, B, and C. A and B are related to the optical absorption coefficient of the photoresist, α and C is the overall rate constant of the exposure reaction. More specifically,

$$\alpha = Am + B$$
$$A = (a_M - a_P)M_0$$
$$B = a_P M_0 + a_R R + a_S S \tag{66}$$

where a_M = molar absorption coefficient of the photoactive compound M
$\quad a_P$ = molar absorption coefficient of the exposure product P
$\quad a_S$ = molar absorption coefficient of the solvent S
$\quad a_R$ = molar absorption coefficient of the resin R
$\quad M_0$ = the PAC concentration at the start of the exposure (i.e., after prebake)
$\quad m = M/M_0$, the relative PAC concentration as a result of exposure

These expressions do not explicitly take into account the effects of prebake on the resist composition. To do so, we can modify Eq. 66 to include absorption by the component X.

$$B = a_P M_0 + a_R R + a_X X \tag{67}$$

where a_X is the molar absorption coefficient of the decomposition product X and the absorption term for the solvent has been neglected. The stoichiometry of the decomposition reaction gives

$$X = M_0' - M_0 \tag{68}$$

Thus,

$$B = a_P M_0 + a_R R + a_x (M_0' - M_0) \tag{69}$$

Let us consider two cases of interest, no bake (NB) and full bake (FB). When there is no prebake (meaning no decomposition), $M_0' = M_0$ and

$$A_{NB} = (a_M - a_P) M_0'$$
$$B_{NB} = a_P M_0' + a_R R \tag{70}$$

We shall define full bake as a prebake that decomposes all PAC. Thus $M_0 = 0$ and

$$A_{FB} = 0$$
$$B_{FB} = a_X M_0' + a_R R \tag{71}$$

Using these special cases in our general expressions for A and B,

$$A = A_{NB} m'$$
$$B = B_{FB} - (B_{FB} - B_{NB}) m' \tag{72}$$

The A parameter decreases linearly as decomposition occurs, and B typically increases slightly.

The development rate is, of course, dependent on the concentration of PAC in the photoresist. However, the product X can also have a large effect on the development rate. Several studies have been performed to determine the composition of the product X [45–47]. The results indicate that there are two possible products and the most common outcome of a prebake decomposition is a mixture of the two. The first product is formed via the reaction 73 and is identical to the product of UV exposure.

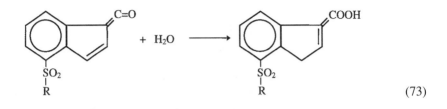

(73)

As can be seen, this reaction requires the presence of water. A second reaction, which does not require water, is the esterification of the ketene with the resin.

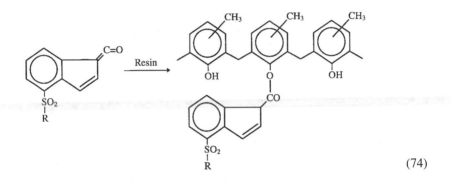

(74)

Both possible products have a dramatic effect on dissolution rate. The carboxylic acid is very soluble in developer and enhances dissolution. The formation of carboxylic acid can be thought of as a blanket exposure of the resist. The dissolution rate of unexposed resist (r_{min}) will increase due to the presence of the carboxylic acid. The dissolution rate of fully exposed resist (r_{max}), however, will not be affected. Since the chemistry of the dissolution process is unchanged, the basic shape of the development rate function will also remain unchanged.

The ester, on the other hand, is very difficult to dissolve in aqueous solutions and thus retards the dissolution process. It will have the effect of decreasing r_{max}, although the effects of ester formation on the full dissolution behavior of a resist are not well known.

If the two mechanisms given in Eq. 73 and 74 are taken into account, the rate equation 64 will become

$$\frac{dM_0}{dt} = -K_1 M_0 - K_2 [H_2O] M_0 \qquad (75)$$

where K_1 and K_2 are the rate constants of Eqs. 73 and 74, respectively. For a given concentration of water in the resist film this reverts to Eq. 64 where

Transmittance

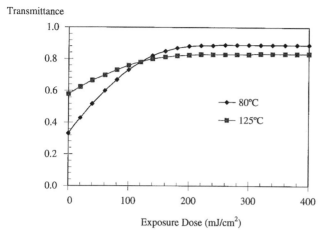

Exposure Dose (mJ/cm^2)

Figure 8 Two transmittance curves for Kodak 820 resist at 365 nm. The curves are for a convection oven prebake of 30 minutes at the temperatures shown. (From Ref. 49.)

$$K_T = K_1 + K_2[H_2O] \qquad (76)$$

Thus, the relative importance of the two reactions will depend not only on the ratio of the rate constants but also on the amount of water in the resist film. The concentration of water is a function of atmospheric conditions and the past history of the resist-coated wafer. Further experimental measurements of development rate as a function of prebake temperature are needed to quantify these effects.

Examining Eq. 72, one can see that the parameter A can be used as a means of measuring m', the fraction of PAC remaining after prebake. Thus, by measuring A as a function of prebake time and temperature, one can determine the activation energy and the corresponding Arrhenius coefficient for the proposed decomposition reaction. Using the technique given by Dill et al. [48], A, B, and C can be easily determined by measuring the optical transmittance of a thin photoresist film on a glass substrate while the resist is being exposed.

Examples of measured transmittance curves are given in Fig. 8, where transmittance is plotted versus exposure dose. The different curves represent different prebake temperatures. For every curve, A, B, and C can be calculated. Figure 9 shows the variation of the resist parameter A with prebake conditions. According to Eqs. 64 and 72, this variation should take the form

$$\frac{A}{A_{NB}} = e^{-K_T t_b} \qquad (77)$$

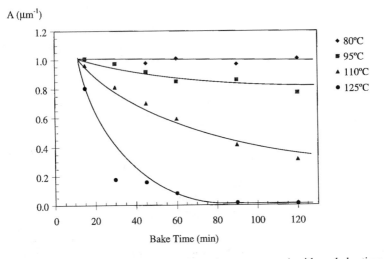

Figure 9   Variation of the resist absorption parameter A with prebake time and temperature for Kodak 820 resist at 365 nm [49].

$$\ln\left(\frac{A}{A_{NB}}\right) = -K_T t_b \tag{78}$$

Thus, a plot of $\ln(A)$ versus bake time should give a straight line with a slope equal to $-K_T$. This plot is shown in Fig. 10. Knowing K_T as a function of temperature, one can determine the activation energy and Arrhenius coefficient from Eq. 65. One should note that the parameters A_{NB}, B_{NB}, and B_{FB} are wavelength dependent, but E_a and A_r are not.

Figure 9 shows an anomaly in which there is a lag time before decomposition occurs. This lag time is the time it took the wafer and wafer carrier to reach the temperature of the convection oven. Equation 64 can be modified to accommodate this phenomenon,

$$m' = e^{-K_T(t_b - t_{wup})} \tag{79}$$

where t_{wup} is the warm-up time. A lag time of about 11 minutes was observed when convection oven baking a ¼-inch-thick glass substrate in a wafer carrier. When a 60-mil glass wafer was used without a carrier, the warm-up time was under 5 minutes and could not be measured accurately in this experiment [49].

Although all the data presented thus far have been for convection oven prebake, the above method of evaluating the effects of prebake can also be applied to hot-plate prebaking.

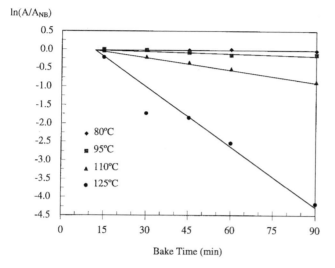

Figure 10 Log plot of the resist absorption parameter *A* with prebake time and temperature for Kodak 820 resist at 365 nm [49].

6.2 Postexposure Bake

Many attempts have been made to reduce the standing wave effect and thus increase line width control and resolution. One particularly useful method is the postexposure, predevelopment bake as described by Walker [50]. A 100°C oven bake for 10 minutes was found to reduce the standing wave ridges significantly. This effect can be explained quite simply as the diffusion of PAC in the resist during a high-temperature bake. A mathematical model that predicts the results of such a postexposure bake (PEB) is described below.

In general, molecular diffusion is governed by Ficke's second law of diffusion, which states (in one dimension)

$$\frac{\partial C_A}{\partial t} = \mathcal{D}\frac{\partial^2 C_A}{\partial x^2} \tag{80}$$

where C_A = concentration of species A
$\mathcal{D}$ = diffusion coefficient of A at some temperature *T*
t = time that the system is at temperature *T*

Note that the diffusivity is assumed to be independent of concentration here. This differential equation can be solved given a set of boundary conditions, i.e., an initial distribution of A. One possible boundary condition is known as the impulse source. At some point x_0 there are *N* moles of substance A and at all other points there is no A. Thus, the concentration at x_0 is infinite. Given this initial distribution of A, the solution to eq. 80 is the Gaussian distribution function.

$$C_A(x) = \frac{N}{\sqrt{2\pi\sigma^2}} e^{-r^2/2\sigma^2} \tag{81}$$

where $\sigma = \sqrt{2\mathcal{D}t}$, the diffusion length, and $r = x - x_0$.

In practice, there are no impulse sources. Instead, we can approximate an impulse source as having some concentration C_0 over some small distance Δx centered at x_0, with zero concentration outside this range. An approximate form of Eq. 81 is then

$$C_A(x) = \frac{C_0 \Delta x}{\sqrt{2\pi\sigma^2}} e^{-r^2/2\sigma^2} \tag{82}$$

This solution is fairly accurate if $\Delta x < 3\sigma$. If there are two "impulse" sources located at x_1 and x_2, with initial concentrations C_1 and C_2 each over a range Δx, the concentration of A at x after diffusion is

$$C_A(x) = \left[\frac{C_1}{\sqrt{2\pi\sigma^2}} e^{-r_1^2/2\sigma^2} + \frac{C_2}{\sqrt{2\pi\sigma^2}} e^{-r_2^2/2\sigma^2} \right] \Delta x \tag{83}$$

where $r_1 = x - x_1$ and $r_2 = x - x_2$.

If there are a number of sources Eq. 83 becomes

$$C_A(x) = \frac{\Delta x}{\sqrt{2\pi\sigma^2}} \sum C_n e^{-r_n^2/2\sigma^2} \tag{84}$$

Extending the analysis to a continuous initial distribution $C_0(x)$, Eq. 84 becomes

$$C_A(x) = \frac{1}{\sqrt{2\pi\sigma^2}} \int_{-\infty}^{\infty} C_0(x - x') e^{-x'^2/2\sigma^2} \, dx' \tag{85}$$

where x' is now the distance from the point x. Equation 85 is simply the convolution of two functions.

$$C_A(x) = C_0(x) * f(x) \tag{86}$$

where

$$f(x) = \frac{1}{\sqrt{2\pi\sigma^2}} e^{-x^2/2\sigma^2}$$

This equation can now be made to accommodate two-dimensional diffusion.

$$C_A(x, y) = C_0(x, y) * f(x, y) \tag{87}$$

where

$$f(x,y) = \frac{1}{\sqrt{2\pi\sigma^2}} e^{-r^2/2\sigma^2}$$

$$r = \sqrt{x^2 + y^2}$$

We are now ready to apply Eq. 87 to the diffusion of PAC in a photoresist during a postexposure bake. After exposure, the PAC distribution can be described by $m(x,z)$, where m is the relative PAC concentration. According to Eq. 87 the relative PAC concentration after a postexposure bake, $m^*(x,z)$, is given by

$$m^*(x,z) = \frac{1}{2\pi\sigma^2} \int\int_{-\infty}^{\infty} m(x-x', z-z') e^{-r'^2/2\sigma^2} dx'dz' \tag{88}$$

In evaluating Eq. 88 it is common to replace the integrals by summations over intervals Δx and Δz. In such a case, the restrictions that $\Delta x < 3\sigma$ and $\Delta z < 3\sigma$ will apply. An alternative solution is to solve the diffusion equation 80 directly, for example, using a finite difference approach.

The diffusion model can now be used to simulate the effects of a postexposure bake. Using a lithography simulator, a resist profile can be generated. By including the model for a postexposure bake, the profile can be generated showing how the standing wave effect is reduced. The only parameter that needs to be specified in Eq. 88 is the diffusion length σ, or equivalently, the diffusion coefficient $\mathcal{D}$ and the bake time t. In turn, $\mathcal{D}$ is a function of the bake temperature T and, of course, the resist system used. Thus, if the functionality of $\mathcal{D}$ with temperature is known for a given resist system, a PEB of time t and temperature T can be modeled. A general temperature dependence for the diffusivity $\mathcal{D}$ can be found using the Arrhenius equation (for temperature ranges that do not traverse the glass transition temperature).

$$\mathcal{D} = \mathcal{D}_0 e^{-E_a/RT} \tag{89}$$

where $\mathcal{D}_0$ = Arrhenius constant (units of nm²/min)
  E_a = activation energy
  R = universal gas constant
  T = temperature in kelvins

Unfortunately, very little work has been done in measuring the diffusivity of photoactive compounds in photoresist.

7   PHOTORESIST DEVELOPMENT

An overall positive resist processing model requires a mathematical representation of the development process. Previous attempts have taken the form of empirical fits to development rate data as a function of exposure [51,52]. The model formulated below begins on a more fundamental level, with a postulated reaction mechanism that then leads to a development rate equation [53]. The rate constants involved can be determined by comparison with experimental data. An enhanced kinetic model with a second mechanism for dissolution inhibition is also presented [54]. Deviations from the expected development rates have been reported under certain conditions at the surface of the resist. This effect, called surface induction or surface inhibition, can be related empirically to the expected development rate, i.e., to the bulk development rate as predicted by a kinetic model.

Unfortunately, fundamental experimental evidence of the exact mechanism of photoresist development is lacking. The model presented below is reasonable, and the resulting rate equation has been shown to describe actual development rates extremely well. However, faith in the exact details of the mechanism is limited by this dearth of fundamental studies.

7.1 Kinetic Development Model

In order to derive an analytical development rate expression, a kinetic model of the development process will be used. This approach involves proposing a reasonable mechanism for the development reaction and then applying standard kinetics to this mechanism in order to derive a rate equation. We shall assume that the development of a diazo-type positive photoresist involves three processes: diffusion of developer from the bulk solution to the surface of the resist, reaction of the developer with the resist, and diffusion of the product back into the solution. For this analysis, we shall assume that the last step, diffusion of the dissolved resist into solution, occurs very quickly so that this step may be ignored. Let us now look at the first two steps in the proposed mechanism. The diffusion of developer to the resist surface can be described with the simple diffusion rate equation, given approximately by

$$r_D = k_D(D - D_S) \tag{90}$$

where r_D is the rate of diffusion of the developer to the resist surface, D is the bulk developer concentration, D_S is the developer concentration at the resist surface, and k_D is the rate constant.

We shall now propose a mechanism for the reaction of developer with the resist. The resist is composed of large macromolecules of resin R along with a photoactive compound M, which converts to product P upon exposure to UV light. The resin is quite soluble in the developer solution, but the presence of the PAC (photoactive compound) acts as an inhibitor to dissolution, making the development rate very slow. The product P, however, is very soluble in developer, enhancing the dissolution rate of the resin. Let us assume that n molecules of product P react with the developer to dissolve a resin molecule. The rate of the reaction is

$$r_R = k_R D_S P^n \tag{91}$$

where r_R is the rate of reaction of the developer with the resist and k_R is the rate constant. (Note that the mechanism shown in Eq. 91 is the same as the "polyphotolysis" model described by Trefonas and Daniels [55].) From the stoichiometry of the exposure reaction,

$$P = M_0 - M \tag{92}$$

where M_0 is the initial PAC concentration (i.e., before exposure).

The two steps outlined above are in series; i.e., one reaction follows the other. Thus, the two steps will come to a steady state such that

$$r_R = r_D = r \tag{93}$$

Equating the rate equations, one can solve for D_S and eliminate it from the overall rate equation, giving

$$r = \frac{k_D k_R D P^n}{k_D + k_R P^n} \tag{94}$$

Using Eq. 92 and letting $m = M/M_0$, the relative PAC concentration, Eq. 94 becomes

$$r = \frac{k_D D(1-m)^n}{k_D / k_R M_0^n + (1-m)^n} \tag{95}$$

When $m = 1$ (resist unexposed), the rate is zero. When $m = 0$ (resist completely exposed), the rate is equal to r_{max} where

$$r_{max} = \frac{k_D D}{k_D / k_R M_0^n + 1} \tag{96}$$

If we define a constant a such that

$$a = k_D / k_R M_0^n \tag{97}$$

the rate equation becomes

$$r = r_{max} \frac{(a+1)(1-m)^n}{a + (1-m)^n} \tag{98}$$

Note that the simplifying constant a describes the rate constant of diffusion relative to the surface reaction rate constant. A large value of a will mean that diffusion is very fast, and thus less important, compared to the fastest surface reaction (for completely exposed resist).

There are three constants that must be determined experimentally, a, n, and r_{max}. The constant a can be put in a more physically meaningful form as follows. A characteristic of some experimental rate data is an inflection point in the rate curve at about $m = 0.2$-0.7. The point of inflection can be calculated by letting

$$\frac{d^2 r}{dm^2} = 0$$

giving

$$a = \frac{(n+1)}{(n-1)}(1 - m_{TH})^n \tag{99}$$

where m_{TH} is the value of m at the inflection point, called the threshold PAC concentration.

This model does not take into account the finite dissolution rate of unexposed resist (r_{min}). One approach is simply to add this term to Eq. 98, giving

$$r = r_{max}\frac{(a+1)(1-m)^n}{a+(1-m)^n} + r_{min} \tag{100}$$

This approach assumes that the mechanism of development of the unexposed resist is independent of the developmented mechanism proposed above. In other words, there is a finite dissolution of resin that occurs by a mechanism that is independent of the presence of exposed PAC.

Consider the case in which the diffusion rate constant is large compared to the surface reaction rate constant. If $a \gg 1$, the development rate equation 100 will become

$$r = r_{max}(1 - m)^n + r_{min} \tag{101}$$

The interpretation of a as a function of the threshold PAC concentration m_{TH} given by Eq. 99 means that a very large a would correspond to a large negative value of m_{TH}. In other words, if the surface reaction is very slow compared to the mass transport of developer to the surface there will be no inflection point in the development rate data and Eq. 101 will apply. It is quite apparent that Eq. 101 could be derived directly from Eq. 91 if the diffusion step were ignored.

7.2   Enhanced Kinetic Development Model

The previous kinetic model is based on the principle of dissolution enhancement. The carboxylic acid enhances the dissolution rate of the resin-PAC mixture. In reality, this is a simplification. There are really two mechanisms at work. The PAC acts to inhibit dissolution of the resin while the acid acts to enhance dissolution. Thus, the rate expression should reflect both of these mechanisms. A new model, call the enhanced kinetic model, was proposed to include both effects [54]:

$$R = R_{resin} \frac{1 + k_{enh}(1-m)^n}{1 + k_{inh}(m)^l} \qquad (102)$$

where k_{enh} is the rate constant for the enhancement mechanism, n is the enhancement reaction order, k_{inh} is the rate constant for the inhibition mechanism, l is the inhibition reaction order, and R_{resin} is the development rate of the resin alone.

For no exposure, $m = 1$ and the development rate is at its minimum. From Eq. 102,

$$R_{min} = \frac{R_{resin}}{1 + k_{inh}} \qquad (103)$$

Similarly, when $m = 0$, corresponding to complete exposure, the development is at its maximum.

$$R_{max} = R_{resin}(1 + k_{enh}) \qquad (104)$$

Thus, the development rate expression can be characterized by five parameters: R_{max}, R_{min}, R_{resin}, n, and l.

Obviously, the enhanced kinetic model for resist dissolution is a superset of the original kinetic model. If the inhibition mechanism is not important, then $l = 0$. For this case, Eq. 102 is identical to Eq. 101 when

$$R_{min} = R_{resin}, \qquad R_{max} = R_{resin}k_{enh} \qquad (105)$$

The enhanced kinetic model of Eq. 102 assumes that mass transport of developer to the resist surface is not significant. Of course, a simple diffusion of developer can be added to this mechanism as was done above with the original kinetic model.

7.3 Surface Inhibition

The kinetic models given above predict the development rate of the resist as a function of the photoactive compound concentration remaining after the resist has been exposed to UV light. There are, however, other parameters that are known to affect the development rate, but which were not included in this model. The most notable deviation from the kinetic theory is the surface inhibition effect. The inhibition, or surface induction, effect is a decrease in the expected development rate at the surface of the resist [56–58]. Thus, this effect is a function of the depth into the resist and requires a new description of development rate.

Several factors have been found to contribute to the surface inhibition effect. High-temperature baking of the photoresist has been found to product surface inhibition and is thought to cause oxidation of the resist at the resist

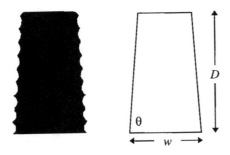

Figure 11   Typical photoresist profile and its corresponding trapezoid.

surface [56–58]. In particular, prebaking the photoresist may cause this reduced development rate phenomenon [56,58]. Alternatively, the induction effect may be the result of reduced solvent content near the resist surface. Of course, the degree to which this effect is observed depends on the prebake time and temperature. Finally, surface inhibition can be induced with the use of surfactants in the developer.

An empirical model can be used to describe the positional dependence of the development rate. If we assume that development rate near the surface of the resist exponentially approaches the bulk development rate, the rate as a function of depth, $r(z)$, is

$$r(z) = r_B\left(1 - \left(1 - r_0\right)e^{-z/\delta}\right) \tag{106}$$

where r_B is the bulk development rate, r_0 is the development rate at the surface of the resist relative to r_B, and δ is the depth of the surface inhibition layer. The induction effect has been found to take place over a depth of about 100 nm [56,58].

8   LINE WIDTH MEASUREMENT

A cross section of a photoresist profile has, in general, a very complicated two-dimensional shape (Fig. 11). In order to compare the shapes of two different profiles, one must find a convenient description for the shapes of the profiles that somehow reflects their salient qualities. The most common description is to model the resist profile as a trapezoid. Thus, three numbers can be used to describe the profile: the width of the base of the trapezoid (line width, w), its height (resist thickness, D), and the angle that the side makes with the base (sidewall angle, θ). Obviously, to describe such a complicated shape as a resist profile with just three numbers is a great, though necessary, simplification. The key to success is to pick a method of fitting a trapezoid to the profile that preserves the important features of the profile, is numeri-

Original Profile   Weighted Profile

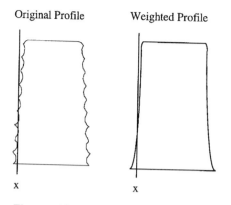

x   x

Figure 12   Determining the weighted resist profile.

cally practical, and as a result is not overly sensitive to slight changes in the profile.

Their are many possible algorithms for measuring the resist profile. One algorithm, called the linear weight method, is designed to mimic the behavior of a top-down line width measurement system. The first step is to convert the profile into a "weighted" profile as follows: at any given x position (i.e., along the horizontal axis), determine the "weight" of the photoresist above it. The weight is defined as the total thickness of resist along a vertical line at x. Figure 12 shows a typical example. The weight at this x position would be the sum of the lengths of the line segments that are within the resist profile. As can be seen, the original profile is complicated and multivalued whereas the weighted profile is smooth and single-valued.

A trapezoid can now be fit accurately to the weighted profile. The simplest type of fit will be called the standard line width determination method: ignoring the top and bottom 10% of the weighted resist thickness, a straight line is fit through the remaining 80% of the sidewall. The intersection of this line with the substrate gives the line width, and the slope of this line determines the sidewall angle. Thus, the standard method gives the best-fit trapezoid through the middle 80% of the weighted profile.

There are cases in which one part of the profile may be more significant than another. For these situations, the one could select the threshold method for determining line width. In this method, the sidewall angle is measured using the standard method, but the width of the trapezoid is adjusted to match the width of the weighted profile at a given threshold resist thickness. For example, with a threshold of 20%, the trapezoid will cross the weighted profile at a thickness of 20% up from the bottom. Thus, the threshold method can be used to emphasize the importance of one part of the profile.

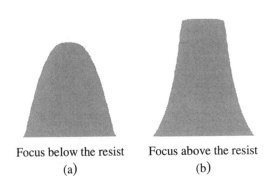

Focus below the resist   Focus above the resist
         (a)   (b)

Figure 13   Resist profiles at the extremes of focus.

The two line width determination methods deviate from one another when the shape of the resist profile begins to deviate from the general trapezoidal shape. Figure 13 shows two resist profiles at the extremes of focus. Using 10% threshold, the line widths of these two profiles are the same. Using a 50% threshold, however, shows profile (a) to be 20% wider than profile (b). The standard line width method, on the other hand, shows profile (a) to be 10% wider than profile (b). Finally, a 1% threshold gives the opposite result, with profile (a) 10% smaller than profile (b). The effect of changing profile shape on the measured line width is further illustrated in Fig. 14, which shows CD versus focus for the standard and 5% threshold CD measurement methods. It is important to note that sensitivity of the measured line width to profile shape is not particular to lithography simulation but is present in any CD measurement system. Fundamentally, this is the result of using the trapezoid model for resist profiles.

Obviously, it is difficult to compare resist profiles when the shapes of the profiles are changing. It is very important to use the line width method (and proper threshold value, if necessary) that is physically the most significant for the problems being studied. If the bottom of the resist profile is most important, the threshold method with a small (e.g., 5%) threshold is recommended. It is also possible to "calibrate" the simulator to a line width measurement system. By adjusting the threshold value used by the simulator, results comparable to actual measurements can be obtained.

9   LUMPED PARAMETER MODEL

Typically, lithography models make every attempt to describe physical phenomena as accurately as possible. However, in some circumstances speed is

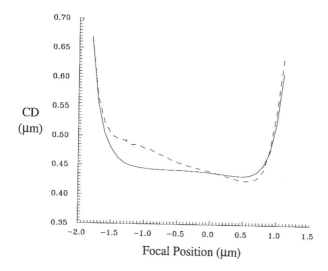

Figure 14 Effect of resist profile shape on line width measurement in a lithography simulator. CD measurement methods are standard (dashed line) and 5% threshold (solid line).

more important than accuracy. If a model is reasonably close to correct and fast, many interesting applications are possible. With this trade-off in mind, the lumped parameter model was developed [59–61].

9.1 Development Rate Model

The mathematical description of the resist process incorporated in the lumped parameter model uses a simple photographic model relating development time to exposure, while the aerial image simulation is derived from the standard optical parameters of the lithographic tool. A very simple development rate model is used based on the assumption of a constant contrast. Before proceeding, however, let us define a few terms needed for the derivations that follows. Let E be the nominal exposure energy (i.e., the intensity in a large clear area times the exposure time), $I(x)$ the normalized image intensity, and $I(z)$ the relative intensity variation with depth into the resist. It is clear that the exposure energy as a function of position within the resist (E_{xz}) is just $E\, I(x)I(z)$ where $x = 0$ is the center of the mask feature and $z = 0$ is the top of a resist of thickness D. Defining logarithmic versions of these quantities,

$$\varepsilon = \ln[E], \qquad i(x) = \ln[I(x)], \qquad i(z) = \ln[I(z)] \tag{107}$$

and the logarithm of the energy deposited in the resist is

$$\ln[E_{xz}] = \varepsilon + i(x) + i(z) \tag{108}$$

The photoresist contrast (γ) is defined theoretically as [62]

$$\gamma = \frac{d \ln r}{d \ln E_{xz}} \tag{109}$$

where r is the resulting development rate from an exposure of E_{xz}. Note that the base e definition of contrast is used here. If the contrast is assumed constant over the range of energies of interest, Eq. 109 can be integrated to give a very simple expression for development rate. In order to evaluate the constant of integration, let us pick a convenient point of evaluation. Let ε_0 be the energy required to just clear the photoresist in the allotted development time, t_{dev}, and let r_0 be the development rate that results from an exposure of this amount. Carrying out the integration gives

$$r(x,z) = r_0 e^{\gamma(\varepsilon + i(x) + i(z) - \varepsilon_0)} = r_0 \left[\frac{E_{xz}}{E_0} \right]^{\gamma} \tag{110}$$

As an example of the use of the above development rate expression and to further illustrate the relationship between r_0 and the dose to clear, consider the standard dose to clear experiment where a large clear area is exposed and the thickness of photoresist remaining is measured. The definition of development rate,

$$r = \frac{dz}{dt} \tag{111}$$

can be integrated over the development time. If $\varepsilon = \varepsilon_0$, the thickness remaining is by definition zero, so that

$$t_{dev} = \int_0^D \frac{dz}{r} = \frac{1}{r_0} \int_0^D e^{-\gamma i(z)} \, dz \tag{112}$$

where $i(x)$ is zero for an open frame exposure. Based on this equation, one can now define an effective resist thickness, D_{eff}, which will be very useful in the derivation of the lumped parameter model that follows.

$$D_{eff} = r_0 t_{dev} e^{\gamma i(D)} = e^{\gamma i(D)} \int_0^D e^{-\gamma i(z)} \, dz = \int_0^D \left[\frac{I(z)}{I(D)} \right]^{-\gamma} dz \tag{113}$$

As an example, the effective resist thickness can be calculated for the case of absorption only causing a variation in intensity with depth in the resist. For such a case, $I(z)$ will decay exponentially and Eq. 113 can be evaluated to give

$$D_{eff} = \frac{1}{\alpha\gamma} \left(e^{\alpha\gamma D} - 1 \right) \tag{114}$$

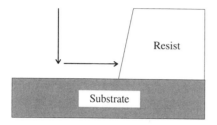

Figure 15 Illustration of segmented development: development proceeds first vertically, then horizontally, to the final resist sidewall.

If the resist is only slightly absorbing so that $\alpha\gamma D \ll 1$, the exponential can be approximated by the first few terms in its Taylor series expansion.

$$D_{\mathrm{eff}} \approx D\left(1 + \frac{\alpha\gamma D}{2}\right) \tag{115}$$

Thus, the effect of absorption is to make the resist seem thicker to the development process. The effective resist thickness can be thought of as the amount of resist of constant development rate that requires the same development time to clear as the actual resist with a varying development rate.

9.2 Segmented Development

Equation 110 is an extremely simple-minded model relating development rate to exposure energy based on the assumption of a constant resist contrast. In order to use this expression, we will develop a phenomenological explanation for the development process. This explanation will be based on the assumption that development occurs in two steps: a vertical development to a depth z, followed by a lateral development to position x (measured from the center of the mask feature) [63] as shown in Fig. 15.

A development ray, which traces out the path of development, starts at the point $(x_0, 0)$ and proceeds vertically until a depth z is reached such that the resist to the side of the ray has been exposed more than the resist below the ray. At this point the development will begin horizontally. The time needed to develop in both vertical and horizontal directions, t_z and t_x, respectively, can be computed from Eq. 110. The development time per unit thickness of resist is just the reciprocal of the development rate.

$$\frac{1}{r(x,z)} = \tau(x,z) = \tau_0 e^{-\gamma(\varepsilon + i(x) + i(z))} \tag{116}$$

where

$$\tau_0 = \frac{1}{r_0} e^{\gamma \varepsilon_0} \tag{117}$$

The time needed to develop to a depth z is given by

$$t_z = \tau_0 e^{-\gamma \varepsilon} e^{-\gamma i(x_0)} \int_0^z e^{-\gamma i(z')} \, dz' \tag{118}$$

Similarly, the horizontal development time is

$$t_x = \tau_0 e^{-\gamma \varepsilon} e^{-\gamma i(z)} \int_{x_0}^x e^{-\gamma i(x')} \, dx' \tag{119}$$

The sum of these two times must equal the total development time.

$$t_{\text{dev}} = \tau_0 e^{-\gamma \varepsilon} \left[e^{-\gamma i(x_0)} \int_0^z e^{-\gamma i(z')} \, dz' + e^{-\gamma i(z)} \int_{x_0}^x e^{-\gamma i(x')} \, dx' \right] \tag{120}$$

9.3 Derivation of the Lumped Parameter Model

The above equation can be used to derive some interesting properties of the resist profile. For example, how would a small change in exposure energy $\Delta \varepsilon$ affect the position of the resist profile x? A change in overall exposure energy will not change the point at which the development ray changes direction. Thus, the depth z is constant. Differentiating Eq 120 with respect to log-exposure energy, the following equation can be derived:

$$\left. \frac{dx}{d\varepsilon} \right|_z = \frac{\gamma t_{\text{dev}}}{\tau(x,z)} = \gamma t_{\text{dev}} r(x,z) \tag{121}$$

Since the x position of the development ray end point is just one half of the line width, Eq. 121 defines a change in critical dimension (CD) with exposure energy. To put this expression in a more useful form, take the log of both sides and use the development rate expression 110 to give

$$\ln\left(\frac{dx}{d\varepsilon} \right) = \ln\left(\gamma t_{\text{dev}} r_0 \right) + \gamma \left(\varepsilon + i(x) + i(z) - \varepsilon_0 \right) \tag{122}$$

Rearranging,

$$\varepsilon = \varepsilon_0 - i(x) - i(z) + \frac{1}{\gamma} \ln\left(\frac{dx}{d\varepsilon} \right) - \frac{1}{\gamma} \ln\left(\gamma t_{\text{dev}} r_0 \right) \tag{123}$$

where ε is the (log) energy needed to expose a feature of width $2x$. Equation 123 is the differential form of the lumped parameter model and relates the CD versus log-exposure curve and its slope to the image intensity. A more useful form of this equation is given below; however, some valuable insight can be gained by examining Eq. 123. In the limit of very large γ, one can see that the CD versus exposure curve becomes equal to the aerial image. Thus, exposure latitude becomes image limited. For small γ, the other terms become significant and the exposure latitude is process limited. Obviously, an image-limited exposure latitude represents the best possible case.

A second form of the lumped parameter model can also be obtained in the following manner. Applying the definition of development rate to Eq. 121 or, alternatively, solving for the slope in Eq. 123 yields

$$\frac{d\varepsilon}{dx} = \frac{1}{\gamma t_{dev} r_0} e^{-\gamma(\varepsilon + i(x) + i(z) - \varepsilon_0)} \tag{124}$$

Before proceeding, let us introduce a slight change in notation that will make the role of the variable ε more clear. As originally defined, ε is just the nominal exposure energy. In Eqs. 122 through 124, it takes the added meaning as the nominal energy that gives a line width of $2x$. To emphasize this meaning, we will replace ε by $\varepsilon(x)$ where the interpretation is not a variation of energy with x, but rather a variation of x (line width) with energy. Using this notation, the energy to just clear the resist can be related to the energy that gives zero line width.

$$\varepsilon_0 = \varepsilon(0) + i(x = 0) \tag{125}$$

Using this relation in Eq. 124,

$$\frac{d\varepsilon}{dx} = \frac{1}{\gamma t_{dev} r_0} e^{-\gamma i(z)} e^{\gamma(\varepsilon(0) - \varepsilon(x))} e^{\gamma(i(0) - i(x))} \tag{126}$$

Invoking the definitions of the logarithmic quantities,

$$\frac{dE}{dx} = \frac{E(x)}{\gamma D_{eff}} \left[\frac{E(0)I(0)}{E(x)I(x)} \right]^{\gamma} \tag{127}$$

where Eq. 113 has been used and the line width is assumed to be measured at the resist bottom (i.e., $z = D$). Equation 127 can now be integrated.

$$\int_{E(0)}^{E(x)} E^{\gamma - 1} \, dE = \frac{1}{\gamma D_{eff}} [E(0)I(0)]^{\gamma} \int_0^x I(x')^{-\gamma} \, dx' \tag{128}$$

giving

$$\frac{E(x)}{E(0)} = \left[1 + \frac{1}{\gamma D_{eff}} \int_0^x \left(\frac{I(x')}{I(0)} \right)^{-\gamma} dx' \right]^{1/\gamma} \tag{129}$$

Equation 129 is the integral form of the lumped parameter model. Using this equation, one can generate a normalized CD versus exposure curve by knowing the image intensity, $I(x)$, the effective resist thickness, D_{eff}, and the contrast, γ.

9.4   Sidewall Angle

The lumped parameter model allows the prediction of line width by developing down to a depth z and laterally to a position x, which is one half of the final line width. Typically, the bottom line width is desired so that the depth chosen is the full resist thickness. By picking different values for z, different x positions will result, giving a complete resist profile. One important result that can be calculated is the resist sidewall slope and the resulting sidewall angle. To derive an expression for the sidewall slope, let us first rewrite Eq. 120 in terms of the development rate.

$$t_{\text{dev}} = \int_0^z \frac{dz'}{r(0,z')} + \int_{x_0}^x \frac{dx'}{r(x',z)} \tag{130}$$

Taking the derivative of this expression with respect to z,

$$0 = \int_0^z \frac{d\tau}{dz} dz' + \frac{1}{r(0,z)} + \int_{x_0}^x \frac{d\tau}{dz} dx' + \frac{1}{r(x,z)} \frac{dx}{dz} \tag{131}$$

The derivative of the reciprocal development rate can be calculated from Eq. 110 or 116,

$$\frac{d\tau}{dz} = -\gamma\tau(x,z)\frac{d \ln\left[E_{xz}\right]}{dz} \tag{132}$$

As one would expect, the variation of development rate with depth into the resist depends on the variation of the exposure dose with depth. Consider a simple example in which bulk absorption is the only variation of exposure with z. For an absorption coefficient of α, the result is

$$\frac{d \ln\left[E_{xz}\right]}{dz} = -\alpha \tag{133}$$

Using Eqs. 132 and 133 in 131,

$$-\alpha\gamma\left(\int_0^z \tau\, dz' + \int_{x_0}^x \tau\, dx'\right) = \frac{1}{r(0,z)} + \frac{1}{r(x,z)}\frac{dx}{dz} \tag{134}$$

Recognizing the term in parentheses as simply the development time, the reciprocal of the resist slope can be given as

$$-\frac{dx}{dz} = \frac{r(x,z)}{r(0,z)} + \alpha\gamma t_{\text{dev}} r(x,z) = \frac{r(x,z)}{r(0,z)} + \alpha\frac{dx}{d\varepsilon} \tag{135}$$

Equation 135 shows two distinct contributors to sidewall angle. The first is the development effect. Because the top of the photoresist is exposed to developer longer than the bottom, the top line width is smaller, resulting in a sloped sidewall. This effect is captured in Eq. 135 as the ratio of the development rate at the edge of the photoresist feature to the development rate at the center. Good sidewall slope is obtained by making this ratio small. The second term in Eq. 135 describes the effect of optical absorption on the resist slope. High absorption or poor exposure latitude will result in a reduction of the resist sidewall angle.

9.5 Results

The lumped parameter model is based on a simple model for development rate and a phenomenological description of the development process. The result is an equation that predicts the change in line width with exposure for a given aerial image. The major advantage of the lumped parameter model is its extreme ease of application to a lithography process. The two parameters of the model, resist contrast and effective thickness, can be determined by the collection of line width data from a standard focus-exposure matrix. These data are routinely available in most production and development lithography processes; no extra or unusual data collection is required. The result is a simple and fast model that can be used as an initial predictor of results or as the engine of a lithographic control scheme.

In addition, the lumped parameter model can be used to predict the sidewall angle of the resulting photoresist profile. The model shows the two main contributors to resist slope: development effects due to the time required for the developer to reach the bottom of the photoresist, and absorption effects resulting in a reduced exposure at the bottom of the resist.

Finally, the lumped parameter model presents a simple understanding of the optical lithography process. The potential of the model as a learning tool should not be underestimated. In particular, the model emphasizes the competing roles of the aerial image and the photoresist process in determining line width control. This fundamental knowledge lays the foundation for further investigations into the behavior of optical lithography systems.

10   USES OF LITHOGRAPHY MODELING

In the 20 years since optical lithography modeling was first introduced to the semiconductor industry, it has gone from a research curiosity to an indispensable tool for research, development, and manufacturing. There are numerous examples of how modeling has had a dramatic impact on the evolution of lithography technology and many more ways in which it has subtly, but undeniably, influenced the daily routines of lithography professionals. There are four major uses for lithography simulation: (1) as a research tool, performing experiments that would be difficult or impossible to do any other way; (2) as a development tool, quickly evaluating options, optimizing processes, or saving time and money by reducing the number of experiments that have to be performed; (3) as a manufacturing tool, for troubleshooting process problems and determining optimum process settings; and (4) as a learning tool, to help provide a fundamental understanding of all aspects of the lithography process. These four applications of lithography simulation are not distinct—there is much overlap among these basic categories.

10.1   Research Tool

Since the initial introduction of lithography simulation in 1974, modeling has had a major impact on research efforts in lithography. Here are some examples of how modeling has been used in research.

Modeling was used to suggest the use of dyed photoresist in the reduction of standing waves [64]. Experimental investigation into dyed resists did not begin until 10 years later [65,66].

After phase-shifting masks were first introduced [67], modeling proved to be indispensable in their study. Levenson et al. [68] used modeling extensively to understand the effects of phase masks. One of the earliest studies of phase-shifting masks used modeling to calculate images for Levenson's original alternating phase mask, then showed how phase masks increased defect printability [69]. The same study used modeling to introduce the concept of the outrigger (or assist slot) phase mask. Since these early studies, modeling results have been presented in nearly every paper published on phase-shifting masks.

Off-axis illumination was first introduced as a technique for improving resolution and depth of focus based on modeling studies [70]. Since then, this technique has received widespread attention and has been the focus of many more simulation and experimental efforts.

Using modeling, the advantages of having a variable numerical aperture, variable partial coherence stepper were discussed [70,71]. Since then, all major stepper vendors have offered variable NA, variable coherence systems. Modeling remains a critical tool for optimizing the settings of these flexible new machines.

The use of pupil filters to enhance some aspects of lithographic performance has, to date, only been studied theoretically using lithographic models [72]. If such studies prove the usefulness of pupil filters, experimental investigations may also be conducted.

Modeling has been used in photoresist studies to understand the depth of focus loss when printing contacts in negative resists [73], the reason for artificially high values of resist contrast when surface inhibition is present [74], the potential for exposure optimization to maximize process latitude [75,76], and the role of diffusion in chemically amplified resists [77]. Lithographic models are now standard tools for photoresist design and evaluation.

Modeling has always been used as a tool for quantifying optical proximity effects and for defining algorithms for geometry-dependent mask biasing [78,79]. Most people would consider modeling to be a required element of any optical proximity correction scheme.

Defect printability has always been a difficult problem to understand. The printability of a defect depends considerably on the imaging system and resist used, as well as the position of the defect relative to other patterns on the mask and the size and transmission properties of the defect. Modeling has proved a valuable and accurate tool for predicting the printability of defects [80,81].

Modeling has also been used to understand metrology of lithographic structures [82–85] and continues to find new applications in virtually every aspect of lithographic research.

One of the primary reasons that lithography modeling has become such a standard tool for research activities is the ability to simulate such a wide range of lithographic conditions. While laboratory experiments are limited to the equipment and materials on hand (a particular wavelength and numerical aperture of the stepper, a given photoresist), simulation gives an almost infinite array of possible conditions. From high numerical apertures to low wavelengths, hypothetical resists to arbitrary mask structures, simulation offers the ability to run "experiments" on steppers that you do not own with photoresists that have yet to be made. How else can one explore the shadowy boundary between the possible and the impossible?

10.2 Process Development Tool

Lithography modeling has also proven to be an invaluable tool for the development of new lithographic processes and equipment. Some of the more common uses include the optimization of dye loadings in photoresist [86,87], simulation of substrate reflectivity [88,89], the applicability and optimization of top and bottom antireflection coatings [90,91], and simulation of the effect of bandwidth on swing curve amplitude [92,93]. In addition, simulation has been used to help understand the use of thick resists for thin-film head manufacture [94] as well as other nonsemiconductor applications.

Modeling is used extensively by makers of photoresist to evaluate new formulations [95,96] and to determine adequate measures of photoresist performance for quality control purposes [97]. Resist users often employ modeling as an aid for new resist evaluations. On the exposure tool side, modeling has become an indispensable part of the optimization of the numerical aperture and partial coherence of a stepper [98–100] and in the understanding of the print bias between dense and isolated lines [101]. The use of optical proximity correction software requires rules on how to perform the corrections, which are often generated with the help of lithography simulation [102].

As a development tool, lithography simulation excels due to its speed and cost-effectiveness. Process development usually involves running numerous experiments to determine optimum process conditions, shake out possible problems, determine sensitivity to variables, and write specification limits on the inputs and outputs of the process. These activities tend to be both time consuming and costly. Modeling offers a way to supplement laboratory experiments with simulation experiments to speed up this process and reduce costs. Considering that a single experimental run in a wafer fabrication facility can take from hours to days, the speed advantage of simulation is considerable. This allows a greater number of simulations than would be practical (or even possible) in the fabrication facility.

10.3 Manufacturing Tool

Although you will find less published material on the use of lithography simulation in manufacturing environments [103–105], the reason is the limited publications by people in manufacturing rather than the limited use of lithography modeling. The use of simulation in a manufacturing environment has three primary goals: to reduce the number of test or experimental wafers that must be run through the production line, to troubleshoot problems in the fab, and to aid in decision making by providing facts to support engineering judgment and intuition.

Running test wafers through a manufacturing line is costly not so much because of the cost of the test but because of the opportunity cost of not running product [106]. If simulation can reduce the time a manufacturing line is not running product even slightly, the return on investment can be significant. Simulation can also aid in reducing the time required to bring a new process on line.

10.4 Learning Tool

Although the research, development, and manufacturing applications of lithography simulation presented above give ample benefits of modeling based on time, cost, and capability, the underlying power of simulation is its ability to act as a learning tool. Proper application of modeling allows the user to learn efficiently and effectively. There are many reasons why this is true. First, the speed of simulation versus experimentation makes feedback much more timely. Since learning is a cycle (an idea, an experiment, a measurement, then comparison with the original idea), faster feedback allows more cycles of learning. Because simulation is very inexpensive, there are few inhibitions and more opportunities to explore ideas. And, as the research application has shown us, there are fewer physical constraints on what "experiments" can be performed.

All of these factors allow the use of modeling to gain an understanding of lithography. Whether learning fundamental concepts or exploring subtle nuances, the value of improved knowledge cannot be overstated.

REFERENCES

1. Dill, F. H., Optical lithography, *IEEE Trans. Electron Devices*, ED-22(7), 440–444 (1975).
2. Dill, F. H., Hornberger, W. P., Hauge, P. S., and Shaw, J. M., Characterization of positive photoresist, *IEEE Trans. Electron Devices*, ED-22(7), 445–452 (1975).
3. Konnerth, K. L., and Dill, F. H., In situ measurement of dielectric thickness during etching or developing processes, *IEEE Trans. Electron Devices*, ED-22(7), 452–456 (1975).
4. Dill, F. H., Neureuther, A. R., Tuttle, J. A., and Walker, E. J., Modeling projection printing of positive photoresists, *IEEE Trans. Electron Devices*, ED-22(7), 456–464 (1975).
5. Oldham, W. G., Nandgaonkar, S. N., Neureuther, A. R., and O'Toole, M., A general simulator for VLSI lithography and etching processes: Part I—Application to projection lithography, *IEEE Trans. Electron Devices*, ED-26(4), 717–722 (1979).
6. Mack, C. A., PROLITH: A comprehensive optical lithography model, *Proc. SPIE*, 538, 207–220 (1985).
7. Goodman, J. W., *Introduction to Fourier Optics*, McGraw-Hill, New York, 1968.
8. Oldham, W. G., Nandgaonkar, S. N., Neureuther, A. R., and O'Toole, M., A general simulator for VLSI lithography and etching processes: Part I—Application to Projection Lithography, *IEEE Trans. Electron Devices*, ED-26(4), 717–722 (1979).
9. Mack, C. A., PROLITH: A comprehensive optical lithography model, *Proc. SPIE*, 538, 207–220 (1985).
10. Dill, F. H., Neureuther, A. R., Tuttle, J. A., and Walker, E. J., Modeling projection printing of positive photoresists, *IEEE Trans. Electron Devices*, ED-22(7), 456–464 (1975).
11. Mack, C. A., Understanding focus effects in submicron optical lithography, *Proc. SPIE*, 922, 135–148 (1988); *Opt. Eng.*, 27(12), 1093–1100 (1988).
12. Bernard, D. A., Simulation of focus effects in photolithography, *IEEE Trans. Semiconductor Manuf.*, 1(3), 85–97 (1988).
13. Mack, C. A., Analytical expression for the standing wave intensity in photoresist, *App. Opt.*, 25(12), 1958–1961 (1986).
14. Bernard, D. A., and Urbach, H. P., Thin-film interference effects in photolithography for finite numerical apertures, *J. Opt. Soc. Am. A*, 8(1), 123–133 (1991).
15. Born, M., and Wolf, E., *Principles of Optics*, 6th ed., Pergamon, Oxford, 1980, pp. 113–117.
16. Cole, D. C., Barouch, E., Hollerbach, U., and Orszag, S. A., Extending scalar aerial image calculations to higher numerical apertures, *J. Vac. Sci. Technol.*, B, 10, 3037–3041 (1992).

17. Flagello, D. G., Rosenbluth, A. E., Progler, C., and Armitage, J., Understanding high numerical aperture optical lithography, *Microelectron. Eng.*, *17*, 105–108 (1992).

18. Mack, C. A., and Juang, C.-B., Comparison of scalar and vector modeling of image formation in photoresist, *Proc. SPIE*, *2440*, 381–394 (1995).

19. Middlehoek, S., Projection masking, thin photoresist layers and interference effects, *IBM J. Res. Dev.*, *14*, 117–124 (1970).

20. Korka, J. E., Standing waves in photoresists, *Appl. Opt.*, *9*(4), 969–970 (1970).

21. Ilten, D. F., and Patel, K. V., Standing wave effects in photoresist exposure, *Image Technol.* 9–14 (Feb/March 1971).

22. Widmann, D. W., Quantitative evaluation of photoresist patterns in the 1µm range, *Appl. Opt.*, *14*(4), 931–934 (1975).

23. Dill, F. H., Optical lithography, *IEEE Trans. Electron Devices*, ED-22(7), 440–444 (1975).

24. Berning, P. H., Theory and calculations of optical thin films, in *Physics of Thin Films* (G. Hass, ed.), Academic Press, New York, 1963, pp. 69–121.

25. Mack, C. A., Analytical expression for the standing wave intensity in photoresist, *Appl. Opt.*, *25*(12), 1958–1961 (1986).

26. Skoog, D. A., and West, D. M., *Fundamentals of Analytical Chemistry*, 3rd ed., Holt, Rinehart, & Winston, New York, 1976, pp. 509–510.

27. Koyler, J. M., et al., Thermal properties of positive photoresist and their relationship to VLSI processing, *Kodak Microelectronics Seminar Interface '79*, 1979, pp. 150–165.

28. Shaw, J. M., Frisch, M. A., and Dill, F. H., Thermal analysis of positive photoresist films by mass spectrometry, *IBM J. Res. Dev.*, *21*, 219–226 (1977).

29. Dill, F. H., Hornberger, W. P., Hauge, P. S., and Shaw, J. M., Characterization of positive photoresist, *IEEE Trans. Electron Devices*, ED-22(7), 445–452 (1975).

30. Mack, C. A., Absorption and exposure in positive photoresist, *Appl. Opt.*, *27*(23), 4913–4919 (1988).

31. Albers, J., and Novotny, D. B., Intensity dependence of photochemical reaction rates for photoresists, *J. Electrochem. Soc.*, *127*(6), 1400–1403 (1980).

32. Herrick, C. E., Jr., Solution of the partial differential equations describing photodecomposition in a light-absorbing matrix having light-absorbing photoproducts, *IBM J. Res. Dev.*, *10*, 2–5 (1966).

33. Diamond, J. J., and Sheats, J. R., Simple algebraic description of photoresist exposure and contrast enhancement, *IEEE Electron Device Lett.* EDL-7(6), 383–386 (1986).

34. Babu, S. V., and Barouch, E., Exact solution of Dill's model equations for positive photoresist kinetics, *IEEE Electron Device Lett.* EDL-7(4), 252–253 (1986).

35. Ito, H., and Willson, C. G., Applications of photoinitiators to the design of resists for semiconductor manufacturing, *ACS Symp. Ser.*, *242*, 11–23 (1984).

36. Seligson, D., Das, S., Gaw, H., and Pianetta, P., Process control with chemical amplification resists using deep ultraviolet and x-ray radiation, *J. Vac. Sci. Technol.*, B6(6), 2303–2307 (1988).

37. Mack, C. A., DeWitt, D. P., Tsai, B. K., and Yetter, G., Modeling of solvent evaporation effects for hot plate baking of photoresist, *Proc. SPIE*, *2195*, 584–595 (1994).

38. Fujita, H., Kishimoto, A., and Matsumoto, K., Concentration and temperature dependence of diffusion coefficients for systems polymethyl acrylate and *n*-alkyl acetates, *Trans. Faraday Soc.*, *56*, 424–437 (1960).

39. Bornside, D. E., Macosko, C. W., and Scriven, L. E., Spin coating of a PMMA/chlorobenzene solution, *J. Electrochem. Soc.*, *138*(1), 317–320 (1991).

40. MacDonald, S. A., et al., Airborne chemical contamination of a chemically amplified resist, *Proc. SPIE*, *1466*, 2–12 (1991).

41. Dean, K. R., and Carpio, R. A., Contamination of positive deep-UV photoresists, *OCG Microlithography Seminar Interface '94*, 1994, pp. 199–212.

42. Ohfuji, T., Timko, A. G., Nalamasu, O., and Stone, D. R., Dissolution rate modeling of a chemically amplified positive resist, *Proc. SPIE*, *1925*, 213–226 (1993).

43. Incropera, F. P., and DeWitt, D. P., *Fundamentals of Heat and Mass Transfer*, 3rd ed., Wiley, New York, 1990.

44. Dill, F. H., and Shaw, J. M., Thermal effects on the photoresist AZ1350J, *IBM J. Res. Dev.*, 21(3), 210–218 (1977).

45. Shaw, J. M., Frisch, M. A., and Dill, F. H., Thermal analysis of positive photoresist films by mass spectrometry, *IBM J. Res. Dev.*, *21*(3), 219–226 (1977).

46. Koyler, J. M., Custode, F. Z., and Ruddell, R. L., Thermal properties of positive photoresist and their relationship to VLSI processing, *Kodak Interface '79*, Nov. 1979, pp. 150–165.

47. Johnson, D. W., Thermolysis of positive photoresists, *Proc. SPIE*, *469*, 72–79 (1984).

48. Dill, F. H., et al., Characterization of positive photoresists, *IEEE Trans. Electron Devices*, *ED-22*(7), 445–452 (1975).

49. Mack, C. A., and Carback, R. T., Modeling the effects of prebake on positive resist processing, *Kodak Microelectronics Seminar Proceedings*, 1985, pp. 155–158.

50. Walker, E. J., Reduction of photoresist standing-wave effects by post-exposure bake, *IEEE Trans. Electron. Devices.*, *ED-22*(7), 464–466 (1975).

51. Dill, F. H., et al., Characterization of positive photoresists, *IEEE Trans. Electron Devices*, *ED-22*(7), 445–452 (1975).

52. Narasimham, M. A., and Lounsbury, J. B., Dissolution characterization of some positive photoresist systems, *Proc. SPIE*, *100*, 57–64 (1977).

53. Mack, C. A., Development of positive photoresist, *J. Electrochem. Soc.*, *134*(1), 148–152 (1987).

54. Mack, C. A., New kinetic model for resist dissolution, *J. Electrochem. Soc.*, *139*(4), L35–L37 (1992).

55. Trefonas, P., and Daniels, B. K., New principle for image enhancement in single layer positive photoresists, *Proc. SPIE*, *771*, 194–210 (1987).

56. Dill, F. H., and Shaw, J. M., Thermal effects on the photoresist AZ1350J, *IBM J. Res. Dev.*, *21*(3), 210–218 (1977).

57. Pampalone, T. R., Novolac resins used in positive resist systems, *Solid State Tech.*, *27*(6), 115–120 (1984).

58. Kim, D. J., Oldham, W. G., and Neureuther, A. R., Development of positive photoresist, *IEEE Trans. Electron Dev.*, *ED-31*(12), 1730–1735 (1984).

59. Hershel, R., and Mack, C. A., Lumped parameter model for optical lithography, in *Lithography for VLSI, VLSI Electronics—Microstructure Science* (R. K. Watts and N. G. Einspruch, eds.), Academic Press, New York, 1987, pp. 19–55.

60. Mack, C. A., Stephanakis, A., and Hershel, R., Lumped parameter model of the photolithographic process, *Kodak Microelectronics Seminar Producings*, 1986, pp. 228–238.

61. Mack, C. A., Enhanced lumped parameter model for photolithography, *Proc. SPIE, 2197*, 501–510 (1994).

62. Mack, C. A., Lithographic optimization using photoresist contrast, *KTI Microlithography Seminar Proceedings*, 1990, pp. 1–12; *Microelectronic. Manuf. Technol.*, *14*(1), 36–42 (1991).

63. Watts, M. P. C., and Hannifan, M. R., Optical positive resist processing II. Experimental and analytical model evaluation of process control, *Proc. SPIE, 539*, 21–28 (1985).

64. Neureuther, A. R., and Dill, F. H., Photoresist modeling and device fabrication applications, in *Optical and Acoustical Micro-Electronics*, Polytechnic Press, New York, 1974, pp. 233–249.

65. Stover, H. L., Nagler, M., Bol, I., and Miller, V., Submicron optical lithography: I-line lens and photoresist technology, *Proc. SPIE, 470*, 22–33 (1984).

66. Bol, I. I., High-resolution optical lithography using dyed single-layer resist, *Kodak Microelec. Seminar Interface '84*, 1984, pp. 19–22.

67. Levenson, M. D., Viswanathan, N. S., and Simpson, R. A., Improving resolution in photolithography with a phase-shifting mask, *IEEE Trans. Electron Devices*, ED-29(12), 1828–1836 (1982).

68. Levenson, M. D., Goodman, D. S., Lindsey, S., Bayer, P. W., and Santini, H. A. E., The phase-shifting mask II. Imaging simulations and submicrometer resist exposures, *IEEE Trans. Electron Devices*, ED-31(6), 753–763 (1984).

69. Prouty, M. D., and Neureuther, A. R., Optical imaging with phase shift masks, *Proc. SPIE, 470*, 228–232 (1984).

70. Mack, C. A., Optimum stepper performance through image manipulation, *KTI Microelectronics Seminar Proceedings*, 1989, pp. 209–215.

71. Mack, C. A., Algorithm for optimizing stepper performance through image manipulation, *Proc. SPIE, 1264*, 71–82 (1990).

72. Fukuda, H., Terasawa, T., and Okazaki, S., Spatial filtering for depth-of-focus and resolution enhancement in optical lithography, *J. Vac. Sci. Technol.*, B9(6), 3113–3116 (1991).

73. Mack, C. A., and Connors, J. E., Fundamental differences between positive and negative tone imaging, *Proc. SPIE, 1674*, 328–338 (1992); *Microlithography World*, *1*(3), 17–22 (1992).

74. Mack, C. A., Lithographic optimization using photoresist contrast, *KTI Microlithography Seminar Proceedings*, 1990, pp. 1–12; *Microelectron. Manuf. Technol.*, *14*(1), 36–42 (1991).

75. Mack, C. A., Photoresist process optimization, *KTI Microelectronics Seminar Proceedings*, 1987, pp. 153–167.

76. Trefonas, P., and Mack, C. A., Exposure dose optimization for a positive resist containing poly-functional photoactive compound, *Proc. SPIE, 1466*, 117–131(1991).

77. Petersen, J. S., Mack, C. A., Sturtevant, J., Myers, J. D., and Miller, D. A., Non-constant diffusion coefficients: Short description of modeling and comparison to experimental results, *Proc. SPIE, 2438*, 167–180 (1995).

78. Mack, C. A., and Kaufman, P. M., Mask bias in submicron optical lithography, *J. Vac. Sci. Technol., B6*(6), 2213–2220 (1988).

79. Shamma, N., Sporon-Fielder, F., and Lin, E., A method for correction of proximity effect in optical projection lithography, *KTI Microelectronics Seminar, Proceedings*, 1991, pp. 145–156.

80. Neureuther, A. R., Flanner, P., III, and Shen, S., Coherence of defect interactions with features in optical imaging, *J. Vac. Sci. Technol., B5*(1), 308–312 (1987).

81. Wiley, J., Effect of stepper resolution on the printability of submicron 5× reticle defects, *Proc. SPIE, 1088*, 58–73 (1989).

82. Milner, L. M., Hickman, K. C., Gasper, S. M., Bishop, K. P., Naqvi, S. S. H., McNeil, J. R., Blain, M., and Draper, B. L., Latent image exposure monitor using scatterometry, *SPIE, 1673*, 274–283 (1992).

83. Bishop, K. P., Milner, L. M., Naqvi, S. S. H., McNeil, J. R., and Draper, B. L., Use of scatterometry for resist process control, *SPIE, 1673*, 441–452 (1992).

84. Milner, L. M., Bishop, K. P., Naqvi, S. S. H., and McNeil, J. R., Lithography process monitor using light diffracted from a latent image, *SPIE, 1926*, 94–105 (1993).

85. Zaidi, S., Prins, S. L., McNeil, J. R., and Naqvi, S. S. H., Metrology sensors for advanced resists, *SPIE, 2196*, 341–351 (1994).

86. Johnson, J. R., Stagaman, G. J., Sardella, J. C., Spinner, C. R., III, Liou, F., Tiefonas, P., and Meister, C., The effects of absorptive dye loading and substrate reflectivity on a 0.5 µm I-line photoresist process, *SPIE*, 1925, 552–563 (1993).

87. Conley, W., Akkapeddi, R., Fahey, J., Hefferon, G., Holmes, S., Spinillo, G., Sturtevant, J., and Welsh, K., Improved reflectivity control of APEX-E positive tone deep-UV photoresist, *SPIE, 2195*, 461–476 (1994).

88. Thane, N., Mack, C., and Sethi, S., Lithographic effects of metal reflectivity variations, *SPIE, 1926*, 483–494 (1993).

89. Singh, B., Ramaswami, S., Lin, W., and Avadhany, N., IC wafer reflectivity measurement in the UV and DUV and its application for ARC characterization, *SPIE, 1926*, 151–163 (1993).

90. Miura, S. S., Lyons, C. F., and Brunner, T. A., Reduction of linewidth variation over reflective topography, *SPIE, 1674*, 147–156 (1992).

91. Yoshino, H., Ohfuji, T., and Aizaki, N., Process window analysis of the ARC and TAR systems for quarter micron optical lithography, *SPIE, 2195*, 236–245 (1994).

92. Flores, G., Flack, W., and Dwyer, L., Lithographic performance of a new generation I-line optical system: A comparative analysis, *SPIE, 1927*, 899–913 (1993).

93. Kuyel, B., Barrick, M., Hong, A., and Vigil, J., 0.5 micron deep UV lithography using a Micrascan-90 step-and-scan exposure tool, *SPIE, 1463*, 646–665 (1991).

94. Flores, G. E., Flack, W. W., and Tai, E., An investigation of the properties of thick photoresist films, *SPIE, 2195*, 734–751 (1994).

95. Iwasaki, H., Itani, T., Fujimoto, M., and Kasama, K., Acid size effect of chemically amplified negative resist on lithographic performance, *SPIE, 2195*, 164–172 (1994).

96. Schaedeli, U., Münzel, N., Holzwarth, H., Slater, S. G., and Nalamasu, O., Relationship between physical properties and lithographic behavior in a high resolution positive tone deep-UV resist, *SPIE*, *2195*, 98–110 (1994).

97. Schlicht, K., Scialdone, P., Spragg, P., Hansen, S. G., Hurditch, R. J., Toukhy, M. A., and Brzozowy, D. J., Reliability of photospeed and related measures of resist performances, *SPIE*, *2195*, 624–639 (1994).

98. Cirelli, R. A., Raab, E. L., Kostelak, R. L., and Vaidya, S., Optimizing numerical aperture and partial coherence to reduce proximity effect in deep-UV lithography, *SPIE*, *2197*, 429–439 (1994).

99. Katz, B., Rogoff, T., Foster, J., Rericha, B., Rolfson, B., Holscher, R., Sager, C., and Reynolds, P., Lithographic performance at sub-300 nm design rules using high NA I-line stepper with optimized NA and σ in conjunction with advanced PSM technology, *SPIE*, *2197*, 421–428 (1994).

100. Luehrmann, P., and Wittekoek, S., Practical 0.35 μm I-line lithography, *SPIE*, *2197*, 412–420 (1994).

101. Deshpande, V. A., Holland, K. L., and Hong, A., Isolated-grouped linewidth bias on SVGL Micrascan, *SPIE*, *1927*, 333–352 (1993).

102. Henderson, R. C., and Otto, O. W., Correcting for proximity effect widens process latitude, *SPIE*, *2197*, 361–370 (1994).

103. Engstrom, H., and Beacham, J., Online photolithography modeling using spectrophotometry and PROLITH/2, *SPIE*, *2196*, 479–485 (1994).

104. Kasahara, J., Dusa, M. V., and Perera, T., Evaluation of a photoresist process for 0.75 micron, G-line lithography, *SPIE*, *1463*, 492–503 (1991).

105. Puttlitz, E. A., Collins, J. P., Glynn, T. M., and Linehan, L. L., Characterization of profile dependency on nitride substrate thickness for a chemically amplified I-line negative resist, *SPIE*, *2438*, 571–582 (1995).

106. Mahoney, P. M., and Mack, C. A., Cost analysis of lithographic characterization: An overview, *Proc. SPIE*, *1927*, 827–832 (1993).

3

Optics for Photolithography

Bruce W. Smith

Rochester Institute of Technology
Rochester, New York

1   INTRODUCTION

Optical lithography involves the creation of relief image patterns through the projection of radiation within or near the ultraviolet (UV)-visible portion of the electromagnetic spectrum. Techniques of optical lithography, or photolithography, have been used to create patterns for engravings, photographs, and printing plates. In the 1960s, techniques developed for the production of lithographic printing plates were utilized in the making of microcircuit patterns for semiconductor devices. These early techniques of contact or proximity photolithography were refined to allow circuit resolution on the order of 3 to 5 μm. Problems encountered with proximity lithography, such as mask and wafer damage, alignment difficulty, and field size, have limited its application for most photolithographic needs. In the mid-1970s, projection techniques minimized some of the problem encountered with proximity lithography and have led to the development of tools that currently allow resolution below 0.25 μm.

Diagrammed in Fig. 1 are generic proximity and projection techniques for photolithography. Figure 1a is a schematic of a proximity setup in which a mask is illuminated and held in close contact with a resist-coated substrate. The illumination system consists of a source and a condenser lens assembly, which provides uniform illumination to the mask. The illumination source outputs radiation in the blue-ultraviolet portion of the electromagnetic spectrum. The mercury–rare gas discharge lamp is a source well suited for photolithography

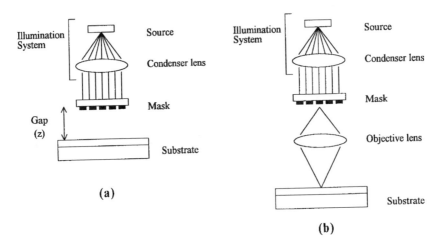

Figure 1 Schematic of optical lithography techniques (a) proximity and (b) projection lithographic systems.

and is almost entirely relied on for production of radiation in the 350–450-nm range. Since output below 365 nm is weak from a mercury or mercury–rare gas lamp, other sources have been utilized for shorter wavelength exposure. The ultraviolet region from 150 to 300 nm is referred to as the deep UV. Although a small number of lithographic techniques operating at these wavelengths have made use of gas discharge lamps, the use of a laser source is an attractive alternative. Several laser sources have potential for delivering high-power deep-ultraviolet radiation for photoresist exposure. A class of lasers that has been shown to be well suited for photolithography are the excimer lasers. Excimer lasers using argon fluoride (ArF) and krypton fluoride (KrF) gas mixtures are most prominent, producing radiation at 193 and 248 nm, respectively. Details of these systems can be found elsewhere. Shown in Figure 1b is a setup for a projection imaging system. The optical configuration for projection microlithography tools most closely resembles a microscope system. Early microlithographic objective lenses were modifications of microscope lens designs, which have now evolved to allow diffraction-limited resolution over large fields at high numerical apertures. Like a proximity system, a projection tool includes an illumination system and a mask but utilizes an objective lens to project images toward a substrate. The illumination system focuses an image of the source into the entrance pupil of the objective lens to provide maximum uniformity at the mask plane.

Both irradiance and coherence properties are influenced by the illumination system. The temporal coherence of a source is a measure of the correlation of the source wavelength to the source spectral bandwidth. As a source spectral bandwidth decreases, its temporal coherence increases. Coherence length, l_c, is related to source bandwidth as:

$$l_c = \lambda^2 / \Delta\lambda$$

Interference effects become sufficiently large when an optical path distance is less than the coherence length of a source. Optical imaging effects such as interference (standing wave) patterns in photoresist become considerable as source coherent length increases.

The spatial coherence of a source is a measure of the phase relationships between photons or wavefronts emitted. A true point source, by definition, is spatially coherent, since all wavefronts originate from a single point. Real sources, however, are less than spatially coherent. A conventional laser, which utilizes oscillation for amplification of radiation, can produce nearly spatially coherent radiation. Lamp sources, such as gas discharge lamps, exhibit low spatial coherence, as do excimer lasers, which require few oscillations within the laser cavity. Both temporal and spatial coherence properties can be controlled by an illumination system. Source bandwidth and temporal coherence are controlled through wavelength selection. Spatial coherence is controlled through manipulation of the effective source size imaged in the objective lens. In image formation, the control of spatial coherence is of primary importance because of its relationship to diffraction phenomena.

Current designs of projection lithography systems include (1) reduction or unit magnification, (2) refractive or reflective optics, and (3) array stepping or field scanning. Reduction tools allow a relaxation of mask requirements, including minimum feature size specification and defect criteria. This in turn reduces the contribution to the total process tolerance budget. The drawbacks for reduction levels greater than 5:1 include the need for increasingly larger masks and the associated difficulties in their processing. Both unit magnification (1:1) and reduction (M:1) systems have been utilized in lithographic imaging system design, each well suited for certain requirements. As feature size and control place high demands on 1:1 technology, reduction tools are generally utilized. In situations in which feature size requirements be met with a unit magnification, such systems may prove superior as mask field sizes, defect criteria, and lens aberrations are reduced. A refractive projection system must generally utilize a narrow spectral band of a lamp-type source. Energy outside this range would be removed prior to the condenser lens system to avoid wavelength-dependent defocus effects or chromatic aberration. Some degree of chromatic aberration correction is possible in a refractive lens system by incorporating elements of various glass types. As wavelengths below 300 nm are pursued for refractive projection lithography, the control of spectral bandwidth becomes more critical. As few transparent optical materials exist at these wavelengths, chromatic aberration correction through glass material selection is difficult. Greater demands are therefore placed on the source, which may be required to deliver a spectral bandwidth on the order of a few picometers. Clearly, such a requirement would limit the application of lamp sources at these wavelengths, leading to laser-based sources as the only alternative for short-wavelength refractive systems. Reflective optical systems (catoptric) or combined refractive-reflective systems (catadioptric) can be used to reduce wavelength influence and reduce source requirements, especially at wavelengths below 300 nm.

To understand the underlying principles of optical lithography, fundamentals of both geometrical and physical optics need to be addressed. Since optical lithography using projection techniques is the dominant technology for current integrated circuit (IC) fabrication, the development of the physics behind projection lithography will be concentrated on in this chapter. Contact lithography will be covered in less detail.

2 IMAGE FORMATION: GEOMETRICAL OPTICS

An understanding of optics in which the wave nature of light is neglected can provide a foundation for further study into a more inclusive approach. Thus geometrical optics will be introduced here, which will allow investigation into valuable information about imaging [1]. This will lead to a more complete study of imaging through physical optics, in which the wave nature of light is considered and interference and diffraction can be investigated.

Both refractive lenses and reflective mirrors play important roles in microlithographic optical systems. The optical behavior of mirrors can be described by extending the behavior of refractive lenses. Although a practical lens will contain many optical elements, baffles, apertures, and mounting hardware, most optical properties of a lens can be understood through the extension of simple single-element lens properties. The behavior of a simple lens will be investigated to gain an understanding of optical systems in general.

A perfect lens would be capable of an exact translation of an incident spherical wave through space. A *positive lens* would cause a spherical wave to converge faster, and a negative lens would cause a spherical wave to diverge faster. Lens surfaces are generally spherical or planar and may have forms including biconvex, planoconvex, biconcave, planoconcave, negative meniscus, and positive meniscus, as shown in Fig. 2. In addition, aspheric surfaces are possible, which may be used in an optical system to improve its performance. These types of elements are generally difficult and expensive to fabricate and are not yet widely used. As design and manufacturing techniques improve, applications of aspherical elements will grow, including their use in microlithographic lens systems.

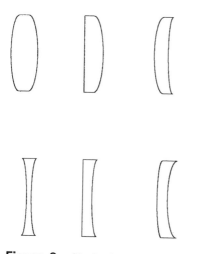

Figure 2 Single-element lens shapes. At top are positive lenses—bi-convex, plano-convex, and meniscus convex. At bottom are negative lenses—bi-concave, plano-concave, and meniscus concave.

2.1 Cardinal Points

Knowledge of the cardinal points of a simple lens is sufficient to understand its behavior. These points, the first and second focal points (F_1 and F_2), the principal points (P_1 and P_2), and the nodal points (N_1 and N_2), lie on the optical axis of a lens, as shown in Fig. 3. The principal planes are also shown here, which contain respective principal points and can be thought of as the surfaces

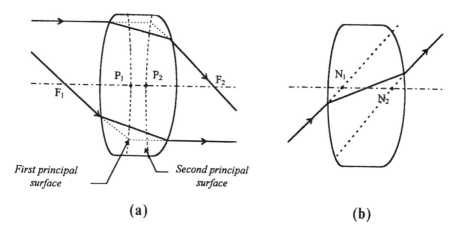

Figure 3 Cardinal points of a simple lens. (a) Focal points (F1 and F2) and principal points (P1 and P2). (b) Nodal points (N1 and N2).

where refraction effectively occurs. Although these surfaces are not truly planes, they are nearly so. Rays that pass through a lens act as if they refract only at the first and second principal planes and not at any individual glass surface. A ray passing through the first focal point (F_1) will emerge from the lens at the right parallel to the optical axis. For this ray, refraction effectively occurs at the first principal plane. A ray traveling parallel to the optical axis will emerge from the lens and pass through the second focal point (F_2). Here, refraction effectively occurs at the second principal plane. A ray passing through the optical center of the lens will emerge parallel to the incident ray and pass through the first and second nodal points (N_1, N_2). A lens or lens system can therefore be represented by its two principal planes and focal points.

2.2   Focal Length

The distance between a lens focal point and corresponding principal point is known as the effective focal length (EFL), as shown in Fig. 4. The focal length can be either positive, when F_1 is to the left of P_1 and F_2 is to the right of P_2, or negative, when the opposite occurs. The reciprocal of the effective focal length ($1/f$) is known as the lens power. The front focal length (FFL) is the distance from the first focal point (F_1) to the leftmost surface of the lens along the optical axis. The back focal length (BFL) is the distance from the rightmost surface to the second focal point (F_2).

The lens maker's formula can be used to determine the effective focal length of a lens, if the radii of curvature of surfaces (R_1 and R_2 for first and second surfaces), lens refractive index (n_i), and lens thickness (t) are known. Several

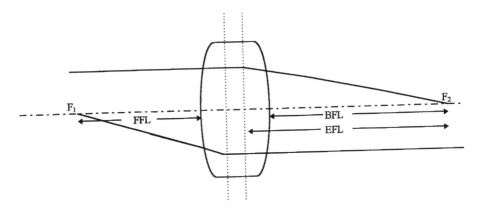

Figure 4   Determination of focal length for a simple lens, front focal length (FFL), back focal length (EFL).

sign conventions are possible. We will generally consider distances measured toward the left as positive. R_1 will be considered positive if its center of curvature lies to the right of the surface and R_2 will be considered negative if its center of curvature lies to the left of the surface. Focal length is determined by:

$$\frac{1}{f} = (n_i - 1)\left[\frac{1}{R_1} - \frac{1}{R_2} + \frac{(n_i - 1)t}{n_i R_1 R_2}\right]$$

2.3 Geometrical Imaging Properties

If the cardinal points of a lens are known, geometrical imaging properties can be determined. A simple biconvex is considered, such as the one shown in Fig. 5, where an object is placed a positive distance s_1 from focal point F_1 at a positive object height y_1. This object can be thought of as consisting of many points that will emit spherical waves to be focused by the lens at the image plane. The object distance (d_1) is the distance from the principal plane to the object, which is positive for objects to the left of P_1. The image distance to the principal plane (d_2), which is positive for an image to the right of P_2, can be calculated from the lens law:

$$\frac{1}{d_1} + \frac{1}{d_2} = \frac{1}{f}$$

For systems with a negative effective focal length, the lens law becomes:

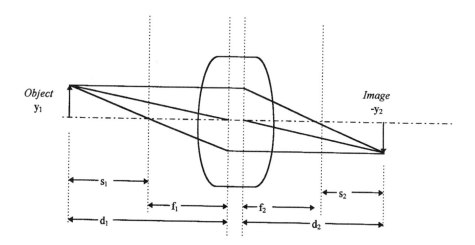

Figure 5 Ray tracing method for finding image location and magnification.

$$\frac{1}{d_1} + \frac{1}{d_2} = -\frac{1}{|f|}$$

The lateral magnification of an optical system is expressed as:

$$m = \frac{y_2}{y_1} = \frac{-d_2}{d_1}$$

where y_2 is the image height, which is positive upward.

The location of an image can be determined by tracing any two rays that will intersect in the image space. As shown in Fig. 5, a ray emanating from an object point, passing through the first focal point F_1, will emerge parallel to the optical axis, being effectively refracted at the first principal plane. A ray from an object point traveling parallel to the optical axis will emerge after refracting at the second principal plane passing through F_2. A ray from an object point passing through the center of the lens will emerge parallel to the incident ray. All three rays intersect at the image location. If the resulting image lies to the right of the lens, the image is real (assuming light emanates from an object on the left). If the image lies to the right, it is virtual. If the image is larger than the object, magnification is greater than unity. If the image is erect, the magnification is positive.

2.4   Aperture Stops and Pupils

The light accepted by an optical system is physically limited by aperture stops within the lens. The simplest aperture stop may be the edge of a lens or a physical stop placed in the system. Figure 6 shows how an aperture stop can limit

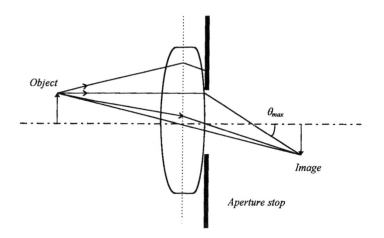

Figure 6   Limitation of lens maximum acceptance angle by an aperture stop.

the acceptance angle of a lens. The numerical aperture (NA) is the maximum acceptance angle at the image plane, determined by the aperture stop.

$$NA_{IMG} = n_i \sin(\theta_{max})$$

Since the optical medium is generally air, $NA_{IMG} \sim \sin(\theta_{max})$. The field stop shown in Fig. 7 limits the angular field of view, which is generally the angle subtended by the object or image from the first or second nodal point. The angular field of view for the image is generally that for the object. The image of the aperture stop viewed from the object is called the entrance pupil, whereas the image viewed from the image is called the exit pupil, as seen in Figs. 8 and 9. As we will see, the aberrations of an optical system can be described by the deviations in spherical waves at the exit pupil coming to focus at the image plane.

2.5 Chief and Marginal Ray Tracing

We have seen that a ray emitted from an off-axis point, passing through the center of a lens, will emerge parallel to the incident ray. This is called the chief ray, which is directed toward the entrance pupil of the lens. A ray that is emitted from an on-axis point and directed toward the edge of the entrance pupil is called a marginal ray. The image plane can, therefore, be found where a marginal ray intersects the optical axis. The height of the image is determined by the height of the chief ray at the image plane, as seen in Fig. 10. The marginal ray also determines the numerical aperture. The marginal and chief rays are related to each other by the Lagrange invariant, which states that the product of

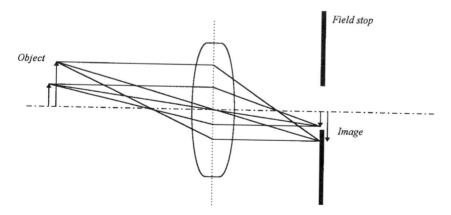

Figure 7   Limitation of angular field of view by a field stop.

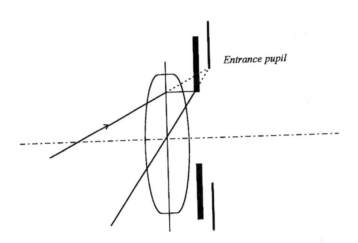

Figure 8 Location of the entrance pupil for a simple lens.

the image NA and image height is equal to the object NA and object height, or $NA_{OBJ}y_1 = NA_{IMG}y_2$. It is essentially an indicator of how much information can be processed by a lens. The implication is that as object or field size increases, NA decreases. To achieve an increase in both NA and field size, system complexity increases. Magnification can now be expressed as:

$$m = \frac{NA_{OBJ}}{NA_{IMG}}$$

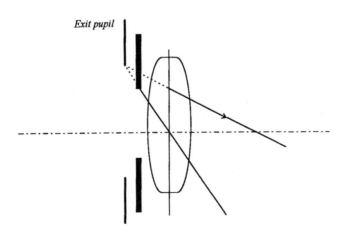

Figure 9 Location of the exit pupil for a simple lens.

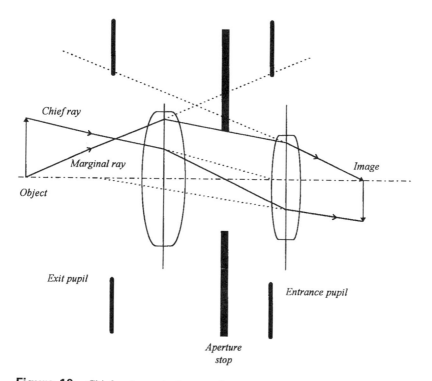

Figure 10   Chief and marginal ray tracing through a lens system.

2.6   Mirrors

A spherical mirror can form images in ways similar to refractive lenses. Using the reflective lens focal length, the lens equations can be applied to determine image position, height, and magnification. To use these equations, a sign convention for reflection needs to be established. Since refractive index is the ratio of the speed of light in vacuum to the speed of light in the material considered, it is logical that a change of sign would result if the direction of propagation was reversed. For reflective surfaces, therefore,

1. Refractive index values are multiplied by −1 upon reflection.
2. The signs of all distances upon reflection are multiplied by −1.

Figure 11 shows the location of principal and focal points for two mirror types: concave and convex. The concave mirror is equivalent to a positive converging lens. A convex mirror is equivalent to a negative lens. The effective focal length is simplified because of the loss of the thickness term and sign changes to:

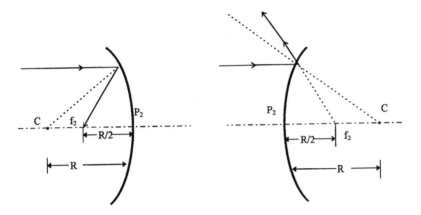

Figure 11   Location of principal and focal points for (a) concave and (b) convex mirrors.

$$f = -\frac{1}{2}R$$

3   IMAGE FORMATION: WAVE OPTICS

Many of the limitations of geometrical optics can be explained by considering the wave nature of light. As we have reasoned that a perfect lens translates spherical waves from an object point to an image point, such concepts can be used to describe deviations from nongeometrical propagation that would otherwise be difficult to predict.

An approach proposed by Huygens [2] allows an extension of optical geometric construction to wave propagation. Through use of this simplified wave model, many practical aspects of the wave nature of light can be understood. Huygens' principle provides a basis for determining the position of a wavefront at any instance based on knowledge of an earlier wavefront. A wavefront is assumed to be made up of an infinite number of point sources. Each of these sources produces a spherical secondary wave, called a wavelet. These wavelets propagate with appropriate velocities, determined by refractive index and wavelength. At any point in time, the position of the new wavefront can be determined as the surface tangent to these secondary waves. Using the concepts of Huygens, electromagnetic fields can be thought of as sums of propagating spherical or plane waves. Although Huygens had no knowledge of the nature of the light wave or the electromagnetic character of light, this approach has allowed analysis without the need to fully solve Maxwell's equations.

The diffraction of light is responsible for image creation in all optical situations. When a beam of light encounters the edge of an opaque obstacle, propagation is not rectilinear, as might be assumed based on assumptions of geometrical shadowing. The resulting variation in intensity produced at some distance from the obstacle is dependent on the coherence of light, its wavelength, and the distance the light travels before being observed. The situation for coherent illumination is shown in Fig. 12. Shown are a coherently illuminated mask and the resulting intensity pattern observed at increasing distances. Such an image in intensity is known as an aerial image. Typically, with coherent illumination, fringes are created in the diffuse shadowing between light and dark, a result of interference. Only when there is no separation between the obstacle and the recording plane does rectilinear propagation occur. As the recording plane is moved away from the obstacle, there is a region in which the geometrical shadow is still discernible. Beyond this region, far from the obstacle, the intensity pattern at the recording plane no longer resembles the geometrical shadow but rather contains area of light and dark fringes. At close distances, where geometric shadowing is still recognizable, near-field diffraction, or Fresnel diffraction, dominates. At greater distances, far-field diffraction, or Fraunhofer diffraction, dominates.

3.1 Fresnel Diffraction: Proximity Lithography

The theory of Fresnel diffraction is based on the Fresnel approximation to the propagation of light and describes image formation for proximity printing

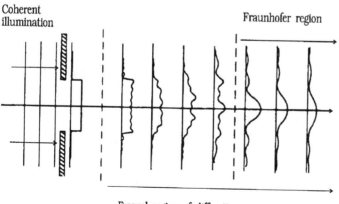

Figure 12 Diffraction pattern of a coherently illuminated mask opening at near (Fresnel) and far (Fraunhofer) distances.

where separation distances between the mask and wafer are normally held to within a few microns [3]. The distribution of intensity resembles that of the geometric shadow. As the separation between the mask and wafer increases, the integrity of an intensity pattern resembling an ideal shadowing diminishes.

Theoretical analysis of Fresnel diffraction is difficult, and Fresnel approximations based on Kirchhoff diffraction theory are used to obtain a qualitative understanding [4]. Since our interest lies mainly with projection systems and diffraction beyond the near-field region, a rigorous analysis will not be attempted here. Instead, analysis of results will provide some insight into the capabilities of proximity lithography.

Fresnel diffraction can be described using a linear filtering approach, which can be made valid over a small region of the observation or image plane. For this analogy, a mask function is effectively frequency filtered with a quadratically increasing phase function. This quadratic phase filter can be thought of as a slice of a spherical wave at some plane normal to the direction of propagation, as shown in Fig. 13. The resulting image will exhibit "blurring" at edges and oscillating "fringes" in bright and dark regions. Recognition of the geometrical shadow becomes more difficult as the illumination wavelength increases, the mask feature size decreases, or the mask separation distance increases. Figure 14 illustrates the situation in which a space mask is illuminated with 365-nm radiation and the separation distance between mask and wafer is 1.8 μm. For relatively large features, on the order of 10 to 15 μm, rectilinear propagation dominates and the resulting image intensity distribution resembles the mask. In order to determine the minimum feature width resolvable, some specification

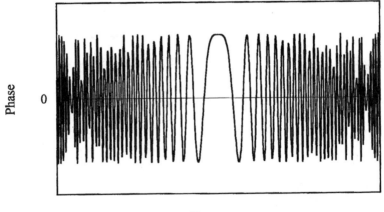

Frequency

Figure 13   A quadratic phase function.

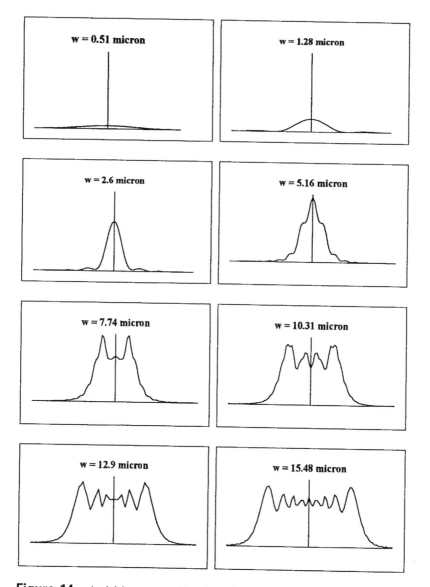

Figure 14 Aerial images resulting from frequency filtering of a slit opening with a quadratic phase function. The illumination wavelength is 365 nm and separation distance is 1.8 μm for mask opening sizes shown.

for maximum intensity loss and line width deviation must be made. These specifications are determined by the photoresist material and processes. If an intensity tolerance of ±5% and a mask space width to image width tolerance of ±20% is acceptable, a relationship for minimum resolution results:

$$w \approx 0.7\sqrt{\lambda s}$$

where w is space width, λ is illumination wavelength, and s is separation distance. As can be shown, resolution below 1 μm should be achievable with separations of 5 μm or less. A practical limit for resolution using proximity methods is closer to 3 to 5 μm because of surface and mechanical separation control as well as alignment difficulties.

3.2 Fraunhofer Diffraction: Projection Lithography

For projection lithography, diffraction in the far-field or Fraunhofer region needs to be considered. No longer is geometric shadowing recognizable; rather fringing takes over in the resulting intensity pattern. Analytically, this situation is easier to describe than Fresnel diffraction. When light encounters a mask, it is diffracted toward the objective lens in the projection system. Its propagation will determine how an optical system will ultimately perform, depending on the coherence of the light that illuminates the mask.

Consider a coherently illuminated single space mask opening, as shown in Fig. 15. The resulting Fraunhofer diffraction pattern can be evaluated by ex-

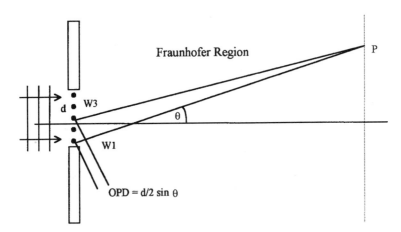

Figure 15 Determination of Fraunhofer diffraction effects for a coherently illuminated single mask opening.

amining light coming from various portions of the space opening. Using Huygens' principle, the opening can be divided into an infinite number of individual sources, each acting as a separate source of spherical wavelets. Interference will occur between every portion of this opening, and the resulting diffraction pattern at some far distance will depend on the propagation direction θ. It is convenient for analysis to divide the opening into two halves ($d/2$). With coherent illumination, all wavelets emerging from the mask opening are in phase. If waves emitted from the center and bottom of the mask opening are considered (labeled w1 and w3), it can be seen that an optical path difference (OPD) exists as one wave travels a distance $d/2 \sin \theta$ farther than the other. If the resulting OPD is one half-wavelength, or any multiple of one half-wavelength, waves will interfere destructively. Similarly, an OPD of $d \sin \theta$ exists between any two waves that originate from points separated by one half of the space width. The waves from the top portion of the mask opening interfere destructively with waves from the bottom portion of the mask when:

$$d \sin \theta = m\lambda \quad (m = \pm 1, \ \pm 2, \ \pm 3, \ ...)$$

where $|m| \leq d/\lambda$. From this equation, the positions of dark fringes in the Fraunhofer diffraction pattern can be determined. Figure 16 is the resulting diffraction pattern from a single space, where a broad central bright fringe exists at positions corresponding to θ = 0 and dark fringes occur where θ satisfies the destructive interference condition.

Although this geometric approach is satisfactory for a basic understanding of Fraunhofer diffraction principles, it cannot do an adequate job of describing the propagation of diffracted light. Fourier methods and scalar diffraction theory provide a description of the propagation of diffracted light through several approximations (previously identified as the Fresnel approximations), specifically [5,6]:

1. The distance between the aperture and the observation plane is much greater than the aperture dimension.

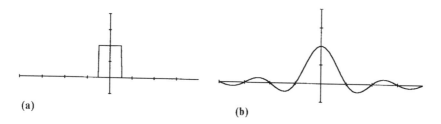

(a)

(b)

Figure 16 (a) A single space mask pattern and (b) its corresponding Fraunhofer diffraction pattern. These are Fourier transform pairs.

2. Spherical waves can be approximated by quadratic surfaces.
3. Each plane wave component has the same polarization amplitude (with polarization vectors perpendicular to the optical axis).

These approximations are valid for optical systems with numerical apertures below 0.6 if illumination polarization can be neglected. Scalar theory has been extended beyond these approximations to numerical apertures of 0.7 [7] and full vector diffraction theory has been utilized for more rigorous analysis [8].

3.3 Fourier Methods in Diffraction Theory

Whereas geometrical methods allow determination of interference minimums for the Fraunhofer diffraction pattern of a single slit, the distribution of intensity across the pattern is most easily determined through Fourier methods. The coherent field distribution of a Fraunhofer diffraction pattern produced by a mask is essentially the Fourier transform of the mask function. If we let $m(x,y)$ be a two-dimensional mask function or electric field distribution across the x-y mask plane and let $M(u,v)$ be the coherent field distribution across the u-v Fraunhofer diffraction plane, then

$$M(u,v) = \mathcal{F}\{m(x,y)\}$$

will represent the Fourier transform operation. Both $m(x,y)$ and $M(u,v)$ have amplitude and phase components. From Fig. 12, we could consider $M(uv)$ the distribution (in amplitude) at the farthest distance from the mask.

The field distribution in the Fraunhofer diffraction plane represents the spatial frequency spectrum of the mask function. In the analysis of image detail, preservation of spatial structure is generally of most concern. For example, the lithographer is interested in optimizing an imaging process to maximize the reproduction integrity of fine feature detail. To separate out such spatial structure from an image, it is convenient to work in a domain of spatial frequency rather than of feature dimension. The concept of spatial frequency is analogous to temporal frequency in the analysis of electrical communication systems. Units of spatial frequency are reciprocal distance. As spatial frequency increases, pattern detail becomes finer. Commonly, units of cycles/mm or mm^{-1} are used, where 100 mm^{-1} is equivalent to 5 μm, 1000 mm^{-1} is equivalent to 0.5 μm, and so forth. The Fourier transform of a function, therefore, translates dimensional (x,y) information into spatial frequency (u,v) structure.

The Fourier Transform

The unique properties of the Fourier transform allow convenient analysis of spatial frequency structure [9]. The Fourier transform takes the general form:

$$F(u) = \int\limits_{-\infty}^{\infty} f(x)e^{-2\pi iux} \, dx$$

for one dimension. Uppercase and lowercase letters are used to denote Fourier transform pairs.

In words, the Fourier transform expresses a function $f(x)$ as the sum of weighted sinusoidal frequency components. If $f(x)$ is a real-valued, even function, the complex exponential ($e^{-2\pi iux}$) could be replaced by a cosine term, $\cos(2\pi ux)$, making the analogy more obvious. Such transforms are utilized but are of little interest for microlithographic applications, since masking functions, $m(x,y)$, will generally have odd as well as even components.

If we revisit the single slit pattern analyzed previously with Fraunhofer diffraction theory, we can see that the distribution of the amplitude of the interference pattern produced is simply the Fourier transform of an even, one-dimensional, nonperiodic, rectangular pulse, commonly referred to as a rect function, rect (x). The Fourier transform of rect(x) is a sinc(u) where:

$$\text{sinc}(u) = \frac{\sin(\pi u)}{\pi u}$$

which is shown in Fig. 16. The intensity of the pattern is proportional to the square of the amplitude, or a $\text{sinc}^2(u)$ function, which is equivalent to the power spectrum. The two functions, rect (x) and sinc(u), are Fourier transform pairs, where the inverse Fourier transform of $F(u)$ is $f(x)$:

$$f(x) = \int\limits_{-\infty}^{\infty} F(u)e^{+2\pi iux} \, du$$

The Fourier transform is nearly its own inverse, differing only in sign.

The scaling property of the Fourier transform is of specific importance in imaging applications. Properties are such that:

$$\mathcal{F}\left(f\left(\frac{x}{b} \right) \right) = |b|F(bu)$$

and

$$\mathcal{F}\left(rect\left(\frac{x}{b} \right) \right) = |b|\text{sinc}(bu)$$

where b is the effective width of the function. The implication of this is that as the width of a slit decreases, the field distribution of the diffraction pattern becomes more spread out with diminished amplitude values. Figure 17 illustrates the effects of scaling on a one-dimensional rect function.

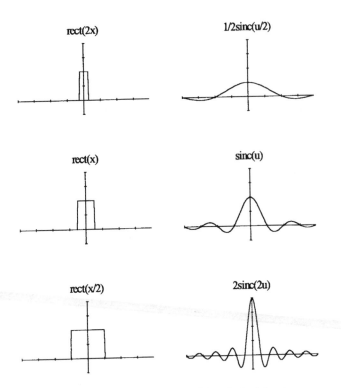

Figure 17   Scaling effects on rect(x) and sinc(u) pairs.

A mask object is generally a function of both x and y coordinates in a two-dimensional space. The two-dimensional Fourier transform takes the form:

$$F(u,v) = \int\limits_{-\infty}^{\infty} \int\limits_{-\infty}^{\infty} f(x,y)e^{-2\pi i(ux+vy)} \, dx \, dy$$

The variables u and v represent spatial frequencies in the x and y directions, respectively. The inverse Fourier transform can be determined in a fashion similar to the one-dimensional case, with a conventional change in sign.

In IC lithography, isolated as well periodic lines and spaces are of interest. We have analyzed diffraction for isolated features through Fourier transform of the rect function. We can analyze diffraction effects for periodic feature types in a similar manner.

Rectangular Wave

Where a single slit mask can be considered as a nonperiodic rectangular pulse, line/space patterns can be viewed as periodic rectangular waves. In Fraunhofer diffraction analysis, this rectangular wave is analogous to the diffraction grating. We choose the rectangular wave function of Fig. 18 as an illustration, where the maximum amplitude is A and the wave period is p, also known as the pitch. This periodic wave can be broken up into components of a rect function, with width ½, and a periodic function that we will call comb(x) where:

$$\text{comb}\left(\frac{x}{p}\right) = \sum_{n=-\infty}^{\infty} \delta(x - np)$$

an infinite train of unit-area impulse functions spaced one pitch unit apart. (An impulse function is an idealized function, with zero width and infinite height, having an area equal to 1.0.) To separate these two functions, rect(x) and comb(x), from the rectangular wave, we need to realize that it is a convolution operation that relates them. Since convolution in the space (x) domain becomes multiplication in frequency:

$$m(x) = \text{rect}\left(\frac{x}{p/2}\right) * \text{comb}\left(\frac{x}{p}\right)$$

$$M(u) = \mathcal{F}\{m(x)\} = \mathcal{F}\left\{\text{rect}\left(\frac{x}{p/2}\right)\right\} \times \mathcal{F}\left\{\text{comb}\left(\frac{x}{p}\right)\right\}$$

By utilizing the transform properties of the comb function:

$$\mathcal{F}\{\text{comb}(x/b)\} = |b|\text{comb}(bu)$$

the Fourier transform of the rectangular wave can be expressed as

$$\mathcal{F}\left\{\text{rect}\left(\frac{x}{p/2}\right) * \text{comb}\left(\frac{x}{p}\right)\right\} = M(u)$$

$$= \frac{A}{2}\text{sinc}\left(\frac{u}{2u_0}\right)\sum_{n=-\infty}^{\infty}\delta(u - nu_0)$$

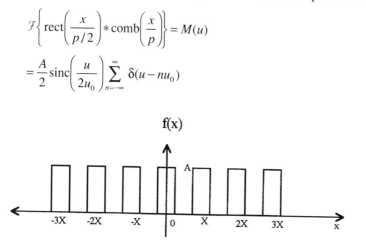

f(x)

Figure 18 A periodic rectangular wave, representing dense mask features.

where $u_0 = 1/p$, the fundamental frequency of the mask grating. The amplitude spectrum of the rectangular wave is shown in Fig. 19, where $A/2 \; \mathrm{sinc}(u/2u_0)$ provides an envelope for the discrete Fraunhofer diffraction pattern. It can be shown that the discrete interference maxima correspond to $d \sin \theta = m\lambda$ where $m = 0, \pm 1, \pm 2, \pm 3$, and so on, where d is the mask pitch.

Harmonic Analysis

We can utilize the amplitude spectrum of the rectangular wave to decompose the function into a linear combination of complex exponentials by assigning proper weights to complex-valued coefficients. This allows harmonic analysis through the Fourier series expansion, utilizing complex exponentials as basis functions. These exponentials, or sine and cosine functions, allow us to represent the spatial frequency structure of periodic functions as well as non-periodic functions. Let us consider the periodic rectangular wave function $m(x)$, of Fig. 18. Since the function is even and real-valued, we can utilize the amplitude spectrum to decompose $m(x)$ into the cosinusoidal frequency components:

$$m(x) = \frac{A}{2} + \frac{2A}{\pi}[\cos(2\pi u_0 x)] - \frac{2A}{3\pi}[\cos(2\pi(3u_0)x)]$$
$$+ \frac{2A}{5\pi}\cos(2\pi(5u_0)x)] - \frac{2A}{7\pi}[\cos(2\pi(7u_0)x)] + \dots$$

By graphing these components in Fig. 20, it becomes clear that each additional term brings the sum closer to the function $m(x)$.

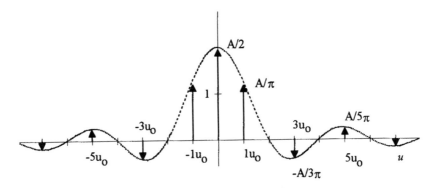

Figure 19 The amplitude spectrum of a rectangular wave, $A/2 \; \mathrm{sinc}(u/2u_0)$. This is equivalent to the discrete orders of the coherent Fraunhofer diffraction pattern.

These discrete coefficients are the diffraction orders of the Fraunhofer diffraction pattern, which are produced when a diffraction grating is illuminated by coherent illumination. These coefficients, which are represented as terms in the harmonic decomposition of $m(x)$ in Fig. 20, correspond to the discrete orders seen in Fig. 19. The zeroth order (centered at $u = 0$) corresponds to the constant DC term $A/2$. At either side are the $\pm$ first orders, where $u_1 = 1/p$. The $\pm$ second orders correspond to $u_2 = \pm 2/p$, and so on. It would follow that if an imaging system was not able to collect all diffracted orders propagating from a mask, complete reconstruction would not be possible. Furthermore, as higher frequency information is lost, fine image detail is sacrificed. There is,

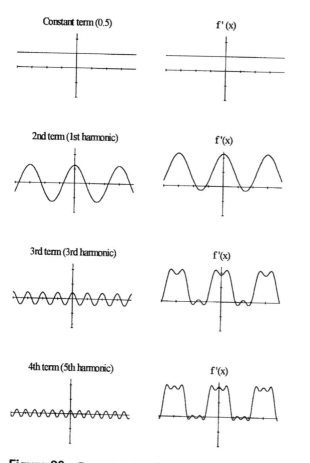

Figure 20   Reconstruction of a rectangular wave (right) using Fourier series expansion.

therefore, a fundamental limitation to resolution for an imaging system determined by its inability to collect all possible diffraction information.

Finite Dense Features

The rectangular wave is very useful for understanding the fundamental concepts and Fourier analysis of diffraction. In reality, however, we deal with finite mask functions rather than such infinite functions as the rectangular wave. The extent by which a finite number of mask features can be represented by an infinite function depends on the number of features present. Consider a mask consisting of five equal line/space pairs, or a five-bar function as shown in Fig. 21. This mask function can be represented before as the convolution of a scaled rect (x) function and an impulse train comb(x). In order to limit the mask function to five features only, a windowing function must be introduced as follows:

$$m(x) = \left[\text{rect}\left(\frac{x}{p/2}\right) * \text{comb}\left(\frac{x}{p}\right) \right] \times \text{rect}\left(\frac{x}{5p}\right)$$

As before, the spatial frequency distribution is a Fourier transform, but now each diffraction order is convolved with a sinc(u) function, scaled appropriately by the inverse width of the windowing function:

$$M(u) = \left[\frac{A}{2}\text{sinc}\left(\frac{u}{2u_0}\right) \sum_{n=-\infty}^{\infty} \delta(u - nu_0) \right] * 5\,\text{sinc}\left(\frac{u}{u_0/5}\right)$$

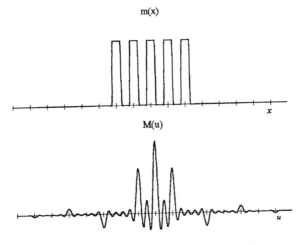

$m(x)$

$M(u)$

Figure 21 A five-bar mask function $m(x)$ and its corresponding coherent spatial frequency distribution $M(u)$.

As more features are added to the five-bar function, the width of the convolved sinc(u) is narrowed. At the limit where an infinite number of features is considered, the sinc(u) function becomes a $\delta(u)$ and the result is identical to the rectangular wave. At the other extreme, if a one-bar mask function is considered, the resulting spatial frequency distribution is the continuous function shown in Fig. 16.

The Objective Lens

In a projection imaging system, the objective lens has the ability to collect a finite amount of diffracted information from a mask, determined by its maximum acceptance angle or numerical aperture. A lens behaves as a linear filter for a diffraction pattern propagating from a mask. By limiting high-frequency diffraction components, it acts as a low-pass filter blocking information propagating at angles beyond its capability. Information that is passed is acted on by the lens to produce a second inverse Fourier transform operation, directing a limited reconstruction of the mask object toward the image plane. It is limited not only by the loss of higher frequency diffracted information but also by any lens aberrations that may act to introduce image degradation. In the absence of lens aberrations, imaging is referred to as diffraction limited. The influence of lens aberration on imaging will be addressed in detail later on. At this point, if an ideal diffraction-limited lens can be considered, the concept of a lens as a linear filter can provide insight image formation.

The Lens as a Linear Filter

If an objective lens could produce an exact inverse Fourier transform of the Fraunhofer diffraction pattern emanating from an object, complete image reconstruction would be possible. A finite lens numerical aperture will prevent this. Consider a rectangular grating where $p \sin \theta = m\lambda$ describes the positions of the discrete coherent diffraction orders. If a lens can be described in terms of a two-dimensional pupil function $H(u,v)$, limited by its scaled numerical aperture, NA/λ, then:

$$H(u,v) = 1 \quad \text{if } \sqrt{u^2 + v^2} < \frac{NA}{\lambda}$$

$$0 \quad \text{if } \sqrt{u^2 + v^2} > \frac{NA}{\lambda}$$

describes the behavior of the lens as a low-pass filter. The resulting image amplitude produced by the lens is the inverse Fourier transform of the mask's Fraunhofer diffraction pattern multiplied by this lens pupil function:

$$A(x, y) = \mathcal{F}\{M(u, v) \cdot H(u, v)\}$$

The image intensity distribution, known as the aerial image, is equal to the square of the image amplitude:

$$I(x, y) = |A(x, y)|^2$$

For the situation described, coherent illumination allows simplification of optical behavior. Diffraction at a mask is effectively a Fourier transform operation. Part of this diffracted field is collected by the objective lens, where diffraction is in a sense "reversed" through a second Fourier transform operation. Any losses incurred through limitations of a lens NA < 1.0 results in less than complete reconstruction of the original mask detail. To extend this analysis for real systems, an understanding of coherence theory is needed.

3.4 Coherence Theory in Image Formation

Much has been written about coherence theory and the influence of spatial coherence on interference and imaging [10]. For projection imaging, three illumination situations are possible that allow the description of interference behavior. These are coherent illumination, where wavefronts are correlated and are able to interfere completely; incoherent illumination, where wavefronts are uncorrelated and unable to interfere; and partial coherent illumination, where partial interference is possible. Figure 22 shows the situation, where spherical wavefronts are emitted from point sources, which can be used to describe coherent, incoherent, and partial coherent illumination. With coherent illumination, spherical waves emitted by a single point source on axis result in plane waves normal to the optical axis when acted upon by a lens. At all positions on the mask, radiation arrives in phase. Strictly speaking, coherent illumination implies zero intensity. For incoherent illumination, an infinite collection of off-axis point sources result in plane waves at all angles ($\pm\pi$). The resulting illumination at the mask has essentially no phase-to-space relationship. For partially coherent illumination, a finite collection of off-axis point sources describes a source of finite extent, resulting in plane waves within a finite angle. The situation of partial coherence is of most interest for lithography, the degree of which will have a great influence on imaging results.

   Through the study of interference, Young's double-slit experiment has allowed an understanding of a great deal of optical phenomenon. The concept of partial coherence can be understood using modifications of Young's double-slit experiment. Consider two slits separated a distance p apart, illuminated by a coherent point source, as depicted in Fig. 23a. The resulting interference fringes are cosinusoidal with frequency $u_0 = 1/p$, as would be predicted using interference theory or Fourier transform concepts of Fraunhofer diffraction (the Fourier

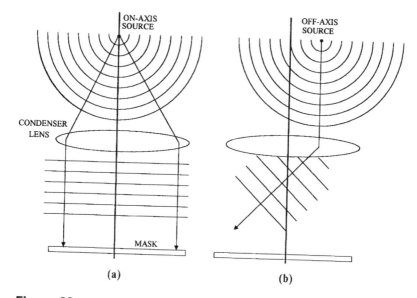

Figure 22 The impact of on-axis (a) and off-axis (b) point sources on illumination coherence. Plane waves result for each case and are normal to the optical axis only for an on-axis point.

transform of two symmetrically distributed point sources or impulse functions is a cosine). Next consider a point source shifted laterally and the resulting phase-shifted cosinusoidal interference pattern, shown in Fig. 23b. If this approach is extended to a number of point sources to represent a real source of finite extent, it can be expected that the resulting interference pattern would be an average of many cosines with reduced modulation and with a frequency u_0, as shown in Fig. 23c. The assumption for this analysis is that the light emitted from each point source is of identical wavelength, or there is a condition of temporal coherence.

3.5 Partial Coherence Theory: Diffracted-Limited Resolution

The concept of degree of coherence is useful as a description of illumination condition. The Abbe theory of microscope imaging can be applied to microlithographic imaging with coherent or partially coherent illumination [11]. Abbe demonstrated that when a ruled grating is coherently illuminated and imaged through an objective lens, the resulting image depends on the lens numerical aperture. The minimum resolution that can be obtained is a function of both the illumination wavelength and the lens NA, as shown in Fig. 24 for co-

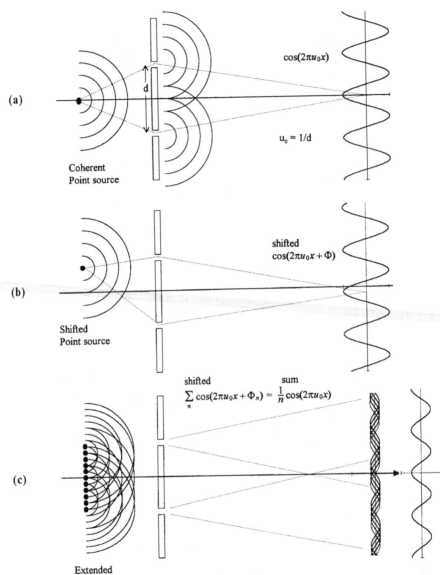

Figure 23 Diffraction patterns from two slits separated by a distance d for (a) coherent illumination, (b) oblique off-axis illumination, and (c) partially coherent illumination.

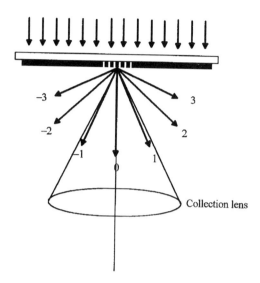

Figure 24 The condition for minimum diffraction limited resolution for a coherently illuminated grating mask.

herent illumination. Since no imaging is possible if no more than the undiffracted beam is accepted by the lens, it can be reasoned that a minimum of the first diffraction order is required for resolution. The position of this first order is determined as:

$$\sin(\theta) = \frac{\lambda}{p}$$

Since a lens numerical aperture is defined as the sine of the half acceptance angle (θ), the minimum resolvable line width ($R = p/2$) becomes:

$$R = \frac{p}{2} = 0.5\frac{\lambda}{NA}$$

Abbe's work made use of a smooth uniform flame source and a substage condenser to form its image in the object plane. To adapt to nonuniform lamp sources, Köhler devised a two-stage illuminating system to form an image of the source into the entrance pupil of the objective lens, as shown in Fig. 25 [12]. A pupil at the condenser lens can control the numerical aperture of the illumination system. As the pupil is closed down, the source size (d_s) and the effective source size (d_s') are decreased, resulting in an increase in the extent of coherency. Thus, Köhler illumination allows control of partial coherence. The degree of partial coherence (σ) is conventionally measured as the ratio of ef-

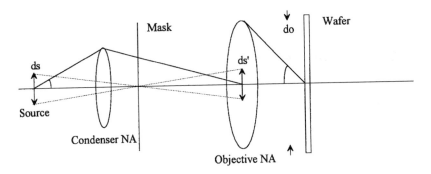

Figure 25   Schematic of Köhler illumination. The degree of coherence (σ) is determined as ds'/do or NA_C/NA_O.

fective source size to full objective aperture size or the ratio of condenser lens NA to objective lens NA:

$$\text{Degree of coherence } (\sigma) = (d_s'/d_o) = (NA_C/NA_o)$$

As σ approaches zero, a condition of coherent illumination exists. As σ approaches one, incoherent illumination exists. In lithographic projection systems, σ is generally in the range 0.3 to 0.9. Values below 0.3 will result in "ringing" in images, fringes which result from coherent interference effects similar to those shown as terms are added in Fig. 20.

Partial coherence can be thought of as taking an incoherent sum of coherent images. For every point within a source of finite extent, a coherent Fraunhofer diffraction pattern is produced which can be described by Fourier methods. For a point source on axis, diffracted information is distributed symmetrically and discretely about the axis. For off-axis points, diffraction patterns are shifted off axis and, as all points are considered together, the resulting diffraction pattern becomes a summation of individual distributions. Figure 26 depicts the situation for a rectangular wave mask pattern illuminated with σ greater than zero. Here, the zeroth order is centered on axis but with a width > 0, a result of the extent of partially coherent illumination angles. Similarly, each higher diffraction order also has width > 0, an effective spreading of discrete orders. The impact of partial coherence is realized when the influence of an objective lens is considered. By spreading the diffraction orders about their discrete coherent frequencies, operation on the diffracted information by the lens produces a frequency averaging effect of the image and loss of image modulation, as seen previously in Fig. 23 for the double-slit example. This image degradation is not desirable when coherent illumination would allow superior image reconstruction. If, however, a situation exists in which coherent illumination of a given

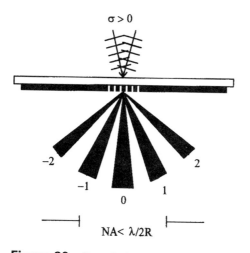

Figure 26 Spread of diffraction orders for partially coherent illumination resolution below 0.5λ/NA becomes possible.

mask pattern does not allow lens collection of diffraction orders beyond the zeroth order, partially coherent illumination would be preferred. Consider a coherently illuminated rectangular grating mask where ± first diffraction orders fall just outside a projection systems lens NA. With coherent illumination, imaging is not possible as feature sizes fall below the $R = 0.5\lambda/NA$ limit. Through use of partially coherent illumination, partial first diffraction order information can be captured by the lens, resulting in imaging capability. Partial coherent illumination, therefore, is desirable as mask features fall below $R = 0.5\lambda/NA$ in size. An optimum degree of coherence can be determined for a feature based on its size, the illumination wavelength, and the objective lens NA. Figure 27 shows the effect of partial coherence on imaging features of two sizes. The first case, Fig. 27a, is one in which aerial images for features are larger than the resolution possible for coherent illumination (here 0.6λ/NA). As seen, any increase in partial coherence above $\sigma = 0$ results in a degradation of the aerial image produced. This is due to the averaging effect of the fundamental cosinusoidal components used in image reconstruction. As seen in Fig. 27b, features smaller than the resolution possible with coherent illumination (0.4λ/NA) are resolvable only as partial coherence levels increase above $\sigma = 0$. It stands to reason that for every feature size and type, there exists a unique optimum partial coherence value that allows the greatest image improvement while allowing the minimum degradation. Focus effects also need to be considered as partial coherence is optimized for. This will be addressed further as depth of focus is considered.

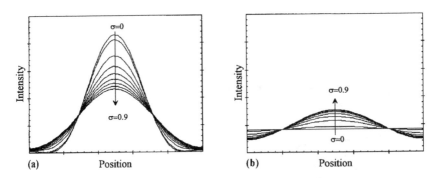

Figure 27   Intensity aerial images for features with various levels of partial coherence. Features corresponding to 0.6λ/NA are relatively large and are shown on the left (a). Small features corresponding to 0.4λ/NA are shown on the right (b).

4   IMAGE EVALUATION

The minimum resolution possible with coherent illumination is that which satisfies:

$$R = 0.5\lambda/\text{NA}$$

which is commonly referred to as the Rayleigh criterion [13]. Through incoherent or partially coherent illumination, resolution beyond this limit is made possible. Methods of image assessment are required to evaluate an image that is transferred through an optical system. As we will see, such methods will also prove useful as an imaging system deviates from ideal and optical aberrations are considered.

4.1   OTF, MTF, and PTF

The optical transfer function (OTF) is often used to evaluate the relationship between an image and the object that produced it [14]. In general, a transfer function is a description of an entire imaging process as a function of spatial frequency. It is a scaled Fourier transform of the point spread function (PSF) of the system. The PSF is the response of the optical system to a point object input, essentially the distribution of a point aerial image.

For a linear system, the transfer function is the ratio of the image modulation (or contrast) to object modulation (or contrast):

$$C_{\text{image}}(u)/C_{\text{object}}(u)$$

where contrast (C) is the normalized image modulation at frequency u:

$$C(u) = (S_{\text{max}} - S_{\text{min}})/(S_{\text{max}} + S_{\text{min}}) \leq 1$$

Here, S is the image or object signal. To fulfill the requirements of a linear system, several conditions must be met. In order to be linear, the input of a system's response to the superposition of two inputs must equal to the superposition of the individual responses. If $\Theta\{f(x)\} = g(x)$ represents the operation of a system on an input $f(x)$ to produce an output $g(x)$, then:

$$\Theta\{f_1(x) + f_2(x)\} = g_1(x) + g_2(x)$$

represents a system linear with superposition. A second condition of a linear system is shift invariance, where a system operates identically at all input coordinates. Analytically, this can be expressed as:

$$\Theta\{f(x - x_0)\} = g(x - x_0)$$

or a shift in input results in an identical shift in output. An optical system can be thought of as shift invariant in the absence of aberrations. Since the aberration of a system changes from point to point, the PSF can vary significantly from a center to an edge field point.

Intensities must add for an imaging process to be linear. In the coherent case of the harmonic analysis of a square wave in Fig. 20, the amplitudes of individual components have been added rather than their intensities. Whereas an optical system is linear in amplitude for coherent illumination, it is linear in intensity only for incoherent illumination. The OTF therefore be can be used as a metric for analysis of image intensity transfer only for incoherent illumination. Modulation is expressed as:

$$M = (I_{max} - I_{min}) / (I_{max} + I_{min})$$

where I is image or object intensity. It is a transfer function for a system over a range of spatial frequencies. A typical OTF is shown in Fig. 28, where modulation is plotted as a function of spatial frequency in cycles/mm. As seen, higher frequency objects (corresponding to finer feature detail) are transferred through the system with lower modulation. The characteristics of the incoherent OTF can be understood by working backward through an optical system. We have seen that an amplitude image is the Fourier transform of the product of an object and the lens pupil function. Here, the object is a point and the image is its PSF. The intensity PSF for an incoherent system is a squared amplitude PSF, also know as an Airy Disk, shown in Fig. 29. Since multiplication becomes a convolution via a Fourier transform, the transfer function of an imaging system with incoherent illumination is proportional to the self-convolution or the autocorrelation of the lens pupil function, which is equivalent to the Fourier transform of its PSF. As seen in Fig. 28, the OTF resembles a triangular function, the result of autocorrelation of a rectangular pupil function (which would be circular in two dimensions). For coherent illumination, the coherent transfer function is proportional to the pupil function

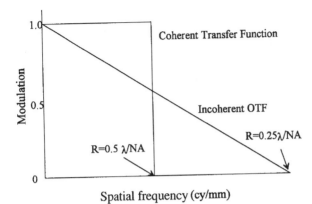

Figure 28 Typical incoherent optical transfer function (OTF) and coherent contrast transfer function (CTF).

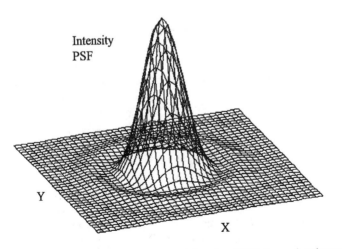

Figure 29 Intensity point spread function (PSF) for an incoherent system.

itself. The incoherent transfer function is twice as wide as the coherent transfer function, indicative that the cutoff frequency is twice that for coherent illumination. The limiting resolution for incoherent illumination becomes:

$$R = 0.25\lambda / \text{NA}$$

Although Rayleigh's criterion for incoherent illumination describes the point beyond which resolution is no longer possible, it does not give an indication of image quality at lower frequencies (corresponding to larger feature sizes). The OTF is a description of not only the limiting resolution but also the modulation at spatial frequencies up to that point.

The OTF is generally normalized to 1.0. The magnitude of the OTF is the modulation transfer function (MTF), which is commonly used. The MTF ignores phase information transferred by the system, which can be described using the phase transfer function (PTF). Because of the linear properties of incoherent imaging, the OTF, MTF, and PTF are independent of the object. Knowledge of the pupil shape and the lens aberrations is sufficient to describe the OTF completely. For coherent and partially coherent systems, there are no such metrics that are object independent.

4.2 Evaluation of Partial Coherent Imaging

For coherent or partially coherent imaging, the ratio of image modulation to object modulation is object dependent, making the situation more complex than for incoherent imaging. The concept of a transfer function can still be utilized, but limitations should be kept in mind. As shown earlier, the transfer function of a coherent imaging system is proportional to the pupil function itself. The cutoff frequency corresponds exactly to the Rayleigh criterion for coherent illumination. For partially coherent systems, the transfer function is neither the pupil function nor its autocorrelation, which results in a more complex situation. The evaluation of images requires a summation of coherent images, correlated by the degree of coherence at the mask. A partially coherent transfer function must include a unique description of both the illumination system and the lens. Such a transfer function is commonly referred to as a cross transfer function or the transmission cross coefficient [15].

For a mask object with equal lines and spaces, the object amplitude distribution can be represented as:

$$f(x) = a_0 + 2 \sum_{n=1}^{\infty} a_n \cos(2\pi nux)$$

where x is image position and u is spatial frequency. From partial coherence theory, the aerial image intensity distribution becomes:

$$I(x) = A + B\cos(2\pi u_0 x) + C\cos^2(2\pi u_0 x)$$

which is valid for $u \geq (1 + \sigma)/3$. The terms A, B, and C are given by:

$$A = a_0^2 T(0,0) + 2a_1^2 [T(u_1, u_2) - T(-u_1, u_2)]$$

$$B = 4a_0 a_1 RE[T(0, u_2)]$$

$$C = 4a_1^2 T(-u_1, u_2)$$

where $T(m_1, n'u_2)$ is the transmission cross coefficient, a measure of the phase correlation at two frequencies u_1 and u_2. Image modulation can be calculated as $M = B/(A + C)$.

The concepts of an MTF can be extended to partially coherent imaging if generated for each object uniquely. Steel [16] developed approximations to an exact expression for the MTF for partially coherent illumination. Such normalized MTF curves (denoted as MTF_p curves) can be generated for various degrees of partial coherence [17], as shown in Fig. 30. In systems with few aberrations, the impact of changes in the degree of partial coherence can be evaluated for any unique spatial frequency. By assuming a linear change in MTF between spatial frequencies u_1 and u_2, a correlation factor $G(\sigma, u)$ can be calculated that relates incoherent MTF_{INC} to partially coherent MTF_p:

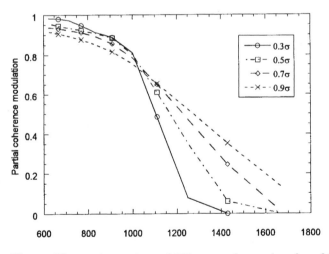

Figure 30 Partially coherent MTF_p curves for σ values from 0.3 to 0.7 for a 365nm, 0.37NA diffraction limited system.

$$u_1 = (1-\sigma)NA/\lambda$$

$$u_2 = (1+0.18\sigma)NA/\lambda$$

$$G(\sigma,u) = \begin{cases} \dfrac{1}{1-(4/\pi)\sin(u\lambda/2NA)} & u \le u_1 \\[3ex] \dfrac{1-(4/\pi)\sin(u_2\lambda/2NA)(u-u_1)/(u_2-u_1)}{1-(4/\pi)\sin(u_2\lambda/2NA)} & u_1 < u < u_2 \\[3ex] <1 & u_2 < u \end{cases}$$

The partially coherent MTF becomes:

$$\mathrm{MTF}_P(\sigma,u) = G(\sigma,u)\mathrm{MTF}_{\mathrm{INC}}(\sigma,u)$$

Using MTF curves such as those in Fig. 30 for a 0.37NA i-line system, partial coherence effects can be evaluated. With partial coherence of 0.3, the modulation at a spatial frequency of 1150 cycles/mm (corresponding to 0.43 μm lines) is near 0.35. Using a σ of 0.7, modulation increases by 71%. At 950 cycles/mm, however (corresponding to 0.53 μm lines), modulation decreases as partial coherence increases. The requirements of photoresist materials need to be addressed to determine appropriate σ values for a given spatial frequency. The concept of critical modulation transfer function (CMTF) is a useful approximation for relating minimum modulation required for a photoresist material. The minimum required modulation for a resist with contrast γ can be determined as:

$$\mathrm{CMTF} = \frac{10^{1/\gamma}-1}{10^{1/\gamma}+1}$$

For a resist material with a γ of 2, a CMTF of 0.52 results. At this modulation, large σ values are best suited for the system depicted in Fig. 30 and resolution is limited to somewhere near 0.38 μm. Optimization of partial coherence will be addressed further as additional image metrics are introduced.

As linearity is related to the coherence properties of mask illumination, stationarity is related to aberration properties across a specific image field. For a lens system to meet the requirements of stationarity, an isoplanatic patch needs to be defined in the image plane where the transfer function and (PSF) does not significantly change. Shannon [18] has describe this region as "much larger than the dimension of the significant detail to be examined on the image surface" but "small compared to the total area of the image." A real lens, therefore, requires a set of evaluation metrics, one for each unique isoplanatic patch. The number of OTFs or other metrics required for any lens will be a function of required performance and financial or technical capabilities. Although a large number of OTFs will better characterize a lens, more than a few may be impractical. Since an OTF will degrade with defocus, a position of best focus is normally chosen for lens characterization.

4.3 Other Image Evaluation Metrics

MTF or comparable metrics are limited to periodic features or gratings of equal lines and spaces. Other metrics may be used for the evaluation of image quality by measuring some aspect of an aerial image with less restriction on feature type. These may include measurements of image energy, image shape fidelity, critical image width, and image slope. Since feature width is a critical parameter for lithography, aerial image width is a useful metric for insight into the performance of resist images. A 30% intensity threshold is commonly chosen for image width measurement [19]. Few of these metrics, though, give an adequate representation of the impact of aerial image quality on resist process latitude.

Through measurement of the aerial image log slope or ILS, an indication of resist process performance can be obtained [20]. Exponential attenuation of radiation through an absorbing photoresist film leads an exposure profile ($\delta e/\delta x$) related to aerial image intensity as:

$$\frac{\delta}{\delta x} = \frac{\delta(\ln I)}{\delta x}$$

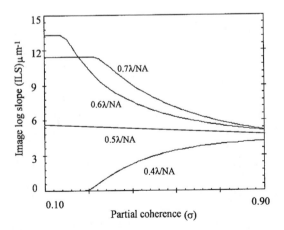

Figure 31 Image log slope (ILS) vs. partial coherence for dense features from 0.4λ/NA to 0.7λ/NA in size.

Since an exposure profile leads to a resist profile upon development, measurement of the slope of the log of an aerial image (at the mask edge) can be directly related to a resist image. Changes in this log aerial image gradient will therefore directly influence resist profile and process latitude. Using ILS as an image metric, aerial image plots such as those in Fig. 27 can be more thoroughly evaluated. Shown in Fig. 31 is a plot of image log slope versus partial coherence for features of size $R = 0.4\lambda/NA$ to $0.6\lambda/NA$. As can be seen, for increasing levels of partial coherence, image log slope increases for features smaller than $0.5\lambda/NA$ and decreases for features smaller than $0.5\lambda/NA$. It is important to notice, however, that all cases converge to a similar image log slope value. Improvements for small features achieved by increasing partial coherence values cannot improve the aerial image in a way equivalent to decreasing wavelength or increasing NA.

To determine to minimum usable ILS value and optimize situations such as the one above for use with a photoresist process, resist requirements need to be considered. As minimum image modulation required for a resist (CMTF) has been related to resist contrast properties, there is also a relationship between resist performance and minimum ILS requirements. As bulk resist properties such as contrast may not be adequately related to process-specific responses such as feature size control, exposure latitude, or depth of focus (DOF), more suitable evaluation methods may be desirable. Resist focus exposure matrices can provide usable depth-of-focus information for a resist-imaging system based on exposure and feature size specifications. Relating DOF to aerial image data for an imaging system can result in determination of a minimum ILS specification. Although ILS is feature size dependent (in units of μm^{-1}), image log slope normalized by multiplying it by the feature width is not. A minimum normalized image log slope (NILS) can then be determined for a resist-imaging system with less dependence on feature size. A convenient rule-of-thumb value for minimum NILS is between 6 and 8 for a single-layer positive resist with good performance.

With image evaluation requirements established, Rayleigh's criterion can be revisited and modified for other situations of partial coherence. A more general form becomes:

$$R = \frac{k_1\lambda}{NA}$$

where k_1 is a process-dependent factor that incorporates everything in a lithography process that is not wavelength or numerical aperture. Its importance should not be minimized, as any process or system modification that allows improvements in resolution effectively reduces the k_1 factor. Diffraction-limited values are 0.25 for incoherent and 0.50 for coherent illumination, as shown earlier. For partial coherence, k_1 can be expressed as:

$$k_1 = \frac{1}{2(\sigma + 1)}$$

where the minimum resolution is that which places the ± first diffraction order energy within the objective lens pupil, as shown in Fig. 26.

4.4 Depth of Focus

Depth of focus needs to be considered along with resolution criteria when imaging with a lens system. Depth of focus is defined as the distance along the optical axis that produces an image of some suitable quality. The Rayleigh depth of focus generally takes the form:

$$\mathrm{DOF} = \pm\frac{k_2\lambda}{\mathrm{NA}^2}$$

where k_2 is also a process-dependent factor. For a resist material of reasonably high contrast, k_2 may be on the order of 0.5. A process specific value of k_2 can be defined by determining the resulting useful DOF after specifying exposure latitude and tolerances. DOF decreases linearly with wavelength and as the square of numerical aperture. As measures are taken to improve resolution it is therefore more desirable to decrease wavelength than to increase NA. Depth of focus is closely related to defocus, the distance along the optical axis from a best focus position The acceptable level of defocus for a lens system will determine the usable DOF. Tolerable levels of this aberration will ultimately be determined by the entire imaging system as well as the feature sizes of interest.

To understand the interdependence of image quality and focus, a wavefront analysis approach is convenient. Aberrations such as defocus can be thought of as deviations from a perfect spherical wave emerging from the exit pupil of a lens toward an image point. This is analogous to working backward through an optical system, where a true point source in image space would correspond to a perfect spherical wave at the lens exit pupil. As shown in Fig. 32, the deviation of an actual wavefront from an unaberrated wavefront can be measured in terms of an optical path difference (OPD). The OPD in a medium is the product of the geometrical path length and the refractive index. For a point object, an ideal spherical wavefront leaving the lens pupil is represented by a dashed line. This wavefront will come to focus as a point in the image plane. Compared to this reference wavefront, a defocused wavefront (one that would focus

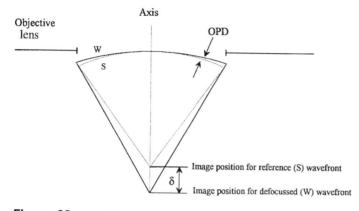

Figure 32 Depiction of optical path error (δ) introduced with defocus. Both reference (S) and defocused (W) wavefronts pass through the center of the objective lens pupil.

at a point some distance from the image plane) introduces error in the optical path distance to the image plane. This error increases with pupil radius. The resulting image will generally no longer resemble a point; instead it will be blurred.

The acceptable DOF for a lithographic process can be determined by relating OPD to phase error. An optical path is best measured in terms of the number (or fraction) of corresponding waves. OPD is realized therefore as a phase-shifting effect or phase error (Φ_{err}), which can be expressed as:

$$\Phi_{err} = \frac{2\pi}{\lambda} OPD$$

By determining the maximum allowable phase error for a process, an acceptable level of defocus can be determined. Consider again Fig. 32. The optical path distance can be related to defocus (δ) as:

$$OPD = \delta(1 - \cos\theta) = \frac{\delta}{2}\left(\sin^2\theta + \frac{\sin^4\theta}{4} + \frac{\sin^6\theta}{8} + \dots\right)$$

$$OPD \approx \frac{\delta}{2}\sin^2\theta = \frac{\Phi_{err}\lambda}{2\pi}$$

for small angles (the Fresnel approximation). Defocus can now be expressed as:

$$\delta = \frac{\Phi_{err}\lambda}{\pi \sin^2\theta} = \left(\frac{\Phi_{err}}{\pi}\right)\frac{\lambda}{NA^2}$$

A maximum phase error term can be determined by defining the maximum allowable defocus that will maintain process specifications. DOF can therefore be expressed in terms of corresponding defocus (δ) and phase error (Φ_{en}/π) terms through use of the process factor k_2:

$$\text{DOF} = \pm \frac{k_2 \lambda}{\text{NA}^2}$$

as seen previously.

If the distribution of mask frequency information in the lens pupil is considered, it is seen that the impact of defocus is realized as zero and first diffraction orders travel different optical path distances. For coherent illumination, the zero order experiences no OPD while the $\pm$ first orders go through a pupil-dependent OPD. It follows that only features that have sufficiently important information (i.e., first diffraction orders) at the edge of the lens aperture will possess a DOF as calculated by the full lens NA. For larger features whose diffraction orders are distributed closer to the lens center, DOF will be substantially higher. For dense features of pitch p, an effective NA can be determined for each feature size, which can subsequently be used for DOF calculation:

$$\text{NA}_{\text{effective}} \sim \frac{\lambda}{p}$$

As an example, consider dense 0.5-μm features imaged using coherent illumination with a 0.50 NA objective lens and 365-nm illumination. The first diffraction orders for these features are contained within the lens aperture at an effective NA of 0.365 rather than 0.50. The resulting DOF (for a k_2 of 0.5) is therefore closer to $\pm$ 1.37 μm rather than to ± 0.73 μm as determined for the full NA.

The distribution of diffraction orders needs to be considered in the case of partial coherence. By combining the wavefront description in Fig. 32 with the frequency distribution description in Fig. 26, DOF can be related to partial coherence, as shown in Fig. 33. For coherent illumination, there is a discrete difference in optical path length traveled between diffraction orders. By using partial coherence, however, there is an averaging effect of OPD over the lens pupil. By distributing frequency information over a broad portion of the lens pupil, the difference in path lengths experienced between diffraction orders is reduced. In the limit of complete incoherence, the zero and first diffraction orders essentially share the same pupil area, effectively eliminating the effects of defocus (which is possible only in the absence of any higher order diffraction terms). This can be seen in Fig. 34, which is similar to Fig. 31 except that a large defocus value has been incorporated. Here it is seen that at low partial coherence values, ILS is reduced with defocus. At high partial coherence levels, however, ILS remains high, indicating that a greater DOF is possible.

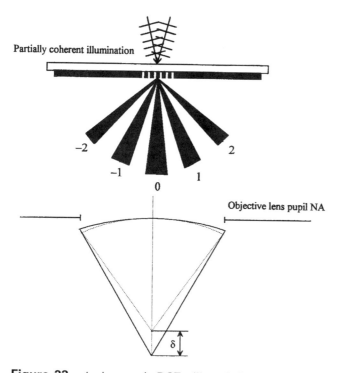

Figure 33 An increase in DOF will result from an increase in partial coherence as path length differences are averaged across the lens pupil. In the limit for incoherent illumination, the zero and first diffraction orders fill the lens pupil and DOF is theoretically infinite (in the absence of higher orders).

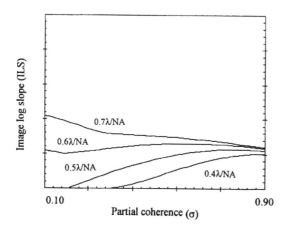

Figure 34 ILS vs. partial coherence for dense features with λ/NA^2 of defocus. Degradation is minimal with higher σ values.

5 IMAGING ABERRATIONS AND DEFOCUS

Discussion of geometrical image formation has so far been limited to the paraxial region, which allows determination of the size and location of an image for a perfect lens. In reality, some degree of lens error or aberration exists in any lens, which causes deviation from this first-order region. For microlithographic lenses, an understanding of the tolerable level of aberrations and interrelationships becomes more critical than for most other optical applications. To understand their impact on image formation, aberrations can be classified by their origin and effects. Commonly referred to as the Seidel aberrations, these include monochromatic aberrations: spherical, coma, astigmatism, field curvature, and distortion, as well as chromatic aberration. A brief description of each aberration will be given along with the effect of each on image formation. In addition, defocus is considered as an aberration and will be addressed. Although each aberration is discussed uniquely, all aberration types at some level will nearly always be present.

5.1 Spherical Aberration

Spherical aberration is a variation in focus as a function of radial position in a lens. Spherical aberration exists for objects either on or off the optical axis. Figure 35 shows the situation for a distant on-axis point object where rays passing through the lens near the optical axis come into focus nearer the paraxial focus than rays passing through the edge of the lens. Spherical aberration can be measured as either a longitudinal (or axial) or transverse (or lateral) error. Longitudinal spherical aberration is the distance from the paraxial focus to the axial intersection of a ray. Transverse spherical aberration is sim-

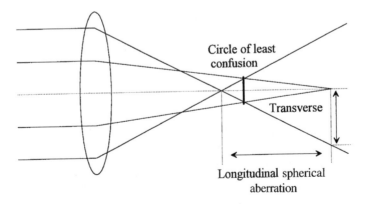

Figure 35   Spherical aberration for an on-axis point object.

ilar but measured in the vertical direction. Spherical aberration is often represented graphically in terms of ray height, as in Fig. 36, where longitudinal error (LA_R) is plotted against ray height at the lens (Y_R). The effect of spherical aberration on a point image is a blurring effect or the formation of a diffuse halo by peripheral rays. The best image of a point object is no longer located at the paraxial focus but instead at the position of the circle of lease confusion. Longitudinal spherical aberration increases as the square of the aperture and is influenced by lens shape. In general, a positive lens will produce an undercorrection of spherical aberration (a negative value) whereas a negative lens will produce an overcorrection. As with most primary aberrations, there is also a dependence on object and image position. As an object changes position, for example, ray paths change, leading to potential increases in aberration levels. If a lens system is scaled up or down, aberrations are also scaled. This scaling would lead to a change in field size but not in numerical aperture. A simple system that is scaled up by 2× with a 1.5× increase in NA, for example, would lead to a 4.5× increase in longitudinal spherical aberration.

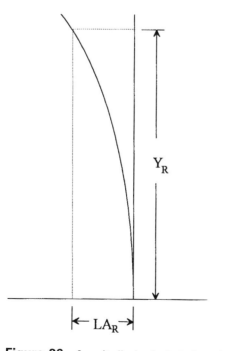

Figure 36 Longitudinal spherical aberration (LA_R) plotted against ray height (Y_R).

5.2 Coma

Coma is an aberration of object points that lie off axis. It is a variation in magnification with aperture that produces an image point with a diffuse comet-like tail. As shown in Fig. 37, rays passing through the center and edges of a lens are focused at different heights. Tangential coma is measured as the distance between the height of the lens rim ray and the lens center ray. Unlike spherical aberration, comatic flare is not symmetric and point image location is sometimes difficult. Coma increases with the square of the lens aperture and also with field size. Coma can be reduced, therefore, by stopping down the lens and limiting field size. It can also be reduced by shifting the aperture and optimizing field angle. Unlike spherical aberration, coma is linearly influenced by lens shape. Coma is positive for a negative meniscus lens and decreases to negative for a positive meniscus lens.

5.3 Astigmatism and Field Curvature

Astigmatism is also an off-axis aberration. With astigmatism present, rays that lie in different planes do not share a common focus. Consider, for instance, a plane that contains the chief ray and the optical axis, known as the tangential plane. The plane perpendicular to this is called the sagittal plane, which also contains the chief ray. Rays in the tangential plane will come to focus at the tangential focal surface, as shown in Fig. 38. Rays in the sagittal plane will come to focus at the sagittal focal surface, and if these two do not coincide, the intermediate surface is called the medial image surface. If no astigmatism exists, all surfaces coincide with the lens field curvature, called the Petzval curvature. Astigmatism does not exist for on-axis points and increases with the

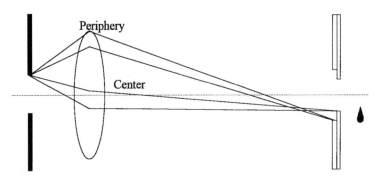

Figure 37 Coma for an off-axis object point. Rays passing through the center and edges of a lens are focused at different heights.

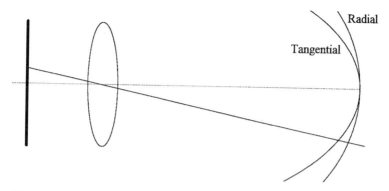

Figure 38 Astigmatism for an off-axis object point. Rays in different planes do not share a common focus.

square of field size. Undercorrected astigmatism exists when the tangential surface is to the left of the sagittal surface. Overcorrection exists when the situation is reversed. Point images in the presence of astigmatism generally exhibit circular or elliptical blur.

Field curvature results in a Petzval surface that is not a plane. This prevents imaging of point objects in focus on a planar surface. Field curvature and astigmatism are closely related and must be considered together if methods of field flattening are used for correction.

5.4 Distortion

Distortion is a radial displacement of off-axis image points, essentially a field variation in magnification. If an increase in magnification occurs as distance from field center increases, a pincushion or overcorrected distortion exists. For a decrease in magnification, barrel distortion results. Distortion is expressed either as a dimensional error or as a percentage. It varies as a third power of field size dimensionally or as the square of field size in terms of percent. The location of the aperture stop will greatly influence distortion.

5.5 Chromatic Aberration

Chromatic aberration is a change in focus with wavelength. Because the refractive index of glass materials is not constant with wavelength, the refractive properties of a lens will vary. Generally, glass dispersion is negative, meaning that refractive index decreases with wavelength. This leads to an increase in refraction for shorter wavelengths and image blurring using multiple wavelengths for imaging. Figure 39 shows a longitudinal chromatic aberration for two wave-

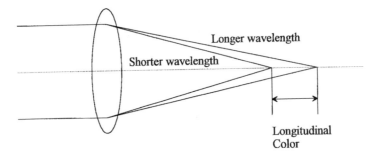

Figure 39   Chromatic aberration for an on-axis point using two wavelengths. For a positive lens, focal length is shortened with decreasing wavelength.

lengths, a measure of the separation of the two focal positions along the optical axis. For this positive lens, there is a shortening of focal length with decreasing wavelength, or undercorrected longitudinal chromatic aberration. The effects of chromatic aberration are of great concern when light is not temporally coherent.

For most primary aberrations, some degree of control is possible by sacrificing aperture or field size. Generally, these methods are not sufficient to provide adequate reduction and methods of lens element combination are utilized. Lens elements with opposite aberration sign can be combined to correct for specific aberrations. Chromatic and spherical aberration can be reduced through use of an achromatic doublet, where a positive element (biconvex) is used in contact with a negative element (negative meniscus or planoconcave). On its own, the positive element possesses undercorrected spherical as well as undercorrected chromatic aberration. The negative element on its own has both overcorrected spherical and overcorrected chromatic aberration. If the positive element is chosen to have greater power as well as lower dispersion than the negative element, positive lens power can be maintained while chromatic aberration is reduced. To address the reduction of spherical aberration with the doublet, the glass refractive index is also considered. As shorter wavelengths are considered for lens systems, the choice of suitable optical materials becomes limited. At wavelengths below 300 nm, few glass types exist and aberration correction, especially for chromatic aberration, becomes difficult.

Although aberration correction can be quite successful through balancing of several elements of varying power, shape, and optical properties, it is difficult to correct a lens over the entire aperture. A lens is corrected for rays at the edge of the lens. This results in either overcorrection or undercorrection in different zones of the lens. Figure 40, for example, is a plot of longitudinal spherical aberration (LA) as a function of field height. At the center of the field, no spherical

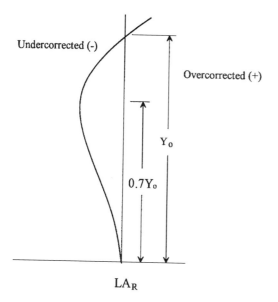

Figure 40   Spherical aberration corrected on-axis and at the edge of the field. Largest aberration (-) is at a 70% zone position.

aberration exists. This lens has been corrected so that no spherical aberration also exists at the edge of the field. Other portions of the field exhibit undercorrection while positions outside the field edge become overcorrected. The worst-case zone here is near 70%, which is common for many lens systems.

Figure 41 shows astigmatism or field curvature plotted as a function of image height. For this lens, there exists one position in the field where tangential and sagittal surfaces coincide, or astigmatism is zero. Astigmatism is overcorrected closer to the axis (relative to the Petzval surface) and it is undercorrected further out.

5.6   Wavefront Aberration Descriptions

For reasonably small levels of lens aberrations, analysis can be accomplished by considering the wave nature of light. As demonstrated for defocus, each primary aberration will produce unique deviations in the wavefront within the lens pupil. An aberrated pupil function can be described in terms of wavefront deformation as:

$$P(r,\theta) = H(r,\theta) \exp\left[i\frac{2\pi}{\lambda} W(r,\theta) \right]$$

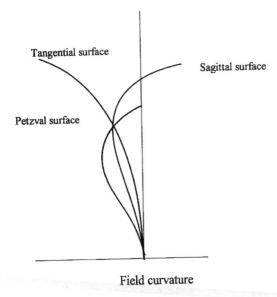

Tangential surface

Sagittal surface

Petzval surface

Field curvature

Figure 41 Astigmatism and field curvature plotted as a function of image height. One field position exists where surfaces coincide.

The pupil function is represented in polar coordinates where $W(r,\theta)$ is the wavefront aberration function and $H(r,\theta)$ is the pupil shape, generally circular. Each aberration can therefore be described in terms of the wavefront aberration function $W(r,\theta)$. Table 1 shows the mathematical description of $W(r,\theta)$ for primary aberrations, spherical, coma, astigmatism, and defocus. As an example, defocus aberration can be described in terms of wavefront deformation. Using Figure 32, the aberration of the wavefront w to the reference wavefront s is the OPD between the two. The defocus wave aberration $W(r)$ increases with aperture as [21]:

$$W(r) = \frac{n}{2}\left(\frac{1}{R_s} - \frac{1}{R_w}\right)r^2$$

where R_s and R_w are radii of two spherical surfaces. Longitudinal defocus is defined as $(R_s - R_w)$. Defocus wave aberration is proportional to the square of the aperture distance, as seen previously.

Shown in Figs. 42 through 45 are three-dimensional plots of defocus, spherical, coma, and astigmatism as wavefront OPD in the lens pupil. The plots represent differences between an ideal spherical wavefront and an aberrated wavefront. For each case, 0.25 waves of each aberration is present. Higher order aberration terms also produce unique and related shapes in the lens pupil.

Table 1 Mathematical Description for Primary
Aberrations and Values of Peak-to-Valley Aberrations

Aberration	$W(r,\theta)$	$W_{p\text{-}v}$
Defocus	Ar^2	A*
Spherical	Ar^4	A
Balanced spherical	$A(r^4-r^2)$	A/4
Coma	$Ar^3\cos\theta$	2A
Balanced coma	$A(r^3-2r/3)\cos\theta$	2A/3
Astigmatism	$Ar^2\cos^2\theta$	A
Balanced astigmatism	$(A/2)r^2\cos2\theta$	A

*The A coefficient represents the peak value of an aberration.

5.7 Zernike Polynomials

Balanced aberrations are desired to minimize the variance within a wavefront. Zernike polynomials describe balanced aberration in terms of a set of coefficients that are orthogonal over a unit circle polynomial [22]. The polynomial can be expressed in Cartesian (x,y) or polar (r,θ) terms and can be applied to

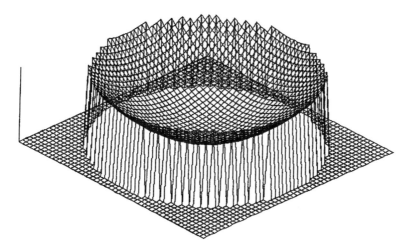

Figure 42 Defocus aberration (r^2) plotted as pupil wavefront deformation. Total OPD is 0.25λ.

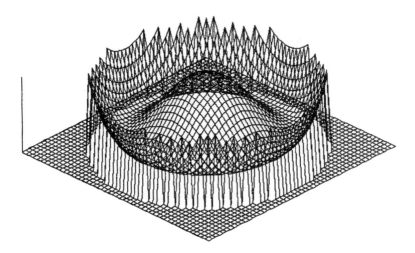

Figure 43   Primary spherical aberration (r^4).

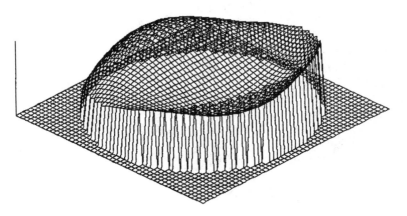

Figure 44   Primary coma aberration ($r^3 \cos\theta$).

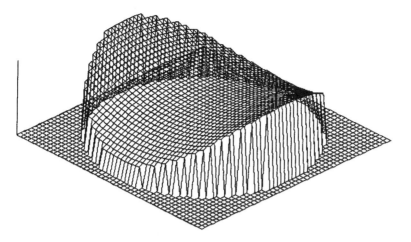

Figure 45 Primary astigmatism ($r^2\cos^2\theta$).

rotationally symmetrical or nonsymmetrical systems. Since these polynomials are orthogonal, each term individually represents a best fit to the aberration data. Generally, fringe Zernike coefficient normalization to the pupil edge is used in lens design, testing, and simulation. Other normalizations do exist, including a renormalizing to the root-mean-square (RMS) wavefront aberration The fringe Zernike coefficients are shown in Table 2, along with corresponding primary aberrations.

5.8 Aberration Tolerances

For OPD values less than a few wavelengths of light, aberration levels can be considered small. Since any amount of aberration results in image degradation, tolerance levels must be established for lens systems, dependent on application. This results in the need to consider not only specific object requirements and illumination but also resist requirements. For microlithographic application, resist and process capability will ultimately influence the allowable lens aberration level.

Conventionally, an acceptably diffraction-limited lens is one that produces no more than one quarter-wavelength ($\lambda/4$) wavefront OPD. For many nonlithographic lens systems, the reduced performance resulting from this level of aberration is allowable. To measure image quality as a result of lens aberration, the distribution of energy in an intensity point spread function (or Airy disk) can

Table 2 Fringe Zernike Polynomial Coefficients and Corresponding Aberrations*

Term	Fringe Zernike Polynomial	Aberration
1	1	Piston
2	$r \cos(\alpha)$	X Tilt
3	$r \sin(\alpha)$	Y Tilt
4	$2r^2 - 1$	Defocus
5	$r^2 \cos(2\alpha)$	3rd Order astigmatism
6	$r^2 \sin(2\alpha)$	3rd Order 45° astigmatism
7	$(3r^3 - 2r) \cos(\alpha)$	3rd Order X coma
8	$(3r^3 - 2r) \sin(\alpha)$	3rd Order Y coma
9	$(6r^4 - 6r^2) + 1$	3rd Order spherical
10	$r^3 \cos(3\alpha)$	
11	$r^3 \sin(3\alpha)$	
12	$(4r^4 - 3R^2) \cos(2\alpha)$	5th Order astigmatism
13	$(4R^4 - 3R^2) \sin(2\alpha)$	5th Order 45° astigmatism
14	$(10r^5 - 12r^3 + 3r) \cos(\alpha)$	5th Order X coma
15	$(10r^5 - 12r^3 + 3r) \sin(\alpha)$	5th Order Y coma
16	$20r^6 - 30r^4 + 12r^2 - 1$	5th Order spherical
17	$r^4 \cos(4\alpha)$	
18	$r^4 \sin(4\alpha)$	
19	$(5r^5 - 4r^3) \cos(3\alpha)$	
20	$(5r^5 - 4r^3) \sin(3\alpha)$	
21	$(15r^6 - 20r^4 + 6r^2) \cos(2\alpha)$	7th Order astigmatism
22	$(15r^6 - 20r^4 + 6r^2) \sin(2\alpha)$	7th Order 45° astigmatism
23	$(35r^7 - 60r^5 + 30r^3 - 4r) \cos(\alpha)$	7th Order X coma
24	$(35r^7 - 60r^5 + 30r^3 - 4r) \sin(\alpha)$	7th Order Y coma
25	$70r^8 - 140r^6 + 90r^4 - 20r^2 + 1$	7th Order spherical
26	$r^5 \cos(5\alpha)$	
27	$r^5 \sin(5\alpha)$	
28	$(6r^6 - 5r^4) \cos(4\alpha)$	
29	$(6r^6 - 5r^4) \sin(4\alpha)$	
30	$(21r^7 - 30r^5 + 10r^3) \cos(3\alpha)$	
31	$(21r^7 - 30r^5 + 10r^3) \sin(3\alpha)$	
32	$(56r^8 - 105r^6 + 60r^4 - 10r^2) \cos(2\alpha)$	9th Order astigmatism
33	$(56r^8 - 105r^6 + 60r^4 - 10r^2) \sin(2\alpha)$	9th Order 45° astigmatism
34	$(126r^9 - 280r^7 + 210r^5 - 60r^3 + 5r) \cos(\alpha)$	9th Order X coma
35	$(126r^9 - 280r^7 + 210r^5 - 60r^3 + 5r) \sin(\alpha)$	9th Order Y coma
36	$252r^{10} - 630r^8 + 560r^6 - 210r^4 + 30r^2 - 1$	9th Order spherical
37	$924r^{12} - 2772r^{10} + 3150r^8 - 1680r^6 + 420r^4 - 42r^2 + 1$	11th Order spherical

*Coefficients are normalized to the pupil edge.

be evaluated. The ratio of energy at the center of an aberrated point image to the energy at the center of a unaberrated point image is known as the Strehl ratio, as shown in Fig. 46. For an aberration-free lens, of course, the Strehl ratio is 1.0. For a lens with $\lambda/4$ OPD, the Strehl ratio is 0.80, nearly independent of the specific primary aberration types present. This is conventionally known as the Rayleigh $\lambda/4$ rule [23]. A general rule of thumb is that the effects on image quality are similar for identical levels of primary wavefront aberration. Table 3 shows the relationship between peak-to-valley (P-V) OPD, RMS OPD, and Strehl ratio. For low-order aberrations, RMS OPD can be related to P-V OPD by:

RMS OPD = (P-V OPD)/3.5

The Strehl ratio can be used to understand a good deal about an imaging process. The PSF is fundamental to imaging theory and can be used to calculate the diffraction image of both coherent and incoherent objects. By convolving a scaled object with the lens system PSF, the resulting incoherent image can be determined. In effect, this becomes the summation of the irradiance distribution of the image elements. Similarly, a coherent image can be determined by

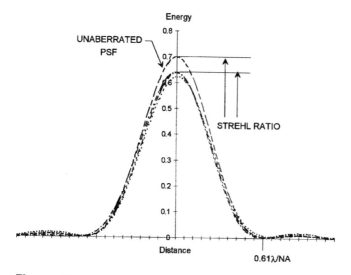

Figure 46   Strehl ratio for an aberrated point image.

Table 3 Relationship Between Peak-to-Valley OPD, RMS OPD, and Strehl Ratio

P-V OPD	RMS OPD	Strehl ratio*
0.0	0.0	1.00
0.25RL = $\lambda/16$	0.018λ	0.99
0.5RL = $\lambda/8$	0.036λ	0.95
1.0RL = $\lambda/4$	0.07λ	0.80
2.0RL = $\lambda/2$	0.14λ	0.4

*Strehl ratios below 0.8 do not provide for a good metric of image quality.

adding the complex amplitude distributions of the image elements. Figure 47 and 48 show the effects of various levels of aberration and defocus on the PSF for an otherwise ideal lens system. Fig. 47a through 47c show PSFs for spherical, coma, and astigmatism aberration at 0.15 λ OPD levels. It is seen that the aberrations produce similar levels of reduced peak intensities. Energy distribution, however, varies somewhat with aberration type. Figure 48 shows how PSFs are affected by these primary aberrations combined with defocus. For each aberration type, defocus is fixed at 0.25 λ OPD.

To extend evaluation of aberrated images for partially coherent systems, the use of the PSF (or OTF) becomes difficult. Methods of aerial image simulation can be utilized for lens performance evaluation. By incorporating lens aberration parameters into a scalar or vector diffraction model, most appropriately through use of Zernike polynomial coefficients, aerial image metrics such as as image modulation or ILS can be used. Figure 49 shows the results of a three-bar mask object imaged through an aberrated lens system at a partial coherence of 0.5. Figure 49a shows aerial images produced in the presence of 0.15 λ OPD spherical aberration with +/- 0.25 λ OPD of defocus. Figure 49b and c show resulting images with coma and astigmatism, respectively. Figure 49d shows the unabberated aerial image through the same defocus range. These aerial image plots suggest that the allowable aberration level will be influenced by resist capability, as more capable resists and processes will tolerate larger levels of aberration.

5.9 Microlithographic Requirements

It is evident from the preceding image plots that the Rayleigh $\lambda/4$ rule may not be suitable for microlithographic applications, where small changes in the aerial image can be translated into photoresist and result in substantial loss of process latitude. To establish allowable levels of aberration tolerances, photoresist requirements need to be considered along with process specifications. For

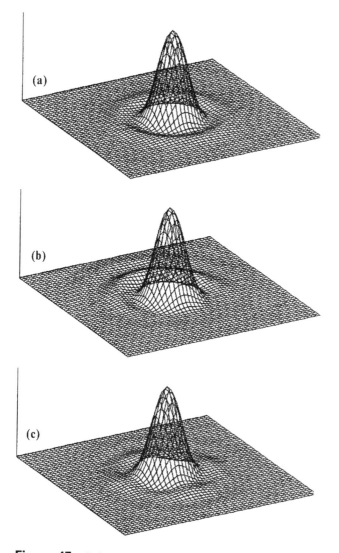

Figure 47   Point spread functions for 0.15 λ of primary (a) spherical aberration, (b) coma, and (c) astigmatism.

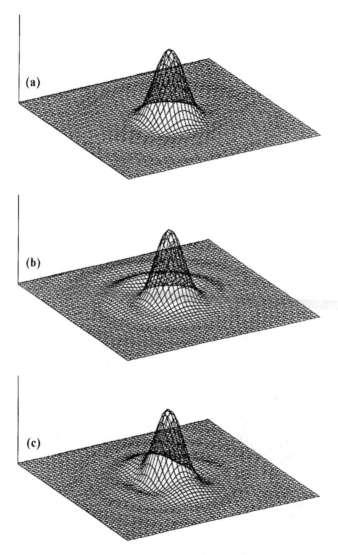

Figure 48 Point spread functions for 0.15 λ of primary aberrations combined with 0.25λ of defocus: (a) spherical aberration, (b) coma, and (c) astigmatism.

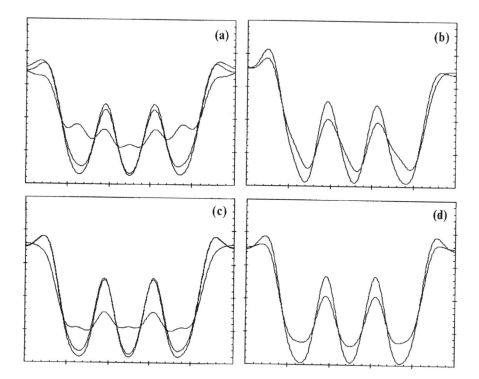

Figure 49 Aerial images for three-bar mask patterns imaged with a partial coherence of 0.5 (a) 0.15 λ OPD of spherical aberration with +/- 0.25λ OPD of defocus. Note that optimal focus is shifted positively. (b) Coma with defocus. Defocus symmetry remains but positional asymmetry is present. (c) Astigmatism with defocus. Optimal focal position is dependent on orientation. (d) Aerial images with no aberration present.

a photoresist with reasonably high contrast and reasonably low NILS requirements, a balanced aberration level of 0.05 λ OPD and a Strehl ratio of 0.91 may be acceptable [24]. As process requirements are tightened, demands on a photoresist process will be increased to maintain process latitude at this level of aberration. It is likely that as shorter wavelength technology is pursued, resist and process demands will require that aberration tolerance levels be reduced further. It is also important to realize that aberrations cannot be strictly considered to be independent as they contribute to image degradation in a lens. In reality, aberrations are balanced with one another to minimize the size of on image point in the image plane. Although asymmetric aberrations (i.e., coma, astigmatism, and lateral chromatic aberration) should be minimized for microlitho-

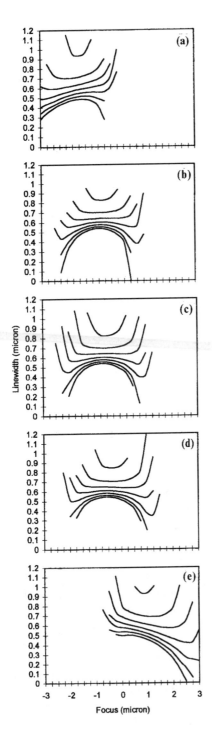

graphic lens application, this may not necessarily be the case for spherical aberration. This is because imaging is not carried out through a uniform medium toward an imaging plane but instead through several material media and within a photoresist layer. Figure 50 shows the effects of imaging in photo-resist with an aberration-free lens using a scalar diffraction model and a positive resist model [25] for simulation. These are plots of resist feature width as a function of focal position for various levels of exposure. Focal position is chosen to represent the resist top surface (zero position) as well as a range below (negative) and above (positive) the top surface. This focus exposure matrix does not behave symmetrically throughout the entire focal range. Change in feature size with exposure is not equivalent for positive and negative defocus amounts, as seen in Figure 50. Figure 50d is a focus-exposure matrix plot for positive resist and an unabberated objective lens. Figure 50a through 50e are plots for systems with various amounts of primary spherical aberration, showing how CD slope and asymmetry is impacted through focus. For positive spherical aberration, an increase in through-focus CD slope is observed while for small negative aberration, a decrease results. For this system, 0.03 λ of negative spherical aberration produces better symmetry and process latitude than with no aberration. The opposite would occur for a negative resist. It is questionable whether such techniques would be appropriate to improve imaging performance since some degree of process dedication would be required.

Generally, a lithographic process is optimized for the smallest feature detail present. Optimal focus and exposure may not coincide for larger features, however. Feature size linearity is therefore also influenced by lens aberration. Figure 51 shows a plot of resist feature size versus mask feature size for various levels of spherical aberration. Linearity is also strongly influenced by photoresist response. These influences of photoresist processes and lens aberration on lithographic performance can be understood by considering the nonlinear response of photoresist to an aerial image. Consider a perfect aerial image with modulation of 1.0 and infinite image log slope, such as that which would result from a collection of all diffraction orders. If this image is used to expose photoresist of any reasonable contrast, a resist image with near-perfect modulation could result. In reality, small feature aerial images do not have unity modulation but instead have a distribution of intensity along the *x-y* plane. Photoresist does not behave linearly to intensity, nor is it a high-contrast-threshold detector. Imaging into a resist film is therefore dependent on the distribution of the aerial image intensity and resist exposure properties. Resist image widths are

Figure 50 Focus-exposure matrix plots for imaging of 0.6 μm dense features, 365nm, 0.5NA, 0.3σ. Spherical aberration levels are (a) -0.2 λ, (b) -0.05λ, (c) -0.03 λ, (d) 0.00λ, (e) +0.20λ.

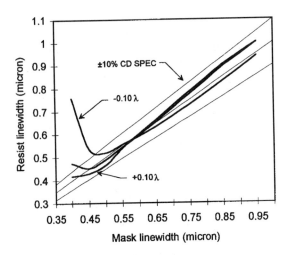

Figure 51 Resist linearity plots from 0.35 to 1.0 μm (with imaging system in Figure 50 for positive resist). Linearity is improved with the presence of positive spherical aberration.

not equal at the top and at the bottom of the resist. Some unique optimum focus and exposure exist for every feature/resist process/imaging system combination, and any system or process changes will affect features differently.

6 OPTICAL MATERIALS AND COATINGS

Several properties of optical materials must be considered in order to effectively design, optimize, and fabricate optical components. These properties include transmittance, reflectance, refractive index, surface quality, chemical and mechanical stability, and purity. Transmittance, reflectance, and absorbance are fundamental material properties that are generally determined by the glass type and structure and can be described locally using optical constants.

6.1 Optical Properties and Constants

Transmittance through an optical element will be affected by the internal absorption of the material and external reflectances at its surfaces. Both of these properties can be described for a given material thickness (*t*) through the complex refractive index:

$$\hat{n} = n(1 + ik)$$

where n is the real component of the refractive index and k is the imaginary component, also known as the extinction coefficient. These constants can be related to a material's dielectric constant (ε), permeability (μ), and conductivity (σ) for real σ and $\varepsilon\alpha\sigma$ as:

$$n^2(1-k^2) = \mu\varepsilon$$

$$n^2 k = \frac{\mu\sigma}{v}$$

Internal transmittance for a homogeneous material is dependent on material absorbance (α) by Beer's law:

$$I(t) = I(0) \exp(-\alpha t)$$

where $I(0)$ is incident intensity and $I(t)$ is transmitted intensity through the material thickness t. Transmittance becomes $I(t)/I(0)$. Transmittance cascades through an optical system through multiplication of individual element transmittance values. Absorbance as expressed by $-(1/t)$ ln(transmission) is additive through an entire system.

External reflection at optical surfaces occurs as light passes from a medium of one refractive index to a medium of another. For materials with nonzero absorption, surface reflection (from air) can be expressed as:

$$R = \left[\frac{[n(1+ik)] \cos \theta_i - n_1 \cos \theta_t}{[n(1+ik)] \cos \theta_i + n_1 \cos \theta_t} \right]$$

where n and n_1 are the medium refractive indices, θ_i is incident angle, and θ_t is transmitted angle. For normal incidence in air this becomes:

$$R = \frac{n^2(1+k^2)+1-2n}{n^2(1+k^2)+1+2n}$$

This simplifies for nonabsorbing materials to:

$$R = \frac{(n-1)^2}{(n+1)^2}$$

Since refractive index is wavelength dependent, transmission, reflection, and refraction cannot be treated as constant over any appreciable wavelength range. The real refractive index for optical materials may behave as shown in Fig. 52, where a large spectral range is plotted and areas of index discontinuity occur. These transitions represent absorption bands in a glass material, which generally occur in the UV and infrared (IR) regions. For optical systems operating in or near the visible region, refractive index is generally well be-

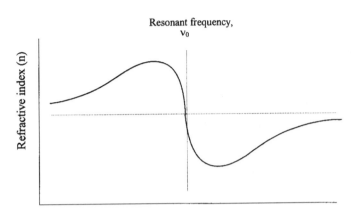

Figure 52   Frequency dependence of refractive index (n). Values approach 1.0 at high and low frequency extremes.

haved and can be described through use of dispersion equations such as a Cauchy equation [26]:

$$n = a + \frac{b}{\lambda^2} + \frac{c}{\lambda^4} + \ldots$$

where the constants a, b, and c are determined by substituting known index and wavelength values between absorption bands. For optical systems operating in the UV or IR, absorption bands may limit the application of many otherwise suitable optical materials.

6.2   Optical Materials Below 300 nm

Optical lithography below 300 nm is made difficult because of the increase in absorption in optical materials. Few transparent materials exist below 200 nm, limiting design and fabrication flexibility in optical systems. Refractive projection systems are possible at these short wavelengths but require consideration of issues concerning aberration effects and radiation damage.

The optical characteristics of glasses in the UV are important when considering photolithographic systems containing refractive elements. As wavelengths below 250 nm are utilized, issues of radiation damage and changes in glass molecular structure become additional concerns. Refraction in insulators is limited by interband absorption at the material's band gap energy, E_g. For 193-nm radiation, a photon energy of $E \sim 6.4$ eV limits optical materials to those with relatively large band gaps. Halide crystals, including CaF_2, LiF, BaF_2, MgF_2,

Table 4 Experimentally Determined Band Gaps and UV Cutoff Wavelengths for Selected Materials

Material	E_γ (eV)	$\lambda_c = hc/E_g$ (nm)
BaF_2	8.6	144
CaF_2	9.9	126
MgF_2	12.2	102
LiF	12.2	102
NaF	11.9	104
SiO_2	9.6	130

and NaF, and amorphous SiO_2 (or fused silica) are the few materials that possess large enough band gaps and have suitable transmission below 200 nm. Table 4 shows experimentally determined band gaps and UV cutoff wavelengths of several halide crystals and fused silica [27]. UV cutoff wavelength is determined as hc/E_g.

The performance of fused silica, in terms of environmental stability, purity, and manufacturability, make it a superior candidate in critical UV applications such as photolithographic lens components, beam delivery systems, and photomasks. Although limiting the number of available materials to fused silica does introduce optical design constraints (for correction of aberrations including chromatic), the additional use of materials such as CaF_2 and LiF does not provide a large increase in design flexibility because of the limited additional refractive index range (n_i at 193 nm for CaF_2 is 1.492, for LiF is 1.521, and fused silica is 1.561 [28]). Energetic particles (such as electrons and x-rays) and short-wavelength photons have been shown to alter the optical properties of fused silica [29]. Furthermore, because of the high peak power of pulsed lasers, optical damage through rearrangement is possible with excimer lasers operating at wavelengths of 248 and 193 nm [30]. Optical absorption and luminescence can be caused by a lack of stoichiometry in the fused silica molecular matrix. Changes in structure can come about through absorption of radiation and energy transfer processes. E' color centers in type III fused silica (wet fused silica synthesized directly by flame hydrolysis of silicon tetrachloride in a hydrogen-oxygen flame [31]) have been shown to exist at 2.7 eV (458 nm), 4.8 eV (260 nm), and 5.8 eV (210 nm) [32].

7 OPTICAL IMAGE ENHANCEMENT TECHNIQUES

7.1 Off-Axis Illumination

Optimization of the partial coherence of an imaging system has been introduced for circular illuminator apertures. By controlling the distribution of diffraction information in the objective lens, maximum image modulation can be obtained. An illumination system can be further refined by considering illumination apertures that are not necessarily circular. Shown in Fig. 53 is a coherently illuminated mask grating imaged through an objective lens. Here, the ± 1 diffraction orders are distributed symmetrically around the zeroth order. As seen earlier in Fig. 33, when defocus is introduced, an OPD between the zeroth and the ± first orders results. The acceptable depth of focus is dependent on the extent of the OPD and the resulting phase error introduced. Figure 54 shows a system in which illumination is obliquely incident on the mask at an angle so that the zeroth and first diffraction orders are distributed on alternate sides of the optical axis. Using reasoning similar to that used for incoherent illumination, it can be shown that the minimum k factor for this oblique condition of partially coherent illumination is 0.25. The illumination angle is chosen uniquely for a given wavelength, NA, and feature size and can be calculated for dense features as $\sin^{-1}(0.5\lambda/d)$ for NA = $0.5\lambda/d$, where d is the feature pitch. The most significant impact of off-axis illumination is realized when considering focal depth. In this case, the zeroth and first diffraction orders now travel an identical path length regardless of the defocus amount. The consequence is a depth of focus that is effectively infinite.

In practice, limiting illumination to allow for one narrow beam or pair of beams leads to zero intensity. Also, imaging is limited to features oriented along one direction in an x-y plane. To overcome this, an annular or ring aperture can be employed that delivers illumination at angles needed with a finite ring width to allow some finite intensity as shown in Fig. 55a. The resulting focal depth is less than

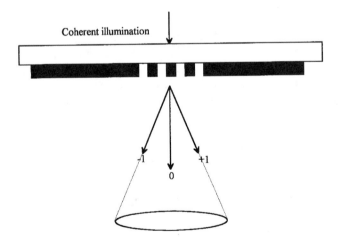

Figure 53 Coherently illuminated mask grating and objective lens. Only 0 and ± 1st diffraction orders are collected.

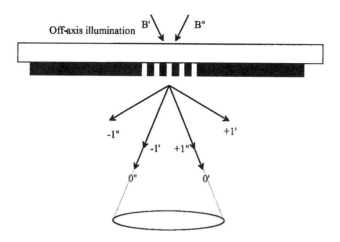

Figure 54   Oblique or off-axis illumination of a mask grating where 0 and 1st diffraction orders coincide in lens pupil.

that for the ideal case but an improvement over a full circular aperture can be achieved. For most integrated circuit applications, features are limited to horizontal and vertical orientation and quadrupole configurations may be more suitable. For the quadrupole configuration shown in Fig. 55b, two beams are optimally off axis for one feature direction while two beams are optimal for the orthogonal orientation. There is an offsetting effect between the two sets of poles for both feature directions. A better configuration is depicted in Fig. 55c, where poles are at diagonal positions oriented 45° to horizontal and vertical mask features. Here, each beam is off axis to all mask features and minimal image degradation occurs.

Either the annular or quadrupole off-axis system would need to be optimized for a specific feature size and would provide nonoptimal illumination for all others. Consider, for instance, features that are larger than those optimal for a given illumination angle. Only at angles corresponding to $\sin^{-1}(0.5\lambda/d)$ do mask frequency components coincide. With smaller features, higher frequency components do not overlap and additional spatial frequency artifacts are introduced. This can lead to a possible degradation of imaging performance. For the optimal quadrupole situation, with poles oriented at diagonal positions, resolution to $0.25\lambda/\mathrm{NA}$ is not possible, as it is with the two-pole or the horizontal/verticle quadrupole. As shown in Figure 56, the minimum resolution becomes $\lambda/(2\sqrt{2}\,\mathrm{NA})$.

Analysis of OAI

To evaluate the impact of off-axis illumination on image improvement, consider the electric field for a binary grating mask illuminated by two discrete beams

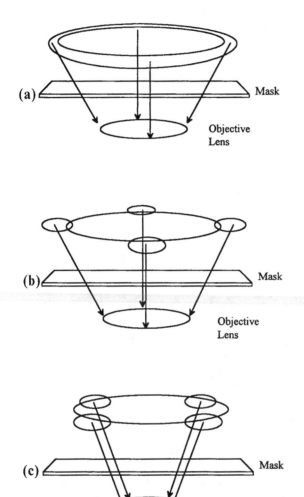

Figure 55 Off-axis illumination schemes for projection imaging (a) annular (b) quadrupole with horizontal and vertical poles, and (c) quadrupole with diagonal poles.

as shown in Fig. 54. The normalized amplitude or electric field distribution can be represented as:

$$A(x) = 0.25\left[2\ \cos\ \theta + \cos\left(\frac{2\pi x}{\lambda} + \theta\right) + \cos\left(\frac{2\pi x}{\lambda} - \theta\right)\right]$$

which can be derived by multiplying the electric field of a coherently illuminated mask by $e^{i\theta}$ and $e^{-i\theta}$ and summing. The resulting aerial image takes the form:

$$I(x)\ \propto\ |E(x)|^2 = \frac{1}{32}\left[6 + 8\ \cos\frac{2\pi x}{\lambda} + 2\ \cos\frac{4\pi x}{\lambda} + 6\ \cos(2\theta) + 4\left(\frac{2\pi x}{\lambda} + 2\theta\right)\right.$$

$$\left. + 4\ \cos\left(\frac{2\pi x}{\lambda} - 2\theta\right) + \cos\ 2\left(\frac{2\pi x}{\lambda} + \theta\right) + \cos\ 2\left(\frac{2\pi x}{\lambda} - \theta\right)\right]$$

The added frequency terms present can lead to improper image reconstruction compared to that for an aerial image resulting from simple coherent illumination:

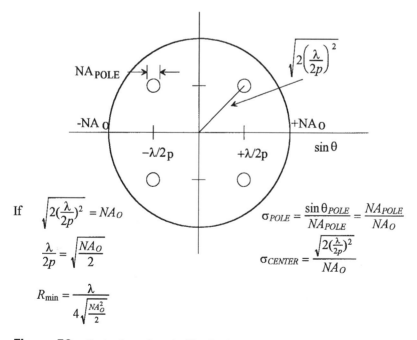

Figure 56 Optimal quadrupole illumination with diagonal poles. Pole size and position can be specified in relative sigma values, σ_{pole} and σ_{center}. Minimum resolution (R_{min}) is also derived.

$$E(x) = \frac{1}{2}\left(1 + \cos\frac{2\pi x}{\lambda}\right)$$

$$I(x) = \frac{1}{8}\left(3 + 4\cos\frac{2\pi x}{\lambda} + \cos\frac{4\pi x}{\lambda}\right)$$

The improvement in the aerial image for two-beam illumination is seen when using a lens with NA $< \lambda/p$. With two-beam illumination, high-frequency artifact terms are not passed by the lens but information beyond the zeroth order is acted upon, expressed:

$$I(x) = \frac{1}{32}\left[5 + 4\ \cos\frac{2\pi x}{\lambda} + 4\ \cos(2\theta) + 4\ \cos\left(\frac{2\pi x}{\lambda} - 2\theta\right) + \cos\ 2\left(\frac{2\pi x}{\lambda} - \theta\right)\right]$$

At the optimum illumination angle, spatial frequency vectors are symmetrical about the optical axis and the aerial image simplifies to:

$$I(x) = \frac{9}{32}\left[1 + \cos\frac{2\pi x}{\lambda}\right]$$

There are no higher "harmonic" frequencies present in the aerial image produced with off-axis illumination. This becomes evident by comparing three-beam interference (0, ± 1st orders) with two-beam interference (0 and 1st orders only). Under coherent illumination, three-beam interference results in a cosine biased by the amplitude of the zeroth order. The amplitude of the zeroth-order bias is less than the amplitude of the first-order cosine, resulting in sidelobes at twice the spatial frequency of the mask features, which is seen in Fig. 20. With off-axis illumination and two-beam interference, the electric field is represented by an unbiased cosine, resulting in a frequency-doubled resolution and no higher frequency effects.

Isolated Line Performance

By considering grating features, optical analysis of off-axis and conventional illumination can be quite straightforward. When considering isolated features, however, discrete diffraction orders do not exist but instead a continuous diffraction pattern is produced. Convolving such a frequency representation with either illumination poles or an annular ring will result in diffraction information distributed over a range of angles. An optimal angle of illumination that will place low-frequency information out at the full numerical aperture of the objective lens will distribute most energy at nonoptimal angles. Isolated line performance is therefore, minimally enhanced by off-axis illumination. Any improvement is reduced significantly also as the pole or ring width is increased. When both dense and isolated features are considered together in a field, it follows that the dense to isolated feature size bias or proximity effect will be affected by off-axis illumination [33]. Figure 57 shows, for instance, the decrease in image CD bias between dense and isolated 0.35-μm features for increasing levels of annular illumination using a 0.55 NA i-line exposure system. As obscuration in the condenser lens pupil is increased (resulting in annular illumination of decreasing ring width), dense to isolated feature size bias decreases. As features approach $0.25\lambda/NA$, however, larger amounts of energy go uncollected by the lens, which may lead to an increase in this bias as seen in Fig. 58.

Off-axis illumination schemes have been proposed by which the modulation of nonperiodic features could be improved [34]. Resolution improvement for off-axis illumination requires multiple mask pattern openings for interference, leading to discrete diffraction orders. Small auxiliary patterns can be added close too an isolated feature to allow the required interference effects. By adding features below the resolution cutoff of an imaging system ($0.2\lambda/NA$ for example), and placing them at optimal distances so that their sidelobes coincide with main feature main lobs ($0.7\lambda/NA$ for instance), peak amplitude and image log slope can be improved [35]. Higher order lobes of isolated feature diffraction patterns can be further enhanced by adding additional $0.2\lambda/NA$ spaces at corresponding distances [36]. Various arrangements are possible, as shown in Fig. 59. Shown here are arrangements for opaque line space patterns, an isolated opaque line, clear line space patterns, and an isolated clear space. The

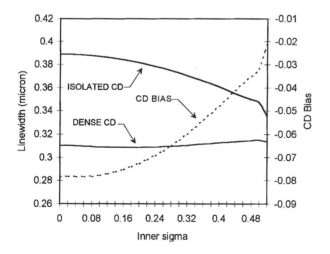

Figure 57 Image CD bias vs. annular illumination. Inner sigma values correspond to the amount of obscuration in the condenser lens pupil. Partial coherence σ (outer) is 0.52 for 0.35 μm features using 365 nm illumination and 0.55NA. Defocus is 0.5 μm. As central obscuration is increased, image CD bias increases.

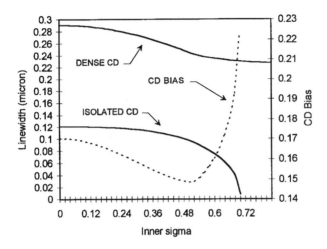

Figure 58   Similar conditions as Figure 57 for 0.22 μm features. Image CD bias is now reversed with increasing inner sigma.

image enhancement offered by using these techniques is realized as focal depth is considered. Figures 60 through 62 show the DOF improvement for a five-bar space pattern through focus. Figure 60 shows aerial images through λ/NA^2 (± 0.74 μm) of defocus for $0.5\lambda/NA$ features using conventional illumination with σ = 0.5. Figure 61 gives results using quadrupole illumination. Figure 62 shows aerial images through focus for the same feature width with auxiliary

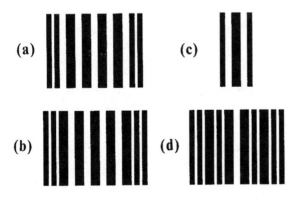

Figure 59   Arrangement for additional auxiliary patterns to improve isolated line and CD bias performance using OAI. (a) opaque dense features, (b) clear dense features, (c) opaque isolated features, and (d) clear isolated features.

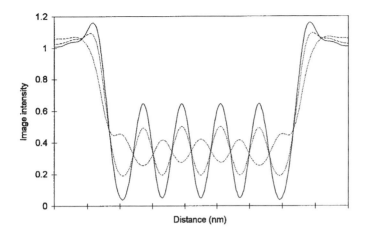

Figure 60 Aerial image intensity for 0.37 μm features through +/- 0.5λ/NA² of defocus using σ = 0.5, 365 nm, and 0.5NA.

patterns smaller than 0.2λ/NA and off-axis illumination. An improvement in DOF is apparent with minimal intensity in the dark field. Additional patterns would be required to increase peak intensity, which may be improved by as much as 20%.

Another modification of off-axis illumination has been introduced that modifies the illumination beam profile [37]. This modified beam illumination tech-

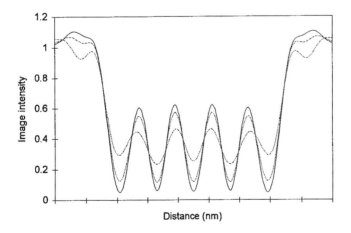

Figure 61 Aerial images as in Figure 60 using OAI.

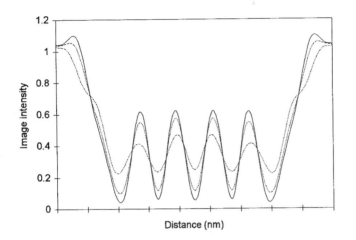

Figure 62   Aerial images for features with 0.08 λ/NA auxiliary patterns and OAI. Note the improvement in minimum intensity of outermost features at greatest defocus.

nique fills the condenser lens pupil with weak quadrupoles, where energy is distributed within and between poles, as seen in Fig. 63. This has been demonstrated to allow better control of DOF and proximity effects for a variety of feature types.

7.2   Phase Shift Masking

Up to this point, control of the amplitude of a mask function has been considered and phase information has been assumed to be nonvarying. It has already been shown that the spatial coherence or phase relation of light is responsible for interference and diffraction effects. It would follow, therefore, that control of phase information at the mask may allow additional manipulation of imaging performance. Consider the situation in Fig. 64, where two rectangular grating masks are illuminated with coherent illumination. The conventional "binary" mask in Fig. 64a produces an electric field which varies from 0 to 1 as a transition is made from opaque to transparent regions. The minimum numerical aperture that can be utilized for this situation is one that captures the zero and ± first diffraction orders or NA≥λ/p. The lens acts on this information to produce a cosinusoidal amplitude image appropriately biased by the zeroth diffraction order. The aerial image is proportional to the square of the amplitude image. Now consider Fig. 64b, where a π "phase shifter" is added (or subtracted) at alternating mask openings which creates an electric field at the mask varying from −1 to +1, where a negative amplitude represents a π phase shift

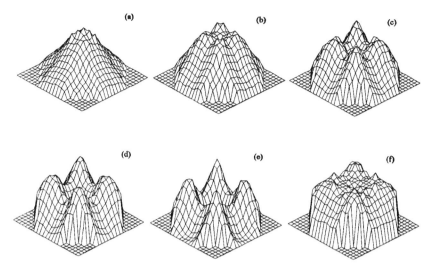

Figure 63 Modified illumination profiles for conventional and OAI. (Reproduced with permission from Ogawa et al., 1994.)

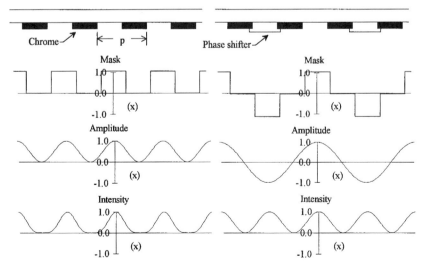

Figure 64 Schematic of (a), a conventional binary mask (b) an alternating phase shift mask. The mask electric field, image amplitude, and image intensity is shown for each.

(a $\pi/2$ phase shift would be 90° out of the paper, $3\pi/2$ would be 90° into the paper, and so forth). Analysis of this situation can be simplified if the phase shift mask function is decomposed into separate functions, one for each state of phase where $m(x) = m_1(x) + m_2(x)$. The first function, $m_1(x)$, can be described as a rectangular wave with a pitch equal to four times the space width:

$$m_1(x) = \text{rect}\left(\frac{x}{p/2}\right) * \text{comb}\left(\frac{x}{2p}\right)$$

The second mask function, $m_2(x)$, can be described as:

$$m_2(x) = \left[\text{rect}\left(\frac{x}{3p/2}\right) * \text{comb}\left(\frac{x}{2p}\right)\right] - 1$$

The spatial frequency distribution becomes:

$$M(u) = \mathcal{F}\{m(x)\} = \mathcal{F}\{m_1(x)\} + \mathcal{F}\{m_2(x)\}$$

which is shown in Fig. 65. It is immediately noticed that the zero term is removed through the subtraction of the centered impulse function, $\delta(x)$. Also, the distribution of the diffraction orders has been defined by a comb(u) function with one

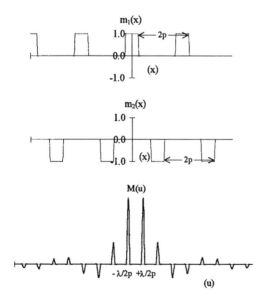

Figure 65   Spatial frequency distribution m(u) resulting from coherent illumination of an alternating phase shift mask, as decomposed into m$_1$(x) and m$_2$(x).

half the frequency required for a conventional binary mask. The minimum lens NA required is that which captures the ± first diffraction orders, or $\lambda/2p$. The resulting image amplitude pupil filtered and distributed to the wafer is an unbiased cosine with a frequency of one half the mask pitch. When the image intensity is considered ($I(x) = |A(x)|^2$), the result is a squared cosine with the original mask pitch. Intensity minimum points are ensured as the amplitude function passes through zero. This "forced zero" results in minimum intensity transfer into photoresist, a situation that will not occur for the binary case as shown.

For coherent illumination, a lens acting on this diffracted information has a 50% decrease in the numerical aperture required to capture these primary orders. Alternatively, for a given lens numerical aperture, a mask that utilizes such alternating aperture phase shifters can produce a resolution twice that possible using a conventional binary mask. Next, consider image degradation through defocus or other aberrations. For the conventional case, the resulting intensity image becomes an average of cosines with decreased modulation. The ability to maintain a minimum intensity becomes more difficult as the aberration level is increased. For the phase-shifted mask case, the minimum intensity remains exactly zero, increasing the likelihood that photoresist can reproduce a usable image.

For the phase-shifted mask, since features one half the size can be resolved, the minimum resolution can be expressed as:

$$R = 0.25\lambda / NA$$

As the partial coherence factor is increased from zero, the impact of this phase shift technique is diminished to a point at which for incoherent illumination no improvement is realized for phase shifting over the binary mask. To evaluate the improvement of phase shift masking over conventional binary masking, we can consider the electric field at the wafer, neglecting higher order terms:

$$E(x) = \cos\left(\frac{\pi x}{\lambda}\right)$$

The intensity in the aerial image is approximated by:

$$I(x) = \frac{1}{2}\left[1 + \cos\frac{2\pi x}{\lambda}\right]$$

which is comparable to that for off-axis illumination. In reality, higher order terms will affect DOF. Phase shift masking may, therefore, result in a lower DOF than for fully optimized off-axis illumination.

The technique of phase shifting alternating features on a mask is appropriately called alternating phase shift masking. Phase information is modified by either adding or subtracting "optical" material from the mask substrate at a thickness that corresponds to a π phase shift [38,39]. Figure 66 shows two wave

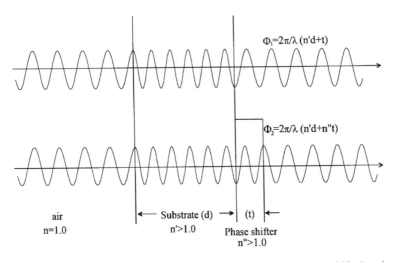

$$\Phi_1 = 2\pi/\lambda \,(\mathrm{n'd+t})$$

$$\Phi_2 = 2\pi/\lambda \,(\mathrm{n'd+n''t})$$

air
n=1.0

← Substrate (d) → (t) ←
n'>1.0   Phase shifter
                 n''>1.0

Figure 66 Diagram of wavetrain propagation through phase shifted and unshifted positions of a mask.

trains traveling through a transparent refracting medium (a glass plate), both in phase on entering the material. The wavelength of light as it enters the medium from air is compressed by a factor proportional to the refractive index at that wavelength. Upon exiting the glass plate into air, the initial wavelength of the wavefronts is restored. If one wave train travels a greater path length than the other, a shift in phase between the two will result. By controlling the relationship between the respective optical path distances traveled over the area of some refracting medium with refractive index n_i, a phase shift can be produced as follows:

$$\Delta\phi = \frac{2\pi}{\lambda}(n_i - 1)t$$

where t is the shifter thickness. The required shifter thicknesses for a π phase shift at 365, 248, and 193 nm wavelengths in fused silica are 3720, 2470, and 1850 Å, respectively. At shorter wavelengths less phase shift material thickness is required. Depending on the mask fabrication technique, this may limit the manufacturability of these types of phase shift masks for short UV wavelength exposures. Generally, a phase shift can be produced by using either thin-film deposition and delineation or direct glass etch methods. Both techniques can introduce process control problems. In order to control phase shifting to within ±5°, a reasonable requirement for low-*k*-factor lithography, i-line phase shifter thickness must be held to within 100 Å in fused silica. For 193-nm lithography, this becomes 50 Å If etching techniques cannot operate within this tolerance level over large mask substrates (in a situation in which an etch stop layer is not present), the application of etched glass phase shift masks for IC production may be limited to longer wavelengths. There also exists a trade-off between phase errors allowed through fabrication techniques and through increasing partial coherence. As partial coherence is increased above zero, higher demands are placed on phase shifter etch control. If etch control ultimately places a limitation on maximum partial coherence allowed, the issue of exposure throughput becomes a concern.

Variations in the alternating phase shift mask have been developed to allow for application to nonrepetitive structures [40]. Figure 67 shows several approaches in which phase-shifting structures are applied at or near the edge of isolated features. These "rim" phase-shifting techniques do not offer the doubling resolution improvement of the alternating approach but does produce a similar forced zero in intensity at the wafer due to a phase transition at feature edges. The advantage of these types of schemes is their ability to be applied to arbitrary feature types. As with the alternating phase shift mask, these rim masks require film deposition and patterning or glass etch processing and may be difficult to fabricate for short UV wavelength applications. In addition, pattern placement

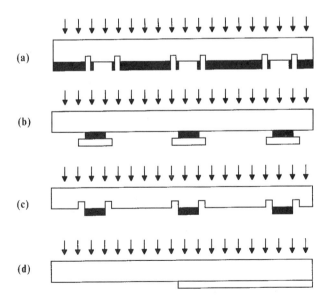

Figure 67 Various phase shift mask schemes (a) etch outriggers, (b) additive rim shifters, (c) etched rim shifters, and (d) chromeless phase shift mask.

accuracy of these features that are sub-0.25 *k* factor in size is increasingly challenging as wavelength decreases.

Other phase shift mask techniques make use of a phase-only transition and destructive interference at edges [41]. A "chromeless" phase edge technique, as shown also in Fig. 67, requires a single mask patterning step and produces intensity minimums at the wafer mask plane at each mask phase transition. When used with a sufficiently optimized resist process, this can result in resolution well beyond the Rayleigh limit. Resist features as small as *k* = 0.20 have been demonstrated with this technique, which introduces opportunities for application especially for critical isolated feature levels. An anomaly of using such structures is the addition of phase transitions at every shifter edge. To eliminate resulting intensity dips produced at these edges, multiple-level masks have been used [42]. After exposure with the chromeless phase edge mask, a binary chrome mask can be utilized to eliminate undesired field artifacts. An alternative way to reduce these unwanted phase edge effects is to engineer into the mask additional phase levels, such as 60° and 120° [43]. To achieve such a phase combination, two phase etch process steps are required during mask fabrication. This may ultimately limit application. Variations on these phase-shifting schemes include a shifter-shutter structure, which allows control over feature width and reduces field artifacts, and a clear field approach using sub-Rayleigh limit grating or checkerboard structures [36].

Each of these phase shift masking approaches requires some level of added mask and process complexity. In addition, none of these techniques can be used universally for all feature sizes, shapes, or parity. An approach that can minimize mask design and fabrication complexity may gain the greatest acceptance for application to manufacturing. An attenuated phase shift mask (APSM) may be such an approach, where conventional opaque areas on a binary mask are replaced with partially transmitting regions (5–15%) that produce a π phase shift with respect to clear regions. This is a phase shift mask approach that has evolved out of x-ray masking, where attenuators inherently possess some degree of transparency [44]. As shown in Fig. 68, such a mask will produce a mask electric field that varies from 1 to 0.1 in amplitude (for a 10% transmitting attenuator) with a shift in phase, represented by a transition from a positive electric field component to a negative. The electric field at the wafer possesses a loss of modulation but retains the phase change and transition through zero. Squaring the electric field results in an intensity with a zero minimum.

Recent work in areas of attenuated phase shift masking has demonstrated both resolution and focal depth improvement for a variety of feature types. Attenuated phase shift mask efforts at 365, 248, and 193 nm have shown a near doubling of focal depth for features on the order of *k* = 0.5 [45,46]. As such technologies are considered for IC mask fabrication, practical materials that can satisfy both the 180° phase shift and the required transmittance at wavelengths

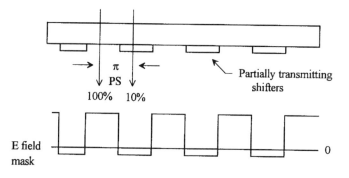

Figure 68 A 10% attenuated phase shift mask. A π phase shift and 10% transmission is achieved in attenuated regions. The zero mask electric field ensures minimum aerial image intensity.

to 193 nm need to be investigated. A single-layer APSM material is most attractive from the standpoint of process complexity, uniformity, and control. The optimum degree of transmission of the attenuator can be determined through experimental or simulation techniques. A maximum image modulation or image log slope is desired while maintaining a minimum printability level of "side-lobes" formed from intensity within shadowed regions. Depending on feature type and size and resist processes, APSM transmission values between 4 and 15% may be appropriate. In addition to meeting optical requirements to allow appropriate phase shift and transmission properties, an APSM material must be able to be patterned using plasma etch techniques, have high etch selectivity to fused silica, be chemically stable, have high absorbance at alignment wavelengths, and not degrade with exposure. These requirements may ultimately limit the number of possible candidates for practical mask application.

Phase shifting in a transparent material is dependent on a film's thickness, real refractive index, and the wavelength of radiation as seen earlier. To achieve a phase shift of 180°, the required film thickness becomes:

$$t = \frac{\lambda}{2(n-1)}$$

The requirements of an APSM material demand that films are absorbing, i.e., that they possess a nonzero extinction coefficient (k). This introduces additional phase-shifting contributions from film interfaces that can be determined by:

$$\Phi = \arg\left(\frac{2n_2^*}{n_1^* + n_2^*}\right)$$

where n_1^* is the complex refractive index $(n + k)$ of the first medium and n_2^* is the complex refractive index of the second [47]. These additional phase terms are nonnegligible as k increases, as shown in Fig. 69. In order to determine the total phase shift resulting from an absorbing thin film, materials and interface contributions need to be accounted for.

To deliver both phase shift and transmission requirements, film absorption (α) or extinction coefficient (k) are considered:

$$\alpha = \frac{4\pi k}{\lambda}$$

where α is related to transmission as $T = e^{-\alpha t}$. In addition, mask reflectivity below 15% is desirable, which can be related to n and k through the Fresnel equation for normal incidence:

$$R = \frac{(n-1)^2 + k^2}{(n+1)^2 + k^2}$$

In order to meet all optical requirements, a narrow range of material optical constants is suitable at a given exposing wavelength. Both chromium oxydinitride– and molybdenum silicon oxynitride–based materials have been used as APSM materials at 365 nm. For shorter wavelength applications, these materials become too opaque. Alternative materials have been introduced that, through modification of material composition or structure, can be tailored for optical performance at wavelengths from 190 to 250 nm [48]. These materials include

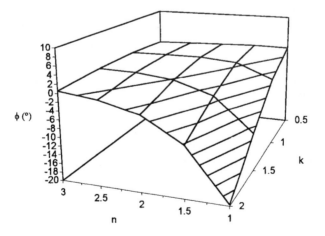

Figure 69   Additional phase terms resulting at interfaces, as a function of n and k.

understoichiometric silicon nitride, aluminum-rich aluminum nitride, and other metal oxides, nitrides, and silicides. The usefulness of these materials in production may ultimately be determined by their ability to withstand short wavelength exposure radiation. In general, understoichiometric films possess some degree of instability, which may result in optical changes during exposure.

7.3 Mask Optimization, Biasing, and Optical Proximity Compensation

When considering one-dimensional imaging, features can often be described through use of fundamental diffraction orders. Higher order information lost through pupil filtering leads to less "square-wave" image reconstruction and a loss of aerial image integrity. With a high-contrast resist, such a degraded aerial image can be used to reconstruct a near-square-wave relief image. When considering two-dimensional imaging, the situation becomes more complex. Whereas mask to image width bias for a simplified one-dimensional case can be controlled via exposure/process or physical mask feature size manipulation, for two-dimensional imaging there are high-frequency interactions that need to be considered. Loss or redistribution of high-frequency information results in such things as corner or contact rounding, which may influence device performance.

Other problems encountered when considering complex mask patterns are the fundamental differences between imaging isolated lines, isolated spaces, contacts, and dense features. The reasons for these differences are manyfold. First, a partially coherent system is not linear in either amplitude or intensity. As we have seen, only an incoherent system is linear in intensity and only a coherent system is linear in amplitude. It should not be expected, therefore, that an isolated line and an isolated space feature are complementary. In addition, photoresist is a nonlinear detector, responding differently to the thresholds introduced by these two feature types. This reasoning can be extended to the concept of mask biasing. At first guess, we may reason that a small change in the size of a mask feature would result in a near-equivalent change in resist feature width, or at least aerial image width. Neither is possible because, in addition to nonlinearity of the imaging system, biasing is not a linear operation.

Differences in image features of various types are also attributed to the fundamental frequency representation of dense versus isolated features. Dense features can be suitably represented by discrete diffraction orders using coherent illumination. Orders are distributed with some width for incoherent and partially incoherent illumination. Isolated features, on the other hand, can be represented as some fraction of a sinc function for coherent illumination, distributed across the frequency plane for incoherent and partially coherent illumination. In terms of frequency information, these functions are very different. Figure 70 shows the impact of partial coherence on dense to isolated feature bias for $0.6\lambda/NA$

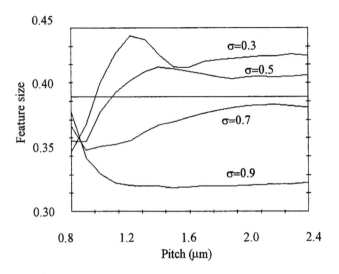

Figure 70   The variation in dense to isolated feature bias with partial coherence. For low σ values, dense features (2× pitch) print smaller than isolated features (6× pitch). For high σ values, the situation is reversed (365 nm, 0.5NA, 0.4 μm lines, positive resist).

features. Dense lines (equal lines and spaces) print smaller than isolated lines for low values of partial coherence. At high partial coherence values, the situation is reversed. There also exists some optimum where the dense to isolated feature bias is near zero. Variations in exposure, focus, aberrations, and resist process will also have effects.

Through characterization of the optical and chemical processes involved in resist patterning, image degradation can be predicted. If the degradation process is understood, small feature biases can be introduced to account for losses. This predistortion technique is often referred to as optical proximity compensation (OPC), which is not a true correction in that lost diffraction detail is not accounted for. Mask biasing for simple shapes can be accomplished with an iterative approach but complex geometry or large fields probably require rule-based computation schemes [49]. Generally, several adequate solutions are possible. Those that introduce the least process complexity are chosen for implementation. Figure 71a shows a simple two-dimensional mask pattern and the resulting simulated resist image for a $k_1 = 0.5$ process. Feature rounding is evident at both inside and outside corners. The image degradation can be quantified by several means. Possible approaches may be to measure linear deviation, area deviation, or radius deviation. Figure 71b shows a biased ver-

(a)

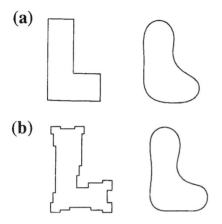

(b)

Figure 71 Simple two-dimensional mask patterns (a) without OPC and the resulting resist image (b) with OPD and the resulting resist image.

sion of the same simple pattern and resulting simulated aerial image. Comparisons of the two images show the improvement realized with such correction schemes. The advantage of these techniques is the relatively low cost of implementation

7.4 Dummy Diffraction Mask

A technique of illumination control at the mask level is possible that offers resolution improvement similar to that for off-axis illumination [50] Here, two separate masks are used. In addition to a conventional binary mask, a second diffraction mask composed of line space or checkerboard phase patterns is created with 180° phase shifting between patterns. Coherent light incident on the diffraction mask is diffracted by the phase grating as shown in Fig. 72. When the phase grating period is chosen so that the angle of diffraction is $\sin^{-1}(\lambda/p)$ the first diffraction orders from the phase mask will deliver illumination at an optimum off-axis angle to the binary mask. There is no energy in the phase diffraction pattern on axis (no DC term) and higher orders have less energy than the first. For a line/space phase grating mask, illumination is delivered to the binary mask as with off-axis two-pole illumination. For a checkerboard phase grating mask, a situation similar to quadrupole illumination results.

A basic requirement for such an approach is that the phase mask and the binary mask are sufficiently far apart to allow far-field diffraction effects from the

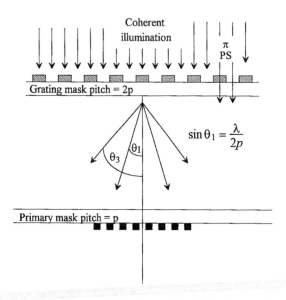

Figure 72   Schematic of a grating diffraction mask used to produce off-axis illumination for primary mask imaging.

phase mask to dominate. This distance is maximized for coherent illumination, on the order of $2p/\lambda$ where $2p$ is the phase mask grating period. As partial coherence is increased, a collection of illumination angles exists. This will decrease image contrast as well as maximum intensity and decrease the required mask separation distance. The tolerance to phase error has been shown to be greater that ±10%. Angular misregistration of 10° may also be tolerable. Resolution capability for coherent illumination is identical to that for alternating phase shift masking and off-axis illumination. This approach is, however, limited to periodic mask features.

7.5   Polarized Masks

We have so far considered the amplitude and phase components of light for design of lithographic masks. Light also possesses polarization characteristics that can be utilized to influence imaging performance [51]. Consider Figs. 19 and 24, where zero and ± first diffraction orders are collected for an equal lines/space object. Here the zeroth-order amplitude is $A/2$ and the ± first-order amplitudes are A/π. For a transverse electric (TE) state of linear polarization, these orders can be represented in terms of complex exponentials as:

zeroth order : $A/2 \begin{pmatrix} 0 \\ 1 \\ 0 \end{pmatrix} \exp[i2\pi/\lambda(0x+0y+1z)]$

+ first order : $A/\pi \begin{pmatrix} 0 \\ 1 \\ 0 \end{pmatrix} \exp[i2\pi/\lambda(ax+0y+cz)]$

−first order : $A/\pi \begin{pmatrix} 0 \\ 1 \\ 0 \end{pmatrix} \exp[i2\pi/\lambda(-ax+0y+cz)]$

For transverse magnetic (TM) polarization, these orders become:

zeroth order : $A/2 \begin{pmatrix} 1 \\ 0 \\ 0 \end{pmatrix} \exp[i2\pi/\lambda(0x+0y+1z)]$

+ first order : $A/\pi \begin{pmatrix} c \\ 0 \\ -a \end{pmatrix} \exp[i2\pi/\lambda(ax+0y+cz)]$

−first order : $A/\pi \begin{pmatrix} c \\ 0 \\ a \end{pmatrix} \exp[i2\pi/\lambda(-ax+0y+cz)]$

As shown previously, the sum of these terms produces the electric field at the wafer plane. The aerial images at the wafer plane for TE and TM polarization become:

$$I_{TE}(x) = \frac{A}{\pi} + \frac{4A}{\pi} \cos^2\left(\frac{2\pi ax}{\lambda}\right) + \frac{2A}{\pi} \cos\left(\frac{2\pi ax}{\lambda}\right)$$

$$I_{TM}(x) = \frac{A}{\pi} + \frac{4A}{\pi^2} \left[a^2 + (c^2 - a^2) \cos^2\left(\frac{2\pi ax}{\lambda}\right)\right] + \frac{2c}{\pi} \cos\left(\frac{2\pi ax}{\lambda}\right)$$

The normalized image log slope (NILS = ILS × line width) for each aerial image becomes:

$$NILS_{TE} = 8$$

$$NILS_{TM} = 8\frac{\sqrt{(1-a^2)}}{1+(16a^2/\pi^2)}$$

The second term in the $NILS_{TM}$ equation is less than one, resulting in a lower resolution value for TM polarization as compared to TE polarization. There can therefore be some benefit to using TE polarization over TM polarization or non-polarized light. Conventionally, polarized light has not been used for optical lithographic systems but recent advances in catadioptric systems do require polarization control. For any system, it would be difficult to illuminate all critical features with TE-only polarization through source control, since feature orientation would be limited to one direction only. The concept of polarization modulation built into a mask itself has been introduced as a potential step for mask modification. This would require the development of new, probably single crystalline, materials and processes. A polarized mask has been proposed as a means of accomplishing optimization of various feature orientations [52,53]. An alternating aperture polarization mask can also be imagined that could produce maximum image contrast.

8 OPTICAL SYSTEM DESIGN

In an ideal lens, the image formed is a result of all rays at all wavelengths from all object points forming image plane points. Lens aberrations create deviations from this ideal and a lens designer must make corrections or compensations. The degrees of freedom available to a designer include material refractive index and dispersion, lens surface curvatures, element thickness, and lens stops. Other application-specific requirements generally lead lens designers toward only a few practical solutions.

For a microlithographic optical system, Köhler illumination is generally used. Requirements for a projection lens are that two images are simultaneously relayed: the image of the reticle and the image of the source (or the illumination exit pupil). The projection lens cannot therefore be separated from the entire optical system; consideration of the illumination optics needs to be included. In designing a lens system for microlithographic work, image quality is generally the primary consideration. Limits must often be placed on lens complexity and size to allow workable systems. The push toward minimum aberration, maximum numerical aperture, maximum field size, maximum mechanical flexibility, and minimum environmental sensitivity has lead to designs that incorporate features somewhat unique to microlithography.

8.1 Strategies for Reduction of Aberrations: Establishing Tolerances

Several classical strategies can be used to achieve maximum lens performance with minimum aberration. These might include modification of material indices and dispersion, splitting the power of elements, compounding elements, using symmetric designs, reducing the effective field size, balancing existing aberrations, or using elements with aspheric surfaces. Incorporating these techniques is often a delicate balancing operation.

Material Characteristics

When available, the use of several glass types of various refractive index values and dispersions allows significant control over design performance. Generally, for positive elements, high-index materials will allow reduction of most aberrations, because of the reduction of ray angles at element surfaces. This is especially useful for the reduction of Petzval curvature. For negative elements, lower index materials are generally favored, which effectively increases the extent to which correcting is effective. Also, a high value of dispersion is often used for the positive element of an achromatic doublet, whereas a low dispersion is desirable for the negative element. For microlithographic applications, the choice of materials that allows these freedoms is limited to those that are transparent at design wavelengths. For g-line and i-line wavelengths, several glass types transmit well, but below 300 nm only fused silica and fluoride crystalline materials can be used. Without the freedom to control refractive index and dispersion, a designer is forced to look for other ways to reduce aberrations. In the case of chromatic aberration, reduction may not be possible and restrictions must be placed on source bandwidth if refractive components are used.

Element Splitting

Aberrations can be minimized or balanced by splitting the power of single elements into two or more components. This allows a reduction in ray angles, which results in a lowering of aberration. This technique is often employed to reduce spherical aberration where negative aberration can be reduced by splitting a positive element and positive aberration can be reduced by splitting a negative element. The selection of the element to split can often be determined through consideration of higher order aberration contributions. Using this technique for microlithographic lenses has resulted in lens designs with a large number of elements.

Element Compounding

Compounding single elements into a doublet is accomplished by cementing the two and forming an interface. This technique allows control of ray paths and allows element properties not possible with one glass type. In many cases, a doublet will have a positive element with a high index combined with a negative element of lower index and dispersion. This produces an achromatized lens component that performs similar to a lens with a high index and very high dispersion. This accomplishes both a reduction in chromatic aberration and a flattening of the Petzval field. Coma aberration can also be modified by taking advantage of the refraction angles at the cemented interface, where upper and

lower rays may be bent differently. The problem with utilizing a cemented doublet approach with microlithographic lenses is again in the suitable glass materials. Most UV and deep-UV glass materials available have a low refractive
index (~1.5), which limits the corrective power of a doublet. This results in a
narrow wavelength band over which an achromatized lens can be corrected in
the UV.

Symmetrical Design

An optical design that has mirror symmetry about the aperture stop is free of
distortion, coma, and chromatic aberration. This is due to an exact cancelling
of aberrations on each side of the pupil. In order to have complete symmetry,
unit magnification is required. Optical systems that are nearly symmetrical can
result in substantial reduction of higher order residuals of distortion, coma, and
chromatic aberration. These systems, however, operate with unit magnification, a requirement for object-to-image symmetry. Since 1× imaging limits
mask and wafer geometry, these systems can be limiting for very high resolution applications but are widely used for larger feature lithography.

Aspheric Surfaces

Most lens designs restrict surfaces to being spherically refracting or reflecting. The freedom offered by allowing incorporation of aspheric surfaces can
lead to dramatic improvements in residual aberration reduction. Problems encountered with aspheric surfaces include difficulties in fabrication, centering,
and testing. Several techniques have been utilized to produce parabolic as
well as general aspheres [54]. Lithographic system designs have started to
take advantage of aspheric elements on a limited basis. The success of these
surfaces may allow lens designs to be realized that would otherwise be
impossible.

Balancing Aberrations

For well-corrected lenses, individual aberrations are not necessarily minimized
but instead balanced with respect to wavefront deformation. The optimum balance of aberration is unique to the lens design and is generally targeted to
achieve minimum OPD. Spherical aberration can be corrected for in several
ways, depending largely on the lens application. When high-order residual aberrations are small, correction of spherical aberration to zero at the edge of the
aperture is usually best, as shown in Fig. 40. Here, the aberration is balanced
for minimum OPD and is best for diffraction-limited systems such as projection lenses. If a lens is operated over a range of wavelengths, however, this correction may result in a shift in focus with aperture size. In this case, spherical
aberration may be overcorrected. This situation would result in a minimum shift
in best focus through the full aperture range, but a decrease in resolution would
result at full aperture.

Chromatic aberration is generally corrected at a 0.7 zone position within the aperture. In this way, the inner portion of the aperture is undercorrected and the outer portion of the lens is overcorrected. Astigmatism can be minimized over a full field by overcorrecting third-order astigmatism and undercorrecting fifth-order astigmatism. This will result in the sagittal focal surface located inside the tangential surface in the center of the field and vice versa at the outside of the field. Petzval field curvature is adjusted so that the field is flat with both surfaces slightly inward.

Correction such as these can be made through control of element glass, power, shape, and position. The impact of many elements of a full lens design make minimization and optimization very difficult. Additionally, corrections such as those discussed operate primarily on third-order aberration. Corrections of higher order and interactions cannot be made with single element or surface modifications. Lens design becomes a delicate process best handled with optical design programs which utilize local and global optimization. Such computational tools allow interaction of lens parameters based on a starting design and an optical designers experience. By taking various paths to achieve low aberration, high numerical aperture, large flat fields, and robust lithographic systems, several lens designs have evolved.

8.2 Basic Lithographic Lens Design

The All-Reflective (Catoptric) Lens

Historically, the 1× ring-field reflective lens used in a scanning mode was one of the earliest projection systems used in integrated circuit manufacture [55]. The reflective aspect of such catoptric systems has several advantages over refractive lens designs. Since most or all of the lens power is in the reflective surfaces, the system is highly achromatized and can be used over a wide range of wavelengths. Chromatic variation of aberrations is also absent. In addition, aberrations of special mirrors are much smaller than those of a refractive element. A disadvantage of a conventional catoptric system, such as the configurations lens shown in Fig. 73, is the obscuration required for imaging. This blocking of light rays close to the optical axis is in effect a low-pass filtered system that can affect image modulation and depth of focus. The 1× Offner design of the ring-field reflecting system gets around this obscuration by scanning through a restricted off-axis annulus of a full circular field, as shown in Fig. 74. This not only eliminates the obscuration problems but also substantially reduces radial aberration variation. Since the design is rotationally symmetrical, all aberrations are constant around the ring. By scanning the image field through this ring, astigmatism, field curvature, and distortion are averaged. It can also be seen that this design is symmetrical on image and object sides. This results in 1× magnification but allows further cancellation of aberration.

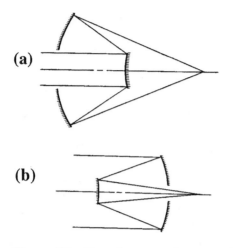

Figure 73 Two-mirror catoptric systems (a) the Schwarzschild configuration, (b) the Cassegrain configuration.

The low power refractive elements in this design are used for correction of astigmatism with field radius which allows this system to be utilized over a wavelength range essentially limited by coatings. These systems have been used at wavelengths from 250 to 450 nm. This design is limited to numerical apertures below 0.35 because of the physical lens sizes needed for large angles. Also,

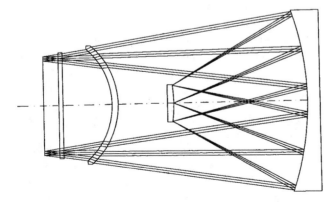

Figure 74 The 1× Offner ring-field reflective lens. (Reproduced with permission from Williamson, 1995.)

vignetting of rays by the secondary mirror forces operation off axis and introduces an increase in aberration level. Mechanically, at larger numerical apertures, reticle and wafer planes may be accessible only by folding the design. Field size is also limited by lens size and high-order aberration. Moreover, unit magnification limits both resolution and wafer size.

The All-Refractive (Dioptric) Lens

Early refractive microlithographic lenses resembled microscope objectives and projection lithography was often performed using off-the-shelf microscope designs and construction. As IC device areas grow, requirements for lens field sizes are increased. Field sizes greater than 25 mm are not uncommon for current IC technology using lens numerical apertures above 0.50. Such requirements have led to the development of UV lenses that operate well beyond λ/4 requirements for diffraction-limited performance, delivering resolution approaching 0.15 μm.

Shown in Fig. 75 is a refractive lens design for use in a 5× i-line reduction system [56]. The design utilizes a large number of low-power elements for minimization of aberration s well as aberration-canceling surfaces. The availability of several glass types at i-line and g-line wavelengths allows chromatic aberration correction of such designs over bandwidths approaching 10 nm. The maximum NA for these lens types is approaching 0.65 with field sizes larger than 30 nm.

Achromatic refractive lens design is not possible at wavelengths below 300 nm and, apart from chromatic differences of paraxial magnification, chromatic aberration cannot be corrected. Restrictions must be placed on exposure sources, generally limiting spectral bandwidth on the order of a few picometers. First-order approximations for source bandwidth based on paraxial defocus of the image by half of the Rayleigh focal depth also show the high dependence on lens NA and focal length. Chromatic aberration can be expressed as:

$$\delta f = \frac{f(\delta n)}{(n-1)}$$

where f is focal length, n is refractive index, and δf is focus error, or chromatic aberration. Combining with the Rayleigh depth of focus condition:

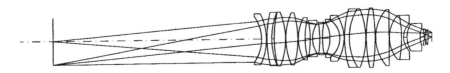

Figure 75 An all-refractive lens design for a 5× i-line reduction system.

$$DOF = \pm 0.5 \frac{\lambda}{NA^2}$$

produces a relationship:

$$\Delta\lambda(FWHM) = \frac{(n-1)\lambda}{2f(dn/d\lambda)NA^2}$$

where $dn/d\lambda$ is the dispersion of the lens material. Lens magnification, m, further affects required bandwidth as:

$$\Delta\lambda(FWHM) = \frac{(n-1)\lambda}{2f(1+m)(dn/d\lambda)NA^2}$$

A desirable chromatic refractive lens from the standpoint of the laser requirements would therefore have a short focal length and a small magnification (high reduction factor) for a given numerical aperture. Requirements for IC manufacture, however, do not coincide. Shown in Fig. 76 is an example of a chromatic refractive lens design [56]. This system utilizes an aspherical lens element, which is close to the lens stop [57]. Because refractive index is also dependent on temperature and pressure, chromatic refractive lens designs are highly sensitive to barometric pressure and lens heating effects.

Catadioptric-Beamsplitter Designs

Both the reflective (catoptric) and refractive (dioptric) systems have advantages that would be beneficial if a combined approach to lens design were utilized. Such a refractive-reflective approach is known as a catadioptric design. Several lens designs have been developed for microlithographic projection lens application. A catadioptric lens design that is similar to the reflective ring-field system is the 4× reduction Offner, shown in Fig. 77 [56]. The field for this lens is also an annulus or ring, which must be scanned for full field imaging. The design uses four spherical mirrors and two fold mirrors. The refractive elements are utilized for aberration correction and their power is minimized, reducing chromatic effects and allowing the lens to be used with an Hg lamp at DUV wavelengths.

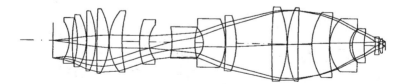

Figure 76   A chromatic all-refracting lens design for a 4× 248 nm system.

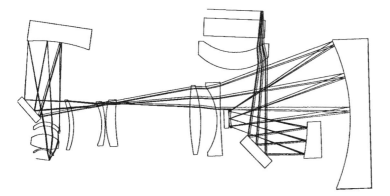

Figure 77   The 4× catadioptric MSI design.

This also minimizes the sensitivity of the design to lens heating and barometric pressure. The drawbacks of this system are its numerical aperture, limited to sub-0.5 levels by vignetting, and the aberration contributions from the large number of reflective surfaces. Alignment of lens elements is also inherently difficult.

To avoid high amounts of obscuration of prohibitively low lens numerical apertures, many lens designs have made use of the incorporation of a beam-splitter Several beamsplitter types are possible. The conventional cube beam-splitter consists of matched pairs of right angle prisms, one with a partially reflecting film deposited on its face, optically cemented. A variation on the cube beamsplitter is a polarizing beamsplitter, as shown in Fig. 78. An incident beam of linearly polarized light is divided with transverse magnetic (TM) and transverse electric (TE) states emerging at right angles. Another possibility is a

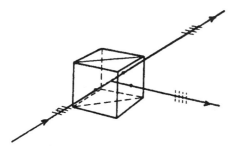

Figure 78   A polarizing beam-splitter. A linearly polarized beam is divided into TM and TE states at right angles.

beamsplitter that is incorporated into a lens element, known as a Mangin mirror, as shown in Fig. 79. Here a partial reflector allows one element to act as both a reflector and a refractor. Although use of a Mangin mirror does require central obscuration, if a design can achieve levels below 10% (radius), the impacts on imaging resolution and depth of focus are minimal [58].

The 4× reduction Dyson shown in Fig. 80 is an example of a catadioptric lens design based on a polarizing beamsplitter [56]. The mask is illuminated with linearly polarized light, which is directed through the lens toward the primary mirror [59]. Upon reflection, a waveplate changes the state of linear polarization, allowing light to be transmitted toward the wafer plane. Variations on this design use a partially reflecting beamsplitter, which may suffer from reduced throughput and a susceptibility coating damage at short wavelengths. Obscuration is eliminated, as is the low-NA requirement of the off-axis designs to prevent vignetting. The beamsplitter is well corrected for operation on axis, minimizing high-order aberrations and the requirement for an increasingly thin ring field for high NA, as with the reduction Offner. The field is square, which can be used in a stepping mode, or rectangular for step and scanning. The simplified system, with only one mirror possessing most of the lens power, leads to lower aberration levels than for the reduction Offner design. This design allows a spectral bandwidth on the order of 5–10 nm, allowing operation with a lamp or laser source.

As seen earlier, at high NA values (above 0.5) for high-resolution lithography, diffraction effects for TE and TM are different. When the vectorial nature of light is considered, a biasing between horizontally oriented and vertically oriented features results. Although propagation into a resist material will reduce this biasing effect [60], it cannot be neglected. Improvements on the reduction Dyson in Fig. 80 have included elimination of the linear polarization effect by incorporating a second waveplate near the wafer plane. The resulting circular polarization removes the H-V biasing possible with linear polarization and also rejects light reflected from the wafer and lens surface, reducing lens flare. Improvements have also increased the NA of the Dyson design, up to 0.7 using

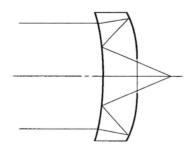

Figure 79 A Mangin mirror-based beam splitter approach to a catadioptric system. A partially reflective surface allows one element to act as a reflector and a refractor.

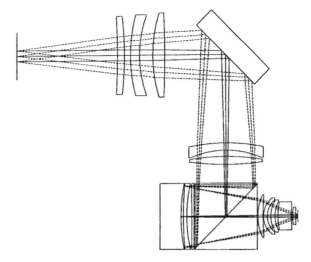

Figure 80   A 4× reduction Dyson catadioptric lens design utilizing a polarizing beam splitter.

approaches including larger NA beamsplitter cubes, shorter image conjugates, increased mirror asphericity, and source bandwidths below 1 nm. This spectral requirement, along with increasingly small field widths to reduce aberration, requires that these designs be used only with excimer laser sources. Designs have been developed for both 248 and 193 nm wavelengths. Examples of these designs are shown in Figs. 81 [61] and 82 [62].

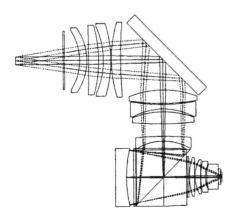

Figure 81   An improved reduction Dyson utilizing a second waveplate to eliminate linear polarization effects at the wafer. (Reproduced with permission from Williamson, 1996.)

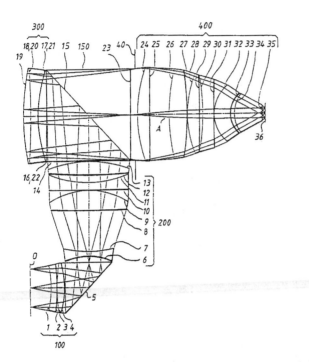

Figure 82 A reduction Dyson approach with the stop behind the beam splitter. Numerical apertures to 0.7 can be achieved with a high degree of collumation. Spectral narrowing is likely needed.

REFERENCES

1. Smith, W., *Modern Optical engineering*, Mc-Graw-Hill, New York, 1966, p. 17.
2. Huygens, C., *Traité de la Lumière*, Leyden, 1690 (English translation by S. P. Thompson, *Treatise on Light*, Macmillan, London, 1912).
3. Fresnel, A., *Ann. Chem. Phys.*, 239 (1816).
4. Goodman, J. W., *Introduction to Fourier Optics*, McGraw-Hill, New York, 1968, p. 57.
5. von Helmholtz, H., *J. Math. 57*, 7 (1859).
6. Kirchhoff, G., *Ann. Phys. 18*, 663 (1883).
7. Cole, D. C., Extending scalar aerial image calculations to higher numerical apertures, J. VAC. SCI. TECHNOL. B 10(6), 3037 (1992).
8. Flagello, D. G., and Rosenbluth, A. E., Lithographic tolerances based on vector diffraction theory, *J. Vac. Sci. Technol. B 10*(6), 2997 (1992).
9. Gaskill, J. D., *Linear Systems, Fourier Transforms and Optics*, Wiley, New York, 1978.

10. Hopkins, H. H., The concept of partial coherence in optics, *Proc. R. Soc., A 208*, 408 (1953).

11. Kingslake, R., *Optical system Design*, Academic Press, London, 1983, p. 196.

12. O'Shea, D. C., *Elements of Modern Optical Design*, Wiley, New York, 1985, p. 113.

13. Lord Rayleigh, *Philos. Mag.* (5), 8, 403 (1879).

14. Hopkins, H. H., Introductory methods of image assessment, *SPIE 274*, 2 (1981).

15. Born, M., and Wolf, E., *Principles of Optics*, Pergamon Press, New York, 1964, p. 530.

16. Steel, W. H., Effects of small aberrations on the images of partially coherent objects, *J. Opt. Soc. Am.*, *47*, 405 (1957).

17. Offner, A., Wavelength and coherence effects on the performance of real optical projection systems, *Photogr. Sci. Eng.*, *23*, 374 (1979).

18. Shannon, R. R., How many transfer functions in a lens? *Opt. Photon. News*, *1*, 40 (1995).

19. Hill, A., Webb, J., Phillips, A., Connors, J., Design and Analysis of a High NA Projection System for 0.35 μm Deep-UV Lithography, *SPIE Vol. 1927*, (1993), 608.

20. Levinson, H. J., Arnold, W. H., *J. Vac. Sci. Technol. B 5*(1), 293 (1987).

21. Mahajan, V., *Aberration Theory Made Simple*, SPIE Press, Bellingham, WA, 1991, p. 8.

22. Zernike, F., *Physica*, *1*, 689 (1934).

23. Lord Rayleigh, *Scientific Papers*, Vol. 1, Dover, New York, 1964, p. 432.

24. Smith, B. W., *First International Symposium on 193 nm Lithography*, Colorado Springs, CO, 1995.

25. PROLITH/2 V. 5.0, FINLE Technologies, 1996.

26. Born, M., and Wolf, E., *Principles of Optics*, Pergamon Press, Oxford, 1980, p. 95.

27. Gan Fuxi, *Optical and Spectroscopic Properties of Glass*, Springer-Verlag, New York, 1992, p. 74.

28. Refractive Index Information (Approximate), Acton Research Corporation, Acton, MA, 1990.

29. Rothschild, M., Ehrlich, D. J., and Shaver, D. C., *Appl. Phys. Lett.*, *55*(13), 1276 (1989).

30. Leung, W. P., Kulkarni, M., Krajnovich, D., and Tam, A. C., *Appl. Phys. Lett.*, *58*(6), 551 (1991).

31. Hyde, J. F., U.S. Patent 2,272,342 (1962).

32. Imai, H., Arai, K., Saito, T., Ichimura, S., Nonaka, H., Vigouroux, J. P., Imagawa, H., Hosono, H., and Abe, Y., in *The Physics and Technology of Amorphous SiO$_2$* (R. A. B. Devine, ed.) Plenum Press, New York, 1988, p. 153.

33. Partlow, W., Thampkins, P., Dewa, P., and Michaloski, P., *SPIE 1927*, 137 (1993).

34. Asai, S., Hanyu, I., and Hikosaka, K., *J. Vac. Sci. Technol. B 10*(6), 3023 (1992).

35. Toh, K., Dao, G., Gaw, H., Neureuther, A., and Fredrickson, L., *SPIE 1463*, 402 (1991).

36. Tamechika, E., Horiuchi, T., Harada, K., *Jpn. J. Appl. Phys. 32*, 5856 (1993).

37. Ogawa, T., Uematsu, M., Ishimaru, T., Kimura, M., and Tsumori, T., *SPIE 2197*, 19 (1994).

38. Kostelak, R., Garofalo, J., Smolinsky, G., and Vaidya, S., *J. Vac. Sci. Technol. B* 9(6), 3150 (1991).
39. Kostelak, R., Pierat, C., Garafalo, J., and Vaidya, S., *J. Vac. Sci. Technol. B 10*(6), 3055 (1992).
40. Lin, B., *SPIE 1496*, 54 (1990).
41. Watanabe, H., Takenaka, H., Todokoro, Y., and Inoue, M., *J. Vac. Sci. Technol. B 9*(6), 3172 (1991).
42. Levensen, M., *Phys. Today 46*(7), 28 (1993).
43. Watanabe, H., Todokoro, Y., Hirai, Y., and Inoue, M., *SPIE 1463*, 101 (1991).
44. Ku, Y., Anderson, E., Shattenburg, and Smith, H., *J. Vac. Sci. Technol. B 6*(1), 150 (1988).
45. Kostelak, R., Bolan, K., and Yang, T. S., *Proc. OCG Interface Conference*, 1993, p. 125.
46. Smith, B. W., and Turget, S., *SPIE Optical/Laser Microlithography VII,* 2197, 201 (1994).
47. Born, M., and Wolf, E., *Principles of Optics*, Pergamon Press, Oxford, 1980, p. 60.
48. Smith, B. W., Butt, S., Alam, Z., Kurinec, S., and Lane, R., *J. Vac. Sci. Technol. B 14*(6), 3719, (1996).
49. Liu, Y., and Zakhor, A., *IEEE Trans. Semicond. 5*, 138 (1992).
50. Yoo, H., Oh, Y., Park, B., Choi, S., and Jeon, Y., *Jpn. J. Appl. Phys. 32*, 5903 (1993).
51. Smith, B. W., Flagello, D., and Summa, J., *SPIE 1927*, 847 (1993).
52. Asai, S., Hanyu, I., and Takikawa, M., *Jpn. J. Appl. Phys., 32*, 5863 (1993).
53. Matsumoto, K., and Tsuruta, T., *Opt. Eng 31*(12), 2656 (1992).
54. Golini, D., Pollicove, H., Platt, G., Jacobs, S., and Kordonsky, W., *Laser Focus World 31*(9), 83 (1995).
55. Offner, A., *Opt. Eng. 14*(2), 130 (1975).
56. Williamson, D. M., by permission.
57. Buckley, J., and Karatzas, C., *SPIE, 1088*, 424 (1989).
58. Bruning, J., *OSA Symposium on Design, Fabrucation, and Testing for sub-0.25 micron Lithographic Imaging*, 1996.
59. Sewell, H., *SPIE 2440*, 49 (1995).
60. Flagello, D., and Rosenbluth, A., *J. Vac. Sci. Technol. B. 10*(6), 2997 (1992).
61. Williamson, D., et al. *SPIE, 2726*, 780 (1996).
62. Fürter, G., Carl-Zeiss-Stiftung, by permission.

4

Krypton Fluoride Excimer Laser for Advanced Microlithography

Palash Das

Cymer, Inc.
San Diego, California

Uday Sengupta

ASIA QUEST Inc.
San Diego, California

The excimer–based stepper is now expected to play a significant role in the manufacturing of ultralarge scale integrated (ULSI) devices requiring sub–0.3 μm design rule features. They will be used in a mix-and match strategy along with high numerical aperture (NA) i-line steppers, scanners, and step-and-scan systems for critical layers in the production of 64-Mb dynamic random access memory (DRAM) generation and beyond of integrated circuit (IC) devices. This is supported by the present availability of a number of production worthy high-NA, wide-field excimer stepper models, along with the recent introduction of several process-worthy and moderate cost, positive-tone deep-ultraviolet (UV) photoresists.

The excimer laser for the stepper, since its introduction in 1987, has evolved from a laboratory instrument to fully production-worthy fabrication line equipment. This chapter will discuss the status of such a laser. We will discuss the operating theory and the design features of an excimer laser—in particular: the discharge chamber, pulsed power spectral narrowing module, and the wavemeter. This chapter will also present some of the latest technical innovations incorporated into the laser that reduce maintenance intervals and increase reliability. Finally, we will present and discuss the performance specifications of a current production lithography excimer laser.

1   INTRODUCTION AND BACKGROUND

Microlithography for advanced ULSI fabrication is now making a transition from using an i-line (365 nm) mercury lamp to a deep-UV excimer laser—krypton fluoride (248 nm)—as the illumination source. This transition is both evolutionary and revolutionary. Evolutionary, because the change from a lamp to a laser will be almost transparent to the IC maker and to the optical designer of the lithography tool. However, the change is revolutionary because of the complexity and the pulsed operation of the laser compared with the simple and continuously operating lamp. The cost of operating a laser is now comparable to that of operating an advanced i-line lamp. The next evolutionary transition would be from the krypton fluoride (KrF) excimer laser to the shorter wavelength argon fluoride (ArF) excimer laser (193 nm). The KrF excimer–based lithography system is now expected to become the primary exposure tool for printing sub–0.3 μm design rule features in IC manufacturing, and the ArF excimer process will be used for sub–0.20 μm features. In what follows, we will discuss primarily the KrF excimer laser. However, the basic physics of excimer lasers is similar. The last section will briefly cover the physics of the ArF laser.

The KrF excimer laser–based lithography tool will be used in a mix-and-match strategy along with high NA i-line steppers beginning with the large-scale production of second-generation 64-Mbit dynamic random access memory ICs and similar devices. Such production is expected to commence by 1997. All major lithography tool manufacturers in 1995 were offering high NA production ready excimer-based steppers or scanners. The availability of robust, process ready, and moderate in cost positive-done deep-UV photoresist also allows a cost-effective transition to excimer-based lithography.

Interest in excimer-based lithography initially emerged in 1986 when it was prematurely assumed that making an i-line stepper lens would not be feasible due to the unavailability of a family of high-transmission optical glass at 365 nm. The IC industry and the stepper makers had envisioned jumping from the g-line directly to the excimer stepper. However, the poor reliability and the high cost of operating an excimer laser at that time forced the stepper makers to reevaluate their assumption about the i-line stepper. As a result, tremendous progress was made in improving the transmission and general quality of glass at 365 nm. By 1989 i-line steppers and the i-line process had become as good as or better than the existing g-line process. The i-line stepper has now emerged as the primary lithography tool for most IC fabrication and it is also expected to be used in the future along with the excimer stepper in a mix-and-match strategy even for sub-0.3 μm IC devices. Another problem which hampered the introduction of excimer lithography for many years was the unavailability of a robust and low-cost positive-tone photoresist. Now, after almost 10 years in development, the excimer lithography process is mature enough to be production worthy. Both the laser and the photoresist are now ready to meet the production challenge.

Advanced lithography tools fall into two categories: (1) an all-refractive lens reduction stepper/scanner or (2) a catadioptric scanning imaging system. Large-field lithography tools in the future will use both refractive and catadioptric scanning schemes.

A refractive reduction lens (×4 or ×5) images the reticle pattern on the wafer through an all-refractive lens system. In a stepper, the entire reticle is imaged on a wafer die site at one time. In a refractive scanner only a thin slice of the reticle is imaged on the wafer through the center—the sweet region—of the lens, while both the reticle and the wafer are moved simultaneously in opposite directions so as to print the entire reticle on a wafer die site. In the latter, lens distortion effects are substantially reduced because only the center (best) portion of the lens is used and any distortion is averaged out over the field by the nature of scanning. Although the lens design and fabrication are simpler in this case, mechanical complexity increases because of the need to move precisely the reticle and the wafer simultaneously. (Note: the reticle has to move four times faster than the wafer (for an ×4 reduction system.) The performance requirements for the laser are also greater for the scanner compared with the laser for a stepper.

Similarly, the catadioptric scanning system images the reticle pattern on the wafer by scanning a slit exposure across the reticle. Once again, both the reticle and the wafer are moved simultaneously in opposite directions to print the full die on the wafer and there is a 4× reduction in image size. However, in this case a mirror is used to image instead of a lens. The performance requirement for the laser in this case is the least stringent.

As is well known, below 300 nm there is only one suitable optical material available for building the stepper lens—fused silica. Other materials, such as CaF_2, MgF_2, or LiF, although transparent in deep UV, are unsuitable because they are crystalline, birefringent, and have high thermal expansion coefficients. An all fused silica stepper lens, as a result, will have no chromatic correction capability. Therefore, the spectral bandwidth of the illumination source has to be reduced and the required bandwidth is a function of the lens numerical aperture. A mercury lamp using filters is incapable of this task; only an optical amplifying medium such as a spectrally narrowed excimer laser will be able to meet all the necessary requirements.

The KrF excimer laser has a natural bandwidth of approximately 300 pm. For a refractive system (NA > 0.5)—either a stepper or a scanner—this bandwidth has to be reduced to below 0.8 pm (Table 1). On the other hand, the cata-

Table 1   Stepper/Scanner Performance and Required Laser Specification

	1st *(1988–89)*	*2nd* *(1990–92)*	*3rd* *(1993–97)*
Stepper/Scanner			
NA	0.35	0.4–0.45	0.40–0.63 (variable)
Field size (nm)	21 Ø	21 Ø, 25 Ø	> 30 Ø
Optical throughput efficiency	5–8%	≥ 10%	≥ 15%
Laser			
Spectral bandwidth: FWHM (pm)	≤ 3	≤ 2.2	≤ 0.8
Spectral bandwidth: 95% energy band (pm)	—	< 7	≤ 3.0
Center wavelength stability (pm)	≤ ± 1	≤ ± 0.5	≤ ± 0.25
Energy variation (σ)	≤ 3.5%	≤ 3%	≤ 2.5%
Power (W)	2–3	4	6–10
Repetition rate (Hz)	200	400	500–1000

dioptric scanning system is able to use the broadband spectral output of the laser. However, for a high-NA (>0.5) catadioptric system some spectral narrowing (~150 pm) is needed.

Incidentally, the excimer laser is almost an ideal illumination source for lithography. The output is spatially incoherent (coherence length approximately 100 to 200 μm) like a lamp, but is spectrally narrow compared with a lamp, which allows a simpler optic and illuminator design. The laser is efficient, 0.6% for a spectrally narrowed and greater than 2% for a broadband laser. It is able to provide precise illumination on command, with no decrease in output power (therefore, no loss in throughput, as is the case with a mercury lamp near the end of its life). The laser is also suited for implementing enhanced illumination schemes, such as quadrupole or annular, with minimal loss of throughput. The laser can be installed remotely, which eliminates any unnecessary thermal loading on the stepper or the enclosure. Finally, the laser operating cost is now comparable to the cost of exchanging mercury lamps in advanced production lithography tools.

To better understand the excimer stepper and the lithography process, it is helpful to establish some simple relationships between laser parameters and corresponding stepper performance. This is done in Table 2, which is self-explanatory and shows a multifaceted relationship between the laser and the stepper. Such is not the case with the mercury arc lamp and the stepper.

Table 2 Laser Parameters Versus Stepper Performance

Spectral bandwidth and spectral energy distribution	$\Rightarrow$ (affects)	Resolution, depth of focus
Relative wavelength stability	$\Rightarrow$	Focal plan stability (long term) Resolution, DOF (short term)
Absolute wavelength stability	$\Rightarrow$	Magnification, distortion
Output power	$\Rightarrow$	Throughput
Repetition rate	$\Rightarrow$	Energy dose accuracy, speckle reduction
Pulse-to-pulse energy stability	$\Rightarrow$	Energy dose accuracy
Beam profile, beam pointing, and beam divergence stability	$\Rightarrow$	Exposure uniformity, illuminator efficiency
Polarization stability	$\Rightarrow$	Illuminator efficiency
Spatial coherence	$\Rightarrow$	Speckle, exposure

In the next section, we discuss the theory, design, and performance of an excimer laser for lithography. All excimer stepper makers today use a common laser, from one laser manufacturer; this chapter therefore focuses primarily on the performance and design of this laser. The basic operating principles of all lithography lasers are, however, similar.

2 EXCIMER LASER

2.1 History

The term "excimer" comes from "excited dimer," a class of molecules that exists only in the upper excited state but not in the ground state. The excimer molecule has a short upper state lifetime, and it decays to the ground state through disassociation while emitting a photon [1]. There are two types of excimers: rare gas excited dimers such as Xe_2 and Kr_2^*, and the rare gas halogens such as XeF^*, $XeCl^*$, KrF^*, and ArF^*. The latter class of excimers are of greater interest because they emit deep-UV photons (351, 308, 248, and 193 nm). The concept of using an excimer molecule as a laser medium was first proposed in 1960 [2]. The first successful rare gas halide lasers were, however, demonstrated in 1975 by several researchers [3,4]. The availability of pulsed energetic electron beams (e-beams) permitted excitation of the rare gas and halogen mixtures to create the so-called e-beam sustained excimer lasers (Fig. 1). In these lasers, a short pulse from a high-power e-beam provides the only source of power to the laser gas. The high efficiencies, about 9% [6], and large energies, 350 J with KrF [7], obtained from these systems revolutionized the availability

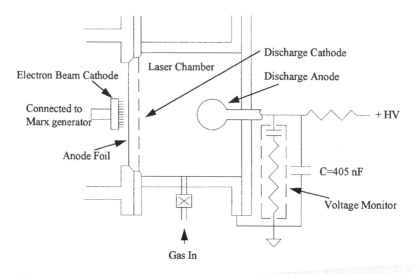

Figure 1 Electron beam sustained KrF laser. Electron beam enters the discharge region through the anode foil. Due to foil heating problems, high-repetition-rate operation is not possible.

of high-energy photon sources in UV. These energetic UV beams found applications in isotope separation, x-ray generation, and spectroscopy [8]. But there were several technical problems associated with optics and beam transport at UV wavelengths, especially at these high energies. In addition, e-beam sustained lasers suffered from self-pinching of the electron beam due to its own magnetic field and from heating, degradation, and rupture of the foil through which electrons enter the discharge region. The repetition rate was also limited to a few pulses a minute. These technical issues limited the growth of e-beam sustained lasers in the commercial environment. Today, all commercial lasers are UV-preionized and discharge pumped. Typically, these lasers operate at low pulse energies (10 to 500 mJ) and high repetition rates (100 to 1000 Hz) but are extremely reliable.

Experience shows that indeed sufficient energy can be extracted from UV-preionized discharge-pumped lasers only if they are pumped using a fast electrical discharge circuit. Because of the short discharge duration, there are only a few photon round trips through the gain medium. As a result, the output beam is somewhat incoherent compared with other lasers. Interestingly, it is this property of incoherence that makes the excimer laser suitable for lithography, because speckle problems are minimal. However, as we shall soon see, the short gain duration also complicates the laser's pulsed power and spectral bandwidth control technology.

The following subsections describe excimer laser operation, physics, and associated technology that makes it all happen. Excimer lasers have evolved significantly over the past two decades. This may be attributed to three separate government-funded programs in the United States, Japan, and Europe. In the United States, the Department of Defense and Department of Energy have funded excimer laser development for isotope separation, laser communication, and materials processing. In Japan, the primary goal of AMM-TRA was to develop excimer lasers for materials processing and machining. In Europe, the JESSI program had goals similar to those of AMMTRA. Today, there are at least three suppliers of KrF excimer lasers optimized for lithography applications—Cymer, Inc. in the United States, Lambda Physik in Germany, and Komatsu in Japan. We focus our attention on their KrF lasers, optimized for microlithography.

2.2 Operation

A typical excimer laser and its associated electrical circuit used for this purpose are shown in Fig. 2. The operating sequence of this circuit is as follows:

1. The power supply is commanded to charge the storage capacitor Cs at a rate faster than the repetition rate of the laser. The inductor L across the laser head prevents the so-called peaking capacitors, Cp, from being charged. The high-voltage switch (thyratron) is open when Cs is charged. Typically Cs is charged to between 12 and 25 kV depending on the desired laser energy.
2. The thyratron is then commanded to commute; i.e., the switch is closed. The closing time for a typical thyratron is about 30 ns, during which the thyratron changes state from an open to a shut switch. The command to commute is generated by the stepper or the scanner.
3. At this point, Cs pulse charges the capacitors Cp at a rate determined by Cs, Cp, and Lm (Fig. 3). A typical charge rate of Cp by Cs is about 100 V/nsec.
4. As Cp charges, its voltage appears between the electrodes, creating high electric fields between them. The gas is ionized because of the electric fields. During this time, there is no current between electrodes (Fig. 3a).
5. When the voltage across Cp reaches a certain threshold, the current through the electrodes increases (Fig. 3a). The current rise is determined by Cp and (Lc + Lm). Depending on the electrode gap, gas mixture, and gas pressure, the voltage on Cp can ring up to a higher voltage than on Cs. Therefore, Cp is referred to as a "peaking" capacitor.

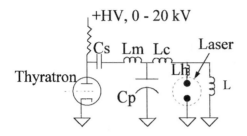

Figure 2   A typical excimer laser and its associated electrical circuit.

6.   Under the right conditions, described later, the discharge forms a medium from which laser energy may be extracted with suitable optics (Fig. 3b). An energy monitor subsystem measures and reports the energy to the laser's controller and to the stepper.

7.   After the termination of the laser pulse, all voltages are rapidly dissipated as heat in the discharge (Fig. 3a and b). The laser is now ready to repeat steps 1 through 7.

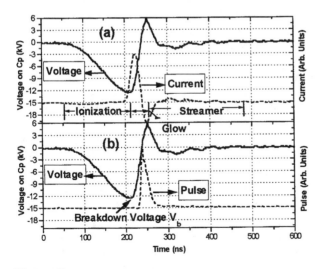

Figure 3   (a) Voltage on peaking capacitors, current through laser discharge, and the three discharge phases. (b) Voltage on peaking capacitors, laser pulse waveforms, and breakdown voltage Vb. The laser pulse occurs only during the glow phase.

2.3 Discharge

Based on the voltage waveform on Cp, the laser discharge may be divided into three distinct phases. These are ionization, glow, and streamer. In the following sections we describe these three phases and explain the evolution of the laser pulse with respect to these phases.

The photochemical reactions during these phases are the following:

$Kr + e^- \rightarrow Kr^* + e^-$	Two-step ionization	(1)	Ionization phase
$Kr^* + e^- \rightarrow Kr^+ + 2e^-$			
$F_2 + e^- \rightarrow F^- + F$	Electron attachment	(2)	
$Kr^* + F_2 + Ne \rightarrow KrF^* + F + Ne,$	KrF* Formation via harpooning collisions	(3)	
$Kr^+ + F^- + Ne \rightarrow KrF^* + Ne$	KrF* Formation via ion channels	(4)	
$KrF^* \rightarrow Kr + F + h\nu$	Spontaneous emission	(5)	Glow phase
$KrF^* + h\nu \rightarrow Kr + F + 2h\nu$	Stimulated emission	(6)	
$KrF^* + F_2 \rightarrow Kr + F + F_2$	KrF* quenching	(7)	
$KrF^* + Kr \rightarrow 2Kr + F$	KrF* quenching	(8)	
$KrF^* + 2Ne \rightarrow Kr + F + Ne$	KrF* quenching	(9)	
$KrF^* + 2Kr \rightarrow Kr_2F^* + Kr$	Tri-atomic excimer formation	(10)	

The harpooning collisions, in which the excited Kr atoms spilt F_2 molecules, and the ion channel reactions are illustrated in Fig. 4.

Ionization Phase

The ionization phase constitutes sequences 3 and 4 discussed above. It lasts for approximately 100–200 nsec depending on the magnitudes of circuit parameters Cs, Cp, and Lm and on the gas mixture and pressure. The ionization phase needs a minimum of 10^6 to 10^8 electrons per cm^3 for its initiation. This is generally achieved through either arcs or coronas that generate deep-UV photons. The photons ionize the gas to create the electron density just prior to the onset of the ionization phase. This process of generating electrons via UV photons is known as preionization and is described in Section 2.2.

During the two-step ionization process (Eq. 1), the electron density in the discharge region multiplies rapidly. The growth of electrons occurs primarily in the region between the electrodes where the electric fields are highest and is moderated only by the loss of electrons due to attachment (Eq. 2). Subsequently, the electron density reaches some 10^{13} per cm^3. At such high electron densities, gas breakdown occurs, resulting in a rapid drop of voltage across the electrodes and a rapid rise of current through the electrodes. The next phase, the glow or discharge phase, is initiated.

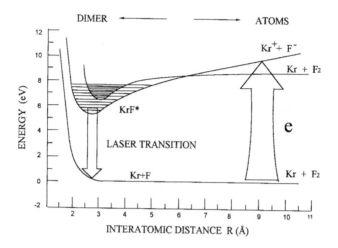

Figure 4 Energy diagram for a KrF* excimer laser. KrF* is formed via two reaction channels. It decays to the ground state via disassociation into Kr and F while emitting a photon at 248 nm.

Glow Phase

During the glow phase, energy from Cp is transferred to the region between the electrodes (sequence 5). The rapid rise of current through the electrodes is controlled only by the magnitude of Cp and (Lh + Lc), i.e., current rise time $\sim 1/\sqrt{(Lh+Lc)Cp}$. This interelectrode region conducts heavily and the upper state KrF* excimer is formed via three-body reactions (Eqs. 3 and 4). Numerical calculations [10] indicate that the ion channel contribution toward the formation of KrF* is about 20% and the balance is from harpooning collisions.

Once the excited krypton fluoride (KrF*) is formed, it can either radiatively decay by spontaneous emissions (Eq. 2.2.5); be quenched (Esq. 2.2.7 through 2.2.10) by collisions with Kr, F_2, and Ne; or radiate photons by stimulated emissions (Eq. 2.2.6). For efficient laser power extraction, the probability of stimulated emission should be much larger than the combined probability of decay by radiative and collisional processes. The ratio of these probabilities is given by ϕ_c/ϕ_s, where ϕ_c and ϕ_s are the cavity and the saturation flux respectively.

The saturation flux, ϕ_s, is defined as [11]

$$\phi_s = \frac{h\nu}{\sigma_s}\left[\frac{1}{\tau_r}+\sum_R K_R N_R\right] \tag{11}$$

where $h\nu$ is the energy of photon at 248 nm, about 5.1 eV; σ_s is the stimulated cross section, ~2.6 Å^2; τ_r is the KrF* lifetime due to spontaneous emission, ~9 ns; K_R is the two-body quenching rate constant; and N_R is the corresponding number density of Kr, F_2, and Ne. Therefore, power extraction can be optimized by minimizing the saturation flux, ϕs. Since both σ_s and τ_r are constants, saturation flux is mainly determined by the gas mixture and concentration.

The cavity flux ϕ_c is determined by four parameters:

1. Gain (g)
2. Loss (α)
3. Reflectivity of laser mirror (R)
4. Length of the discharge (L)

The gain coefficient, g, is defined by:

$$g = \sigma_s N_{KrF*} \tag{12}$$

It can be increased by increasing the KrF* density in the discharge during the glow phase.

The loss is primarily due to transient species during the discharge and absorption of KrF radiation by F_2

$F_2 + h\nu \rightarrow 2F$	photodissociation	(13)
$F^- + h\nu \rightarrow F + e^-$	photodetachment	(14)
$Kr_2^+ + h\nu \rightarrow 2Kr$	ionic absorption	(15)
$Kr_2F* + h\nu \rightarrow 2Kr + F$	triatomic excimer absorption	(16)

Fresnel reflections, absorption, and scattering of radiation by laser windows also contribute to the losses. But their contribution can be minimized by using Brewster angles of incidences on optical surfaces. Therefore, for a given gas mixture (i.e., fixed ϕ_s), the radiation extraction efficiency (η_{ext}) can be calculated from the following equation [11]:

$$\eta_{ext} = \frac{2(1-\sqrt{R})}{(1+\sqrt{R})} \left\{ \frac{1}{\alpha L - \frac{1}{2}\ln R} - \frac{1}{gL} \right\} \tag{17}$$

Most commercial lasers, optimized for lithography operation, operate with a gain-to-loss ratio (g/α) of 5 and a gL product of 5. The optimum reflectivity (Fig. 5) is therefore between 10 and 20%.

During the glow phase, the voltage across the electrodes is approximately a constant, albeit only for a short duration, 20 to 30 nsec. This voltage is often referred to as the discharge voltage (V_d) or glow voltage. The V_d may be calculated from E/P, where E is the electric field between the electrodes and P is the total gas pressure, via:

$$V_d = \frac{E}{P}H \tag{18}$$

where H is the spacing between the electrodes. The magnitude of E/P depends on the gas mixture [12]. Table 3 lists the contribution of the component gases

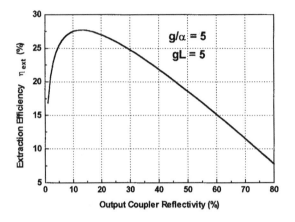

Figure 5 The maximum extraction efficiency of a typical KrF laser occurs when the reflectivity of the mirror is about 10–20%.

to the E/P used in a typical commercial laser. The discharge voltage is then calculated by simply summing the contributions from the individual component gases. For examples, for an electrode spacing of 2 cm, at a pressure of 3 atm (i.e., 2280 torr) of 2.2 torr of F_2, 23 torr of Kr, and 2255 torr of Ne, the discharge voltage V_d is (4.0 kV due to F_2 + 1.1 kV due to Kr + 3.4 kV due to Ne) 8.5 kV.

It is advantageous to lengthen the duration of the glow phase as it permits greater deposition and extraction of energy, or, more important, the energy may be deposited less rapidly. A lower rate of energy deposition reduces the discharge peak currents, thus increasing the optical pulse duration. An increase in the pulse duration eases design requirements for spectral narrowing. Experimental evidence [12], coupled with theoretical modeling of excimer discharges [17], indicates that the glow phase duration can be increased by decreasing the F_2 concentration and by decreasing the number density of electrons at the onset of the glow phase. The glow phase is initiated by the ionization phase, during

Table 3 Contribution of the Gases to the E/P of KrF Lasers

Gas	E/P (kV/cm-torr)
Ne	7.5×10^{-4}
Kr	2.4×10^{-2}
Ar	1.0×10^{-2}
F2	0.9

Source: Ref. 12.

which the electron density increases as the field (or voltage) across the electrodes increases. Therefore, to a large extent, the number density of electrons at the onset of glow phase depends on the voltage across the electrodes just before the initiation of the glow phase (V_b in Figure 3b). Thus, it is possible to increase the glow phase time by reducing the peek voltage V_b across the electrodes and by reducing the concentration of F_2 [10]. These facts form some of the critical design rules for the laser designer.

Streamer Phase

After the glow phase, the discharge degenerates into streamers or arcs and the optical intensity drops. As compared with the glow phase, during which energy is deposited uniformly over the electrode surface, during the streamer phase energy deposition is localized. The total energy deposited in the streamer phase is generally a very small fraction of that deposited during the glow phase (Fig. 6). Nevertheless, because of its localized nature, the energy density (and corresponding current density) on the electrodes is very high. The high current density heats the electrode surface, causing it to vaporize. Some other deleterious effects of the streamer phase include the loss of fluorine due to continuous electrode passivation after each pulse, increase in discharge cross section due to electrode erosion, and creation of metal fluoride dust due to the chemical reaction of fluorine and hot metal vapor. The energy dissipated during this phase in

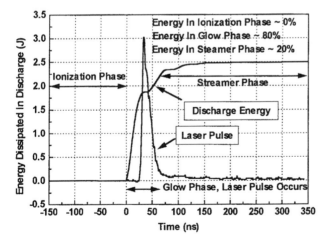

Figure 6   Energy dissipated in the electrode region during the three phases of the discharge. No energy is dissipated during ionization phase. Most energy is dissipated during the glow phase, but the small fraction that is dissipated in the ionization phase is detrimental to the laser electrodes.

the electrodes can be minimized by maximizing power transfer from the peaking capacitors to the glow phase. The streamer phase is detrimental but is almost impossible to eliminate in any practical system. Later, we will describe a novel circuit that recovers part of the residual energy in the circuit after the glow phase instead of dissipating it in the streamer phase.

2.4 Preionization

Ultraviolet preionization of excimer lasers has been the subject of much investigation. Pioneering investigations by Taylor [12] and Treshchalov and Peet [13] showed that achieving discharge stability is dependent upon two main criteria: (1) a very uniform initial electron density in the discharge region and (2) achieving a minimum preionization electron density. This threshold density is dependent upon gas mixture and pressure, the concentration of F_2 and electronegative impurities, electrode shape, profile, and voltage rise time. The uniformity of initial electron density in the discharge depends on the method of preionization. Two kinds of preionization are used in KrF lasers—spark and corona (Fig. 7).

Spark

In this method, an array of sparks is located near and along the length of the discharge electrodes. These sparks provide a very high level of preionization and the resultant electron density far exceeds the required minimum. The sparks are connected to the peaking capacitors Cp, thereby preventing the complexity of additional preionizer circuitry. But it is difficult to achieve sufficient uniformity due to the discrete and finite sparks, resulting in increased discharge instability. In addition, the discharge current that passes through the peaking capacitors also passes through the pins. This causes excessive erosion of the pins and promotes chemical reactions with laser gas that can cause a rapid burn-up of F_2. At high repetition rates, the spark electrodes can become a source of localized heating of the laser gas and cause index gradients. The direction of

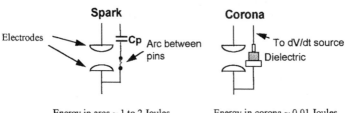

Figure 7   Some common methods of UV preionization in lithography lasers.

the beam in such an optically nonuniform medium changes as the index of refraction changes, resulting in the so-called pointing instability of the beam. Furthermore, a variation in preionizer gaps lead to nonsimultaneous firing of the pins and increased beam pointing instability.

Corona

A corona preionizer consists of two electrodes of opposite polarity with a dielectric in between. As in spark preionization, the corona preionizer is located along the length of the discharge electrodes. When one of the corona preionizer electrodes is charged with respect to the other electrode, a corona discharge develops on the surface of the dielectric and in the gas near the electrodes. The level of preionization can be increased by increasing the dielectric constant and by increasing the rate of rise in voltage. Although corona preionization is considered to be a relatively weaker source of preionization electrons compared with the spark preionizer, it is nevertheless very uniform due to the continuous nature of the preionizer design (as compared with discrete sparks). Also, problems due to spark preionizer erosion are nonexistent in corona preionization.

Theoretical estimates [14] show that under the weak preionization condition, the voltage rise time across the discharge electrodes should be of the order of 1 kV/ns. This is much faster than the 100 V/ns shown in Fig. 4. The question is, why do corona-preionized KrF lasers work? A possible explanation [15] is that for lasers using F_2 as the halogen, electron attachment produces F ions within a few nanoseconds. For homogeneous discharge development, some of these weakly attached electrons become available through collisional detachment as the discharge voltage promotes acceleration. This collisional detachment process partially offsets the electron loss due to electron attachment and compensates for the weak preionization, which could explain why corona-preionized KrF lasers work.

2.5 Laser Design Considerations

How do the aforementioned discussions affect the design of the laser? To the laser designer, the discharge voltage, V_d, is the key parameter. This parameter determines the electrode spacing, as pressure, and range of operating voltage on the peaking capacitors C_p. The analysis will proceed as follows.

Prior to the initiation of the ionization phase, the storage capacitor C_s is charged to a DC voltage V_1. The charging current bypassses the peaking capacitors C_p as the electrode gap is nonconductive during this time. When the thyratron commutes, C_s pulse charges C_p. The voltage on peaking capacitors V_2 also appears across the electrodes.

After a time $t = \tau_\delta$ (ionization time), the number density of electrons reach a certain threshold, at which time the gap between the electrodes breaks down into the glow phase. The electron density depends, as mentioned before, on the gas mixture and on the voltage on C_p at breakdown, V_b.

During the ionization phase, the rate at which the C_s pulse charges C_p is determined by the time derivative of the following equation:

$$V_2 = -\frac{\beta V_1}{\beta + 1}(1 - \cos \omega t) \quad \text{for } t < \tau_\delta \tag{19}$$

where

$$\beta = \frac{C_s}{C_p}, \quad C = \frac{C_p C_s}{C_p + C_s}, \quad \omega = \frac{1}{\sqrt{LmC}}$$

V_2 = voltage on C_p, and L_m = main loop inductance. Therefore, for a given C_p and C_s, the rate of voltage rise across C_p is controlled by L_m. A typical value of β is between 1.1 and 1.5, and that of L_m is between 100 to 300 nH. The designer adjusts β, L_m, and the gas mixture such that energy transfer between C_s and C_p is nearly complete when the voltage across the electrodes breaks down. At that moment, the ratio of the energy on C_p and C_s is $4\beta/(\beta + 1)^2$. This is the fraction of the stored energy stored in C_s transferred to C_p. Inductance L_m is large enough that C_s cannot deliver charge directly to the discharge because of the short duration of its glow phase (< 30 nsec). The residual energy in C_s rings in the circuit after the glow phase until this energy is damped in the discharge and circuit elements.

However, the aforementioned requirements will not automatically guarantee high efficiency or energy. The designer has to tackle the other issues (most of which are very complex) to operate the laser at its highest efficiency. Some of the issues are electrode profile, electrode gap (H), and total loop inductance in the head ($L_c + L_h$), where L_c is stray circuit inductance and L_h is the laser head inductance. The L_h is proportional to the electrode gap, gas mixture and pressure (P), and materials that come in contact with laser gas. It can be shown [16] that if the breakdown voltage is twice the discharge voltage, that is,

$$V_b = 2V_d \tag{20}$$

then the discharge impedance matches the impedance of the discharge circuit, and the power transfer efficiency to the discharge is maximal. The designer normally tries to operate the laser so that Eq. 20 is approximately satisfied. Under these conditions, the power transferred (P_d) to the discharge is

$$P_d = \sqrt{C_p}\left(\frac{E}{P}\right)^2 \frac{P^2 H^2}{\sqrt{L_c + L_h}} \tag{21}$$

Therefore, for a given volume, a large H favors strong discharge pumping. But Eq. 21 presents contradictory messages. For instance, when the discharge volume is fixed, increasing H will lead to an increase in L_h that would decrease the power transferred to the discharge. An increase in C_p would increase the power transferred to the discharge, but this increase is accompanied by an increase in

L_c that would tend to decrease the transferred power. The discharge E/P may be optimized, which is done by optimizing the gas mixture. The designer often faces several conflicting issues and the design is based on such considerations as line narrowed or broadband, reliability, costs, and mechanical constraints.

3 SYSTEM DESCRIPTION

The lithography excimer laser system consists of the following major modules:

1. Laser chamber
2. Pulsed power module
3. Optical resonator
4. Optical diagnostics
5. Control unit
6. Peripheral support subsystems

A module-level layout of Cymer, Inc. ELS-5000 laser is shown in Fig. 8. In the following sections, we will describe the design considerations and details of these modules.

3.1 Chamber

The discharge chamber is a pressure vessel, designed to hold several atmospheres of a mixture of corrosive and inert gases (Fig. 8). These vessels are designed to known safety standards. The chamber is usually quite massive, between 50 to 100 kg, and designed for convenient access for service and replacement. The key components in the chamber are described below.

Electrodes

The electrodes determine the discharge width, which in turn determines the beam size. Typically, electrode widths are 20 to 25 mm, electrode gaps are 15 to 25 mm, and lengths are 500 to 800 mm. The electrodes are profiled to produce discharges that are less than 5 mm wide. The cathode is supported by an insulating structure, since it is connected to the high voltage, and the anode is attached to the metal chamber as it is at the ground potential. The choice of electrode material is critical in operating the laser reliably. These electrodes are often made from brass, although recently much effort [17] has been made to find other electrode materials that are compatible with F_2 and have low erosion under electron and ion bombardment.

Preionizer

The preionization is performed by corona discharges or spark discharges located on either side of the discharge region. Preionizer technology is quite complex and is highly proprietary information to any laser manufacturer. In the case of spark preionization, the material for the spark pin is brass. The di-

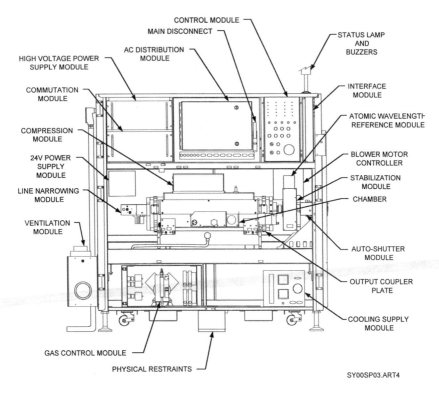

Figure 8 System view of Cymer, Inc. model ELS-5000.

electric material used in corona preionization has a high dielectric constant, high dielectric strength, and is compatible with fluorine. Sapphire or other forms of alumina is used. The electrodes of the corona preionizer are normally made from brass.

Blower and Magnetically Coupled Drive System

Since the laser is pulsed (500 to 1000 Hz), it is essential to clear the discharge region between pulses—a task performed by a tangential blower, which is magnetically coupled to an external drive source. The rotational speed of the blower determines the flow speed of the gas between the electrodes. The clearing ratio (F) is defined as

$$F = \frac{\text{flow speed}}{W_{\text{d}} \times \text{repetition rate}} \tag{22}$$

where W_{d} is the discharge width. Usually, a clearing ratio of 3 is adequate to obtain stable discharges. In practice, it is found that the clearing ratio has an impact on the laser's pulse-to-pulse energy stability, and a ratio of 5 or 6 is preferred. An approach to high F is to increase the rotational speed of the blower. In practice, it is found that higher blower speeds result in bearing failures and an increase in the complexity and size of the magnetic coupling and motor. The flow ducting in the chamber is optimized to maximize the flow speed between the electrodes without increasing the blower speed.

Heat Exchanger and Heaters

The laser's efficiency is highest at a particular empirically determined gas temperature, between 35 and 45°C. The laser chamber is maintained at this temperature by external heaters. During normal operation, the water flow through the laser's heat exchanger and the current to the heaters are regulated to maintain optimum laser gas temperature. It is observed that the laser's beam properties (size, divergence, direction) are affected by gas temperature. Stable gas temperature helps stabilize the laser's beam properties.

Because the area of the finned heat exchange is much larger than the area of the chamber itself, its material of construction is very important. The materials should be compatible with F_2, and should passivate easily in F_2. Minute leaks in the heat exchanger can be disastrous to the laser. Nickel-plated copper or nickel heat exchangers are commonly used.

Metal Fluoride Trap

The metal fluoride dust created by erosion of the electrode settles everywhere inside the chamber including (in the case of spark preionization) laser windows, which leads to an increase in optical losses. This problem is solved by implementing a dust trapping/window protection system as an integral part of the chamber (metal fluoride trap in Fig. 8). The metal fluoride dust is collected by means of an electrostatic precipitator inside the trap. A small amount of laser gas is extracted from the chamber and is passed over negatively charged high-field wires to trap the dust. The dust-free gas is then released over the windows to keep them clean. The gas is driven through the precipitator by the differential pressure built up inside the laser chamber due to the high-velocity flow. In addition, the windows are changed according to a specified maintenance schedule (typically every 1 billion pulses).

Materials of Construction

Loss of fluorine due to the formation of volatile fluorine compounds is the primary cause of laser performance degradation. Therefore, the chambers use particular metals and avoid the use of organic (although chemically resistant) materials such as Kynar, Teflon, or Viton. All these materials contaminate the laser gas, particularly in the presence of electrical discharge, fluorine, and ionic fluorine. As a consequence, gaseous contaminants such as CF_4, COF_2, SiF_4, CO_2, HF, and SF_6 are pervasive in laser chambers that use such organic materials. These contaminants have several detrimental effects; they (1) absorb photons at 248 nm and thus reduce efficiency, (2) contaminate and etch windows, (3) decrease gas life, (4) increase electrode erosion, and (5) worsen pulse-to-pulse energy stability. To overcome this problem, some excimer lasers employ a cryogenic gas reprocessor to freeze out the gaseous contaminants. However, not all contamination can be removed in this manner (such as CF_4). A recent breakthrough in laser chamber design [17,18] resulted in a chamber with useful gas lifetime of several hundred million pulses with a single gas fill. The key feature of the laser chamber is the use of corrosion-resistant ceramics and specialized carbon- and silicon-free alloys to avoid formation of contaminants like SiF_4 and CF_4, which are detrimental to laser performance even at low parts-per-million levels. Compared to standard nickel-plated aluminum, these materials improve laser gas lifetime. Chemical nickel plating is known as a coating that includes various contaminants and is therefore not considered. Extremely erosion-resistant materials are selected for all discharge components. The laser electrodes are made from sputter- and corrosion-resistant copper alloy. Clean-room assembly criteria and multistep passivation procedures are followed in assembling the chamber. In one case, with one gas fill and cryogenic gas puri-fication, a 500-Hz line-narrowed laser operated for 250 million pulses [17]. In another, with optimized pulsed power, the gas life was greater than 750 M pulses, without a gas processor [18].

3.2   Pulsed Power

The pulsed power module converts line voltage to DC voltage and then to a short high-voltage pulse. Since line voltage and high voltage are involved, the construction of the module is monitored very closely by plant safety engineers. The module is designed around safety guidelines detailed by SEMI S2-93 or similar standards. Also, the peak currents in the discharge are very high (20 to 30,000 amperes!). Therefore, extra precaution is exercised in containing the radiofrequency noise generated by the current to within confines of the pulsed power and chamber. The pulsed power module consists of the following key components.

High-Voltage Power Supply

It is a well-regulated capacitor charging high-voltage power supply with a regulation of < 0.3%. Such tight regulation is required to improve the pulse-to-pulse energy stability of the laser. Functionally, the capacitor charging power supplies convert 50/60 Hz AC input power to regulated high-voltage DC. This is done by converting the AC frequency to a high frequency (20 to 40 kHz) and then converting the high frequency to high-voltage DC by a transformer and rectifier assembly. Since the frequencies involved in switching and voltage conversion are much higher than line frequency, the overall efficiency of these power supplies is very high—typically 80 to 90%. Over the past few years, the regulation, reliability, and safety of these power supplies have improved considerably, so they require very little, if any, maintenance.

Pulse-Forming Network

The DC energy stored in a capacitor charged by the high-voltage power supply is transformed into a pulse by a combination of capacitors, inductors, saturable inductors (or magnetic switches), and a switch. If the network switches at high voltages, then the switch is a thyratron. If the network switches at low voltage (< 1000 V), the switch is a silicon-controller rectifier (SCR).

The capacitors are connected in a low-inductance configuration. They are the so-called doorknob capacitors, made from strontium titanate or barium titanate. The capacitor technology has kept up with the requirements of laser industry, and today these capacitors can be purchased in various forms to suit the design of the lasers from TDK or Murata.

The saturable inductors are inductors that can change from a state of high inductance to low inductance. A high inductor holds off pulsed voltage due to its high impedance until the inductor saturates. The inductance is proportional to the permeability of the inductor core material. The cores of these inductors are constructed from various forms of iron that exhibit a very high permeability until the magnetic flux (which depends on the current through the inductor) inside them reaches a certain critical value. Then their permeability drops to a very low value. Typically, the permeability drops from about 10,000 to 1. Since the inductor switches by merely switching its state, it is called a "passive" switch, as compared to a thyratron or SCR, where active charge transfer occurs between the electrodes. Therefore, the life of such a switch is almost limitless. Manufacturers of saturable iron include Allied Chemicals, Hitachi, and TDK, and they are sold under commercial names such as Metglas and Finemet.

A thyratron is a hot-cathode, gas-filled, high-voltage shorting switch. The problem of depositing a few joules (2 to 4 J per pulse) at 15 to 20 kV in 20 to 30 nsec is not trivial. The problem is amplified by the fact that the energy deposition is at high voltages, requiring a very fast high-voltage switch. The thyratron switches several thousands of amperes of current very quickly (i.e., very large change in current with time) at high repetition rates. Thyratrons were originally developed for radar applications in which the peak current and rise time requirements were significantly less stringent. However, under laser conditions, these thyratrons have a lifetime of 100 to 200 million pulses, or just about 50 hours of operation at 1 kHz.

Over the past few years, commercial suppliers have used several techniques to increase the thyratron lifetime. By joint technical collaboration between laser manufacturers and thyratron manufacturers [19], techniques were developed to understand the processes that degrade thyratron performance. It was found that as the thyratrons aged, their conduction losses increased (Fig. 9). The losses are a function of the input energies to the laser, and at typical lithography laser inputs the losses could be as high as 25%, rendering the thyratron unusable. The

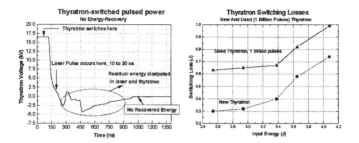

Figure 9   Thyratron switching losses are significant and increase with thyratron life.

increases in thyratron losses were attributed the reduction in cathode emission of the thyratron. An alternative cathode technology coupled with a modified anode structure resulted in a new thyratron (EEV's model CX 1626) with a lifetime greater than 5 billion pulses.

A more effective approach [17] is the use of pulse compression techniques in which the thyratron's peak current and current rise time correspond to those in a radar application. The resulting long pulse is not suitable for a KrF laser. Therefore, magnetic switches are used to compress the pulse, resulting in a high-peak, high-rise-time pulse for the laser. Figure 10 shows a typical two-stage magnetic pulse compression technique. The HV supply charges the main storage capacitor Cs. When the thyratron is switched, the current pulse width and the current rise time are controlled by Cs, C1, and L. Typically, the current pulse width is about 1 μsec. As C1 charges up, charging of C2 is blocked by the saturable core SR1. The core SR1 is designed to hold off a certain voltage for a certain time, at which point is saturates. The saturation point of SR1 is selected so that the transfer of charge from Cs to C1 is nearly complete. The saturated inductance of SR1 is selected so that the charge time of C2 by C1 is shorter, by a factor of 3 to 4 (i.e., about 250 to 300 nsec). Similarly, Cp is charged in a shorter time, ~100 nsec.

The advantage of this technique for thyratron lifetime is obvious. The thyratron is never exposed to the laser discharge, resulting in its long life (> 1 billion pulses). Also, if the pulse compression technique is extended, it might be possible to replace the thyratron completely with a solid-state device that has a limitless lifetime. However, the disadvantage of the pulse compression technique is that each stage must handle the energy required for the following stages plus its losses. If the materials of the saturable inductors are not selected carefully, the losses per stage can be very high. Typically, a two-stage compression circuit will lose 25% of the energy deposited in Cs. For high-repetition-rate operation, these losses can be a significant problem.

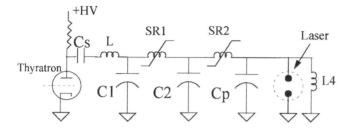

Figure 10 Simplified schematic of magnetic pulse compression circuit. SR1 and SR2 are saturable inductors. L and L4 are inductors. Cs, C1, C2, and Cp are capacitors.

In an extension of the magnetic pulse compression technique the thyratron is replaced by an all-solid-state switch [18] shown schematically in Fig. 11. The SSPPM is divided into two submodules—the commutation module and the compression module (Fig. 8). The 20 kV power supply used in the thyratron system is replaced by a 1-kV supply. The thyratron switch is replaced by an SCR switch that does not feed Cp directly but instead switches the energy of C0 into a pulse compression circuit formed by C1, C2, C3, a step-up transformer, and three saturable inductors [20]. The operation of this circuit is as follows. The DC charge stored on C0 is switched through the SCR and the inductor L0 into C1. The saturable inductor, L1, holds off the voltage on C1 for approximately 2.5 μs and then becomes conducting, allowing the transfer of charge from C1 to C2. The second saturable inductor, L2, holds off the voltage on C2 for approximately 500 ns and then allows the charge on C2 to flow through the primary of 1:20 step-up transformer. The output from the step-up transformer is stored on C3 until the saturable inductor L3 becomes conducting in approximately 100–150 nsec. The charge is then finally transferred through L3 into Cp and laser discharge occurs. The voltage waveform on Cp, shown in Fig. 12, closely matches the shape of that

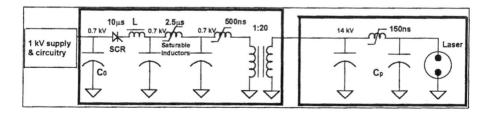

Figure 11 Simplified schematic of SCR-switched pulsed power for use with KrF lasers. (Courtesy of Cymer, Inc.)

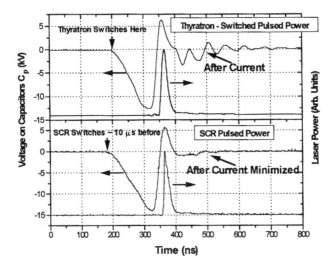

Figure 12   Voltage waveform on peaking capacitors with a thyratron-switched and SCR-switched pulsed power unit.

produced by an equivalent thyratron-switched pulsed power module, except that the one waveform exhibits little or no after-ringing.

The increased complexity of the solid-state pulsed power module is compensated for by the elimination of the expensive and short-lived thyratron. An additional and important feature of the SSPPM is the recovery of the energy reflected from the laser chamber (Fig. 13). With the SSPPM, the energy reflected by the laser chamber due to impedance mismatch no longer rings back and forth between the SSPPM and the laser chamber. The SSPPM circuit is designed to transmit this reflected energy all the way back through the pulse-forming network into C0. Upon recovery of this energy onto C0, the SCR switches off, ensuring that this captured energy remains on C0. Thus, regardless of the operating voltage, gas mixture, or chamber conditions, the voltage waveform across the laser electrodes exhibits the behavior of a well-tuned system. This performance is maintained over all laser operating conditions, resulting in improved chamber and gas life (Fig. 14).

Today, no lithography laser manufacturer separates pulsed power and chamber development. The long-term reliability of a lithography laser is as much dependent on the chamber as it is on its pulsed power. Some other key parameters, such as the laser's energy stability, are also dependent on the chamber design and pulsed power.

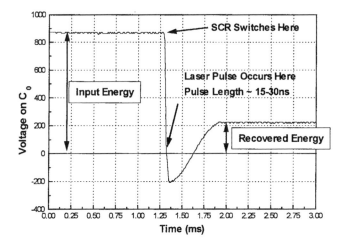

Figure 13 Voltage on C_0 indicates recovered energy from previous pulse for following pulse.

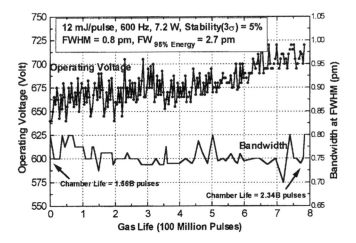

Figure 14 By a combination of solid-state pulsed power and laser chamber optimization, nearly 800 million pulses can be obtained with a single gas fill. No gas processor was used in this case. During operation, the laser maintained all beam parameters. (Data courtesy of Dr. William Partlo and Dr. Igor Fomenkov, Cymer, Inc.)

3.3   Optical Resonator

A plane-plane resonator is the most commonly used design for lithography lasers. The resultant highly multimode, divergent output is perfect for this application. The reflectivity of output coupler is typically 10 to 20%. The total reflector is a part of the line-narrowing optics of the laser. The optical assembly is mounted on an ultrastable assembly that is not sensitive to changes in environment such as temperature and vibrations. The resonator assembly is complicated by the fact that the spectral output of the laser should be much narrower than the laser's natural line width.

Spectral Narrowing

The bandwidth, full width at half-maximum (FWHM), of a free-running KrF excimer laser is approximately 300 pm. As discussed earlier, an excimer stepper requires the output of the laser to be spectrally narrowed between 0.8 and 3 pm, FWHM, depending on the NA of the lens. It should be noted that the integrated energy spectrum and the spectral width at 95% energy are more critical to stepper performance than the FWHM value. However, most users find it convenient to talk about FWHM instead of spectral width at 95% energy.

Spectral narrowing of a KrF laser is complicated by its short pulse duration (10 to 15 nsec, FWHM) and UV wavelength. The short pulse results in very high intracavity power ($\sim$1 MW/cm^2), and the short wavelength can thermally distort optical materials due to their high absorption coefficient at 248 nm. Also, the total number of round trips through the resonator (which includes the line-narrowing optical elements) for a typical laser is small, about three to four. If the single-pass bandwidth through the resonator is denoted by $\Delta\lambda_1$, then the final line width $\Delta\lambda_f$ after n passes is given by [21]:

$$\Delta\lambda_f = \frac{\Delta\lambda_1}{\sqrt{n}} \tag{23}$$

Therefore, the single-pass bandwidth of the optical system should be, at most, a factor of 2 higher than the final line width. in fact, time-resolved spectral measurements [22] indicate that the spectral line width could decrease by a factor of 2 from the start of the pulse to the tail of the pulse. Therefore, the efficiency of converting the broadband spectrum to a line-narrowed spectrum (i.e., from 300 pm to < 1 pm) of the optical system must be very high.

The common technique of line narrowing the KrF laser is by introducing wavelength disperse optical elements in the resonator. Three types of disperse elements can be used: prisms, etalons, and gratings [23]. Prisms do not provide enough dispersion and are thus unsuitable. Etalons are highly dispersive and efficient for spectrally narrowing an excimer laser [24]. In fact, many of the earlier lithography excimer lasers used a pair of etalons for spectral narrowing.

However, etalons suffer from two major shortcomings: thermal drift and coating damage. Both of these problems limit the use of etalons in a conventional optical setup for spectral narrowing. This problem was, however, solved by placing the etalons in a secondary optical branch in a novel polarization-coupled resonator configuration [25]. But this system is fairly complex and difficult to implement.

The use of a high dispersive grating in a Littrow configuration is the simplest and most effective spectral line-narrowing technique (Fig. 15). Because the grating is a dispersive element, the line width is proportional to the beam divergence. To get a narrow line width, a small beam divergence is required. Hence, two slits and three prism beam expanders are inserted in the laser resonator. Only one grating is tuned to control the wavelength. Since a grating is more stable than an etalon, the wavelength drift is much smaller and can be easily compensated for by tuning the grating. But the presence of apertures in the resonator limits the size of the laser gain region. Therefore, optimum conversion from non-line-narrowed to line-narrowed output requires a narrow discharge. The narrow electric discharge limits the output energy of the laser and decreases the lifetime of the electrodes. However, the problems are surmountable, and today lithography lasers operate between 500 and 1000 Hz, at 10–12 mJ per pulse and with a line width of 0.8 pm to 0.9 pm [26].

Another practical technique combines an etalon, prism, and a Littrow grating [27]. The grating is used for coarse narrowing and the etalon is used for fine narrowing. Because the grating is thermally stable, the wavelength drift is minimized. The prism beam expanders decrease the light intensity on the etalon by 80% and the wavelength drift of the etalon is minimized. In a variation of the aforementioned technique [17], the resonator keeps the radiation intensity

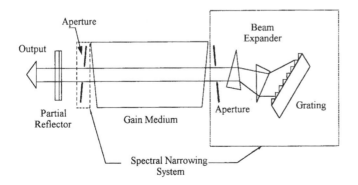

Figure 15 Spectral narrowing of a KrF excimer laser using a grating and prism. The prism is used to expand the beam. The aperture controls the bandwidth.

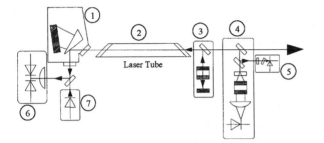

Figure 16 Optical setup for a prism, grating, and etalon line-narrowing system. 1, Tuning block with grating and prism beam expander; 2, laser tube with Brewster window; 3, front optics module with partial reflector, IC-etalon, total reflector; 4, bandwidth/wavelength monitor; 5, energy monitor module; 6, synchronization module; 7, pilot laser.

on the etalon very low because it is located in a separate branch of the laser resonator (Fig. 16). The line width of the laser is < 0.9 pm and the stability of the wavelength is ± 15 pm.

As the need for narrower and narrower spectral bandwidth increases for higher NA lenses, optical quality of the dispersive elements for spectral narrowing has to improve accordingly. Small deviations from flatness or material homogeneity cause wavefront errors and spectral broadening. The KrF gain medium amplifies these errors, which results in an increase in bandwidth. The selection of defect-free optics, therefore, becomes critical. However, the problem of minor wavefront curvature (which causes an increase in bandwidth) can be solved in a novel way by introducing a small concave or convex) curvature in the grating [26]. This is accomplished by physically bending the grating by means of a clamp and screw arrangement. The radius of curvature thus introduced into the grating could be between 0.5 and 10 km. This method allows one to achieve very narrow spectral bandwidths (< 1 pm) with good efficiency (i.e., about 40% of the free-running laser energy is converted to a bandwidth of 0.8 pm).

3.4 Optical Diagnostics

The lithography process is sensitive to several beam parameters. Experience has shown that some of these parameters do not change with time (or age of the laser). Therefore, they are normally measured once, just prior to integration of the laser to the stepper. The properties that do not change are:

1. Bean profile, beam pointing, and beam divergence stability
2. Polarization stability
3. Spatial coherence

One property that does change, and is very critical to the process, but is measured just prior to stepper integration is the spectral energy distribution. As we will discuss later, continuous measurement of this parameter is not practical.

The properties that change and are measured continuously during laser operation are the following:

1. Spectral bandwidth and spectral energy distribution
2. Relative wavelength stability
3. Absolute wavelength stability
4. Output energy and repetition rate
5. Pulse-to-pulse energy stability

In the following sections we will discuss the instrumentation used to measure some of the beam parameters. We will focus our attention on wavelength and bandwidth measurement (see Ref. 28 for techniques for measuring other beam parameters).

Wavelength Measurement

The center wavelength of the lithography laser output radiation has to be stabilized in order to (1) maintain focus at the wafer plane and, to a lesser degree, (2) minimize any change in magnification. Drift in center wavelength, however, affects the focal plane stability more severely than magnification. The variation of the central wavelength at the start of a burst of pulses is also important. In the following sections, we will describe a wavemeter that measures most of the spectral requirements for lithography. The wavemeter measures the wavelength and tunes the line-narrowing optics (etalon or grating) to compensate for any deviation from target wavelength.

The wavemeter used for a production lithography laser has to be compact and yet meet the requirements of good relative accuracy, low long-term drift, and good absolute precision with reference to some known standard (such as atomic absorption or emission line) and must be rugged enough to be transportable. The requirement in each case is $< \pm 0.15$ pm. Furthermore, the wavelength measurement has to be insensitive to changes in the ambient temperature or pressure. In addition, the wavemeter should be capable of measuring the spectral bandwidth (FWHM) with an accuracy of ± 0.15 pm several times a second. The operating range of this wavemeter, on the other hand, can be relatively small, 248.35 ± 0.300 nm. The wavelength is measured using a combination of a grating and an etalon (Fig. 17). The grating and the etalons are used, respectively, for coarse and fine measurements. The output from the grating spectrometer is imaged in the central region of a 1024-element silicon photodiode array, and the fringe pattern from the etalon is imaged on the two sides (Fig. 18). The central image from the etalon is blocked intentionally. The wavelength is determined by measuring the diameter of the etalon fringe pattern and the position of the coarse grating output.

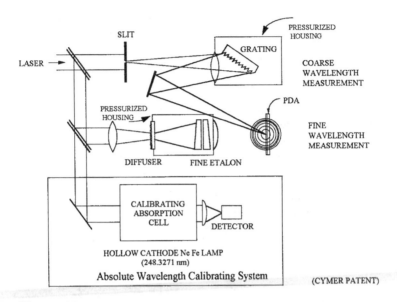

Figure 17   Wavemeter based on etalon and grating. Grating is used for coarse measurement, while the etalon does the fine measurement. Absolute wavelength calibration is done off-line in the factory.

The diameter D_p of the pth fringe from the center fringe is related to the wavelength via the following equation:

$$D_p^2 = 4f^2\lambda(p-1+\varepsilon)/(\mu h), \quad p = 1, 2, \dots \tag{24}$$

where μ is the refractive index of the air in the etalon gap at wavelength λ, ε is the fractional order number at the center fringe pattern, f is the focal length of the imaging lens, and h is the etalon gap. As is well known, the etalon fringe pattern is identical for wavelengths separated by multiples of its free spectral range (FSR), typically 20 pm for such applications. The grating measurement is used to determine the wavelength to within the FSR of the etalon and then Eq. 24 is used to determine the exact wavelength with respect to the wavelength determined by the grating. In practice, the wavemeter is calibrated at the factory with reference to some standard such as a hollow cathode Ne-Fe lamp, which has an absorption peak at 248.3271 nm.

From Eq. 24, we see that a small change in wavelength translates to a change in the diameter of the fringe. For wavelength change less than the FSR of the etalon, the etalon is capable of tracking the wavelength of the laser and stabilizing the laser wavelength. The coarse grating is used to eliminate any possible error or discrepancy in the laser wavelength drift of greater than the FSR of the etalon.

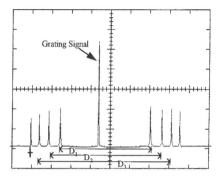

Figure 18 Fringe pattern from a grating and an etalon imaged on a 1024-element photodiode array. The central fringe of the etalon is blocked. The diameters D_1, D_2, and D_3 of the etalon fringes are used to determine laser wavelength.

In this wavemeter, the resolution of the grating measurement is ± 0.5 pm and its long-term accuracy is ± 0.5 pm. The etalon, on the other hand, has a resolution of ± 0.1 pm and long-term accuracy of ± 0.15 pm. Experience has shown that these wavemeters can be made stable to within ± 0.5 pm. Furthermore, to eliminate ambient pressure–dependent changes, both the grating and the etalon are housed inside individual pressurized housings. Temperature stability is achieved by using very low thermal expansion coefficient etalon spacers and good thermal management of the etalon housing.

In some wavemeters [29], the need for ultrastable optics to achieve absolute wavelength stability is eliminated by incorporating an absolute reference inside the wavemeter. Light from a mercury (Hg) lamp at 253.7 nm is compared to the KrF light through an optical system as shown in Fig. 19. The optical system creates two etalon fringe patterns corresponding to two wavelengths, which are compared at the photodiode array. Since the fringes from the Hg etalon correspond to a known wavelength, the wavelength from KrF laser can be calculated. Therefore, in this wavemeter, the wavelength is measured by comparison to a known standard.

Bandwidth Measurement

The bandwidth of the laser output is measured from the etalon fringe pattern. A fringe nestled between two other fringes provides a scale to measure the laser bandwidth directly from the fringe bandwidth. This pattern is used to determine the spectral bandwidth of the laser. If the etalon used has a finesse ($F = 30$), then the etalon resolution or bandwidth is FSR/F = 0.67 pm. Therefore, the measurement of the spectral bandwidth (FWHM) from the etalon fringe pattern width is not strictly correct; the fringe measurement has to be deconvolved for the etalon bandwidth.

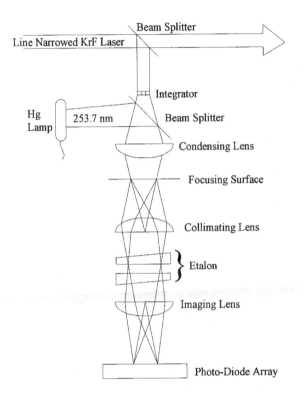

Line Narrowed KrF Laser

Beam Splitter

Hg Lamp

253.7 nm

Integrator

Beam Splitter

Condensing Lens

Focusing Surface

Collimating Lens

Etalon

Imaging Lens

Photo-Diode Array

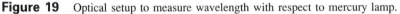

Figure 19   Optical setup to measure wavelength with respect to mercury lamp.

Spectral Energy Distribution

The fringe pattern does not provide a good idea of the spectral energy content in the wings. In fact, a good understanding of background optical noise levels (due to scattering in the optical instruments) and electronic offsets (within the data acquisition system) is necessary in order to compute accurately the spectrally integrated energy. At present, metrological instruments are not available to make such sensitive measurements. Instead, one has to build a high-resolution spectrometer [30] with noise levels of the order of 10^{-4}. The impact of the spectrometer's small but finite resolution (0.22 pm) is small while measuring the FWHM and even smaller in the 95% integrated energy (Figs. 20, 21).

Wavelength Control

The wavelength information obtained from the wavemeter is used to control the laser wavelength by changing the angle of illumination on the grating in the line-narrowing module. In practice, the grating is mounted on a microstepper, and its angle is scanned as the wavelength is measured. This process is slow

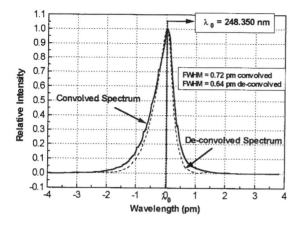

Figure 20 ELS-4000F laser line shape and width, measured with a high-resolution grating spectrometer, at 12 mJ, 600 Hz.

(several hundred milliseconds) and cannot compensate for the wavelength shift phenomenon described below.

The technology for measuring laser wavelength and spectral bandwidth is now well understood. However, what is somewhat less understood is the effect in which the wavelengths of the first few pulses in a string of laser pulses deviate from the target wavelength typically by a fraction of a picometer. This ef-

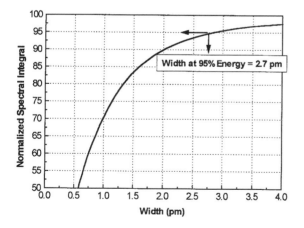

Figure 21 High-resolution grating spectrometer scan of Cymer model ELS-4000F laser. Measurements were made at 12 mJ; 600 Hz. (Data provided by Dr. Igor Fomenkov, Cymer, Inc.)

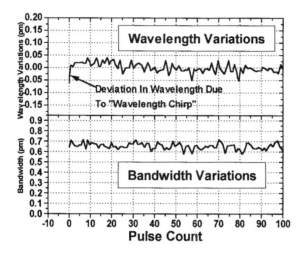

Figure 22 The wavelength chirping phenomenon results in a shift of the laser's wavelength during the first few pulses in a burst. The bandwidth variations are negligible. (Data courtesy of Dr. Igor Fomenkov, Cymer, Inc.)

fect is called "wavelength chirping" [31]. Experimental investigations of this phenomenon indicate that a strong coupling of the laser gas flow, discharge location, and spectral profile and center wavelength exists. Apparently, a small discharge shift occurs during the first few pulses in the burst, resulting in the wavelength chirp. The discharge, gas flow, and line-narrowing optics can be modified to reduce this effect, and the process of optimization of the line-narrowing optics includes minimization of wavelength chirping. The chirp is about 0.06 pm for the first pulse and a rapid decrease for the subsequent pulses (Fig. 22). But the effective 95% bandwidth calculated by integrating all the spectral profiles of a 40-shot burst is increased by only 1% due to the chirping phenomenon. This result indicates that the chirp, at this level, has an insignificant effect on stepper performance.

3.5 Control Unit

The microprocessor-based laser controllers play a significant role in monitoring and improving the laser performance. In fact, some fundamental deficiencies in the laser are overcome by using smart or self-learning software. The following example [32] will illustrate the role of the laser controller in controlling a key performance parameter of the laser.

The step-and-repeat lithography process has many steps, such as wafer loading, prealignment, exposure, and stepping of die (Fig. 23). After the laser has warmed up (typically 10 seconds to 15 minutes) and is the standby state, the laser may be

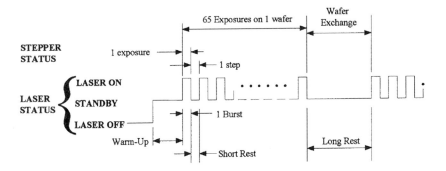

Figure 23 Operating mode of a step-and-repeat lithography laser.

operated in short bursts of pulses separated by rest periods. During the short burst, the die is exposed. This burst is followed by a short rest, typically 1 second, corresponding to stepping from chip to chip. The long bursts, typically several tens of seconds long, correspond to wafer exchange or reticle exchange.

The burst mode makes the laser operation unstable in energy and spectral performance at the beginning of a few or few tens of pulses of each burst. figure 24a shows the pulse energy stability of the first burst after 15 seconds standby time in constant-voltage operation (i.e., the input energy to the laser was constant). It can be seen that the variation in energy is most severe during the first few pulses of the burst. After the first few pulses, the energy of the subsequent pulses is more well behaved, implying that the energy can be stabilized by simply adjusting the voltage (i.e., input energy). The reason for the transient phenomena during the start of the burst is not known. It is believed that during the rest period, the population of some unknown transient species is negligible, but as the laser fires, these species are created. The population of these species rapidly reaches equilibrium after few pulses. The transient effect is more pronounced after a long rest period than a short rest period.

The pulse-to-pulse energy stability determines the minimum number of pulses for proper dose control accuracy [33]. It affects the quality and the repeatability of the pattern of resist. Fortuitously, it has been observed that the transient behavior during the start of the burst is fairly repeatable. Therefore, as the laser steps through its bursts, with the short rest in between burst, the energy stability is approximately the same. Similarly, the transient behavior after long rest periods is also the same. The laser's control system software is used to study and learn this transient behavior. After few bursts (during learning period), the control software knows about the transient behavior and accordingly biases the laser's operating voltage to compensate for the high-energy pulses during the beginning of the burst. In Fig. 24b we see the burst mode be-

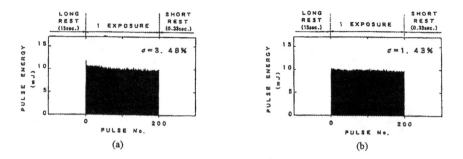

Figure 24   (a) Pulse-to-pulse energy stability without control at the beginning of 65-exposure train. (b) Pulse-to-pulse energy stability when the laser operates with "spike killer" at the beginning of 65-exposure train.

havior of the laser after the control software has learned about the behavior and has compensated for it during the beginning of the burst. As one can see, the stability has improved by a factor of 2.

The control system also plays an important role in performing system diagnostics and in maintaining stable fluorine concentration is the laser gas mixture [34].

3.6   Peripheral Support Subsystems

The AC distribution module, the vacuum pump module, the cabinet ventilation (Fig. 8), and the gas distribution module are some examples of the peripheral support subsystems of the laser. Until recently, their role in making lithography production worthy has largely been ignored. But with new product safety guidelines being enforced on semiconductor equipment manufacturers, the situation has changed considerably. The design and construction of support subsystems are scrutinized more carefully and have to comply with more than one safety/design standard. Some of these safety/design standards are:

1. SEMI S2-93
2. IBM non-product equipment standard
3. IBM gas safety standard
4. SEMI F-15 gas tracer standard
5. UL-5417 for electric motors
6. UL-499 for heaters
7. UL-508 for industrial controls
8. UL-1012 for electrical safety
9. CDRH 21CFR for radiation safety
10. CE

Laser manufacturers are quickly adapting their designs to these standards.

4 LASER PERFORMANCE AND MAINTENANCE

4.1 Performance Specifications

The performance specifications for a lithography laser are determined by the requirements of the stepper, resist, characteristics, and throughput issues. As seen in Table 1, as the stepper performance has progressed, the requirements on the laser have become more stringent. The latest stepper models suitable for sub-0.4 μm resolution in production are equipped with a variable NA lens (0.35 to > 0.5), variable coherence illuminator (0.3 to 0.7), and a large exposure field capability (> 21 × 21 mm²). Furthermore, several process-worthy, modest cost, deep-UV positive-tone resists, with a sensitivity between 30 and 60 mJ/cm², are now commercially available. The excimer lasers commonly used in these steppers are the Cymer laser, series ELS-4000 and ELS-5000, Komatsu KLES-G6 (10 mJ, 6 W, 0.8 pm, FWHM) and Lambda Physik LITHO (13.3 mJ, 600 Hz, < 0.9 pm FWHM). Performance specifications for Cymer's ELS-4000F and ELS-5000 are shown in Table 4. A detailed system configuration and layout of ELS-4000 are shown in Fig. 25. The ELS-5000 was introduced a year after ELS-4000. Their differences highlight the rapidly changing requirements in this industry.

4.2 Laser Reliability and Maintenance

The subject of laser reliability has been discussed for many years. Only recently, major technical innovations have been made that have improved the reliability of these lasers. These innovations include solid-state switched pulsed

Table 4 ELS-4000F and ELS-5000 Typical Performance Specifications

Specification	ELS-4000F	ELS-5000
Center wavelength	248.35 nm	248.35 nm
Wavelength tuning range	± 150 pm	± 150 pm
Repetition rate	600 Hz	1000 Hz
Pulse energy	12 mJ	10 mJ
Power	7.2 W	10.0 W
Spectral bandwidth (FWHM)	0.8 pm	0.8 pm
Band for 95% energy	< 3 pm	< 3 pm
Pulse-to-pulse energy variations (1 σ)	< 2.5%	< 2.5%
Wavelength drift over 8 hours	± 0.25 pm	± 0.25 pm
Wavelength drift over 6 months	± 0.25 pm	± 0.25 pm
Gas life	50 M pulses	100 pulses

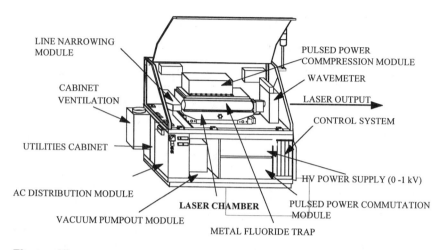

Figure 25   Cymer, Inc. model EX-4000F for stepper/scanner applications.

power circuits and long-life, metal and ceramic laser chambers. As a result of these continuous improvements, the cost of operation of these lasers has decreased substantially, and they are now comparable to the use of i-line mercury lamps. However, unlike lamps, which are discarded after use, lasers have to be maintained and laser subsystems have to be refurbished.

Before we discuss maintenance schedules, it is useful to estimate the laser usage during actual production. It is worth noting that unlike a mercury lamp, the laser is operating only during exposure. The model used to estimate laser usage is based on a resist sensitivity of 50 mJ/cm^2 and an optical throughput efficiency of 16%, both fairly typical values. As a result, laser usage during production will be approximately 2×10^9 pulses (Table 5) in 1 year.

Scheduled maintenance intervals for Cymer's ELS-5000 are given in Table 6. Note that except for gas exchange and fluorine trap replacement, other ac-tion items call for checking performance before proceeding to replace the part or the module. The intervals shown here are for reference. For higher stepper uptime and availability, laser maintenance will generally be synchronized to coincide with scheduled stepper maintenance. The operating cost for the laser today is approximately $30,000 for 1000 million pulses (Fig. 26) and is expected to decrease by an additional 20–30% in the future. As one can see, the operating cost for ELS-5000 (and other lasers) is dominated by the cost of laser chamber replacement. An incremental improvement

Table 5 Estimated Laser Usage During Production

Resist sensitivity	40 mJ/cm²
Field size	952 mm²
Laser power	10 W
Repetition rate	1000 Hz
Energy density at wafer	0.16 mJ/cm²
Exposure time/Field	254 ms
Number of pulses per wafer	8378
Wafer size	200 mm
Wafer throughput	90 W/hr
Laser pulses per hour	7.54×10^5
Average utilization [over 1 year (8670 hr)]	70%
Pulses per year	4.6×10^9

in chamber reliability or chamber replacement costs [35] will lead to a significant decrease in the cost of operation (Fig. 27). The reliability of the laser, in terms of mean time between failures (MTBF), now exceeds 1000 hours, and the uptime or availability of a properly maintained laser is better than 95%.

Table 6 ELS-5000 Maintenance Schedule

Activity	Interval in pulses
Gas exchange	100 M or 5 days
Fluorine trap	250 refills
Window inspection/clean[a]	> 1000 M
Optics inspection/exchange[a]	> 1000 M
Inspect, recalibrate, and qualify laser[a]	> 1000 M
Laser chamber (min)[b]	> 2500 M
Line-narrowing module (min)[b]	> 3000 M
Wavemeter module	> 5000 M

[a]Check baseline performance: voltage versus energy, bandwidth. Recalibrate if necessary.
[b]Phototest: resolution versus DOF.

Cost Per 1 Billion Pulses, Calculated Over 10 Billion Pulses

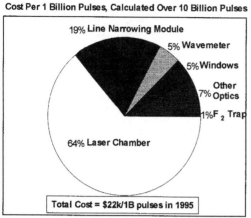

Figure 26 Cost of operation of ELS-5000. The cost is dominated by the cost of chamber replacement. (Data courtesy of Cymer, Inc.)

5 ARGON FLUORIDE EXCIMER LASER

The conversion of a KrF laser to an ArF laser is quite simple—replace krypton with argon. The principle of operation of a ArF laser is also very similar to that of a KrF laser. However, there are several key differences between the two

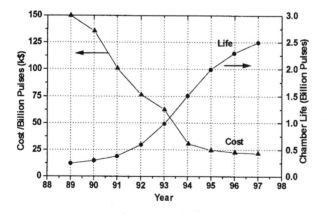

Figure 27 The cost of ownership of a lithography KrF laser has rapidly decreased as the chamber life has increased. (From Ref. 35.)

lasers, all which tend to make the ArF laser less production worthy than KrF. The differences between ArF and KrF are summarized below.

Property or Performance	KrF	ArF
Laser efficiency	For optimized KrF, about 3%.	For optimized ArF, about 1.5%. Implies more input power for same output.
Repetition rate	1-kHz KrF lasers available in January 1996.	The maximum from the same laser is about 600 Hz before the onset of discharge instabilities.
Losses	Transient species created in the discharge absorb at 248 nm, but these species are short-lived and their absorption is small.	The Schumann-Runge absorption bands of molecular oxygen and atomic carbon absorption are at 193 nm (Fig. 28). These are easily created in the discharge and they tend to reduce laser output significantly.
Optical losses	At the energy density for lithography, CaF_2 and fused silica materials have excellent life. Optical losses are not considered to be a problem.	Both CaF_2 and fused silica form absorptive color centers (Fig. 29). Fused silica also undergoes densification, resulting in change of refractive index. Therefore, optical losses are very high.
Line narrowing efficiency	Approximately 40% of laser's free running output (FWHM ~ 300 pm) can be converted to line-narrowed output (FWHM ~ 1 pm).	The conversion efficiency is much smaller, about 25% (Table 7).
Cost of operation or standard maintenance intervals	Cost of operation is determined by chamber life.	The cost of operation is determined by all subsystems (Table 8).

6 SUMMARY AND OUTLOOK

The krypton fluoride excimer laser for lithography, after a difficult beginning, is now a production worthy, fab-line qualified manufacturing tool. It is now able to meet all the stepper and process requirements in terms of performance,

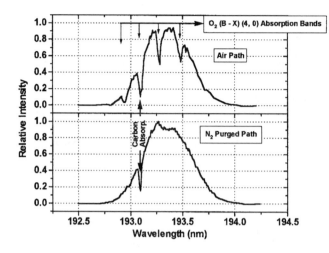

Figure 28   Spectrum of the free-running ArF laser, after propagation through 1 m of air and with nitrogen. Several P and R rotational lines of the (4, 0) vibrational band of oxygen are noted, along with the carbon absorption line at 193.09005 nm (From Ref. 28.)

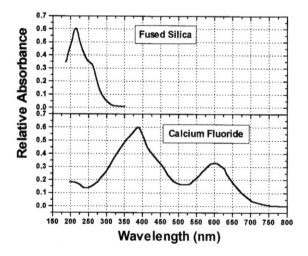

Figure 29   Both fused silica and calicium fluoride form absorptive color centers upon irradiation at 193 nm. (From Ref. 36.)

Table 7   Cymer, Inc. ELS-5000A ArF Lasers for Microlithography Research

Specification	Free running	Partially narrowed	Fully narrowed
Wavelength	193 nm	193 nm	193 nm
Bandwidth	Free running	≤50 pm	< 0.7 pm
Pulse energy	20 mJ	7 mJ	5 mJ
Repetition rate	1000 Hz	1000 Hz	1000 Hz
Power	20 W	7 W	5 W

reliability, and operating costs. Improvements in system design and engineering were responsible for this.

Lithography needs for sub-0.3 μm resolution, such as 64 M DRAM, will be met by i-line and excimer steppers. The excimer stepper will be used for some critical layers. The steppers for sub-0.3 μm resolution employ lenses with NA < 0.6 and a field size exceeding 21 × 21 mm². The laser for this should have a spectral bandwidth of < 0.8 pm (FWHM) with an output power of 6–10 W. These lasers are available today and can satisfactorily meet the technical specifications and the cost-of-operation goals. Following krypton fluoride, an argon fluoride (193 nm) excimer lithography is expected to push the limits of optical lithography below 0.2 μm resolution. One would expect that transition from 248 nm to 193 nm would be easy. However, today ArF technology has several technical barriers that need to be solved.

ACKNOWLEDGMENTS

We would like to thank all the scientists and engineers at Cymer for their contributions to this chapter and for their contributions to excimer laser technology for microlithography.

Table 8   Cymer, Inc. ELS-5000A ArF Laser Maintenance Intervals (in Pulses)

Gas exchange	30 million
Window exchange	100 million
Laser chamber exchange	1000 million
Pulse power module exchange	10,000 million
Wavemeter module exchange	1000 million
Line-narrowing module exchange	500 million

REFERENCES

1. Krauss, M., and Mies, F. H., *Excimer Lasers* (C. K. Rhodes, ed.), Springer-Verlag, New York, 1979.
2. Houtermans, F. G., *Helv. Phys. Acta*, *33*, 933 (1960).
3. Searles, S. K., and Hart, G. A., *Appl. Phys. Lett*, *27*, 243 (1975).
4. Brau, C. A., and Ewing, J. J., *Appl. Phys. Lett*, *27*, 435 (1975).
5. Simazaki, H., Nakamura, S., Obara, M., and Fujioka, T., *Excimer Lasers—1983* (C. K. Rhodes, H. Egger, and H. Pummer, eds.), American Institute of Physics, New York, 1983.
6. Rockni, M., Mangano, J. A., Jacobs, J. H., and Hsia, J. C., *IEEE J. Quantum Electron.*, *QE-14*, 464 (1978).
7. Hunter, R., 7th Winter Colloquium on High Power Visible Lasers, Park City, Utah, 1977.
8. Rhodes, C. K., and Hoff, P. W., *Excimer Lasers* (C. K. Rhodes, ed.), Springer-Verlag, New York, 1979.
9. Sengupta, U. K., Opt. Eng. *32*, 2410 (1993).
10. Sze, R., *IEEE J. Quantum Electron.*, *QE-15*, 1338 (1979).
11. Shaw, M. J., in *Physics of Laser Resonators* (D. R. Hall and P. E. Jackson, eds.), Adam Hilger, 1989.
12. Taylor, R. S., *Appl. Phys.*, *B41*, 1 (1986).
13. Treschchalov, A. B., and Peet, V. E., *IEEE J. Quantum Electron.*, *24* (1988).
14. Lin, S. C., and Levatter, J. I., *Appl. Phys. Lett.*, *34*, 8, (1979).
15. Hsia, J., *Appl. Phys. Lett.*, *30*, 101 (1977).
16. Rothe, D. E., Wallace, C., and Petach, T., *Excimer Lasers—1983* (C. K. Rhodes, H. Egger, and H. Pummer, eds.), American Institute of Physics, New York, 1983.
17. Coutts and Webb, *J. Appl. Phys.*, *59*, 704 (1986); Patzel, R., Kleinschmidt, J., Rebhan, U., Franklin, J., and Endert, H., *SPIE Symposium on Optical/Laser Microlithography VIII*, *2440*, 101 (1995).
18. Partlo, W., Sandstrom, R., Fomenkov, I., and Das, P., *SPIE Symposium on Optical/Laser Microlithography VIII*, *2440*, 90 (1995).
19. Das, P., Sengupta, U., Pirrie, C., Robinson, P., and Weatherup, C., *ISLOE Proceedings*, 1993.
20. Birx, D. L., and Ball, D. G., Lawrence Livermore Laboratories Tech. Doc. UCID-18831, Nov. 1980.
21. Barnes, J., Barnes, N., and Miller, G., *IEEE J. Quantum Electron.*, *24*(6), 1029 (1988).
22. Sandstrom, R., private communication, Cymer Laser Technologies, April 1995.
23. Wakabayahi, O., Kowaka, M., and Kobayashi, Y., *SPIE Symposium on Microlithography VI*, *1463*, 617 (1991).
24. Mckee, T. J., *Can. J. Phys.*, *63*, 214 (1985).
25. Furuya, N., Ono, T., Horiuchi, N., Yamanaka, K., and Miyata, T., *SPIE Symposium on Optical/Laser Microlithography III*, *1264*, 520 (1990).
26. Sandstrom, R., U.S. Patent 5,095,492 (1992).
27. Wakabayahi, O., Kowaka, M., and Kobayashi, Y., *SPIE Symposium on Microlithography VI*, *1463*, 617 (1991).

28. Sandstrom, R., *SPIE Symposium on Optical/Laser Microlithography IV, 1463,* 610 (1993).
29. Wakabayahi, O., Kowaka, M., and Kobayashi, Y., *SPIE Symposium on Microlithography VI, 1463,* 617 (1991).
30. Fomenkov, I. V., and Sandstrom, R., *SPIE Symposium on Optical/Laser Microlithography VI, 1927,* 64 (1993)
31. Ishihara, T., Sandstrom, R., Reiser, C., and Sengupta, U., *SPIE Symposium on Optical/Laser Microlithography V, 674,* 473 (1992).
32. Kowaka, M., Kobayashi, Y., Wakabayashi, O., Itoh, N., Fujimoto, J., Ishihara, T., Nakarai, H., Mizoguchi, H., Amada, Y., and Nozue, Y., *SPIE Symposium on Optical/Laser Microlithography VI, 1927,* 241 (1993)
33. Miyaji, A., Suzuki, K., and Atsumi, S., International Lasers/Applications, Technical Proceedings, 36 (1991).
34. Das, P., and Larson, D., U.S. Patent 5,377,215 (1994).
35. Wittekoek, S., Sematech Deep UV Lithography Workshop, Austin, Texas, 1995.
36. Sedlacek, J. H. C., and Rothschild, M., *SPIE, 1835,* 80 (1992).

5

Alignment and Overlay

Gregg M. Gallatin

SVG Lithography
Wilton, Connecticut

1 INTRODUCTION

This chapter discusses the problem of alignment in an exposure tool and its net result, overlay. Relevant concepts are described and standard industry terminology is defined. The discussion has purposely been kept broad and tool nonspecific. The content should be sufficient to make understanding the details and issues of alignment and overlay in particular tools relatively straightforward.

We will use the following convention: orthogonal Cartesian in-plane wafer coordinates are (x,y) and the normal to the wafer or out-of-plane direction will be the z axis.

2 OVERVIEW AND NOMENCLATURE

As discussed in other chapters, integrated circuits are constructed by successively depositing and patterning layers of different materials on a silicon wafer. The patterning process consists of a combination of exposure and development of photoresist followed by etching and doping of the underlying layers and deposition of another layer. This process results in a complex and, on the scale of microns, very nonhomogeneous material structure on the wafer surface.

Typically each wafer contains multiple copies of the same pattern called "fields" arrayed on the wafer in a nominally rectilinear distribution known as the "grid." Often, but not always, each field corresponds to a single "chip."

The exposure process consists of projecting the image of the next layer pattern onto (and into) the photoresist that has been spun onto the wafer. For the integrated circuit to function properly each successive projected image must be accurately matched to the patterns already on the wafer. The process of determining the position, orientation, and distortion of the patterns already on the wafer and then placing them in the correct relation to the projected image is termed "alignment." The actual outcome, i.e., how accurately each successive patterned layer is matched to the previous layers, is termed "overlay."

The alignment process requires, in general, both the translational and rotational positioning of the wafer and/or the projected image as well as some distortion of the image to match the actual shape of the patterns already present. The fact that the wafer and the image need to be positioned correctly to get one pattern on top of the other is obvious. The requirement that the image often needs to be distorted to match the previous patterns is not at first obvious but is a consequence of the following realities. No exposure tool or aligner projects an absolutely perfect image. All images produced by all exposure tools are slightly distorted with respect to their ideal shape. In addition, different exposure tools distort the image in different ways. Silicon wafers are not perfectly flat or perfectly stiff and any tilt or distortion of the wafer during exposure, either fixed or induced by the wafer chuck, results in distortion of the printed patterns. Any vibration or motion of the wafer relative to the image that occurs during exposure and is unaccounted for or uncorrected by the exposure tool will "smear" the image in the photoresist. Thermal effects in the reticle, the projection optics, and/or the wafer will also produce distortions.

The net consequence of all this is that the shape of the first-level pattern printed on the wafer is not ideal and all subsequent patterns must, to the extent possible, be adjusted to fit the overall shape of the first-level printed pattern. Different exposure tools have different capabilities to account for these effects, but, in general, the distortions or shape variations that can be accounted for include x and y magnification and skew. These distortions, when combined with translation and rotation, make up the complete set of linear transformations in the plane. They are defined and discussed in detail in the Appendix.

Since the problem is to match successively the projected image to the patterns already on the wafer and not simply to position the wafer itself, the exposure tool must effectively be able to detect or infer the relative position, orientation, and distortion of both the wafer patterns themselves and the projected image. The wafer patterns are always measured directly, whereas the image position orientation and distortion are sometimes measured directly and sometimes inferred from the reticle position after a baseline reticle-to-image calibration has been performed.

2.1   Alignment Marks

It is difficult to sense directly the circuit patterns themselves and therefore alignment is accomplished by adding fiducial marks, known as alignment marks, to the circuit patterns. These alignment marks can be used to determine the reticle position, orientation, and distortion and/or the projected image position, orientation, and distortion. They can also be printed on the wafer along with the circuit pattern and hence can be used to determine the wafer pattern position, orientation, and distortion. Alignment marks generally consist of one or more clear or opaque lines on the reticle, which then become "trenches" or "mesas" when printed on the wafer. But more complex structures such as gratings, which are simply periodic arrays of trenches and/or mesas, and checkerboard patterns are also used. Alignment marks are usually located either along the edges of "kerf" of each field or a few "master marks" are distributed across the wafer. Although alignment marks are necessary, they are not part of the chip circuitry and therefore, from the chip maker's point of view, they waste valuable wafer area or "real estate." This drives alignment marks to be as small as possible, and they are often less than a few hundred micrometers on a side. In principle, it would be ideal to align to the circuit patterns themselves, but this has so far proved to be very difficult to implement in practice. The circuit pattern printed in each layer is highly complex and varies from layer to layer. This approach therefore requires an adaptive pattern recognition algorithm. Although such algorithms exist, their speed and accuracy are not equal to those obtained with simple algorithms working on signals generated by dedicated alignment marks.

2.2   Alignment Sensors

In order to "see" the alignment marks, alignment sensors are incorporated into the exposure tool, with there generally being separate sensors for the wafer, the reticle, and/or the projected image itself. Depending on the overall alignment strategy, these sensors may be entirely separate systems or they may be effectively combined into a single sensor. For example, a sensor that can see the projected image directly would nominally be "blind" with respect to wafer marks and hence a separate wafer sensor is required. But a sensor that "looks" at the wafer through the reticle alignment marks themselves is essentially performing reticle and wafer alignment simultaneously and hence no separate reticle sensor is necessary. Note that in this case the positions of the alignment marks in the projected image are being inferred from the positions of the reticle alignment marks and a careful calibration of reticle to image positions must have been performed before the alignment step.

Also, there are two generic system-level approaches for incorporating an alignment sensor into an exposure tool, termed "through the lens" and "not through the lens" or "off axis." In the through-the-lens (TTL) approach the aligment sensor looks through the same or mostly the same optics that are used to project the aerial image onto the wafer. In the not-through-the-lens (NTTL) approach the alignment sensor uses its own optics, which are completely or mostly separate from the image projection optics. The major advantage of TTL is that to some extent it provides common-mode rejection of optomechanical instabilities in the exposure tool. That is, if the projection optics move, then, to first order, the shift in the position of the projected image at the wafer plane matches the shift in the image of the wafer as seen by the alignment sensor. This cancelation to some extent desensitizes alignment with respect to optomechanical instabilities. The major disadvantage of TTL is that it requires the projection optics to be simultaneously good for exposure as well as alignment. Since alignment and exposure generally do not work at the same wavelength, the exposure imaging capabilities of the projection optics must be compromised to allow sufficiently accurate performance of the alignment sensor. The net result is that neither the projection optics nor the alignment sensor is providing optimum performance. The major advantage of the NTTL approach is precisely that it decouples the projection optics and alignment sensor, allowing each to be independently optimized. Also, since an NTTL sensor is independent of the projection optics, it is compatible with different tool types such as i-line, deep ultraviolet (DUV), and extreme ultraviolet (EUV). Its main disadvantage is that optomechanical drift is not automatically compensated and hence the alignment sensor to projected image "baseline" must be recalibrated on a regular basis, which can reduce throughput. The TTL approach requires the same projected image to alignment sensor calibration to be made, but it does not need to be repeated as often.

Furthermore, as implied above, essentially all exposure tools use sensors that detect the wafer alignment marks optically. That is, the sensors project light at one or more wavelengths onto the wafer and detect the scattering/diffraction from the alignment marks as a function of position in the wafer plane. Many types of alignment sensor are in common use and their optical configurations cover the full spectrum from simple microscopes to heterodyne grating interferometers. Also, since different sensor configurations operate better or worse on given wafer types, most exposure tools "sport" more than one sensor configuration to allow for good overlay on the widest possible range of wafer types. Finally, there are two generic sensor archetypes: "scanning, and "staring." A staring sensor has a spatially resolved finite field of view. That is, it produces some type of spatially resolved "image" of the area around and including an alignment mark and thus can just "stare" at the wafer to collect alignment data. An ordinary microscope is a simple example of a staring sensor. A scanning sensor does not simultaneously collect spatially resolved information. It effectively sees only the net signal from a single point, line, or area on the wafer. In order to collect spatial information, either the sensor must physically scan the wafer or some parameter such as the phase of the illuminating light must be varied so that sensor is able to see spatial features on the wafer. A sensor that projects a pattern of light such as a single line onto the wafer and detects only the total scatter/diffraction from a matching pattern on the wafer must physically move the projected pattern with respect to the wafer, i.e., scan the wafer, to produce spatially dependent data. Some grating sensors project multiline patterns onto the wafer, which they effectively cause to move or scan by varying the relative phase of the illuminating waves. An overview of the various types of alignment sensor is given below. Detailed descriptions of some specific sensors can be found in Refs. 1–9.

2.3 Alignment Strategies

The overall job of an alignment sensor is to determine the position of each of a given subset of all the alignment marks on a wafer in a coordinate system fixed with respect to the exposure tool. These position data are then used in either of two generic ways, termed "global" and "field-by-field," to perform alignment. In global alignment the marks in only a few fields are located by the alignment sensor(s) and the data are combined in a best-fit sense to determine the optimium alignment of all the fields on the wafer. In field-by-field alignment the data collected from a single field are used to align only that field. Global alignment is usually both faster, because not all the fields on the wafer are located, and less sensitive to noise, because it combines all the data together to find a best overall fit. But, since the results of the best fit are used in a feedforward or dead reckoning approach, it does rely on the overall optomechanical stability of the exposure tool.

Alignment is generally implemented as a two-step process; that is, a fine alignment step with an accuracy of tens of nanometers follows an initial coarse alignment step with an accuracy of microns. When a wafer is first loaded into the exposure tool, the uncertainty in its position in exposure tool coordinates is often on the order of several hundred microns. The coarse alignment step uses a few large alignment targets and has a capture range equal to or greater than the initial wafer position uncertainty. The coarse alignment sensor is generally very similar to the fine alignment sensor in configuration, but in some cases these two sensors can be combined into two modes of operation of a single sensor. The output of the coarse alignment step is the wafer position to within several microns, which is within the capture range of the fine alignment system. Sometimes a "zero" step known as "prealignment" is performed in which the edge of the wafer is detected mechanically or optically so that it can be brought into the capture range of the coarse alignment sensor.

2.4 Alignment Versus Leveling and Focusing

Alignment requires positioning the wafer in all six degrees of freedom: three translation and three rotation. But adjusting the wafer so that it lies in the projected image plane, i.e., leveling and focusing the wafer, which involves one translational degree of freedom (motion along the optic axis) and two rotational degrees of freedom (orienting the plane of the wafer to be parallel to the projected image plane), is generally considered separate from alignment. Only in-plane translation (two degrees of freedom) and rotation about the projection optic axis (one degree of freedom) are commonly meant when referring to alignment. The reason for this separation in nomenclature is the difference in accuracy required. The accuracy required for in-plane translation and rotation generally needs to be on the order of several tens of nanometers or about 20 to 30% of the minimum feature size or critical dimension (CD) to be printed on the wafer. Current state-of-the-art CD values are on the order of several hundred nanometers and thus the required alignment accuracy is less than 100 nm. On the other hand, the accuracy required for out-of-plane translation and rotation is related to the total usable depth of focus of the exposure tool, which is generally close to the CD value. Thus out-of-plane focusing and leveling the wafer require less accuracy than in-plane alignment. Also, the sensors for focusing and leveling are usually completely separate from the "alignment sensors," and focusing and leveling do not usually rely on patterns on the wafer. Only the wafer surface needs to be sensed.

2.5 Field and Grid Distortion

As discussed above, along with in-plane rigid body translation and rotation of the wafer, various distortions of the image may be required to achieve the necessary overlay. The deviation of the circuit pattern in each field from its ideal rectangular shape is termed field distortion. Along with field distortion it is usually necessary to allow for grid distortion, i.e., deviations of the field centers from the desired perfect rectilinear grid. Both the field and grid distortions can be separated into linear and nonlinear terms as discussed in the Appendix. Depending on the location and number of alignment marks on the wafer, most exposure tools are capable of accounting for some or all of the linear components of field and grid distortion.

Although all the as-printed fields on a given wafer are nominally distorted identically, in reality the amount and character of the distortion of each field vary slightly from field to field. If the lithographic process is sufficiently well controlled, this variation is generally small enough to ignore. It is this fact that makes it possible to perform alignment using the global approach.

As mentioned above, different exposure tools produce different specific average distortions of the field and grid. In other words, each tool has a unique distortion signature. A tool aligning to patterns that it printed on the wafer will on average be better able to match the distortion in the printed patterns than a different tool with a different distortion signature. The net result is that the overlay will be different in the two cases, with the "tool-to-itself" overlay (i.e., the result of a tool aligning to patterns that it printed) being generally several tens of nanometers better than when one tool aligns to the patterns printed by a different tool, the "tool-to-tool" result. Ideally, one would like to make all tools have the minimum distortion, but this is not necessary. All that is really necessary is to match the distortion signatures of all the tools that will be handling the same wafers. This can be done by tuning the tools to match a single "master tool," or they can be tuned to match their average signature.

2.6 Wafer Versus Reticle Alignment

Although both the reticle and wafer alignments must be performed accurately, wafer alignment is usually the bigger contributor to alignment errors. The main reason is the following: a single reticle is used to expose many wafers. Thus, once the reticle alignment marks have been "calibrated" they do not change, whereas the detailed structure of the wafer alignment marks varies in multiple and unpredictable ways not only from wafer to wafer but also across a single wafer. Just as real field patterns are distorted from their ideal shape, the material structure making up the trenches and/or mesas in real alignment marks is distorted from its ideal shape. Thus the width, depth, side wall slope, etc., as well as the symmetry, of the trenches and mesas vary from mark to mark. The effect of this variation in mark structure on the alignment signal from each mark is called "process sensitivity." The ideal alignment system, i.e., combination of optics and algorithm, would be the one with the least possible process sensitivity. The result of all this is that the major fundamental limitation to achieving good overlay is almost always associated with wafer alignment. Furthermore, most projection optical systems reduce or demagnify the reticle image at the wafer plane and thus less absolute accuracy is generally required to position the reticle itself.

3 OVERLAY ERROR CONTRIBUTORS

The overall factors that effect overlay are the standard ones of measurement and control. The position, orientation, and distortion of the patterns already on the wafer must be inferred from a limited number of measurements and the position orientation and distortion of the pattern to be exposed must be controlled using a limited number of adjustments. For actual results of particular tools see Refs. 10–12. Here we present simply a list of the basic sources of error.

Measurement

1. Alignment system: Noise and inaccuracies in the ability of the alignment system to determine the positions of the alignment marks. This includes not only the alignment sensor itself but also the stages and laser gauges that serve as the coordinate system for the exposure tool, as well as the calibration and stability of the alignment system axis to the projected image, which is true for both NTTL and TTL. It also includes the electronics and algorithm that are used to collect and reduce the alignment data to field and grid terms. Finally, it must be remembered that the alignment marks are not the circuit pattern and the exposure tool is predicting the circuit pattern position, orientation, and distortion from the mark positions. Errors in this prediction due to the nonperfection of the initial calibration of the mark-to-pattern relationship or changes in the relationship due to thermal and/or mechanical effects and simplifications in algorithmic representation, such as the linear approximation to the nonlinear distortion, all contribute to overlay error.
2. Projection optics: Variations and/or inaccuracies in the determination of the distortion induced in the projected pattern by the optical system. Thermomechanical effects change the distortion signature of the optics. At the nanometer level this signature is also dependent on the actual aberrations of the projection optics, which cause features with different line widths to print at slightly different positions. In tool-to-itself overlay the optical distortion is nominally the same for all exposed levels, so this effect tends to be minimal in this case. In tool-to-tool overlay the difference in the optical distortion signatures of the two different projection optics is generally not trivial and thus can be a significant contributor to overlay errors.
3. Illumination optics: Nontelecentricity in the source pupil when coupled with focus errors and/or field nonflatness will produce image shifts and/or distortion. Variation in the source pupil intensity across the field can also shift the printed alignment mark position with respect to the circuit position.
4. Reticle: Reticle metrology errors, i.e., errors in the mark-to-pattern position measurements. Variation in the mark-to-pattern position caused by reticle mounting and/or reticle heating. Particulate contamination of the reticle alignment marks can also shift the apparent mark position.

Control

1. Wafer stage: Errors in the position and rotation of the wafer stage, both in plane and out of plane, during exposure contribute to overlay errors. Also, wafer stage vibration contributes. These are rigid body effects. There are also non–rigid body contributors such as wafer and wafer stage heating,

which can distort the wafer with respect to the exposure pattern, and chucking errors, which "stretch" the wafer in slightly different ways each time it is mounted.

2. Reticle stage: Essentially all the same considerations as for the wafer stage apply to the reticle stage but with some slight mediation due to the reduction nature of the projection optics.

3. Projection optics: Errors in the magnification adjustment cause pattern mismatch. Heating effects can alter the distortion signature in uncontrollable ways.

3.1 Measuring Overlay

Overlay is measured simply by printing one pattern on one level and a second pattern on a consecutive level and then measuring, on a stand-alone metrology system, the difference in the position, orientation, and distortion of the two patterns. If both patterns are printed on the same exposure tool the result is tool-to-itself overlay and if they are printed on two different exposure tools the result is tool-to-tool overlay.

The stand-alone metrology system consists basically of a microscope for viewing the patterns, connected to a laser gauge-controlled stage for measuring their relative positions. The most common pattern is a square inside a square, which is called "box-in-box," and its 45° rotated version, called "diamond-in-diamond." The shift of the inner square with respect to the outer square is the overlay at that point in the field. The results from multiple points in the field can be expressed as field magnification, skew, and rotation, and the average position of each field can be expressed as grid translation, magnification, skew, and rotation.

4 PRECISION, ACCURACY, THROUGHPUT, AND SENDAHEADS

Ideally, alignment should be fast and accurate. As a minimum it needs to be repeatable and precise.

Alignment should be fast because lithography is a manufacturing technology and not a science experiment. Thus there is a penalty to be paid if the alignment process takes too long: the number of wafers produced per hour decreases. This leads to a trade-off between alignment accuracy and alignment time. Given sufficient time, it is possible, as least in principle, to align essentially any wafer with arbitrary accuracy. But as the allowed time gets shorter the accuracy achievable will in general decrease.

Due to a combination of time constraints, alignment sensor nonoptimality, and excess mark structure variation it is sometimes possible only to achieve repeatable and precise alignment. But since accuracy is also necessary for overlay, a predetermined correction factor or "offset" must be applied to such alignment results. The correction factor is most commonly determined using a "sendahead" wafer. That is, a wafer that has the nominal alignment mark structures printed on it is aligned and exposed and the actual overlay in terms of the difference between the desired exposure position, rotation, and distortion and the actual exposure position, rotation, and distortion is measured. These measured differences are then applied as an offset directly to the alignment results on all subsequent wafers of that type, which effectively cancels out the alignment error seen by the sensor. For this approach to work, the alignment process must produce repeatable results so that measuring the sendahead wafer is truly indicative of how subsequent wafers will behave. Also, it must have sufficient precision to satisfy the overlay requirements once the sendahead correction has been applied.

5 THE FUNDAMENTAL PROBLEM OF ALIGNMENT

The fundamental job of the alignment sensor is to determine, as rapidly as possible, the positions of a set of alignment marks in exposure tool coordinates to the required accuracy. Here, the word "position" nominally refers to the center of the alignment mark. To put the accuracy requirement in perspective, it must be remembered that the trenches and/or mesas that make up an alignment mark are on the order of the critical dimension or larger; thus the alignment sensor must be able to locate the center of an alignment mark to a very small fraction of the mark dimensions.

Now, if the alignment mark itself, including any overcoat layers such as photoresist, is perfectly symmetric about its center and the alignment sensor is perfectly symmetric, then the center of the alignment signal corresponds exactly to the center of the alignment mark. Thus only for the case of perfect symmetry does finding the center of the signal correspond to finding the center of the alignment mark. If the mark and/or the alignment sensor is in any way not perfectly symmetric, the signal center will not be coincident with the mark center and finding the signal center does not mean you have found the mark center. This is the fundamental problem of alignment.

Noise also causes the detected signal to be asymmetric. But if the signal is sufficiently sampled and the data are reduced appropriately, then, within limits, the effect of noise on the determination of the signal center can be made as small as necessary, leaving only the systematic variations in signal shape to contend with. The relation between the true mark center and the signal center can be determined by solving Maxwell's equations for each particular mark structure and sensor configuration. The result of such an analysis is a sensitive function of the details of the mark structure and the sensor configuration. Generally, the details of the mark structure and its variation both across a wafer and from wafer-to-wafer are not well known, and the results of such calculations have so far been used only for sensitivity studies and off-line debugging of alignment problems.

As discussed above, when the offset between the true mark center and the signal center is too large to ignore, it can be determined by using sendahead wafers. The overlay on a sendahead wafer is measured and applied as a fixed offset or correction to the mark positions found by the alignment sensor on subsequent wafers on the same type. Thus sendaheads effectively provide an empirical solution as opposed to an analytic solution to the difference between the true and measured mark positions. But sendaheads take time and cost money, and thus chip manufacturers would very much prefer to work with alignment systems that do not require sendaheads. Over the years, tool manufacturers have generally improved the symmetry of the alignment sensors and increased the net signal-to-noise ratio of the data to meet the tighter overlay requirements associated with shrinking CD values. There have also been significant improvements in wafer processing. But whereas in the past the dominant contributor to alignment error may well have been the sensor itself, now inherent mark asymmetry in many cases is an equal or dominant contributor. The economic benefit of achieving the required overlay with no sendaheads is nontrivial but requires the development of a detailed understanding of process-induced mark asymmetries. The development of such a knowledge base would allow the design of robust alignment sensors, algorithms, and strategies. Another way to look at this is the following. In effect, a nonsymmetric mark has no well-defined center and the tool user must be able to define what he means by it if the tool is to meet overlay. In the past this was done using sendaheads. In the future it will be done using accurate models of how the signal distorts as a function of known mark asymmetries.

5.1 Alignment Mark Modeling

The widths, depths, and thicknesses of the various "blocks" of material that make up an alignment mark are usually between a few tenths and several times the sensing wavelength in size. In this regime geometrical and physical optics are both at best rough approximations and only a reasonably rigorous solution to Maxwell's equation for each particular case will be able to make valid predictions of signal shape, intensity, and mark offset. This is illustrated in Fig. 1. Because of the overall complexity of wave propagation and boundary condition

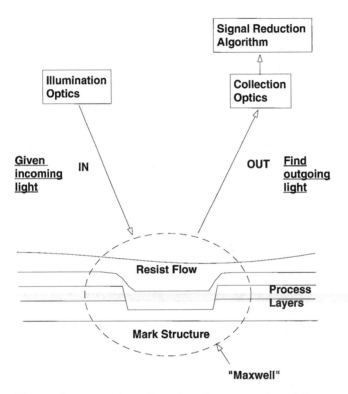

Figure 1 The basic problem that alignment mark modeling must solve is to determine the outgoing distribution of light as a function of the incoming distribution. (See text for detailed discussion.)

matching in an average alignment mark, it is essentially impossible to predict intuitively how the light will scatter and diffract from a given mark structure. Thus to understand the details of why a particular mark structure produces a particular signal shape and a particular offset requires solving Maxwell's equations for that structure. Also, the amplitude and phase of the light scattered or diffracted in a particular direction depends sensitively on the details of the mark structure. Variations in the thickness or shape of a given layer by as little as 10 nm or in its index by as little as 1% can significantly alter the alignment signal shape and position. Thus, again, to understand what is happening requires detailed knowledge of the actual three-dimensional mark structure as well as its variation in real marks.

In general, all the codes and algorithms used for the purpose of alignment mark modeling are based on rigorous techniques for solving multilayer grating diffraction problems, and they essentially all couch the answer in the form of a "scattering matrix," which is nothing but the optical transfer function of the alignment mark. It is beyond the scope of this discussion to describe in detail the various forms that these algorithms take, and we refer the reader to the literature for details. Although we will not discuss how a scattering matrix is computed, it is worth understanding what a scattering matrix is and how it can be used to determine alignment signals for different sensor configurations.

The two key aspects of Maxwell's equations and the properties of the electromagnetic field that we will need are the following:

1. The electromagnetic field is a vector field. That is, the electric and magnetic fields have a magnitude and a direction. The fact that light is a vector field, i.e., has polarization states, should not be ignored when analyzing the properties of alignment marks as this can, in some cases, lead to completely erroneous results.
2. Light obeys the wave equation, i.e., it propagates. But it must also obey Gauss' law. In other words, Maxwell's equations contain more physics than just the wave equation.

It is convenient to use the natural distinction between wafer in-plane directions, x and y, and the out-of-plane direction or normal to the wafer, z, to define the two basic polarization states of the electromagnetic field, which we will refer to as TE, for tangential electric, and TM, for tangential magnetic. For TE polarization the electric field vector, $\mathbf{E}$, is tangent to the surface of the wafer; that is, it has only x and y components, $\mathbf{E} = \hat{e}_x E_x + \hat{e}_y E_y$. For TM polarization the magnetic field vector, $\mathbf{B}$, is tangent to the surface of the wafer; that is, it has only x and y components, $\mathbf{B} = \hat{e}_x B_x + \hat{e}_y B_y$ (see Fig. 2). We use the convention that $\hat{e}_x, \hat{e}_y$, and $\hat{e}_z$ are the unit vectors for the x, y, and z directions, respectively. We can work with just the electric field for both polarizations, since the corresponding magnetic field can be calculated from it, and use the notation $\mathbf{E}_{TE}$ for the TE polarized waves and $\mathbf{E}_{TM}$ for the TM polarized waves.

For completeness, Maxwell's equations, in MKS units, for a homogeneous static isotropic nondispersive nondissipative medium, take the form

$$\boldsymbol{\partial} \cdot \mathbf{E} = 0$$

$$\boldsymbol{\partial} \cdot \mathbf{B} = 0$$

$$\boldsymbol{\partial} \times \mathbf{E} = -\partial_t \mathbf{B}$$

$$\boldsymbol{\partial} \times \mathbf{B} = \frac{n^2}{c^2} \partial_t \mathbf{E}$$

where n is the index of refraction and c is the speed of light in vacuum.

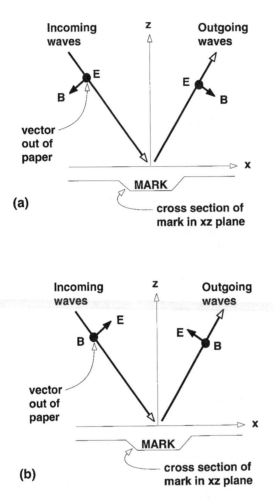

Figure 2 The most convenient pair of basic polarization states are the so-called (a) TE and (b) TM configurations. In either case in two dimensions the full vector form of Maxwell's equation reduces to a single scalar partial differential equation for these two polarization states.

The wave equation follows directly from Maxwell's equations and is given by

$$\left(\frac{n^2}{c^2}\partial_t^2 - \partial^2\right)\mathbf{E}\,(\mathbf{x},t) = 0$$

$$\left(\frac{n^2}{c^2}\partial_t^2 - \partial^2\right)\mathbf{B}\,(\mathbf{x},t) = 0$$

We use the notation $\partial_t = \partial/\partial t$, $\boldsymbol{\partial} \equiv \boldsymbol{\nabla} = \hat{e}_i \partial_i = \hat{e}_x \partial_x + \hat{e}_y \partial_y + \hat{e}_z \partial_z = \hat{e}_x \partial/\partial x + \hat{e}_y \partial/\partial y + \hat{e}_z \partial/\partial z$, $\boldsymbol{\partial}^2 = \boldsymbol{\partial} \cdot \boldsymbol{\partial} = \partial_x^2 + \partial_y^2 + \partial_z^2$ where the $\cdot$ indicates the standard dot product of vectors; i.e., for two vectors $\mathbf{A}$ and $\mathbf{B}$ we have $\mathbf{A} \cdot \mathbf{B} = A_x B_x + A_y B_y + A_z B_z \equiv \Sigma_i A_i B_i$ with i taking the "values" x, y, z. To simplify the notation, we will use the summation convention in which repeated indices are automatically summed over their appropriate range. This allows us to drop the summation sign, Σ, so that $\mathbf{A} \cdot \mathbf{B} = A_i B_i$. Also, using the summation convention we can write $\mathbf{A} = \hat{e}_i A_i$ and $\mathbf{B}$ and $\hat{e}_i B_i$, etc. The cross-product of $\mathbf{A}$ and $\mathbf{B}$, which is denoted by $\mathbf{A} \times \mathbf{B}$, is defined by $\hat{e}_i \varepsilon_{ijk} A_j B_k$ where ε_{ijk} with i, j, k taking the "values" x, y, z is defined by $\varepsilon_{xyz} = \varepsilon_{yzx} = \varepsilon_{zxy} = +1$, $\varepsilon_{zyx} = \varepsilon_{yxz} = \varepsilon_{xzy} = -1$, with all other index combinations being zero. So, for example, $\boldsymbol{\partial} \times \mathbf{E} = \hat{e}_x(\partial_y E_z - \partial_z E_y) + \hat{e}_y(\partial_z E_x - \partial_x E_z) + \hat{e}_z(\partial_x E_y - \partial_y E_x)$.

The Gauss law constraint is

$$\boldsymbol{\partial} \cdot \mathbf{E}\,(\mathbf{x},t) = \boldsymbol{\partial} \cdot \mathbf{B}\,(\mathbf{x},t) = 0$$

The solution to the wave equation can be written as a four-dimensional Fourier transform, which is nothing but a linear superposition of plane waves of the form $e^{i\hat{\mathbf{p}} \cdot \hat{\mathbf{x}} - i\omega t}$. These are plane waves because their surfaces of constant phase, i.e., the positions $\mathbf{x}$ that satisfy $\mathbf{p} \cdot \mathbf{x} - \omega t = $ constant, are just planes. The unit vector $\hat{p} = \mathbf{p}/|\mathbf{p}|$ defines the normal to these planes or wavefronts, and for ω positive, the wavefronts propagate in the $+\hat{p}$ direction with speed $v = \omega/p$. The wavelength λ is related to $\mathbf{p}$ by $p = |\mathbf{p}| = \sqrt{\mathbf{p}^2} = \sqrt{p_i p_i} = \sqrt{p_x^2 + p_y^2 + p_z^2} = 2\pi/\lambda$, and the frequency, f, in hertz is related to the radian frequency ω by $\omega = 2\pi f$. Combining these relations with the speed of propagation yields $v = 2\pi f/(2\pi/\lambda) = \lambda f$. We will take ω to be positive throughout the analysis.

Substituting a single unit-amplitude plane wave electric field $\mathbf{E} = \hat{\varepsilon} e^{i\hat{\mathbf{p}} \cdot \hat{\mathbf{x}} - i\omega t}$ into the wave equation with $\hat{\varepsilon}$ a unit vector representing the polarization direction of the electric field, we find that $\mathbf{p}$ and ω must satisfy

$$-\frac{n^2}{c^2}\omega^2 + \mathbf{p}^2 = 0$$

This is the dispersion relation in a medium of index n.

Substituting $\mathbf{E} = \hat{\varepsilon} e^{i\hat{\mathbf{p}} \cdot \hat{\mathbf{x}} - i\omega t}$ into the Gauss law constraint yields

$$\boldsymbol{\partial} \cdot (\hat{\varepsilon} e^{i\mathbf{p} \cdot \mathbf{x} - i\omega t}) = i\mathbf{p} \cdot \hat{\varepsilon} e^{i\mathbf{p} \cdot \mathbf{x} - i\omega t} = 0$$

which is satisfied by demanding that $\hat{p} \cdot \hat{\varepsilon} = 0$. That is, for a single plane wave the electric field vector must be perpendicular to the direction of propagation. Note that this requires $\hat{\varepsilon}$ to be a function of $\hat{p}$.

Substituting $\mathbf{E} = \hat{\varepsilon} e^{i\hat{\mathbf{p}} \cdot \hat{\mathbf{x}} - i\omega t}$ into the particular Maxwell equation $\partial_t \mathbf{B} = -\boldsymbol{\partial} \times \mathbf{E}$, where $\times$ denotes a cross-product, yields

$$\partial_t \mathbf{B} = -i\mathbf{p} \times \hat{\varepsilon} e^{i\mathbf{p} \cdot \mathbf{x} - i\omega t}$$

$$= -ip(\hat{p} \times \hat{\varepsilon}) e^{i\mathbf{p} \cdot \mathbf{x} - i\omega t}$$

$$= -i\omega \left(\frac{n}{c}\right)(\hat{p} \times \hat{\varepsilon}) e^{i\mathbf{p} \cdot \mathbf{x} - i\omega t}$$

where we have used $p = \omega n/c$, which follows from the dispersion relation. The solution to this equation is

$$\mathbf{B} = \left(\frac{n}{c}\right)(\hat{p} \times \hat{\varepsilon}) e^{i\mathbf{p} \cdot \mathbf{x} - i\omega t}$$

which shows that $\mathbf{E}$ and $\mathbf{B}$ for a single plane wave are in phase with one another. They propagate in the same direction. $\mathbf{B}$ has units which differ from those of $\mathbf{E}$ by the factor n/c. Also, $\mathbf{B}$ is perpendicular to both $\hat{p}$, the direction of propagation, and $\hat{\varepsilon}$, the polarization direction of the electric field. Note that $\hat{\varepsilon} \times (\hat{p} \times \hat{\varepsilon}) = \hat{p}$ and so $\mathbf{E} \times \mathbf{B}$ points in the direction of propagation of the wave.

For the purpose of modeling the optical properties of alignment marks it is convenient to separate $\mathbf{p}$ into the sum of two vectors, one parallel and one perpendicular to the wafer surface. The parallel or tangential vector will be written as $\boldsymbol{\beta} = \hat{e}_x \beta_x + \hat{e}_y \beta_y$ and the perpendicular vector as $-\gamma \hat{e}_z$ for waves propagating toward the wafer, i.e., generally in the $-z$ direction and $+\gamma \hat{e}_z$ for waves propagating away from the wafer, i.e., generally in the $+z$ direction. We will refer to $\boldsymbol{\beta}$ as the tangential propagation vector. The magnitude of $\boldsymbol{\beta}$ is related to the angle of incidence or the angle of scatter by $|\boldsymbol{\beta}| = nk \sin(\theta)$ with θ the angle between the propagation vector $\mathbf{p}$ and the z axis. Using this notation for the components of $\mathbf{p}$, the dispersion relation takes the form $\beta^2 + \gamma^2 - (n^2/c^2)\omega^2 = 0$, which gives $\gamma(\boldsymbol{\beta}) = \sqrt{n^2 k^2 - \boldsymbol{\beta}^2}$ where $k \equiv \omega/c = 2\pi/\lambda$ with λ the wavelength in vacuum. The γ is purely real (for n real) and $|\boldsymbol{\beta}| < nk$, which corresponds to propagating waves, i.e., $e^{\pm i\gamma z}$ is an oscillating function of z, whereas for $|\boldsymbol{\beta}| > nk$, γ becomes purely imaginary, $\gamma = i|\gamma|$ and $e^{\pm i\gamma z} = e^{\mp |\gamma| z}$, which is exponentially decaying or increasing with z and correponds to evanescent waves.

Since the wave equation is linear, a completely general solution for $\mathbf{E}$ can be written as a superposition of the basic plane wave solutions.

$$\mathbf{E}(\mathbf{x}, t) = \underbrace{\int \left[\hat{\varepsilon}_{TE}(\hat{\beta}) a_{TE}(\boldsymbol{\beta}, k) + \hat{\varepsilon}_{TM}(\hat{\beta}) a_{TM}(\boldsymbol{\beta}, k)\right] e^{i\boldsymbol{\beta} \cdot \boldsymbol{\rho} + i\gamma z - ickt} d^2\beta \, dk}_{\equiv \mathbf{E}_{out} = \text{outgoing, i.e., mark scattered/diffracted waves}}$$

$$+ \underbrace{\int \left[\hat{\varepsilon}_{TE}(\hat{\beta}) b_{TE}(\boldsymbol{\beta}, k) + \hat{\varepsilon}_{TM}(\hat{\beta}) b_{TM}(\boldsymbol{\beta}, k)\right] e^{i\boldsymbol{\beta} \cdot \boldsymbol{\rho} + i\gamma z - ickt} d^2\beta \, dk}_{\equiv \mathbf{E}_{in} = \text{incoming, i.e., sensor illumination waves}}$$

where we have explicitly indicated the contributions from TE and TM waves and $\rho = \hat{e}_x x + \hat{e}_y y$ is the in-plane position.

The outgoing waves, E_{out} are those that have been scattered or diffracted by the alignment mark. Different sensor configurations collect and detect different portions of E_{out} in different ways to generate alignment signal data. The functions $a_{TE}(\beta, k)$ and $a_{TM}(\beta, k)$ are the amplitudes, respectively, of the TE and TM outgoing waves with tangential propagation vector β and frequency $f = k/2\pi c$. The incoming waves, E_{in} are the illumination, that is the distribution of light that the sensor projects onto the wafer. Different sensor configurations project different light distributions, i.e., different combinations of plane waves onto the wafer. The functions $b_{TE}(\beta, k)$ and $b_{TM}(\beta, k)$ are the amplitudes, respectively, of the TE and TM incoming waves with tangential propagation vector β and frequency $f = k/2\pi c$.

Because Maxwell's equations are linear (we are not concerned with nonlinear optics) the incoming and outgoing waves are linearly related to one another. This relation can conveniently be written in the form

$$\underbrace{\begin{pmatrix} a_{TE}(\beta,k) \\ a_{TM}(\beta,k) \end{pmatrix}}_{\text{Outgoing waves}} = \int \underbrace{\begin{pmatrix} S_{EE}(\beta,\beta') & S_{EM}(\beta,\beta') \\ S_{ME}(\beta,\beta') & S_{MM}(\beta,\beta') \end{pmatrix}}_{\text{Mark scattering matrix} \equiv S} \cdot \underbrace{\begin{pmatrix} b_{TE}(\beta',k) \\ b_{TM}(\beta',k) \end{pmatrix}}_{\text{Incoming waves}} d^2\beta'$$

Each element of S is a complex number that can be interpreted as the coupling from a particular incoming wave to a particular outgoing wave. See Fig. 3 for the physical representation of S in two dimensions. For example, $S_{EE}(\beta, \beta')$ is the coupling from the incoming TE wave with tangential propagation vector β' to the outgoing TE wave with tangential propagation vector β. In the same way $S_{EM}(\beta, \beta')$ is the coupling from the incoming TM wave at β' to the outgoing TE wave at β. Note that since elements of S are complex numbers and complex numbers have an amplitude and a phase, the elements of S account for both the amplitude of the coupling, i.e., how much outgoing wave one will have for an incoming wave of a given amplitude, and for the phase shift that occurs when incoming waves are coupled to outgoing waves. Note that for stationary and optically linear media there is no cross-coupling of different temporal frequencies, $f_{in} = f_{out}$ or equivalently $k_{in} = k_{out}$. The diagonal elements of S with respect tangential propagation vector are those for which $\beta = \beta'$ and these elements correspond to specular reflection from the wafer. The off-diagonal elements, i.e., those with $\beta' \neq \beta$, are nonspecular waves, i.e., the waves that have been scattered or diffracted by the alignment mark. The value of each element of S depends on the detailed structure of the mark, that is, on the thicknesses, shapes, and indices of refraction of all the material "layers" that make up the alignment marks as well as on the wavelength of the light. It is important to note that

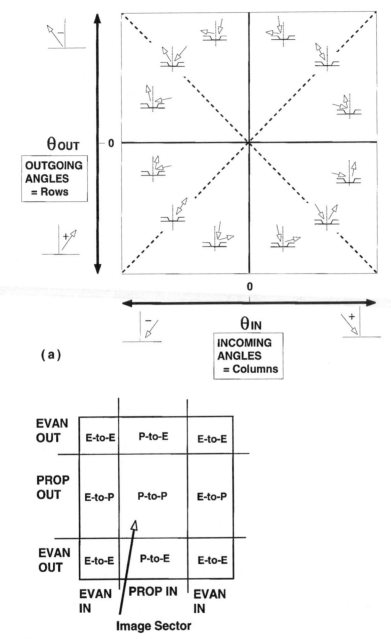

(a)

(b)

Figure 3   (a) The physical meaning of the elements of the scattering matrix. The different elements in the matrix correspond to different incoming and outgoing angles of

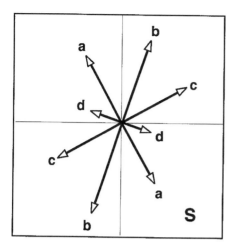

Figure 4 A perfectly symmetric alignment mark has a scattering matrix which is perfectly centro-symmetric. That is, elements at equal distance but opposite directions from the center of the matrix ($\vec{\beta} = \vec{\beta}' = 0$) are equal as indicated.

a symmetric mark requires the scattering matrix to be centro-symmetric. This is illustrated in Fig. 4.

It follows from this that the scattering matrix must be computed for each particular mark structure and for each wavelength of use, but once this matrix has been computed, the alignment signals that are generated by that mark for all possible sensor configurations that use the specified wavelengths are completely contained in S. For example, the difference between brightfield and darkfield collection numerical apertures [NA = sin (θ)] is shown in Fig. 5.

propagation of plane waves. (b) To generate valid solutions to Maxwell's equation requires including evanescent as well as propagating waves.

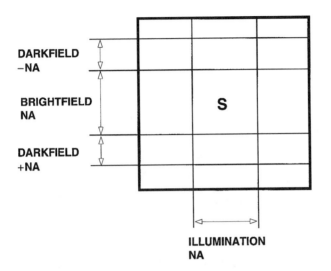

Figure 5 In all cases, the complete optical properties of the alignment mark are contained in the scattering matrix and all alignment sensors simply combine the rows and columns of this matrix in different ways. The above diagram shows a simple example of this. The brightfield illumination and collection numerical apertures (NA) coincide whereas the darkfield range does not. The darkfield range is a combination of waves with more positive (+NA) and negative (−NA) numerical apertures than the illumination.

6   BASIC OPTICAL ALIGNMENT SENSOR CONFIGURATIONS

This section describes in very general terms the various basic configurations that an alignment sensor can take and the nominal signal shapes that it will produce. As mentioned in the first section only optical sensors are considered, that is, sensors that project light onto the wafer and detect the scattered or diffracted light.

The purpose of the alignment sensor is to detect the position of an alignment mark, so no matter what the configuration of the alignment sensor, the signal it produces must depend in one way or another on the mark position. Thus it follows that all alignment sensors, in a very general sense, produce a signal that can be considered to represent some sort of image of the alignment mark. This image can be thoroughly conventional as in a standard microscope or it can be rather unconventional as in a scanned grating interference sensor.

Simplified diagrams of several different basic configurations are included for completeness. The simplicity of these diagrams is in stark contrast to the schematics of real alignment systems, whose complexity almost always belies the very simple concept they embody.

The following are common differentiators among alignment basic alignment sensor types.

Scanning versus staring: A staring sensor simultaneously detects position-dependent information over a finite area on the wafer. A standard microcope is an example of a staring sensor. The term "staring" comes directly from the idea that all necessary data for a single mark can be collected with the sensor simply staring at the wafer. A scanning sensor, on the other hand, can effectively see only a single point on the wafer and hence must be scanned either mechanically or optically to develop the full wafer position-dependent signal. Mechanical scanning may amount simply to moving the wafer in front of the sensor. Optical scanning can be accomplished by changing the illuminating light in such a way as to move the illimuminating intensity pattern on the wafer. Optical scanning may involve the physical motion of some element in the sensor itself, such as a steering mirror, or it may not. For example, if the illumination spectrally contains only two closely spaced wavelengths, then for certain optical configutions, the intensity pattern of the illumination will automatically sweep across the wafer at a predictable rate.

Bright-field versus dark-field: All sensors illuminate the mark over some range of angles. This range can be large as in an ordinary microscope or it can be small as in some grating sensors. If the angle over which the sensor detects the light scattered or diffraced from the wafer is the same as the illumination angle, it is called bright-field detection. The reason for this terminology is that for a flat wafer with no mark the specularly reflected light will be collected and hence the signal is bright where the mark is not. In a mark region light will be scattered out of the illumination angle range and hence marks send less light to the detectors and appear dark relative to the nonmark areas. In dark-field detection the scatter or diffraction angles that are detected are distinctly different from the illumination angles. In this case, specular light is not collected and so a nonmark area appears dark and the mark itself appears bright.

Phase versus amplitude: Since light is a wave, it carries both phase and amplitude information and sensors that detect only the amplitude or only the phase or some combination of both have been and are being used for alignment. A simple microscope uses both because the image is essentially the Fourier transform of the scattered or diffracted light and the Fourier transform is a result of both the amplitude and phase information. A sensor that senses the position of the interference pattern generated by the light scattered at two distinct angles is detecting only the phase, whereas a sensor that looks only at the total intensity scattered into a specific angle or range of angles is detecting only the amplitude.

Diagrams of various basic sensor configurations are shown in Figs. 6–10.

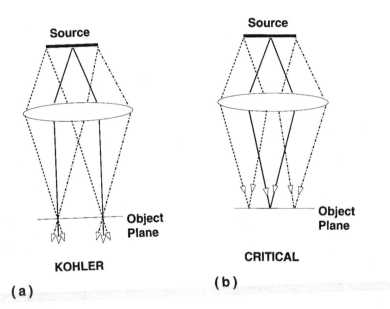

Figure 6 There are two generic forms of illumination: (a) Kohler and (b) critical. For Kohler illumination each point in the source becomes a plane wave at the object. For critical illumination each point in the source is a point at the object.

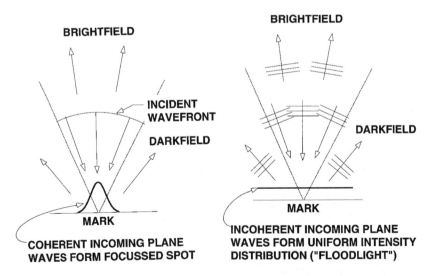

Figure 7 This diagram illustrates the two generic illumination coherence configurations that are in common use. Specifically it shows the difference between coherent and incoherent illumination with the same numerical aperture.

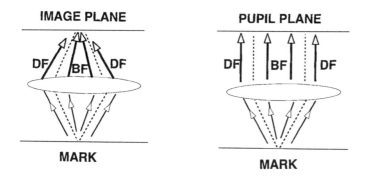

Figure 8 This diagram illustrates the two generic light collection configurations that are in common use. (BF = brightfield, DF = darkfield)

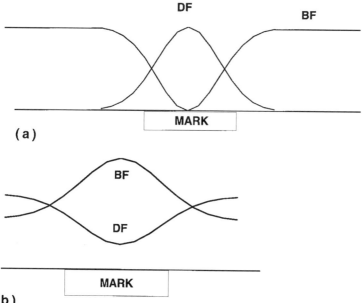

Figure 9 (a) The curves indicate signal intensity. The nomenclature "brightfield" (BF) and "darkfield" (DF) refers to the intensity that the sensor will produce when looking at a perfectly flat wafer with no alignment mark present. In brightfield (darkfield), the range of incoming and outgoing plane wave angles is (is not) the same. Generally a mark will appear dark in a bright background in brightfield imaging and bright in a dark background in darkfield imaging. (b) If the background area is very rough compared to the mark, then the scatter may actually be less from the mark than from the background, and the brightfield and darkfield signals will appear reversed as shown.

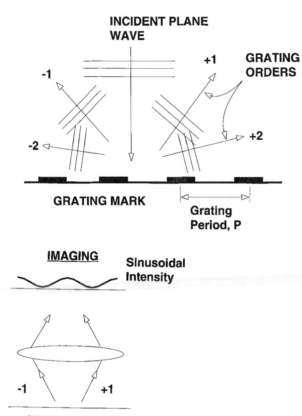

Figure 10   This is the generic configuration of a grating alignment sensor. The upper figure shows angular distribution of the grating orders is given by the grating equation, as shown, with $\beta = (2\pi/\lambda) \sin (\theta)$, where λ is the wavelength and θ is the angle of propagation as measured with respect to the normal of the wafer surface. If only the +1 and −1 grating orders are collected the "image" produced is purely sinusoidal as shown in the lower figure.

7   ALIGNMENT SIGNAL REDUCTION ALGORITHMS

Only when process offsets are known a priori or are measured using sendaheads does the alignment problem default to finding the signal centroid itself. In this section we will assume that this is the case. If the only degrading influence on the signal were zero-mean Gaussian white noise, then the optimum algorithm for determining the signal centroid is to correlate the signal with itself and find the position of the peak of the output. Equivalently, because the derivative, i.e., the slope, of a function at its peak is zero, we can correlate the signal with its derivative and find the position where the output of the correlation crosses through zero. One proof that this is the optimal algorithm involves using the technique of maximum likelihood. Below we present a different derivation that starts with the standard technique of finding the centroid or center of mass of the signal and shows that the optimum modification to it in the presence of noise results in an autocorrelation algorithm, even for non-zero-mean noise.

Wafer alignment signals are generated by scattering or diffracting light from an alignment mark on the wafer. For nongrating marks the signal from a single alignment mark will generally appear as one or perhaps several localized "bumps" in the alignment sensor signal data. As discussed above, the real problem is to determine the center of the alignment mark from the signal data. If sufficient symmetry is present in both the alignment sensor and the alignment mark structure itself, this reduces to finding the centroid or "center of mass" of the signal. For grating marks the signal is often essentially perfectly periodic and usually sinusoidal with perhaps an overall slowly varying amplitude envelope. In this case the "centroid" can be associated with the phase of the periodic signal as measured relative to a predefined origin. In general, all of the algorithms discussed below can be applied to periodic as well as isolated signal bumps. But for periodic signals the Fourier algorithm is perhaps the most appropriate. In all cases there may be some known offset based on a sendahead wafer or on some baseline tool calibration that must be added to the measured signal centroid to shift it to match the mark center.

Clearly, real signals collected from real wafers will be corrupted by noise and degraded by the asymmetry present in real marks and real alignment sensors. Since the noise contribution can be treated statistically, it is straightforward to develop algorithms that minimize on average its contribution to the final result. If this were the only problem facing alignment, then simply increasing the number of alignment marks scanned would allow overlay to become arbitrarily accurate. But, as noted in Section 5, process variation both across a wafer and from wafer to wafer changes not only the overall signal amplitude but also the mark symmetry and hence the signal symmetry. This effect is not statistical and is currently not predictable. Therefore, other than trying to make the algorithm as insensitive to signal level and asymmetry as possible and potentially using sendaheads, there is not much that can be done.

It is simplest to proceed with the general analysis in continuum form. For completeness, the adjustments to the continuum form that must be made to use discrete, i.e., sampled, data are briefly discussed. These adjustments are straightforward but tedious and somewhat tool dependent. Thus they are only briefly described. Also, we will work in one dimension since x and y values are generally computed separately anyway. Finally, the portions of the signal representing alignment marks can be positive bumps in a nominally zero background, as would occur in darkfield imaging, or can be negative bumps in a nominally nonzero background, as would occur in brightfield imaging. For simplicity we will make the tacit assumption that we are dealing with darkfield-like signals. In the grating case the signals are generally sinusoidal, which can be viewed either way, and we will treat this case separately.

Let $I(x)$ be a perfect, and hence symmetric, signal bump (or bumps) as a function of position, x. The noise, $n(x)$, will be taken to be additive, white (i.e., uncorrelated), and spatially and temporally stationary (i.e., constant in space and time).

When a new wafer is loaded and a given alignment mark is scanned, the mark and hence the signal will be translated by an unknown amount s relative to some predetermined origin of the coordinate system. Thus, the actual detected signal $D(x)$ is given by $I(x)$ shifted a distance s, that is, $D(x) = I(x - s)$. It is the purpose of the alignment sensor to determine the value of s from the detected signal. The position of the centroid or center of mass of the signal is defined as

$$C = \frac{\int xD(x)dx}{\int D(x)dx} = \frac{\int xI(x-s)\,dx}{\int I(x-s)\,dx}$$

This is illustrated in Fig. 11.

To show that $s = C$ so that we can find s simply by computing the centroid, let $y = x - s$; then

$$C = \frac{\int (y+s)I(y)\,dy}{\int I(y)\,dy} = \underbrace{\frac{\int yI(y)\,dy}{\int I(y)\,dy}}_{=0} + s\underbrace{\left(\frac{\int I(y)\,dy}{\int I(y)\,dy}\right)}_{=1}$$

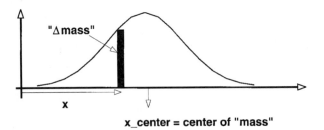

x_center = center of "mass"

Figure 11 The "center of mass" algorithm estimates the mark center, x_center, by multiplying the distance from the origin, x, by the signal intensity at x then summing this result over a specified range and dividing by the total area under the intensity curve in the same range.

The first term vanishes because

$$\int y I(y)\, dy = \int [(\text{odd}) \times (\text{even})]\, dy = 0$$

and we are assuming symmetric signals and limits of integration, which for all practical purposes can be set to $\pm\infty$. Thus

$$s = C$$

and the shift position can be found by computing the centroid.

In the presence of noise the actual signal is the pure signal, shifted by the unknown amount s, with noise added:

$$D(x) = I(x-s) \rightarrow D(x) = I(x-s) + n(x)$$

Below we discuss standard algorithms for computing a value for C from the measured data $D(x)$, which, based on the above discussion, amounts to estimating the value of s, which we will label s_E. Along with using the measured data, some of the algorithms also make use of a priori knowledge of the ideal signal shape $I(x)$.

The digitally sampled real data are not continuous and we will use the convention $D_i = D(x_i)$ to label the signal values measured at the sample positions x_i where $i = 1, 2, \ldots, N$ with N the total number of data values for a single signal.

7.1   Threshold Algorithm

Consider an isolated single bump in the signal data that represents an "image" of an alignment mark. The threshold algorithm attempts to find the bump centroid by finding the midpoint between the two values of x at which the bump has a given value called, obviously, the threshold. In the case in which the signal contains multiple bumps representing multiple alignment marks, the algorithm can be applied to each bump separately and the results can be combined to produce an estimate of the net bump centroid.

For now, let $D(x)$ consist of a single positive bump plus noise, and let D_T be the specified threshold value. Then, if the bump is reasonably symmetric and smoothly varying and D_T has been chosen appropriately, there will be two and only two values of x, call them x_L and x_R, that satisfy

$$D_T = D(x_L) = D(x_R)$$

The midpoint between x_L and x_R, which is simply the average of x_L and x_R, is taken as the estimate for s, i.e.,

$$s_E = \tfrac{1}{2}(x_L + x_R)$$

See Fig. 12.

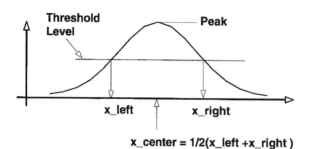

Figure 12 The threshold algorithm estimates the mark center, x_center by finding the midpoint between the threshold crossover positions x_left and x_right.

As shown below, this algorithm is very sensitive to noise because it uses only two points out of the entire signal. A refinement that eliminates some of this noise dependence is to average the result from multiple threshold levels. Taking $D_{T_1}, D_{T_2}, \ldots, D_{T_N}$ to be N different threshold levels with $s_{E_1}, s_{E_2}, \ldots s_{E_N}$ being the corresponding centroid estimates for the levels, the net centroid is taken to be

$$s_E = \frac{1}{N}(s_{E_1} + s_{E_2} + \cdots + s_{E_N})$$

This definition of s_E weights all the N threshold estimates equally. A further refinement of the multiple-threshold approach is to weight the separate threshold results nonuniformly. This weighting can be based on intuition and/or modeling and/or experimental results which indicate that certain threshold levels tend to be more reliable than others. In this case

$$s_E = w_1 s_{E_1} + w_2 s_{E_2} + \cdots + w_N s_{E_N}$$

where $w_1 + w_2 + \cdots + w_N = 1$.

Noise Sensitivity of the Threshold Algorithm

Noise can lead to multiple threshold crossovers and it is generally best to pick the minimum threshold value to be greater than the noise level. This is of course signal dependent, but a minimum threshold level of 10% of the peak bump value is reasonable. Also, since a bump has zero slope at its peak, noise will completely dominate the result if the threshold level is set too high. Generally the greatest reasonable threshold level that should be used is on the order of 90% of the bump peak.

The sensitivity of s_E to noise can be determined in the following way. Let x_{L0} and x_{R0} be the true noise-free threshold positions, that is,

$$I(x_{L0}) = I(x_{R0}) = D_T$$

Now let Δ_L and Δ_R be the deviations in threshold position caused by noise so that the $x_L = x_{L0} + \Delta_L$ and $x_R = x_{R0} + \Delta_R$. Substituing this into the threshold equation and assuming the Δ's are small gives

$$D_T = D(x_L) = I(x_{L0} + \Delta_L) + n(x_{L0} + \Delta_L)$$
$$\approx I(x_{L0}) + I'(x_{L0})\Delta_L + n(x_{L0}) + n'(x_{L0})\Delta_L$$

and

$$D_T = D(x_R) = I(x_{R0} + \Delta_R) + n(x_{R0} + \Delta_R)$$
$$\approx I(x_{R0}) + I'(x_{R0})\Delta_R + n(x_R) + n'(x_{R0})\Delta_R$$

where the prime on $I(x)$ and $n(x)$ indicates differentiation with respect to x. Using $I(x_{L0}) = I(x_{R0}) = D_T$ and solving for the Δ's yields

$$\Delta_L = \frac{n(x_{L0})}{I'(x_{L0}) + n'(x_{L0})}$$

$$\Delta_R = \frac{n(x_{R0})}{I'(x_{R0}) + n'(x_{R0})}$$

The temptation at this stage is to assume that n' is much smaller than I', but for this to be true the noise must be highly correlated as a function of x; that is, it cannot be white. The derivative of uncorrelated noise has a root-mean-square (rms) slope of infinity. The discrete nature of real sampled data will mitigate the "derivative" problem somewhat, but still, in order to obtain reasonable answers using this algorithm, the noise must be well behaved.

Assuming the $n(x)$ is smooth enough so that we can make the approximation $n' \ll I'$ gives

$$s_E = \frac{x_L + x_R}{2} + \frac{n(x_{L0})}{2I'(x_{L0})} + \frac{n(x_{R0})}{2I'(x_{R0})}$$

The rms error in s_E, call it σ_s in the single threshold algorithm as a function of the rms noise σ_n, assuming the noise is spatially stationary and uncorrelated from the left to the right side of the bump and that $I'(x_{L0}) = I'(x_{R0}) \equiv I'$, is then

$$\sigma_s = \frac{\sigma_n}{\sqrt{2I'}}$$

This result shows explicitly that the error will be large in regions where the slope I' is small and thus it is best to choose the threshold to correspond to large slopes. If the results from N different threshold levels are averaged and the slope I' is essentially the same at all the threshold levels, then

$$\sigma_s \cong \frac{\sigma_n}{\sqrt{2NI'}}$$

Discrete Sampling and the Threshold Algorithm

For discretely sampled data only rarely will any of the D_i correspond exactly to the threshold value. instead there will be two positions on the left side of the signal and two positions on the right where the D_i values cross over the threshold level. Let the i values between which the crossover occurs on the left be i_L and $i_L + 1$ and on the right i_R and $i_R + 1$: then the actual threshold positions can be determined by linear interpolation between corresponding sample positions. The resulting x_L and x_R values are then given by

$$x_L = \frac{x_{i_{L+1}} - x_{i_L}}{D_{i_{L+1}} - D_{i_L}}(D_T - D_{i_L}) + x_{i_L}$$

$$x_R = \frac{x_{i_{R+1}} - x_{i_R}}{D_{i_{R+1}} - D_{i_R}}(D_T - D_{i_R}) + x_{i_R}$$

7.2 Correlator Algorithm

The correlator algorithm is somewhat similar to the variable weighting threshold algorithm in that it uses most or all of the signal data but nominally not uniformly. The easiest approach to deriving the correlator algorithm is to minimize the noise contribution to the determination of C as given by the integration above.

It is obvious that in the presence of additive noise the centroid integration should be restricted to the region where the signal bump is located. Integrating over regions where there is noise but no bump simply corrupts the result. In other words, there's no point to integrating where the mark isn't. We can limit the integration range by including a function $f(x)$ in the integrand that is nonzero only over a range that is about equal to the bump width. The centroid calculation then takes the general form

$$C = \int f(x)D(x)\,dx$$

Of course, $f(x)$ must be centered close to the actual bump centroid position for this to work. This can be accomplished in several ways. For example, an approximate centroid position x_0 could first be determined using a simple algorithm such as the threshold algorithm. The function $f(x)$ is then shifted by this amount by letting $f(x) \to f(x - x_0)$ so that there is now significant overlap between it and the bump. The value of C computed via the integration is then the bump centroid position estimate, s_E, as measured relative to the position x_0. Or, in an alternative approach, $f(x)$ could progressively be shifted by small increments and the centroid computed for each case. In this case, when the bump is far from center of $f(x)$, there is little or no overlap between between the two and the output of the integration will be small with the main contribution coming from noise. But as $f(x)$ is shifted close to the bump they will begin to overlap and the magnitude of the integral will increase. The sign of the result depends on the relative signs of $f(x)$ and the bump in the overlap region. As the $f(x)$ is shifted through the bump, the magnitude of the integral will first increase to a peak and then decrease and pass through zero and become negative as $f(x)$ moves through the bump centroid, and eventually increase back to just the noise contribution as the overlap decreases to zero. Mathematically this process takes the form of computing

$$C(x_0) = \int f(x - x_0)D(x)\,dx$$

for all values of x_0 in the signal range. The value of $C(x_0)$ is the estimate of the centroid position measured relative to the shift position x_0, that is, $C(x_0) = s_E - x_0$. The point is that the integral provides a valid estimate of position only when there is significant overlap between the bump and $f(x)$. This occurs in the region where the magnitude of the integration passes through zero with the optimum overlap being exactly when the bump is centered at x_0 so that $C(x_0) = s_E - x_0 = 0$, from which it follows that $s_E = x_0$. Thus the algorithm takes the form of correlating $f(x)$ with $D(x)$ with the best estimate of the centroid position, s_E, being given by the value of x_0 that produces the exact zero crossing in the integration.

The optimum form of the function $f(x)$ is that which minimizes the noise contribution to C in the region of the zero crossing. In the presence of noise we rewrite the centroid calculation as

$$C(x_0) = \int f(x - x_0)D(x)\,dx$$
$$= \int f(x - x_0)I(x - s)\,dx + \int f(x - x_0)n(x + x_0)\,dx$$
$$= \int f(x)I(x - (s - x_0))\,dx + \int f(x)n(x + x_0)\,dx$$

where in the last step we have changed integration variables by letting $(x - x_0)$ be replaced by x.

Assuming that the bump centroid, s, is close to x_0, that is, $s - x_0$ is much less than the width of the signal, we can write

$$C(x_0) = \int f(x)\,(I(x) - (s - x_0)I'(x))\,dx + \int f(x)n(x + x_0)\,dx$$

where $I'(x) \equiv \partial I(x)/\partial x$. In order to have a nonbiased estimate of the centroid position measured relative to x_0, i.e., a nonbiased estimate of the value of $s - x_0$, the value of $C(x_0)$ as given above must equal the true value, $s - x_0$, that is obtained in the absence of noise. Taking the statistical expectation value with respect to the noise gives

$$\langle C(x_0) \rangle = \int f(x)I(x)\,dx - (s - x_0)\int I'(x)f(x)\,dx + \int f(x)\langle n(x + x_0)\rangle\,dx$$

Letting $\langle n(x + x_0) \rangle \equiv \langle n \rangle$ = constant we get

$$\langle C(x_0) \rangle = \int f(x)I(x)\,dx - (s - x_0)\int I'(x)f(x)\,dx + \langle n \rangle \int f(x)\,dx$$

In order to have $\langle C(x_0) \rangle = s - x_0$, $f(x)$ must satisfy the following set of equations:

$$\int f(x)I(x)\,dx = 0$$

$$\int I'(x)f(x)\,dx = -1$$

$$\int f(x)\,dx = 0$$

The first and last of these conditions demand that $f(x)$ be an antisymmetric, i.e., an odd, function of x. The second condition is consistent with this because $I'(x)$ is antisymmetric since we have assumed $I(x)$ is symmetric. But, in addition, it specifies the normalization of $f(x)$. We can satisfy all three equations if we write $f(x)$ in the form

$$f(x) = -\frac{a(x)}{\int I'(x)a(x)\,dx}$$

where $a(x)$ is an antisymmetric function.

To determine the optimum form for $a(x)$ we minimize the expectation value of the noise-to-signal ratio. The last term in the formula for $C(x_0)$ is the noise and the second term is the signal. Substituting these terms and the above form for $f(x)$ and taking the expectation value, we get

$$\left\langle \frac{\text{noise}}{\text{signal}} \right\rangle = \left\langle \frac{\left[\int a(x)n(x)\,dx\right]^2}{\left[\int a(x)I'(x)\,dx\right]^2} \right\rangle$$

after using $\langle n(x)n(x') \rangle = \sigma^2 \delta(x - x')$ as required for white noise. To find the function $a(x)$ that minimizes $\langle \text{noise/signal} \rangle$, replace $a(x)$ with $a(x) + \Delta a(x)$ in the above result, expand in powers of $\Delta a(x)$, and demand that the coefficient of $\Delta a(x)$ to the first power vanish. After some manipulation this yields the following equation for $a(x)$:

$$a(x) = I'(x)\frac{\int [a(x)]^2\,dx}{\int a(x)I'(x)\,dx}$$

The solution to this equation is simply

$$a(x) = I'(x)$$

and so

$$f(x) = \frac{I'(x)}{\int (I'(x))^2 \, dx} = \text{stationary white noise optimum correlation function}$$

This is the standard result: The optimum correlator is the derivative of the ideal bump shape. If instead of finding the zero-cross position after correlating with the derivative, we correlated the signal with the ideal bump shape and searched for the peak in the result, then this is the standard matched-filter approach as used in many areas of signal processing.

The same result can also be derived using the method of least squares. The mean square difference between $D(x)$ and $I(x - s)$ is given by

$$\int [D(x) - I(x-s)]^2 \, dx$$

To minimize this requires finding s_E such that

$$0 = \left[\frac{\partial}{\partial s} \int [D(x) - I(x-s)]^2 \, dx \right]_{s = s_E}$$

Taking the derivative inside the integral, and using the fact $\int I(x)I'(x)dx = 0$ if I vanishes at the endpoints of the integration, gives

$$0 = \int I'(x - s_E)D(x) \, dx$$

This is the same result as above but without the normalization factor. This derivation was presented many years ago by Robert Hufnagel.

Note that at the peak of the bump the derivative is zero, whereas at the edges the slope has the largest absolute value. Using the derivative of the bump as the weighting function in the correlation shows explicitly that essentially all of the information about the bump centroid comes from its edges with essentially no information coming from its peak. Simply put, if the signal is shifted a small amount, the largest change in signal value occurs in the regions with the largest slope, i.e., the edges, and there is essentially no change in the value at the peak. The edges are therefore the most sensitive to the bump position and hence contain the most position information. This is illustrated for a stepwise correlator, i.e., a stepwise approximation to $I'(x)$ in Fig. 13.

The above result assumes that the only degrading influence on the signal is stationary white noise, i.e., spatially uncorrelated noise with position-independent statistics. With some effort the stationarity and uncorrelated restrictions can be removed and the corresponding result for correlated nonstationary noise can be derived. But that is not the problem. The problem is that generally noise is not the dominant degrading influence on the alignment signal, process variation is. Thus the above result provides only a good starting

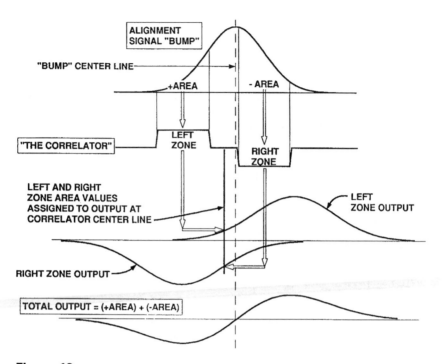

Figure 13 The correlator algorithm estimates the mark center as the position which has equal areas in the left and right zones under the signal "bump". The algorithm computes the area difference, as shown, as a function of position and the estimated mark center corresponds to the position of the zero crossing.

point for picking a correlator function. To achieve the optimum insensitivity to process variations this result currently must be fine-tuned based on actual signal data. In future, if sufficient understanding of the effect of symmetric and asymmetric process variation on alignment structures is developed, the optimum correlator for particular cases can be designed from "first principles."

The correlator algorithm can clearly be implemented in software but it can also be implemented directly in hardware, where it takes the form of a "split detector." That is, consider two detectors placed close to one another with their net width being approximately equal to the expected bump width. The voltage from each detector is proportional to the area under the portion of the signal that it intercepts. When these two voltages are equal then, assuming identical detectors, the signal center is exactly in the middle of the two detectors. If a simple circuit is used to produce the voltage difference then, just as above, a zero crossing indicates the signal center. Note that the detectors uniformly weight the signal that they intercept rather than weighting by the derivative of the signal. Thus the split detector approach is equivalent to a lumped correlator algorithm where the smoothly varying signal derivative has been replaced by two rectangular steps.

Noise Sensitivity of the Correlator Algorithm

In the presence of noise the value of s is still determined by finding the value of x_0 for which $C(x_0)$ is zero. From above this amounts to

$$C(x_0) = 0 = \int f(x)I(x)\, dx - (s - x_0) \int I'(x)f(x)\, dx + \int f(x)n(x + x_0)\, dx$$

Using $\int f(x)I(x)\, dx = 0$ and $\int I'(x)f(x)\, dx = -1$, we find

$$(s - x_0) = \int f(x)n(x + x_0)\, dx$$

which is in general not equal to zero and amounts to the error in s_E for the particular noise function $n(x)$. Using the form for $f(x)$ given above and calculating the rms error σ_s in s_E assuming spatially stationary noise yields

$$\sigma_s = \sqrt{\frac{\iint I'(x_1)I'(x_2)\langle n(x_1)n(x_2)\rangle\, dx_1\, dx_2}{\left[\int (I'(x))^2\, dx\right]^2}}$$

For the case in which the noise is uncorrelated so that $\langle n(x_1)n(x_2)\rangle = \sigma_n^2\delta(x_1 - x_2)$, this reduces to

$$\sigma_s = \frac{\sigma_n}{\sqrt{\int (I'(x))^2\, dx}}$$

This result shows explicitly again that the error in s_E is larger when the slope of the ideal bump shape is small. Note that $\langle n(x_1)n(x_2)\rangle = \sigma_n^2\delta(x_1 - x_2)$ requires σ_n to have units of $I \times \sqrt{\text{length}}$ because the delta function has units of $1/\text{length}$ and $n(x)$ has units of I.

Discrete Sampling and the Correlator Algorithm

First, for discrete sampling the integration is replaced by summation, i.e.,

$$C(x_0) = \int f(x - x_0)D(x)\, dx \rightarrow C_{i_0} = \sum_i f_{i-i_0}D_i$$

Second, as with the threshold algorithm, discrete sampling means that only rarely will an exact zero crossing in the output of the correlation occur exactly at a sample point. Usually two consequtive values of i_0 will straddle the zero crossing, that is, C_{i0} and $C_{i0 + 1}$ are both small but have opposite signs so that the true zero crossing occurs between them. If f_i is appropriately normalized, then both C_{i0} and $C_{i0 + 1}$ provide valid estimates of the signal bump centroid position as measured relative to the i_0 and $i_0 + 1$ positions, respectively, with both results being equally valid. Assuming that $i = 0$ corrsponds to the origin of the coordinate system and Δx is the sample spacing, then the two estimates are $s_E = C_{i0} + i_0\Delta x$ and $s_E = C_{i0 + 1} + (i_0 + 1)\Delta x$, respectively. Averaging the two results yields a better estimate given by

$$s_E\left(i_0 + \tfrac{1}{2}\right)\Delta x + \tfrac{1}{2}\left(C_{i_0} + C_{i_0+1}\right)$$

This result is exactly equivalent to linear interpolation of the zero-cross position from the two bounding values, since proper normalization of $f(x)$ is equivalent to making the slope of the curve equal to unity.

7.3 Fourier Algorithm

This algorithm is based on Fourier analyzing the signal. It is perhaps most straightforward to apply it to signals that closely approximate sinusoidal waveforms, but it can in fact be applied to any signal. We discuss the algorithm first for nonsinusoidal signals and then show the added benefit that accrues when it is applied to sinusoidal signals such as would be produced by a grating sensor (see Ref. 19).

Assuming that $I(x)$ is real and symmetric, its Fourier transform

$$\tilde{I}(\beta) \equiv \frac{1}{\sqrt{2\pi}} \int_{-\infty}^{+\infty} I(x)e^{i\beta x}\, dx$$

is real and symmetric, i.e.,

$$\tilde{I}(\beta) = \tilde{I}^{*}(\beta): \quad \text{real}$$

$$\tilde{I}(\beta) = \tilde{I}(-\beta): \quad \text{symmetric}$$

The parameter β is the spatial frequency in radians/(unit length) $= 2\pi \times$ cycles/(unit length), and "*" indicates complex conjugation.

The Fourier transform of the measured signal, $\tilde{D}(\beta)$, is related to $\tilde{I}(\beta)$ by a phase factor,

$$\tilde{D}(\beta) \equiv \frac{1}{\sqrt{2}} \int_{-\infty}^{+\infty} D(x)e^{i\beta x}\, dx$$

$$\equiv \frac{1}{\sqrt{2}} \int_{-\infty}^{+\infty} I(x - s)e^{i\beta x}\, dx$$

$$\equiv \frac{1}{\sqrt{2}} \int_{-\infty}^{+\infty} I(x')e^{i\beta(x'+s)}\, dx'$$

$$= e^{i\beta s}\tilde{I}(\beta)$$

where in the first step we have used $D(x) = I(x - s)$ as given above and in the second step we have changed variables, letting $x' = x + s$.

Remembering that $\tilde{I}(\beta)$ is real, we can then calculate s by scaling the arctangent of the ratio of the imaginary to the real component of the Fourier transform as follows:

$$s = \frac{1}{\beta} \arctan\left(\frac{\mathrm{Im}\left(\tilde{D}(\beta)\right)}{\mathrm{Re}\left(\tilde{D}(\beta)\right)}\right)$$

This can be proved by first noting that since $\tilde{I}(\beta)$ is real we have $\mathrm{Im}(\tilde{D}(\beta)) = \sin(\beta s)\tilde{I}(\beta)$ and $\mathrm{Re}(\tilde{D}(\beta)) = \cos(\beta s)\tilde{I}(\beta)$. Therefore $\tilde{I}(\beta)$ cancels in the ratio, leaving $\sin(\beta s)/\cos(\beta s) = \tan(\beta s)$. Then taking the arctangent and dividing by the spatial frequency, β, leaves the shift, s, as desired.

There are several interesting aspects of the above equation. Although the right-hand side can be evaluated for different values of β, they all yield the same value of s. Thus in the absence of any complicating factors such as noise or inherent signal asymmetry, any value of β can be used and the result will be the same.

Noise Sensitivity of the Fourier Algorithm

In the presence of noise the Fourier transform of the signal data takes the form

$$\tilde{D}(\beta) = e^{i\beta s}\tilde{I}(\beta) + \tilde{n}(\beta)$$

Substituting this form for $\tilde{D}(\beta)$ into the result given above for s yields

$$s(\beta) = \frac{1}{\beta} \arctan\left(\frac{\tilde{I}(\beta)\sin(\beta s) + \mathrm{Im}[\tilde{n}(\beta)]}{\tilde{I}(\beta)\cos(\beta s) + \mathrm{Re}[\tilde{n}(\beta)]}\right)$$

where s is now a function of β as indicated. That is, different β values will yield different estimates for s. The best estimate will be obtained from a weighted average of the different s values. This weighted average can be written as

$$s_E = \int f(\beta)s(\beta)\, d\beta$$

$$= \int \frac{f(\beta)}{\beta} \arctan\left(\frac{\tilde{I}(\beta)\sin(\beta s) + \mathrm{Im}[\tilde{n}(\beta)]}{\tilde{I}(\beta)\cos(\beta s) + \mathrm{Re}[\tilde{n}(\beta)]}\right) d\beta$$

$$\approx s \int f(\beta)\, d\beta + \int \frac{f(\beta)}{\beta} \frac{(\cos(\beta s)\,\mathrm{Im}[\tilde{n}(\beta)] - \sin(\beta s)\,\mathrm{Re}[\tilde{n}(\beta)])}{\tilde{I}(\beta)}\, d\beta$$

In the last step we have assumed that $f(\beta)$ is large in regions where the signal-to-noise ratio is large, that is, $\tilde{I} > \tilde{n}$, and it is essentially zero in regions where the signal-to-noise ratio is small, that is, $\tilde{I} < \tilde{n}$. Assuming zero-mean noise so that $\langle \tilde{n}(\beta) \rangle = 0$, we must have $\int f(\beta)\, d\beta = 1$ for s_E to be equal to the true answer, s, on average, that is, so that $\langle s_E \rangle = s$. The error in s_E is then given by the second term and we have

$$\sigma_s^2 = \int \frac{f(\beta_1)}{\beta_1 \tilde{I}(\beta_1)} \frac{f(\beta_2)}{\beta_2 \tilde{I}(\beta_2)} \left\langle \begin{array}{l} (\cos(\beta_1 s)\, \mathrm{Im}[\tilde{n}(\beta_1)] - \sin(\beta_1 s)\, \mathrm{Re}[\tilde{n}(\beta_1)]) \\ \times (\cos(\beta_2 s)\, \mathrm{Im}[\tilde{n}(\beta_2)] - \sin(\beta_2 s)\, \mathrm{Re}[\tilde{n}(\beta_2)]) \end{array} \right\rangle d\beta_1\, d\beta_2$$

Using the fact that $n(x)$ is real gives $\mathrm{Re}[\tilde{n}(\beta)] = \tfrac{1}{2}[\tilde{n}(\beta) + \tilde{n}(-\beta)]$ and $\mathrm{Im}[\tilde{n}(\beta)] = \tfrac{1}{2i}[\tilde{n}(\beta) - \tilde{n}(-\beta)]$. Assuming $n(x)$ is uncorrelated, that is, $\langle n(x)n(x') \rangle = \sigma_n^2 \delta(x - x')$, it follows that

$$\langle \mathrm{Re}[\tilde{n}(\beta_1)]\, \mathrm{Re}[\tilde{n}(\beta_2)] \rangle = \frac{\sigma_n^2}{2}[\delta(\beta_1 - \beta_2) + \delta(\beta_1 - \beta_2)]$$

$$\langle \mathrm{Im}[\tilde{n}(\beta_1)]\, \mathrm{Im}[\tilde{n}(\beta_2)] \rangle = \frac{\sigma_n^2}{2}[\delta(\beta_1 - \beta_2) - \delta(\beta_1 - \beta_2)]$$

$$\langle \mathrm{Re}[\tilde{n}(\beta_1)]\, \mathrm{Im}[\tilde{n}(\beta_2)] \rangle = 0$$

Substituting this above and assuming $f(\beta) = f(-\beta)$ yields

$$\sigma_s^2 = \sigma_n^2 \int \left(\frac{f(\beta)}{\beta \tilde{I}(\beta)} \right)^2 d\beta$$

We can find the optimum form for $f(\beta)$ by letting $f(\beta) = a(\beta)/\int d\beta\, a(\beta)$ so that $\int d\beta f(\beta) = 1$ is automatically satisfied, then replacing a with $a + \Delta a$ and expanding in powers of Δa, and finally demanding that the first order in Δa terms vanish for all Δa. This yields the following relation:

$$\int \frac{a(\beta)\Delta a(\beta)}{\left(\beta \tilde{I}(\beta)\right)^2} d\beta = \left(\frac{\int \Delta a(\beta) d\beta}{\int a(\beta) d\beta} \right) \int \left(\frac{a(\beta)}{\beta \tilde{I}(\beta)} \right)^2 d\beta$$

which is satisfied by letting $a(\beta) = (\beta \tilde{I}(\beta))^2$, which then gives

$$f(\beta) = \frac{\left(\beta \tilde{I}(\beta)\right)^2}{\int \left(\beta \tilde{I}(\beta)\right)^2 d\beta}$$

Substituting this above then gives

$$s_E = \frac{1}{\int \left(\beta \tilde{I}(\beta)\right)^2 d\beta} \int \beta \left(\tilde{I}(\beta)\right)^2 \arctan\left(\frac{\mathrm{Im}\left[\tilde{D}(\beta)\right]}{\mathrm{Re}\left[\tilde{D}(\beta)\right]} \right) d\beta$$

$$\sigma_s = \frac{\sigma_n}{\sqrt{\int \left(\beta \tilde{I}(\beta)\right)^2 d\beta}}$$

Thus the optimum weighting is proportional to the power spectrum of the signal $\tilde{I}^2$ as one would expect when the noise is uncorrelated. Also, the β factor shows that there is no information about the position of the bump for $\beta \sim 0$. This is simply a consequence of the fact that $\beta = 0$ corresponds to a constant value in x which carries no centroid information. Finally, $I'(x)$ in Fourier or β space is given by $i\beta\tilde{I}(\beta)$ and thus σ_s has the same basic form in both the correlator and Fourier algorithms. Note that $\langle n(x)n(x')\rangle = \sigma_n^2\delta(x - x')$ requires σ_n to have units of $I \times \sqrt{\text{length}}$, because the delta function has units of 1/length and $n(x)$ has units of I. This is exactly what is required for σ_s, to have units of length, since $\tilde{I}$ has units of $I \times$ length.

Like the correlator algorithm, the Fourier algorithm can also be derived using least squares. Substituting the Fourier transform representations

$$I(x) = \frac{1}{\sqrt{2\pi}} \int \tilde{I}(\beta)e^{-i\beta x}d\beta$$

$$D(x) = I(x - s_0)$$

$$= \frac{1}{\sqrt{2\pi}} \int \tilde{I}(\beta)e^{-i\beta(x-s_0)}d\beta$$

into the least squares integral $\int [D(x) - I(x - s)]^2 \, dx$, taking a derivative with respect to s and setting the result equal to zero for $s = s_E$ yields

$$0 = \int \beta\left|\tilde{I}(\beta)\right|^2 \sin[\beta(s_E - s_0)]$$

Using $\sin[\beta(s_E - s_0)] \cong \beta(s_E - s_0)$ for s_E close to s_0 and $\beta s_0 = \arctan$ $(\text{Im}[\tilde{D}(\beta)]/\text{Re}[\tilde{D}(\beta)])$, we obtain the same result as above.

Discrete Sampling and the Fourier Algorithm

The main effect of having discretely sampled rather than continuous data is to replace all the integrals in the above analysis with sums, i.e., replace true Fourier transforms with discrete Fourier transforms (DFTs) or their fast algorithmic implementation, fast Fourier transforms (FFTs).

Application of the Fourier Algorithm to Grating Sensors

In many grating sensors and in some nongrating sensors the pure mark signal is not an isolated bump but a sinusoid of a specific known frequency, say β_0, multiplied possibly by a slowly varying envelope function. The information about the mark position in this case is encoded in the phase of the sinusoid. The total detected signal will, as usual, be corrupted by noise and other effects, which in general adds sinusoids of all different frequencies, phases, and amplitudes to the pure β_0 sinusoid. But, since we know that the mark position information is contained only in the β_0 frequency component of the signal, all the other frequency components can simply be ignored in a first approximation.

They are useful only as a diagnostic for estimating the goodness of the signal. That is, if all the other frequency components are small enough that the signal is almost purely a β_0 sinusoid, then the expectation is that the mark is clean and uncorrupted and the noise level is low, in which case one can have high confidence in the mark position predicted by the signal. On the other hand, if all the other frequency components of the signal are as large as or larger than the β_0 frequency component, it is likely that the β_0 frequency component is severely corrupted by noise and the resulting centroid prediction is suspect.

Using the above result for computing s from the Fourier transform of the signal but using only the β_0 frequency component in the calculation yields

$$ s = \frac{1}{\beta_0} \arctan\left(\frac{\mathrm{Im}\left(\tilde{D}(\beta_0)\right)}{\mathrm{Re}\left(\tilde{D}(\beta_0)\right)}\right) $$

and in the presence of noise we have

$$ s_E = \frac{1}{\beta_0} \arctan\left(\frac{\tilde{I}(\beta_0)\,\sin(\beta_0 s) + \mathrm{Im}[\tilde{n}(\beta_0)]}{\tilde{I}(\beta_0)\,\cos(\beta_0 s) + \mathrm{Re}[\tilde{n}(\beta_0)]}\right) $$

$$ \simeq s + \frac{\cos(\beta_0 s)\,\mathrm{Im}[\tilde{n}(\beta_0)] - \sin(\beta_0 s)\,\mathrm{Re}[\tilde{n}(\beta_0)]}{\tilde{I}(\beta_0)} $$

for $\bar{n}(\beta_0) \ll \tilde{I}(\beta_0)$. The effect of noise on the grating result is given by

$$ \sigma_s^2 = \frac{\sigma_n^2}{\sqrt{\left(\beta_0 \tilde{I}(\beta_0)\right)^2 \Delta\beta}} $$

where $\Delta\beta$ is the spatial frequency resolution of the sensor.

8   GLOBAL ALIGNMENT ALGORITHM

The purpose of the global alignment algorithm is to combine all the separate alignment mark position measurements into an optimum estimate of the correctable components of the field and grid distortions along with the overall grid and field positions. These "correctable" components generally consist of some or all of the linear distortion terms described in the Appendix. The linear components of the average field distortion are referred to collectively as "field terms." The position of a given reference point in each field, such as the field center, defines the "grid," and these points will also have some amount of rotation, magnification, skew, etc. with respect to the expected grid. The linear components of the grid distortion are referred to collectively as "grid terms." In global fine alignment, where the alignment marks on only a few fields on the wafer are measured, both field and grid terms need to be determined from the alignment data to perform overlay. In field-by-field alignment, where each field is aligned based only on the data from that field, the grid terms are not directly relevant. Here we consider only global fine alignment. To be most general we will solve for all six linear distortion terms discussed in the Appendix: x and y translation, rotation, skew, x magnification, and y magnification. Note that not all exposure tools can correct for all these terms and thus the algorithm must be adjusted accordingly. We will consider a generic alignment system that measures and returns the x and y position values of each of N_M alignment marks in each of N_F fields on a wafer. Let $m = 1, 2, \ldots, N_M$ label the marks in each field and $f = 1, 2, \ldots, N_F$ label the fields. We will use the following matrix-vector notation for position, as measured with respect to some predefined coordinate sysmtem fixed with respect to the exposure tool.

$$r_{mf} = \begin{pmatrix} x_{mf} \\ y_{mf} \end{pmatrix} = \text{expected position of mark } m \text{ in field } f$$

$$r'_{mf} = \begin{pmatrix} x'_{mf} \\ y'_{mf} \end{pmatrix} = \text{measured position of mark } m \text{ in field } f$$

$$R_f = \begin{pmatrix} X_f \\ Y_f \end{pmatrix} = \text{expected position of field } f \text{ reference point}$$

$$R'_f = \begin{pmatrix} X'_f \\ Y'_f \end{pmatrix} = \text{measured position of field } f \text{ reference point}$$

To be explicit we must now choose a reference point for each field. It is the difference between the measured and expected positions of this reference point that defines the translation of the field. A suitable choice would be the center of the field but this is not necessary. Basically any point within the field can be used, but this is not to say that all points are equal in this regard. Different choices will result in different noise propagation and round-off error in any real implementation, and the reference point must be chosen to minimize these effects to the extent necessary. We will take the center of mass of the mark positions to be the reference point; i.e., we define the position of the reference point of field f by

$$R_f = \frac{1}{N_M} \sum_m r_{mf}$$

If the alignment marks are symmetrically arrayed around a field, then R_f as defined above is the field center.

The analysis is simplified if we assume that the field terms are defined with respect to the field reference point; that is, field rotation, skew, and x and y magnification do not affect the position of the reference point. This can be done by writing

$$r_{mf} = R_f + d_m$$

which effectively defines d_m as the position of mark m measured with respect to the reference point. The field terms are applied to d_m and the grid terms to R_f. Combining the previous two equation yields the following constraint:

$$\sum_m d_m = 0$$

Remember that the inherent assumption of the global fine alignment algorithm is that all the fields are identical and so d_m does not require a field index, f. But the measured d_m values will vary from field to field, and so we have for the measured data

$$r'_{mf} = R'_f + d'_{mf}$$

The implicit assumption of global fine alignment is that, to the overlay accuracy required, we can write

$$r'_{mf} = T + G \cdot R_f + F \cdot d_m + n_{mf}$$

where R_f and d_m are the expected grid and mark positions and

$$T = \begin{pmatrix} T_x \\ T_y \end{pmatrix} = \text{grid translation}$$

$$G = \begin{pmatrix} G_{xx} & G_{xy} \\ G_{yx} & G_{yy} \end{pmatrix} = \text{grid rotation skew and mag matrix}$$

$$F = \begin{pmatrix} F_{xx} & F_{xy} \\ F_{yx} & F_{yy} \end{pmatrix} = \text{field rotation skew and mag matrix}$$

See the Appendix for the relationship between the matrix elements and the geometric concepts of rotation, skew, and magnification. The term n_{mf} is noise that is nominally assumed to have a zero-mean Gaussian probability distribution and is uncorrelated from field to field and from mark to mark. The field translations are, by definition, just the shifts of the reference point of each field and so are given by

[Translation of field f] $= T + G \cdot R_f$

$$= \begin{pmatrix} T_x \\ T_y \end{pmatrix} + \begin{pmatrix} G_{xx} & G_{xy} \\ G_{yx} & G_{yy} \end{pmatrix} \cdot \begin{pmatrix} X_f \\ Y_f \end{pmatrix}$$

Throughout this analysis the + and · indicate standard matrix addition and multiplication, respectively.

In the equation for r'_{mf} the unknowns are the field and grid terms. The expected positions and the measured positions are known. Thus the equation must be inverted to solve for the combined field and grid terms, which amounts to 10 nominally independent numbers (2 from the translation vector and 4 each from the grid and field matrices). The nominal independence of the 10 terms must verified in each case because some exposure tools and/or processes will, for example, have no skew (so that term is explicitly zero) or the grid and field isotropic magnification terms will automatically be equal. We will take all 10 terms to be independent for the remainder of this discussion. Appropriate adjustment of the results for dependent or known terms is straightforward.

Solving for the 10 terms from the expected and measured position values is generally done using some version of a least-squares fit. The least-squares approach, in a strict sense, applies only to Gaussian-distributed uncorrelated noise. Since real alignment measurements are often corrupted by "flyers" or "outliners," i.e., data values that are not part of a Gaussian probability distribution, some alteration of the basic least-squares approach must be made to eliminate or at least reduce their effect on the final result. This is an age old problem that is discussed very clearly in Ref. 20. The optimum approach that needs to be applied in a particular case must be determined from the statistics of the measured data including overlay results. Finally, it is not the straightforward software implementation of the least-squares solution derived below that is difficult, it is all the ancillary problems that must be accounted for in any real application, such as the determination and elimination of flyers, allowing for missing data, determining when more fields are needed and which fields to add, etc.

For the purposes of understanding the basic concept of global alignment we will simply assume a single iteration of the standard least-squares algorithm in the derivation given below.

Substituting the matrix-vector form for the field and grid terms into the equation for r'_{mf}, rearranging terms, and separating out the x and y components yields

$$n_{xmf} = x'_{mf} - T_x - X_f G_{xx} - Y_f G_{xy} - d_{xm} F_{xx} - d_{ym} F_{xy}$$

and

$$n_{ymf} = y'_{mf} - T_y - X_f G_{yx} - Y_f G_{yy} - d_{xm} F_{yx} - d_{ym} F_{yy}$$

The x and y terms can be treated separately and with the equations written again in matrix-vector form, but clustered this time with respect to the grid and field terms, we have for the x equations

$$\underbrace{\begin{pmatrix} n'_{x11} \\ n'_{x21} \\ n'_{x31} \\ \vdots \\ n'_{xN_M N_F} \end{pmatrix}}_{\text{error} \equiv \varepsilon_x} = \underbrace{\begin{pmatrix} x'_{11} \\ x'_{21} \\ x'_{31} \\ \vdots \\ x'_{N_M N_F} \end{pmatrix}}_{\text{data} \equiv D_x} - \underbrace{\begin{pmatrix} 1 & X_1 & Y_1 & d_{x1} & d_{y1} \\ 1 & X_1 & Y_1 & d_{x2} & d_{y2} \\ 1 & X_1 & Y_1 & d_{x3} & d_{y3} \\ \vdots & \vdots & \vdots & \vdots & \vdots \\ 1 & X_{N_F} & Y_{N_F} & d_{xN_M} & d_{yN_M} \end{pmatrix}}_{A} \cdot \underbrace{\begin{pmatrix} T_x \\ G_{xx} \\ G_{xy} \\ F_{xx} \\ F_{xy} \end{pmatrix}}_{\text{unknowns} \equiv U_x}$$

and for the y equations

$$\underbrace{\begin{pmatrix} n'_{y11} \\ n'_{y21} \\ n'_{y31} \\ \vdots \\ n'_{yN_M N_F} \end{pmatrix}}_{\text{error} \equiv \varepsilon_y} = \underbrace{\begin{pmatrix} y'_{11} \\ y'_{21} \\ y'_{31} \\ \vdots \\ y'_{N_M N_F} \end{pmatrix}}_{\text{data} \equiv D_y} - \underbrace{\begin{pmatrix} 1 & X_1 & Y_1 & d_{x1} & d_{y1} \\ 1 & X_1 & Y_1 & d_{x2} & d_{y2} \\ 1 & X_1 & Y_1 & d_{x3} & d_{y3} \\ \vdots & \vdots & \vdots & \vdots & \vdots \\ 1 & X_{N_F} & Y_{N_F} & d_{xN_M} & d_{yN_M} \end{pmatrix}}_{A} \cdot \underbrace{\begin{pmatrix} T_y \\ G_{yx} \\ G_{yy} \\ F_{yx} \\ F_{yy} \end{pmatrix}}_{\text{unknowns} \equiv U_y}$$

Using the indicated notation, the above equations reduce to

$$\varepsilon_x = D_x - A \cdot U_x$$

and

$$\varepsilon_y = D_y - A \cdot U_y$$

The standard least-squares solution is found by minimizing the sum of the squares of the errors, which can be written as

$$\varepsilon_x^T \cdot \varepsilon_x = (D_x - A \cdot U_x)^T \cdot (D_x - A \cdot U_x)$$

and

$$\varepsilon_y^T \cdot \varepsilon_y = (D_y - A \cdot U_y)^T \cdot (D_y - A \cdot U_y)$$

where the superscript T indicates the transpose. Taking derivatives with repect to the elements of the unknown vectors, i.e., taking derivatives one by one with respect to the field and grid terms, and setting the results to zero to find the minimum yields, after some algebra, the following result.

$$U_x = \left(A^T \cdot A \right)^{-1} \cdot A^T \cdot D_x$$

and

$$U_y = \left(A^{\mathrm{T}} \cdot A\right)^{-1} \cdot A^{\mathrm{T}} \cdot D_y$$

where the superscript −1 indicates the matrix inverse and T indicates the transpose.

Note that the A matrix is fixed for a given set of fields and marks. Thus the combination $(A^{\mathrm{T}} \cdot A)^{-1} \cdot A^{\mathrm{T}}$ can be computed for a particular set of fields and marks and the result can simply be matrix multiplied against the column vector of x and y data to produce the best-fit field and grid terms. Alignment is then performed by using these data in the $r_{mf} = T + G \cdot R_f + F \cdot d_m$ equation in a feedforward sense to compute the position, orientation, and linear distortion of all the fields on the wafer.

9 APPENDIX

Let x and y be standard orthogonal Cartesian coordinates in two dimensions. Consider an arbitrary combination of translation, rotation, and distortion of the points in the plane. This will carry each original point (x,y) to a new position, (x',y'), i.e.,

$$x \to x' = f(x,y)$$
$$y \to y' = g(x,y)$$

The functions f and g can be expressed as power series in the x and y coordinates with the form

$$x' = f(x,y) = T_x + M_{xx}x + M_{xy}y + Cx^2 + Dxy + \cdots$$
$$y' = g(x,y) = T_y + M_{yx}x + M_{yy}y + Ey^2 + Fxy + \cdots$$

where the T, M, C, D, E, F, ... coefficients are all constant, i.e., independent of x and y.

The T terms represent a constant shift of all the points in the plane by the amount T_x in the x direction and T_y in the y direction. The M terms represent shifts in the coordinate values that depend linearly on the original coordinate values. The remaining C, D, E, F, and higher order terms all depend nonlinearly on the original coordinate values. Using matrix-vector notation we can then write the above two equations as a single equation of the form

$$\begin{pmatrix} x' \\ y' \end{pmatrix} = \underbrace{\begin{pmatrix} T_x \\ T_y \end{pmatrix}}_{\text{Constant}} + \underbrace{\begin{pmatrix} M_{xx} & M_{xy} \\ M_{yx} & M_{yy} \end{pmatrix} \cdot \begin{pmatrix} x \\ y \end{pmatrix}}_{\text{Linear term}} + \begin{pmatrix} \text{nonlinear} \\ \text{terms} \end{pmatrix}$$

where the $+$ and $\cdot$ indicated standard matrix addition and multiplication, respectively.

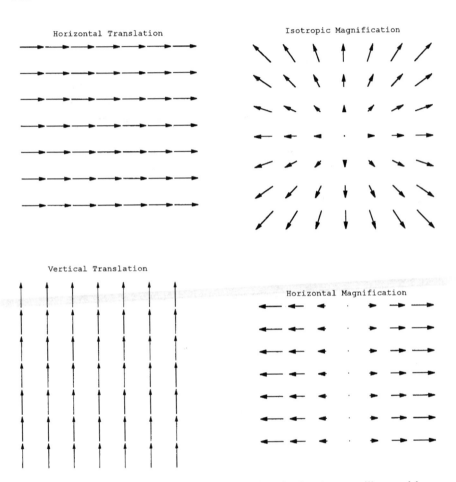

Figure 14   The various standard linear distortions in the plane are illustrated here. As discussed in the text, various combination of rotation skew and magnification can be used as a complete basis set for linear distortion. For example, it is clear that isotropic magnification is the equal weight linear combination of horizontal and vertical magnification and rotation is the equal weight linear combination of horizontal and vertical skew.

Vertical Magnification

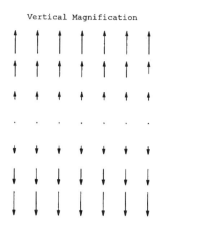

Horizontal Skew

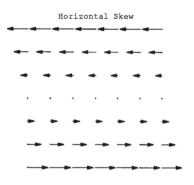

Vertical Skew

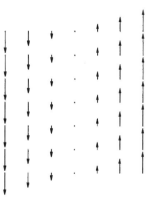

Rotation

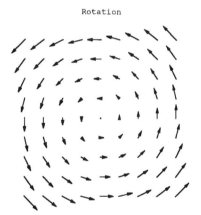

Figure 14 Continued.

The constant term is a translation that has separate x and y values. The linear term involves four independent constants, M_{xx}, M_{xy}, M_{yx}, and M_{yy}. These can be expressed as combinations of the more geometric concepts of rotation, skew, x magnification (x-mag) and y magnification (y-mag). Each of of these "pure" transformations can be written as a single matrix:

$$\text{Rotation} = \begin{pmatrix} \cos(\theta) & -\sin(\theta) \\ \sin(\theta) & \cos(\theta) \end{pmatrix}$$

$$\text{Skew} = \begin{pmatrix} 1 & 0 \\ \sin(\psi) & 1 \end{pmatrix}$$

$$x\text{-Mag} = \begin{pmatrix} m_x & 0 \\ 0 & 1 \end{pmatrix}$$

$$y\text{-Mag} = \begin{pmatrix} 1 & 0 \\ 0 & m_y \end{pmatrix}$$

Here θ is the rotation angle and ψ is the skew angle both measured in radians, and m_x and m_y are the x and y magnifications, respectively, both of which are unitless. Both skew and rotation are area preserving because their determinants are equal to unity, whereas x-mag and y-mag change the area by factors of m_x and m_y, respectively.

Skew has been defined above to correspond geometrically to a rotation of just the x axis by itself, i.e., x-skew. Instead of using rotation and x-skew we could have used rotation and y-skew or the combination x-skew and y-skew. Similarly, instead of using x-mag and y-mag the combinations isotropic magnification, i.e., "iso-mag," and x-mag or iso-mag and y-mag could have been used. Which combinations are chosen is purely a matter of convention.

The net linear tranformation matrix, M, can be written as the product of the mag, skew, and rotation matrices. Since matrix multiplication is not commutative, the exact form that M takes in this case depends on the order in which the separate matrices are multiplied. But, since most distortions encountered in an exposure tool are small, we need to consider only the infinitesimal forms of the matrices, in which case the result is commutative.

Using the approximations

$$\cos(\phi) \cong 1$$

$$\sin(\phi) \cong \phi$$

$$m_x = 1 + \mu_x$$

$$m_y = 1 + \mu_y$$

and then expanding to first order in all the small terms, θ, ψ, μ_x, and μ_y, we get

$$M = (x - \text{mag}) \cdot (y - \text{mag}) \cdot (\text{skew}) \cdot (\text{rotation})$$

$$= \begin{pmatrix} m_x & 0 \\ 0 & 1 \end{pmatrix} \cdot \begin{pmatrix} 1 & 0 \\ 0 & m_y \end{pmatrix}$$

$$\cdot \begin{pmatrix} 1 & 0 \\ \sin(\psi) & 1 \end{pmatrix} \cdot \begin{pmatrix} \cos(\theta) & -\sin(\theta) \\ \sin(\theta) & \cos(\theta) \end{pmatrix}$$

$$= \begin{pmatrix} m_x \cos(\theta) & -m_x \sin(\theta) \\ m_y(\sin(\theta) + \sin(\psi) \cos(\theta)) & m_y(\cos(\theta) - \sin(\psi) \sin(\theta)) \end{pmatrix}$$

$$\cong \begin{pmatrix} 1 + \mu_x & -\theta \\ \theta + \psi & 1 + \mu_y \end{pmatrix}$$

$$\cong \underbrace{\begin{pmatrix} 1 & 0 \\ 0 & 1 \end{pmatrix}}_{\text{Identity matrix}} + \begin{pmatrix} \mu_x & -\theta \\ \theta + \psi & \mu_y \end{pmatrix}$$

Thus the transformation takes the infinitesimal form

$$\begin{pmatrix} x' \\ y' \end{pmatrix} \cong \begin{pmatrix} x \\ y \end{pmatrix} + \underbrace{\begin{pmatrix} T_x \\ T_y \end{pmatrix} + \begin{pmatrix} \mu_x & -\theta \\ \theta + \psi & \mu_y \end{pmatrix} \cdot \begin{pmatrix} x \\ y \end{pmatrix}}_{\cong \begin{pmatrix} \Delta_x \\ \Delta_y \end{pmatrix}}$$

REFERENCES

1. Flanders et. al., A new interferometric alignment technique, *Appl. Phys. Lett., 31,* 426 (1977).
2. Bouwhuis and Wittekoek, Automatic alignment system for optical projection printing, *IEEE Tran. on Elect. Dev.,* ED-26, 723 (1979).
3. Bealieu and Hellebrekers, Dark field technology: a practical approach to local alignment, *SPIE, 772,* 142 (1987).
4. Tabata and Tojo, High-precision interferometric alignment using checker grating, *J. Vac. Sci. Technol., B7,* 1980 (1989).
5. Suzuki and Une, An optical-heterodyne alignment technique for quarter-micron x-ray lithography, *J. Vac. Sci. Technol., B7,* 1971 (1989).
6. Uchida, et al., A mask-to-wafer alignment and gap setting method for x-ray lithography using gratings, *J. Vac. Sci. Technol., B9,* 3202 (1991).
7. Chen, et al., Experimental evaluation of the two-state alignment system, *J. Vac. Sci. Technol., B9,* 3222 (1991).
8. D. H. Kim, K. H. Lee, Y. H. Oh, J. H. Lee, H. B. Chung, H. J. Yoo, Baseline error-free non-TTL alignment system using oblique illumination for wafer steppers, *2440-82,* Electronics and Telecommunications Research Institute, Korea.

9. R. Sharma, N. D. Katarla, V. N. Ojha, A. K. Kanjilal, R. Narain, V. T. Chitnis, Photolithographic mask aligner based on modified moiré technique, *2440-83*, National Physical Lab. (India); Y. Uchida, Aichi Institute of Technology, Japan.
10. Cronin and Gallatin, Microscan II overlay error analysis, *SPIE, 2196*, (1994).
11. N. Magome, H. Kawai, Total overlay analysis for designing future aligner, *2440-80*, Nikon Corp., Japan.
12. Starikov, et. al., Accuracy of overlay measurements: tool and asymmetry effects, *Opt. Eng., 31*, 1298 (1992).
13. Yuan and Strojwas, Modeling optical microscope images of integrated-circuit structures, *J. Opt. Soc. Am., A8*, 778 (1991).
14. Yuan, et. al., *SPIE, 1088*, 392 (1989).
15. Bobroff and Rosenbluth, Alignment errors from resist coating topography, *J. Vac. Sci. Technol., B6*, 403 (1988).
16. Gallatin, et. al., Modeling the images of alignment marks under photoresist, *SPIE, 772*, 193, (1987).
17. Gallatin, et. al., Scattering matrices for imaging layered media, *J. Opt. Soc. Am., A5*, 220 (1988).
18. Gamelin, et al., Exploration of scattering from topography with massively parallel computers, *J. Vac. Sci. Technol., B7*, 1984 (1989).
19. Gatherer and Meng, Frequency domain position estimation for lithographic alignment, *Proc. IEEE Int'l. Conf. Acoustics, Speech and Signal Proc.* (April, 1993).
20. Branham, *Scientific Data Analysis*, Springer-Verlag, (1990).

6

Electron Beam Lithography Systems

Geraint Owen and James R. Sheats

Hewlett-Packard Laboratories
Palo Alto, California

1 INTRODUCTION

Lithography using beams of electrons to expose the resist was one of the earliest processes used for integrated circuit fabrication, dating back to 1957 [1]. Today essentially all high-volume production, even down to sub-half-micrometer feature sizes, is done with optical techniques, due to the advances in stepper technology described thoroughly elsewhere in this volume. Nevertheless, electron beam systems continue to play two vital roles, which will in all probability not diminish in importance for the foreseeable future. First, they are used to generate the masks that are used in optical exposure systems (as well as x-ray systems), and second, they are used in the low-volume manufacture of ultrasmall features for very high performance devices, as described by Dobisz et al. in Chapter 13. In addition, however, there is some activity in so-called mix-and-match lithography, in which the e-beam system is used to expose one or a few levels with especially small features, and optical systems are used for the rest. Thus it is possible that as feature sizes move below about 0.18 μm (where optical techniques face substantial obstacles that will certainly take some years of research to overcome), electron beam systems might play a role in advanced manufacturing despite their throughput limitations as serial exposure systems. For these reasons it is important for the lithographer to have some knowledge of the operation of e-beam exposure systems, even though it is expected that optical lithography will continue to be the dominant manufacturing technique.

This chapter provides an introduction to such systems. It is intended to have sufficient depth for the reader to understand the basic principles of operation and design guidelines, without attempting to be a principal source for a system designer or a researcher pushing the limits of the technique. The treatment is based on a monograph by Owen [2], which the reader should consult for more detail, as well as background information and historical aspects. processing details (including discussion of currently available resists) and aspects unique to ultrasmall features (sub-100 nm) are covered in Chapter 13.

2   THE ELECTRON OPTICS OF ROUND-BEAM INSTRUMENTS

2.1   General Description

Figure 1 is a simplified ray diagram of a hypothetical scanned-beam electron lithography instrument, in which lenses have been idealized as thin optical elements. The electron optics of a scanning electron microscope [3] would be similar in many respects.

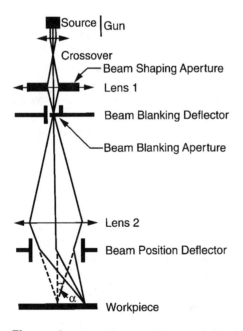

Figure 1   Simplified ray diagram of the electron optical system of a hypothetical round-beam electron lithography system.

Electrons are emitted from the source, whose crossover is focused onto the surface of the workplace by two magnetic lenses. The numerical aperture is governed by the beam shaping aperture. This intercepts current emitted by the gun that is not ultimately focused onto the spot. In order to minimize the excess current flowing down the column, the beam shaping aperture needs to be placed as near as possible to the gun and, in extreme cases, may form an integral part of the gun itself. This is beneficial because it reduces electron-electron interactions, which have the effect of increasing the diameter of the focused spot at the workpiece. A second benefit is that the lower the current flowing through the column, the less opportunity there is for polymerizing residual hydrocarbon or siloxane molecules and forming insulating contamination films on the optical elements. If present, these can acquire electric charge and cause beam drift and loss of resolution.

A magnetic or electrostatic deflector is used to move the focused beam over the surface of the workpiece; this deflector is frequently placed after the final lens. The beam can be turned off by a beam blanker, which consists of a combination of an aperture and a deflector. When the deflector is not activated, the beam passes through the aperture and exposes the workpiece. However, when the deflector is activated, the beam is diverted, striking the body of the aperture.

A practical instrument would incorporate additional optical elements, such as alignment deflectors and stigmators. The arrangement shown in the figure is only one possible configuration for a scanned-beam instrument. Many variations are possible; a number of instruments, for example, have three magnetic lenses.

If the beam current delivered to the workpiece is I, the area on the wafer to be exposed is A, and the charge density to be delivered to the exposed regions (often called the "dose") is Q, it then follows that the total exposure time is

$$T = QA / I \tag{1}$$

Thus, for short exposure times, the resist should be as sensitive as possible and the beam current should be as high as possible.

The beam current is related to the numerical aperture (α) and the diameter of the spot focused on the substrate (d) by the relationship

$$I = \beta \left(\frac{\pi d^2}{4} \right) \left(\pi \alpha^2 \right) \tag{2}$$

where β is the brightness of the source. In general, the current density in the spot is not uniform but consists of a bell-shaped distribution; as a result, d corresponds to an "effective" spot diameter. Note that the gun brightness and the numerical aperture need to be as high as possible to maximize current density.

Depending on the type of gun, the brightness can vary by several orders of magnitude (see Section 2.2): a value in the middle of the range is 10^5 A cm^{-2} sr^{-1}. The numerical aperture is typically about 5×10^{-3} rad. Using these values, and assuming a spot diameter of 0.5 μm, Eq. 2 predicts a beam current of about 15 nA, a value that is typical for this type of lithography system.

For Eq. 2 to be valid the spot diameter must be limited only by the source diameter and the magnification of the optical system. This may not necessarily be the case in practice because of the effects of geometric and chromatic aberrations and electron-electron interactions.

The time taken to expose a chip can be calculated using Eq. 1. As an example, a dose of 10 μC cm^{-2}, a beam current of 15nA, and 50T coverage of a 5 × 5 mm^2 chip will result in a chip exposure time of 1.4 minutes. A 3-in.-diameter wafer could accommodate about 100 such chips, and the corresponding wafer exposure time would be 2.3 hr. Thus, high speed is not an attribute of this type of system, particularly bearing in mind that many resists require doses well in excess of 10 μC cm^{-2}. For reticle making, faster electron resists with sensitivities of up to 1 μC cm^{-2} are available: however, their poor resolution precludes their use for direct writing.

Equation 1 can also be used to estimate the maximum allowable response time of the beam blanker, the beam deflector, and the electronic circuits controlling them. In this case, A corresponds to the area occupied by a pattern pixel; if the pixel spacing is 0.5 μm, then $A = 0.25 \times 10^{-12}$ m^2. Assuming a resist sensitivity of 10 μC cm^{-2} and a beam current of 15 nA implies that the response time must be less than 1.7 μsec. Thus, the bandwidth of the deflection and blanking systems must be several MHz. Instruments that operate with higher beam currents and more sensitive resists require correspondingly greater bandwidths.

Since the resolution of scanned-beam lithography instruments is not limited by diffraction, the diameter of the disk of confusion (Δd) caused by a defocus error Δz is given by the geometrical optical relationship:

$$\Delta d = 2\alpha\Delta z. \tag{3}$$

Thus, if the angular aperture is 5×10^{-3} rad and the allowable value of Δd is 0.2 μm, then $\Delta z < 20$ μm. This illustrates the fact that, in electron lithography, the available depth of focus is sufficiently great that it does not affect resolution.

2.2 Electron Guns

The electron guns used in scanning electron lithography systems are similar to those used in scanning electron microscopes (for a general description see, for example, Oatley [3]). There are four major types: thermionic guns using a tungsten hairpin as the source, thermionic guns using a lanthanum hexaboride source, tungsten field emission guns, and tungsten thermionic field emission (TF) guns.

Thermionic guns are commonly used, being simple and reliable. The source of electrons is a tungsten wire, bent into the shape of a hairpin, which is self-heated to a temperature of 2300–2700° by passing a DC current through it. The brightness of the gun and the lifetime of the wire depend strongly on temperature. At lower heater currents, the brightness is of the order of 10^4 A cm^{-2} sr^{-1}, and the lifetime is of the order of 100 hr. At higher heating currents, the brightness increases to about 10^5 A cm^{-2} sr^{-1}, but the lifetime decreases to a value of the order of 10 hr (see, for example, Broers [4] and Wells [5]). Space charge saturation prevents higher brightnesses from being obtained. (The brightness values quoted here apply to beam energies of 10–20 keV.)

Lanthanum hexaboride is frequently used as a thermionic emitter by forming it into a pointed rod and heating its tip indirectly using a combination of thermal radiation and electron bombardment [4]. At a tip temperature of 1600°C and at a beam energy of 12 keV, Broers reported a brightness of over 10^5 A cm^{-2} sr^{-1} and a lifetime of the order of 1000 hr. This represents an increase in longevity of a factor of two orders of magnitude over a tungsten filament working at the same brightness. This is accounted for by the comparatively low operating temperature, which helps to reduce evaporation. Two factors allow lanthanum hexaboride to be operated at a lower temperature than tungsten. The first is its comparatively low work function (approximately 3.0 eV as opposed to 4.4 eV). The second, and probably more important, factor is that the curvature of the tip of the lanthanum hexaboride rod is about 10 µm, whereas that of the emitting area of a bent tungsten wire is an order of magnitude greater. As a result, the electric field in the vicinity of the lanthanum hexaboride emitter is much greater, and the effects of space charge are much less pronounced.

Because of its long lifetime at a given brightness, a lanthanum hexaboride source needs to be changed only infrequently, which is a useful advantage for electron lithography because it reduces the downtime of a very expensive machine. A disadvantage of lanthanum hexaboride guns is that they are more complex than tungsten guns, particularly as lanthanum hexaboride is extremely reactive at high temperatures, which makes its attachment to the gun assembly difficult. The high reactivity also means that the gun vacuum must be better than about 10^{-6} torr if corrosion by gas molecules is not to take place.

In the field emission gun, the source consists of a wire (generally of tungsten), one end of which is etched to a sharp tip with a radius of curvature of approximately 1 µm. This forms a cathode electrode, the anode being a coaxial flat disk that is located in front of the tip. A hole on the axis of the anode allows the emitted electrons to pass out of the gun. To generate a 20-keV beam of electrons, the potential difference between the anode and cathode is maintained at 20 kV, and the spacing is chosen so as to generate an electric field of about 10^9 V m^{-1} at the tip of the tungsten wire. At this field strength, electrons within the wire are able to tunnel through the potential barrier at the tungsten-vacuum interface, after which they are accelerated to an energy of 20 keV. An additional electrode is frequently included in the gun structure to control the emission current. (A general review of field emission has been written by Gomer [6].)

The brightness of a field emission source at 20 keV is generally more than 10^7 A cm^{-2} sr^{-1}. Despite this very high value, field emission guns have not been extensively used in electron lithography because of their unstable behavior and their high-vacuum requirements. In order to keep contamination of the tip and damage inflicted on it by ion bombardment to manageable proportions, the gun vacuum must be about 10^{-12} torr. Even under these conditions, the beam is severely affected by low-frequency flicker noise, and the tip must be reformed to clean and repair it at approximately hourly intervals. Stille and Astrand [7] converted a commercial field emission scanning microscope into a lithography instrument. Despite the use of a servo system to reduce flicker noise, dose variations of up to 5% were observed.

The structure of a TF gun is similar to that of a field emission gun, except that the electric field at the emitting tip is only about 10^8 V m^{-1} and that the tip is heated to a temperature of 1000–1500°C. Because of the Schottky effect, the apparent work function of the tungsten tip is lowered by the presence of the electric field. As a result, a copious supply of electrons is emitted thermionically at comparatively low temperature. The brightness of a typical TF gun is similar to that of a field emission gun (at least 10^7 A cm^{-2} st^{-1}), but the operation of a TF gun is far simpler. Because the tip is heated, it tends to be self-cleaning and a vacuum of 10^{-9} torr is sufficient for stable operation. Flicker noise is not a serious problem, and lifetimes of many hundreds of hours are obtained, tip reforming being unnecessary. A description of this type of gun is given by Kuo and Siegel [8], and an electron lithography system using a TF gun is described below.

A thermionic gun produces a crossover whose diameter is about 50 μm, whereas field emission and TF guns produce crossovers whose diameters are of the order of 10 nm. For this reason, to produce a spot diameter of about 0.5 μm, the lens system associated with a thermionic source must be demagnifying, but that associated with a field emission or TF source needs to be magnifying.

2.3 The Beam Blanker

The function of the beam blanker is to switch on and off the current in the electron beam. To be useful, a beam blanker must satisfy three performance criteria.

1. When the beam is switched "off," its attenuation must be very great; typically a value of 10^6 is specified.
2. Any spurious beam motion introduced by the beam blanker must be very much smaller than the size of a pattern pixel; typically the requirement is for much less than 0.1 μm of motion.
3. The response time of the blanker must be very much less than the time required to expose a pattern pixel; typically this implies a response time of much less than 100 nsec.

In practice, satisfying the first criterion is not difficult, but careful design is required to satisfy the other two, the configuration of Fig. 1 being a possible scheme. An important aspect of its design is that the center of the beam blanking deflector is confocal with the workpiece.

Figure 2 is a diagram of the principal trajectory of electrons passing through an electrostatic deflector. The real trajectory is the curve *ABC*, which, if fringing fields are negligible, is parabolic. At the center of the deflector, the trajectory of the deflected beam is displaced by the distance *B'B*. The virtual trajectory consists of the straight lines *AB'* and *B'C*. Viewed from outside, the effect of the deflector is to turn the electron trajectory through the angle φ about the point *B'* (the center of the deflector). If, therefore, *B'* is confocal with the workpiece, the position of the spot on the workpiece will not change as the deflector is activated, and performance criterion 2 will be satisfied (the angle of incidence will change, but this does not matter).

The second important aspect of the design of Fig. 1 is that the beam blanking aperture is also confocal with the workpiece. As a result, the cross section of the beam is smallest at the plane of the blanking aperture. Consequently, when the deflector is activated (shifting the real image of the crossover from *B'* to *B*), the transition from "on" to "off" occurs more rapidly than it would if the aperture were placed in any other position. This helps to satisfy criterion 3.

The blanking aperture is metallic, and so placing it within the deflector itself would, in practice, disturb the deflecting field. As a result, the scheme of

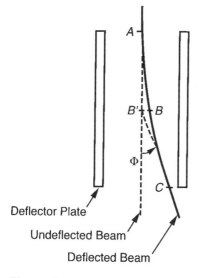

Figure 2   The principal trajectory of electrons passing through an electrostatic deflector.

Fig. 1 is generally modified by placing the blanking aperture just outside the deflector; the loss in time resolution is usually insignificant.

An alternative solution has been implemented by Kuo et al. [9]. This is to approximate the blanking arrangement of Fig. 2 by two blanking deflectors one above and one below the blanking aperture. This particular blanker was intended for use at a data rate of 300 MHz, which is unusually fast for an electron lithography system, and so an additional factor, the transit time of the beam through the blanker structure, became important.

Neglecting relativistic effects, the velocity *(v)* of an electron traveling with a kinetic energy of *V* electron volts is

$$v = \left(\frac{2qV}{m} \right)^{1/2} \tag{4}$$

(*q* being the magnitude of the electronic charge and *m* the electronic mass). Thus the velocity of a 20-keV electron is approximately 8.4×10^7 m s^{-1}. Tbe length of the blanker of Kuo et al. [9] in the direction of travel of the beam was approximately 40 mm, giving a transit time of about 0.5 nsec. This time is significant compared with the pixel exposure time of 3 nsec and, if uncorrected, would have resulted in a loss of resolution, caused by the partial deflection of the electrons already within the blanker structure when a blanking signal was applied.

To overcome the transit time effect, Kuo et al. [9] inserted a delay line between the upper and lower deflectors. This arrangement approximated a traveling wave structure in which the deflection field and the electron beam both moved down the column at the same velocity, eliminating the possibility of partial deflection.

2.4   Deflection Systems

Figure 3 is a diagram of a type of deflection syvstem widely used in scanning electron microscopes, the "prelens double-deflection" system. The deflectors D1 and D2 are magnetic coils that are located behind the magnetic field of the final magnetic lens. In a frequently used configuration, L1 and L2 are equal, and the excitation of D2 is arranged to be twice that of D1, but acting in the opposite direction. This has the effect of deflecting the beam over the workpiece but not shifting the beam in the principal plane of the final lens, thus keeping its off-axis aberrations to a minimum. The size of this arrangement may be gauged from the fact that L1 typically lies between 50 and 100 mm.

The prelens double-deflection system is suitable for use in scanning electron microscopes (SEMs) because it allows a very small working distance (*L*) to be used (typically, *L* is less than 10 mm in SEM). This is essential in microscopy because spherical aberration is one of the most important factors limiting the resolution, and the aberration coefficient increases rapidly with working distance. Thus, the prelens double-deflection system allows a high ultimate reso-

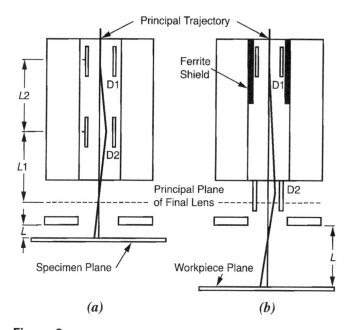

Figure 3   (a) A prelens double-deflection system, a type of deflector commonly used in scanning electron microscopes. (b) An in-lens double-deflection system, a type of deflector that is used in scanning electron lithography instruments. Note that the working distance (L) is made greater in (b) than it is in (a) because spherical aberration is not a limiting factor in scanning electron lithography; the longer working distance reduces the deflector excitation necessary to scan the electron beam over distances of several millimeters. The purpose of the ferrite shield in (b) is to reduce eddy current effects by screening D1 from the upper bore of the final lens.

lution (10 nm or better) to be achieved, but generally only over a limited field (about $10 \times 10 \ \mu m^2$). Outside this region, off-axis deflection aberrations enlarge the electron spot and distort the shape of the scanned area.

Although this limited field coverage is not a serious limitation for electron microscopy, it is for electron lithography. In this application, the resolution required is comparatively modest (about 100 nm), but it must be maintained over a field whose dimensions are greater than $1 \times 1 \ mm^2$. Furthermore, distortion of the scan field must be negligible.

Early work in scanning electron lithography was frequently carried out with converted SEM using prelens double deflection. Chang and Stewart [10] used such an instrument and reported that deflection aberrations degraded its resolution to about 0.8 μm at the periphery of a $1 \times 1 \ mm^2$ field at a numerical aperture of 5×10^{-3} rad. However, they also noted that the resolution could be maintained at better than 0.1 µm throughout this field if the focus and stigmator controls were manually readjusted after deflecting the beam. In many modem systems, field curvature and astigmatism are corrected in this way, but under computer control, the technique being known as "dynamic correction" (see, for example, Owen [11].

Chang and Stewart [10] also measured the deflection distortion of their instrument. They found that the nonlinear relationship between deflector current and spot deflection caused a positional error of 0.1 µm at a nominal deflection of 100 µm. The errors at larger deflections would be very much worse, because the relationship between distortion errors and nominal deflection consists of a homogeneous cubic polynomial under the conditions used in scanning electron lithography. Deflection errors are often corrected dynamically in modern scanning lithography systems by characterizing the errors before exposure, using the laser interferometer as the calibration standard. During exposure, appropriate corrections are made to the excitations of the deflectors.

Owen and Nixon [12] carried out a case study on a scanning electron lithography system with a prelens double-deflection system. On the basis of computer calculations they showed that the source of off-axis aberrations was the deflection system, the effects of lens aberrations being considerably less serious. In particular, they noted that the effects of spherical aberration were quite negligible. This being the case, they went on to propose that, for the purposes of electron lithography, postlens deflection was feasible, At working distances of several centimeters, spherical aberration would still be negligible for a well-designed final lens, and there would be sufficient room to incorporate a single deflector between it and the workpiece.

A possible configuration was proposed and built, the design philosophy adopted being to correct distortion and field curvature dynamically and optimize the geometry of the deflection coil so as to minimize the remaining aberrations. Amboss [13] constructed a similar deflection system that maintained a resolution of better than 0.2 µm over a 2×2 mm^2 scan field at a numerical aperture of 3×10^{-3} rad. Calculations had indicated that the resolution of this system should have been 0.1 µm, and Amboss attributed the discrepancy to imperfections in the winding of the deflection coils.

A different approach to the design of low-aberration deflection systems was proposed by Ohiwa et al. [14]. This "in-lens" scheme, illustrated in Fig. 3b, is an extension of the prelens double-deflection system, fro which it differs in two respects.

1. The second deflector is placed within the polepiece of the final lens, with the result that the deflection field and the focusing field are superimposed.
2. In a prelens double-deflection system, the first and second deflectors are rotated by 180° about the optic axis with respect to each other. This rotation angle is generally not 180° in an in-lens deflection system.

Ohiwa et al. showed that the axial position and rotation of the second deflector can be optimized to reduce the aberrations of an in-lens deflection system to a level far lower than would be possible with a prelens system. The reasons for this are as follows.

1. Superimposing the deflection field of D2 and the lens field creates what Ohiwa et al. termed a "moving objective lens." The superimposed fields form a rotationally symmetrical distribution centered not on the optic axis but on a point whose distance from the axis is proportional to the magnitude of the deflection field. The resultant field distribution is equivalent to a magnetic lens which, if the sytstem is optimized, moves in synchronism with the electron beam deflected by D1 in such a way that the beam always passes through its center.
2. The rotation of DI with respect to D2 accounts for the helical trajectories of the electrons in the lens field.

A limitation of this work was that the calculations involved were based, not on physically realistic lens and deflection fields, but on convenient analytic approximations. Tbus, although it was possible to give convincing evidence that the scheme would work, it was not possible to specify a practical design. This limitation was overcome by Munro [15], who developed a computer program that could be used in the design of this type of deflection system. Using this program, Munro designed a number of postlens, in-lens, and prelens deflection systems. A particularly promising in-lens configuration was one that had an aberration diameter of 0.15 μm after dynamic correction when covering a 5×5 mm^2 field at an angular aperture of 5×10^{-3} rad and a fractional beam voltage ripple of 10^{-4}.

Because the deflectors of an in-lens deflection system are located near metallic components of the column, measures have to be taken to counteract eddy current effects. The first deflector can be screened from the upper bore of the final lens by inserting a tubular ferrite shield as indicated in Fig. 3b [16]. This solution would not work for the second deflector, because the shield would divert the flux lines constituting the focusing field. Chang et al. [17] successfully overcame this problem by constructing the lens pole pieces not of soft iron but of ferrite.

Although magnetic deflectors are in widespread use, electrostatic deflectors have several attributes for electron lithography. In the past, they have rarely been used because of the positional instability that has been associated with them, caused by the formation of insulating contamination layers on the surface of the deflection plates. However, improvements in vacuum technology now make the use of electrostatic deflection feasible.

The major advantage of electrostatic over magnetic deflection is the comparative ease with which fast response times can be achieved. A fundamental reason for this is that, to exert a given force on an electron, the stored energy density associated with an electrostatic deflection field (U_E) is always less than that associated with a magnetic deflection field (U_M). If the velocity of the electrons within the beam is v and that of light in free space is c, the ratio of energy densities is

$$\frac{U_E}{U_M} = \left(\frac{v}{c}\right)^2 \tag{5}$$

Thus, an electrostatic deflection system deflecting 20-keV electrons stores only 8% as much energy as a magnetic deflection system of the same strength occupying the same volume. It follows that the output power of an amplifier driving the electrostatic system at a given speed needs to be only 8% of that required to drive the magnetic system.

Electrostatic deflection systems have attractions in addition to their suitability for high-speed deflection.

1. They are not prone to the effects of eddy currents or magnetic hysteresis.
2. The accurate construction of electrostatic deflection systems is considerably easier than of magnetic deflection systems. This is so because electrostatic deflectors consist of machined electrode plates, whereas magnetic deflectors consist of wires that are bent into shape. Machining is an operation that can be carried out to close tolerances comparatively simply, whereas bending is not.

An electron lithography system that uses electrostatic deflection is described below.

Computer-aided techniques for the design and optimization of electrostatic, magnetic, and combined electrostatic and magnetic lens and deflection systems have been described by Munro and Chu [18–21].

The thyratron is then commanded to commute; i.e., the switch is closed. The closing time for a typical thyratron is about 30 ns, during which the thyratron changes state from an open to a shut switch. The command to commute is generated by the stepper or the scanner.

2.5 Electron-Electron Interactions

The mean axial separation between electrons traveling with a velocity v and constituting a beam current I is

$$\Delta = \frac{qv}{I} = \frac{1}{I}\left(\frac{2q^3V}{m}\right)^{1/2} \tag{6}$$

In a scanning electron microscope the beam current may be 10 pA, and for 20-keV electrons this corresponds to a mean electron-electron spacing of 1.34 m. Because the length of an electro optical column is about 1 m, the most probable number of electrons in the column at any given time is less than one, and electron-electron interactions are effectively nonexistent.

In a scanning lithography instrument, however, the beam current has a value between 10 nA and 1 μA, corresponding to mean electron spacings between 1.34 mm and 13.4 μm. Under these circumstances electron-electron interactions are noticeable. At these current levels, the major effect of the forces between electrons is to push them radially, thereby increasing the diameter of the focused spot. (In heavy current electron devices, such as cathode-ray tubes or microwave amplifiers, the behavior of the beam is analogous to the laminar flow of a fluid, and electron-electron interaction effects can be explained on this basis. However, the resulting theory is not applicable to lithography instruments, in which the beam currents are considerably lower.)

Crewe [22] has used an analytic technique to estimate the magnitude of interaction effects in lithography instruments and has shown that the increase in spot radius is given approximately by

$$\Delta r = \frac{1}{8\pi\varepsilon_0} \left(\frac{m}{q} \right)^{1/2} \frac{LI}{\alpha V^{3/2}} \tag{7}$$

In this equation, a represents the numerical aperture of the optical system, L represents the total length of the column, m and q are the mass and charge of an electron, and ε_0 is the permittivity of free space. Note that neither the positions of the lenses nor their optical properties appear in Eq. 7; it is only the total distance from source to workpiece that is important. For 20-keV electrons traveling down a column of length 1 m and numerical aperture 5×10^{-3} rad, the spot radius enlargement is 8 nm for a beam current of 10 nA, which is negligible for the purposes of electron lithography. However, at a beam current of 1 μA, the enlargement would be 0.8 μm, which is significant. Thus, great care must be taken in designing electron optical systems for fast lithography instruments that utilize comparatively large beam currents. The column must be kept as short as possible, and the numerical aperture must be made as large as possible.

Groves et al. [23] have calculated the effects of electron-electron interactions using, not an analytic technique, but a Monte Carlo approach. Their computations are in broad agreement with Crewe's equation. Groves et al. also compared their calculations with experimental data, obtaining reasonable agreement.

3   AN EXAMPLE OF A ROUND-BEAM INSTRUMENT: EBES

The EBES (electron-beam exposure system) was designed and built primarily for mask making for optical lithography on a routine basis. It had a resolution goal of 2-μm line widths and was designed in such a way as to achieve maximum reliability in operation rather than pushing the limits of capability.

The most unusual feature of this machine was that the pattern was written by moving the mask plate mechanically with respect to the beam. The plate was mounted on an X-Y table that executed a continuous raster motion, with a pitch (separation between rows) of 128 μm. If the mechanical raster were executed perfectly, each point on the mask could be accessed if the electron beam were scanned in a line, 128 μm long, perpendicular to the long direction of the mechanical scan. However, in practice, since mechanical motion of the necessary accuracy could not be guaranteed, the actual location of the stage was measured using laser interferometers, and the position errors were compensated for by deflecting the beam appropriately. As a result, the scanned field was 140×140 μm, sufficient to allow for errors of ± 70 μm in the x direction and ± 6 μm in the y direction.

The advantage of this approach was that it capitalized on well-known technologies. The manufacture of the stage, although it required high precision, used conventional mechanical techniques. The use of laser interferometers was well established. The demands made on the electron optical system were sufficiently inexacting to allow the column of a conventional SEM to be used, although it had to be modified for high-speed operation [16].

Since EBES was not intended for high-resolution applications it was possible to use resists of comparatively poor resolution but high sensitivity, typically 1 μC cm^{-2}. At a beam current of 20 nA, Eq. 1 predicts that the time taken to write an area of 1 cm^2 would be 30 sec (note that the exposure time is independent of pattern geometry in this type of machine). Therefore the writing time for a 10×10 cm^2 mask or reticle would be about 1.4 hr, regardless of pattern geometry. For very large scale integrated (VLSI) circuits, this is approximately an order of magnitude less than the exposure time using an optical reticle generator.

Because of its high speed, it is practicable to use EBES for making masks directly, without going through the intermediate step of making reticles [24]. However, with the advent of wafer steppers, a major use of these machines is now for the manufacture of reticles, and they are in widespread use. The writing speeds of later models have been somewhat increased, but the general principles remain identical to those originally developed.

4   SHAPED-BEAM INSTRUMENTS

4.1   Fixed Square-Spot Instruments

Although it is possible to design a high-speed round-beam instrument with a data rate as high as 300 MHz, it is difficult and its implementation is expensive. Pfeiffer [25] proposed an alternative scheme that allows patterns to be written at high speeds using high beam currents, but without the need for such high data rates. In order to do this, he made use of the fact that the data supplied to a round-beam machine are highly redundant.

The spot produced by a round-beam machine is an image of the gun crossover, modified by the aberrations of the optical system. As a result, not only is it round, but also the current density within it is nonuniform, conforming to a bell-shaped distribution. Because of this, the spot diameter is often defined as the diameter of the contour at which the current density falls to a particular fraction of its maximum value, this fraction typically being arbitrarily chosen as ½ or $1/e$. In order to maintain good pattern fidelity, the pixel spacing (the space between exposed spots) and the spot diameter must be relatively small compared with the minimum feature size to be written. A great deal of redundant information must then be used to specify a pattern feature (a simple square will be composed of many pixels).

Pfeiffer and Loeffler [26] pointed out that electron optical systems could be built that produced not round, nonunifom spots, but square, uniformly illuminated ones. Thus, if a round-spot instrument and a square-spot instrument operate at the same beam current and expose the same pattern at the same dose, the data rate for the square-spot instrument will be smaller than that for the round-spot instrument by a factor of n^2, where n is the number of pixels that form the side of a square. Typically $n = 5$ to get adequate uniformity, and the adoption of a square-spot scheme will reduce a data rate of 300 MHz to 12 MHz, a speed at which electronic circuits can operate with great case.

To generate a square, uniformly illuminated spot, Pfeiffer and Loeffler [27] had used Kohler's method of illumination, a technique well known in optical microscopy (see, for example, Born and Wolf [26]). The basic principle is illustrated in Fig. 4a. A lens (L1) is interposed between the source (S) and the plane to be illuminated (P). One aperture (SA1) is placed on the source side of the lens, and another (BA) is placed on the other side. 'Tbe system is arranged in such a way that the following optical relationships hold.

1. The planes of S and BA are confocal.
2. The planes of SA1I and P are confocal.

Under these circumstances the shape of the illuminated spot at P (2) is similar to that of SA1, but demagnified by the factor d1/d2. (For this reason SA1 is usually referred to as a spot shaping aperture.) The numerical aperture of the imaging system is determined by the diameter of the aperture BA. Thus, if SA1 is a square aperture, a square patch of illumination (2) will be formed at P, even though the aperture BA is round. 'The uniformity of the illumination stems from the fact that all trajectories emanating from a point such as s on the source are spread out to cover the whole of (2). When Koehler's method of illumination is applied to optical microscopes, a second lens is used to ensure that trajectories from a given source point impinge on P as a parallel beam. However, this is unnecessary for electron lithography.

Pfeiffer [25] and Mauer et al. [28] have described a lithography system, the EL1, that used this type of illumination. It wrote with a square spot nominally

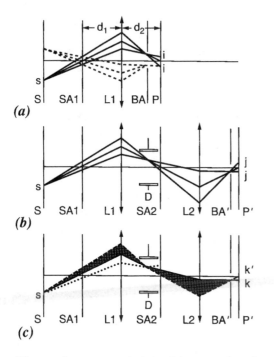

Figure 4   (a) The principle of the generation of a square, uniformly illuminated spot, using Koehler's method of illumination. (b) The extension of the technique to the generation of a rectangular spot of variable dimensions, with the spot shaping deflected D unactivated. (c) As for (b), but with D activated.

measuring 2.5×2.5 μm containing a current of 3 μA. Because of the effects of electron-electron interactions, the edge acuity of the spot was 0.4 μm. Tbe optical system was based on the principles illustrated in Fig. 4a but was considerably more complex, consisting of four magnetic lenses. The lens nearest the gun was used as a condenser, and the spot shaping aperture was located within its magnetic field. This aperture was demagnified by a factor or 200 by the three remaining lenses, the last of which was incorporated in an in-lens deflection system.

The EL1 lithography instrument was used primarily for exposing interconnection patterns on gate array wafers. It was also used as a research tool for direct writing and for making photomasks [29].

4.2   Shaped Rectangular-Spot Instruments

A serious limitation of fixed square-spot instruments is that the linear dimensions of pattern features are limited to integral multiples of the minimum feature size. For example, using a 2.5×2.5 μm square spot, a 7.5×5.0 μm rectangular feature can be written, but a 8.0 × 6.0 μm feature cannot. An extension of the square-spot technique that removed this limitation was proposed by Fontijn [30] and first used for electron lithography by Pfeiffer [31].

The principle of the scheme is illustrated in Fig. 4b. In its simplest form, it involves adding a deflector (D), a second shaping aperture (SA2), and a second lens (L2) to the configuration of Fig. 4a. The positions of these additional optical components are determined by the following optical constraints.

1. SA2 is placed in the original image plane, P.
2. The new image plane is P', and L2 is positioned so as to make it confocal with the plane of SA2.
3. The beam shaping aperture BA is removed and replaced by the deflector D. The center of deflection of D lies in the plane previously occupied by BA.
4. A new beam shaping aperture BA' is placed at a plane conjugate with the center of deflection of D (i.e., with the plane of the old beam shaping aperture BA).

SA1 and SA2 are both square apertures, and their sizes are such that a pencil from s that just fills SA1 will also just fill SA2 with the deflector unactivated. This is the situation depicted in Fig. 4b and under these circumstances, a square patch of illumination, jj, is produced at the new image plane P'.

Figure 4c shows what happens when the deflector is activated. The unshaded portion of the pencil emitted from a does not reach P', because it is intercepted by Sa2. However, the shaded portion does reach the image plane, where it forms a uniformly illuminated rectangular patch of illumination kk'. By altering the strength of the deflector, the position of k' and hence the shape of the illuminated patch can be controlled. Note that since the center of deflection of D is confocal with BA', the beam shaping aperture does not cause vignetting of the spot as its shape is changed. Only one deflector is shown in the figure; in a practical system there would be two such deflectors mounted perpendicular to each other so that both dimensions of the rectangular spot could be altered.

Weber and Moore [29] built a machine, the EL2, based on this principle, which was used as a research tool. Several versions were built, each with slightly different performance speficiations. The one capable of the highest resolution used a spot whose linear dimensions could be varied from 1.0 to 2.0 μm in increments of 0.1 μm. A production version of the EL2, the EL3, was built by Moore et al. [32]. The electron optics of this instrument were similar to those of the EL2, except that the spot shaping range was increased from 2:1 to 4:1. A version of the EL3 that was used for 0.5-μm lithography is described by Davis et al. [33]. In this instrument, the spot current density was reduced from 50 to 10 A cm^{-2} and the maximum spot size to 2 × 2 μm to reduce the effects of electron-electron interactions.

Equation 1 cannot be used to calculate the writing time for a shaped-beam instrument because the beam current is not constant, but varies in proportion to the area of the spot. A pattern is converted for exposure in a shaped-spot instrument by partitioning it into rectangular "shots." The instruments writes the pattern by exposing each shot in turn, having adjusted the spot size to match that of the shot. The time taken to expose a shot is independent of its area and is equal too Q/J (Q being the dose and J the current density within the shot), and so the time taken to expose a pattern consisting of N shots is

$$T = NQ/J. \tag{8}$$

Thus, for high speed, the following requirements are necessary.

1. The current density in the spot must be as high as possible.
2. In order to minimize the number of pattern shots, the maximum spot size should be as large as possible. In practice, a limit is set by electron-electron interactions that degrade the edge acuity of the spot at high beam currents.
3. Tbe pattern conversion program must be efficient at partitioning the patter into as few shots as possible, given the constraint imposed by the maximum shot size.

In a modern ultrahigh-resolution commercial system such as that manufactured by JEOL, the area that can be scanned by the beam before moving the stage is of the order of 1×1 mm, and the minimum address size (pixel size) can be chosen to be 5 or 25 nm.

5   ELECTRON BEAM ALIGNMENT TECHNIQUES

5.1   Pattern Registration

The first step in writing a wafer directly is to define registration marks on it. Commonly, these are grouped into sets of three, each set being associated with one particular chip site. The registration marks may be laid down on the wafer in a separate step before any of the chip levels are written, or they may be written concurrently with the first level of the chip.

Pattern registration is necessary because no lithography instrument can write perfectly reproducibly. Several factors, discussed in detail in the following, can lead to an offset of a given integrated circuit level from its intended position with respect to the previous one.

1. *Loading errors.* Wafers are generally loaded into special holders for exposure. Frequently, the location and orientation of a wafer are fixed by a kinematic arrangement of three pins. However, the positional errors associated with this scheme can be substantial fraction of 1 mm, and the angular errors can be as large as 1°.

2. *Static and dynamic temperature errors.* Unless temperature is carefully controlled, thermal expansion of the wafer can cause these to be significant. The thermal expansion coefficient of silicon is 8×10^{-6} °C^{-1}, and over a distance of 50 mm this corresponds to a shift of 0.4 µm for a 1°C change. When two pattern levels are written on a wafer at two different temperatures, but the wafers are in thermal equilibrium in each case, a static error results. If, however, the wafer is not in thermal equilibrium while it is being written, a dynamic error results whose magnitude varies as the temperature of the wafer changes with time.

3. *Substrate height variations.* These are important because they give rise to changes in deflector sensitivity. For example, consider a postlens deflector, nominally 100 mm above the substrate plane and deflecting over a 5×5 mm scan field. A change of 10 µm in the height of the chip being written results in a maximum pattern error of 0.25 µm. Height variations can arise from two causes. The first is nonperpendicularity between the substrate plane and the undetected beam, which makes the distance between the deflector and the portion of the substrate immediately below it a function of stage position. The second cause is curvature of the wafer. Even unprocessed wafers are bowed, and high-temperature processing steps can change the bowing significantly. The deviations from planarity can amount to tens of micrometers.

4. *Stage yaw.* The only type of motion that a perfect stage would execute would be linear translation. However, when any real stage is driven, it will rotate slightly about an axis perpendicular to its translational plane of motion. Typically, this motion, called yaw, amounts to several arcseconds. The positional error introduced by a yaw of 10″ for a 5×5 mm chip is 0.24 µm.

5. *Beam position drift.* The beam in a lithography instrument is susceptible to drift, typically amounting to a movement of less than 1 µm in 1 hr.

6. *Deflector sensitivity drift.* The sensitivities of beam deflectors tend to drift, due to variations in beam energy and gain changes in the deflection amplifiers. This effect can amount to a few parts per million in 1 hr.

By aligning the pattern on registration marks, exact compensation is made for loading errors, static temperature errors, substrate height variations, and yaw, all of which are time independent. Usually dynamic temperature errors, beam position drift, and deflector sensitivity drift are reduced to negligible levels by pattern registration because, although they are time dependent, the time scales associated with them are much greater than the time taken to write a chip.

A typical alignment scheme would consist of a "coarse" registration step followed by a "fine" registration step. The procedures are in general quite similar to those used in optical lithography, which are discussed at length in Chapters 1 and 5. Here we concentrate on aspects unique to electron lithography, primarily having to do with the nature of the alignment detection signals.

Using the wafer flat (or some other mechanical factor, in the case of non-standard substrates), a coarse positioning is carried out and the wafer scanned (not at high resolution) in the area of an alignment mark. Assuming it is detected, the coordinates of its center (with reference to an origin in the machine's system) are now known, and an offset is determined from the coordinates specified for it in the pattern data.

This level of accuracy is still inadequate for pattern writing, but it is sufficient to allow the fine registration step to be carried out. One purpose of fine registration is to improve the accuracy with which the coarse registration compensated for loading errors. In addition, it compensates for the remaining misregistration errors (temperature errors, substrate height variations, stage yaw, beam position drift, and deflector sensitivity drift). Because these will, in general, vary from chip to chip, fine registration is carried out on a chip-by-chip basis. Each chip is surrounded by three registration marks. Since the residual errors after coarse registration are only a few micrometers, the chip marks need to be only about 100 μm long. The steps involved in fine registration could be as follows.

1. The pattern data specify coordinates corresponding to the center of the chip. These are modified to account for the wafer offset and rotation measured during the coarse registration step. The stage is moved accordingly, so as to position the center of the chip under the beam.
2. The electrom beam is deflected to the positions of the three alignment marks in turn, and each mark is scanned. In this way the position of each of the three marks is measured.
3. The pattern data are transformed linearly so as to conform with the measured positions of the marks, and the pattern is then written onto the chip.

This procedure is repeated for each chip on the wafer.

Numerous variations of the scheme described here exist. A serious drawback of this scheme is that it works on the assumption that each chip corresponds to a single scanned field. A registration scheme described by Wilson et al. [34] overcomes this limitation, allowing any number of scanned fields to be stitched together to write a chip pattern, making it possible to write chips of any size.

5.2 Alignment Mark Structures

Many types of alignment mark have been used in electron lithography, including pedestals of silicon or silicon dioxide, metals of high atomic number, and trenches etched into the substrate. The last type of mark is frequently used and will be considered here as an example to demonstrate how alignment signals are generated. A common method of forming trenches is by etching appropriately masked silicon wafers in aqueous potassium hydroxide. Wafers whose top

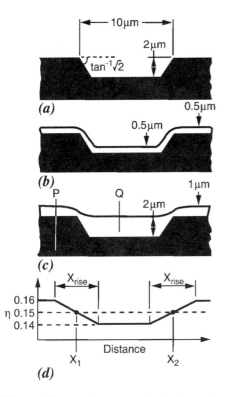

Figure 5 (a) A cross-sectional view of an alignment mark consisting of a trench etched into silicon. The wall angle of $\tan^{-1}\sqrt{2}$ is the result of the anisotropic nature of the etch. (b) Coverage of the trench by a film of resist that has little tendency to "planarize." (c) Coverage by a resist that has a strong tendency to planarize. (d) The variation of backscatter coefficient η as a function of position for the situation depicted in (c).

surface corresponds to the [100] plane are normally used for this purpose. The etching process is anisotropic, causing the sides of the trenches to be sloped, as illustrated in Fig. 5a. Typically, the trench is 10 μm wide and 2 μm deep.

The way in which the resist film covers a trench depends on the dimensions of the trench, the material properties of the resist, and the conditions under which the resist is spun onto the wafer. Little has been published on this subject, but from practical experience it is found that two extreme cases exist.

1. If the resist material shows little tendency to planarize the surface of the wafer and is applied as a thin film, the situation depicted in Fig. 5b arises. The resist forms a uniform thin film, whose top surface follows the shape of the trench faithfully.

2. If, on the other hand, a thick film of a resist that has a strong tendency to planarize is applied to the wafer, the situation shown in Fig. 5c results. The top surface of the resist is nearly flat, but the thickness of the resist film increases significantly in the vicinity of the trench.

Tbe mechanisms for the generation of alignment mark signals are different in these two cases.

5.3 Alignment Mark Signals

The electrons emitted when an electron beam with an energy of several keV bombards a substrate can be divided into two categories.

1. Tbe secondary electrons are those ejected from the substrate material itself. They are of low energy, and their energy distribution has a peak at an energy of a few eV. By convention, it is assumed that electrons with energies below 50 eV are secondaries.
2. The backscattered electrons are primaries that have been reflected from the substrate. For a substrate of silicon (atomic number $Z = 14$), their mean energy is approximately 60% of that of the primary beam [35].

The electron collectors used in scanning electron microscopes are biased at potentials many hundreds of volts above that of the specimen in order to attract as many secondary electrons as possible. As a consequence, it is these electrons that dominate the formation of the resulting image. Everhart et al. [36] explain why this is done:

> . . . the paths of (back-scattered) electrons from the object to the collector are substantially straight, whilst those of secondary electrons are usually sharply curved. It follows that (back-scattered) electrons cannot reveal detail of any part of the object from which there is not a straight-line path to the collector, while secondary electrons are not subject to this limitation. Thus, secondary electrons provide far more detail when a rough surface is under examination.

However, this argument does not apply to the problem of locating a registration mark, which is a comparatively large structure whose fine surface texture is of no interest. Consequently, no discrimination is made against backscattered electrons in alignment mark detection and, in fact, it is these electrons that contribute most strongly to the resulting signals. Backscattered electrons may be collected either by using a scintillator-photomultiplier arrangement or by using a solid-state diode as a detector. This is a popular collection scheme and is usually implemented by mounting an annular diode above the workpiece. Wolf et al. [37] used a solar cell diode 25 mm in diameter, with a 4-mm-diameter hole in it through which the primary electron beam passed, the total solid angle subtended at the workpiece being 0.8 sr. Detectors of this type are insensitive to secondary electrons, because they are not sufficiently energetic to penetrate down to the depletion region that is under the surface; the threshold energy for penetration is generally several hundred eV. The gain of the detector varies linearly with excess energy above the threshold, the gradient of the relationship being approximately 1 hole–electron pair per 3.5 eV of beam energy.

A useful extension of this technique (see, for example, Reimer, 1984) is to split the detector into two halves. When the signals derived from the two halves are subtracted, the detector responds primarily to topographic variations on the substrate: this mode is well suited for detecting the type of mark depicted in Fig. 5b. When the signals are added, the detector responds to changes in the backscattered electron coefficient (η). It is found that the type of mark shown in Fig. 5c is best detected in this mode, because the values of η at locations such as P and Q are significantly different, whereas the topographic variations are small.

The backscattering coefficients of composite samples consisting of thin films supported on bulk substrates have been studied by electron microscopists (see, for example, Niedrig [38]. It is found that the composite backscattering coefficient varies approximately linearly from a value corresponding to the substrate material (η_s) for very thin films to a value corresponding to the film material (η_F) for very thick films. The value η_F is achieved when the film thickness is greater than about half the electron range in the film material.

A silicon substrate has a backscattering coefficient $\eta_S = 0.18$ (see, for example, Reed, 1975). The widely used electron resist poly(methyl methacrylate) (PMMA) has the chemical formula $C_5O_2H_8$ and its mass concentration averaged atomic number is 6.2; as a rough approximation it can be assumed that its backscattering coefficient is equal to that of carbon, i.e., that $\eta_F = 0.07$. The density of PMMA is 1.2 g cm^{-3}, and the data of Holliday and Sternglass [39] imply that the extrapolated range of 20-keV electrons in the material is about 8 μm. From these values. it follows that the backscattering coefficient of bulk silicon is reduced by roughly 0.02 for every 1 μm of PMMA covering it. A similar result has been calculated by Aizaki (1979) using a Monte Carlo technique.

Figure 5d is a sketch of the variation of η along the fiducial mark depicted in Fig. 5c. It has been assumed that at P and Q, well away from topographical changes, η has the values 0.16 and 0.14, respectively. Tbe change in η caused by the sides of the trench is assumed to occur linearly over a distance of x_{rise} 5 μm. The exact form of the transition depends on the shape of the trench, the way the resist thickness changes in its vicinity, the range of electrons in the resist and, most important, their range in silicon. (The extrapolated range of 20-keV electrons in silicon is about 2 μm.) Since a split backscattered electron detector connected in the "adding" mode responds to changes in η, Fig. 5d also represents the signal collected as a well-focused electron beam is scanned over the registration mark. Despite the simplifying assumptions that have been made, this sketch is representative of the signals that are obtained in practice.

5.4   The Measurement of Alignment Mark Position

A threshold technique is frequently used to measure the position of an alignment mark. In Fig. 5d, for example, the threshold has been set to correspond to $\eta = 0.15$, an the position of the center of the trench is $x = (x_1 = x_2)/2$. The accuracy with which x_1 and x_2 can be measured is limited by electrical noise. of which there are three major sources:

1.   The shot noise associated with the primary electron beam
2.   The noise associated with the generation of backscattered electrons
3.   The noise associated with the detector itself

Wells et al. [40] analyzed the effects of shot noise and secondary emission noise on alignment accuracy. Their theory may be adapted to deal with backscatter noise by replacing the coefficient of secondary emission by the backscattering coefficient η. With this modification, the theory predicts that the spatial accuracy with which a threshold point such as x_1 or x_2 may be detected is

$$\Delta x = \left(\frac{128 q x_{\text{rise}}}{m^2 HQ} \frac{1+\eta}{\eta} \right)^{1/3} \tag{9}$$

The quantities appearing in this equation are defined as follows.

1. Δx is the measure of the detection accuracy. It is defined such that the probability of a given measurement being in error by more than Δx is 10^{-4}.
2. x_{rise} is the rise distance of the signal. A value of 5 μm is assumed in Fig. 5d.
3. η is the mean backscattering coefficient. A value of 0.15 is assumed.
4. m is the fractional change in signal as the mark is scanned. In Fig. 5d, $m = 0.02/0.15$ [this symbol not found] 0.13.
5.   It is assumed that the beam oscillates rapidly in the direction perpendicular to the scan direction with an amplitude $(1/2)H$. In this way, the measurement is made, not along a line, but along a strip of width H. A typical value is $H = 10$ μm.
6. Q is the charge density deposited in the scanned strip.

Equation 9 indicates that a compromise exists between registration accuracy (Δx) and charge density (Q) and that Δx may be made smaller than any set value provided that Q is large enough. For 0.5-μm lithography, an acceptable value of Δx could be 0.1 μm. To achieve this level of accuracy, Eq. 9 predicts that a charge density $Q = 2300$ μC cm^{-2} has to be deposited. This calculation illustrates the point made earlier: Since electron resists require doses in the range 1–100 μC cm^{-2} for exposure, pattern features cannot be used as registration marks.

Wells et al. pointed out that a threshold detection scheme is wasteful, because it uses only the part of the alignment signal that corresponds to the immediate vicinity of the threshold point. If the complete waveform is used, all the available information is utilized. and the charge density necessary to achieve an accuracy of Δx is reduced by the factor $\Delta x/x_{rise}$. In the case of the example considered above, this would reduce Q from 2300 to 46 μC cm^{-2}. One way in which the complete waveform can be utilized is to use a correlation technique to locate the alignment mark; such schemes have been described by Cumming [41], Holburn et al. [42], and Hsu [43].

5.5 Machine and Process Monitoring

Although a modern commercial electron lithography exposure system comes with a great deal of computer control, close system monitoring is essential for obtaining optimum performance. Table 1 shows a set of tests that have been found useful for a high-resolution system operating in an R&D mode. In addition, a weekly alignment monitor is run using an electrical test pattern. The first level consists of standard van der Pauw pads connected to resistors oriented in the X and Y directions. The second level cuts a slot in the resistor, dividing it in two equal parts. The difference between resistance values gives the amount of misalignment.

Table 1 Tests for a High-Resolution Electron Lithography System

Feature	*Evaluation tool and purpose*
25-step incremental dose pads in two versions: large and small shot sizes	Optical/Nanospec—at lowest resolving dose, beam current density distribution visible in pad section; track thickness vs. dose for resist shelf/film life
25-step incremental dose line/space features from 0.1 to 0.5 μm	SEM—determine shot-butting quality for fine-line exposures (0.2 μm); line width vs. dose
Single- and four-field grid pattern	System mark detection—measure field gain/distortion
10 × 10 array of single crosses	System mark detection—measure stage accuracy
Mask mode field butting	Optical—measure verniers to determine needed corrections
Aligned overlay test pattern	Optical—measure verniers to determine needed corrections
Custom	Add any feature needed for special exposures

6 THE INTERACTION OF THE ELECTRON BEAM WITH THE SUBSTRATE

6.1 Power Balance

Consider a silicon substrate, coated with a film of PMMA 0.5 μm thick, with an electron beam of energy 20 keV and current 1 μA impinging on the top surface of the resist; the power flowing is 20 mW. Part of this power is dissipated chemically and thermally in the resist, part thermally in the substrate, and the remainder leaves the substrate.

The energy loss as the beam passes in the forward direction through the resist can be calculated using the Thomson-Whiddington law, expressed by Wells [44] as

$$E_A^2 - E_B^2 = b'z \tag{10}$$

with $b' = 6.9 \times 10^9 \left(\rho E_A^{0.5} / Z^{0.2} \right)$

Here, E_A is the energy (in eV) of the electrons as they enter the resist, and E_B is the mean energy as they exit it; z is the thickness (in cm) of the resist film, while the density of the resist is ρ g cm^{-2} and its effective atomic number is Z. Since the resist film is thin, it is assumed that the number of electrons absorbed or generated within it is negligible. The mean energy loss that occurs within the resist film in this "forward" direction is $\Delta E_f = E_A - E_B = 1.04$ keV, and the power dissipated by the beam as it passes through the resist is given by

$$P_f = I_B \Delta E_f \tag{11}$$

which for the conditions cited above is 1 mW.

The beam penetrates into the silicon, and a fraction $\eta = 0.18$ of the electron current is backscattered out of the substrate into the resist. The data of Bishop [35] indicate that the mean energy of the backscattered electrons is 60% of the incident energy (19.0 keV in this case) and so the power dissipated in the substrate is 16.9 mW.

The backscattered electrons pass through the resist film toward the surface, in the "backward" direction. It is assumed that the number of electrons absorbed or generated within the resist film is negligible, so the electrons constitute a current ηI_B. Although the mean electron energy as they enter the resist (11.4 keV) is known, one cannot use the Thomson-Whiddington law to calculate the energy lost in the resist film, ΔE_B, for two reasons: first, the spread of electron energies at C is wide (unlike that at A), and second, the directions of travel of the backscattered electrons are not, in general, normal to the resist-substrate interface.

The ΔE_B may be estimated from the results of Kanter [45], who investigated the secondary emission of electrons from aluminium ($Z = 13$). He proposed that because of the lower energies and oblique trajectories of electrons backscattered from the sample, they would be a factor β more efficient at generating secondary electrons at the surface then was the primary beam. Kanter's estimated value for β was 4.3, and his experimentally measured value was 4.9. Since secondary electron generation and resist exposure are both governed by the rate of energy dissipation at the surface of the sample, and since the atomic numbers of aluminium ($Z = 13$) and silicon ($Z = 14$) are nearly equal, it is reasonable to assume that these results apply to the exposure of resist on a silicon wafer. Thus

$$\Delta E_B = \beta \Delta E_f \tag{12}$$

where P is expected to have a value between 4 and 5. The power dissipated in the resist film by the backscattered electrons is

$$P_b = \eta I_B \Delta E_b = \eta \beta I_B \Delta E_f \tag{13}$$

Comparing Eqs. 11 and 13, P_b/P_f is given by the ratio

$$\eta_e = \frac{P_b}{P_f} = \eta \beta \tag{14}$$

It is generally acknowledged that for silicon at a beam energy of 20 keV, η lies between 0.7 and 0.8, corresponding to $\beta = 4$. (A number of experimental measurements of η_e have been collated by Hawryluk [46]; these encompass a range of values varying from 0.6 to 1.0.) If it is assumed that $\beta = 4.0$, then the mean energy lost by the backscattered electrons as they pass through the resist film is $E_b = 4.16$ keV.

Thus, in this example, of the incident power in the beam, approximately 5% is dissipated in the resist by forward-traveling electrons, approximately 4% is dissipated in the resist by backscattered electrons, 85% id dissipated as heat in the substrate, and the remaining 7% leaves the workpiece as the kinetic energy of the emergent backscattered electrons.

The quantity that controls the change in solubility of a resist is the total energy absorbed per unit volume (energy density), ε J m^{-3}. Assuming that the energy is absorbed uniformly in a resist layer of thickness z, this is related to the exposure dose Q by the expression

$$\varepsilon = \frac{\Delta E_f (1 + \eta_e)}{z} Q \tag{15}$$

For the example considered in this section, Eq. 15 indicates that an exposure dose of 1 μC cm^{-2} corresponds to an absorbed energy densitiy of 3.6×10^7 J cm^{-3}.

6.2 The Spatial Distribution of Energy in the Resist Film

Monte Carlo techniques have been used to investigate the interactions of electrons with matter in the context of electron probe microanalysis and scanning electron microscopy by Bishop [35], Shimizu and Murata [47], and Murata et al. [48]. Kyser and Murata [49] investigated the interaction of electron beams with resist films on silicon using the same method, pointing out that its conceptual simplicity and the accuracy of the physical model were useful attributes.

Monte Carlo calculations indicate that the lateral distribution of energy dissipated by the forward-traveling electrons at the resist-silicon interface may be approximated closely as a Gaussian. Broers (1981a) has noted that the standard deviation computed in this way may be expressed as σ_f (measured in μm) where

$$\sigma_f = \left(\frac{9.64z}{V}\right)^{1.75} \tag{16}$$

where V (measured in keV) is the energy of the incident electron beam and z (measured in μm) is the thickness of the resist film. For 20-keV electrons penetrating 0.5 μm of resist, Eq. 16 predicts that $\sigma_f = 0.08$ μm. Thus, forward scattering is not a serious limitation until one reaches the "nanolithography" regime discussed in Chapter 13, in which case such techniques as thin resist films and electron beams with energies greater than 20 keV are used, as discussed extensively there.

The electrons backscattered from the substrate expose the resist film over a region with a characteristic diameter σ_b, which is approximately twice their range in the substrate. Monte Carlo simulation techniques have been extensively used to simulate electron backscattering. Shimizu and Murata applied this technique to compute the backscatter coefficient and the lateral distribution of electrons backscattered from aluminium at a beam energy of 20 keV. Their calculations showed that $\eta = 0.18$ and that the electrons emerged from a circular region 4 μm in diameter. Since silicon and aluminium are adjacent elements in the period table, the results for silicon are almost identical.

In the context of electron lithography, it is important that the volume in the resist within which the forward-traveling electrons dissipate their energy is very much smaller than that within which the backscattered electrons dissipate theirs. The comparatively diffuse backscattered energy distribution determines the contrast of the latent image in the resist, and the more compact forward-scattered energy distribution determines the ultimate resolution.

7 ELECTRON BEAM RESISTS AND PROCESSING TECHNIQUES

Poly(methyl methacrylate) (PMMA), which was one of the first resists used with electron lithography, is still commonly used because of its high resolution and because it is one of the best known and understood positive e-beam resists.

Its primary disadvantages are very low sensitivity and poor etch resistance under many important plasma conditions. Some positive resists that eliminate these problems are now available, but their process sensitivities are much greater; they are based on the acid catalysis phenomena described at length in Chapter 7.

Traditional negative-acting resists possessed far higher sensitivities (because only one crosslink per molecule is sufficient to insolubilize the material), but at the expense of resolution. The resists were developed in a solvent appropriate for the noncrosslinked portion, and the crosslinked material would be swelled by this solvent, often touching neighboring patterns and resulting in extensive pattern distortion. As a result, they were limited to feature sizes greater than about 1 μm. The introduction of Shipley's acid-catalyzed novolak-based resist (SAL-601 or its subsequent versions) was a major advance, because it gives excellent resolution and good process latitude, with etch resistance similar to that of conventional optical resists. Even though it relies on crosslinking for its action, it avoids the swelling problem because, being a novolak (phenolic-type polymer, with acidic hydrogen), it is developed in aqueous base in essentially the same manner as positive optical novolak resists. Water is not a good solvent for the polymer, and so no swelling occurs. (For an extensive discussion of the mechanism of development of novolak and phenolic resists, see Chapter 7.)

Much of the discussion of resist processing at nanolithography dimensions in Chapter 13 is also relevant to high-resolution e-beam lithography, and the reader should consult this material for further details and references.

8 THE PROXIMITY EFFECT

8.1 Description of the Effect

Tbe proximity effect is the exposure of resist by electrons backscattered from the substrate, constituting a background on which the pattern is superimposed. If this background were constant, it would create no lithographic problem other than a degradation in contrast that, although undesirable, would be by no means catastrophic. However, the background is not constant, and the serious consequence of this was observed in positive resists by Chang and Stewart [10]: "Several problems have been encountered when working at dimensions of less than 1 μm. For example, it has been found that line width depends on the packing density. When line spacing is made less than 1 μm, there is a noticeable increase in the line width obtained when the spacing is large."

Figure 6 illustrates the way in which the proximity effect affects pattern dimensions. In Fig. 6a it is assumed that an isolated narrow line (for example, of width 0.5 μm) is to be exposed. The corresponding energy density distribution is shown in Fig. 6d. The energy density deposited in the resist by forward-traveling electrons is ε, and the effects of lithographic resolution and forward scattering on

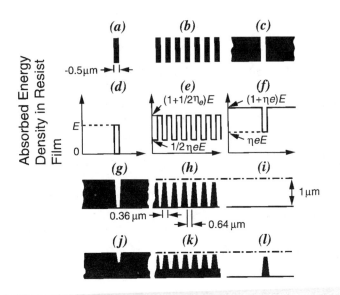

Figure 6 The influence of the proximity effect on the exposure of (a) an isolated line, (b) equally spaced lines and spaces, and (c) an isolated space (exposed regions are denoted by shading). The absorbed energy densities are shown in (d), (e), and (f). The profiles of the resist patterns are shown in (g), (h), and (i) after development time appropriate for the isolated space. The shapes of the developed resist patterns have been drawn to be roughly illustrative of what would be observed in practice.

the edge acuity of the pattern have been ignored. Because the width of the isolated line is a fraction of 1 μm and the characteristic diameter of the backscattered electron distribution (σ_b) is several μm. the backscattered energy density deposited in the resist is negligibly small.

This, however, is not the case for the exposure of the isolated space depicted in Fig. 6c. Since the width of the space is much smaller than σ_b, it is a good approximation to assume that the pattern is superimposed on a uniform background energy density $\eta_e\varepsilon$, as is shown in Fig. 6f. Figure 6b and e deal with an intermediate case—an infinite periodic array of equal lines and spaces. Here, the pattern is superimposed on a background energy density of $\eta_e\varepsilon/2$.

Thus, the energy densities corresponding to exposed and unexposed parts of the pattern are strongly dependent on the nature of the pattern itself. This leads to difficulties in maintaining the fidelity of the pattern during development. In the drawings in Fig. 6g–i it has been assumed that a development time has been chosen that allows the isolated line (g) to develop out to the correct dimensions. However, because the energy densities associated with the isolated space are appreciably higher, this pattern may well be so overdeveloped at the end of this time that it has completely disappeared (i). The problem may not be so drastic for the equal lines and spaces, for which the energy densities have lower values. Nevertheless. the lines will be overdeveloped: in (h) they are depicted (arbitrarily) as having a width of 0.36 μm, not the required 0.5 μm.

The situation cannot be improved by reducing the development time. Figures 6j–l illustrate what happens if the patterns are developed for a time appropriate for the isolated space. Although this is now developed out to the correct dimension, the isolated line and equal line and space patterns are inadequately developed.

In general, because of the proximity effect, any one of these types of pattern may be made to develop out to the correct dimensions by choosing an appropriate development time. However, it is impossible to develop them all out to the correct dimensions simultaneously. Although the proximity effect poses serious problems, it does not constitute a fundamental resolution limit to electron lithography. A number of methods for compensating for the effect, or at least reducing the gravity of the problems, have been devised. These are described below. It should be noted that this discussion changes significantly when feature sizes reach sub-100 nm dimensions, and these effects are described in Chapter 13.

8.2 Methods of Compensating for the Proximity Effect

The most popular form of proximity effect compensation is probably dose correction. To implement this method, the dose delivered by the lithography instrument is varied in such a way as to deposit the same energy density in all exposed regions of the pattern. With reference to Fig. 6, this situation occurs if the dose delivered to the isolated line (a) is increased by the factor $(1 + \eta_e)$ and that to the lines of the line and space pattern (b) by a factor of $(1 + \eta_e)(1 = \eta_e/2)^{-1}$. If this is done, all three types of pattern will develop out to approximately the correct dimensions after the same development time (that appropriate for the isolated space in Fig. 6c.

The dose correction scheme was first proposed by Chang et al. [50], who applied it to a vector scan round-beam lithography instrument, variations in dose being obtained by varying the speed with which the beam was scanned over the substrate. Submicrometer bubble devices were successfully made in this way, and because of the simplicity and highly repetitive nature of the pattern, the calculation of the necessary dose variations was not arduous. However, for complex, nonrepetitive patterns, the dose calculations become involved, making the use of a computer to carry them out essential. The calculations are time consuming and therefore expensive to carry out, several hours of CPU time sometimes being necessary, even when using large, fast computers. A set of programs designed for this purpose has been described by Parikh [51], and these have since become widely used.

Parikh's algorithm involves a convolution of the pattern data with the inverse of the response function associated with electron backscattering. In order to make the computation tractable, the approximations made are considerable. Kern [52] has pointed out that the dose compensation calculations can be carried out exactly and more conveniently in the spatial frequency domain using a Fourier transform technique. Further analysis of dose compensation algorithms has been published by Owen [53,54].

Another popular form of compensation is shape correction. This would be applied to the patterns of Fig. 6 by decreasing the widths of the exposed lines in (b), increasing the width of the isolated space in (e), and developing the pattern for a time appropriate for the isolated line pattern in (a). In practical applications, the magnitudes of the shape corrections to be applied are determined empirically from test exposures. For this reason, this technique is generally applied only to simple, repetitive patterns for which the empirical approach is not prohibitively time consuming.

A correction scheme that involves no computation other than reversing the tone of the pattern has been described by Owen and Rissman [55]. The scheme is implemented by making a correction exposure in addition to the pattern exposure. The correction exposure consists of the reversed field of the pattern and is exposed at a dose a factor $\eta_e(1 + \eta_e)^{-1}$ less than the pattern dose using a beam defocused to a diameter a little less than σ_b. The attenuated, defocused beam deposits an energy density distribution in the resist that mimics the backscattered energy density associated with a pattern pixel. Since the correction exposure is the reverse field of the pattern exposure, the combination of the two produces a uniform background energy density, regardless of the local density of the pattern. If this correction technique were applied to the pattern of Fig. 6, all pattern regions would absorb an energy density $(1 + \eta_e)\varepsilon$ and all field regions an energy density of $\eta_e\varepsilon$. These are identical to the exposure levels of a narrow isolated space (to which a negligible correction dose would have been applied). As a result, after development, all the patterns (a), (b), and (c) would have the correct dimensions.

It has been reported that the use of beam energies much greater than 20 keV (e.g., 50 keV) reduces the proximity effect, and experimental and modeling data have been presented to support this claim (see, for example, Neill and bull [56]. At first sight, it would seem that the severity of the proximity effect should not be affected by increasing the beam energy, as there is good evidence that this has a negligible effect on η_e [57].

A possible explanation for the claimed reduction of the proximity effect at high energies hinges on the small size of the test patterns on which the claims are based. At 20 keV, the range of backscattered electrons in silicon is about 2 μm, and at 30 keV it is about 10 μm [39]. A typical test structure used for modeling or experimental exposure may have linear dimensions of the order of a few μm. As a result, at 20 keV nearly all the backscattered electrons generated during exposure are backscattered into the pattern region itself. However, at 50 keV, the electrons are backscattered into a considerably larger region, thereby giving rise to a lower concentration of backscattered electrons in the pattern region. Thus, the use of a high beam energy will reduce the proximity effect is the linear dimensions of the pattern region are considerably smaller than the electron range in the substrate.

A more general explanation, which applies to pattern regions of any size, is statistical. At 20 keV, a given point on a pattern receives backscattered energy from a region about 4 μm in diameter, whereas at 50 keV it would receive energy from a region about 20 μm in diameter. It is therefore to be expected that the variation in backscattered energy from point to point should be less at 50 keV than at 20 keV, since a larger area of the pattern is being sampled at the higher beam energy. Consequently, because the proximity effect is caused by point-to-point variations in backscattered energy density, it should become less serious at higher beam energies.

ACKNOWLEDGMENTS

We thank Judith Seeger for contributing the information on routine machine performance monitoring.

REFERENCES

1. Buck, D. A., and Shoulders, K. *Proceedings Eastern Joint Computer Conference*, New York, ATEE, 1957, p. 55.
2. Owen, G., *Rep. Prog. Phys.*, **48,** 795 (1985).
3. Oatley, C. W., *The Scanning Electron Microscope*, Cambridge University Press, Cambridge, UK, 1972, chapters 2 and 3.
4. Broers, A. N., *J. Sci. Instrum. (J. Phys. E)*, **2,** 272 (1969).
5. Wells, O. C., *Scanning Electron Microscopy*, McGraw-Hill, New York, 1974, table 4.
6. Gomer, R., *Field Emission and Field Ionization*, Harvard University Press, Cambridge, MA, chapters 1 and 2.
7. Stille, G., and Astrand, B., *Phys. Scr.*, **18,** 367 (1978).
8. Kuo, H. P., and Siegel, B. M., in *Electron and Ion Beam Science and Technology, 8th International Conference* (R. Bakish, ed.), The Electrochemnical Society, Princeton, NJ, 1978, pp. 3–10.
9. Kuo, H. P., Foster, J., Haase, W., Kelly, J., and Oliver, B. M., in *Electron and Ion Beam Science and Technology, 10th International Conference$* (R. Bakish, ed.), The Electrochemical Society, Princeton, NJ–91.
10. *Chang, T. H. P., and Stewart, A. D. G., in* Proceedings 10th Symposium on Electron, Ion and Laser Beam Technology (L. Marton, ed.), IEEE, San Francisco, 1969, p. 97.

400 Owen and Sheats

11. Owen, G., *J. Vac. Sci. Technol.* **19,** 1064 (1981).
12. Owen, G., and Nixon, W. C., *J. Vac. Sci. Technol.,* **10,** 983 (1973).
13. Amboss, K., *J. Vac. Sci. Technol.,* **12,** 1152 (1975).
14. Ohiwa, H., Goto, E., and Ono, A., *Electron. Commun. Jpn.,* **54B,** 44 (1971).
15. Munro, E., *J. Vac. Sci. Technol,* **12,** 1146 (1975).
16. Lin, L. H., and Beauchamp, H. L., *J. Vac. Sci. Technol.,* **10,** 987 (1973).
17. Chang, T. H. P., Speth, A. J., Ting, C. H., Viswanathan, R., Parikh, M., and Munro, E., in *Electron and Ion Beam Science and Technology, 7th International Conference* (R. Bakish, ed.), The Electrochemical Society, Princeton, NJ, 1982, pp. 376–391.
18. Munro, E., and Chu, H. C., *Optik,* **60,**, 371 (1982).
19. Munro, E., and Chu, H. C., *Optik,* **61,** 1 (1982).
20. Chu, H. C., and Munro, E., *Optik,* **61,** 121 (1982).
21. Chu, H. C., and Munro, E., *Optik,* **61,** 213 (1982).
22. Crewe, A. V., *Optik,* **52,** 337 (1978).
23. Groves, T., Hammon, D. L, and Kuo, H., *J. Vac. Sci. Technol,* **16,** 1680 (1979).
24. Pease, R. F. W., Ballantyne, J. P., Henderson, R. C., Voshchenkov, M., and Yau, L. D., *IEEE Trans. Electron Dev.,* **ED-22,** 393 (1975).
25. Pfeiffer, H. C., *J. Vac. Sci. Technol.,* **12,** 1170 (1975).
26. Pfeiffer, H. C., and Loeffler, K. H., *Proceedings 7th International Conference on Electron Microscopy,* Societé Française de Microscopie Electronique, 1970, pp. 63–64.
27. Born, M., and Wolf, E., *Principles of Optics,* Pergamon, Oxford, 1975.
28. Mauer, J. L., Pfeiffer, H. C., and Stickel, W., *IBM J. Res. Dev.,* **21,** 514 (1977.
29. Weber, E. V., and Moore, R. D., *J. Vac. Sci. Technol.,* **16,** 1780 (1979).
30. Fontijn, L. A., *Ph.D. thesis,* Delft University Press, Delft, 1972.
31. Pfeiffer, H. C., *J. Vac. Sci. Technol.,* **15,** 887 (1978).
32. Moore, R. D., Caccoma, G. A., Pfeiffer, H. C., Weber, E. V., and Woodard, O. C., *J. Vac. Sci. Technol.,* **19,** 950 (1981).
33. Davis, D. E., Gillespie, S. J., Silverman, S. L., Stickel, W., and Wilson, A. D., *J. Vac. Sci. Technol.,* **B1,** 1003 (1983).
34. Wilson, A. D., Studwell, T. W., Folchi, G., Kern, A., and Voelker, H., in *Electron and Ion Beam Science and Technology, 8th International Conference* (R. Bakish, ed.), The Electrochemical Society, Princeton, NJ, 1978, pp. 198–205.
35. Bishop, H. E., *Br. J. Appl. Phys.,* **18,** 703 (1967).
36. Everhart, T. E., Wells, O. C., and Oatley, C. W., *J. Electron. Control,* **7,** 97 (1959).
37. Wolf, E. D., Coane, P. J., and Ozdemir, F. S., *J. Vac. Sci. Technol.,* **6,** 1266 (1975).
38. Niedrig, H., *Opt. Acta,* **24,** 679 (1977).
39. Holliday, J. E., and Sternglass, E. J., *J. Appl. Phys.,* **30,** 1428 (1959).
40. Wells, O. C., *IEEE Trans. Electron Dev.,* **ED-12,** 556 (1965).
41. Cumming, D., *Microcircuit Engineering 80, Proceedings International Conference on Microlithography,* Delft University Press, Delft, 1981, pp. 75–81.
42. Holburn, D. M., Jones, G. A. C., and Ahmed, H., *J. Vac. Sci. Technol.,* **19,** 1229 (1981).
43. Hsu, T. J., *Hewlett Packard J.,* **32(5),** 34 (1981).

44. Wells, O. C., *Scanning Electron Microscopy*, McGraw-Hill, New York, 1974, section 3.2.1.
45. Kanter, H., *Phys. Rev.*, **121**, 681 (1961).
46. Hawryluk, R. J., *J. Vac. Sci. Technol.*, **19**, 1 (1981).
47. Shimizu, R., and Murata, K., *J. Apply. Phys.*, **42**, 387 (1971).
48. Murata, K., Matsukawa, T., and Shimizu, R., *Jpn. J. Appl. Phys.*, **10**, 678 (1971).
49. Kyser, D. F., and Murata, K., in *Electron and Ion Beam Science and Technology, 6th International Conference* (R. Bakish, ed.), The Electrochemical Society, Princeton, NJ, 1974, pp. 205–223.
50. Chang, T. H. P., Wilson, A. D., Speth, A. J., and Kern, A., in *Electron and Ion Beam Science and Technology, 6th International Conference* (R. Bakish, ed.), The Electrochemical Society, Princeton, NJ, 1974, pp. 580–588.
51. Parikh, M., *J. Appl. Phys.*, **50**, 4371 (1979).
52. Kern, D. P., in *Electron and Ion Beam Science and Technology, 9th International Conference* (R. Bakish, ed.), The Electrochemical Society, Princeton, NJ, 1980, pp. 326–329.
53. Owen, G., *J. Vac. Sci. Technol.*, **B8**, 1889 (1990).
54. Owen, G., *Opt. Eng.*, **32**, 2446 (1993).
55. Owen, G. and Rissman, P., *J. Appl. Phys.*, **54**, 3573 (1983).
56. Neill, T. R., and Bull, C. J., *Microcircuit Engineering 80, Proceedings International Conference on Microlithography,* Delft University Press, Delft, 1981, pp. 45–55.
57. Jackel, L. D., Howard, R. E., Mankiewich, P. M., Craighead, H. G., and Epworth, R. W., *Appl. Phys. Lett.*, **45**, 698 (1994).

7

X-Ray Lithography

Takumi Ueno

Hitachi Ltd.
Ibaraki-ken, Japan

James R. Sheats

Hewlett-Packard Laboratories
Palo Alto, California

1   INTRODUCTION

The use of a very short wavelength electromagnetic wave, i.e., x-ray, has an a priori obvious potential for high-resolution patterning. Almost a quarter-century has passed since x-ray lithography was described in 1972 by Spears and Smith [1]; in this time many research institutes have been concerned with its development. However, the application of x-ray lithography to real production environments has not yet materialized. The main reason for this delay is that optical lithography has been doing much better than expected two decades ago. When x-ray lithography was proposed, the resolution limit of optical lithography was considered to be 2–3 μm. Today one does not have much difficulty in fabricating half-micrometer patterns with a current i-line reduction projection aligner. Machines with large numerical aperture (NA) lenses and short-wavelength irradiation have been designed to obtain better resolution. Developments in resist processes and resist materials for high resolution have extended the use of optical lithography.

X-ray lithography is a novel technology requiring an entirely new combination of source, mask, resist, and alignment system. It is said that "quantum jumps" are required on each front for practical use of x-ray lithography [2]. Therefore, there has been reluctance to consider x-ray lithography as an alternative to optical lithography. In view of these difficulties and continued encroachment by optical lithography, it is not unreasonable to ask whether x-ray lithography still has a future.

It is difficult to tell how far the resolution of optical lithography can be extended. However, it is not easy in practice to obtain patterns much smaller than the irradiation wavelength, unless such an exotic technique as wavefront engineering including interference lithography [3,4] is utilized. Therefore, provided that the device-related problems of scaling integrated circuits to lateral dimensions smaller than around 0.15 μm are solved, some means are required of doing lithography at dimensions smaller than can be provided by conventional light sources and optics (where by "conventional" we mean to include both lamps and lasers and optics that look like the mirrors and lenses discussed in Chapter 2 of this book). It is necessary to continue research on x-ray lithography to provide one possible solution to this demand. Another solution, or family thereof, is discussed in Chapter 13 on ultrahigh-resolution electron beam lithography and proximal probe lithography. Each of these methods has associated with it a set of advantages and disadvantages, and despite the many years of research that have gone before, it is to be expected that many more years will be required to determine which will be the most appropriate for high-volume, high-yield manufacturing of ultralarge-scale integrated circuits (ULSICs).

Because x-ray lithography has not reached the stage of practical application, this chapter will be of a somewhat different nature than most of the rest of the book (it shares this feature to some extent with Chapter 13). Many questions must be answered before a practical system can be described and a practitioner's "handbook" is written. The present work attempts to provide a general introduction to what is known and to give some indication of probable future directions. As in any research effort, many surprises may be in store. An excellent recent overview of current research is given by Smith et al. [5].

2 CHARACTERISTICS OF X-RAY LITHOGRAPHY

The x-ray lithography system proposed by Spears and Smith [1] is proximity printing as shown in Fig. 1. Although there have been reports on reduction projection x-ray lithography (see Section 8), the focus here is mainly on x-ray proximity printing, for which the technology is at this point most highly developed.

The advantages of 1:1 x-ray lithography are summarized as follows based on the reported literature (although some are controversial as described below).

1. By using soft x-rays, wavelength-related diffraction problems, which limit the resolution of optical lithography, are effectively reduced. _
2. High-aspect-ratio pattern fabrication can be achieved due to the transparency of resist film to x-rays.
3. Many defect-causing particles in the light optics regime are transparent to x-rays.

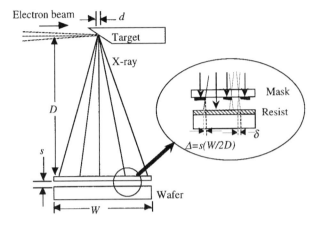

Figure 1 Schematic diagram of an x-ray lithography system.

4. There is a possibility of high throughput because large areas can be irradiated.
5. Large depth of focus gives good process latitude.
6. There is practically no field size limitation.
7. Unwanted scattering and reflection are negligible, because the index of refraction in the x-ray spectral region is about the same for all materials (close to unity) [5]. This eliminates the standing-wave effect and other reflection-based problems that plague optical lithography.

3 FACTORS AFFECTING THE SELECTION OF X-RAY WAVELENGTH

It is generally accepted that the x-ray wavelength lies in the range from 10 to 0.1 nm and it overlaps with the ultraviolet region in the longer wavelength region and with γ-rays in the shorter wavelength region. However, although x-rays cover a wide spectral range, the region of wavelengths for x-ray lithography is rather limited. The limited choice of materials for masking determines this wavelength range.

The absorption coefficient for mask materials as a function of wavelength is shown in Fig. 2 [6]. A mask with a reasonable contrast ratio is necessary to obtain good definition of x-ray images. According to Spears and Smith [1], the wavelength must be longer than 0.4 nm to obtain 90% x-ray absorption using the most highly absorbing material (Au, Pt, Ta, W, etc.) with 0.5 μm thickness. On the other hand, substrate materials (Be, Si, SiC, Si_3N_4, BN, and organic polymers) restrict the usable wavelength to be less than 2 nm to transmit more than 25% of the incident x-rays (see Fig. 2). Thus, the wavelength range is lim-

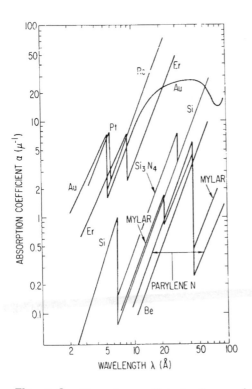

Figure 2   Absorption coefficients of some of the most absorbing and most transparent materials for x-rays.

ited to $0.4 < \lambda < 2$ nm. A plot of contrast ratios [related to the modulation transfer function (MTF), of the mask] as a function of Au thickness for four different wavelengths is shown in Fig. 3 [6].

Because x-rays are generated under vacuum, a "vacuum window" separating the vacuum from the exposing area is needed. The material (Be) for this window also dictates the wavelength range of x-rays. Although exposure systems under vacuum have been proposed, wafer handling would be complicated.

As will be discussed in the next section, the range of photoelectrons and diffraction effect limit the resolution. The effects of photoelectron range and diffraction on resolution are depicted in Fig. 4 [7]. The range of photoelectrons is smaller for longer wavelengths, while the diffraction effect is smaller for shorter wavelengths. The optimum wavelength for x-ray lithography seems to be around 1 nm.

It is known that the absorption coefficient varies strongly with wavelength. Organic resist materials mainly consist of C, H, and O, and absorption coefficients for these elements are higher in the longer wavelength region and lower

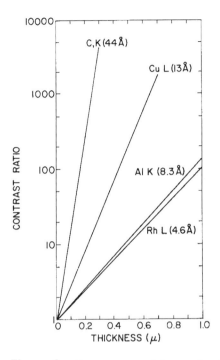

Figure 3 X-ray contrast of Au as a function of Au thickness for four different wavelengths (bremsstrahlung neglected) [6].

in the shorter one. Therefore, the longer wavelength is desirable for higher resist sensitivity. The amount of absorbed energy is closely related to resist sensitivity, which will be described in Section 7.

In summary, the materials for x-ray masks are of the utmost importance in determining the wavelength range $0.4 < \lambda < 2$ nm.

4 RESOLUTION OF X-RAY LITHOGRAPHY

4.1 Geometrical Factors

A typical exposure system for x-ray lithography using an electron beam bombardment source is schematically depicted in Fig. 1. The opaque part of the mask casts shadows onto the wafer below. The edge of the shadow is not absolutely sharp because of the finite size of the x-ray source d (diameter of focal spot of electrons on the anode) at a distance D from the mask. If the gap between mask and wafer is called s, the penumbral blur δ is given by

$$\delta = s(d/D) \tag{1}$$

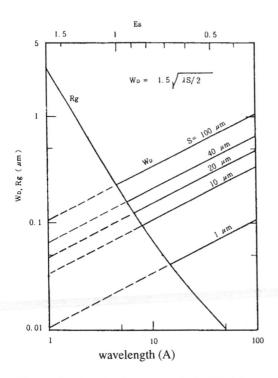

Figure 4   Relation between resolution W_0 and x-ray wavelength λ. The effect of photoelectron range R_g and mask-wafer gap S on resolution as a function of the wavelength is also shown [7]. E_s is the synchrotron storage ring energy (in MeV) to give the corresponding x-ray wavelength (see Section 5.2).

Smaller gap and smaller x-ray source size lead to a smaller penumbra. Small size and high intensity are important factors for developing x-ray sources. The incident angle of x-rays on the wafer varies from 90° at the center of wafer to $\tan^{-1}(2D/W)$ at the edge of the wafer diameter W. The shadows are slightly longer at the edge by an amount Δ that is given by

$$\Delta = s(W/2D) \tag{2}$$

The smaller gap and larger D give the smaller Δ. A full wafer exposure system can be adopted when this geometrical distortion is acceptable. Otherwise, a step-and-repeat exposure mode is necessary.

4.2 Effect of Secondary Electrons

Three processes are involved in the absorption of x-rays: Compton scattering, the generation of photoelectrons, and the formation of electron-positron pairs.

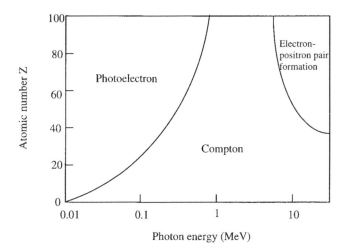

Photon energy (MeV)

Figure 5 Main contribution of photon-atom interaction as a function of atomic number and photon energy.

The magnitude of the three processes depends strongly on x-ray energy and atomic number as shown in Fig. 5 [8]. The electron-positron pair formation is possible at x-ray energies above 1.02 MeV. The energies of the x-ray quanta in x-ray lithography are lower than 10 keV. For such energies the cross section for the photoelectric effect is about 100 times larger than that for Compton scattering. Therefore, only the effect of the photoelectrons needs to be considered.

The absorption of an x-ray by an atom is an inner-shell excitation followed by emission of the photoelectron (Fig. 6). In the simplest picture, when an x-ray photon is absorbed, a photoelectron is generated with kinetic energy E_p where

$$E_p = E_x - E_b \tag{3}$$

Here E_x is the energy of the x-ray photon and E_b is the binding energy required to release an electron from an atom, as calculated by assuming that the final state of the atom has the same electronic configuration as it had before ionization. In reality, there is some "relaxation," which is a consequence of many-electron configuration interaction effects, which results in the emitted electron having a slightly greater energy than it otherwise would have [9]. This relaxation energy is the order of a few eV, while E_b is of the order of several hundred eV.

The vacancy that is created in the atom is filled quickly and the energy E_b is distributed to the surroundings via either an Auger electron or fluorescent radiation. Usually the vacancy is filled by an electron from the next higher level and the energy released is a fraction smaller than E_b. X-ray fluorescence occurs at a wavelength slightly longer than the wavelength corresponding to the absorption

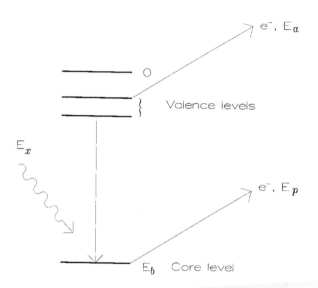

Figure 6   Schematic energy diagram showing the general processes involved in x-ray absorption. Core ionization results in the emission of a photoelectron of energy E_p, and the filling of this core level by an internal transition of energy $E_b - E_{val}$ gives rise to an Auger electron of energy E_a (which may or may not come from exactly the same level as the one filling the core).

edge. The ratio of the probability for Auger emission to fluorescence for light elements is approximately 9:1. Hence for light elements 90% or more of the binding energy is transferred to the surroundings by Auger electrons. These electrons produced by the photoelectric effect and the Auger process cause excitation and ionization in the resist film, leading to chemical changes in polymers. Hence the range of these electrons is related to the resolution of exposed patterns.

The range of electrons in poly(methyl methacrylate) (PMMA) films as a function of electron energy is shown in Fig. 7 [1], based on conventional electron energy loss analysis. The energies of the characteristic copper, aluminum, and molybdenum x-rays are indicated for comparison. The first attempt to measure the the range of photoelectrons in a lithographic experiment was carried out by Feder et al. [6]. They measured the maximum penetration depth of x-ray generated electrons from a heavy metal layer into PMMA resist. The effective range was determined by the experimental arrangement shown in Fig. 8. The erbium film evaporated on the resist film acted as an x-ray absorber and electron generator to expose the resist. After the exposure the erbium film was removed and the resist was developed. In Fig. 8 a plot of the change in resist film thickness as a function of development time is also shown. In all cases the initial stages of development showed a rapid decrease in thickness followed by a

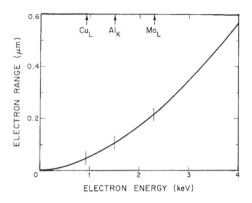

Figure 7 Characteristic electron range as a function of electron energy for a typical polymer film (ρ = 1 g/cm^3) [1].

normal development curve representative of PMMA. They considered that extrapolation of the normal part of the curve gives the effective range of electrons.

It is clear from this figure that the effective range of electrons depends on the wavelength of x-rays: the range is smaller for longer wavelength. Although the energy of photoelectrons from Er would be different from the energy of photoelectrons from C and O, the ranges are much smaller than expected values shown in Fig. 7. The resolution of this apparent discrepancy comes in part from considering that the spatial distribution of deposited energy is affected by the source of electrons [10]. The Auger electrons are shorter ranged: the standard deviation of the Gaussian distribution for C (290 eV) is 3 nm and for O (530 eV) 6 nm; these ranges are, of course, independent of the photon energy. The associated photoelectrons have longer ranges but deposit their energy more diffusely.

Several factors enter into the increase in resolution over that suggested by the nominal range data in Fig. 7. Lower energy leads to larger elastic scattering cross sections, thus helping confine the electrons [10]. Inelastic scattering mean free paths tend to be smallest (for most materials) in the vicinity of 100 eV [9]. Finally, it is important to realize that the definition of "range" is not a precise value; what counts is resist development. Resist development is in general not a linear function of exposure dose, and it may be possible to develop features correctly in the presence of a low level of "background" exposure. It has been shown experimentally that 30-nm line widths can be produced with good fidelity in PMMA resist using an x-ray wavelength of 0.83 nm, with a corresponding maximum photoelectron range of 40–70 nm [11], and Smith et al. [5] suggest that feature sizes down to 20 nm are feasible using wavelengths of 1 nm and longer.

In x-ray lithography, one should take into account the effects of photoelectrons and Auger electrons near the interface of the resist and the silicon substrate. Ticher and Hundt [12] have reported the depth profile of the deposited energy of photo-

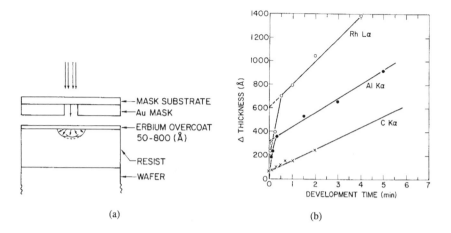

(a)   (b)

Figure 8   Schematic showing the measurement of effective range of electrons generated by x-ray exposure (a). The incident x-rays transmitted through the mask are incident
on a resist film coated with erbium. Removal of erbium and development of the resist film
will give the depth of the electrons. The depth of the developed exposed area in resist is
plotted as a function of development time (b). The intercepts on the vertical axis represent
the maximum penetration depth of electrons as measured in the developed resist [6].

electrons and Auger electrons generated in the resist and silicon by Al_K (0.83 nm)
and Rh_L x-rays (0.43 nm). The angular distributions of the electrons are important
in calculating the distribution of energy transferred. The Auger electrons have a
spherical or isotropic distribution from their starting point, whereas the photoelectrons generated by x-rays with energies below 10 keV are preferentially emitted
perpendicular to the impinging x-rays. Whereas for Al_K radiation the electrons
from the silicon have only a minor influence on the deposited energy profile, the
electrons generated by Rh_L in the silicon can give a high contribution to the energy density at the resist-silicon interface even in the unexposed area as shown in
Fig. 9. This difference was attributed to the larger electron range for Rh_L than for
Al_K radiation. The calculated energy density curves for Rh_L and Al_K radiation are
in good agreement with the resist profile after development. Some simulations
[13–15] have shown that it is important to expose with a wavelength above the
absorption edge of silicon, i.e., $\lambda > 0.7$ nm, because of photoelectrons originating
in the substrate and propagating back into the resist.

Photoelectrons are also generated from the absorber on the mask by the absorption of the incident radiation. These electrons cause unwanted exposure
on the resist, which deteriorates the mask contrast and system resolution.
These photoelectrons can be eliminated by coating the mask with an organic
layer.

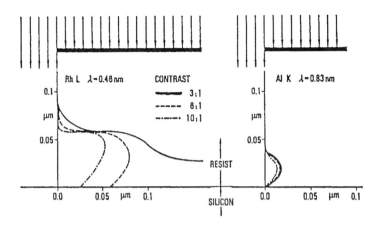

Figure 9 Effect of the secondary (photo- and Auger) electrons on the deposited energy in a resist film near the resist-substrate interface. Lines of constant energy density $(D(x,z)/D_0 = 0.5)$ near the bottom of the resist layer are plotted for various contrast values for Rh_L and Al_K radiation [12].

4.3 Diffraction Effect

In proximity x-ray printing, diffraction must be carefully considered even though diffraction in x-ray lithography is smaller than that in optical lithography. The minimum line width W_{min} is related to the mask-sample gap s by

$$W_{min} = [s\lambda / \alpha]^{1/2} \tag{4}$$

where λ is the source wavelength and α is the reciprocal of the square of the so-called Fresnel number [5]. Both accurate calculation (using Maxwell's equations and the real dielectric properties of the absorber) and experiment [16–18] show that an α value as large as 1.5 can be used if the spatial coherence of the source is optimized, which turns out to be $\beta = \delta/W_{min} \sim 1.5$ (δ being the penumbral edge blur due to the finite source size as defined in eq. (1), equivalent to a measure of spatial coherence). Under these conditions, edge ringing (rapid spatial variations in transmitted intensity close to the mask edge) is eliminated at the expense of a less abrupt edge transition [5]. The image quality is nevertheless sufficient to print a 100-nm pitch electrode pattern with high fidelity using 1.32-nm x-rays at $s = 2.7$ μm, with an exposure latitude of at least 2.3 × [18]. Extension of these results by the foregoing analysis suggests that a gap of 15 μm will suffice for 100-nm features using 1-nm radiation and a source subtending 3.5 mrad (as viewed from the substrate [5].

Figure 4 is a plot of minimum feature size versus mask-sample gap. Smith and co-workers [5] have found it possible to routinely achieve controlled gaps of 5 μm and smaller in a research setting; this would yield ~ 60–70-nm or smaller features. Whether this can be done in manufacturing has not yet been demonstrated. Factors to be considered are the cleanliness and flatness of both substrate and mask. Features below about 30–40 nm require mask-substrate contact. Again, there remains a gap between what has been demonstrated in a research mode and high-volume manufacturing.

5   X-RAY SOURCES

5.1   Electron Beam (EB) Bombardment X-Ray Sources

X-ray radiation produced by bombardment of material with accelerated electrons has been utilized as an x-ray source since the discovery of x-rays. When an accelerated electron (several tens of keV) impinges on the target, two types of radiation are produced. One is continuous radiation primarily produced from interactions with nuclei; the electron emits energy when it experiences the strong electric field near the nucleus (bremsstrahlung). The other is characteristic radiation (x-ray fluorescence); when the incident electron energy is high enough, it can cause inner-shell excitation followed by the emission of characteristic lines. A typical x-ray spectrum generated by EB bombardment is shown in Fig. 10 [19], which shows sharp high-intensity characteristic radiation and broad low-intensity bremsstrahlung. Although it is primarily the characteristic radiation that is used for x-ray lithography, the influence of the continuous radiation on exposure dose cannot be neglected. The energy of the characteristic line is determined by the materials used as a target.

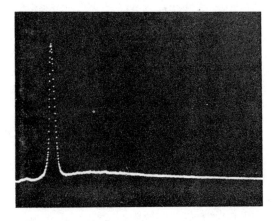

Figure 10   X-ray emission spectrum from Pd with electron beam bombardment. [From Ref. 19.]

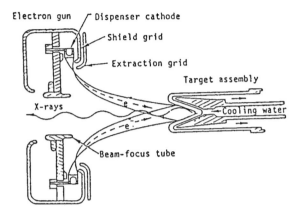

Figure 11 Schematic view of electron gun and target Gaines-type assembly for x-ray generation [20].

A Gaines-type x-ray source is shown in Fig. 11 [20]. This source has an inverted cone geometry providing a large surface area with a minimum (and symmetric) projected spot. At the same time, the inverted cone acts as an excellent blackbody absorber for electrons. The cathode of the electron gun is ring shaped and masked from the view of the target, since it is necessary to prevent evaporated cathode material from being deposited on the targets. The target is cooled by high-velocity water flow.

5.2 Synchrotron Orbit Radiation (SOR)

Synchrotron orbit radiation is a very intense and well-collimated x-ray source. It has received a great deal of attention as a source for x-ray lithography since the report by Spiller et al. [21]. Synchrotron radiation is emitted when a relativistic electron experiences an acceleration perpendicular to its direction of motion. The characteristics of SOR are summarized as follows [21]:

1. The radiation is a broad continuum, spanning the infrared through the x-ray range.
2. The intensity of the flux is several orders of magnitude larger than that of conventional EB bombardment sources.
3. The radiation is collimated vertically and its divergence is small (a few mrad).
4. The radiation is horizontally polarized in the orbital plane (electron trajectory plane).
5. The source is clean in an ultrahigh vacuum.
6. The radiation can be considered pulsed, because bursts of radiation are seen from the circular motion.

Characteristics 2 and 3 are utilized in x-ray lithography. The high radiation intensity can reduce the exposure time. The small divergence of SOR essentially eliminates the problem of geometrical distortion, which imposes severe constraints on mask-to-wafer positioning with conventional x-ray sources as discussed above. The spectral distribution and intensity of synchrotron radiation are dependent on electron energy, magnetic field, and orbital radius of the deflection magnet. As described in Section 3 on the selection of x-ray wavelength, the wavelength region for x-ray lithography is determined by mask contrast and mask substrate material. Therefore, the electron energy and magnetic field of SOR should be optimized to offer a desirable spectral distribution and intensity for x-ray lithography.

Although the SOR is a collimated beam and the effective source size is small, the x-ray beam is rectangular or slitlike in shape at some distance from the source. The emitted radiation is horizontally uniform but very nonuniform vertically. To get enough exposure area, several methods have been reported [22]: a wafer was moved with a mask during exposure, a mirror that scans the reflected light vertically was oscillated, and the electrons were oscillated in the storage ring.

Other disadvantages of synchrotron radiation are large physical dimension and high cost. Although several attempts to design compact SOR sources to reduce the construction cost have been reported [22], it still requires in the vicinity of a billion dollars for a system. The cost per beam port can be reduced by using a multiport system, which might then be cost-competitive with optical lithography exposure systems. However, at least two SOR sources are necessary in case of shutdown.

5.3   Plasma X-Ray Sources

Several attempts to obtain high-intensity x-ray emission from extremely high-energy plasmas have been made. Devices capable of producing such plasmas rely on the ability to deliver energy to a target more rapidly than it can be carried away by loss processes. Several devices capable of producing a dense high-temperature plasma by electric discharge and laser pulse irradiation have been reported.

Economou and Flanders [23] reviewed the gas-puff configuration reported by Stalling et al. [24], which is shown in Fig 12. This consists of a fast valve and supersonic nozzle. When the valve is fired, the gas expands through the nozzle and forms a hollow cylinder at the nozzle exit. A high, pulsed current is driven through the gas cylinder, causing the gas to ionize. The magnetic pressure induced by current through the resulting plasma cylinder leads to collapse onto the axis, forming a dense, hot plasma that is a strong x-ray source.

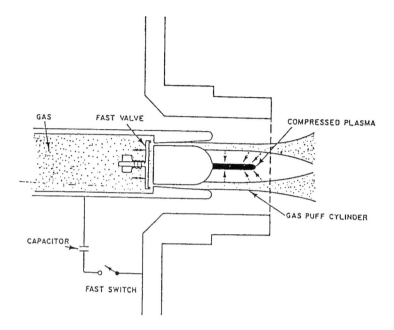

Figure 12 Schematic representation of the gas puff configuration. The fast-acting gas release valve and the shaped nozzle form a cylinder of gas. A discharge current through the gas causes the cylinder collapse, forming the plasma x-ray source [23].

For a laser plasma source, either an infrared or ultraviolet laser is used with pulses varying from 50 psec to 10 nsec. The beam focused on the target (10^{14} W/cm^2 is needed) creates a plasma of high enough temperature to produce blackbody radiation [25]. The conversion efficiency from laser energy to x-ray photons is higher than that of electron impact excitation, but the conversion efficiency from electric energy to laser is low. The advantage of this approach is that the power supply can be positioned away from the aligner, preventing electromagnetic interference.

6   X-RAY MASKS

6.1   Mask Fabrication

One of the most difficult technologies in x-ray lithography is the mask fabrication. In proximity x-ray lithography, production, inspection, and repair of x-ray masks are the most problematic aspects. X-ray masks consist of a thin membrane as a substrate, x-ray absorber patterns, and a frame to protect the membrane. The x-ray mask uses a very thin membrane as substrate instead of the glass substrate used for photomask, because no material is highly transparent to x-rays. Materials currently investigated as membranes include SiC, SiN, and Si. X-ray absorber materials are mostly Au, Ta, and W, which define the circuit pattern on the membrane. These resist patterns are fabricated by electron beam lithography.

Examples of x-ray mask fabrication schemes for an Au additive process and a Ta subtractive process are shown in Fig. 13. The additive process indicates the plating of x-ray absorber on the resist patterned membrane, while the subtractive process indicates etching the x-ray absorber using the resist patterns as an etching mask. X-ray mask fabrication using an additive method includes deposition of membrane film on a silicon wafer, back-etching the silicon to the membrane film, glass frame attachment, deposition of Cr for plating base, resist coating, pattern formation by electron beam lithography, Au plating (additive process), and finally resist removal. In the subtractive method [26], after deposition of SiN film for the membrane and Ta film for the absorber, resist patterns are formed on the Ta film by electron beam lithography. The patterns are first transferred to SiO_2, and then SiO_2 patterns are transferred to the Ta film by dry etching. Finally, the silicon substrate is etched from the back side to the membrane. It is difficult to relax the stress of the membrane in both additive and subtractive processes.

Optical lithography has extended its resolution capability down to 0.25 μm, and the use of the ArF excimer laser (193 nm) as a light source, along with wavefront engineering, may have the potential for resolution approaching the 0.1-μm level. Therefore, the issues of x-ray masks for sub-100 nm, i.e., nanolithography, are especially important. X-ray lithography in this realm requires absorber patterns near 0.1 μm fabricated on the mask membrane in 1:1 dimension precisely. An x-ray wavelength of ~ 1 nm is used as discussed earlier. The difference in absorption coefficient of the material on the mask must provide the image contrast. To obtain appropriate mask contrast, the absorber thickness must be 0.5 to 1 μm as described before. These structures become more difficult to fabricate due to the high aspect ratio as the minimum feature size becomes smaller. In addition, these precise high-aspect-ratio patterns should be maintained with low distortion on the thin film membrane. However, the aspect ratio problem can be alleviated to some extent if one can use a thinner absorber film with expectation of a phase shift effect, because it was reported that a thinner absorber (0.3 to 0.35 μm) can improve the image quality by letting some of the x-ray radiation pass through in the same manner as a "leaky chrome" optical phase shift mask [27,28].

These masks are remarkably robust mechanically; they can, for example, withstand 1 atmosphere of pressure [5]. They are, however, subject to distortion by radiation damage, the supporting frame, and by the stress in the ab-

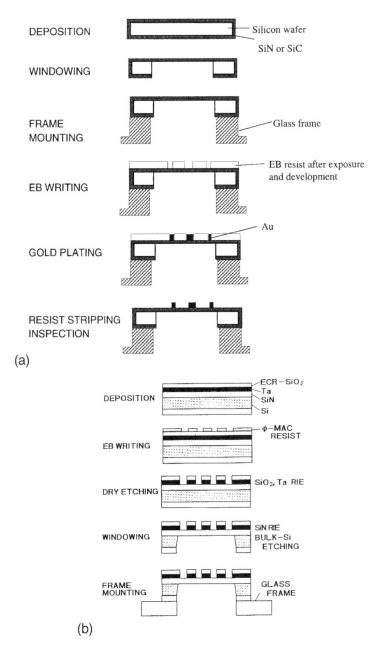

Figure 13 X-ray mask fabrication processes. The glass frame and membrane (nominally 1 μm thick) must be flat to submicrometer specifications in order to be useful in high-resolution proximity printing. In reproducible laboratory processing, 3-cm-diameter masks have been made that are flat to 250 nm or better, enabling gaps below 5 μm [5].

sorber film. The first of these problems appears negligible for SiC and Si masks but has not yet been fully solved for SiN_x.

The issue of absorber stress is the most critical one and has yet to be adequately addressed in a way that is compatible with high-volume manufacturing, although stress-free masks have been made. Smith et al. [5] discuss these issues in depth and give additional references.

6.2 Mask Patterning

Absorber patterns are usually made by electron beam lithography, although a variety of techniques have been proposed and investigated, including also photolithography, interferometric lithography, x-ray lithography (i.e., mask replication), and ion-beam lithography [5]. However, most of the electron beam exposure machines currently used are unable to meet the requirement for very accurate pattern size and beam placement needed to pattern features below 0.2 μm.

In the subtractive method, resist pattern formation is carried out on the x-ray absorber materials of high atomic number, such as Ta and W, which usually show a higher backscattering effect than those of low atomic number. The backscattering causes electron energy deposition in unwanted areas (proximity effect, as discussed in Chapter 6), resulting in pattern size variation. The proximity correction during electron beam exposure makes the electron beam exposure more complicated. With the additive approach, a very thin plating base is patterned, minimizing the backscattering problem. Care must be taken, however, to avoid pinholes in this film.

A second important problem associated with e-beam patterning arises from e-beam scan distortion and stitching errors. Conventional e-beam systems do not have feedback to maintain precise positioning of the beam relative to the interferometrically controlled stage. Research is currently in progress to address this problem [5].

X-ray lithography has been shown to be sufficiently well controlled that it is capable of producing replicas from a master mask with adequate fidelity; thus it is feasible for the original pattern generation using electron beams to be carried out with greater precision (and at correspondingly higher cost) than for optical masks without sacrificing cost-effectiveness for the overall process.

6.3 Mask Alignment

Although Taniguchi et al. [29] demonstrated several years ago a misalignment detectivity of ~5 nm using an interferometric scheme, such techniques have not achieved 3σ alignments close to their detectivity. As with any alignment procedure, the performance with "real-world" wafers is inferior to that obtained under carefully controlled conditions. The difficulties of achieving alignment of successive layers to within 70 Å (25% of a 30-nm critical feature size) are formidable with any technique. Electron beam lithography (the nanometer application of which is discussed in Chapter 13) has some advantage in that, since it is a direct write process, the precision of detection of alignment marks is in general not substantially worse than the resolution itself. X-ray lithography must rely on optical techniques, and it is a major design challenge to provide a set of signals whose fidelity is not degraded unacceptably by the various reflective and scattering effects present in integrated circuit wafers.

7   X-RAY RESIST MATERIALS

Requirements for x-ray resists strongly depend on x-ray sources and lithographic processes. A variety of multilayer resist systems, as well as the conventional single-layer resist process, have been extensively studied [30]. A simple single-layer resist is desirable for practical use in x-ray lithography to be compatible with the existing process for optical lithography. A single-layer resist process requires a resist with high resolution as well as high dry-etch resistance.

7.1   Factors Determining Sensitivity of X-Ray Resists

The absorption of a photon is the first step of photochemical or radiation-induced chemical reactions in the resist film. X-ray energy absorption is given by Beer's law

$$I = I_0 e^{-\mu_m \rho l} \tag{5}$$

where I_0 is the intensity of incident x-rays, I the intensity of x-rays after penetration through a thickness l of a homogeneous material having a mass absorption coefficient μ_m for x-rays, and ρ the bulk density of the material. Therefore, the mass absorption coefficient for a polymer, μ_{mp}, is given by

$$\mu_{mp} = \frac{\sum A_i \mu_{mi}}{\sum A_i} \tag{6}$$

where A_i and μ_{mi} are the atomic weight and mass absorption coefficient, respectively. The percent of x-rays absorbed in a polymer can be calculated from the relation

$$\% \text{ absorbed} = (I_0 - I)/I_0 = 1 - e^{-\mu_m \rho l} \tag{7}$$

For these calculations, values for μ_m in Table 1 [30] can be used. For example, absorption fractions of x-ray energy by a high-resolution electron beam resist poly(methyl methacrylate) (PMMA) with 1-μm thickness are only 3.1 and 1.7% for Mo (5.14 Å) and Pd (4.36 Å) x-rays, respectively. Improvement in

Table 1 Mass Absorption Coefficients of Selected Elements [30]

		μ_m (cm^2/g)					
Element	Z	Pd 4.36 Å	Rh 4.60 Å	Mo 5.41 Å	Si 7.13 Å	Al 8.34 Å	Cu 13.36 Å	C 44.70 Å
C	6	100	116	184	402	627	2714	2373
N	7	155	180	285	622	970	4022	3903
O	8	227	264	416	908	1415	5601	6044
F	9	323	376	594	1298	2022	6941	8730
Si	14	1149	1337	2115	279	423	1959	36980
P	15	1400	1630	2579	371	564	2405	41280
S	16	1697	1975	232	483	733	3079	47940
Cl	17	2013	197	301	628	953	3596	50760
Br	35	1500	1730	2649	3680	1456	3101	32550
Fe	26	630	726	1118	2330	3536	10690	13300
Sn	50	675	772	1160	2318	3437	9623	6332
Tl	81	1083	1213	1032	1904	2697	6276	13030
Most absorbing elements		Cl S Br P Si Heavy atoms	S Br P Si Heavy atoms	Br P Si Heavy atoms F	Br Heavy atoms F O Cl	Heavy atoms F Br O N	Heavy atoms F O N Cl	Cl S P Si Heavy atoms
Least absorbing elements		C N O	C N Cl	C S N	Si P C	Si P C	Si P C	C N O

sensitivity of x-ray resists is not an easy task because of the low deposited energy of x-rays in the resist film. As can be seen in Table 1, the mass absorption coefficients for halogen atoms and metals have larger values for 4–15-Å x-rays. Therefore, incorporation of these atoms into polymers is an effective approach to increasing x-ray absorption. Since the Cl atom strongly absorbs Pd (4.36 Å) x-rays, there was a report on Cl-containing acrylate polymers, poly(2,3-dichloro-1-propylacrylate) (DCPA) by Bell Laboratories workers [31]. The absorption fraction for DCPA is at most 9.9% for Pd (4.36 Å) x-rays. On the other hand, absorption fractions of 1 μm of AZ-1350J photoresist are 70 and 40% for i-line (365 nm) and g-line (436 nm), respectively. More than 90% of the x-ray energy penetrates through the resist film, whereas in optical lithography about half of the incident light can be utilized. The sensitivity is generally described by the incident energy instead of absorbed energy. The sensitivity of diazonaphthoquinone-novolak photoresist is about 100 mJ/cm^2. This means that an x-ray resist should be more than five times as sensitive as a conventional photoresist as far as absorbed energy in a resist film is concerned.

Photo- and Auger electrons produced following absorption of x-rays in a resist film cause chemical change leading to differential solubility behavior. Therefore, chemical reactions induced by x-ray irradiation are similar to those induced by electron beam irradiation. Most electron beam resists can be used as x-ray resists. In addition, x-ray sensitivity shows a linear relation with electron beam sensitivity, as shown in Fig. 14 [32].

7.2 Trends in X-Ray Resists

Since the electron sensitivity shows a good correlation with x-ray sensitivity, positive-working resists using radiation-induced chain scission–type polymers such as PMMA and negative-working resists using crosslinking-type polymers can be used. However, for drastic improvement in sensitivity, the recent trend in x-ray resists has been to use a photoinduced chain reaction system as described in "chemical amplification" [33] in the chapter on chemistry of photo-resists (Chapter 8). The chemical amplification system utilizes strong acids produced from acid generator photodecomposition to catalyze the reaction of acid-sensitive groups either in the polymer backbone or on the side chain. Since the chemical amplification system utilizes the drastic change in solubility for aqueous base developer, it shows high-resolution capability. Device fabrication using x-ray lithography has been demonstrated using chemical amplification resists [26, 34–36]. Generally, a deprotection reaction is used for positive resists and an acid-hardening

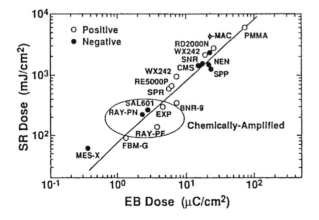

Figure 14 Relation of x-ray sensitivity with electron sensitivity for various resists [32].

reaction of melamine derivatives is used for negative ones. One of the disadvantages of this type of resist is acid diffusion into unexposed areas. The range of the diffusion depends on the process conditions, especially postexposure baking temperature, and has been investigated in detail [34] (see also Chapter 8).

8 X-RAY PROJECTION SYSTEMS

8.1 Mirror-type Reduction Projection Systems

Workers at AT&T Bell Laboratories demonstrated an x-ray reduction projection exposure system based on Schwarzschild reflection type 20:1 reduction in 1990 (Fig. 15) [37] and achieved 0.1-μm line and space patterns, which cannot be obtained by photolithography. Since then, much attention has been focused on reduction x-ray lithography again, although reduction projection systems were already reported by workers at Lawrence Livermore National Laboratory [38] and NTT [39]. The x-ray reduction projection system can be accepted as an extension of the projection system (steppers) used in the present photolithography. Minimum feature size on the mask can be several times larger than that for proximity printing.

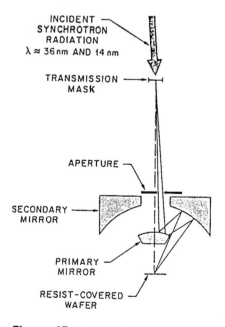

Figure 15   Schematic diagram showing the Schwarzschild objective used with an eccentric aperture and off-axis illumination [37].

The difficulty in x-ray reduction systems is the fabrication of mirrors. Aspherical multilayer mirrors are necessary to reduce the number of mirrors, and the thickness of each layer is only a few tens of angstroms. Since the wavefront error of these mirrors is required to be less than $\lambda/14$, extremely precise thickness control is needed, and higher accuracy is needed for shorter wavelength. A multilayer mirror is prepared by periodical vapor deposition of dielectrics with different refractive indices. The pitch of dielectrics determines the wavelength of maximum reflectivity and the accuracy of the pitch determines the reflectivity.

The requirements for resists for the reduction projection system are different because of the different exposure wavelength. The use of wavelengths shorter than 10 nm is limited by the present status of multilayer mirror fabrication. Most of the materials have high absorption coefficients in this wavelength region. The extinction of x-rays along the film thickness is a severe problem for image formation at around 10 nm wavelength. The workers at AT&T Bell Laboratories demonstrated pattern formation with a three-layer resist process using PMMA as an imaging layer.

Smith et al. [5] have recently described some interesting concepts involving the use of Fresnel zone plates for projection x-ray nanolithography; in one manifestation the exposure requires no mask.

9 CONCLUSIONS

X-ray lithography carries the potential for resolution at the limit of conceivable device structures that depend on the bulk properties of matter (i.e., larger than the scale of individual molecules or small aggregates). However, the advantages described above sometimes give rise to disadvantages. Since the refractive index of x-rays is near one (which minimizes unwanted scattering and interference effects), optical elements for x-rays are limited to mirrors and Fresnel zone plates. It is, therefore, difficult to collimate or focus the x-rays. Since the transmittance of the resist film is high (which gives rise to exposures that are very uniform vertically and allowing high aspect ratios), only several percent of the energy is deposited in the resist film. This high transmittance requires extremely high resist sensitivity to avoid x-ray damage of the devices and to maintain adequate throughput. The proximity printing requires a system to control the gap between mask and wafer. This gap also gives rise to such problems as penumbra and magnification, and the x-ray source size cannot be neglected. For the application of x-ray lithography to actual ULSI fabrication, alignment technology should also be established. Above all, x-ray mask fabrication is a most difficult issue for actual use of x-ray lithography. It is always difficult to predict the limitation of minimum feature size that can be fabricated with optical lithography. There is no doubt, however, that the obstacles for x-ray lithography described above should be overcome before the end of the optical lithography era.

As always in a fundamentally commercial endeavor, economics will make the final determination of what technology is brought to fruition, since it is the cost per device that is the primary driver for the continued minaturization of integrated circuits. Although it seems rather likely that these problems will be solved, their solutions must be achieved at a cost lower than that offered by other technologies that may mature with larger features, but whose costs may be steadily lowered by continuous aggressive engineering efforts. For the next several years, the foregoing discussion should provide useful guidelines to allow the interested reader to monitor the research activity in this field.

REFERENCES

1. Spears, E., and Smith, H. I., *Electron Lett.*, **8**, 102 (1972); Spears, E. and Smith, H. I., *Solid State Technol.*, **15**(7), 21 (1972).
2. Fay, B., Tai, L., and Alexander, D., *Proc. SPIE*, **537**, 57 (1985).
3. Smith, H. I., *Proc. IEEE*, **62**, 1361 (1974).
4. Terasawa, T., and Okazaki, S., *IEICE Trans. Electron.*, **E76-C**, 19 (1993).
5. Smith, H. I., Schattenburg, M. L., Hector, S. D., Ferrera, J., Moon, E. E., Yang, I. Y., and Burkhardt, M., *Microelectron. Eng.*, **32**, 143 (1996).
6. Feder, R., Spiller, E., and Topalian, J., *J. Vac. Sci. Technol.*, **12**, 1332 (1975); Feder, R., Spiller, E., and Topalian, J., *Polym. Eng. Sci*, **17**, 385 (1977).
7. Atoda, N., *Hoshasenkagaku (Radiation Chem.)*, **19**, 41 (1984); Atoda, N., *Proceedings of International Conference on Advances in Microelectronic Devices and Processing*, p. 109, 1994.
8. Watanbe, T., in *Hoshasen to genshi bunshi (Radiation Effect on Atoms and Molecules)* (S. Shida, ed.), Kyoritsu, 1966, p. 30.
9. Woodruff, D. P., and Delchar, T. A., *Modern Techniques of Surface Science*, Cambridge University Press, Cambridge, UK, 1986.
10. Ocola, L. E., and Cerrina, F., *J. Vac. Sci. Technol.*, **B11,**, 2839 (1993).
11. Early, K., Schattenburg, M. L., and Smith, H. I., *Microelectron. Eng.*, **11**, 317 (1990).
12. Tischer, P., and Hundt, E., *Proc. 8th Symp. Electron Ion Beam Sci. Technol.*, **78-5**, 444 (1987).
13. Murata, K., *J. Appl. Phys.*, **57**, 575 (1985); Murata, K., Tanaka, M., and Kawata, H., *Optik*, **84**, 163 (1990).
14. Ocola, L. E., and Cerrina, F., *J. Vac. Sci, Technol.*, **B11**, 2839 (1993).
15. Ogawa, T., Mochiji, K., Soda, Y., and Kimura, T., *Jpn. J. Appl. Phys.*, **28**, 2070 (1989).
16. Hector, S. D., Schattenburg, M. L., Anderson, E. H., Chu, W., Wong, V. V., and Smith, H. I., *J. Vac. Sci. Technol.*, **B10**, 3164 (1992).
17. Guo, J. Z. Y., Ceffina, F., Difabrizio, E., Luciani, L., Gentili, M., and Gerold, D., *J. Vac. Sci. Technol.*, **B10**, 3150 (1992).
18. Chu, W., Smith, H. I., and Schattenburg, M. L., *Appl. Phys. Lett.*, **59**, 1641 (1991).
19. Leslie, B., Neukermans, A., Simon, T., and Foster, J., *J. Vac. Sci. Technol.*, **B1**, 1251 (1983).
20. Gaines, J. L., and Hansen, R. A., *Nucl. Instrum. Methods*, **126**, 99 (1975).

21. Spiller, E., Eastman, D. E., Feder, R., Grobman, W. D., Gudat, W., and Topalion, J., *J. Appl. Phys.*, **47**, 5450 (1976).
22. Heuberger, A., *Solid State Technol.*, **29**(2), 93 (1986); Wilson, M. N., Smith, A. I., Kempson, V. C., Purvis, A. L., Anderson, R. J., Townsend, M. C., Jorden, A. R., Andrew, D. E., Suller, V. P., and Poole, M. W., *Jpn. J. Appl. Phys.*, **29**, 2620 (1990).
23. Economou, N. P., and Flanders, D. C., *J. Vac. Sci. Technol.*, **19**, 868 (1981).
24. Stalling, C., Childers, K., Roth, I., and Schneider, R., *Appl. Phys. Lett.*, **35**, 524 (1979).
25. Hoffman, A. L., Albrecht, G. F., and Crawford, E. A., *J. Vac. Sci. Technol*, **B3**, 258 (1985).
26. Deguchi, K., *J. Photopolym. Sci. Technol.*, **4**, 445 (1993).
27. Somemura, Y., Deguchi, K., Miyoshi, K., and Matsuda, T., *Jpn. J. Appl. Phys.*, **31**, 4221 (1992); Somemura, Y., and Deguchi, K., *Jpn. J. Appl. Phys.*, **31**, 938 (1992).
28. Xiao, J., Kahn, M., Nachman, R., Wallance, J., Chen, Z., and Cerrina, F., *J. Vac. Sci. Technol.*, **B12**, 4038 (1994).
29. Ishihara, S., Kanai, M., Une, A., and Suzuki, M., *J. Vac. Sci. Technol.*, **B6**, 1652 (1989).
30. Taylor, G. N., *Solid State Technol.*, **23**(5), 73 (1980); Taylor, G. N., *Solid State Technol.*, **27**(6), 124 (1984).
31. Taylor, G. N., Coquin, G. A., and Somek, S., *Polym. Eng. Sci.*, **17**, 420 (1977).
32. Deguchi, K., *ULSI lithography no kakushin (Innovation of ULSI Lithography)*, Science Forum, 1994, p. 245.
33. Ito, H., and Willson, C. G., *Polym. Eng. Sci.*, **23**, 1012 (1983); Ito, H., and Willson, C. G., Polymers in electronics, *ACS Symp. Ser.*, **242**, 11 (1984).
34. Nakamura, J., Ban, H., Deguchi, K., and Tanaka, A., *Jpn. J. Appl. Phys.*, **30**, 2619 (1991).
35. DellaGardia, R., Wasik, C., Puisto, D., Fair, R., Liebman, L., Rocque, J., Nash, S., Lamberti, A., Collini, G., French, R., Vampatella, B., Gifford, G., Nastasi, V., Sa, P., Volkringer, F., Zell, T., Seeger, D., and Warlaumont, J., *Proc. SPIE*, **2437**, 112 (1995).
36. Fujii, K., Yoshihara, T., Tanaka, Y., Suzuki, K., Nkajima, T., Miyatake, T., Miyatake, E., Orita, E., and Ito, K., *J. Vac. Sci. Technol.*, **B12**, 3949 (1994).
37. Bjorkholm, J. E., Borkor, J., Eicher, L., Freeman, R. R., Gregus, J., Jewell, T. E., Mansfield, W. M., MacDowell, A. A., Raab, E. L., Silftvast, W. T., Szeto, L. H., Dennant, D. M., Waskiewicz, W. K., White, D. L. Windt, D. L., Wood, O. R., II, and Bruning, J. H., *J. Vac. Sci. Technol.*, **B8**, 1509 (1990).
38. Hawryluk, A. M., and Seppala, L G., *J. Vac. Sci. Technol.*, **B6**, 2162 (1988).
39. Kinoshita, H., Kurihara, K., Ishii, Y., and Torii, Y., *J. Vac. Sci. Technol.*, **B7**, 1648 (1989).

8

Chemistry of Photoresist Materials

Takumi Ueno

Hitachi Ltd.
Ibaraki-ken, Japan

1 INTRODUCTION

The design requirements of successive generation of very large scale integrated (VLSI) circuits have led to a reduction in lithographic critical dimensions. The aim of this chapter is to discuss the progress of the resists for present and future lithography. It is worthwhile describing the history and the trend of lithography and resists. It can be recognized from Fig. 1.1 that the second turning point of resist materials will come soon [1]. The first turning point was the replacement of a negative resist composed of cyclized rubber and a bisazide by a positive photoresist composed of a diazonaphthoquinone (DNQ) and a novolak resin. This was induced by the change of exposure system from a contact printer to a g-line (436 nm) reduction projection step-and-repeat system, the so-called stepper. The cyclized rubber system has poor resolution due to swelling during the development and low sensitivity due to lack of absorption at the g-line. The DNQ-based positive photoresist shows sensitivity at the g-line and high resolution using alkali aqueous development.

Performance of the g-line stepper was improved by increasing the numerical aperture (NA). Then shorter wavelength i-line (365 nm) lithography was introduced. DNQ-novolak resist can still be used for i-line lithography; therefore, much effort has been made to improve the resolution capability of DNQ-novolak resist as well as depth-of-focus latitude. The effect of novolak resin and the

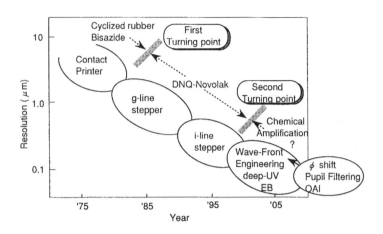

Figure 1 Development trend of lithography and resists.

chemical structure of DNQ on dissolution inhibition capability has been investigated mainly to get high dissolution contrast, which will be discussed in Section
2. Progress in this type of resist and an i-line stepper is remarkable, achieving
resolution below the exposure wavelength of the i-line (0.365 μm). However,
i-line lithography has difficulty accomplishing 0.3-μm processes [64M dynamic
random access memory (DRAM)], even using a high-NA i-line stepper in conjunction with a DNQ-novolak resist.

Several competing lithographic technologies have been proposed for the future: wavefront engineering of the i-line, deep-ultraviolet (deep-UV) lithography,
and electron beam lithography [2]. The wavefront engineering includes off-axis
illumination (OAI), pupil filtering, and phase-shifting lithography (discussed in
Chapter 2). OAI basically utilizes two fluxes with interference betweeen +1 or
−1 order diffracted light and 0-order light at the image plane: +1 or −1 order diffracted light is not used for imaging, resulting in lower intensity than in conventional imaging. In pupil filtering [3], resolution capability and depth of focus
of the hole pattern can be improved at the expense of light intensity of the image
plane. DNQ-novolak resists can be used for OAI and pupil filtering, although
higher sensitivity is necessary. For phase-shifting lithography, bridging of patterns at the end of the line- and space-patterns occurs when a positive resist is
used [4]. Therefore, negative resists with high sensitivity and high resolution are
required. In deep-UV lithography positive and negative resists with high sensitivity, high resolution, and high transmittance at the exposure wavelength are
needed. The discussion of future lithography includes chemical amplification resists, surface imaging resists, and ArF excimer laser resists.

2 DIAZONAPHTHOQUINONE (DNQ)-NOVOLAK POSITIVE PHOTORESISTS

The positive photoresist composed of DNQ and novolak resin is the workhorse for semiconductor fabrication [5]. It is surpsing that this resist has a resolution capability below the exposure wavelength of the i-line (365 nm). In this section the photochemical reaction of DNQ and improvement of the resist performance by newly designed novolak resins and DNQ inhibitors are discussed.

2.1 Photochemistry of DNQ

The Wolff rearrangement reaction mechanism of DNQ was proposed by Süs [6] in 1942 as shown in Scheme 1. It is surprising that the basic reaction was already established a half-century ago, although Süs [6] suggested the chemical structure of the final product, 1-indenecarboxylic acid, which was corrected to 3-indenecarboxylic acid [7]. Packansky and Lyerla [7] showed direct spectroscopic evidence of 1-indenoketene intermediate formation at 77 K using infrared (IR) spectroscopy. Similar results were also reported by Hacker and Turro [8]. Packansky and Lyerla [7] also investigated the reaction of ketene intermediates using infrared and carbon-13 nuclear magnetic resonance spectroscopy. The reactivity of ketene depends on the conditions as shown in Scheme 2. Under ambient conditions, ketene reacts with water trapped in the novolak resin to yield 3-indenecarboxylic acid. However, UV exposure in vacuo results in ester formation via ketene-phenolic OH reaction.

Vollenbroek et al. [9,10] also investigated the photochemistry of 2,1-diazonaphthoquinone (DNQ)-5-(4-cumylphenyl)-sulfonate and DNQ-4-(4-cumylphenyl)-sulfonate using photoproduct analysis. They confirmed that the photoproduct of DNQ is indenecarboxylic acid and its dissolution in aqueous base gives the formation of indenyl carboxylate dianion, which decarboxylates in several hours. They found out that films of mixtures of novolak and indenecarboxylic acid showed no difference in dissolution rate compared with that of exposed photoresist.

Many attempts to detect the intermediates in the photochemistry of DNQ by using time-resolved spectroscopy have been reported. Nakamura et al. [11] de-

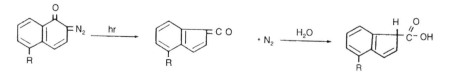

Scheme 1 Photolysis mechanism for DNQ-PAC proposed by Süs.

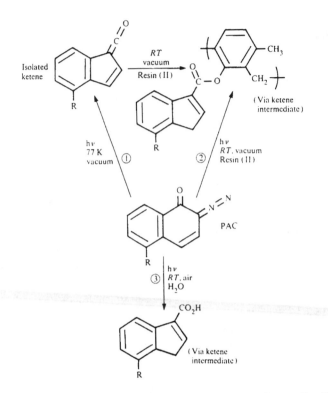

Scheme 2   UV-induced decomposition pathways for DNQ-PAC in a novolak resin.

tected a strong absorption intermediate at 350 nm, which was assigned as a ketene intermediate formed by DNQ sulfonic acid in solution. Shibata et al. [12] observed transient absorption at 350 nm of hydrated ketene as a intermediate of DNQ-5 sulfonic acid. Similar results were also reported by Barra et al. [13] and Andraos et al. [14] Tanigaki and Ebbsen [15] observed an oxirene intermediate as a precursor of ketene, which was also confirmed by spectroscopic analysis in an Ar matrix at 22.3 K. It is still controversial whether ketocarbene is a reaction intermediate [9], but the existence of the ketene intermediate has been confirmed. Since most of the attempts to detect the intermediates were performed in solution, further studies are needed to confirm the reactioin intermediates in the resist film. Sheats [16] described reciprocal failure, intensity dependence on sensitivity, in DNQ-novolak resists with 364-nm exposure, which is postulated to involve the time-dependent absorbance of the intermediate ketene.

2.2   Improvement in Photoresist Performance

Novolak Resins

A group at Sumitomo Chemical has made a systematic study of novolak resin to improve performance of the positive resists [17–22]. It is generally accepted that a resist with high sensitivity gives low film-thickness retention of the unexposed area after development and low heat resistance (Fig. 2). Novolak resins have been designed with a molecular structure and a molecular weight different from those of existing materials, although control of synthesis in novolak resin is considered to be difficult due to poor reproducibility. They investigated the relation between lithographic performance and the characteristics of novolak resins such as the isomeric structure of cresol, the position of the methylene bond, the molecular weight, and the molecular weight distribution (Fig. 3). To clarify the lithographic performance, it is attempted ot measure the dissolution rate of unexposed and exposed resist. It is not always easy to judge improvement in contrast by γ-value in exposure characteristic curves where the remaining film thickness after development is plotted as a function of the logarithm of exposure dose. Since the difference in dissolution rate between exposed and unexposed is two to five orders of magnitude, the measurement of dissolution rate made the difference in resist performance clearer than that of the exposure characteristics curves used in the early work [17].

With increasing molecular weight, the dissolution rate of novolak rein (R_n) and unexposed (R_0) and exposed (R_p) resist decreases as shown in Fig. 4. Therefore, the contrast remains almost constant for change in molecular weight of novolak resin [19].

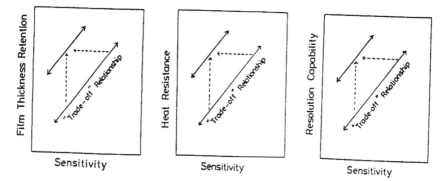

Figure 2   Trade-off relationships for various performances of a photoresists. Dotted line indicates the improvement of the performance.

(1) Molecular Weight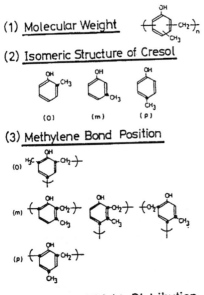

(2) Isomeric Structure of Cresol

(o)   (m)   (p)

(3) Methylene Bond Position

(o)

(m)

(p)

(4) Molecular Weight Distribution

Figure 3 Factors of novolak resins that influence resist characteristics.

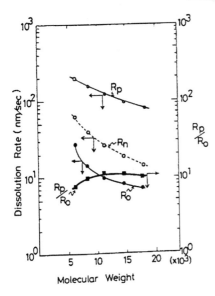

Figure 4 Effect of molecular weight of novolak resins on dissolution rates. The resists composed of novolak resins were synthesized from m-cresol (80%) and p-cresol (20%) and 3HBP-DNQ ester, where 3HBP is 2,3,4,-trihydroxybenzophenone. R_n, dissolution rate of novolak resins; R_0, dissolution rate of unexposed film; R_p, dissolution rate of exposed (60 mJ/cm^2 film.

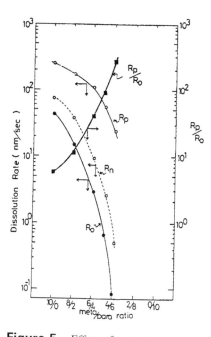

Figure 5 Effect of *meta-* to *para*-cresol ratio in novolak resins on dissolution rates. The molecular weights of these novolak resins are almost the same. R_n, R_0, and R_p are as defined in the word of Fig. 4.

When the para-meta ratio of novolak resin increases, dissolution rates of novolak resin (R_n) and the resist films of unexposed (R_0) and exposed (R_p) resist decrease (Fig. 5). [19] However, the decrease in dissolution rate of unexposed resist is larger than that of the exposed region for novolak resin with a high para-meta ratio. Therefore, the resist contrast was improved using novolak resin with a high para-meta ratio at the expense of its sensitivity. The decrease in dissolution rate with a high *p*-cresol content may be ascribed to high polymer regularity and rigidness leading to slow diffusion of the developer.

Figure 6 shows the dependence of dissolution rate on the S_4 value of *m*-cresol novolak resin, which represents the ratio of unsubstituted carbon-4 in the benzene ring of cresol to carbon-5, which indicates the fraction of ortho-ortho methylene bonding: high ortho bonding [19]. With increasing S_4 value, the content of type (B) structure increases in novolak resin. The dissolution rate of unexposed resist (R_0) shows a drastic decrease with increasing S_4 value as shown in Fig. 6, while the dissolution rate of novolak (R_n) resin decreases slightly. It should be noted that the dissolution rate of the exposed area remains constant for various S_4 values. Therefore, a high-contrast resist is obtained without sensitivity loss using a novolak resin with a high S_4 value. Azo coupling of

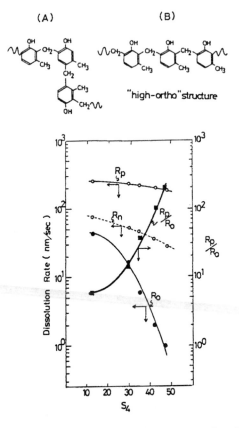

Figure 6   Effect of content of "unsubstituted carbon-4 in benzene ring of cresol", S_4, in novolak resins synthesized from *m*-cresol on dissolution rates. The molecular weights of these novolak resins are almost the same.

novolak resin with diazonaphthoquinone via base-catalytic reaction during development as shown in Scheme 3 can explain the difference in resist performance with S_4 value. High-ortho novolak has more vacant para positions than a normal novolak resin, and these vacant positions enhance the electrophilic azo coupling reaction.

The effect of the molecular weight distribution of novolak resin on resist performance is shown in Fig. 7 [18]. The dissolution rate of novolak resin increases with increasing molecular weight distribution (M_w/M_n). The discrimination between exposed and unexposed area is large at a certain M_w/M_n value, indicating that the optimum molecular weight distribution gives high-contrast resist.

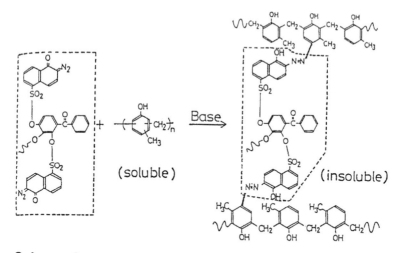

Scheme 3   Dissolution inhibition azo coupling reaction of DNQ-PAC with novolak resin.

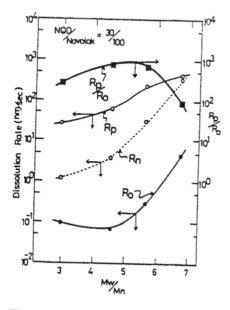

Figure 7   Effect of molecular weight distribution of novolak resins on dissolution rates. The molecular weights of these novolak resins are almost the same.

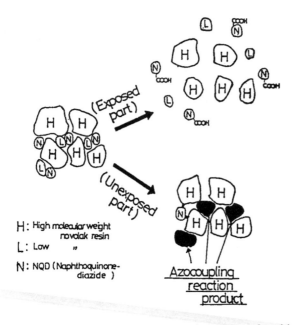

Figure 8   Stone wall model for development of positive photoresist.

On the basis of their systematic studies of novolak resins, Hanabata et al. [19] proposed the "stone wall" model for positive photoresist with alkali development as shown in Fig. 8. In exposed parts, indenecarboxylic acid formed by exposure and low-molecular-weight novolak resin dissolve first into the developer. This increases the surface contact area of high-molecular-weight novolak with the developer, leading to dissolution promotion. In unexposed areas, the azo coupling reaction of low-molecular-weight novolak resin with DNQ retards the dissolution of low-molecular-weight resin. This stone wall model gave clues to designing a high-performance positive photoresist in their following works.

They extended the study on novolak resins by synthesizing from various alkyl (R) substituted phenolic compounds including phenol, cresol, ethylphenol, and butylphenol, and copolymers of these were investigated to see the effect of their composition on the resist performance [20]. The requirements for resists were that the dissolution rate of exposed areas should be larger than 100 nm/s and the dissolution rate ratio of exposed to unexposed area should be larger than 10. To meet the requirements, they proposed the selection principles of phenol compounds for novolak resin synthesis: (1) the average carbon number in substituent R per one phenol nucleus must be 0.5–1.5 ($0.5 < [C]/[OH] < 1.5$); (2) the ratio of para-unsubstitution R with respect to OH group must be 50%.

The Sumitomo group tried to clarify the roles of individual molecular weight parts of novolak resin: low-molecular-weight (150–500), middle-molecular-weight (500–5000) and high-molecular-weight (> 5000) novolak in resist performance [21]. It was found that a novolak resin with a low content of middle-molecular-weight component shows high performance such as resolution, sensitivity and heat resistance. Then the tandem-type novolak resin shown in Fig. 9 was proposed.

The advantage of tandem-type novolak resins can be explained again by the stone wall model. The low-molecular-weight novolaks and DNQ molecules are stacked between high-molecular-weight novolaks. In exposed areas, dissolution of indenecarbokylic acid and low-molecular-weight novolaks promotes dissolution of high-molecular-weight novolaks due to increased surface contact with the developer. In unexposed areas, the azo coupling reaction of DNQ compounds with low-molecular-weight novolaks retards the dissolution.

Therefore, phenolic compounds can be used instead of low-molecular-weight novolaks, if the compounds have moderate hydrophobicity and azo coupling capability with DNQ. Hanabata et al. [22] showed high-performance characteristics of the resists composed of phenolic compounds, high-molecular-weight novolaks, and a DNQ compound with high heat resistance.

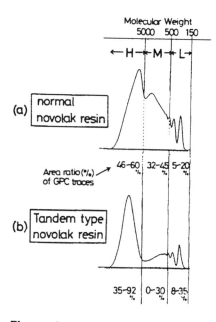

Figure 9 Gel permeation chromatography traces of a normal novolak and tandem-type novolak resin.

Studies of the effects of novolak molecular structures on resist performance have also been reported by several groups. Kajita et al. [23] of JSR investigated the effect of novolak structure on dissolution inhibition by DNQ. They found that the use of meta-methyl substituted phenols, especially 3,5-dimethylphenol, is effective in obtaining a higher ratio of intra- to intermolecular hydrogen bonds and the ratio can be controlled by selecting the phenolic monomer composition. Interaction between ortho-ortho units of novolak resin and the DNQ moiety of the PAC plays an important role in dissolution inhibition in alkali development. It was found that naphthalenesulfonic acid esters without the diazoquinone moiety also showed dissolution inhibition. This dissolution inhibition effect also depended on the structure of the novolak resin, indicating the importance of interaction between the naphthalene moiety and the novolak resin. They propsoed a host-guest complex composed of a DNQ moiety and a cavity or channel formed with aggregation of several ortho-ortho linked units as shown in Fig. 10, where the complex is formed via electrostatic interaction.

Honda et al. [24] proposed the dissolution inhibition mechanism called "Octopus Pot" of novolak-PAC interaction and the relationship between novolak microstructure and DNQ inhibitor. The mechanism involves two steps. The first step is a static molecular interaction between novolak and DNQ via macromolecular complex formation during spin coating. A secondary dynamic effect during the development process enhances the dissolution inhibition via formation of cation complexes having lower solubility.

The addition of DNQ to novolak caused the OH band shift to a higher frequency (blue shift) in infrared (IR) spectra, which suggests a disruption of the

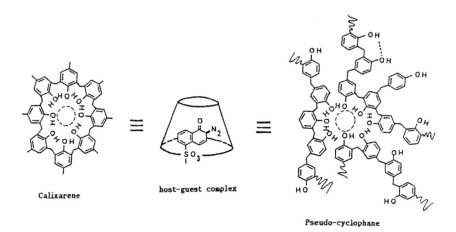

Calixarene   host-guest complex   Pseudo-cyclophane

Figure 10   Host-guest complex model for dissolution inhibition of a photoresist.

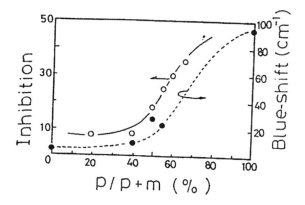

Figure 11 Correlation of dissolution inhibition and blue shift with *p*-cresol content in *m/p*-cresol novolaks. The *x* axis indicates the *p*-cresol content in the feedstock for novolak synthesis. The inhibition was defined as the ratio of dissolution rate of the synthesized novolak to that of unexposed resist that was formulated with this novolak and 4HBP-DNQ ester, where 4HBP is 2,3,4,4'-tyetrahydroxybenzophenone (average esterification level = 2.75), The ester content in solid film is 20 wt. %.

novolak hydrogen bonding by the inhibitor and concomitant hydrogen bonding with the inhibitor. The magnitude of the blue shift increases monotonically with the dissolution inhibition capability as shown in Fig. 11. An increase in *p*-cresol content in *m/p*-cresol novolaks leads to an increase in ortho-ortho bonding because only ortho positions are available for reaction on the *p*-cresol nucleus. The magnitude of the blue shift for *p*-cresol trimer was found to be dependent on the DNQ concentration and goes through a maximum at a mole ratio (*p*-cresol to DNQ) of 18. This suggests that a complex involving six units of *p*-cresol trimer and one molecule of DNQ is formed, probably through intermolecular hydrogen bonding. The "Octopus Pot" model of the macromolecular complex is depicted schematically in Fig. 12.

To improve the dissolution inhibition effect, Honda et al. [25] synthesized novolak resin with a *p*-cresol trimer sequence of novolak incorporated into a polymeric chain; they copolymerized *m*-cresol with a reactive precursor, which was prepared by attaching two units of *m*-cresol to the terminal ortho position of *p*-cresol trimer. This kind of novolak can exhibit a higher degree of dissolution inhibition at a lower content of DNQ-PAC.

The secondary dynamic effect of dissolution chemistry during development was investigated for a series of novolak resins with different structures with various quarternary ammonium hydroxides [26,27]. Phenolic resins used were (1) conventional *m-p*-cresol (CON), (2) high ortho, ortho *m/p*-cresol novolak oligomer (hybrid pentamer; HP), (3) high ortho, ortho *m/p*-cresol made by poly-

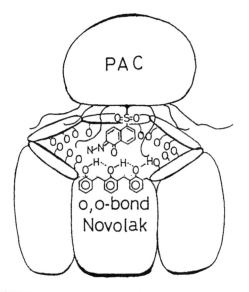

Figure 12 Schematic Octopus Pot model of macromolecular complex of ortho-ortho bonded novolak microstructure with DNQ-PAC.

merization of HP with *m*-cresol (HON), (4) novolak from xylenol feedstock (PAN), and (5) polyvinylphenol (PVP). The ultraviolet (UV) spectral change as a function of dissolution time is shown in Fig. 13. The absorbance at 282 nm decreases with decreasing novolak film thickness. A new absorption band appeared at 305 nm that was assigned to the cation complex between novolak and tetramethylammonium cation. (Fig. 14) The relation between cation complex formation rate and dissolution rate of HP is shown in Fig. 15 for three types of quarternary ammonium hydroxide. The dissolution rate can be monitored by absorption at 282 nm of the aromatic absorption band of novolak resin. The rate of the complex formation is approximately the same as the rate of dissolution when using a water rinse. This evidence supports cation diffusion as the rate-determining step for dissolution. The CON and HON novolaks relatively quickly build up a high concentration of quarternary ammonium complex, while PAN shows slower formation of the complex despite lower molecular weight than in CON novolak as shown in Fig. 16. Since the cation diffusion typically controls dissolution, polymer flexibility and microstructure exert a strong influence on cation diffusion rate. The effects of developer cations have also been studied by other workers [27,28].

Studies described above suggest that the dissolution behavior of novolak resins is quite important in developing positive photoresists. To understand the

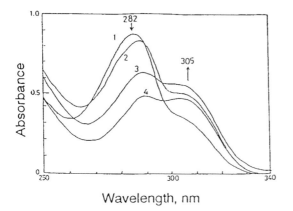

Wavelength, nm

Figure 13 UV absorption spectral change of hybrid pentamer (HP, see Fig. 15) film with development time with 0.262 N tetramethylammonium hydroxide solution. Development time: (1) 50 sec; (2) 100 sec, (3) 200 sec; (4) 500 sec. [From Ref. 26.]

dissolution mechanism, theoretical and experimental studies of dissolution behavior of phenolic resins have been made [28–34].

DNQ

Next we should consider the effect of chemical structures of DNQ inhibitors on resist performance. The effect should be investigated in correlation with novolak structures. DNQ compounds are usually synthesized by the esterification

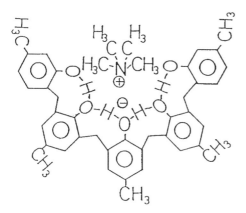

Figure 14 Schematic structure of tetramethylammonium ion complex of hybrid pentamer (HP, see Fig. 15). [From Ref. 26.]

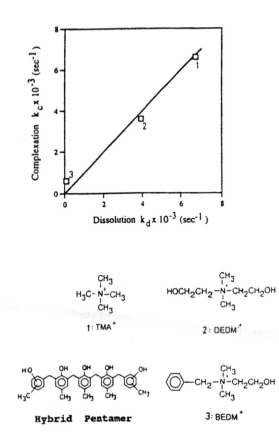

Figure 15 Correlation of cation complex formation rate to the dissolution rate with hybrid pentamer.

reaction of phenol compounds with DNQ sulfonyl chloride, and many DNQ-PACs are reported. Kishimura and co-workers [35] have reported on the dissolution inhibition effect of DNQ-PACs derived from polyhydroxybenzophenones and several *m*-cresol novolak resins. The number of DNQ moieties in the resist film and the average esterification value of DNQ-PACs were the same for each type of ballast molecule. The distance between DNQ moieties in the DNQ-PAC and the degree of dispersion of DNQ moieties in the resist film are important in enhancing the dissolution inhibition effect.

Tan et al. [36] of Fuji Photo Film described DNQ-sulfonyl esters of novel ballast compounds. The PAC structure was designed to minimize the background absorption at 365 nm and enable a resist formation to be optimized with low PAC loading. They proposed 3,3,3',3'-tetramethyl-1,1'-spiroindane-5,6,7,5',6',7'-hexol (Fig. 17) as a polyhydroxy ballast compound.

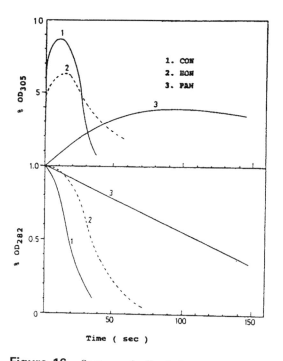

Figure 16 Spctroscopic dissolution rate monitoring (SDRM) curves of various types of novolak films in 0.262 N TMAH solution. (1) CON, a conventional *m*/*p*-cresol novolak; (2) HON, a high ortho-ortho *m*/*p*-cresol novolak made by polymerization of hybrid pentamer (HP, see Fig. 15) with *m*-cresol; (3) PAN, a novolak made from xylenol feedstock. [From Ref. 26.]

Nemoto et al. [37] of JSR investigated the effect of DNQ proximity and the hydrophobicity of a variety of trifunctional PACs on the dissolution characteristic of positive photoresist. They found that the new index $L \times RT$ is linearly related to dissolution inhibition for various novolak resins as shown in Fig. 18, where L is the average distance between DNQ groups in PAC molecules estimated by molecular arbital (MO) calculation and RT is the retention time in re-

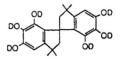

Figure 17 DNQ-PAC made from 3,3,3'3'-tetramethyl-1,1'-spiroindane-5,6,7,5',6',7'-hexol polyhydroxy ballast compound, where D is 2,1-diazonaphthoquinone-5-sulfonyl.

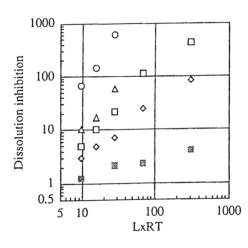

Figure 18   Influence of the resin structure on the relation between the dissolution inhibition and $L \times RT$ (see text). (○) 73MX35 novolak resin synthesized from 7/3 molar ratio of *m*-cresol to 3,5-xylenol; (△) 82MX35 novolak resin synthesized from 8/2 molar ratio of *m*-cresol to 3,5-xylenol; (□) 91MX35 novolak resin synthesized from 9/1 molar ratio of *m*-cresol to 3,5-xylenol; (◇) 100M novolak resin synthesized from *m*-cresol; (■) polyhydroxystyrene. [From Ref. 37.]

verse high-performance liquid chromatographic (HPLC) measurements. RT can be a measure of hydrophobicity of the PAC.

Similar results were reported by Uenishi et al. [38] of Fuji Photo Film. They used model backbones without hydroxy groups and fully esterified DNQ-PACs. The inhibition capability was found to be correlated with the retention time on reverse-phase HPLC, a measure of hydrophobicity, and with the distance of the DNQ moiety of DNQ-PACs.

The Fuji Photo Film group extended their investigation of PAC structure effects on dissolution behavior to include the effects of the number of unesterified OH groups of DNQ-PAC on image performance [39]. PACs generally lose their inhibition capability with increasing number of unesterified OH groups compared to fully esterified PACs, whereas certain particular PACs still remained strongly inhibiting even when an OH was left unesterified. Such PACs lost inhibition when one more OH was left unesterified (Fig. 19) and gave large dissolution discrimination upon exposure, which results in a high resolution resist. DNQ-PACs with steric crowding around OH groups seem to be the structural requirement in addition to hydrophobicity and remote DNQ configuration. The PAC provides good solubility in resist solvent. Hanawa et al. [40] also proposed PACs obtained by selective esterification of OH groups of ballast molecule with steric hindrance OH groups

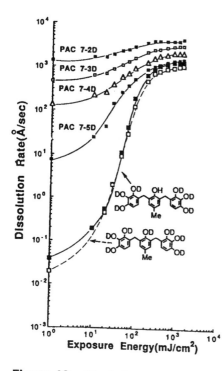

Figure 19 Dissolution rate change with exposure dose for DNQ-PAC with different esterifcation degree. [From Ref. 39.]

(Fig. 20) [41]. These PACs give higher sensitivity, γ-value, and resolution than those of fully esterified PACs. Hindered OH groups are effective for scum-free development.

Workers from IBM and Höchst-Celanese reported a DNQ-PAC derived from phenolphthalein that showed advantageous scumming behavior: even at high

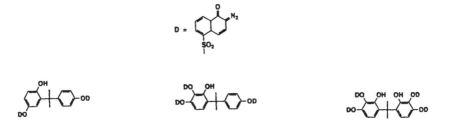

Figure 20 DNQ-PACs with steric hindrance OH groups obtained by selective esterification of OH groups with DNQ-sulfonylchlorides. [From Ref. 40.]

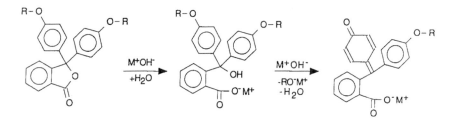

Scheme 4   Lactone ring opening during alkali development.

defocus, the patterns did not web or scum as is usually observed [42]. It may be due to a base-catalyzed hydrolysis of the lactone ring that leads to a more soluble photoproduct as shown in Scheme 4.

A polyphotolysis model [43] for DNQ resists stimulated study of PAC molecules. The model suggests that more DNQ groups in a single PAC molecule improve the resist contrast. Some results support the model but some does not. Hanawa et al. [40] reported that two DNQs in a PAC showed a contrast similar to that of three DNQs in a PAC. Uenishi et al. [39] also investigated the effect of number of DNQs in a single PAC and number of OH groups unesterified. Although the number of DNQs in a PAC is important for improving the contrast in some cases, it is not simple because the distance of DNQ groups and hydrophobicity of the PAC also affect the dissolution inhibition capability as described above.

2.3   Perspective of DNQ Resists

As described above, an enormous amount of data of novolak resins and DNQ compounds has been accumulated. Several models such as the stone wall model of the Sumitomo group, the host-guest model of the JSR, and the Octo-pus Pot model of OCG were proposed to explain the dissolution behavior of high-performance photoresists. There are some agreements and contradictions between them. Naphthalene sulfonyl groups play a major role in novolak dissolution inhibition for both reports by Honda et al. (OCG) [24] and Kajita et al. (JSR) [23]. It is generally accepted that high-ortho novolak shows high inhibition effect by DNQ-PAC. For base-induced reaction, Hanabata et al. (Sumitomo Chemical) [19] reported azo coupling, while Honda et al. [24] concluded that azo coupling cannot explain the high dissolution inhibition effect for high-ortho novolak. However, the models proposed above are instructive for understanding resist performance and giving clues for development of high-performance resists.

Table 1 shows a summary of the Sumitomo group's work on novolak resins. Although these results are impressive, they were obtained under cer-

Table 1 Effect of Five Factors of Novolak Resins on Dissolution Rates and Resist Performance: (0), Improvement; (x), Deterioration; (↑), Increase; (↓), Decrease; and (→), No Change

Factors	Disolution rate Unexposed (R_p)	Exposed (R_0)	R_pR_0 ratio	Sensitivity	Film thick. retention	Heat resist	Resolution
Molecular weight MW:↑	→ (0)	→ (x)	↑	→ (0)	← (0)	←	↑
Isomeric structure of cresol para:↑	→ (0)	→ (x)	← (0)	→ (x)	← (0)	← (0)	← (0)
Methylene bond position S_4:↑	→ (0)	↑	← (0)	↑	← (0)	→ (x)	← (0)
Molecular weight distribution M_w/M_n:↑	↓↑ (x)	← (0)	↑↓ (0)	↑↓ (0)	↑↓ (0)	↑↓ (0)	↑↓ (0)
NQD/novolak ratio:↑	→ (0)	(x)	← (0)	(x)	← (0)	← (0)	← (0)

tain conditions. For example, the S_4 effect was investigated for novolaks obtained from *m*-cresol. Therefore, the effects of *m/p*-cresol and molecular weight and molecular weight distribution were not given. Effects of combinations of various novolak resins and DNQ-PAC on resist performance were not fully understood. Further study of these effects may improve the resist performance.

3 CHEMICAL AMPLIFICATION RESIST SYSTEMS

Deep-UV lithography is one of several competing candidates for future lithography to obtain resolution below 0.30 μm. DNQ-based positive photoresists are not suitable for deep-UV lithography, due to both absorption and sensitivity. Absorption of both novolak resins and DNQ-PACs is high and does not bleach at around 250 nm, resulting in resist profiles with severely sloping sidewalls. Much attention has been focused on chemical amplification resist systems, especially for deep-UV lithography. These resits are advantageous because of high sensitivity, which is important because the light intensity of deep-UV exposure tools is lower than that of conventional i-line steppers.

In chemical amplified resist systems, a single photoevent initiates a cascade of subsequent chemical reactions. The resists are generally composed of an acid generator that produces acid upon exposure to radiation and acid-labile compounds or polymers that change the solubility in the developer by acid-catalyzed reactions. As shown in Fig. 21, the photogenerated acid catalyzes the chemical reactions that change the solubility in a developer. The change from insoluble to soluble is shown. The quantum yield for the acid-catalyzed reaction is the product of the quantum efficiency of acid generation multiplied by the catalytic chain length. In chemically amplified resists, acid generation is the only photochemical event. Therefore, it is possible to design the acid-labile base polymer with high transmittance in the deep-UV region. Since the small amount of acid can induce many chemical events, it is expected that yields of acid-catalyzed reaction along the film thickness can be alleviated even for a concentration gradient of photogenerated acid along the film thickness. Another important point about chemically amplified resist systems is the drastic polarity change by the acid-catalyzed reaction, which can avoid swelling during the development and give high contrast.

Many chemical amplification resist systems have been proposed since the report by the IBM group [44,45]. Most of these are based on acid-catalyzed reactions [46–51], althogh some with base-catalyzed reactions have been reported [52,53]. Here, acid generators and resists are classified by acid-catalyzed reaction and discussed.

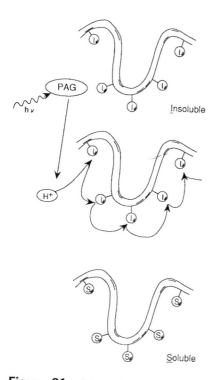

Figure 21 Schematic representatin of a positive chemically amplified resist.

3.1 Acid Generators

Onium Salts

Most well-known acid generators are onium salts such as iodonium and sulfonium salts, which were invented by Crivello [54]. The photochemistry of diaryl iodonium and triaryl sulfonium salts has been studied in detail by Hacker and Dektar [55–59]. The primary products formed upon irradiation of diphenyiodonium salts are iodobenzene, iodobiphenyl, acetanilide, benzene, and acid, as shown in Scheme 5 [55]. The reaction mechanism for product formation from diaryliodonium salts is shown in Scheme 6, where the bar indicates reaction in a cage. The mechanism for direct photolysis in solution can be described by three types of processes; in-cage reactions, cage-escape reactions, and termination reactions. The photolysis products are formed by heterolysis of diaryliodonium salts to phenyl cation and iodobenzene and also by homolysis to phenyl radical and iodobenzene radical cation. Direct photolysis favors product formation by a heterolytic cleavage pathway. In-cage recombination produces

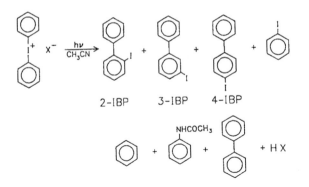

Scheme 5   Photoproducts from diphenyliodonium salts.

iodobiphenyl, while cage-escaped reaction produces iodobenzene, acetanilide, and benzene.

Direct photolysis of triphenyl sulfonium salts produces new rearrangement products: phenylthiobiphenyl, along with diphenylsulfide, as shown in Scheme 7 [56]. The reaction mechanism is shown in Scheme 8. The heterolytic cleavage gives phenyl cation and diphenyl sulfide, whereas homolytic cleavage gives te singlet phenyl radical and diphenylsulfinyl radical cation pair. These pairs of intermediates then produce the observed photoproducts by an in-cage recombination mechanism, leading to phenylthiobiphenyl. Diphenylsulfide is formed by direct photolysis in either an in-cage or a cage-escape reaction. Other products are formed by cage-escape or termination reactions.

The difference in photolysis of onium salts in the solid state and in solution has been studied from the viewpoint of cage and cage-escape reactions [58]. Photolysis of triphenylsulfonium salts in the solid state shows a remarkable

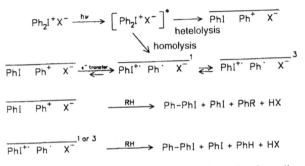

Scheme 6   Mechanism of product formation from direct photolysis of diphenyliodonium salts. The bars indicate in-cage reactions.

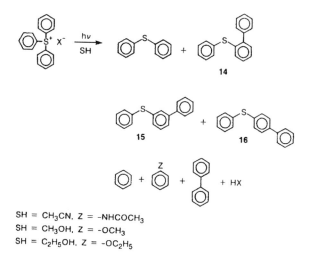

SH = CH₃CN, Z = -NHCOCH₃
SH = CH₃OH, Z = -OCH₃
SH = C₂H₅OH, Z = -OC₂H₅

Scheme 7 Photoproducts from direct irradiation of triphenylsulfonium salts.

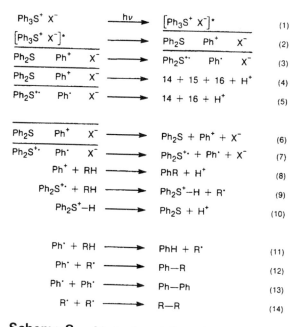

Scheme 8 Mechanism of direct photolysis of triphenylsulfonium salts. The bars indicate in-cage reactions.

counterion dependence and a cage/escape ratio as high as 5:1 is observed, while the ratio in solution is about 1:1. In the solid state, a cage-escape reaction with solvent and termination processes involving solvent cannot occur. Since the environment is rigid, in-cage recombination processes are favored. Thus for the nonnucleophilic MF_n (PF_6, AsF_6, SbF_6, etc.) and triflate anions ($CF_3SO_3^-$), the in-cage recombination to give phenylthiobiphenyls predominates.

Photolysis of onium salts in polymer matrix, poly(*t*-butoxycarbonyloxy-styrene) (tBOC-PHS), was studied [59]. Environments with limited diffusion favor the recombination reaction to yield in-cage products. tBOC-PHS films are such an environment, but there are fewer in-cage products than expected. This can be explained if sensitization of an onium salt by excited tBOC-PHS occurs.

Mckean et al. [60,61] measured the acid generation efficiency in several polymer matrices using the dye titration method. The quantum yield from triphenylsulfonium salts in poly(4-butoxycarbonyloxystyrene) (PtBOC-PHS) is lower than that in solution. The acid generation efficiency from triphenylsulfonium salts in polystyrene, poly(4-vinylanisole), and poly(methyl methacrylate) was measured. They pointed out that the compatibility of sulfonium salts and the polymer matrix with respect to polarity effects the acid generation efficiency.

Halogen Compounds

Halogen compounds such as tricholoromethyl-*s*-triazene have been known as free radical initiators for photopolymerization [46,62]. These halogen compounds were also used as acid generators for an acid-catalyzed solubilization composition [63]. Homolytic cleavage of the carbon-halogen bond produces a halogen atom radical followed by hydrogen abstraction, resulting in the formation of hydrogen halide acid, as shown in Scheme 9 [64].

Calbrese et al. [65] found that the halogenated acid generator, 1,3,5-tris(2,3-dibromopropyl)-1,3,5-triazine-(1*H*,3*H*,5*H*)trione, could be effectively sensitized to 365 and 436 nm using electron-rich sensitizers. They proposed a mechanism for sensitization involving electron transfer from excited sensitizer to photoacid generators in these systems (Scheme 10). The energetics of electron transfer are described by Eq. 1:

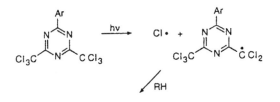

Scheme 9   Mechanism of acid formation from trichloromethyl triazene.

(1) $\qquad$ SH $\xrightarrow{h\nu}$ SH*

(2) $\qquad$ SH* + RX $\longrightarrow$ SH$^{+\cdot}$ + RX$^{-\cdot}$

(3) $\qquad$ $\begin{cases} \text{RX}^{-\cdot} \longrightarrow \text{R}^{\cdot} + \text{X}^{-} \\ \text{SH}^{+\cdot} \longrightarrow \text{S}^{\cdot} + \text{H}^{+} \end{cases}$

Scheme 10 Acid formation mechanism from halogen compounds via electron transfer reaction.

$$\Delta G = E(\text{SH}/\text{SH}^{+\cdot}) - E(\text{RX}^{-}\cdot/\text{RX}) - E_{00}(\text{SH}-\text{SH}^*) - C \qquad (1)$$

in which ΔG is the free enthalpy, $E(\text{SH}/\text{SH}^{+\cdot})$ is the energy required to oxidize the sensitizer, $E(\text{RX}^{-}/\text{RX})$ is the energy required to reduce the acid generator, $E_{00}(\text{SH-SH}^*)$ is the electronic energy difference between the ground state and excited state sensitizer, and C is te coulomb interaction of the ion pair produced. Electrochemical redox potentials and spectroscopic data support this mechanism [65]. Based on similar data for *p*-cresol as a model for phenolic resins in these resists, light absorbed by the resin when such resists are exposed to deep UV may contribute to the sensitivity via electron transfer from the resin to brominated isocyanate to produce an acid.

o-Nitrobenzyl Esters

Houlihan and co-workers [66] have described acid generators based on 2-nitrobenzylsulfonic acid esters. As shown in Scheme 11, the mechanism of the

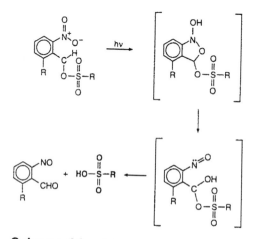

Scheme 11 Mechanism of acid formation from *o*-nitrobenzyl esters.

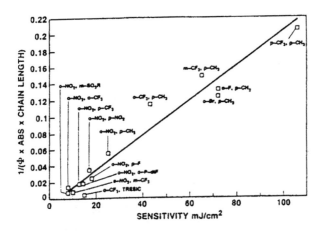

Figure 22 Plot of the lithographic sensitivity versus $1/(\Phi \times$ catalytic chain length $\times$ ABS/μm). Φ is the quantum yield of acid generation, ABS absorbance of the resist film.

photoreaction of nitrobenzyl ester involves insertion of an excited nitro group oxygen into a benzylic carbon-hydrogen bond. Subsequent rearrangement and cleavage generate nitrosobenzaldehyde and sulfonic acid. They also made a study of thermal stability and acid generation efficiency on varying the substituents on 2-nitrobenzylbenzenesulfonates [67,68]. A plot of the reciprocal of quantum yield of acid generation, catalytic chain length, and absorbance per micrometer was made versus sensitivity (Fig. 22) A reasonably linear plot over the whole range of esters is obtained, indicating that three basic parameters in Fig. 22 determine the resist sensitivity [68].

p-Nitrobenzyl Esters

Yamaoka and co-workers [69] have described *p*-nitrobenzylsulfonic acid esters such as *p*-nitrobenzyl-9,10-diethoxyanthracene-2-sulfonate as a bleachable acid precursor. Photodissociation of the *p*-nitrobenzyl ester proceeds via intramolecular electron transfer from the excited singlet state of the 9,10-diethoxyanthracene moiety to the *p*-nitrobenzyl moiety followed by heterolytic bond cleavage at the oxygen-carbon bond of the sulfonyl ester as shown in Scheme 12, where dimethoxyanthracene-2-sulfonate is described. This mechanism was supported by the fact that the transiwnt absorption assigned to dimethoxyanthracene-2-sulfonate radical cation and nitrobenzyl radical anion are detected in laser spectroscopy [70].

Alkylsulfonates

Ueno et al. have shown that tris(alkylsulfonyloxy)benzene can act as a photoacid generator upon deep-UV [71] and electron beam irradiation. [72] Schlegel et al. [73] found that 1,2,3-tris(methanesulfonyloxy)benzene (MeSB) gives a high

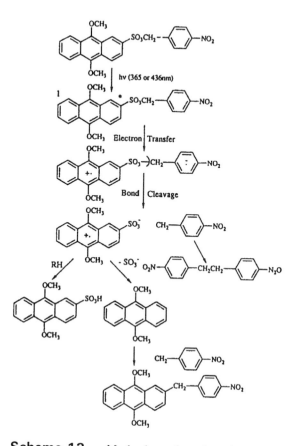

Scheme 12   Mechanism of product formation from direct photolysis of *p*-nitrobenzyl-8,10-dimethoxyanthracene-2 sulfonate.

quantum yield (number of acid moieties generated per photon absorbed in a resist film) when utilized in a novolak resin. The quantum yield would be more than 10 when calculated on the basis of the number of photons absorbed only by the sulfonate. This strikingly high quantum efficiency can be explained in terms of the sensitization mechanism from excited novolak resin to the sulfonates, presumably via electron transfer reaction as shown in Scheme 13 [74].

This mechanism was supposed by the following model experiment. When tBOC-BA is deprotected with a photogeneraed acid in the resist composed of bisphenol A protected with *t*-butoxycarbonyl (tBOC-BA), cellulose acetate as a base polmyer, and MeSB, absorbance at 282 nm increases due to bisphenol A formation, which can be used as a "detector" for the acid-catalyzed reaction. Since cellulose acetate shows no absorption at the exposure wavelength (248 nm), there

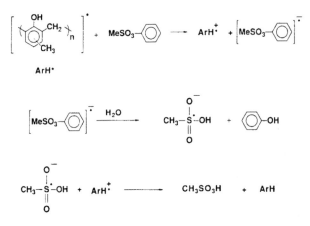

Scheme 13   Mechanism of sulfonic acid generation from alkylsulfonates by electron transfer reaction.

is no possibility of sensitization from excited polymer to MeSB, leading to negligible change of absorbance at 248 nm. On the contrary, when trimethylphenol (TMP) as a model compound of a novolak resin was added to the system, the deprotection reaction proceeded; the absorbance at 282 nm increased with exposure time as well as content of TMP as shown in Fig. 23. In addition, it was found that spectral sensitivity resembles that of the absorption spectra of novolak resin (Fig. 24), indicating sensitization by novolak resin. The effect of chemical structure on acid generation efficiency has been measured for various alkylsulfonates of pyrogallol backbone (Fig. 25), and methanesulfonates of mono-, di-, and trihydroxybenzenes and their isomers [75]. The difference in number of sulfonyl groups per benzene ring may affect the reduction potential or electron affinity of sulfonates, leading to a change in rates of electron transfer reactions. The quantum yield for sulfonates is higher for smaller alkyl size. The acid generation efficiency is higher for methanesulfonates derived from trihydroxybenzenes than those from dihydroxybenzene and monohydrozybenzene derivatives.

α-Hydroxymethylbenzoin Sulfonic Acid Esters

Röchert et al. [76] described α-hydroxymethylbenzoin sulfonic acid esters as photoacid generators. Irradiation of the sulfonic acid ester to an excited triplet state leads to fragmentation via an α-cleavage (Norrish type I) into two radical intermediates as shown in Scheme 14 [76,77]. The bonzoyl radical is stabilized via H abstraction to yield a (substituted) benzylaldehyde almost quantitatively. The second radical intermediate is stabilized via cleavage of the carbon-oxygen bond, which is linked to the sulfonyl moiety ($-CH_2-OSO_2-$) and forms the respective acetophenone and sulfonic acid. The photoacid generating efficiency

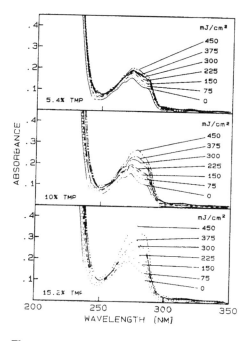

Figure 23 Absorption spectra of resists MeSB/TMP/tBOC-BA/CA = 5/x/15/80-x (weight ratio) after a sequence coating-exposure-baking 80°C/10 minutes with different exposure doses. MeSB, 1,2,3-tris(methanesulfonyloxy)benzene; TMP, trimethylphenol; tBOC-BA, bisphenol A protected with t-butoxycarbonyl; CA, cellulose acetate. Film thickness ~1.5 μm.

of this type of sulfonate is compared with those of bis(arylsufonyl)diazomethane (BAS-DM), 1,2,3-tris(methanesulfonyloxy)benzene (MeSB) and 2,1-diazonaphthoquinone-4-sulfonate (4-DNQ) using the tetrabromophenol blue indicator technique. The order of acid generating efficiency is BAS-DM > α-hydroxymethylbenzoin sulfonic acid esters ~ MeSB > 4-DNQ.

α-Sulfonyloxyketones

α-Sulfonyloxyketones were reproted to be acid generators in chemical amplification resist systems by Onishi et al. [78] The photochemistry of α-sulfonyl-oxyketones is shown in Scheme 15 [79]. *p*-Toluenesulfonic acid is liberated after photoreduction.

Diazonaphthoquinone-4-sulfonate (4-DNQ)

1,2-Diazonaphthoquinone-4-sulfonate can be used as an acid generator [80–82]. The photochemistry of 1,2-diazonaphthoquinone-4-sulfonate shown in Scheme 16 was proposed by Buhr et al. [80]. It is expected that the reaction follows its classical pathway starting from diazonaphthoquinone via the Wolff-rearranged

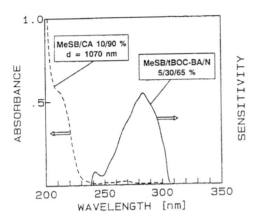

Figure 24 Solid line: spectral sensitivity curves of the resist MeSB/tBOC-BA/ novolak in the deep-UV region. The ordinate scale corresponds to logarithmic decrease of dose values. dotted line: absorption spectrum of MeSB in cellulose film.

ketene to the indene carboxylic acid. In polar media, possibly with proton catalysis, the phenol ester moiety can be elimiated, leading to sulfene, which adds water to generate the sulfonic acid. This reaction mechanism was also supported by Vollenbroek et al. [10]. 4-DNQ acid generators were used for acid-catalyzed crosslinking of image reversal resists [80,81] and for an acid-catalyzed deprotection reaction [82].

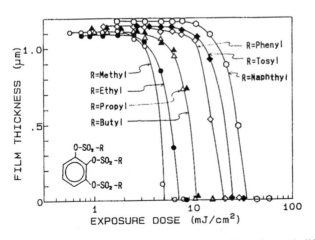

Figure 25 Exposure characteristic curves for resists with different sulfones. Novolak resin/tBOC-BA/a sulfonate = 100/13.3/1.65 (mol ratio).

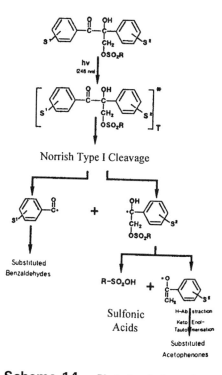

Norrish Type I Cleavage

Substituted
Benzaldehydes

R-SO₂OH

Sulfonic
Acids

Substituted
Acetophenones

Scheme 14   Photochemical reaction mechanism of α-hydroxymethylbenzoin sulfonic acid esters.

Iminosulfonates

Iminosulfonates, which produce sulfonic acids upon irradiation, are generally synthesized from a sulfonyl chloride and an oxime derived from ketones. Shirai and co-workers [83,84] proposed the reaction mechanism (Scheme 17). On irradiation with UV light the cleavage of -O-N = bonds of iminosulfonates and the subsequent abstraction of hydrogen atoms led to the formation of sulfonic acids accompanying the formation of azines, ketones, and ammonia.

N-Hydroxyimidesulfonates

The photodecomposition of *N*-tosylphthalimide (PTS) [85] to give an acid is outlined in Scheme 18 [86,87]. Irradiation to deep-UV light leads to homolytic cleavage of the N-O bond, giving a radical pair. The pair can either collapse to regenerate the starting PTS or undergo cage escape. Hydrogen abstraction from the polymeric matrix by the toluenesulfonyl radical gives toluenesulfonic acid. An alternative mechanism involves electron transfer from the excited state polymer or other aromatic species to PTS to form a radical cation–radical anion

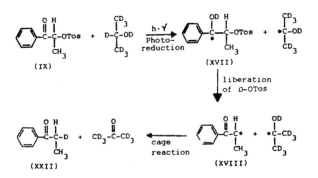

Scheme 15   Photochemical reaction mechanism of α-sulfonyloxy ketones.

pair. The PTS radical anion will be protonated, followed by decomposing homolytically to give toluenesulfonatyl radical. As in the mechanism for direct
photolysis, the sulfonatyl radical abstracts a hydrogen atom from the medium
to give a protic acid.

α,α'-Bisarylsulfonyl Diazomethanes

Pawlowski and co-workers [88] have reported the nonionic acid generators
α,α'-bisarylsulfonyl diazomethanes, which generate sulfonic acids upon deep-
UV irradiation. They analyzed photochemical products of α,α'-bis(4-*t*-
butylphenylsulfonyl) diazomethane in acetronitrile-water solution using HPLC
and proposed the photochemical reaction mechanism shown in Scheme 19
[88,89]. The mechanism of acid generation is that the intermediate carbene
formed during photolytic cleavage of nitrogen rearranges to a highly reactive
sulfene, which then adds water present in the solvent mixture to give the
sulfonic acid (8a). The main product is 4-*t*-butylphenyl thiosulfonic acid

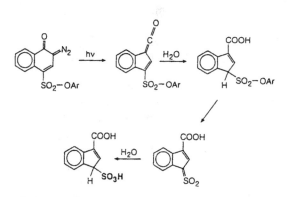

Scheme 16   Sulfonic acid formation from direct photolysis of DNQ-4-sulfonates.

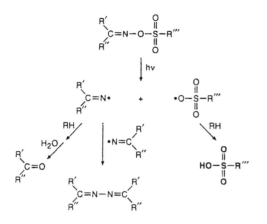

Scheme 17   Photochemistry of iminosulfonates.

4-*t*-butylphenyl ester (4a), probably formed via elimination of nitrogen and carbon dioxide from the parent compound. Although 4a does not contribute to the acid-catalyzed reaction, it is known that thiosulfonic acid esters undergo a thermally induced acid- or base-catalyzed decomposition reaction to yield the respective disulfones and sulfinic acids.

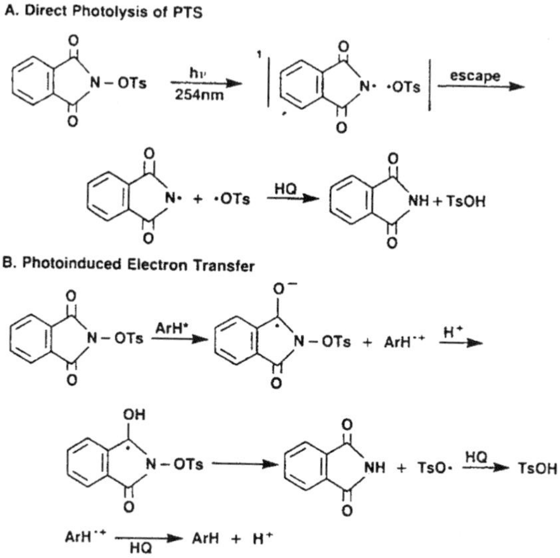

A. Direct Photolysis of PTS

B. Photoinduced Electron Transfer

Scheme 18   Mechanism of sulfonic acid formation from photolysis of *N*-hydroxy-imidesulfonates.

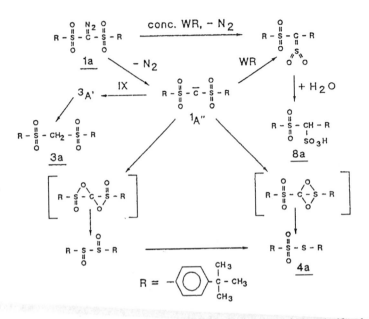

Scheme 19   Photodecomposition mechanism of α,α'-bisarylsulfonyl diazomethanes.

Disulfones

The reaction mechanism for disulfones is shown in Scheme 20 [90]. Homolytic cleavage of the S-S bond is followed by hydrogen abstraction, yielding two equivalents of sulfinic acid. Quantum yield of the photolysis of disulfone compounds in THF solution were determined to be in the range of 0.2 to 0.6 depending on chemical structures.

3.2   Acid-Catalyzed Reaction

Deprotection Reaction

Protection of reactive groups is a general method in synthesis [91]. There are several protecting groups for the hydroxy group of polyhydroxystyrene.

tBOC Group.   The IBM group has reported resist systems based on acid-catalyzed thermolysis of the side-chain *tert*-butoxycarbonyl (tBOC) protecting group [44]. A resist formualted with poly(*p-t*-butoxycarbonyloxystyrene) (tBOC-PHS) and an onium salt as a photoacid generator has been described [44,45]. The acid produced by photolysis of an onium salt catalyzes acidolysis of the tBOC group, which converts tBOC-PHS to poly(hydroxystyrene) (PHS) as shown in Scheme 21. Since the photogenerated acid is not con-

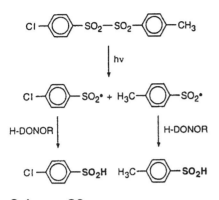

Scheme 20 Photodecomposition mechanism of disulfones.

sumed in the deprotection reaction, it serves only as a catalyst. This system is called chemical amplification.

The exposed part is converted to polar polymer, which is soluble in polar solvents such as alcohols or aqueous base, whereas the unexposed area remains nonpolar. This large difference in polarity between exposed and unexposed areas gives a large dissolution contrast in the developer, which also allows negative or positive images depending on the developer polarity. Development with a polar solvent selectively dissolves the exposed area to give a positive tone image. Development with a nonpolar solvent dissolves the unexposed area to give a negative tone image. Since this resist is based on the polarity change, there is no evidence of the swelling that is present in resists of the gel forma-

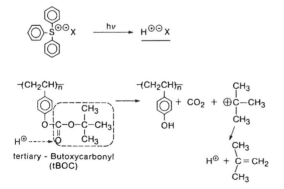

Scheme 21 Chemically amplified resist using acid-catalyzed tBOC deprotection reaction.

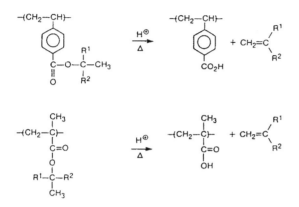

Scheme 22   Acid-catalyced deprotection ($A_{AL}-1$ acidolysis) for polarity change.

tion such as cyclized rubber-based negative resists. The swelling phenomena cause pattern deformation and result in limited resolution.

Since the tertiary butyl ester group is sensitive to $A_{AL}1$-type hydrolysis (acid-catalyzed unimolecular alkyl cleavage) [92] in a reaction that does not require a stoichiometric amount of water, reactions related to the *t*-butyl group described in Scheme 22 have been reported to apply to resist systems [93].

Workers at AT&T proposed a series of copolymers of *tert*-butoxycarbonyloxystyrene and sulfur dioxide prepared by radical polymerization [94]. The sulfone formulation exhibits both improved sensitivity and high contrast. It is expected that chain degradation of the matrix polymer results in a chemically amplified resist with improved sensitivity. They also prepared a new terpolymer, poly[(*tert*-butoxycarbonyloxy)styrene-co-acetoxystyrene-co-sulfone] and found that the acetoxy group can be cleaved from acetoxystyrene monomer in aqueous base solution as shown in Scheme 23 [95]. This cleavage occurs only when sulfone is incorporated into the copolymer in the appropriate amounts. It is expected that this base-catalyzed cleavage during development enhances the solubility of the exposed area where the tBOC group is removed by acid. Incorporation of 50 wt. % acetoxystyrene into the polymer reduces the weight loss ~18% in the sold film, while poly[(*tert*-butoxycarbonyloxy)styrene sulfone] shows 40% loss. The reduction of weight loss is advantageous for adhesion.

A disadvantage of onium salts such as diaryliodonium and triarylsulfonium salts is strong dissolution inhibition for alkali development. In order to improve the solubility of onium salts into the developer, Schwalm [96] proposed a unique photoacid generator that completely converts to phenolic products upon irradiation as shown in Scheme 24. They synthesized sulfonium salts containing acid-labile tBOC protecting group in the same molecule. After irradiation, unchanged

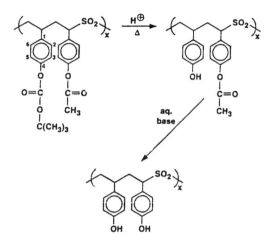

Scheme 23   Acid-catalyzed deprotection reaction during postexposure baking and base-catalyzed cleavage during development.

hydrophobic initiator and hydrophobic photoproducts are formed besides the acid, but upon thermal treatment acid-catalyzed reaction converts all these compounds to phenolic products, resulting in enhanced solubility in aqueous base.

Kawai et al. [97] described a chemically amplified resist composed of partially tBOC-protected monodisperse PHS as a base polymer and tBOC-protected

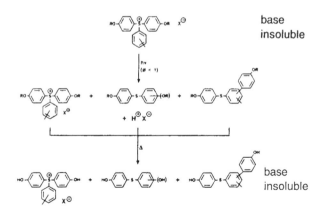

R =   acid labile group

Scheme 24   Reaction mechanism of tBOC-protected acid generator.

bisphenol A as a dissolution inhibitor and a photoacid generator. They reported that the use of monodisperse polymer and optimization of tBOC protection degree improved resolution capability and surface inhibition.

Three component resists using tBOC-protected compounds as dissolution inhibitors in combination with a photoacid generator and a phenolic resin have been reported by several groups [98–101]. Aoai et al. [102] studied systematically the effect of the chemical structures of the backbone of tBOC compounds on dissolution inhibition capability Similar chemical structural effects are observed as reported in DNQ compounds. The tBOC compounds with a large distance between tBOC groups and high hydrophobicity show a high dissolution inhibition effect.

Workers at Toshiba [103], Nihon Kayaku [104], and NTT [105] reported 1-(3*H*)-isobenzofuranone derivatives protected with tBOC as a new type of dissolution inhibitor. The concept of this resist system is shown in Fig. 26. These inhibitors decomposed by acid-catalyzed thermal reaction. In addition, the lactone rings of the decomposed products were cleaved by base-catalyzed reaction in the developer, which may enhance the dissolution rate of exposed area.

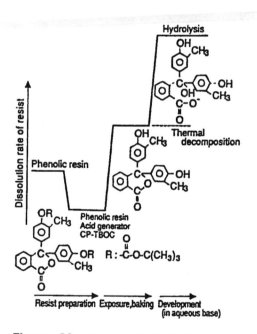

Figure 26 Concept of dissolution rate enhancement during development. tBOC compounds that show dissolution inhibition are deprotected by acid-catalyzed reaction. The deprotected compounds with lactone ring are cleaved by base-catalyzed reaction during development, leading to dissolution enhancement of the exposed region.

THP Group. The tetrahydropyranyl (THP) group can be used as a protecting group of PHS [63,106]. The deprotection reaction of the THP group has been investigated in detail by Sakamizu et al. [107]. The proposed mechanism is shown in Scheme 25. A proton first attacks the phenolic oxygen to produce PHS and a carbocation 1. This carbocation 1 can react with water from the atmosphere or trapped in novolak to give 2-hydroxytetrahydropyran or lose a proton to give 3,4-hydropyran. 2-Hydroxy tetrahydropyran is a hemiacetal and is in equilibrium with 5-hydroxypentanal.

A fully THP protected PHS (THP-M) suffered from poor developability in aqueous base when THP-M was used as a base polymer. The effect of the deprotection degree on dissolution rate was investigated by Hattori et al. [108]. As shown in Fig. 27, 30% protection was enough for negligible dissolution for alkali development. It should be noted that deprotection from 100% to 30% cannot induce a change in dissolution in 2.38% tetramethylammonium hydroxide solution. Optimization of the protection degree can provide alkali-developable two-component resists for KrF lithography (Fig. 28). As shown in Fig. 29, it is difficult to deprotect THP groups completely for both high (92%) and low (20%) protection with THP-M. It should be noted that 20% THP-protecteed THP-M gives a product of lower protected degree at the fully exposed region than 92% THP-protected THP-M. Therefore, it is expected that THP-M with a low degree of protection reduces the surface inhibition due to a high yield of alkali-soluble hydroxy groups.

Other polymers incorporating the THP protecting group have been reported. Taylor et al. [109] evaluated copolymers of benzyl methacrylate and tetrahydropyranyl methacrylate as deep-UV resists. Kikuchi and co-workers [110] described copolymers of styrene and tetrahydropyranyl methacrylate. Terpolymers of *N*-hydroxybenzyl methacrylamide, tetrahydropyranyloxystyrene, and acrylic

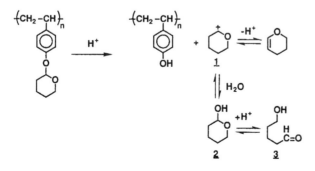

Scheme 25   Acid-catalyzed deprotection reaction of tetrahydropyranyl-protected polyhydroxystyrene (THP-M).

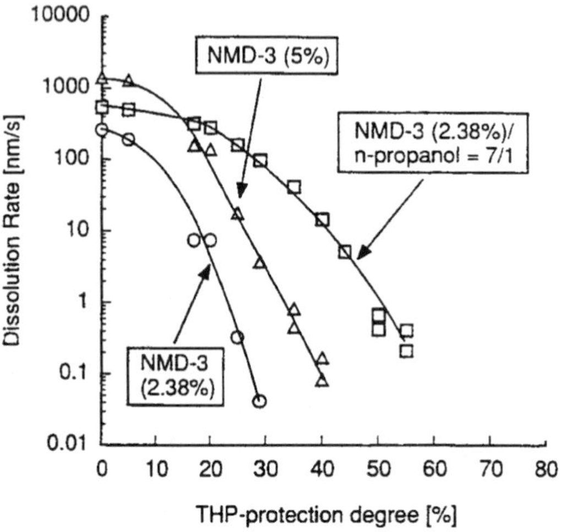

NMD-3 (5%)

NMD-3 (2.38%)/
n-propanol = 7/1

NMD-3
(2.38%)

Dissolution Rate [nm/s]

THP-protection degree [%]

Figure 27   Dissolution rate of THP (tetrahydropyranyl)-protected polyhydroxysty-rene, THP-M as a function of THP protection degree for various developers. NMD, tetra-methylammonium hydroxide aqueous solution.

acid were applied to deep-UV resists, which showed good adhesion to silicon substrates and high glass transition temperatures [111].

Trimethylsilyl Group.   Early work on the trimethylsilyl group as a protecting group was done by Cunningham and Park [112]. Yamaoka et al. [113] made preliminary experiments on the rate of acid-catalyzed hydrolysis for a series of

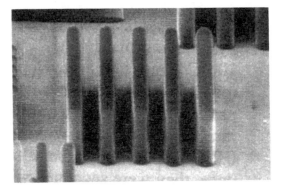

Figure 28   Line and space patterns of 0.3 μm using a resist composed of partially THP-protected polyhydroxystyrene (THP-M) and an onium salt.

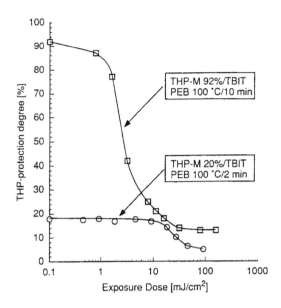

THP-M 92%/TBIT
PEB 100 °C/10 min

THP-M 20%/TBIT
PEB 100 °C/2 min

Figure 29 Change in THP protection degree with exposure dose for THP-Ms of low protection degree (20%) and high protection degree (92%). The deprotection degree was determined by IR after postexposure baking.

alkylsilylated and arylsilylated phenols. The order of the rate is shown in Fig. 30. It is likely that the rate of hydrolysis is governed by the steric hindrance of the trisubstituted silyl group rather by an electronic induction effect, because no obvious correlation between the rate of the hydrolysis and Hammet's values of the silylating substituents is observed. Among the silylating substituents studied, trimethylsilyl group was chosen as a protecting group for polyhydroxystyrene (PHS) because of high rate of hydrolysis and good stability, and the highest rate of hydrolysis was obtained for dimethylsilyl group. They reported a resist using trimethylsilyl-protected PHS combined with *p*-nitrobenzylsulfonate as an acid generator [114].

Phenoxyethyl Group. Phenoxyethyl was proposed as a protecting group of PHS by Jiang and Bassett [115]. As shown in Scheme 26, phenol is produced from the protection group via acid-catalyzed cleavage as well as production of PHS. Since phenol is very soluble in aqueous base, it acts as a dissolution promoter in exposed areas. In addition, phenol is not volatile under lithographic conditions, resulting in smaller film thickness loss than with the tBOC system.

Cyclohexenyl Group. Poly[4-(2-cyclohexenyloxy)-3,5-dimethylstyrene] has been prepared for a dual tone imaging system [116]. Poly[4-(2-cyclohexenyloxy)

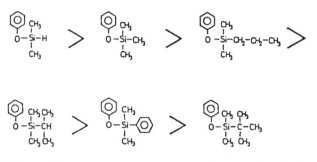

Figure 30   Order of acid-catalyzed hydrolysis rates for alkyl- and arylsilylated phenols.

styrene] is less attractive due to the occurrence of some Claisen rearrangement and of other side reactions as shown in Scheme 27. On the contrary the polymer with ortho position methylation is deprotected easily due to limiation of the side reaction by blocking the reaction site.

t-Butoxycarbonylmethyl Group.   It is generally accepted that carboxylic acid shows higher dissolution promotion than the hydroxy group of phenol. It is expected that the deprotected polymer containing carboxylic acid acts as a dissolution accelerator in aqueous base. However, poly(vinylbenzoic acid) shows high absorbance at 248 nm. To avoid strong absorption of the benzoyl group, Onishi et al. [118] reported partially *t*-butoxycarbonylmethyl-protected PHS, which involves a methylene group between phenyl and carboxylic acid. The reaction mechanism is shown in Scheme 28. Another advantage is that *t*-butoxycarbonylmethyl-protected PHS gave no phase separation after development in film, which is encountered in tBOC-protected PHS.

Depolymerization

Polyphthalaldehyde (PPA).   Ito and Willson [119] reported acid-catalyzed depolymerization of polyaldehydes as a first stage of chemical amplificatioin resists. Polyphthalaldehyde is classified as O,O-acetal, which will be described later. The polymerization of polyaldehyde is known to be an equilibrium

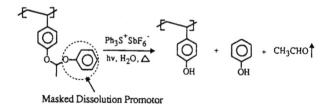

Masked Dissolution Promotor

Scheme 26   Acid-catalyzed reaction of poly(4-(1-phenoxyethoxy)styrene).

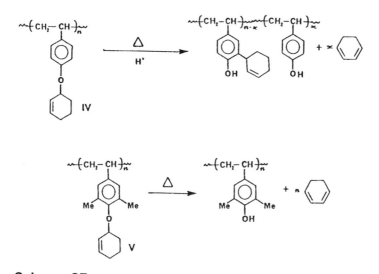

Scheme 27 Acid-catalyzed reaction of cyclohexyl-protected polyhydroxystyrene and methyl-substituted polyhydroxystyrene.

process of quite low ceiling temperature (T_c). Above T_c the monomer is more stable thermodynamically than its polymer. During polymerization at low temperature, end capping by alkylation or acylation terminates the equilibrium process and renders the polymer stable at about 200°C. Although polymers of aliphatic aldehydes are highly crystalline substances that are not soluble in common organic solvents, polyphthalaldehyde (PPA) provides noncrystalline materials that are high soluble and can be coated to provide clear isotropic films of high quality. The T_c of PPA is about –40°C. The resist composed of PPA and an onium salt can give positive tone images without subsequent processes. This is called self-development imaging. As shown in Scheme 29, the acid generated from onium salts catalyzes the cleavage of the main chain acetal bond. Once the bond is cleaved above the ceiling temperature, the materials spontaneously

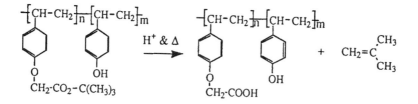

Scheme 28 Chemical structure of BCM-PHS and its acid-catalyzed thermolysis.

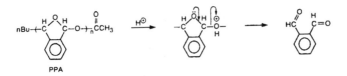

Scheme 29   Acid-catalyzed depolymerization of polyphthalaldehyde.

depolymerize to monomers. PPA can be used as a dissolution inhibitor of no-volak resin in a three-component system. The photogenerated acid induces de-polymerization of PPA, resulting in loss of dissolution inhibition capability to give a positive image.

Although PPA materials are sensitive self-developing resists, they have drawbacks such as liberation during exposure of volatile materials that could damage the optics of exposure tools and poor dry-etching resistance. Ito et al. [120,121] found that poly(4-chlorophthalaldehyde) does not spontaneously de-polymerize upon exposure to radiation but requires a postexposure bake step to obtain a positive relief image, which can avoid damage to optics. This system is called thermal development, as distinguished from self-development.

O,O- and N,O-acetals.   Workers at Höchst AG reported three-component chemical amplification resist systems, using acid-catalyzed depolymerization of *O,O-* and *N,O-*acetals [122,123]. The reaction mechanism is shown in Schemes 30 and 31, respectively. Poly-*N,O-*acetal is protonated at the oxygen atom and liberates an alcohol, XOH. The intermediate formation of a carbocation is the rate-limiting step in hydrolysis and its stability is influenced by mesomeric and inductive effects of the substituents R_1 and R_2. It is noteworthy that the libera-

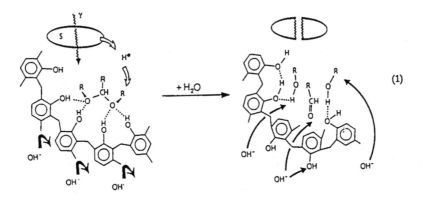

Scheme 30   Acid-catalyzed depolymerization of acetals leading to their loss of dissolution inhibition capability.

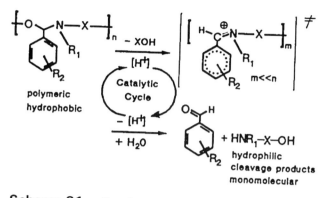

Scheme 31 Reaction mechanism of acid-catalyzed *N,O*-actal hydrolysis.

tion of XOH causes a decrease in molecular weight of an inhibitor and that cleavage products like alcohols and aldehydes show strong dissolution promotion. Since the novolak resin suffers from strong absorption at 248 nm, they developed methylated polyhydroxystyrene, poly(4-hydroxystyene-co-3-methyl-4-hydroxystyrene), as a base resin that shows a reasonable dissolution inhibition effect [124–126].

Polysilylether. The silicon polymer containing silylether groups in the main chain is hydrolyzed by acid and degraded to low-molecular-weight compounds [127,128]. This polymer can be used as a dissolution inhibitor of a novolak resin in a three-component system. As shown in Scheme 32, the decomposition of the polymer includes protonation of oxygen, a nucleophilic attack of water to the Si atom, the cleavage of the Si-O bond, and reproduction of the proton, resulting in depolymerization and loss of inhibition capability. Investigation of the effect of chemical structure around silylether groups in the polymer on the hydrolysis rate indicated that the rate decreases with increasing bulkiness of alkyl group and alkoxy groups.

Polycarbonate and Others. Fréchet et al. [129–134] have designed, prepared, and tested dozens of new imaging materials based on polycarbonates, polyethers, and polyesters that are all susceptible to acid-catalyzed depolymerization. The reaction mechanism of polycarbonates is E_1-like elimination, shown in Scheme 33. The protonation of the carbonyl group of a carbonate is followed by cleavage of the adjacent allylic carbon-oxygen bond to produce two fragments: a fragment containing a monoester of carboxylic acid, 2a, and another containing an allylic carbocation moiety, 2c. Elimination of a proton from this carbocationic moiety results in regeneration of the acid catalyst and formation of terminal diene-containing fragment 2b. The unstable monoester of carbonic acid, 2a, decarboxylates, releasing a terminal alcohol fragment, 2d. The process continues at

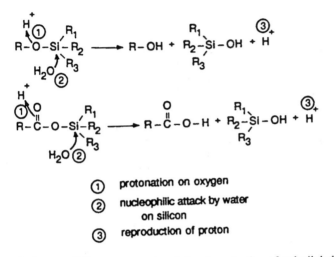

① protonation on oxygen
② nucleophilic attack by water
   on silicon
③ reproduction of proton

Scheme 32   Acid-catalyzed depolymerization of polysilylethers.

other carbonate sites with complete breakdown of the polymer chain resulting in eventual release of benzene, additional carbon dioxide, and a diol. The protons initially generated by irradiation are not consumed in the process.

Crosslinking and Condensation

Acid Hardening of Melamine Derivatives.   Negative tone resists based on acid-hardenig resin (AHR) chemistry are three-component systems composed of a novolak resin, a melamine crosslinking agent, and a radiation-sensitive acid generator [135–138]. The reaction leading to decrease in dissolution rate in alkali aqueous solution via crosslinking is shown in Scheme 34. The protonated

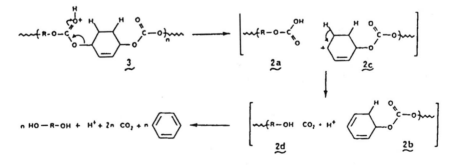

Scheme 33   Acid-catalyzed depolymerization of polycarbonates.

ACID GENERATION STEP:

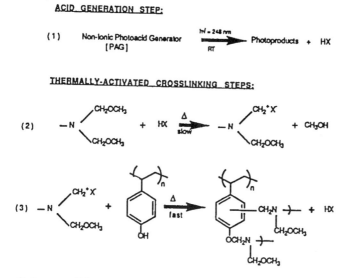

Scheme 34 Acid hardening mechanism in phenolic resins.

melamine liberates a molecule of alcohol upon heating to leave a nitrogen-stabilized carbonium ion. Alkylation of novolak then occurs at either the phenolic oxygen (O-alkylation) or a carbon on the aromatic ring (C-alkylation) and a proton is regenerated. There are several reactive sites on the melamine, allowing it to react more than once per molecule to give crosslinked polymer. The difference in dissolution rate between exposed and unexposed is quite high as reported by Liu et al. [139]. The acid-hardening type resists have been widely evaluated as resists for deep-UV and electron beam lithography. Effects of molecular weight and molecular weight distribution of base resins, such as novolak or PHS, have been investigated [140–142].

Electrophilic Aromatic Substitution. Fréchet et al. [143–148] applied another acid-catalyzed reaction, electrophilic aromatic substitution, to negative resists. The reaction mechanism is shown in Scheme 35. The photogenerated acid reacts with a latent electrophile, such as a substituted benzylacetate, to produce a carbocationic intermediate while acetic acid is liberated. The carbocationic intermediate then leads to electrophilic reaction with neighboring aromatic moieties, regenerating a proton. One application to chemical amplification is a resist composed of copolymers containing a latent electrophile, and an electron-rich aromatic moiety, and a photoacid generator. The copolymers of 4-vinylbenzylacetate and 4-vinylphenol are prepared. An alternative approach is to use a polyfunctional low-molecular-weight latent electrophile in a three-component system including a photoacid generator and a phenolic polymer (Fig. 31).

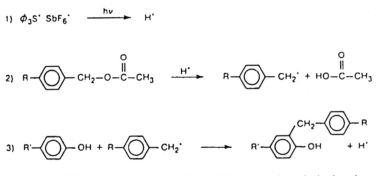

Scheme 35   Acid-catalyzed electrophilic aromatic substitution in a negative chemically amplified resist.

Another type of polyfunctional latent electrophile acting as crosslinker, polyfunctional alcohol, has also been reported [146–149]. Its reaction mechanism is shown in Scheme 36.

Cationic Polymerization.   The chain reaction character of the epoxy group in acid-catalyzed ring-opening polymerization (crosslinking) can be used to obtain negative resists [150]. The use of epoxy-novolak resins is well known in negative resist systems but is limited by poor resolution due to image swelling when developed with organic solvent [151,152]. Conley et al. [153] reported a resist using certain classes of polyepoxide and monomeric epoxide compounds as crosslinkers for alkaline-soluble phenolic resin to get a nonswelling resist. They showed that use of bis-cyclohexane epoxide as a crosslinker results in high sensitivity, high resolution, and excellent resistance to thermal ring-opening polymerization, while some epoxy compounds show sensitivity to the acidity of phenolic resin even at room temperature.

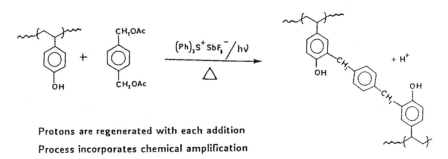

Figure 31   Crosslinking via nonpolymeric multifunctional latent electrophile.

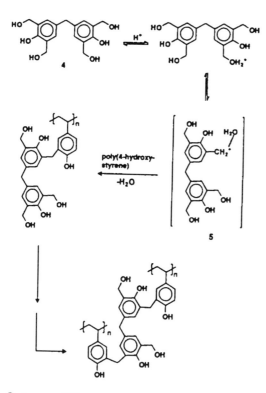

Scheme 36 Cross-linking reaction using acid-catalyzed electrophilic aromatic substitution.

Silanol Condensation. Silanol compounds udnergo condensation to form siloxane in the presence of acid (Scheme 37). It was already reported that silanols can act as dissolution promoters in a novolak resin in the design of a silicon-containing resist with oxygen plasma etching resistance for two-layer resist systems [154]. Therefore, it is expected that the acid-catalyzed reaction produces a dissolution inhibitor, siloxane, that can be applied to a negative resist [155–157]. The resist based on acid-catalyzed silanol condensation consists of diphenylsilanediol, a photoacid generator, and a novolak resin. As shown in Fig. 32, the dissolution rate of the film increases with increase in silanol content, while the exposed film shows a drastic decrease in dissolution rate after baking. The acid-catalyzed products in this system are expected to be siloxane oligomers, which were confirmed by IR spectroscopy and gel permeation chromatography. This acid-catalyzed reaction can be applied to i-line phase-shifting

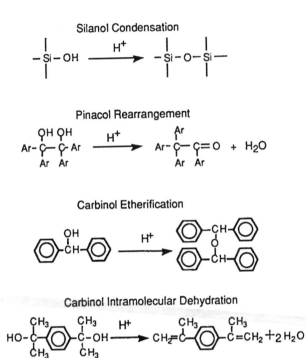

Scheme 37 Acid-catalyzed reactions for polarity change in negative chemically amplified resists.

lithography [156] when an i-line sensitive photoacid generator is used (Fig. 33). A similar system was also reported by McKean et al. [158].

Shiraishi et al. [157] investigated the dissolution inhibition mechanism in a novolak matrix to explain the following interesting experimental results. The resist film fully exposed and baked showed a very small dissolution rate (< 0.03 nm/sec). However, the recoated film after dissolving the exposed film in the casting solvent showed a large dissolution rate. As shown in Fig. 34, hydrophilic silanol groups of silanol compounds surround the hydrophilic hydroxy groups of novolak resin matrix in the equilibrium state. When radiation-induced acid-catalyzed condensation takes place at a hydrophilic site, siloxanes are produced that surround the hydroxy group and shield or block the dissolution in alkali. When this metastable-state film is once dissolved and recoated from solution, hydrophobic siloxanes are surrounded by the hydrophilic sites of novolak resin, resulting in poor dissolution inhibition effect. The insolubilization mechanism of silanol condensation is noncrosslinking but is affected by the site or orientation of silanol condensation products.

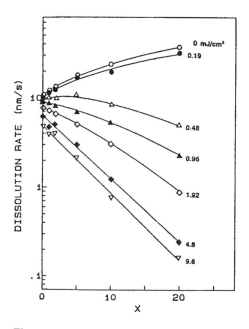

Figure 32   Effect of Ph$_2$Si(OH)$_2$ concentration and exposure dose on dissolution rates. The resist is composed of a novolak resin, Ph$_2$Si(OH)$_2$, and Ph$_3$S$^+$CF$_3$SO$_3^-$. The dissolution rates were measured after postexposure baking.

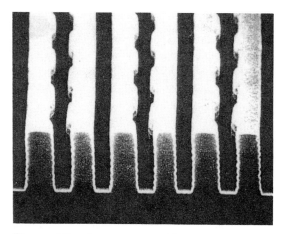

Figure 33   Space patterns of 0.3 μm of the resist using acid-catalyzed condensation of diphenylsilanediol. Exposure carried out with an i-line stepper in conjunction with a phase-shifting mask.

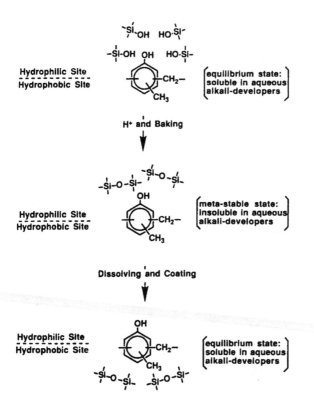

Figure 34 Model of dissolution promotion and inhibition mechanism in the resist composed of a novolak resin, $Ph_2Si(OH)_2$, and $Ph_3S^+CF_3SO_3^-$. Silanol compounds, which surround OH groups of novolak resin, promote dissolution. OH groups are blocked by siloxanes produced by acid-catalyzed condensation of silanols, leading to dissolution inhibition. [From Ref. 157.]

Polarity Change

Although the resist based on silanol condensation shows high resolution capability and high sensitivity, it causes the problem of SiO_x residue formation by oxygen plasma removal processes. Uchino et al. [159–162] designed and tested several types of acid-catalyzed reaction that can be applied to negative resists as shown in Scheme 6.37. The basic concept is the same as that of silanol condensation: A carbinol acts as a dissolution promoter in novolak resin while acid-catalyzed reaction products act as a dissolution inhibitor. Ito and co-workers [163] called these systems "reverse polarity."

Pinacol rearrangement using acid-catalyzed dehydration of pinacols was applied to an alkali-developable resist [159,160]. The resist system was composed of a pinacol compound used as a dissolution inhibition precursor, an onium salt, and a novolak resin. The insolubilization mechanism for the acid-catalyzed reaction of hydrobenzoin in a phenolic matrix is shown in Schemes 37 and 38. Hydrobenzoin converts to diphenylacetaldehyde (Scheme 37), which reacts with hydrobenzoin to form 2,2-diphenyl-4,5-diphenyl-1,3-dioxolane (Scheme 38), resulting in dissolution inhibition. Sooriyakumaran et al. [163] have independently reported a resist system using a polymeric pinacol and benzopinacol.

Use of acid-catalyzed etherification of carbinols gives alkali-developable, highly sensitive negative resists [161]. Certain carbinols can be dissolution promoters of novolak resin, whereas acid-catalyzed products inhibit novolak dissolution in aqueous base. One example of the system consists of diphenylcarbinol (DPC), *m,p*-cresol novolak resin, and diphenyliodonium triflate. The reaction mechanism for insolutilization to alkali dveloper is shown in Scheme 39. In lightly exposed regions bimolecular etherification of DPC occurs, and in the heavily exposed region DPC reacts with novolak resin to form *o*-diphenylmethyl novolak resin.

Intramolecular dehydration of the α-hydroxypropyl group was used for a negative chemical amplification resist in deep-UV [164] and i-line phase-shifting lithography (Fig. 35) [162]. Polymers or compounds with an α-hydroxypropyl group are soluble in aqueous base, and acid-catalyzed intramolecular dehydration reactions (Scheme 6.37) produce dissolution inhibition.

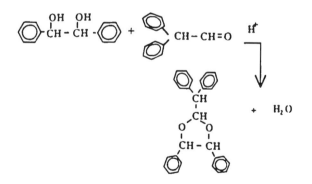

Scheme 38   Reaction of hydrobenzoin with diphenylacetaldehyde. Hydrobenzoin is converted to diphenylacetaldehyde in the presence of acid. Then diphenylacetaldehyde reacts with hydrobenzoin to form 2,2-diphenyl-4,5-diphenyl-1,3-dioxolane, resulting in dissolution inhibition.

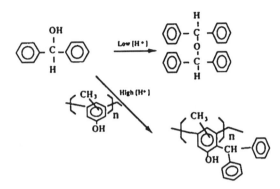

Scheme 39   Acid-catalyzed reaction mechanism of diphenylcarbinol (DPC) in phenolic resin. In lightly exposed regions, bimolecular etherification of DPC occurs, while in the highly exposed region DPC reacts with novolak resin to form *o*-diphenylmethyl novolak resin.

3.3   Route for Actual Use of Chemically Amplified Resists

Chemically amplified resists described above can be summarized as shown in Fig. 36. Some of them have bene extensively evaluated for actual use in deep-UV lithography including KrF excimer laser lithography. It is very difficult to select resists from the commercially available resists, because many things have to be taken into consideration, such as sensitivity, resolution, depth of focus, heat resistance, dry-etch resistance, shelf life, and impurity. In addition, the

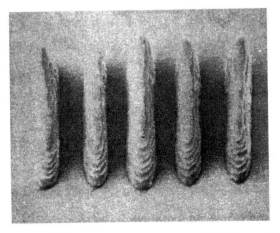

Figure 35   Line and space patterns of 0.275 μm of the resist using acid-catalyzed intramolecular dehydration of a carbinol exposed to i-line using a phase-shifting mask.

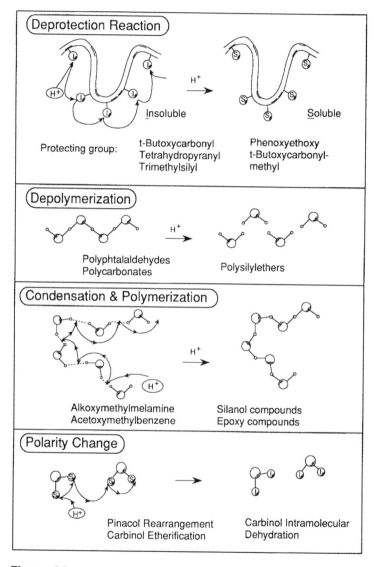

Figure 36 Acid-catalyzed reactions for chemically amplified resists.

compositions of commercially available resists are not disclosed. For positive resists, however, acid-catalyzed deprotection reaction is one of the candidates. In particular, there have been many reports on resists using tBOC protecting group. As for negative resists, resists using acid hardening of melamines from Shipley have been widely accepted.

Process people always compare the chemically amplified resists with DNQ-novolak resists currently used. The sensitivity required for KrF lithography is not a critical issue, as far as acid-catalyzed reactions are used. At present, it is considered that optimum sensitivity is in the range 20 to 50 mJ/cm^2 for KrF excimer laser lithography. Resolution limitation of chemically amplified resists used in KrF lithography is usually better than that of DNQ-novolak resists used for line lithography, although more DOF latitude is required. The dry-etch resistance of chemically amplified resists is similar to that of DNQ-novolak resists, as a phenolic resin is used as a base polymer. Acid-hardening type negative resist is expected to show high dry-etch resistance, as exposed areas are crosslinked.

The main issues for chemically amplified resists are some intrinsic problems associated with acid-catalyzed reactions. Chemically amplified resists are susceptible to process conditions such as airborne contamination, baking conditions, and delay time between exposure and postexposure baking (postexposure delay). Underlying substrates sometimes influence the resist profile. The shelf life is also a critcal issue compared with DNQ-based resists. Most positive chemically amplified resists suffer from line width shift and/or formation of an insolubilization layer or "T-top" profiles (Fig. 37), depending on the postexposure delay. Although it was reported that the delay effect of acid-hardening type negative resists is better than that of the positive ones [141], one should pay attention to process stability. Here factors causing problems are classified into acid diffusion, airborne contamination, and solvent uptake of polymers, although these factors affect the resist performance together.

Figure 37   Typical T-top profiles of a positive chemically amplified resist.

Acid Diffusion

Acid catalysis utilizes a reaction induced by acid diffusion in the resist film, but too much diffusion causes resolution capability to deteriorate. It is critical to understand acid diffusion in the chemically amplified resists in order to improve resolution and line width control and understand the reaction mechanism. Acid diffusion is similar to general diffusion phenomena in polymers [165]. The factors that determine acid diffusion length are baking temperature, residue content of casting solvent, acid size, and matrix polymer properties, such as glass transition temperature and protection degree.

Acid diffusion has been systematically investigated by Schlegel and coworkers [166] using a simple technique, shown in Fig. 38. The exposed film containing photogenerated acid is transferred on a positive chemically amplified resist. The photogenerated acid diffuses into the underlying resist during the subsequent baking process, which causes acid-catalyzed reaction resulting

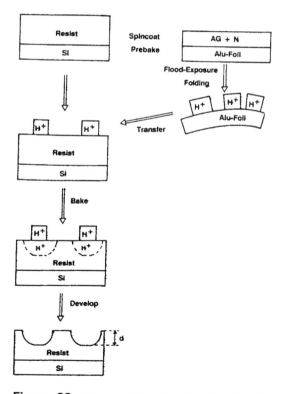

Figure 38 Process scheme for determination of the diffusion range of photogenerated acid in a positive resist.

in an increase in dissolution rate in aqueous base developer. After the development, the depth of the hole is measured to give the diffusion range of a photogenerated acid. The advantage of this method is an exact boundary condition of acid concentration before diffusion; a constant higher acid concentration exists in the transferred exposed film, while no acid exists in the underlying film before baking. The systematic experiment shows that acid diffusion strongly depends on baking temperature, especially after spin coating. Acid diffusion is influenced by the amount of residual casting solvent and the glass transition temperature of the resist film. In order to minimize the diffusion range, a higher prebaking temperature and a lower postexposure baking temperature than the glass transition temperature are recommended.

Other studies on determination of acid diffusion based on an electrochemical method, a contact replication method using x-ray lithography [167], a method using a water-soluble layer [168], and measurement of line width change [169] have been also reported. The acid diffusion range was diminished as the prebaking temperature was raised or postexposure baking was reduced.

Airborne Contamination

In a typical clean room, chemically amplified resists tend to suffer from instability of line width, which is manifested as T-top (Photo 4). MacDonald et al. [170,171] investigated the cause of T-top formation and line width change induced by holding after exposure. The experimental apparatus to investigate the effect of contaminated air on the T-top formation is shown in Fig. 39. Their conclusion is that a surface skin is formed by neutralization of photogenerated acid with airborne contaminant such as hexamethyldisilazane, N-methylpyrrolidone (NMP), and base from paint, adhesive, etc.

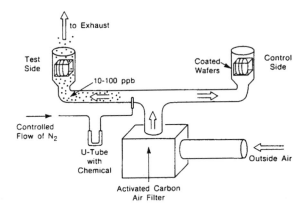

Figure 39 Dynamic flow system used to generate contaminated air.

The airborne contamination problem has been alleviated to some extent by purifying the enclosing atmosphere using activated charcoal filters, which allows the manufacture of 1 Mbit DRAM by deep-UV lithography [172]. The contamination was also protected by application of a protective overcoat. Some approaches for the overcoat were reported [173–175].

N-Methylpyrrolidone Uptake

To study the effect of residual casting solvent on the diffusion rate of the contaminant into chemically amplified resist films, Hinsberg et al. [176–178] directly measured NMP uptake by a series of thin polymer films containing known amounts of residual casting solvent. The reasons for choosing NMP are that (1) it is widely used as a casting and stripping solvent in semiconductor manufacturing, (2) performance degradation of chemical amplified resists has been observed on exposure to a low concentration of NMP vapor, and (3) it is readily available from a commercial source. The amount of residual solvent after bake was determined by a radiochemical method. The NMP uptake was determined by mixing airborne methyl-^{14}C-*N*-methylpyrrolidone into the airstream. There is no simple relationship between the solvent content in the film and its ability to absorb NMP. Although the amount of casting solvent residue clearly increases with increasing polarity, the NMP uptake behavior does not follow a similar trend. However, NMP uptake seems to be influenced by polymer structure.

Therefore, NMP vapor absorption properties of various polymer materials were studied under identical conditions [178]. The NMP contents following storage in an NMP airstream were measured and plotted as a function of solubility parameter and glass transition temperature as shown in Fig. 40. It is seen that polymers with extremely high polarity and low polarity show lower NMP uptake polymers with a solubility parameter δ similar to that of NMP show higher NMP uptake. When the glass transition temperature of a polymer is lower than the baking temperature, NMP uptake of the polymer is negligible. These results suggest that design rules for chemically amplified resists are that the resist polymers should be baked at a temperature higher than their glass transition temperature and that the solubility parameters of the polymers should be different from those of NMP.

3.4 Improvement in Process Stability

Additives

Some additives to solve the delay problems were investigated by BASF workers [179]. Expected reactions of additives with airborne contaminants, usually base, are shown in Scheme 40. Among the additives, sulfonic acid esters and disulfones showed promising results.

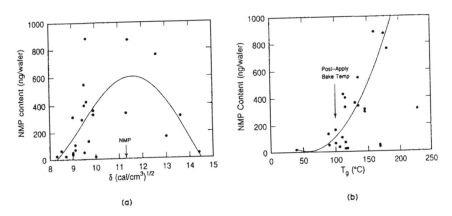

(a)   (b)

Figure 40   (a) Amount of NMP* absorbed under equivalent conditions by various polymers as a function of solubility parameter δ of the polymer. (b) Amount of NMP* absorbed under equivalent conditions by various polymers, as a function of the glass transition temperature (T_g) of the polymer.

Przybilla and co-workers [180] of Höchst proposed a photosensitive base that loses basicity upon irradiation. The basic concept is shown in Fig. 41. In the exposed region acid is generated and at the same time a base is decomposed. When the acid diffuses into unexposed areas, it is neutralized by a photosensitive base. It was reported that this impvoes the line width stability for process conditions.

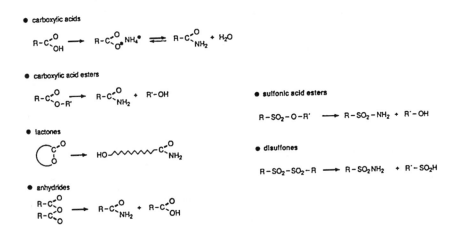

Scheme 40   Expected reaction of additives with airborne contaminations.

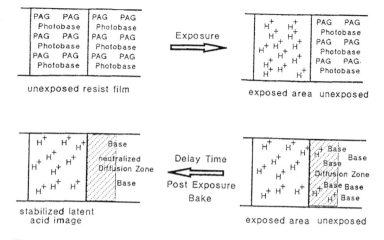

Figure 41 Concept of process stability using a photosensitive base. [From Ref. 180.]

Polymer End Groups

The reaction of the tBOC resists was based on acid-catalyzed deprotection chemistry. Although this reaction was expected to be independent of the molecular weight of a tBOC-PHS, a difference in tBOC deprotection yield was observed for different molecular weights of the polymer [181]. As shown in Fig. 42, the deprotection yield (OH transmittance decrease at 3500 cm^{-1}) for molecular weight 63,000 is higher than that for molecular weight 11,000. This difference may be explained in terms of the different concentration of poisoning CN end group derived from 2,2-azobis(isobutyronitrile) (AIBN): as the molecular weight becomes lower, the end group concentration becomes higher. When tBOC-PHS prepared by radical polymerization using benzoyl peroxide (BPO) or living anionic polymerization with *sec*-butyllithium was used, a higher extent of acid-catalyzed deprotection reaction was observed compared with the polymer obtained by radical polymerization with AIBN initiator. Polymer end groups are important in maximizing the performance of chemical amplification resists.

Tg of Polymers

As described above, the NMP uptake is governed primarily by the glass transition temperature; lower T_g polymer films absorb much less NMP due to better annealing. Ito and co-workers [182] proposed chemical amplification resists formulated with lower T_g *meta*-tBOC-PHS for environmental stabilzation. It was observed that *meta*-tBOC-PHS resists are more resistant to postexposure

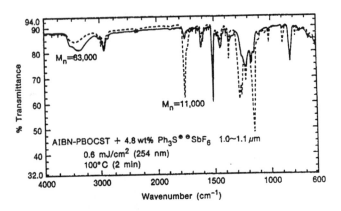

Figure 42   IR spectra of tBOC resists consisting of tBOC-protected polyhydroxy-styrene (PBOCST) of different molecular weights and $Ph_3S^+SbF_6^-$. PBOCST is obtained by radical polymerization with AIBN. The exposure dose is 0.6 mJ/cm² and postexposure bake was at 100°C for 2 minutes. [From Ref. 181.]

delay than the *para*-tBOC-PHS counterparts, when prebake after spin coating is performed at ~ 100°C. This was ascribed to the reduced free volume when the polymer is prebaked at a higher temperature than its T_g. The reduction of the free volume has been confirmed by measuring refractive indices of the two isomer films by a waveguide technique [182].

However, lowering T_g is not the best solution, as low-T_g resists suffer from serious thermal flow during high-temperature processes. It is necessary to design an environmental robust resist system that can be processed at a high temperature to obtain good annealing. it is not easy to design such polymers using partially protected PHS, for example, with tBOC, because these polymers thermally decompose by acidity of the phenol hydroxy group at a lower temperature than fully protected polymers. On the other hand, T_g of partially protected polymers is higher than that of fully protected polymers due to the hydrogen-bonding interaction of the unprotected hydroxy group [183,184]. Therefore, Ito and co-workers [183] showed the design concept of ESCAP (environmental stable chemically amplification positive resist), compared of a thermally and hydrolytically stable resin and a thermally stable photoacid generator: a copolymer of 4-hydroxystyrene (HOST) with *t*-butylacrylate (TBA) and camphorsulfonyloxynaphthalimide (CSN) as an organic nonionic acid generator (Fig. 43). With ESCAP a bake temperature of 150°C or above can be employed. Using this resist, they showed 2-hour stability for postexposure delay.

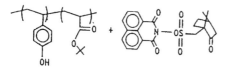

Figure 43 The compositions of ESCAP (environmentally stable chemical amplification positive resist).

4 SURFACE IMAGING

The demand for improved resolution requires imaging systems wiht increasingly higher aspect ratios and better line width control over topography. Line width control and resist profile strongly depend on substrate steps and reflectivity of substrates. Depth of focus (DOF) latitude is another critical issue. The use of shorter wavelengths in photolithography is one of the candidates for obtaining smaller feature sizes. Absorption of the base polymer matrix increases in the deep-UV region, which affects the image profile in the resist film. In ArF excimer laser lithography, the absorption coefficient at 193 nm of aromatic polymers is so high that light absorption is confined to the top ~0.1 μm for polymers. On the other hand, the cost-effectiveness of manufacturing integrated circuits is pushing conventional single-layer resist processes. One solution to the demands described above is surface imaging.

Surface imaging utilizes the chemical change of a surface layer upon exposure to radiation. If a dry etch–resistant material can be selectively incorporated into the surface layer of the exposed or unexposed region, the subsequent oxygen lasma etching affords pattern formation. In surface imaging, the thick layer can be used to cover the substrate topography and reaction is induced only in the surface region. Therefore, the effects of the topography, reflection of substrates, and interference in the resist film on pattern profile and line width control are expected to be minimized. If the substrate topography is planarized with resist film, fine patterns can be obtained even in a limited DOF condition.

4.1 Gas-Phase Functionalization

Taylor and co-workers [185,186] of AT&T Bell Laboratories first demonstrated the surface imaging called gas-phase functionalization. The concept is depicted in Fig. 44. Reactive groups A convert to product groups P upon irradiation. Next the exposed film is treated with a reactive gas MR ocontaining reactive groups R and inorganic atoms M. The atoms can form nonvolatile compounds MY that are resistant to removal under oxygen reactive ion etching conditions

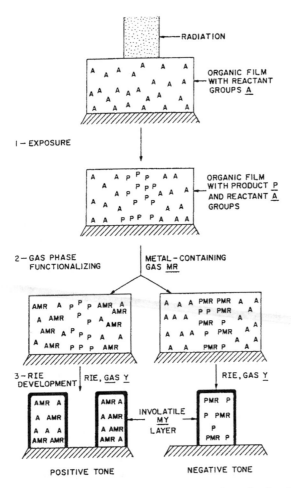

Figure 44 Schematic representation of gas-funtionalized plasma-developed resists showing (1) exposure of a material with reactive groups A, (2) conversion of such groups to product group P, and (3) selective functionalization of either A or P with metal-containing reagent MR, where M is metal and R stands for reactive or inert groups or atoms. (4) Reactive ion etch development using gas Y forming nonvolatile compounds MY and volatile AY, PY, and host Y compounds. [From Ref. 185.]

using gas Y. When MR reacts with A, positive-tone patterns can be obtained. Negative-tone patterns can be obtained by selecting MR that reacts with P.

The radiation-initiated reactions studied in the resist were creation and destruction of unsaturation (olefins, etc.) [185]. They used diborane as an inorganic functionalizing reagent, which efficiently reacts with electron-rich C=C double bonds to form organoboranes. Formation of both positive- and negative-tone patterns was achieved using chloroacrylate homopolymers or copolymers with allylacrylate containing 12–15% unsaturation.

They also described positive-acting resists based on a bisazide and a cyclized poly(isoprene) base polymer, functionalized with gaseous inorganic halides [186]. Upon irradiatino, a bisazide loses two molecules of nitrogen to give a dinitrene intermediate. The nitrene can crosslink a double bond of polyisoprene to give aziridine or inset into a carbon-hydrogen bond to give a secondary amine. Inorganic halides, such as silicon tetrachloride ($SiCl_4$) and tin tetrachloride ($SnCl_4$), are known to react with secondary amines, which are converted to volatile organic and inorganic compounds. In unexposed areas, azide-inorganic halide complexes are converted to a metal oxide layer. Then the subsequent oxygen RIE gave a positive relief image.

4.2 DESIRE

Coopmans and Roland [187,188] proposed DESIRE (diffusion-enhanced silylating resist), whose process flow is depicted in Fig. 45. After UV exposure, selective silylation takes place in the exposed area. During dry development by

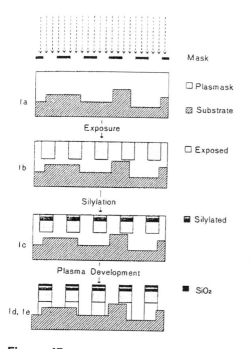

Figure 45 Process for DESIRE (diffusion-enhanced silylating resist). [From Ref. 187.]

oxygen plasma, silylated parts rapidly form a silicon dioxide–rich layer that retards further etching, while the unexposed region can be etched away by the anisotropic process, which results in a negative-type relief image. There have been increased reports including germylation [189,190] since this work. The effect of chemical structure of silylating agents has also been evaluated in the DESIRE process [191,192].

Visser et al. [193] studied the mechanism of selective silylation of resists composed of DNQ compounds and a novolak resin using IR spectroscopy and Rutherford backscattering spectrometry. The model proposed is that some DNQs can act as physical crosslinkers between polymer chains via the formation of hydrogen bonds, whereas the corresponding indenecarboxylic acids cannot. It was found that during silylation a swollen layer is formed with a sharp front separating it from the unreacted resin.

To obtain a positive tone image, the esterification reaction of photogenerated ketene from diazopiperidine with phenolic resin under a dry nitrogen atmosphere is used in image reversal processes (Fig. 46) [194]. The number of hydroxy groups of the phenolic resin is decreased by esterification in exposed areas, resulting in blocking the reaction with silylating reagents. The following flood exposure renders the diffusitivity for silylating reagents of unexposed areas in the first patternwise exposure, leading to a positive tone.

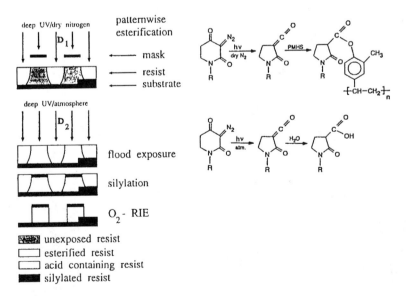

Figure 46   Imaging reversal of DESIRE process.

The resists containing azides were also utilized for positive tone [195]. The exposed area reduces the reactivity with silylating reagents by using crosslinking of polymers to decrease diffusitivity, whereas unexposed areas can react with the silylating reagent.

4.3   Liquid-Phase Sylilation

Sezi et al. [196,197] of Siemens reported a resist that can be silylated in a standard puddle development track at room temperature. The resist is composed of an anhydride-containing copolymer and a DNQ compound. The silylation can be performed with an aqueous solution of bis-aminosiloxane in water and dissolution promoter. During the silylation film thickness increases: swelling occurs. It is difficult to explain the fast silylation (20 nm/sec) by an increase in the free volume generated through molecular rearrangement and release of nitrogen molecules with the photolysis of DNQ. Salt formation between indene carboxylic acid (ICA) and the primary amine moiety of aminosiloxane may induce the dissolution of the salt in the aqueous phase. After the dissolution of ICA in the exposed area into the aqueous phase, free space is created in the surface area where aminosiloxane molecules can diffuse into and can react with ICA or/and the anhydride groups of the base resin (Fig. 47). The latter led to formation of amide and carboxylic acid bound to the resin backbone. Although crosslinking and dissolution compete during silylation, crosslinking was confirmed in the exposed region, whose layer cannot be dissolved in any solvent. Liquid-phase silylation was also reported by other groups [192,198,199].

4.4   Use of Chemical Amplification

MacDonald et al. [200] have reported a negative-tone oxygen plasma–developable resist system that utilizes the change in chemical reactivity of the exposed area. The concept is outlined in Fig. 48 for a resist composed of tBOC-PHS and a photoacid generator. Ultraviolet exposure and subsequent heating initiate acid-catalyzed deprotection of the tBOC group to yield a phenolic hydroxy group. Since hexamethyldisilazane (HMDS) and (dimethylamino)trimethylsilane (DMATMS) are known to react with the phenolic hydroxy group and correspondingly not to react with tBOC-PHS, treating the exposed film with DMATMS vapor selectively incorporates an organosilicon species into the exposed region of the film. When the silylated film is exposed to oxygen plasma, the regions of the film that do not contain the organosilicon species are etched to the substrate and those containing silicon are not etched, resulting in a negative relief image.

They also have described a gas-phase image reversal process that generates a positive tone, plasma-developable image for a chemically amplified system

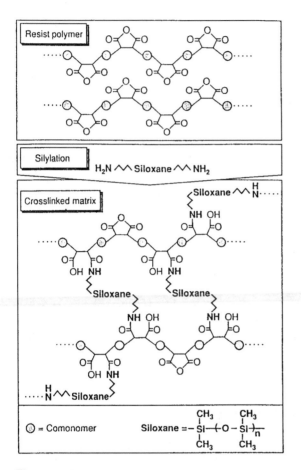

Figure 47 Silylation of an anhydride-containing polymer with a bis-aminosiloxane in the aqueous phase.

[201]. The process is shown in Fig. 49. The phenolic hydroxy groups that are produced by image exposure react with an organic reagent (which must not contain Si, Ge, Ti, etc.) to form a product that is thermally stable and unreactive toward silylation. Flood exposure and baking convert the remaining tBOC-PHS to PHS. These hydroxy groups react with the silylating agent to selectively incorporate silicon. When the film is exposed to oxygen plasma, the regions that do not contain the organosilicon species are etched to the substrate, resulting in a positive-tone relief image.

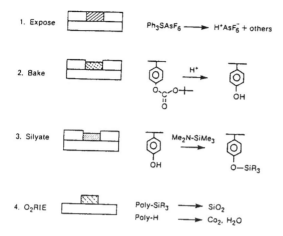

Figure 48 Negative-tone dry development process using chemically amplified resist.

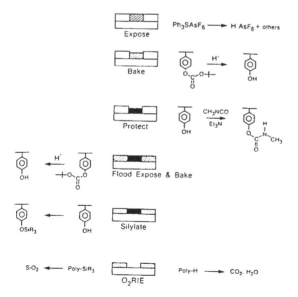

Figure 49 Positive-tone dry development process using imaging reversal of chemically amplified resist.

Workers at Philips [202] and Shipley [203] reported resists composed of phenolic resin, hexamethoxymethylmelamine as a crosslinker, and a photoacid generator. Photogenerated acid causes an acid-catalyzed condensation during postexposure baking, leading to crosslinking of phenolic resin as described in the previous section. A gaseous silylating reagent can diffuse selectively into unexposed areas to react with hydroxy groups of phenolic resin, whereas its diffusion is limited in exposed crosslinked area. This gas-phase modification of exposed polymer film, followed by reactive oxygen ion etching, leads to a positive-tone relief image. The other negative resists using acid-catalyzed reaction such as electrophilic aromatic substitutions of 1,2,4,5-tetra(acetoxymethyl)benzene can also be applied to gas-phase silylation, plasma-developable resists [204].

4.5   Factors That Influence Pattern Formation

Although surface imaging has several advantages for future lithography, some factors should be discussed for actual use: silylation, plasma etching, and removal of silylated resists. In the silylation process, it is important to control the diffusion of silylating reagents, as the swelling by the diffused reagent may cause pattern deformation. There is also a possiblity that silylation occurs in undesirable regions where the diffusion of silylating reagent is limited. Therefore, silylation selectivity is dependent on silylating reagents and process conditions such as reaction temperature and gas pressure.

During oxygen plasma treatment, silicon oxide–rich layer formaton competes with etching including sputtering in the silylated region. SiO_x formation depends on the silicon concentration and its distribution along the film thickness. Plasma etching conditions are a key to determine the selectivity of the etching. Although the regions where silicon is not incorporated are to be etched away, "grass" of the sputtered silicon oxide to the substrate may cause residue problems.

5   RESISTS FOR ArF LITHOGRAPHY

For 193-nm lithography, deep-UV resists cannot be used as currently formulated. The aromatic polymers are not suitable because of their high absorption coefficients at 193 nm. Several approaches to obtaining resists with improved transmittance at 193 nm have been reported. Use of acrylic polymers as base resins combined with acid-catalyzed reaction has been reported.

Allen et al. [205] demonstrated patterning with 193 nm exposure using acrylic polymers and a photoacid generator, which was initially developed for printed circuit board technology. The acrylic polymers are terpolymers of methylmethacrylate, *t*-butylmethacrylate, and methacrylic acid (Fig. 50). The photogenerated acid induces acid-catalyzed deprotection of the *t*-butyl group to

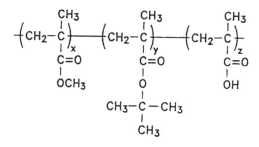

Figure 50 Acrylic terpolymer of methyl methacrylate (MMA), *t*-butyl methacrylate (TBMA), and methacrylic acid (MAA) for ArF excimer laser lithography.

yield polymethacrylic acid. Carboxylic acid polymer is soluble in aqueous base, resulting in a positive image.

A disadvantage of acrylic polymers is poor dry-etch resistance. In order to improve the dry-etch resistance, workers at Fuitsu [206,207] proposed alicyclic polymers containing adamantane or norbornane groups (Fig. 51). The alicyclic component without a conjugated double bond is desirable for transmittance at 193 nm and improved dry-etch resistance compared with aliphatic methacrylate such as poly(methyl methacrylate) (PMMA) or poly(*tert*-butyl methacrylate). They prepared a copolymer of *tert*-butyl methacrylate and adamantyl methacry-

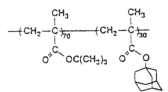

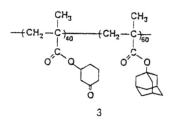

3

Figure 51 Acrylic polymers containing dry etch–resistant adamantyl group for ArF resists.

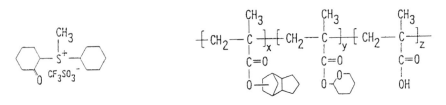

Figure 52 High-transmittance alkylsulfonium salt as an acid generator and a methacrylate terpolymer for ArF resists.

late as a base polymer for ArF excimer laser lithographhy. A similar approach for an ArF resist composed of poly(norbornyl methacrylate) and dicyclohexyldisulfone was reported by workers at Matsushita [208]. Although it was reported that the dry-etch resistance of these polymers is compatible with that of DNQ-novolak resists, it is to be noted that the dry-etch resistance is always dependent on etching conditions, such as etching gas, pressure and flow rate of the etching gas, apparatus, power, shape and size of electrodes, and pumping rate.

Nakano et al. [209] of NEC reported an alkylsulfonium salt, cyclohexylmethyl-(2-oxocyclohexyl)sulfonium triflate (Fig. 52) as an acid generator, which shows high transmittance at 193 nm. A methacrylate terpolymer, poly(tricyclodecanylmethacrylate-co-tetrahydropyranyl methacrylate-co-methacrylic acid) (Fig. 52), was synthesized and used as a base polymer. They obtained a negative image using a resist composed of the above and organic solvent developer.

Workers at Toshiba [210] found that the compounds containing the naphthalene moiety afford lower absorption coefficient at 193 nm than those with the

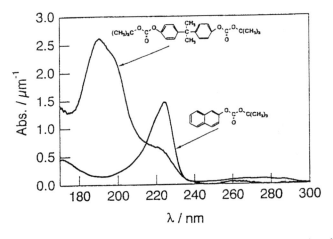

Figure 53 Visible-UV absorption spectra of tBOC-protected naphthol and bisphenol A. [From Ref. 210.]

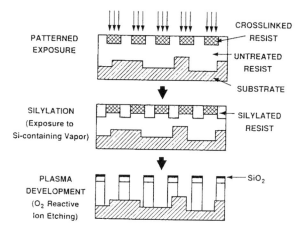

Figure 54   Schematic process flow for 193-nm process. [From Ref. 211.]

phenyl group (Fig. 53). This is ascribed to a shift of λ_{max} (wavelength of absorption maximum) induced by conjugation extension from benzene to naphthalene. This finding leads to resists containing the naphthalene moiety rather than phenyl groups.

Using the high absorbance at 193 nm of phenolic polymers, Hartney et al. [211,212] described surface imaging based on silylation. Irradiation at 193 nm produces direct crosslinking in phenolic polymers near the surface (Fig. 54). The crosslinking prevents diffusion of organosilicon reagent to generate silylation selectivity. Subsequent oxygen plasma treatment forms a etch-resistant silicon oxide mask in the silylated area and etches the unsilylated areas to give a positive-tone image.

6 NEW APPROACHES OF CONTRAST ENHANCEMENT DURING DEVELOPMENT

Contrast enhancement during development using reaction of base with base-labile compounds, such as DNQ sulfonic acid ester of phenolphthalein [42], tBOC-protected phenolphthalein [103,104] (Fig. 26), and polymers containing acetoxystyrene [95] have been reported. Uchino et al. [213] proposed a new contrast enhancement method using contrast-boosted resists (CBRs), which consist of a phenolic resin, a photoactive compound, and a base-labile compound. The concent of a negative CBR is shown in Fig. 55. The CBR offers high resolution because the photochemically induced solubility difference between exposed and unexposed areas is enhanced by the reaction of a base-labile water-repellent compound with base. In an exposed area, the photochemically

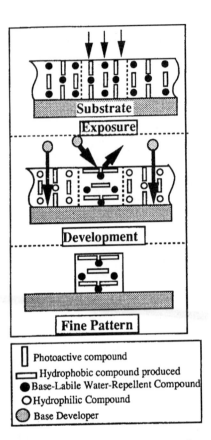

Figure 55 Schematic representation of contrast enhancement during development for negative CBR (contrast-boosted resist). [From Ref. 213.]

produced hydrophobic compounds and the water-repellent compound work together to retard permeability of base developer penetrating into the resist. Thus, the exposed area of the CBR is completely insolublized in the developer. On the other hand, the base developer permeates into the unexposed area of CBR and converts the water-repellent compound into hydrophilic compound that gives no dissolution inhibition in a phenolic resin. Therefore, CBRs exhibit a large contrast compared with conventional resists.

Uchino and co-workers [213] investigated halomethyl ketones listed in Table 2 as water-repellent compounds in a negative resist composed of 4,4'-diazido-3,3 dimethoxybiphenyl and *m,p*-cresol novolak resin. Expected products by reaction of halomethyl ketones in aqueous base are hydroxymethyl ketones. It is interesting to note from Fig. 56 that tris(bromoacetyl)benzene

Table 2 Base-Labile Water-Repellent Compounds for CBR

Compound	Name	Chemical structure
Bromoacetyl benzene	BAB	$COCH_2Br$
p-Bis(bromoacetyl)benzene	*p*-BBAB	$COCH_2Br$ / $COCH_2Br$
m-Bis(bromoacetyl)benzene	*m*-BBAB	$COCH_2Br$ / $COCH_2Br$
1,3,5-Tris(bromoacetyl)benzene	TBAB	$COCH_2Br$, BrH_2COC, $COCH_2Br$
1,3,5-Tris(dibromoacetyl)benzene	TDBAB	$COCHBr_2$, Br_2HCOC, $COCHBr_2$
1,3,5-Tris(chloroacetyl)benzene	TCAB	$COCH_2Cl$, ClH_2COC, $COCH_2Cl$

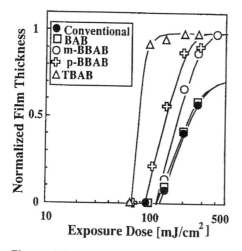

Figure 56 Sensitivity curves of negative CBRs using halomethylaryl ketones with a different number of bromoacetyl groups on a benzene ring. The exposure was carried out with i-line. The resist composition is 4,4′-diazido-3,3′-dimethoxybiphenyl/halo-methylaryl ketone/novolak = 10/20/100 (weight ratio).

gives higher sensitivity and contrast than bis- and monobromoacetylbenzenes. It suggests that change of three bromoacetyl (water-repellent) groups to hydroxyacetyl (hydrophilic) groups is necessary for high contrast enhancement. The concept can be also applied to positive resists.

7 CONCLUSION

The resists for present and future lithography have been described. The strong demand for reduction of minimum feature size will replace the DNQ-novolak positive resists with chemical amplification resists for deep-UV lithography. This demand also requires more precise line width control and higher aspect ratios over substrate topography. More precise control of process and environmental conditions is necessary. Although some of the chemical amplification resists described above show promising results, continuous effort to improve the process stability and shelf life is necessary in cooperation with process people. In ArF excimer laser lithography, surface imaging and the single-layer process using chemical amplification resists will be the candidates. In the the surface imaging processes, line width control associated with surface functionalization and dry development will be a critical issue. To use a chemical amplification resist, the transmittance of the resist and dry etching durability will be a trade-off.

REFERENCES

1. Ueno, T., Shiraishi, H., Uchino, S., Sakamizu, T., and Hattori, T., *J. Photopolym. Sci. Technol.*, *7*, 397 91994).
2. Okazaki, S., *Appl. Surf. Sci.*, *70/71*, 603 (1993).
3. Fukuda, H., Terasaea, T., and Okazai, S., *J. Vac. Sci. Technol.*, *9*, 3113 (1991).
4. Fukuda, H., Imai, A., Terasawa, T., and Okazaki, S., *IEEE Trans. Electron Devices*, *ED-38*, 67 (1991).
5. Dammel, R., *Diazonaphthoquinone-Based Resists*, SPIE tutorial text TT 11, SPIE Optical Engineering Press, 1993.
6. Süs, O. *Justus Liebigs Ann. Chem.*, *556*, 65 (1994).
7. Packansky, J., and Lyerla, J. R., *IBM J. Res. Dev.* 23, 42 (1979); Packansky, J., *Polym. Eng. Sci.*, *20*, 1049 (1980).
8. Hacker, N. J., and Turro, N. J., *Tetrahedron Lett.*, *23*
9. Vollenbroek, F. A., Nijssen, W. P. M., Mutsaers, C. M. J., Geomini, M. J. H. J., Reuhman, M. E., and Visser, R. J., *Polym. Eng. Sci.*, *29*, 928 (1989).
10. Vollenbroek, F. A., Mutsears, C. M. J., and Nijssen, W. P. M., *ACS Polym. Mater. Sci. Eng.*, *61*, 283 (1989).
11. Nakamura, K., Udagawa, S., and Honda, K., *Chem. Lett.*, 763 (1972).
12. Shibata, T., Koseki, K., Yamaoka, T., Yoshizawa, M., Uchiki, H., and Kobayashi, T., *J. Phys. Chem.*, *92*, 6269 (1988).

13. Barra, M., Fisher, T. A., Cernigliaro, G. J., Sinta, R., and Scaiano, J. C., *J. Am. Chem. Soc.*, *114*, 2680 (1992).
14. Andraos, J., Chiang, Y., Huang, C.-G., Kresge, A. J., and Scaiano, J. C., *J. Am. Chem. Soc*, *115*, 10605 (1993).
15. Tanigaki, K., and Ebbsen, T. W., *J. Am. Chem. Soc.*, *109*, 5883 (1989); Tanigaki, K., and Ebbsen, T. W., *J. Phys. Chem.*, *93*, 4531 (1989).
16. Sheats, J., *IEEE Trans. Electron Devices*, *ED-35*, 129 (1988).
17. Furuta, A., Hanabata, M., and Uemura, Y., *J. Vac. Sci. Technol. B4*, 430 (1986); Hanabata, M., Furuta, A., and Uemura, Y., *Proc. SPIE*, *631*, 76 (1986); Hanabata, M., Furuta, A., and Uemura, Y., *Proc. SPIE*, *771*, 85 (1987).
18. Hanabata, M., Uetani, Y, and Furuta, A., *Proc. SPIE*, *920*, 349 (1988).
19. Hanabata, M., Uetani, Y., and Furuta, A., *J. Vac. Sci. Technol. B7*, 640 (1989).
20. Hanabata, M., and Furuta, A., *Proc. SPIE*, *1262*; 476 (1990).
21. Hanabata, M., Oi, F., and Furuta, A., *Proc. SPIE*, *1466*, 132 (1991).
22. Hanabata, M., Oi, F., and Furuta, A., *Polym. Eng. Sci.*, 1494 (1992).
23. Kajita, T., Ota, T., Nemoto, H., Yumoto, Y., and Miura, T., *Proc. SPIE*, *1466*, 161 (1991).
24. Honda, K., Beauchemin, B. T. Jr., Hurditch, R. J., Blankeney, A. J., Kawabe, K., and Kokubo, T, *Proc. SPIE*, *1262*, 493 (1990).
25. Honda, K., Beauchemin, B. T. Jr., Fitzgerald, E. A., Jeffries, A. T., Tadros, S. P. III, Blankeney, A. J., Hurditch, R. J., Tan, S., and Sakaguchi, S., *Proc. SPIE*, *1466*, 141 (1991).
26. Honda, K., Beauchemin, B. T. Jr., Hurditch, R. J., Blankeney, A. J., and Kokubo, T., *Proc. SPIE*, *1672*, 305 (1992); Honda, K., Blankeney, A. J., Hurditch, R. J., Tan, S., and Kokubo, T., *Proc. SPIE*, *1925*, 197 (1993).
27. Hinsberg, W. D., and Guitierrez, M. L., Kodak Microelectronics Interface Seminar, Nov. 1983.
28. Shuang, J.-P., Kewi, T. K., and Reiser, A., *Proc. SPIE*, *1086*, 74 (1989).
29. Yeh, T.-F., Shih, H.-Y., Reiser, A., Toukhy, M. A., and Beauchemin, B. T. Jr., *J. Vac. Sci.* Technol. B, *10*, 715 (1992).
30. Yeh, T.-F., Shih, H.-Y., and Reiser, A., *Macromoleules*, *25*, 5345 (1992).
31. Yeh, T.-F., Reiser, A., Dammel, R. R., Pawlowski, G., and Röchert, H., *Macromolecules*, *26*, 3862 (1993).
32. Shih, H.-Y., Yeh, T.-F., Reiser, A., Dammel, R. R., Merrem, H. J., and Pawlowski, G., *Macromolecules*, *27*, 3330 (1994).
33. Hattori, T., Ueno, T., Shiraishi, H., Hayashi, N., and Iwayanagi, T., *Jpn. J. Appl. Phys.*, *30*, 3215 (1991).
34. Dammel, R. R., Rahman, M. D., Lu, P. H., Canize, A., and Elango, V., *Proc. SPIE*, *2195*, 542 (1994).
35. Kishimura, S., Yamaguchi, A., Yamada, Y., and Nagata, H., *Polym. Eng. Sci.*, *32*, 1550 (1992).
36. Tan, S., Sakaguchi, S., Uenishi, K., Kawabe, Y., Kokubo, T., and Hurditch, R. J., *Proc. SPIE*, *1262*, 513 (1991).
37. Nemoto, H., Inomata, K., Ota, T., Yumoto, Y., Miura, T., and Chaanya, H., *Proc. SPIE*, *1672*, 305 (1992).

38. Uenishi, K., Kawabe, Y., Kokubo, T., and Blakeney, A., *Proc. SPIE*, *1466*, 102 (1991).
39. Uenishi, K., Sakaguchi, S., Kawabe, Y., Kokubo, T., Toukhy, M. A., Jeffries, A. T. III, Slater, S. G., and Hurditch, R. J., *Proc. SPIE*, *1672*, 262 (1992).
40. Hanawa, R., Uetani, Y., and Hanabata, M., *Proc. SPIE*, *1672*, 231 (1992); Hanawa, R., Uetani, Y., and Hanabata, M., *Proc. SPIE*, *1925*, 227 (1993).
41. Hanabata, M., *Adv. Mater. Opt. Electron.*, *4*, 75 (1994).
42. Brunsvold, W., Eib, N., Lyons, C., Miura, S., Plat, M., Dammel, R., Evans, O., Rahman, M. D., Jain, S., Lu, P., and Ficner, S., *Proc. SPIE*, *1672*, 273 (1992).
43. Trefonas, P., III, and Danielss, B. K., *Proc. SPIE*, *771*, 194 (1987).
44. Ito, H., Willson, C. G., and Fréchet, J. M. J., Paper presented at the 1982 Symposium on VLSI Technology, Oiso, Japan, Sept. 1982; Ito, H., Willson, C. G., and Fréchet, J. M. J., U.S. Patent 4,491,628 (1985).
45. Ito, H., and Willson, C. G., *ACS Symp. Ser.*, *242*, 11 (1983).
46. Steppan, H., Buhr, G., and Vollman, H., *Angew. Chem. Int. Ed. Engl.*, *21*, 455 (1982).
47. Iawyanagi, T., Ueno, T., Nonogaki, S., Ito, H., and Willson, C. G., *Adv. Chem. Ser.*, *218*, ch. 3 (1988).
48. Lingnau, J., Dammel, R., and Theis, J., *Solid State Technol.*, *32* (9), 105 (1989); Lingnau, J., Dammel, R., and Theis, J., *Solid State Technol.*, *32* (10), 107 (1989).
49. Sheats, J. R., *Solid State Technol.*, *33* (6), 79 (1990).
50. Lamola, A. A., Szmanda, C. R., and Thackeray, J. W., *Solid State Technol.*, *34* (8), 53 (1990).
51. Reichmanis, E., Houlihan, F. M., Nalamasu, O., and Neenan, T. X., *Chem. Mater.*, *3*, 394 (1991).
52. Cameron, J. F., and Fréchet, J. M. J., *J. Org. Chem.*, *55*, 5918 (1990).
53. Willson, C. G., Cammeron, J. F., MacDonald, S. A., Niesert, C.-P., Fréchet, J. M. J., Leung, M. K., and Ackman, A., *Proc. SPIE*, *1925*, 354 (1993).
54. Crivello, J. V., *Polym. Eng. Sci.*, *23*, 953 (1983); Crivello, J. V., *Adv. Polym. Sci.*, *62*, 1 (1984).
55. Hacker, N. P., and Dektar, J. L., *J. Org. Chem.*, *55*, 639 (1990); *ACS Polym. Mater. Sci. Eng.*, *61*, 76 (1989).
56. Hacker, N. P., and Dektar, J. L., *J. Am. Chem. Soc.*, *112*, 6004 (1990).
57. Dektar, J. L., and Hacker, N. P., *J. Photochem. Photobiol. A. Chem.*, *46*, 233 (1989).
58. Hacker, N. P., Leff, D. V., and Dektar, J. L., *Mol. Cryst. Liq. Cryst.*, *183*, 505 (1990).
59. Hacker, N. P., and Welsh, K. M., *Macromolecules*, *24*, 2137 (1991).
60. McKean, D. R., U., Schaedeli, U., and MacDonald, S. A., *ACS Symp. Ser.*, *412*, 27 (1989).
61. McKean, D. R., Schaedeli, U., Kasai, P. H., and MacDonald, S. A., *ACS Polym. Mater. Sci. Eng.*, *61*, 81 (1989).
62. Buhr, G., European Patent Appl. EP 0 137 452 (1985 Hoechst AG.)
63. Smith, G. H., and Bonham, J. A., U.S. Patent 3,779,778 (1973).
64. Buhr, G., Dammel, R., and Lindley, C., *Polym. Mater. Sci. Eng.*, *61*, 269 (1989).
65. Calabrese, G., Lamola, A., Sinta, R., and Thackeray, J., *Polymer for Microelectronics*, Kodansha, 435 (1990).

66. Houlihan, F. M., Schugard, A., Gooden, R., and Reichmanis, E., *Macromolecules*, *21*, 2001 (1988).
67. Neenan, T. X., Houlihan, F. M., Reichmanis, E., Kometani, J. M., Bachman, B. J., and Thompson, L. F., *Proc. SPIE*, *1086*, 2 (1989).
68. Houlihan, F. M., Neenan, T. X., Reichmanis, E., Kometani, J. M., and Chin, T., *Chem. Mater.*, *3*, 462 (1991).
69. Yamaoka, T., Nishiki, M., Koseki, K., and Koshiba, M., *Polym. Eng. Sci.*, *29*, 856 (1989).
70. Naitoh, K., Yoneyama, K., and Yamaoka, T., *J. Phys. Chem.*, *96*, 238 (1992).
71. Ueno, T., Shiraishi, H., Schlegel, L., Hayashi, N., and Iwayanagi, T., in *Polymers for Microelectronics Science and Technology* (Tabata, Y., Mita, I., Nonogaki, S., Horie, K., and Tagawa, S., eds.), Kodansha, Tokyo, (1990), p. 413.
72. Shiraishi, H., Hayashi, N., Ueno, T., Sakamizu, T., and Murai, F., *J. Vac. Sci. Technol. B*, *9*, 3343 (1991).
73. Schlegel, L., Ueno, T., Shiraishi, H., Hayashi, N., and Iwayanagi, T., *Chem. Mater.*, *2*, 299 (1990).
74. Skamizu, T., Yamaguchi, H., Shiraishi, H., Murai, F., and Ueno, T., *J. Vac. Sci. Technol. B*, *11*, 2812 (1993).
75. Ueno, T., Schlegel, L., Hayashi, N., Shiraishi, H., and Iwayanagi, T., *Polym. Eng. Sci.*, *32*, 1511 (1992).
76. Röschert, H., Eckes, Ch., and Pawlowski, G., *Proc. SPIE*, *1925*, 342 (1993).
77. Berner, G., Kirchmayr, R., Rist, G., and Rutsch, W., J. Rad. Cur., 10 (1986).
78. Onishi, Y., Niki, H., Kobayashi, Y., Hayase, R. H., and Oyasato, N., *J. Photopolym. Sci. Technol.*, *4*, 337 (1991).
79. Berner, G., Kirchmayr, R., Rist, G., and Rutsch, W., *J. Radiation Cur.*, 10 (1986).
80. Buhr, G., Lenz, H., and Scheler, S., *Proc. SPIE*, *1086*, 117 (1989).
81. Grunwald, J. J., Gal, C., and Eidelman, S., Proc. SPIE, 1262, 444 (1990).
82. Hayase, R., Onishi, Y., Niki, H., Oyasato, N., and Hayase, S., *J. Electrochem. Soc.*, *141*, 3141 (1994).
83. Shirai, M., Masuda, T., Tsunooka, M., and Tanaka, M., *Makromol. Chem. Rapid Commun.*, *5*, 689 (1984).
84. Shirai, M., and Tsunooka, M., *J. Photopolym. Sci. Technol.*, *3*, 301 (1990).
85. Renner, C. A., U. S. Patent, 4,371,605 (1980 DuPont).
86. Brunsvold, W., Kwong, R., Moontgomery, W., Moreau, W., Sachdev, H., and Welsh, K., *Proc. SPIE*, *1262*, 162 (1990).
87. Brunsvold, W., Montgomery, W., and Hwang, B., *Proc. SPIE*, *1262*, 162 (1990).
88. Pawlowski, G., Dammel, R., Lindley, C., Merrem, H.-J., Röschert, H., and Lingau, J., *Proc. SPIE*, *1262*, 16 (1990).
89. Poot, A., Delzenne, G., Pollet, R., and Laridon, U., *J. Photogr. Sci.*, *19*, 88 (1971)
90. Aoai, T., Umehara, A., Kamiya, A., Matsuda, N., and Aotani, Y., *Polym. Eng. Sci.*, *29*, 887 (1989).
91. Green, T. W., *Protective Groups in Organic Synthesis*, Wiley, New York, 1981.
92. March, J., *Advances in Organic Chemistry*, 3rd ed., Wiley, New York, 1985, p. 334; Ingold, *Structure and Mechanism in Organic Chemistry*, 2nd ed., Cornell University Press, Ithaca, NY, 1969.
93. Ito, H., *Jpn. J. Appl. Phys.*, *31*, 4273 (1992).

94. Tarascon, R. G., Reichmanis, E., Houlihan, F., Schugard, A., and Thompson, L., *Polym. Eng. Sci.*, *29*, 850 (1989).

95. Kometani, J. M., Galvin, M. E., Heffner, S. A., Houlihan, F. M., Nalamasu, O., Chin, E., and Reichmanis, E., *Macromolecules*, *26*, 2165 (1993).

96. Schwalm, R., *ACS Polym. Mater. Sci. Eng.*, *61*, 278 (1989).

97. Kawai, Y., Tanaka, A., and Matsuda, T., *Jpn. J. Appl. Phys.*, *31*, 4316 (1992).

98. O'Brien, M. J., *Polym. Eng. Sci.*, *29*, 846 (1989).

99. McKean, D. R., MacDonald, S. A., Johnson, R. D., Clecak, N. J., and Willson, C. G., *Chem. Mater.*, *2*, 619 (1990).

100. Kumada, T., Kubota, S., Koezuka, H., Hanawa, T., Kishimura, S., and Nagata, H., *J. Polym. Sci. Technol.*, *4*, 469 (1991).

101. Ban, H., Nakamura, J., Deguchi, K., and Tanaka, A., *J. Vac. Sci. Technol. B*, *9*, 3387 (1991).

102. Aoai, T., Yamanaka, T., and Kokubo, T., *Proc. SPIE*, *2195*, 111 (1994).

103. Kihara, N., Ushirogouchi, U., Tada, T., Naitoh, T., Saitoh, S., and Sasaki, O., *Proc. SPIE*, *1672*, 194 (1992).

104. Koyanagi, H., Umeda, S., Fukunaga, S., Kitaori, T., and Nagasawa, K., *Proc. SPIE*, *1672*, 125 (1992).

105. Ban, H., Nakamura, J., Deguchi, K., and Tanaka, A., *J. Vac. Sci. Technol. B*, *12*, 3905 (1994).

106. Hesp, S. A. M., Hayashi, N., and Ueno, T., *J. Appl. Polym. Sci.*, *42*, 877 (1991).

107. Sakamizu, T., Shiraishi, H., Yamaguchi, H., Ueno, T., and Hayashi, N., *Jpn. J. Appl. Phys.*, *31*, 4288 (1992).

108. Hattori, T., Schlegal, L., Imai, A., Hayashi, N., and Ueno, T., *Opt. Eng.*, *32*, 2368 (1993).

109. Taylor, G. N., Stillwagon, L. E., Houlihan, F. M., Wolf, T. M., Sogah, D. Y., and Hertler, W. R., *J. Vac. Sci. Technol. B*, *9*, 3348 (1991); Taylor, G. N., Stillwagon, L. E., Houlihan, F. M., Wolf, T. M., Sogah, D. Y., and Hertler, W. R., *Chem. Mater.*, *3*, 1031 (1991).

110. Kikuchi, H., Kurata, N., and Hayashi, K., *J. Polym. Sci. Technol.*, *4*, 357 (1991).

111. Mertesdorf, C., Nathal, B., Munzel, N., Holzwarth, H., and Schacht, H. Th., *Proc. SPIE*, *2195*, 246 (1994).

112. Cunningham, W. C., Jr., and Park, C. E., *Proc. SPIE*, *771*, 32 (1987).

113. Yamaoka, T., Nishiki, M., Koseki, K., and Koshiba, M., *Polym. Eng. Sci.*, *29*, 856 (1989).

114. Murata, M., Takahashi, T., Koshiba, M., Kawamura, S., and Yamaoka, T., *Proc. SPIE*, *1262*, 8 (1990).

115. Jiang, Y., and Bassett, *ACS Polym. Mater. Sci. Eng.*, *66*, 41 (1992).

116. Fréchet, J. M. J., Eichler, E., Gauthier, S., Kryczka, B., and Willson, C. G., *ACS Symp. Ser.*, *381*, 155 (1989).

117. Ito, H., Pederson, L. A., Chiong, K. N., Sonchik, S., Tai, C., *Proc. SPIE*, *1086*, 11 (1989).

118. Onishi, Y., Oyasato, N., Niki, H., Hayase, R. H., Kobayashi, Y., Sato, K., and Miyamura, M., *J. Polym. Sci. Technol.*, *5*, 47 (1992).

119. Ito, H., and Willson, C. G., *Polym. Eng. Sci.*, *23*, 1013 (1983).

120. Ito, H., Ueda, M., and Schwalm, R., *J. Vac. Sci. Technol. B*, *6*, 2259 (1988).

121. Ito, H., and Schwalm, R., *J. Electrochem. Soc.*, *136*, 241 (1989).
122. Lingnau, J., Dammel, R., and Theis, J., *Polym. Eng. Sci.*, *29*, 874 (1989).
123. Röschert, H., Przybilla, K.-J., Spiess, W., Wegenroth, H., and Pawlowski, G., *Proc. SPIE*, *1672*, 33 (1992).
124. Mckean, D. R., Hinsberg, W. D., Sauer, T. P., Willson, C. G., Vicari, R., Gordon, D. J., *J. Vac. Sci. Technol. B*, *8*, 1466 (1990).
125. Przybilla, K.-J., Röchert, H., Spiess, W., Eckes, C., Pawlowski, G., and Dammel, R., *Proc. SPIE*, *1466*, 174 (1991).
126. Pawlowski, G., Sauer, T., Dammel, R., Gordon, D. J., Hinsberg, W., McKean, D., Lindley, C. R., Merrem, H.-J., Röschert, H., Vicari, R., and Willson, C. G., *Proc. SPIE*, *1262*, 391 (1990).
127. Aoai, T., Umehara, A., Kamiya, A., Matsuda, N., and Aoai, Y., *Polym. Eng. Sci.*, *29*, 887 (1989).
128. Aoai, T., Aotani, Y., and Umehara, A., *J. Photopolym. Sci. Technol.*, *3*, 389 (1992).
129. Fréchet, J. M. J., Bouchard, F., Houlihan, F., Kryczka, B., and Willson, C. G., *ACS Polym. Mater. Sci. Eng.*, *53*, 263 (1985).
130. Fréchet, J. M. J., Iizawa, T., Bouchard, F., and Stanciulescu, M., *ACS Polym. Mater. Sci. Eng.*, *55*, 299 (1986).
131. Fréchet, J. M. J., Eichler, E., Stanciulescu, M., Iizawa, T., Bouchard, F., Houlihan, F. M., and, Willson, C. G., *ACS Symp. Ser.*, *346*, 138 (1987).
132. Fréchet, J. M. J., Stanciulescu, M., Iizawa, T., and Willson, C. G., *ACS Polym. Mater. Sci. Eng.*, *60*, 170 (1989).
133. Fréchet, J. M. J., Willson, C. G., Iizawa, T., Nishikubo, T., Igarashi, K., and Fahey, J., *ACS Symp. Ser.*, *412*, 100 (1989).
134. Fréchet, J. M. J., Fahey, J., Willson, C. G., Iizawa, T., Igarashi, K., and Nishikubo, T., *ACS Polym. Mater. Sci. Eng.*, *60*, 174 (1989).
135. Feely, W. E., Imhof, J. C., and Stein, C. M., *Polym. Eng. Sci.*, *26*, 1101 (1986).
136. Burns, A., Luethje, H., Vollenbroek, F. A., and Spiertz, E. J., *Microelctron. Eng.*, *6*, 467 (1987).
137. Röschert, H., Dammel, R., Eckes, Ch., Meier, W., Przybilla, K.-J., Spiess, W., and Pawlowski, G., *Proc. SPIE*, *1672*, 157 (1992).
138. Thackeray, J. W., Orsula, G. W., Pavelchek, E. K., Canistro, D., Bogan, L. E., Berry, A. K., and Graziano, K. A., *Proc. SPIE*, *1086*, 34 (1989).
139. Liu, H.-Y., de Grandpre, M. P., and Feely, W. E., *J. Vac. Sci. Technol B 6*, 379 (1988).
140. Thackeray, J. W., Orsula, G. W., Rajaratnam, M. M., Sinta, R., Herr, D., and Pavelchek, E. K., *Proc. SPIE*, *1466*, 39 (1991).
141. Allen, M. T., Calabrese, G. S., Lamola, A. A., Orsula, G. W., Rajaratnam, M. M., Sinta, R., and Thackeray, J. W., *J. Photopolym. Sci. Technol.*, *4*, 379 (1991).
142. Yamaguchi, A., Kishimura, S., Tsujita, K., Morimoto, H., Tsukamoto, K., and Nagata, H., *J. Vac. Sci. Technol. B*, *11*, 2867 (1993).
143. Fréchet, J. M. J., Matuszczak, S., Stoever, H. D. H., Willson, C. G., and Reck, B., *ACS Symp. Ser.*, *412*, 74 (1989).
144. Stoever, H. D. H., Matuszczak, S., Willson, C. G., and Fréchet, J. M. J., *Macromolecules*, *24*, 1741 (1993).

145. Fahey, J. T., and Fréchect, J. M. J., *Proc. SPIE*, *1466*, 67 (1991).
146. Lee, S. M., Fréchect, J. M. J., and Willson, C. G., *Macromolecules*, *27*, 5154 (1994).
147. Lee, S. M., and Fréchet, J. M. J., *Macromolecules*, *27*, 5160 (1994).
148. Lee, S. M., Matuszczak, S., and Fréchet, J. M. J., *Chem. Mater.*, *6*, 1796 (1994).
149. Kajita, T., Kobayashi, E., Tsuji, A., and Kobayashi, Y., *Proc. SPIE*, *1925*, 133 (1993).
150. Dubois, J. C., Eranian, A., and Datamanti, E., 8th International Conference on Electron and Ion Science and Technology, Seattle, 1978, p. 303.
151. Ito, H., and Willson, C. G., *ACS Symp. Ser.*, *242*, 11 (1983).
152. Hatzakis, M., Stewart, K. J., Shaw, J. M., and Rishton, S. A., *J. Electrochem. Soc.*, *138*, 1076 (1991).
153. Conley, W., Moreau, W., Perreault, S., Spinillo, G., Wood, R., Gelorme, J., and Martino, R., *Proc. SPIE*, *1262*, 49 (1990).
154. Toriumi, M., Shiraishi, H., Ueno, T., Hayashi, N., Nonogaki, S., Sato, F., and Kadota, K., *J. Electrochem. Soc.*, *134*, 936 (1987).
155. Ueno, T., Shiraishi, H., Hayashi, N., Tadano, K., Fukuma, E., and Iwayanagi, T., *Proc. SPIE*, *1262*, 26 (1990).
156. Hayashi, N., Tadano, K., Tanaka, T., Shiraishi, H., Ueno, T., and Iwayanagi, T., *Jpn. J. Appl. Phys.*, *29*, 2632 (1990).
157. Shiraishi, H., Fukuma, E., Hayashi, N., Tadano, K., and Ueno, T., *Chem. Mater.*, *3*, 621 (1991).
158. McKean, D. R., Clecak, N. J., and Pederson, L. A., *Proc. SPIE*, *1262*, 110 (1990).
159. Uchino, S., Iwayanagi, T., Ueno, T., and Hayashi, N., *Proc. SPIE*, *1466*, 429 (1991).
160. Uchino, S., and Frank, C. W., *Polym. Eng. Sci.*, *32*, 1530 (1992).
161. Uchino, S., Katoh, M., Sakamizu, T., and Hashimoto, M., *Microelectron. Eng.*, *18*, 341 (1992).
162. Ueno, T., Uchino, S., Hattori, K. T., Onozuka, T., Shirai, S., Moriuchi, N., Hashimoto, M., and Koibuchi, S., *Proc. SPIE*, *2195*, 173 (1994).
163. Sooriyakumaran, R., Ito, H., and Mash, E. A., *Proc. SPIE*, *1466*, 419 (1991).
164. Ito, H., Sooriyakumaran, R., Maekawa, Y., and Mash, E. A., *ACS Polym. Mater. Sci. Eng.*, *66*, 45 (1992).
165. Crank, J., and Park, G. S., eds., *Diffusion in Polymers*, Academic Press, New York, 1969.
166. Schlegel, L., Ueno, T., Hayashi, N., and Iawyanagi, T., *J. Vac. Sci. Technol. B*, *9*, 278 (1991); Schlegel, L., Ueno, T., Hayashi, N., and Iwayanagi, T., *Jpn. J. Appl. Phys.*, *30B*, 3132 (1991).
167. Nakamura, J., Ban, H., Deguchi, K., and Tanaka, A., *Jpn. J. Appl. Phys.*, *30*, 2619 (1991).
168. Asakawa, K., *J. Photopolym. Sci. Technol.*, *6*, 505 (1993).
169. Fedynyshyn, T. H., Thackeray, J. W., Georger, J. H., and Denison, M. D., *J. Vac. Sci. Technol. B*, *12*
170. MacDonald, S. A., Clecak, N. J., Wendt, H. R., Willson, C. G., Snyder, C. D., Knors, C. J., Deyoe, N. B., Maltabes, J. G., Morrow, J. R., McGuire, A. E., and Holmes, S. J., *Proc. SPIE*, *1466*, 2 (1991).

171. MacDonald, S. A., Hinsberg, W. D., Wendt, H. R., Clecak, N. J., Willson, C. G., and Snyder, C. D., *Chem. Mater.*, *5*, 348 (1993).

172. Maltabes, J. G., Homes, S. J., Morrow, J. R., Barr, R. L., Hakey, M., Reynolds, G., Willson, C. G., Clecak, N. J., MacDonald, S. A., Ito, H., *Proc. SPIE*, *1262*, 2 (1990).

173. Nalamasu, O., Reichmanis, E., Cheng, M., Pol, V., Kometani, J. M., Houlihan, F. M., Nenan, T. X., Bohrer, M. P., Mixon, D. A., Thompson, L. F., and Takemoto, C., *Proc. SPIE*, *1466*, 13 (1991).

174. Kumada, T., Tanaka, Y., Kubota, S., Koezuka, H., Ueyama, A., Hanawa, T., and Morimoto, H., *Proc. SPIE*, *1925*, 31 (1993).

175. Oikawa, A., Santoh, N., Miyata, S., Hatakenaka, Y., Tanaka, H., and Nakagawa, K., *Proc. SPIE*, *1925*, 92 (1993).

176. Hinsberg, W. D., MacDonald, S. A., Clecak, N. J., and Snyder, C. D., *Proc. SPIE*, *1672*, 24 (1992).

177. Hinsberg, W. D., MacDonald, S. A., Clecak, N. J., and Snyder, C. D., *Proc. SPIE*, *1925*, 43 (1993).

178. Hinsberg, W. D., MacDonald, S. A., Clecak, N. J., and Snyder, C. D., *Chem. Mater.*, *6*, 481 (1994).

179. Funhoff, D. J. H., Binder, H., and Schwalm, R., *Proc. SPIE*, *1672*, 46 (1992).

180. Przybilla, K.-J., Kinoshita, Y., Masuda, S., Kudo, T., Suehira, N., Okazaki, H., Pawlowski, G., Padmanabam, M., Röchert, H., and Spiess, W., *Proc. SPIE*, *1925*, 76 (1993).

181. Ito, H., England, W. P., and Lundmark, S. B., *Proc. SPIE*, *1672*, 2 (1992).

182. Ito, H., England, W. P., Sooriyakumaran, R., Clecak, N. J., Breyta, G., Hinsberg, W. D., Lee, H., and Yoon, D. Y., *J. Photopolym. Sci. Technol.*, *6*, 547 (1993).

183. Ito, H., Breyta, G., Hofer, D., Sooriyakumaran, R., Petrillo, K., and Seeger, D., *J. Photopolym. Sci. Technol.*, *7*, 433 (1994).

184. Paniez, P. J., Rosilio, C., Mouanda, B., and Vinet, F., *Proc. SPIE*, *2195*, 14 (1994).

185. Taylor, G. N., Stillwagon, L. E., and Venkatesan, T., *J. Electrochem. Soc.*, *131*, 1658 (1984).

186. Wolf, T. M., Taylor, G. N., Venkatesan, T., and Kraetsch, R. T., *J. Electrochem. Soc.*, *131*, 1664 (1984).

187. Coopman F., and Roland, B., *Proc. SPIE*, *631*, 34 (1986).

188. Coopman, F., and Roland, B., *Solid State Technol.*, *30* (6), 93 (1987).

189. Fujioka, H., Nakajima, H., Kishimura, S., and Nagata, H., *Proc. SPIE*, *1262*, 554 (1990).

190. Yoshida, Y., Fujioka, H., Nakajima, H., Kishimura, S., and Nagata, H., *J. Photopolym. Sci. Technol.*, *4*, 49 (1991).

191. Baik, K.-H., Van den hove, L., Goethals, A. M., Op de Beeck, M., and Roland, B., *J. Vac. Sci. Technol. B*, *8*, 1482 (1990).

192. Shaw, J. M., Hatzakis, M., Babich, E. D., Paraszczak, J. R., Witman, D. F., Stewart, K. J., *J. Vac. Sci. Technol. B*, *7*, 1709 (1989).

193. Visser, R.-J., Schellekens, J. P. W., Reuhman-Huisken, M. E., and Van Ijzendoorn, L. J., *Proc. SPIE*, *771*, 111 (1987).

194. Mutsaers, C. M. J., Nijssen, W. P. M., Vollenbroek, F. A., and Kraakman, P. A., *J. Vac. Sci. Technol. B, 10*, 729 (1992).

195. Yang, B.-J. L., Yang, J.-M., and Chiong, K. N., *J. Vac. Sci. Technol. B, 7*, 1729 (1989).

196. Sezi, R., Sebald, M., Leuscher, R., Ahne, H., Birkle, S., and Borndoefer, *Proc. SPIE, 1262*, 84 (1990).

197. Sebald, M., Berthold, J., Beyer, M., Leuscher, R., Nooelschner, Ch., Scheler, U., Sezi, R., Ahne, H., and Birkle, S., *Proc. SPIE, 1466*, 227 (1991).

198. Baik, K.-H., Van den hove, L., and Roland, B., *J. Vac. Sci. Technol. B, 9*, 3399 (1990).

199. Babich, E., Paraszczak, J., Gelorme, J., McGouey, R., Brady, M., Nunes, R., and Smith, R., *Microelectron. Eng., 13*, 47 (1991).

200. MacDonald, S. A., Schlosser, H., Ito, H., Clecak, N. J., and Willson, C. G., *Chem. Mater., 3*, 435 (1991).

201. MacDonald, S. A., Schlosser, H., Ito, H., Clecak, N. J., Willson, C. G., and Fréchet, J. M. J., *Chem. Mater., 4*, 1346 (1992).

202. Schellekens, J. P. W., and Visser, R.-J., *Proc. SPIE, 1086*, 220 (1989).

203. Thackeray, J. W., Bohland, J. F., Orsula, G. W., Ferrari, J., *J. Vac. Sci. Technol. B, 7*, 1620 (1989).

204. Fahey, J., Fréchet, J. M. J., and Schcham-Diamand, Y., *J. Mater. Chem., 4*, 1533 (1994).

205. Allen, R. D., Wallraff, G. M., Hinsberg, W. D., and Simpson, L. L., *J. Vac. Sci. Technol. B, 9*, 3357 (1991).

206. Kaimoto, Y., Nozaki, K., Takechi, S., and Abe, N., *Proc. SPIE, 1672*, 66 (1992).

207. Nozaki, K., Kaimoto, Y., Takahashi, M., Takechi, S., and Abe, N., *Chem. Mater., 6*, 1492 (1994).

208. Yamashita, K., Endo, M., Sasago, M., Nomura, N., Nagano, H., Mizuguchi, S., Ono, T., and Sato, T., *J. Vac. Sci. Technol. B, 11*, 2692 (1993).

209. Nakano, K., Maeda, K., Iwasa, S., Yano, J., Ogura, Y., and Hasegawa, E., *Proc. SPIE, 2195*, 194 (1994).

210. Naito, T., Asakawa, K., Shida, N., Ushirogouchi, T., and Nakase, *Jpn. J. Appl. Phys., 33*, 7028 (1994).

211. Hartney, M. A., Johnson, D. W., and Spencer, A. C., *Proc. SPIE, 1466*, 238 (1991).

212. Hartney, M. A., Horn, M. W., Kunz, R. R., Rothschild, M., and Shaver, D. C., *Microlithography World, May/June*, 16 (1992).

213. Uchino, S., Ueno, T., Migitaka, S., Tanaka, T., Kojima, K., Onozuka, T., Moriuchi, N., and Hashimoto, M., *Proceedings Reg. Tech. Conference Photopolymers*, SPE, Ellenville, New York, 1994, p. 306.

9

Resist Processing

Bruce W. Smith

Rochester Institute of Technology
Rochester, New York

1 INTRODUCTION

For the most part, conventional single-layer photoresists have been based on components with two primary functions. Whether considering older bis-arylazide *cis*-polyisoprene resists, diazonapthoquinone (DNQ)/novolac g/i-line resists, or chemically amplified polyhydroxystyrene (PHS) deep-UV (DUV) resists, an approach has been utilized wherein a base resin material is modified for sensitivity to exposure by a photoactive compound or through photoinduced chemical amplification. The resist base resin is photopolymeric in nature and is responsible for etch resistance, adhesion, coat-ability, and bulk resolution performance. These resins generally do not exhibit photosensitivity on the order required for integrated circuit (IC) manufacturing. Single-component polymeric resists have been utilized for microlithography, including methacrylates, styrenes, and other polymers or copolymers, but sensitization is generally low and limited to exposures at very short ultraviolet (UV) wavelengths or with ionizing radiation. Inherent problems associated with low absorbance and poor radiation resistance (required, for example, during ion implantation or plasma etching steps) generally limit the application of these types of resists to low volumes or processes with unique requirements.

Sensitization of photoresist materials has been accomplished by several methods. In the case of conventional g/i-line resists, a chemical modification of a base-insoluble photoactive compound (PAC), the diazonaphthoquinone, to a base-soluble photoproduct, indene carboxylic acid (ICA), allows an increase in aqueous base solubility. For chemically amplified PHS-based resists, exposure of a photoacid generator (PAG) leads to the production of an acid, which subsequently allows polymer deprotection (positive behavior) or crosslinking (negative behavior). Other similar processes have been developed (as discussed in Chapter 8) and may involve additional components or mechanisms.

For any resist system, the thermodynamic properties of polymeric resins play an important role in processibility. During the coating, exposure, and development processes of a resist, an understanding of the thermodynamic properties is desirable, as the glass transition temperature (T_g) of a polymer influences planarizability, flow, and diffusion. Although reasonably high T_g values may be desirable, glassy materials with values above 200°C are not suitable because of poor mechanical performance. Once three-dimensional resist features are formed, however, a thermoset material may be desired in which the polymer does not flow with temperature and a T_g essentially does not exist. This ensures the retention of high-aspect-ratio features through subsequent high-temperature and high-energy processes. By appropriate engineering of bake steps during single-layer resist processing, the control of polymer thermoplastic and thermoset properties can be made possible. For negative resists, the situation is inherently simplified. Coated negative resists are thermoplastic in nature, with a well-defined T_g range. Upon exposure and subsequent secondary reactions, crosslinking leads to a networked polymer that will not flow with temperature. At some high temperature of decomposition (T_d) the polymer will break down and begin to lose significant volume. Imaging steps are therefore responsible for the production of thermally stable resist features. Operations are often included in the processing of positive resists that can accomplish similar thermal stability enhancements.

This chapter addresses the critical issues involved in the processing of single-layer resists materials. Process steps to be discussed include:

Resist stability, contamination, and filtration
Substrate priming
Resist coat
Soft bake
Exposure
Postexposure bake
Development
Swing effects
Hard bake and postdevelopment treatment

The step-by-step process flow for DNQ/novolac resists has been covered elsewhere, and the reader is directed to these references for additional description [1–3]. Specific details are given here for positive DNQ/novolac resists and both positive and negative DUV chemically amplified resists based on PHS.

2 RESIST STABILITY, CONTAMINATION, AND FILTRATION

2.1 DNQ/Novolac Resist Stability and Filtration

DNQ/novolac resists have proved to be robust materials with respect to sensitivity to thermodynamic and aging effects while stored in uncast form. A resist shelf life of several months can be expected with no significant change in lithographic performance. As resists are considered for application in production, the stability of materials at various points of the process also needs to be considered.

For DNQ/novolac resists, aging can lead to an increase in absorption at longer wavelengths. Resist materials are susceptible to several thermal and acid/base (hydrolytic) reactions when stored [4]. These include thermal degradation of the DNQ to ICA followed by acid-induced azo dye formation and azo coupling of the DNQ and novolac. A characteristic "red darkening" results from this coupling, induced by the presence of acids and bases in the resist. Although long-wavelength absorbance is altered by this red azo dye, the impact on UV absorbance and process performance is most often negligible. Degradation mechanisms can also result in crosslinking, leading to an increase in high-molecular-weight components. Hydrolysis of DNQ may occur to form more soluble products and hydrolysis of solvents is possible, which can lead to the formation of acids [5]. The practical limitation of shelf life for DNQ/novolac resists is generally on the order of 6 months to 1 year. Once coated, resist films can absorb water and exhibit a decrease in sensitivity, which can often be regained through use of a second soft bake step. As will be described, process delays for chemically amplified PHS resists are much more critical than for DNQ/novolac materials.

A larger problem encountered when storing DNQ/novolac resists is sensitizer precipitation. With time, DNQ PAC can fall out of solution, especially at high temperatures. These crystallized precipitates can form most readily with high loading levels of DNQ. In addition, resist particulate levels can be increased by the formation of gel particles, a result of acid-induced novolac crosslinking via thermal decomposition of DNQ. Any of these routes to particulate formation can lead to levels exceeding that measured by the resist manufacturer. Because of this, point-of-use filtration has become common practice for most production applications to ensure photoresist consistency [6]. Resist materials are commonly filtered at a level of approximately 25% of the minimum geometry size. As the geometry size approaches sub-0.35 µm, filtration requirements may approach 0.05 µm. Such ultrafiltering will have an impact on how resists can be manufactured and used. Filtration speed is dramatically reduced and material preparation becomes more costly. Similar concerns can exist for pump throughput during resist dispensing. Fractionation of a resist material can also occur, resulting in the removal of long polymer chains and a change in process performance. To illustrate this, consider an i-line resist (DNQ/novolac) with a molecular weight on the order of $10–20 \times 10^3$ g/mol (number average). The resulting average polymer chain size is nearly 5 to 6 nm with a maximum as large as 40 nm. In highly concentrated resist formulations (>30 wt. %), intertwisting of polymers can result in chain sizes greater than 80 nm. If such a resist is filtered to 0.05 μm, the largest polymer chains can be removed. As technology progresses toward smaller feature resolution, it is clear that particulate and filtration issues need to be carefully considered.

2.2 Stability Issues for Chemically Amplified PHS Resists

Filtration concerns for i-line resists are extended to deep UV lithography as PHS resists are considered. As sub-0.25 μm geometry is pursued, the issue of ultrafiltering becomes an increasingly important problem. In addition, environmental stability issues are present for many chemically amplified resists (CARs) that are not issues for DNQ/novolac resists, especially for resists based on acid-catalyzed reactions and PHS resins. Ion exchange methods are conventionally used to reduce ion contamination levels in resists below 50 ppb. Ionic contamination reduction in both positive and negative CAR systems needs to be carefully considered. Deprotection of acid-labile components can result from reaction with cationic exchange resins. The catalytic acid produced upon exposure of these resists is also easily neutralized with base contamination at ppb levels. These contaminants can include such things as ammonia, amines, and NMP, which are often present in IC processing environments [7]. Any delay between exposure and postexposure bake (PEB) can result in a decrease in sensitivity and the formation of a less soluble resist top layer or "T-top."

To reduce the likelihood of base contamination of these resists, several improvements have been made in resist formulations. One method explored to reduce acid loss is the use of low-activation-energy (E_a) polymers with highly reactive protection groups. These resists are sufficiently active that deprotection can occur immediately upon exposure, significantly reducing the sensitivity to PEB delay effects [8,9]. Additives have also been incorporated into DUV PHS resists to improve their robustness to contamination effects [10,11] and resist topcoating approaches have been introduced [12]. By coating a thin water-soluble transparent polymeric film over a resist layer, protection from airborne contamination can be made possible. This "sealing" layer is removed prior to development with a water rinse. Although such a solution leads to minimal additional process complexity, it is still desirable to use resist techniques that do not require additional material layers. An alternative route for the reduction of contamination effects is the use of high-activation-energy resist materials. By reducing the reactivity of a resist, much higher bake processes are allowed. Increasing the bake temperatures above a polymer's T_g results in a densification of the photoresist. This leads to a significant decrease in the diffusion rate of airborne base contamination prior to or after exposure [13,14]. These high-E_a resists also require that a photoacid generator be chosen that can withstand high temperatures. Other methods used to reduce base contamination of acid-acatalyzed resists include the use of activated charcoal air filtration during resist coating exposure, and development operations [15]. This is now considered a requirement for processing of PHS CAR resists. Environmental base contamination can be neutralized and further reduced by adding weak acids to these filters.

The stability or shelf life of PHS-based resists is also influenced by the structure of polymer protective groups. This is especially true for low-activation-energy (high-reactivity) resists, for which the liability of protective groups may decrease usable resist shelf life. Conversely, the more stable protective groups utilized with high-activation-energy (low-reactivity) resists lead to a higher degree of stability.

3 RESIST ADHESION AND SUBSTRATE PRIMING

Adequate adhesion of photoresist to a wafer surface is critical for proper process performance. Resist adhesion failure can occur not only during photolithography operations but also in subsequent etch, implant, or other masking steps. Negative resists are less prone to adhesion failure, as crosslinking results in a networked polymer that is bound to the wafer surface. Positive resists (especially phenolic-based materials such as novolac or PHS resists) are more likely to be single-polymer chains and rely on weaker physical and chemical forces for adhesion. Etch process undercutting can often result from inadequacies at the resist interface, resulting in loss of etch line width control. The causes of resist adhesion failure are generally related to dewetting of a photoresist film. This can result from a large discordance between the surface tension of the wafer and that of the resist material, especially when coating over silicon oxide. Silicon dioxide is an especially difficult layer to coat over because it provides a hydrophilic surface (water attracting) to a hydrophobic resist (water repelling). The surface tension of thermal silicon dioxide may be on the order of 15 dynes/cm^2, whereas the surface tension of phenolic resists in casting solvent may be near 30 dynes/cm^2. Surface defects can also cause adhesion failure as surface free energy can result in dewetting.

Methods of adhesion promotion can be used for most silicon oxide layers, whether thermally grown, deposited, native, or glasslike. Chemical passivation of these surfaces is generally carried out using silylating priming agents, which act to modify the wafer surface. Some benefit can be realized with priming of layers other than oxides if techniques promote a closer matching of material surface tension. Alkylsilane compounds are generally used to prime oxide surfaces, leading to a lowering of surface hydrophilicity. The most commonly used silane-type adhesion promoter is hexamethyldisilazane (HMDS). Other similar promoters are available, including trimethylsilyldiethylamine (TMSDEA), which can be more effective but also less stable, resulting in lower shelf and coated lifetimes. Reduction of substrate surface tension is carried out in two stages, as shown in Fig. 1. Shown here is a silicon oxide surface with adsorbed water and OH groups. An initial reaction of water with an alkylsilane (HMDS) produces an inert hexamethyldisiloxane and ammonia, resulting in a dehydrated surface. Further reaction with HMDS produces a trimethylsilyl-substituted hydroxyl or oxide species and unstable trimethylsilylamine. With heat, this unstable compound reacts with other surface hydroxyl groups to produce further ammonia and a trimethylsiloxy species. The process continues until steric hindrance (via the large trimethylsilyl groups) inhibits further reaction.

Surface priming using HMDS, TMSDEA, or similar agents can be carried out in either liquid- or vapor-phase modes. In either case, elevated process temperatures (~100°C) must be reached to complete the priming reaction. Substrates should be cleaned prior to application using UV ozone, HF dip, plasma,

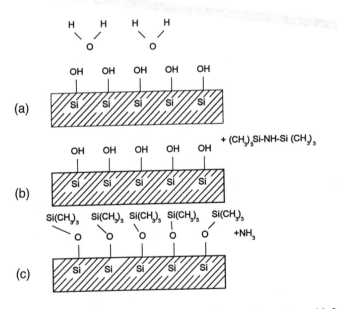

Figure 1 Adhesion promotion of a silicon oxide surface with HMDS surface priming. The substrate is first dehydrated upon reaction with silane promoter. Further reaction with heat leads to a hydrophobic surface.

or other "oxidative" cleaning methods. Adhesion of photoresist to silicon nitride or deposited oxide layers can be enhanced by using an oxygen/ozone plasma treatment. Priming agents are generally best applied using vapor prime methods, either in line or in batch vacuum ovens. Uniformity and reduced chemical usage make this more attractive than liquid methods.

Overpriming of a wafer surface can result in dewetting and lead to further adhesion problems. This can occur with repeated treatment or by using excessive vapor times. Problems are often noticed in isolated substrate areas, depending on device topography or condition. A phenomenon known as resist "popping" can also occur as a result of overpriming; in this case high-fluence exposure (such as that encountered with heavy UV overexposure in ion implantation steps) can cause failure of weakened resist adhesion. Deposition of resist debris onto adjacent substrate areas can result. Measurements of resist surface tension using water contact angle techniques can identify such overpriming problems. Remedies include the use of shorter priming times, resist solvents with lower surface tension, double resist coating steps, or a pretreatment of the wafer surface with the resist casting solvent. Oxygen or ozone plasma treatments can also correct an overprimed wafer surface and allow repriming under more appropriate conditions.

The strength of adhesion bonds between a photoresist and a substrate has also been shown to influence the T_g and thermal expansion coefficient of a thin film. The impact is greatest as resist films approach 1000 Å thicknesses [16].

4 RESIST COATING

4.1 Resist Spin Coating Techniques and Control

Photoresist can be dispensed by several methods, including spin coating, spray coating, and dip coating. The most widely used methods for coating resist onto wafer substrates are spin coating methods. During spin coating, resist is dispensed onto a wafer substrate (either statically or dynamically), accelerated to a final spin speed, and cast to a desired film thickness. Variations on this process have been suggested, including the use of a short-term high-speed initial coating step followed by a slow drying stage [17]. Spin coating processes use the dynamics of centrifugal force to disperse a polymeric resist material over the entire wafer surface. The flow properties (rheology) of the resist influence the coating process and need to be considered to achieve adequate results [18]. In addition, solvent transport through evaporation occurs, which can result in an increase in resist viscosity and shear thinning, affecting the final film properties. As a resist-solvent material is spin cast, the film thickness decreases uniformly, at a rate dependant on the spin speed (ω), kinematic viscosity (υ), solids concentration (c), solvent evaporation rate (e), and initial film thickness, expressed by the following rate equations:

$$\frac{dS}{dt} = \frac{-c2\omega^2 h^3}{3\upsilon} \tag{1}$$

$$\frac{dL}{dt} = (1-c)\frac{2\omega^2 h^3}{3\upsilon} - e \tag{2}$$

where dS/dt and dL/dt are rate of change of solids (S) and solvents (L), respectively [19]. The results are shown in Fig. 2 for a 1-μm film, where both solids and solvent volumes are plotted against spin time. Initially, concentration changes little as resist spread dominates. When the resist thickness drops to one third of its original value, evaporation dominates and solvent content reaches its final value. The high viscosity of the resist eliminates further flow.

The primary material factors that influence spin-coated film properties include the resist polymer molecular weight, solution viscosity, and solvent boiling point (or vapor pressure). Primary process factors include wafer spin speed, acceleration, temperature, and ambient atmosphere. The thickness of a resist film can be modified to some extent through control of the rotation speed of

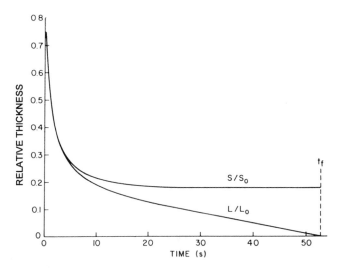

Figure 2 Calculated time dependance during spin coating on the volume of solids (S) and solvent (L) per unit area normalized to initial values. When the resist thickness drops to one third of its original value, evaporation dominates and the solvent content reaches its final value. (From Ref. 19.)

the substrate. Resist thickness is inversely proportional to the square root of spin speed (ω):

$$\text{Thickness} \propto \frac{1}{\sqrt{\omega}} \qquad (3)$$

To achieve large thickness changes, modification of the resist solution viscosity is generally required, as coating at excessively low or high speeds results in poor coating uniformity. At excessively high speeds, mechanical vibration and air turbulence result in high levels of across-wafer nonuniformity. At low spin speeds, solvent loss of the resist front as it is cast over the substrate results in a situation of dynamic resist viscosity, also resulting in high levels of nonuniformity. The optimal spin speed range is dependent on wafer size. Wafers up to 150 mm can be coated at rotation speeds on the order of 4000 to 5000 RPM. Larger substrates require lower speeds.

The optimum coating thickness for a resist layer is determined by the position of coherent interference nodes within the resist layer. Standing waves (see Section 9) resulting from reflections at the resist/substrate interface result in a regular distribution of intensity from the top of the resist to the bottom. This distribution results in a "swing" in the required clearing dose (E_0) for a resist, as shown in Fig. 3. Three curves are shown, for polysilicon, silicon nitride (1260 Å), and silicon dioxide (3700 Å) coated substrates. A general upward trend in E_0 is seen as resist thickness increases. This is due to the residual nonbleachable absorp-

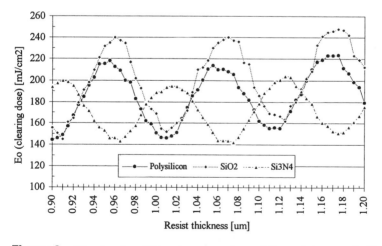

Figure 3   Clearing dose (E_0) swing curves for an i-line resist over polysilicon, silicon dioxide (3700Å), and silicon nitride (1260Å). The increasing trend in required dose is a function of residual absorption. Conditions of minimum interference leads to maximum E_0 values but minimal scumming.

tion of the resist, which can be significant. (For a resist with a residual absorption of 0.10 μm^{-1}, the intensity at the bottom of a 1-μm resist layer is 90% of that experienced at the top.) In addition to this E_0 trend, sensitivity oscillates from minimum to maximum values with thickness. Within one swing cycle, an exposure dose variation of 32% exists for the polysilicon substrate, 27% for silicon nitride, and 36% for silicon dioxide. When resist is coated over a dielectric layer, such as silicon dioxide, silicon nitride, or an antireflective coating (ARC), there will be a shift in the phase of E_0 oscillations. Analysis of swing behavior may therefore be unique for various lithographic levels. Coated thickness optimization can be performed using these swing curves, determined experimentally through open frame exposure of resist coated within a small range of thicknesses. Lithographic modeling can aid in generation of such relationships using knowledge of the resist refractive index, absorption properties (possibly dynamic), exposure wavelength, and resist/substrate reflectivity.

Inspection of the E_0 swing curve in Fig. 3 suggests several possibilities for resist thickness, of which only a few are desirable. For polysilicon, there is a minimum dose requirement at a thickness of ~1.01 μm, where constructive interference occurs, and there is maximum intensity at the resist base. At a resist thickness over polysilicon of ~1.06 μm, destructive interference leads to a maximum E_0 requirement. Other alternatives might include positions on either side of these values (between nodes). Thicknesses corresponding to these midnodal positions allow the least amount of coating process latitude, as small deviations from the targeted film thickness lead to significant changes in dose requirements. Greater latitude exists at maximum interference positions, where there is a minimum requirement for exposure dose, which may be an attractive choice. Small changes in film thickness result only in small E_0 variations but the direction of these changes is toward higher clearing dose values. The result may be scumming of resist features resulting from underexposure, a situation that is unacceptable. The best choice for targeted film thickness may be at a corresponding interference minimum, where small thickness changes result in a small decrease in the dose requirement. Slightly lower throughput may result (generally not a gating factor in today's exposure operations) but this will ensure no resist scumming related to underexposure. Image fidelity at the top surface of a resist film is also influenced by film thickness and positions on the interference curve. By coating at a midnodal thickness, top surface rounding or T-topping can result (see the Section 9 for further discussion).

During spin coating, a large amount of resist "free volume" can be trapped within a resist layer. A simplified free-volume model of molecular transport can be quite useful for correlation and prediction of diffusion properties of resist materials [20,21]. (The reader is directed to Refs. 20 and 21 for a detailed discussion of diffusion in polymer-solvent systems.) Volumetric expansion enhances polymer chain mobility and acts similarly to the addition of plasticizers. The resist's glass transition temperature (T_g) is lowered and the dissolution properties of novolac- and PHS-based resist can be increased [22]. Coating-induced free volume has been shown to affect acid diffusion as well and becomes a concern when considering reduction of airborne base contamination and postexposure delay.

4.2 Solvent Contribution to Film Properties

Residual casting solvent can act as a plasticizer and can reduce the T_g of a resist. Resist solvent content has been shown to be dependent on film thickness. A 1000 Å resist film may, for example, exhibit 50% more solvent retention than a 10,000 Å film. Figure 4 shows residual solvent in PHS polymer films coated at thicknesses of 12,000 Å and 1100 Å. Only near the resist T_g (135°C) does the solvent content for the 1100 Å film approach that of the thicker film. Table 1 shows diffusion coefficients for PGMEA solvent in the same PHS film thicknesses, determined by diffusion analysis during 2 hours of baking. These results may be due to a smaller degree of inter- or intramolecular hydrogen bonding in thinner films [23–25], which can allow a stronger polymer interaction with the casting solvent and lower solvent evaporation rates. A higher solvent content leads to an increased dissolution rate and increased diffusivity levels. When considering various resist solvent systems, it might also be expected that lower boiling point (T_b) solvents would lead to lower solvent

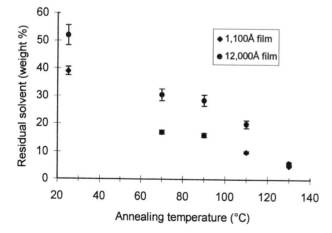

Figure 4 Bake temperature dependence of residual PGMEA solvent in 1,100Å and 12,000Å spin cast films annealed for 1300 minutes. (From Ref. 24.)

Table 1 Diffusion Coefficients of PGMEA Solvent
in PHS Films for 2 Hours of Baking

	Diffusion coefficient (cm²/s)	
Temperature	0.11-µm film	1.2-µm film
70°C	4.2×10^{-14}	1.2×10^{-12}
90°C	9.4×10^{-14}	4.4×10^{-12}
110°C	1.1×10^{-13}	1.4×10^{-11}

retention than higher T_b solvents. The opposite, however, has been demonstrated [26]. PGMEA, for instance, has a boiling point of 146°C and an evaporation rate of 0.34 (relative to *n*-butyl acetate). Ethyl lactate has a higher T_b of 154°C and an evaporation rate of 0.29. Despite its lower boiling point, PGMEA is more likely to be retained in a resist film. The reason for this is a skin formation that results from rapid solvent loss during the coating process [27]. The resist viscosity at the surface increases more rapidly for PGMEA as solvent is exhausted, leading to more residual solvent remaining throughout the resist film. If a resist film is then baked at temperatures below the bulk T_g, densification of surface free volume is allowed only at the top surface of the film and is prevented throughout the bulk. Entrapped solvent therefore leads to an apparent surface induction effect, which can be reduced only if the resist is baked above its T_g. Because solvent content plays an important role in determining the ultimate glass transition temperature of the resist (and therefore its dissolution properties), any postcoating incorporation of solvents can also have an adverse impact on performance. Such additional solvent may be encountered, for instance, when using an edge bead removal process based on acetone, ethyl lactate, pentanone, or other organic solvents.

4.3 Substrate Contribution to Resist Contamination

Continuous improvements have been made in the materials and processes used for DUV PHS chemically amplified resists to reduce top-surface base contamination effects. An additional contamination problem occurs when processing PHS resists over some substrates. Resists coated over Si_3N_4, BPSG, SOG, Al, and TiN have seen shown to initiate a substrate contamination effect that can result in resist scumming or "footing." With TiN substrates, the problem has been attributed to surface N^{-3} and TiO_2, which can act to neutralize photogenerated acid, resulting in a lowering of the dissolution rate at the resist/substrate interface [28]. Sulfuric acid/hydrogen peroxide and oxygen plasma pretreatments have been shown to reduce contamination effects when coating over Si_3N_4 and other problematic substrates [29].

4.4 Edge Bead Removal

After a spin-coating process, a bead of hardened resist exists at the edge of a wafer substrate. Formation of this edge bead is caused in part by excessive resist drying and can result in resist accumulation up to 10 times the thickness of the coated film. Elimination of this edge bead is required to reduce contamination of process and exposure tools. Solvent edge bead removal (EBR) techniques can be utilized to remove this unwanted resist by spraying a resist solvent on the back side of the wafer substrate. Surface tension allows removal of a 2–3-mm resist edge from the front resist surface while removing any back side resist coating. Acetone, ethyl lactate, and pentanone are possible solvent choices for edge bead removal processes.

5 RESIST BAKING—SOFTBAKE

5.1 Goals of Resist Baking

Baking processes are used to accomplish several functions and generally alter the chemical and/or physical nature of a resist material. Goals of resist baking operations may include the following, which are accomplished at various stages during resist processing:

Solvent removal
Stress reduction
Planarization
Reduction of resist voids
Reduction of standing waves
Polymer crosslinking and oxidation
Polymer densification
Volatilization of sensitizer, developer, and water
Induction of (acid) catalytic reactions
Sensitizer/polymer interactions

Polymeric resist resins are thermoplastic in nature, more amorphous than crystalline, and have glass transition temperatures in the 70 to 180°C range. Thermal flow properties are taken advantage of during processing, in which baking steps at or near the T_g allow some degree of fluid-like resist behavior. In a fluid-like state, stress in a coated film can be reduced and diffusion of solvents, sensitizer, and photoproducts is enhanced. At high resist baking temperatures, sensitizer and polymer decomposition can occur. A proper choice of the baking temperature, time, and method must therefore take into account the evaporation and diffusion properties of solvents, decomposition temperature of PAC or PAG, and diffusion properties of the photoinduced acid and base contaminants for chemically amplified resist materials.

5.2 Resist Solvent and T_g Considerations

There is a relationship between a solvent's evaporation rate or boiling point and the residual solvent content in a resist film. Obtaining such a relationship is difficult, however, because residual solvent is highly dependent on the T_g of the resist. If a baking process does not sufficiently reach the resist T_g, it is difficult to remove solvent to levels below a few percent [30]. The resist T_g therefore plays an important role in the evaporation mechanisms of resist solvent removal. Solvent removal has been shown to occur in two stages. The first stage is the diffusion of solvent molecules at temperatures near T_g and their accumulation at the film surface. The second stage is the evaporation of these adsorbed molecules at higher temperatures, dependent on hydrogen bonding properties.

No compaction would be expected if baking temperatures above the resist bulk T_g values were not reached. In fact, soft bake temperatures 10–20°C below a bulk resist T_g are frequently employed with quite successful results. The reason for this is that the T_g of a resist film is not identical to that of bulk resist. It may actually be a great deal lower. This can be explained by the concept of resist free volume, which is minimized if soft bake temperatures above the bulk T_g value are used. If resists are baked more than 5–10°C below the actual resist film T_g, compaction of this intrinsic free volume generally cannot occur [31].

Several resist material factors affect coated PHS film flow properties and may be modified for optimum CAR performance. In general:

Blocking of phenolic groups in PHS generally results in a lowering of T_g, a consequence of the decrease in hydrogen bonding between phenolic groups. A 40–50°C decrease in polymer flow temperature (T_f) has been reported with 25% blocking of PHS [32].

By modifying the molecular weight of the PHS polymer, 20–25°C of the loss in T_g or T_f due to blocking can be regained.

As the number of phenolic groups is increased (relative to t-BOC protective groups), the deprotection temperature is reduced.

As the number of phenolic groups is increased, T_g is also increased.

These relationships can result is a difficult situation if the deprotection temperature is forced lower than the resist T_g. Further manipulation may be possible through the use of copolymerization or by introducing additional hydrogen bonding sites.

There is a trade-off in determining the optimal soft bake temperature. A high soft bake temperature is desired so that the resist film T_g approaches that of the bulk, which leads to the best thermal performance. But at lower soft bake temperatures, an increase in postexposure acid diffusion is made possible, allowing a reduction in standing waves. To accommodate a lower soft bake temperature, a higher postexposure bake (PEB) may be needed to achieve adequate thermal and plasma etch performance properties (see Section 7 for additional description).

5.3 Softbake

Resist films are coated from a polymer solution, making solvent reduction of a coated film a primary action of soft bake (or prebake). Other consequences of soft baking include a reduction of free volume and polymer relaxation, which have been suggested to be important phenomena that affect resist process performance [33]. Prior to coating, photoresist contains between 65 and 85% solvents. Once cast, the solvent content is reduced to 10–20% and the film can still be considered in a "liquid" state. If it was exposed and processed at this point, several adverse consequences would result. At this high solvent level, the film is tacky and highly susceptible to particulate contamination, which can be transferred through handling to subsequent steps. Also, inherent stress resulting from casting a thin film leads to adhesion problems. The most significant impact resulting from the elimination of a soft bake step is lack of dissolution discrimination between exposed and unexposed resist. With such high solvent levels, the expanded resist volume allows a high degree of dissolution regardless of the state of inhibition, protection, acceleration, or crosslinking. Ideally, a solvent content of a few percent would be desirable. Further densification could then be allowed to control the small molecular diffusion properties. To achieve this, the baking operation must approach the boiling point of the casting solvent (on the order of 140°C for conventional solvent systems). At this elevated temperature, decomposition of the resist sensitizer is likely to occur since DNQ decomposition temperatures are on the order of 100–120°C. Some residual solvent may also be desirable for DNQ/novolac to allow water diffusion and conversion of ketene to ICA. Complete solvent removal at prebake is therefore not attempted; instead adequate removal to allow the best exposure and dissolution properties is targeted. Figure 5 shows the development rate versus soft bake temperature for a DNQ/novolac resist. Four zones exist: (I) a no-bake zone where residual solvent and dissolution rates are high; (II) a low-temperature zone (up to 80°C) where the dissolution rate is reduced due to solvent removal; (III) a midtemperature zone (80–110°C) where DNQ is thermally converted to ICA, leading to an increase in development rate; and (IV) a high-temperature zone (>120°C) where film densification occurs, DNQ is further decomposed, and water is removed, leading to an increase in inhibition rather than acceleration. Also, at these temperatures, oxidation and crosslinking of the novolac begin [34].

Whereas a prebake for DNQ/novolac is required to bring the resist to a state suitable for subsequent exposure and development, control to ±1°C is generally adequate to ensure consistent lithographic performance. This is not the case for chemically amplified resists based on PHS, however. Because acid diffusion is an integral part of both positive and negative acid-catalyzed resist, control of polymer composition and density is critical. Consideration for soft bake differs for high-, mid-, and low-E_a CAR resists depending on the reactivity of the resist to acid-induced deprotection. Resists with a moderate activation energy (E_a) had

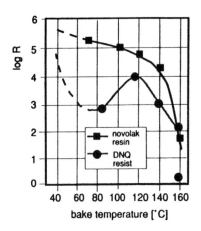

Figure 5   The influence of prebake temperature on dissolution rate (Å/min) for a novolac resin and a DNQ/novolac resist. Prebake time is 30 minutes, developer is 0.25N KOH. (From Ref. 34)

been the conventional route to positive CAR resists. By making use of resists with lower reactivity (high E_a), elevated baking processes above the polymer T_g (~150°C) allow maximum densification and reduction of the diffusion of acid-neutralizing contaminants. This resist design concept also reduces acid diffusion, which can result in an increase in resolution capability [35].

5.4   Resist Baking Methods

The preferred method of resist bake for IC applications utilizes conduction on a vacuum hot plate, usually in line with the entire resist process. Convection baking is another option, performed in an oven and generally used in a batch mode. Loading effects, slow recovery, and poor air circulation uniformity present problems for convection baking with current resist process demands. Microwave and infrared (IR) baking methods have been utilized to a limited extent, but the practicality of these methods is limited because of substrate incompatibility and process control. Both temperature and uniformity control are important for baking processes, the latter becoming most critical as chemically amplified resist requirements are considered. To achieve uniformity, careful consideration of the vacuum plate baking mechanics is required, including temperature uniformity, airflow, and cycle time. To meet the high demands of wafer-to-plate contact across an entire wafer, strict requirements are also placed on contamination control and resist edge bead removal.

Figure 6 shows the mechanisms involved during the first 10 seconds of baking on a vacuum hot plate. Figure 6a shows that the temperature of the wafer

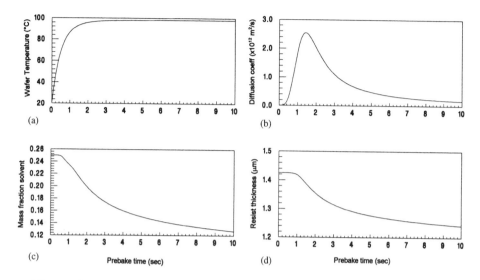

Figure 6 Mechanisms involved during the first ten seconds of hot plate baking of a resist. (a) Rise in wafer temperature; (b) solvent loss; (c) diffusivity; and (d) typical thickness change. [From Mack, C. A. et al., *Proc. SPIE, 2195*, 584 (1994)].

increases with a rapid rise during the first seconds of baking and levels off after 3 seconds. Figure 6b illustrates the solvent loss during this time, which continues to decrease well out to 10 seconds and beyond. Figure 6c shows the impact of baking time on diffusivity, which rises during the initial few seconds and then decreases. Figure 6d shows a typical change in resist thickness during baking, which decreases as the resist density increases.

6 PHOTORESIST EXPOSURE

6.1 Resist Exposure Requirements

Exposure of photoresist involves the absorption of radiation and subsequent photochemical change, generally resulting in a modification of dissolution properties. The absorption characteristics of a photoresist largely influence its resolution and process capabilities. Resists based only on exponential attenuation of radiation (i.e., with no mechanism for photobleaching or chemical amplification) can be limited by a maximum allowable contrast, sidewall angle and ultimate resolution. This is because of the inherent absorption trade-off required when imaging into a resist film. Both maximum transmission (to reach to the bottom of the resist) and maximum absorption (to achieve the highest sensitivity) are desired. There is therefore an optimum resist absorbance value for any resist thickness.

If a resist film has a thickness t and dt is the thickness of the bottommost portion of the resist, the intensity transmitted through the film thickness to dt can be determined from Beer's law:

$$I = I_0 e^{-\varepsilon mt} \tag{4}$$

where ε is the molar extinction coefficient of the sensitizer, and m is the molar concentration. The energy density absorbed at the bottom of the resist is

$$E = I_0 e^{-\varepsilon mt}(1 - e^{-\varepsilon mdt})/dt \tag{5}$$

Since dt is small, $e^{-\varepsilon mdt}$ can be approximated as $I - \varepsilon mdt$ and

$$E = I_0 \varepsilon m e^{-\varepsilon mt} \tag{6}$$

which is maximized when $\varepsilon mt = 1$. Converting to absorbance:

$$\text{Absorbance} = \log_{10} e \cdot \varepsilon mt = 0.434 \tag{7}$$

This is the optimum absorbance for a resist film regardless of thickness. In other words, higher absorption is desired for thinner resists and lower absorption is desired for thicker films. Resists for which chemical amplification or photobleaching is used introduce mechanisms that allow deviation from these constraints. The absorbance of a PAG for chemically amplified resist can be quite low because of the high quantum yield resulting from acatalytic reactions. Photobleaching resists (such as DNQ/novolacs) exhibit dynamic absorption properties, which can allow increased transmission toward the base of a resist film. For these resists, other absorption considerations are required.

The dynamic absorption that exists for DNQ occurs as exposure leads to a more transparent ICA photoproduct. This bleaching phenomenon can be described in terms of Dill absorption parameters A, B, and C [36]. The A parameter describes the exposure-dependent absorption of the resist, the B parameter the exposure-independent absorption, and C the rate of absorption change or bleaching rate. For a DNQ/novolac resist, the C parameter is conveniently related directly to resist sensitivity, since photobleaching corresponds to the conversion of the photoactive compound (PAC) to the photoproduct. (See Chapter 2 for a more detailed discussion of parameter characterization and modeling.) The choice of a specific DNQ compound for mid-UV lithography needs to include evaluation of the unique A, B, and C parameters at the wavelength of exposure. It is generally desirable to have low exposure-independent absorption (B parameter) to achieve maximum exposure efficiency to the bottom of a resist layer. Several approaches exist to minimize residual B parameter absorption of DNQ/novolac resists [37]. These have included the use of highly transparent backbones for multifunctional PACs and binding of the sensitizer to the novolac polymer. A large C parameter is also desirable for maximum sensitivity. Figure 7 shows absorbance spectra for two DNQ/novolac resists. Based only on the evaluation of the absorption prop-

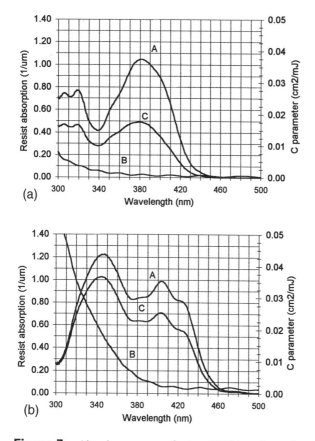

Figure 7 Absorbance curves for two DNQ/novolac resists showing Dill A, B, and C parameters. Resist (a) exhibits lower residual absorption (B parameter) at 365 nm while resist (b) has higher bleachable absorbance and speed (A and C parameters) at 436 nm. (From Prolith/2 V.5.0, 1997.)

erties of these two resists, it can be expected that the resist with a smaller B parameter and larger A and C parameters may perform better (at a specific exposure wavelength) in terms of sensitivity, sidewall angle, and contrast.

Chemical amplification is another avenue that exists to improve the absorption characteristics of a resist. With quantum efficiencies several orders of magnitude higher than what can be achieved for direct photomodified resists, only a small amount of photon absorption is needed. This can be quantified in terms of A and B parameters, which may be on the order of 0.30 μm^{-1} compared with the 0.90 μm^{-1} levels encountered with i-line materials. The downside of such high transparency for resist materials is the increased opportunity for substrate reflection to degrade performance. These effects can be manifested as a line width variation over reflective steps (notching) and a sidewall standing wave. Figure 8 shows standing waves resulting from the coherent interference of incident and reflected radiation within a resist layer. Reduction of these standing waves is crucial in order to retain critical dimension (CD) control. This can be dealt with in either resist exposure or process stages and is ordinarily addressed in both. To reduce standing wave effects during exposure, the reflected contribution to exposure must be controlled. This can be accomplished by incorporating a dye in the resist formulation. Dyes such as coumarin or curcumin compounds have been used as additives to DNQ/novolac resists and are very effective at reducing the reflected exposure contribution in a resist layer at g-line and i-line wavelengths. By adding a dye, the exposure-independent absorption (B parameter) is increased. The result will be a decrease in reflection effects and standing waves but also a decrease in the amount of energy transferred toward the bottom of the resist. This will result in a decrease in sidewall angle, resist contrast, and sensitivity. Dyed resist for i-line use is therefore usually limited to highly reflective, noncritical layers.

Dyes that play a role in the chemistry of a resist system have also been introduced. By transferring the energy absorbed by a dye to the photosensitive component of a resist (for instance, through energy transfer or photoinduced electron transfer mechanisms), an active dye can allow reduction of reflection effects while maintaining sensitivity and resolution. This has been accom-

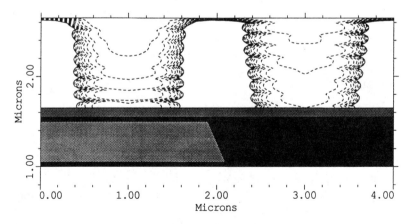

Figure 8   Resist standing waves resulting from coherent interference of incident and reflected radiation within a resist layer. Standing wave phase and amplitude is dependant on the underlying substrate.

plished in chemically amplified PHS resists [38]. The resultant increase in the resist *B* parameter in this case leads to an increase in photoinduced chemical activity, yielding minimal loss in resist performance. Loading of such photoactive dyes can be determined from the preceding analysis for static absorption resists. Resist absorbance on the order of 0.434 could be expected to be best suited for optimal throughput. An alternative to dye incorporation is the use of an anti-reflective layer below the resist. The requirements of current IC processes will soon demand that substrate reflectivity be reduced to levels below 1% for critical layers. The use of such antireflective coatings (ARCs) has become a popular practice for i-line and DUV lithography and is discussed in more detail in Chapter 10.

6.2 Resist Exposure and Process Performance

The sensitivity (E_0) described earlier is a bulk resist characteristic that is useful for resist process comparisons or non-feature-specific process optimization. Resist E_0 swing curves allow for instance the determination of optimum coating thickness values. Monitoring of clearing dose requirements is also useful for characterization of exposure or development uniformity. Through the use of an exposure response curve, as shown in Fig. 9, two additional bulk resist parameters can be obtained that allow further process characterization. Normalized

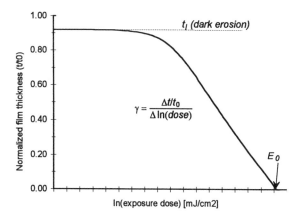

Figure 9   Normalized thickness as a function of $\log_e$-exposure for a positive resist of a given thickness, exposed and developed under specific process conditions. An area of linearity exists in the logarithmic relationship, which can be characterized using a single contrast term (γ). Resist clearing dose (E_0) is the point on the exposure dose axis where normalized thickness becomes zero and the normalized thickness loss (t_l) is an indication of the amount of resist erosion that occurs in unexposed regions.

thickness (normalized to initial predevelopment thickness) is plotted as a function of $\log_e$ exposure for a positive resist of a given thickness, exposed and developed under specific process conditions. An area of linearity exists in the logarithmic relationship, which can be characterized using a single contrast term:

$$\gamma = \frac{\Delta t / t_0}{\Delta \ln(\text{dose})} \tag{8}$$

where t is thickness and t_0 is the initial coating thickness. Resist sensitivity or clearing dose (E_0) is the point on the exposure dose axis at which the normalized thickness becomes zero. A third parameter that is useful for describing resist capability is a normalized thickness loss parameter (t_1), which is an indication of the amount of resist erosion that occurs in unexposed regions (also called dark erosion). An exposure response curve can be generated uniquely for any resist/development process or can be obtained from a more general development rate curve, described in greater detail in Section 8. Figure 10 shows a development rate curve, where resist dissolution rate is plotted as a function of $\log_e$ exposure dose for a positive resist. As exposure is increased, the dissolution rate increases. The linearity of this relationship can be realized on a log-log plot, but a lognormal plot is used here to demonstrate the relationship between a development rate and exposure response curve. Plotted along with dissolution rate in Fig. 10 is an exposure response curve for this resist coated at 9000 Å and developed for 60 seconds.

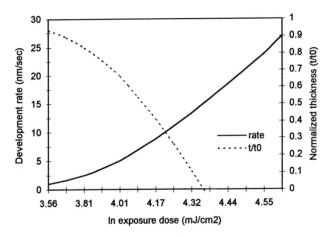

Figure 10   Resist dissolution rate (nm/sec) plotted as a function of $\log_e$ exposure dose for a positive resist. Plotted also is an exposure response curve for this resist coated at 9000 Å and developed for 60 seconds.

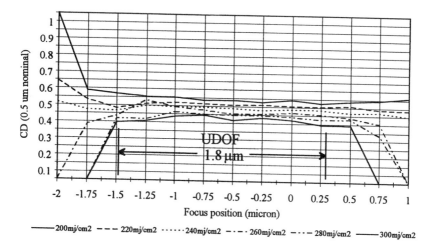

Figure 11 A focus exposure matrix for 0.5 μm dense line features in a positive i-line resist over polysilicon using a numerical aperture of 0.45 and partial coherence of 0.60. Resulting usable depth of focus (UDOF) is 1.8 μm for a CD specification of ± 10% and an exposure latitude requirement of 20%. The corresponding k_2 value for this single layer resist process is near 0.5.

6.3 Exposure and Process Optimization

In order to determine the optimum exposure dose (or range of doses) for a resist process, bulk resist characterization needs to be augmented with feature-specific characterization. To accomplish this, process specifications must be defined uniquely for each feature type and size, mask level, substrate, resist, and process. This is often a difficult task, because definition of an optimum process requires operation at a near-optimum level. The task is therefore an iterative one that can often be made easier through the use of lithographic simulation tools.

Consider the focus-exposure matrix in Fig. 11. Here 0.5-μm dense lines are imaged into an i-line resist with a projection system at a partial coherence of 0.5. Resist CD is plotted against focal position for a series of exposure dose values. The nominal focus setting is labeled 0.0 and is typically at a point near 30% from the top surface, depending on the resist refractive index and to a lesser extent NA and σ (for high NA values). At this position, there is an optimum exposure dose for printing a biased mask CD to its targeted size (see Chapter 3 for a description of mask biasing). As focal position is changed, the feature no longer prints at the target value; it is either too small or too large. The adverse influence of overexposure or underexposure is also increased. This can be understood by considering an aerial image as it is varied through focus, as shown in Fig. 12. At best focus, a relatively large range of exposure variation can be tolerated. As defocus increases, a small amount of overexposure can result in a large amount of energy in shadow areas. Underexposure can result in insufficient energy in clear areas. An exposure must be chosen, therefore, to allow the greatest range of usable focus that results in a CD that remains within the specified target range. More appropriately, a specification is placed on the required exposure latitude to account for within-field and field-to-field non-uniformities. Together with tolerance limits on CD, a resulting usable depth of focus (UDOF) can be determined. For instance, for a ±10% exposure latitude requirement and a ±10% specification on CD, the optimum exposure from Fig. 11 is 240 mJ/cm^2 and the UDOF is near 1.8 µm. The resulting UDOF needs to be evaluated with respect to device topography. It should also be noted that any change is resist process will influence the depth of focus. Any process enhancement methods, whether optical or chemical, have the potential to improve focal depth. These can include the use of reflection suppression (e.g., with an ARC), modified PEB, enhancements of contrast, and improvements in developer selectivity. For evaluation purposes, it is convenient to express a normalized UDOF through use of the Raleigh DOF k_2 factor:

$$k_2 = \frac{(UDOF)(NA^2)}{2\lambda} \tag{9}$$

The corresponding k_2 factor for the focus-exposure matrix of Fig. 11 is near 0.5. Generally, single-layer resist processes can produce k_2 in the range of 0.4 to 0.6.

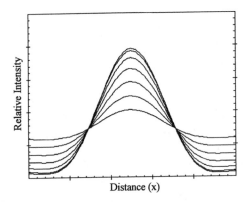

Figure 12 Through focus aerial images for ± 1λ/NA^2 of defocus. Images with no defocus can tolerate a large exposure variation. As defocus is increased, the choice of optimum exposure becomes more critical.

If a resulting k_2 does not correspond to UDOF values large enough for device topography, techniques of planarization may be required. Polymeric planarization is one alternative but is generally not considered to be robust enough to allow adequate process latitude for high-resolution IC applications. Chemical mechanical polishing (CMP) techniques, in which substrate surfaces are polished to reduce topography, are becoming commonplace in many IC process operations. From lithographic standpoint, CMP can be considered as operation that allows improvements in focal depth, CD tolerance, and exposure dose control.

A focus-exposure matrix can also be generated for resist sidewall angle, although this is a much more difficult task than for CD. Figure 13a shows sidewall angle focus-exposure matrix and Fig. 13b shows the corresponding array of resist feature profiles. At an optimum exposure dose value, the base CD of the features remains tightly controlled. At negative values of focus (corresponding to the bottom of the resist), there is a widening at the base of features. At positive focus values (toward the lens), feature thinning occurs. In order to evaluate the impact of these changes through focus and exposure, subsequent etch process selectivity and isotropy need to be considered. If overexposure or underexposure is used to tune CD over topography (corresponding to a shift in focal position), it is likely that the resulting feature sidewall angle will not be adequate. A growing trend in sidewall angle specification is >85°.

From these types of feature-specific process evaluation techniques, it can be understood why it is difficult to increase exposure throughput for a resist without adversely affecting overall performance. For features large enough that aerial image modulation is high (i.e., there is little energy in shadow regions and sufficient energy in clear areas), there will exist a good deal of exposure latitude and UDOF so that some degree of exposure tuning is possible. As features approach $R = 0.5\lambda/NA$ in size, the situation becomes challenging for conventional binary masking and single-layer resists.

Line width linearity has already been discussed as it applies to optical imaging systems. Photoresist materials also behave with a nonlinear response to exposure, which can be seen in the exposure response and development rate curves in Figs. 9 and 10. These nonlinearities can be used to the advantage of the lithographic process. Because the modulation needed for small features is much lower than for large features, it would be expected that a resist that reacted linearly to exposure would do a poor job of faithfully reproducing mask features below $1\lambda/NA$ in size. By tailoring the exposure and dissolution response properties of a resist to operate in a specific desirable nonlinear fashion (nonlinearity itself does not imply added capability), the linearity of the entire lithographic process can be improved. Figure 14 shows a plot of resist CD versus mask CD for an i-line resist process. Only as features approach 0.45 μm in size does the linear relationship between the mask and the resist

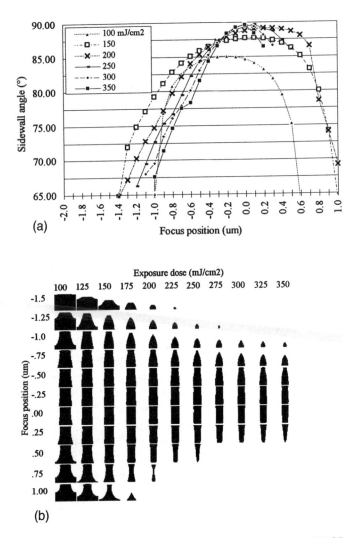

Figure 13 (a) A sidewall angle focus exposure matrix. UDOF can be determined from a sidewall angle specification and exposure latitude requirements. (b) Corresponding array of resist feature profiles.

feature begin to break down. Features in this region require unique mask biasing in order to print to their targeted size. The situation becomes more complex as various feature types are considered and resist linearity down to the minimum size of device geometry is desirable.

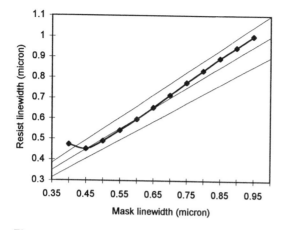

Figure 14 Plot of mask CD vs. resist CD for an i-line resist process. As features approach 0.45 μm, the linear relationship between mask and resist feature begins to break down. Features in this region require unique mask biasing in order to print to their targeted size.

7 POSTEXPOSURE BAKE

A postexposure bake (PEB) of DNQ/novolac resist brings about chemical and physical actions similar to those for prebake. By subjecting resist films to a predevelopment bake step at a temperature higher than that used during prebake, some DNQ decomposition prior to exposure can be reduced. By baking exposed resists at temperatures on the order of 5–15°C higher than prebake temperatures, solvent content can be reduced from 4–7% (prior to exposure) to 2–5%. Whereas prebake is generally performed to bring the resist into region II in Fig. 5, the elevated temperatures used for PEB places the resist toward region III. The most beneficial consequence of a PEB step is, however, not an extended action of earlier bake steps but instead a significant impact on standing wave reduction via thermal flow [39]. During exposure over a reflective substrate, coherent interference produces a distribution of intensity within the resist film. The nodal spacing is a function of the resist refractive index (n_i) and wavelength:

$$\text{Distance between nodes} = \frac{\lambda}{2n_i} \tag{10}$$

The amplitude of the resist standing wave will be affected by absorbance of the resist (α) (which may be dynamic if resist bleaching occurs), resist thickness (t), and reflectance at the resist-air (R_1) and resist-substrate (R_2) interfaces [40] resulting in a swing effect where

Standing wave "swing" $= 4\sqrt{R_1 R_2} \exp(-\alpha t)$ \hfill (11)

Interface reflectance values (R_1 and R_2) are determined from the complex refractive index values of the media involved:

$$\text{Reflectance} = \left(\frac{n_a^* - n_b^*}{n_a^* + n_b^*} \right)^2 \hfill (12)$$

In addition to resist and substrate contributions to interference effects, exposure source characteristics need to be considered. The coherence length (l_c) for a radiation source is determined on the basis of the source wavelength (λ) and bandwidth ($\Delta\lambda$) as

$$l_c = \frac{\lambda^2}{\Delta\lambda} \hfill (13)$$

As the resist thickness approaches the source coherent length, interference effects (standing waves) become negligible. A typical coherence length for i-line stepper tools may be on the order of 10 μm. For a 248-nm lamp-based step-and-scan system, l_c may be on the same order, but as excimer laser lithography is pursued, a 10^3–10^4 factor increase occurs. Although it is not expected that resist would be coated to thicknesses approaching 10 μm or more, the analysis offers insight into the increasingly critical concern with standing wave control. Considered together with the higher transparency (low α) of chemically amplified resist, it becomes obvious that resist imaging over reflective substrates using an excimer laser source would be difficult without employing means of control or compensation.

To demonstrate the impact that a PEB step can have on resist standing waves, consider Fig. 15. Unexposed regions of photoresist contain photoactive compound, exposed regions contain photoproduct, and the boundary between them is determined by the constructive and destructive interference nodes of the exposure standing wave. If the resist temperature is raised near or above its T_g, the PAC can effectively diffuse through the polymer matrix and produce an averaging effect across the exposed/unexposed boundary. This PAC diffusion is a function of the resist T_g, the PAC size and functionality, bake time and temperature, remaining solvent concentration, resist free volume, and (for DNQ/novolac, for instance) any binding between the PAC and the resin. Figure 16 shows the resist standing wave pattern as a function of the PAC diffusion length.

For chemically amplified resists based on thermally induced acid reactions, PEB is used to accomplish critical chemical stages and must be considered nearly as critical as exposure in terms of control, uniformity, and latitude requirements. The concept of a bake "dose" control is a convenient comparative metric to exposure dose control for acid-catalyzed deprotection (positive resists) or crosslinking (negative resists). An Arrhenius relationship exists between PEB

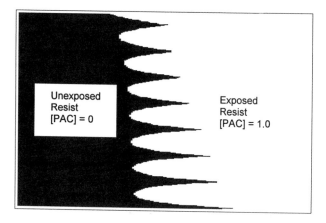

Figure 15   Distribution of photoactive compound (PAC) as a result of standing wave resist exposure. Unexposed regions of photoresist contain PAC, exposed regions contain photo-product. As the resist temperature is raised near or above its T_g, the PAC can effectively diffuse through the polymer matrix to reduce effective standing wave in the developed resist sidewall.

and exposure, such as that shown in Fig. 17 [41]. Here, log exposure dose is plotted against 1/PEB, from which an effective E_a can be determined. Whereas exposure uniformity on the order of ~1% is a current requirement for resist exposure tools, it can be expected that PEB control should be at least as critical. The rate of these reactions is a function of the acid concentration, the activation energy of the protected polymer, the diffusivity of the acid, and the PEB conditions.

Acid diffusion in PHS chemically amplified resists is generally on the order of 50 to a few hundred angstroms, limited by resolution requirements. If neutralization of acid occurs, the exposed resist dissolution rate decreases. If environmental contamination occurs after exposure and prior to PEB, a thin, less soluble inhibition layer forms on the top surface of the resist, which results in the formation of a characteristic T-top upon development, as shown in Fig. 18. Any delay between exposure and PEB (known as postexposure delay, PED) allows this phenomenon to occur. Early material PED time requirements were on the order of a few minutes. Newer resists may allow delays up to several hours. It is important to realize, however, that acid neutralization can begin immediately upon exposure and performance must be evaluated for the specific resist process conditions and process tolerances. Low-E_a resists do not require elevated PEB temperatures for reaction, which can minimize the control requirements for this process step. These resists cannot tolerate high baking temperatures, which may introduce additional stability problems. Choice of the

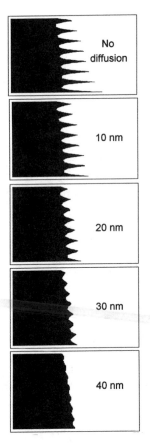

Figure 16 Simulated standing wave pattern in developed resist as a function of increasing PAC diffusion length.

PAG is less critical, allowing choices with smaller cross sections than those needed for high-activation-energy materials. Diffusion properties are also based on size and should be evaluated uniquely for resists of either category.

When determining PEB requirements for deprotection, postexposure solvent content and polymer density also need to be taken into consideration. Temperature control on the order of 0.1°C may be required, with uniformity needs on the same order over wafer diameters approaching 300 mm. Material improvements may relax this requirement somewhat, but control to a few tenths of a degree can be expected as an upper limit.

An additional improvement brought about through the use of a PEB step is a potential increase in resist development rate properties, specifically the dis-

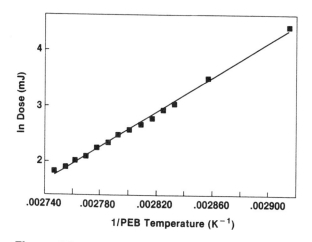

Figure 17 Arrhenius plot of resist sensitivity vs. PEB temperature for a DUV CAR resist. Dose required to print 0.5 μm lines with a 90 second bake is plotted against 1/PEB temperature. An effective activation energy can be calculated from such a plot (130 kJ/mole in this case). (From Ref. 41.)

solution rate log slope (DLS) as discussed in the development section [42]. This occurs as a result of the decrease in resist dissolution rate especially at the resist surface, which is more pronounced in some resists than in others. By reducing the surface dissolution rate, unexposed film erosion can be reduced, resulting in an increase in sidewall slope and an improvement in process latitude. This surface modification is a result of solvent loss and a possible surface "skin" effect, enhanced by resist modification at elevated temperatures.

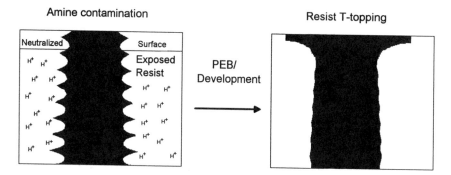

Figure 18 Environmental amine contamination of a chemically amplified (PHS) resist resulting in "T-top" formation after development.

For optimal process performance, PEB processes for chemically amplified PHS resists cannot be considered separately from soft bake steps. There are trade-offs between high and low levels of each. During soft bake of a chemically amplified PHS-based resist, standing waves can be reduced through use of lower temperatures, which allow an increase in acid diffusion across the exposed/unexposed resist boundary. To reduce T-top formation, a high PEB is also desirable. Through use of high PEB temperatures, deprotection can occur even with some degree of reduced acid concentration at the resist top surface. This low soft bake, high PEB combination can result in additional undesirable phenomena. When the resist film is allowed to retain a relatively low T_g, pattern deformation can result from rapid PHS deprotection and subsequent gas evolution at high PEB temperatures. A stepwise PEB has been suggested as a possible solution [43]. An initial low-temperature stage removes protective groups from the bulk of the resist with minimum deformation. A high-temperature stage follows to enhance top surface deprotection and reduce T-top formation.

As discussed earlier, intrinsic or added free volume will affect the glass transition and dissolution properties and deprotection mechanisms of phenolic-based photoresists. The CAR deprotection reaction itself has also been shown to contribute additional free volume [44]. Exposure or PEB-induced variation in resist density can affect dissolution uniformity and CD control. This added influence of exposure and PEB can lead to complex relationships and increased control requirements. The deprotection and densification mechanisms can best be separated in resist systems with low activation energies.

8 RESIST DEVELOPMENT

Resist systems based on solvent development, such as crosslinking bis-arylazide *cis*-polyisoprene negative resists, require some degree of swelling to allow removal of soluble polymer chains or fragments [45]. To keep resist pattern deformation to a minimum, a series of solvents is generally needed for development, with careful consideration of kinetic and thermodynamic properties [46]. The development of resists based on novolac, PHS, or other phenolic resins involves similar dissolution stages but does not require such adverse swelling for dissolution [47–49].

8.1 Dissolution Kinetics of Phenolic Resin Resists

In novolac resins, a narrow penetration zone is formed as water and hydroxyl groups are incorporated in the novolac matrix. This zone is rate limited and does not encompass the entire resist layer, allowing dissolution of resist with minimal swelling. Following the formation of this intermediate layer, phenol is deprotonated and the resulting phenolic ion reacts with water. The negative charge of the phenolate ion is balanced by the developer cations. Upon sufficient conversion of phenol groups, the polymer is soluble in aqueous alkaline developer. A three-zone model has also been suggested, as shown in Fig. 19 [50]. These zones exist during novolac development:

1. A gel layer containing water, TMAH (base), and partially ionized novolac. The thickness of this layer depends on agitation, novolac microstructure, and the developer cation.
2. A penetration zone with a low degree of ionization. The thickness of this zone also depends on the novolac structure as well as the developer cation size and hydrophobicity.
3. Unreacted bulk novolac resist.

The resulting dissolution rate of a resist material is determined by the formation of the gel and penetration layers and the subsequent dissolution of the gel layer into developer.

In DNQ/novolac resists, exposure of the PAC leads to photoproduction of ICA, which acts as a dissolution accelerator. First-order kinetic models for development are based on this mechanism (see, for instance, Chapter 2). DNQ in sufficiently high concentrations (5–25 wt. %) also acts as a dissolution inhibitor to the phenolic novolac resin, decreasing its hydrophilic nature (enhanced development models described in Chapter 2 also account for this phenomenon). This inhibition effect can also be accomplished with other compatible compounds and is not limited to DNQ. It might be reasoned that a similar mechanism would exist for PHS resins, but this is not the case. Although

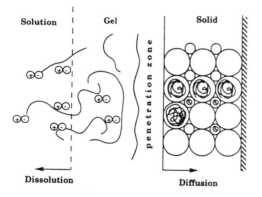

Figure 19 Diagram of a three zone novolac dissolution model with a gel layer containing water, base, and hydrated, partially ionized novolac chains; a penetration zone; and unreacted novolac. (From Ref. 50.)

the dissolution of novolac can be decreased when combined with DNQ by as much as two orders of magnitude, the high dissolution rate of PHS is not significantly reduced. This can be explained by considering the hydrophilic nature of both materials. Novolac is for the most part a hydrophobic resin with hydrophilic sites created when developer reacts with hydroxyl groups. These phenolate ion positions allow a diffusion path for development. The sites of hydroxyl groups are only potential hydrophilic sites, which can be tied up or isolated by the polymer's large aromatic rings. PHS is a vinyl polymer with no aromatic rings in the backbone. Hydroxyl groups exist in a "corkscrew" configuration along the polymer chain, allowing very effective diffusion paths and extremely high dissolution rates.

The dissolution kinetics of chemically amplified resists based on PHS are also quite different from those for DNQ/novolac. Whereas the dissolution of novolac resins is determined by two competitive reactions (inhibition by the DNQ and acceleration resulting from the developer-induced deprotonation of the novolac), there is one primary rate-determining stage for two-component PHS chemically amplified resists. A similar developer-induced deprotonation of phenolic hydroxyl groups has been shown to dominate for negative resists, whereas developer penetration into hydrophobic t-BOC-protected PHS is rate determining for positive resists [51].

8.2   Development and Dissolution Rate Characterization

Development of conventional resist materials is based on imagewise dissolution discrimination. To understand and optimize photoresist development, it is necessary to characterize exposure-dependent dissolution properties. As discussed earlier, the extraction of development rate and exposure relationships allows tremendous insight into the imaging capabilities of a resist process. Shown in Fig. 20 is a family of normalized thickness versus development time curves for a resist material exposed at various dose levels. Such curves can be obtained using laser interferometry techniques and separate substrate exposure [52,53] or a single substrate and multiple exposures [54]. A development rate versus exposure curve such as that in Fig. 21 can be produced from a family of these dissolution curves. To characterize fully the dissolution properties of a resist throughout its entire thickness, a rate curve may not suffice, because development rate is a function of resist thickness. Surface inhibition reduces the development rate significantly at the top surface of the resist. Figure 22 shows a development rate versus resist thickness curve demonstrating that development rate increases from the top surface of the resist toward the bottom.

When development rate and exposure are plotted in a log-log fashion, as shown in Fig. 23, a linear region exists that can be described in terms of a development rate log slope (DLS):

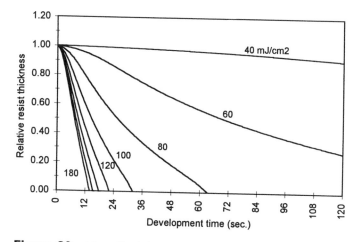

Figure 20 Normalized film thickness versus development time curves for resist exposed at 40 to 180 mJ/cm². Selection of single development time values can lead to development rate vs. relative exposure curves.

$$\text{DLS} = \frac{\partial \ln(\text{dev. rate})}{\partial \ln(\text{dose})} \tag{14}$$

Dissolution rate contrast can be expressed as

$$\text{Contrast} = \frac{R_{max}}{R_{min}} \tag{15}$$

where R_{max} and R_{min} are the maximum and the minimum development rate, respectively. Together, DLS and dissolution rate contrast are effective measures

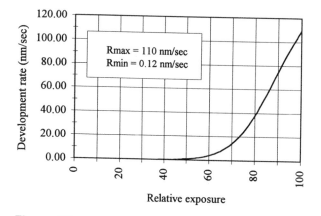

Figure 21 A development rate vs. relative exposure curve from Figure 20.

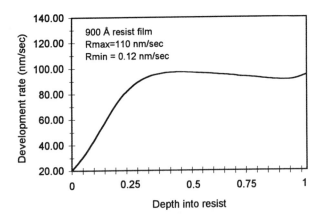

Figure 22   A development rate vs. resist thickness curve, showing distribution of dissolution properties through a resist film.

of the dissolution properties of a resist material. High levels of both metrics are desirable. Control of the resist and development properties can be used can be used to some extent to influence performance. A moderate contrast value near 10,000 is generally sufficient. As developer normality is changed, R_{max} and R_{min} are both affected (as long as base concentration does not fall below a critical level, pH ~12.5), but their ratio and the shape of the curve remain fairly constant [55]. The R_{max} is primarily a function of the polymer itself. Major resist, sensitizer, and solvent factors that influence development rate include:

Polymeric structure
PAC/PAG/inhibitor structure
PAC/PAG/inhibitor concentrations (DNQ loading >20%)
Protection ratio (PHS protection ratio >25%)
Solvent concentration
Polymeric molecular weight (>1.3 × 10⁴ g/mol)
Polydispersity (<3)
Developer composition (metal ion vs. TMAH)
Developer cation size and concentration
Resist surfactant
Resist dissolution inhibition/acceleration state
Developer surfactant

Hydroxyl group positions on PHS polymer also affect the dissolution rate, a function of hydrogen bonding and steric hindrance with the polymer backbone

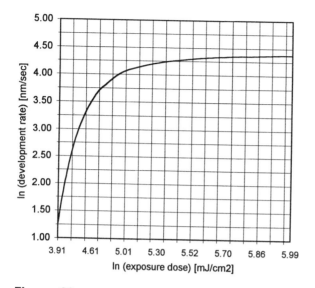

Figure 23 Log development rate vs. log exposure dose. Dissolution rate performance can be evaluated in terms of the slope of the linear region of the curve and the R_{max}/R_{min} ratio.

[56]. Copolymers of 2- and 4-hydroxystyrene have been shown to allow control of PHS dissolution properties.

8.3 Developer Composition

Phenolic resin–based resists can be developed using buffered alkaline solutions such as sodium metal silicates. These metal silicate developers yield a maximum development rate and low dark erosion, compared with most other developer choices. Possible metal ion contamination of devices has nearly eliminated the use of this class developer, however, in favor of metal ion–free tetramethylammonium hydroxide (TMAH). Furthermore, standardization of TMAH developer formulations is becoming widespread, as it is more economical and allows better quality control if there are no requirements for coexistence of several developer types. The larger cross section of TMAH compared with NaOH leads to lower development rates, which may result in lower working sensitivities. TMAH developer concentrations in the range of 0.2 to 0.3 N allow sufficient sensitivity with high contrast and minimum erosion. A 0.26 N solution is becoming a standard for U.S. and overseas resist processing.

In addition to TMAH, surfactants are added to a developer to reduce development time and scumming. Surfactants are used as additives to photoresists, chemical etchants, and developers to improve surface activity or wetting. TMAH developers often employ surfactants at the ppm level to reduce surface tension. Surfactants are especially useful for improving the dissolution of small-surface-area features such as contacts or small space features. By increasing the effective wetting of the developer, scumming problems can be minimized and overexposure- or overdevelopment-induced process biases can be reduced. Also, through the use of developer surfactants, initial development inhibition at the resist surface can be reduced. Additives used for resist developers are mainly of the nonionic variety with hydrophilic and hydrophobic structural characteristics, such as ethylene oxide/propylene oxide block polymer segments with molecular weights near 1000. Concentrations may be up to 800 ppm or 0.05 wt. %. Surface tension decreases as the concentration of surfactants increases until a critical micelle concentration (CMC) is reached. This CMC level represents an equilibrium state at which aggregation begins. Very small changes in the structure of surfactant molecules have been shown to result in large changes in resist development performance. The number and location of hydroxyl groups in the molecular structure of the surfactant determine the activity of surface dissolution during development [57]. The behavior of developer surfactants also depends on resist material properties. Resists that have a larger degree of surface hydrophobicity benefit most from surfactant additives and have been shown to be less dependent on surfactant type. The benefits gained for a particular resist therefore depend on unique resist and surfactant properties and interactions. Figure 24 shows how surface agents acting at a resist/developer interface enhance the surface activity by decreasing surface free energy [58].

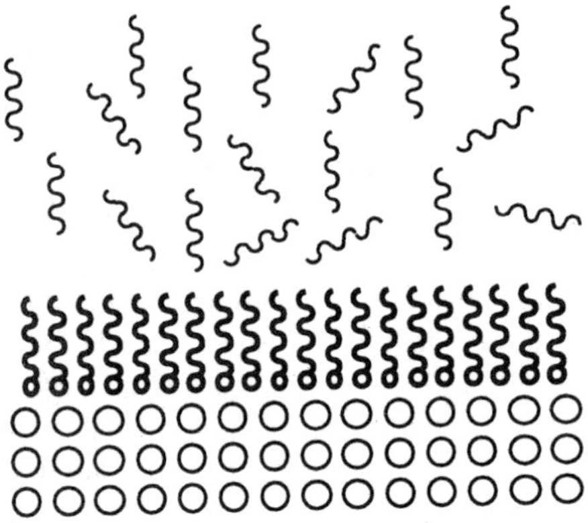

Figure 24   Orientation of surface molecules (center) at a hydrophobic (top) / hydrophilic (bottom) interface. The surfactant molecules are oriented so as to lower the interfacial free energy. (From Ref. 58.)

In addition to the chemical composition of the developer, the concentrations of hydroxyl ions, developer cations, and anions have been shown to strongly influence the dissolution rate of pure novolac films [59]. As the cation concentration is increased, a linear increase in dissolution rate occurs at a constant pH, apparently independent of anion concentration [60]. The structure of the developer cation and anion will determine the maximum allowable concentration before a decrease in dissolution rate begins. Along with the dissolution dependence on the size of the developer cation, its hydrophilicity and the T_g of the partially ionized novolac also influence the development rate [61].

Development temperature is important and requires tight control. This is true not only for the bulk development reservoir and plumbing but also for the development bowl and development atmosphere. The rate of dissolution for TMAH developers follows an Arrhenius relationship:

$$k = A_0 e^{-Ea/RT} \tag{16}$$

with an apparent negative activation energy (E_a) [62]. The reason for this is a highly exothermic sequence of deprotonation steps. A decrease in development temperature results in increased activity, which can seem counterintuitive. This is not the case for development with NaOH or developers with similar chemistry, since no exothermic reactions exist.

8.4 Development Methods

Resist dissolution properties are highly dependent on the development method employed. Development methods commonly used for conventionally coated wafer substrates include static immersion, continuous spray with slow rotation (~500 RPM), and stationary or slow rotation puddle development.

Spray development involves one or more spray nozzles to dispense developer toward the wafer substrate. Processes using ultrasonic atomization of developer allow relatively low velocity dispersion and minimal adiabatic cooling effects during the dispensing. For conventional spray development, the resist dissolution rate has been shown to be relatively insensitive to spray nozzle pressure but linearly dependent on spin speed [63]. With ultrasonic spray development, dissolution variation and resist erosion can result from poor control of the nozzle spray pattern. Dissolution rate and uniformity are also dependent on the uniformity of the spray pattern directed toward the wafer. To minimize nonuniformities, wafer chuck rotation must be carefully controlled at fairly low speeds (100–500 RPM) to ensure adequate developer replenishment. It is for these reasons, along with the excessive developer volume dispensed during processing, that puddle processes are now most common for high-volume production.

Puddle development techniques can improve the tool-to-tool matching of development processes. In addition, the control of puddle development processes over time is significantly better. For optimal performance, flow is kept low to reduce variations in development rate at the edge of the wafer. The dispensed volume of developer should also be kept low to minimize chemical costs and back side wetting but not so low as to cause localized nonuniformities or scumming. The dispensed volume should be carefully controlled to ensure full and uniform coverage of the entire resist surface. During a puddle development process, slow rotation or single rotation may be used to disperse trapped air and provide agitation. If a surfactant-free developer is used, an increase in dispensing pressure may be required to enhance resist wetting.

There are several trade-offs to consider when making a choice between spray, puddle, and immersion methods. Although immersion development can lead to minimum erosion by physical removal of resist, it is not well suited to the in-line processing that now dominates in production. During puddle development, chemical activity decreases with time as the small developer volume becomes exhausted, a situation that is not encountered during immersion processing. There is a more subtle difference between these two techniques as the depletion of developer additives is considered. At ppm levels, surfactants can be exhausted during static immersion development, significantly changing the chemical nature of the developer with time. Since puddle development introduces fresh chemistry for every wafer, consistent wafer-to-wafer development can be ensured. A multiple-puddle method of development [64] is now commonplace in wafer processing and usually involves two development stages. The process consists of dispensing developer onto a wafer and allowing it to remain for a short time (10–20 seconds). It is then spun off and a second puddle is formed and allowed to complete the process (20–30 seconds). Although such multiple-puddle processes serve to replenish developer to the resist, the effect that makes this technique most attractive is an inhibition that occurs between development cycles. The dissolution of unexposed or partially exposed resist will be preferentially slowed at the location of the resist front after the end of the first development step. This phenomenon can be enhanced if rinse and spin-dry steps are added between development cycles [65]. The inhibition may be a result of base-induced oxidation or azo coupling of the novolac. It has also been suggested that a surface modification occurs with interrupted development and an increase in surface energy can enhance resist dissolution discrimination [66]. Multiple development step processing has been also reported and variations on these techniques are now widespread [67]. Intermediate development baking processes have also been investigated [68]. Figure 25 shows resist film thickness plotted as a function of exposure dose for double-puddle and warm-air intermediate development baking processes. Resist contrast is effectively increased with the use of the warm-air bake.

It is important to rinse remaining chemicals from the wafer surface after development because inadequate removal can result in high defect levels. Not

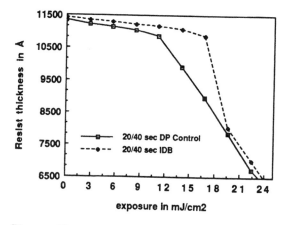

Figure 25 Resist film thickness vs. exposure dose for interrupted double puddle (DP) development and for 50°C warm water intermediate development bake (IDB) showing improvement in resist contrast with IDB. (From Ref. 68.)

only a top-side rinse but also a back side rinse is needed to remove developer and contaminants that could be transferred to subsequent process steps.

8.5 Development Rate Comparison of I-Line and DUV Resists

Although similarities exist between the dissolution properties of DNQ/novolac and PHS-based chemically amplified resists, comparison of these materials demonstrates salient differences in their performance and capabilities. Development rate curves are the tools best suited for this type of comparison. Shown in Fig. 26 are development rate curves for an i-line DNQ/novolac resist, a negative DUV chemically amplified resist, and a positive DUV chemically amplified resist [69]. The negative DUV resist is a three-component acid hardening resist based on a phenolic resin (PHS), a melamine crosslinker, and a photoacid generator [70]. The positive DUV resist is a t-BOC-protected PHS and a photoacid generator [71]. The rate curve for the i-line resist (Fig. 26a) shows a nonlinear dissolution rate that can be divided into three regions. The ability of this resist to achieve high contrast (γ) is evident from the steep development rate log slope (DLS). A large development rate contrast (R_{max}/R_{min}) also exists, leading to high sensitivity and low erosion properties. Figure 27a shows an Arrhenius plot for this resist, where three distinct regions also exist: (I) a high-dose, low-temperature region where E_a is small and positive, (II) an intermediate region where E_a is negative and decreasing, and (III) a low-dose, high-temperature region where E_a is positive and comparatively large. These re-

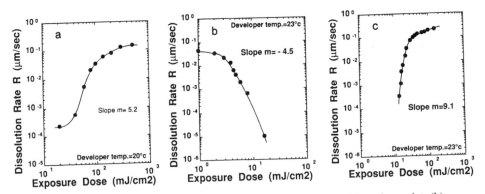

Figure 26 Log development rate curves for (a) an i-line DNQ/novolac resist; (b) a negative DUV chemically amplified resist; and (c) a positive DUV chemically amplified resist. Slope is the development rate log slope (DSL). (From Ref. 69.)

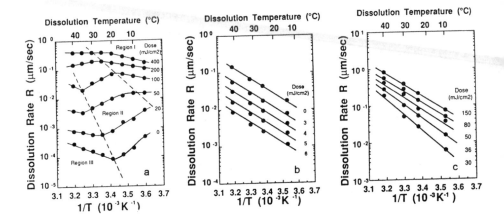

Figure 27 Arrhenius plots for the three resists in Figure 26; (a) shows an Arrhenius plot for the i-line resist where three distinct regions exist: (I) a high dose/low temperature region where E_a is small and positive, (II) an intermediate region where E_a is negative and decreasing, and (III) a low dose/high temperature region where E_a is positive and comparatively large; (b) shows a constant E_a for the negative CAR and suggests that only one reaction mechanism governs development rate; and (c) suggests also a single dissolution mechanism for the positive CAR but a saturation of E_a appears to exist at higher doses where nation of hydroxyl groups at the PHS becomes rate determining, similar to the mechanism for the negative resist. (From Ref. 69.)

sults can be compared with the development rate curves for the negative DUV resist (Fig. 26b and 27b). In this case, a moderately high DLS exists, and when compared with the i-line resist, it would be expected to coincide with worse lithographic performance. The Arrhenius plot shows a constant E_a and suggests that only one reaction mechanism governs development rate. Figure 26c and 27c show plots for the positive DUV resist. The DLS value is much greater than that for either the i-line or the negative resist. The Arrhenius plot also suggests a single dissolution mechanism, but a saturation of E_a appears to exist at higher doses. At these high doses, deprotonation of hydroxyl groups at the PHS becomes rate determining, as in the mechanism for the negative resist. Figure 28 shows the proposed dissolution model for the positive DUV chemically amplified resist. Figure 29a and 29b show development rate curves for a three-component positive DUV resist, which includes an additional dissolution inhibitor and various t-BOC protection levels and molecular weights [72]. Shown in Fig. 30 are plots of dissolution rate and log slope as a function of inhibitor concentration for a three-component PHS chemically amplified resist [73]. Increasing both the protection ratio and the inhibitor concentration results in higher R_{max}/R_{min} contrast and DLS values. Strong surface inhibition effects can limit the practical levels. The optimum protection ratio from Fig. 30 is on the order of 30–35% with an inhibitor concentration of 3%. PAG structure modification, molecular weight polydispersity, and polymer end groups can allow further improvements.

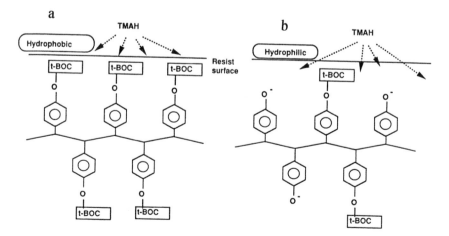

Figure 28   A proposed dissolution model for positive DUV chemically amplified resist derived from Arrhenius plot analysis. Two situations are considered: (a) before deblocking where TMAH penetration is prevented by strong hydrophobicity and (b) after deblocking. (From Ref. 69.)

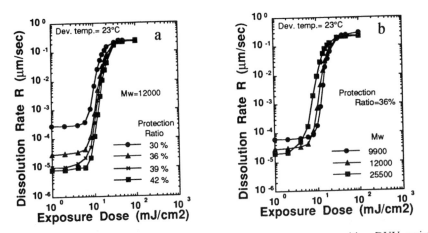

Figure 29 Development rate curves for a three component positive DUV resist, which includes an additional dissolution inhibitor and various t-BOC protection levels and molecular weights. (From Ref. 72.)

Preferential dissolution conditions for positive PHS chemically amplified resists can be summarized. A high R_{max}/R_{min} contrast is desirable, but not so high as to result in severe resolution of sidewall standing waves (some low contrast behavior is desired to reduce sensitivity to small oscillations in intensity at threshold levels). Since R_{max} is primarily a function of the polymeric resin, maximizing the R_{max}/R_{min} dissolution contrast ration generally involves reduction of

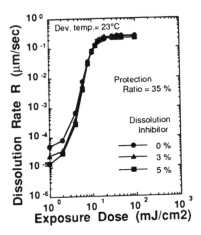

Figure 30 Plots of dissolution rate and log-slope plotted as a function of protection ratio for a three component PHS chemically amplified resist. (From Ref. 73.)

unexposed resist erosion. As shown earlier, a ratio above 10,000 is desirable but probably no greater than 50,000 should be expected. A large DLS is more important and can be controlled to some extent by the resin molecular weight.

9 E_0 AND CD SWING CURVE

Coherent interference resulting from substrate reflectivity will result in a swing of intensity distributed within a resist film. This will correlate to variations in clearing dose (E_0) and CD throughout a resist layer. The swing in E_0 is dependent only on the coherent interference of radiation within the film and can be predicted on the basis of knowledge of the coupling efficiency between the resist and the exposure variation. The only requirement for predicting the E_0 swing is that the distribution and conversion efficiency of the sensitizer reaction be known, making it independent of resist dissolution characteristics. In other words, only the photospeed of the resist influences the E_0 swing. Figure 31 shows the relationship between the E_0 swing ratio and exposure clearing dose (E_0) for several resist systems [74]. The swing ratio has been calculated from eq. 11. Since higher bleaching efficiency leads to higher resist sensitivities, the relationship shown in Fig. 31 makes sense from the standpoint of resist absorbance. Increased nonbleachable absorbance will lead to lower swing ratios, as can be demonstrated by adding a dye to a resist. Figure 32 is a plot of E_0 swing versus exposure-independent resist absorbance (*B* parameter). As resist absorbance increases, swing decreases.

The independence of E_0 swing on resist dissolution, along with the ease with which E_0 values can be measured, makes it an effective method for resist coat

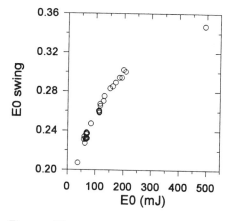

Figure 31 Plot of normalized E_0 verticle swing versus E_0 for several hypothetical resist systems. (From Ref. 74.)

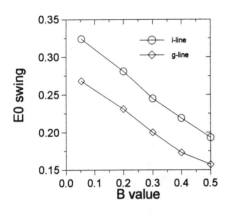

Figure 32 The effect of residual absorption (B parameter) on E_0 swing at constant sensitivity for g-line and i-line exposure. (From Ref. 74.)

characterization, as seen in Section 4. The swing in CD is not so straightforward, as it is influenced by the resist process and dissolution properties. Resist process exposure latitude (or the amount of allowable over- or underexposure) can have a significant influence on CD swing, which can be predicted from the relationship

$$\text{CD swing} = \frac{E_0}{E_L{}^x} \tag{17}$$

where E_L is exposure latitude and x is an empirically determined exponent, on the order of 2.5 for a reasonably fast photoresist.

Secondary swing effects are also present in a resist process. These include swings in resist contrast (γ) and surface contour effects. These secondary effects are a result of the spatial position of a standing wave node at the top surface of the resist. If there is a destructive interference node near the top surface of the resist, a surface induction effect will result, leading to an increase in γ. Figure 33 shows how this can be manifested. At resist thicknesses slightly greater than that corresponding to an optimum maximum exposure (1.18 µm), PAC concentration is increased at the top surface of the resist, resulting in T-top formation. This results in a significant loss of linearity, compared with the optimized condition. At thicknesses slightly less than 1.18 µm, there is a decrease in PAC concentration, resulting in top rounding. These surface effects occur at regular swing periods. The extent to which these secondary surface effects influence a resist process depends on how exposure requirements are affected. Surface effects influence clearing dose (E_0) more strongly than they influence dose to size ($E_{1:1}$) The exposure margin (EM), which is a ratio of these doses,

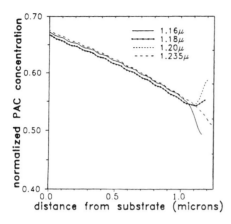

Figure 33 Calculated PAC distribution (at the mask edge) following PEB for four film thicknesses. (From Ref. 74.)

$$EM = \frac{E_{1:1}}{E_0} \tag{18}$$

is a measure of the overexposure requirements for a resist and is a good indicator of mask linearity [75]. Surface-induced swings in E_0 lead to corresponding swings in EM. Resists that demonstrate large surface induction effects during development are most susceptible to these secondary swing effects.

10 POSTDEVELOPMENT BAKING AND RESIST TREATMENT

Postdevelopment baking is often utilized to remove remaining casting solvent, developer, and water within the resist. Baking above the resist's T_g also improves adhesion of the resist to the substrate. Because photosensitivity is no longer required, the baking temperature can be elevated toward the solvent boiling point (T_b), effectively eliminating the solvent from the resist and allowing maximum densification. For DNQ/novolac resist, any remaining DNQ can lead to problems in subsequent process steps. If the still sensitized resist is subjected to a high-energy exposure (such as ion implantation), rapid release of nitrogen can result from radiolysis of DNQ. In a densified resist film, the nitrogen cannot easily diffuse outward and may result in localized explosive resist popping, dispersing resist particles on the wafer surface. Baking above the DNQ T_d after development is therefor desired to volatilize the PAC.

Novolac resins generally suffer from thermal distortion (during subsequent high-temperature processes) more than PHS polymers. PHSs used for DUV resists have T_g values on the order of 140–180°C; the T_g values for novolac resins are in the 80–120°C range. Elevated baking temperatures also result in oxidation and crosslinking of the novolac, producing more "thermoset" materials with flow temperatures higher than the original resist T_g (and less well defined). The temperatures required to accomplish this, however, are above the resist T_g, allowing the flow of patterned features in the process. Novolac resins with T_g values above 130°C are now commonly used and higher T_g resists have been introduced [76].

To enhance the thermal properties of DNQ/novolac resists, the UV crosslinking properties of novolac can be utilized. Although the efficiency is quite low, novolac resin can be made to crosslink at DUV wavelengths. This is facilitated at high temperatures. The high optical absorbance of novolac at wavelengths below 300 nm (absorbance $\gg 1~\mu m^{-1}$) prevents crosslinking to substantial depths. If patterned resist features are subjected to DUV exposure at temperatures above 150°C, a thermally stabilized surface crust can be formed. By elevating the temperature of the "DUV cure" process, oxidation of the bulk of the resist feature can be accomplished. The process is outlined in Fig. 34. The now networked re-

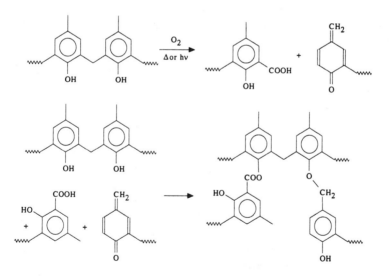

Figure 34   Radical reactions and oxidations induced in novolac from DUV curing. DUV hardening is effective in the presence of oxygen or with no oxygen (in nitrogen for instance) through self-oxidizing of novolac. Removal of DUV cured novolac can be difficult and particulate contamination can occur from rapid nitrogen outgassing at high exposure levels.

sist features can then withstand thermal processes up to 210°C without significant resist flow.

11 RESIST PROCESSING OUTLOOK

As improvements are made to existing resist technology, some process constraints may be reduced. In reality, however, the demand for reduction in geometry size will increase the requirements of process control. Optimum lithographic performance demands that resist processing factors be considered along with any optics-related advances, hence the process dependent "k" factor in the resolution scaling equation. As shorter wavelength technologies are considered, new resist materials need to be developed. The capability of these new resists cannot simply be comparable to that of existing materials but must allow performance that will scale with targeted resolution. Single-layer resist materials for 193-nm lithography have been under development for some time. Beyond this optical wavelength technology, little work has been done. Current i-line and DUV resist materials are impressive predecessors that will lead to extremely high process demands. The cost of ownership of new resist technologies is also an issue of great concern as DUV and 193-nm wavelength exposure is considered. The cost of resist materials and processing equipment may be the largest cost factor involved in a new lithographic technology. This leads to pursuit of not only methods for minimizing chemical materials and preparation costs but also methods for reducing the consumption of resist and processing materials. Resist volumes of less than 4 cm^3 for 200–300-mm wafers are desirable. Material and equipment methods for reducing volume to these levels will serve to reduce lithographic costs as well as impact on environmental safety and health (ESH).

At some point, it can be expected that single-layer resists may not be capable of meeting all needs. This is already seen with the application of antireflective layers to either the top or bottom surface of i-line and DUV resists. As optical and process-related solutions begin to fall short, alternative resist approaches such as top surface imaging may become more practical. Once implemented for manufacturing, these techniques will require a new set of process considerations. Bulk material properties become less of a concern and the demands of dry (plasma) processing may dominate. Regardless of future resist technology, there is assurance that current resists based on DNQ/novolac and chemically amplified PHS will remain in high volume for many years [77].

REFERENCES

1. Thompson, L. F., Wilson, C. G., and Bowden, M. J., *Introduction to Microlithography*, American Chemical Society, Washington, DC, 1994, Chapter 4.
2. Moreau, W., *Semiconductor Lithography*, Plenum, New York, 1988.

3. Dammel, R., *Diazonapthoquinone-Based Resists*, SPIE, Bellingham, WA, 1993, Chapter 5.
4. Moreau, W., *Semiconductor Lithography*, Plenum, New York, 1988, p. 49.
5. Katzisyma, L., *Russ. Chem. Rev.*, *35*, 388 (1966).
6. Asaumi, S., Futura, M., and Yokota, A., *Proc. SPIE*, *1672*, 616 (1992).
7. Hinsberg, W. D., et al., *Proc. SPIE*, *1925*, 43 (1993).
8. Huang, W., et al., *Proc. SPIE*, *2195*, 37 (1994).
9. Nalamasu, O., et al., *ACS Symp. Ser.*, *614*, 4 (1995).
10. Roschert, H., et al., *Proc. SPIE*, *1672*, 33 (1992).
11. Funhoff, D. J. H., Binder, H., and Schwalm, R., *Proc. SPIE*, *1672*, 46 (1992).
12. Nalamasu, O., et al., *J. Vac. Sci. Technol. B*, *10*(6), 2536 (1992).
13. Ito, H., et al., *J. Photopoly. Sci. Technol.*, *7*, 433 (1994).
14. Conley, W., et al., *Proc. SPIE*, *2724*, 34 (1996).
15. McDonald, S. A., *Proc. SPIE*, *1466*, 2 (1991).
16. van Zanten, J. H., Wallace, W. E., and Wu, W. L., *Phys. Rev. E.*, *53*, R2053 (1996).
17. Lyons, D., and Beauchemin, B. T., *Proc. SPIE*, *2438*, 726 (1995).
18. Bornside, D. E., Macosko, C. W., and Scriven, L. E., *J. Imag, Tech.*, *13*, 123 (1987).
19. Meyerhofer, D., *J. Appl. Phys.*, *49*(7), 3993 (1978).
20. Fujita, H., *Adv. Polym. Sci.*, *3*, 1 (1961).
21. Vrentas, J. S., *J. Polym. Sci. Polym. Phys. Ed.*, *15*, 403 (1977).
22. Pain, L., LeCornec C., Roilio, C., and Paniez, P. J., *Proc. SPIE*, *2724*, 100 (1996).
23. Rao, V., Hinsberg, W. D., Frank, C. W., and Pease, R. F. W., *Proc. SPIE*, *2195*, 596 (1994).
24. Frank, C. W., Rao, V., Despotopoulou, M. M., Pease, R. F. W., Hinsberg, W. D., Miller, R. D., and Rabolt, J. F., *Science*, *273*, 912 (1996).
25. Schlegel, L., Ueno, T., Hayashi N., and Iwayanagi T., *J. Vac. Sci. Technol. B*, *9*, 278 (1991).
26. Beauchemin, B., Ebersol, C. E., and Daraktchiev, I., *Proc. SPIE*, *2195*, 613 (1994).
27. Salamy, T. E., et al., *Proc. Electrochem. Soc.*, *90*(1), 36 (1990).
28. Dean, K. R., Carpio, R. A., and Rich, G. K., *Proc. SPIE*, *2438*, 514 (1995).
29. Chun, J., Bok, C., and Baik, K., *Proc. SPIE*, *2724*, 92 (1996).
30. Fields, E., Clarisse, C., and Paniez, P. J., *Proc. SPIE*, *2724*, 460 (1996).
31. Paniez, P. J., Rosilio, C., Monanda, B., and Vinet, F., *Proc. SPIE*, *2195*, 14 (1994).
32. Sinta, R., Barclay, G., Adams, T., and Medeiros, P., *Proc. SPIE*, *2724*, 238 (1996).
33. Paniez, P. J., Festes, G., and Cholett, J. P., *Proc. SPIE*, *1672*, 623 (1992).
34. Koshiba, M., Murata, M., Matsui, M., and Harita, Y., *Proc. SPIE*, *920*, 364 (1988).
35. Ito, H., et al., *Proc. SPIE*, *2438*, 53 (1995).
36. Dill, F. H., et al., *IEEE Trans. Electr. Dev.*, *ED-22*, 440 (1975).
37. Dammel, R., *Diazonapthoquinone-Based Resists*, SPIE Pres, Bellingham, WA, 1993, p. 19.
38. Sturdevant, J., Conley, W., and Webber, S., *Proc. SPIE*, *2724*, 273 (1996).
39. Shaw, J. M., and Hatzakis, M., *IEE Trans. Electr. Dev.*, *ED-25*, 425 (1978).
40. Brunner, T., Proc. SPIE 1463, 297 (1991).
41. Sturdevant, J., Holmes, S., and Rabidoux, P., *Proc. SPIE*, *1672*, 114 (1992).
42. Toukhy, M. A., and Hansen, S. G., *Proc. SPIE*, *2195*, 64 (1994).

43. Tanabe, T., Kobayashi, Y., and Tsuji, A., *Proc. SPIE, 2724*, 61 (1996).
44. Pain, L., Le Cornec, C., Rosilio, C., and Paniez, P. J., *Proc. SPIE, 2724*, 100 (1996).
45. Überreiter, K., and Asmussen, F., *J. Polym. Sci., 57*, 187 (1962).
46. Novembre, A. E., and Hartney, M. A., *Proc. SPE Photopolym. Conf.*, Ellenvile, New York (1985).
47. Huang, J. P., Kwei, T. K., and Reiser, A., *Proc. SPIE, 1086*, 74 (1989).
48. Reiser, A., *Photoreactive Polymers*, Wiley Interscience, New York, 1989, pp. 211–223.
49. Shih, H., Yeu, T., and Reiser, A., *Proc. SPIE, 2195*, 514 (1994).
50. Honda, K., Blakeney, A., and Hurditch, R., *Proc. SPIE, 1925*, 197 (1993).
51. Itani, T., Itoh, K., and Kasama, K., *Proc. SPIE, 1925*, 388 (1993).
52. Konnerth, K. L., and Dil, F. H., *IEEE Trans. Electron, Devices, ED-22*, 453 (1975).
53. Chowdhury, S. D., Alexander, D., Goldman, M., Kukas, A., Farrar N., Takemoto, C., and Smith, B. W., *Proc. SPIE, 2438*, 659 (1995).
54. For instance, the Perkin Elmer Development Rate Monitor (DRM).
55. Arcus, R. A., *Proc. SPIE, 631*, 124 (1986).
56. Dammel, R. R., et al., *Proc. SPIE, 2195*, 542 (1994).
57. Shimomura, S., Shimada, H., Au, R., Miyawaki, M., and Ohmi, T., *Proc. SPIE, 1925*, 602 (1993).
58. Flores, G., and Loftus, J., *Proc. SPIE, 1672*, 328 (1992).
59. Henderson, C. L., et al., *Proc. SPIE, 2724*, 481 (1996).
60. Henderson, C., et al., *Proc. SPIE, 2724*, 481 (1996).
61. Honda, K., Blakeney A., and Hurdith, R., *Proc. SPIE, 1925*, 197 (1993).
62. Garza, C. M., Szmanda, C. R., and Fischer, R. L., *Proc. SPIE, 920*, 321 (1988).
63. Marriott, V., *Proc. SPIE, 394*, 144 (1983).
64. Moreau, W., *Semiconductor Lithography*, Plenum Press, New York, Ch. 10, (1988).
65. Moreau, W. M., Wilson, A. D., Chiong, K. G., Petrillo, K., and Hohn, F., *J. Vac. Sci. Technol. B, 6*, 2238 (1988).
66. Fadda, E., Amblard, G. M., Weill, A. P., and Prola, A. *Proc. SPIE, 2195*, 576 (1994).
67. Yoshimura, T., Murai, F., Shiraishi, H., and Okazaki, S., *J. Vac. Sci. Technol. B, 6*, 2249 (1990).
68. Damarakone, N., Jaenen, P., Van den Hove, L., and Hurditch, R. J., *Proc. SPIE, 1262*, 219 (1990).
69. Itani, T., Itoh, K., and Kasama, K., *Proc. SPIE, 1925* 388 (1993).
70. Thackeray, J. W., et al., *Proc. SPIE, 1086*, 34 (1989).
71. Nalamasu, O., et al., *Proc. SPIE, 1262*, 32 (1990).
72. Itani, T., Iwasaki, H., Fujimoto, M., and Kasama, K., *Proc. SPIE, 2195*, 126 (1994).
73. Itani, T., Iwasaki, H., Yoshin, H., Fujimoto, M., and Kasama, K., *Proc. SPIE, 2438*, 91 (1995).
74. Hansen, S. G., Hurdich, R. J., and Brzozowy, D. J., *Proc. SPIE, 1925*, 626 (1993).
75. Hansen, S. G., and Wang, R. H., *J. Electrochem. Soc., 140*, 166 (1993).
76. Toukhy, M. A., Sarubbi, T. R., and Brzozowy, D. J., *Proc. SPIE, 1466*, 497 (1991).
77. Smith, B. W., *Opt. Photon. News, 8*(3), 23 (1997).

10
Multilayer Resist Technology

Bruce W. Smith

Rochester Institute of Technology
Rochester, New York

Maureen Hanratty

Texas Instruments
Dallas, Texas

1   INTRODUCTION

As higher resolution approaches to microlithography are pursued, conventional single-layer resist materials may fail to meet all process requirements. Multilayer resist techniques have been investigated for several years, but advances in single-layer technology have generally postponed their insertion into high-volume production operations. As long as single-layer resist materials can meet requirements for high-aspect-ratio resolution, photosensitivity, plasma etch resistance, planarization, depth of focus, reflection control, and critical dimension (CD) control, they will be preferred over most multiple-layer or pseudo-multiple-layer techniques. This becomes increasingly difficult and, at some point, the lithographer needs to consider the advantages of dividing the functions of a single-layer resist into separate layers. The fewer layers the better, and the ultimate acceptance of any multilayer technique will be determined by the simplicity of the overall process.

In order to understand the potential advantages of multiple-layer lithographic materials and processes, the general requirements of a photoresist should first be addressed. Although most resist requirements have existed for many generations of integrated circuit processing, the importance of a number of issues has recently increased dramatically.

1.1 Resist Sensitivity

Because resist sensitivity directly affects process throughput, it is a fundamental consideration for the evaluation of resist process capability. In general, resist sensitivity can be shown to be proportional to thickness. For a direct photochemical (not chemically amplified), nonbleaching resist material, this is an exponential relationship, determined by resist absorption and chemical quantum efficiency. However, as resist bleaching mechanisms are considered (as with the photochemical conversion of diazonapthoquinone to indene carboxylic acid), dynamic absorption exists, which introduces some additional considerations to this exponential decay. With chemically amplified resists, quantum efficiency is sufficiently high that the dependence of sensitivity on resist thickness becomes less of an issue and other considerations become more of a concern.

1.2 Depth of Focus

The dependence of depth of focus on lens numerical aperture and wavelength can be expressed as

$$\text{DOF} = \pm k_2 \frac{\lambda}{\text{NA}^2} \tag{1}$$

where λ is wavelength, NA is numerical aperture, and k_2 is a process-dependent factor, determined by process specification and requirements (a typical value for k_2 for a single-layer resist may be near 0.5, as shown in Chapter 9). As optical lithographic technology is pushed toward sub-200 nm wavelengths at numerical apertures greater than 0.6, DOF may fall below 0.5 μm. This presents an interesting challenge for substrate topography and photoresist thickness issues. With such a small useful DOF and without the use of some method of planarization, it is not easily predictable just how large a fraction of this range could be consumed by photoresist thickness.

1.3 Limitations of Resist Aspect Ratio

The physical and chemical nature of a polymeric resist material will determine its limitations for high-aspect-ratio patterning. In addition, the complex nature of development and process chemistry will influence limitations. An aspect ratio less than 3:1 is common for conventional single-layer resists. The limit to how fine the resolution can be for a single-layer resist of a given thickness is influenced to a large extent by polymer flow properties including glass transition temperature (T_g) and melting point (T_m). Because thermoplastic polymeric behavior is desired during processing, in which photoresist materials can go through cycles of heating, flowing, and cooling, they generally possess T_g values in the 70 to 180°C range. Materials of lower T_g will inherently be capable of lower aspect ratio imaging.

1.4 Reflection and Scattering Effects

Imaging over reflective substrates such as metal or polysilicon can allow significant intensity variation within a resist film. High levels of reflectivity can produce overexposure, manifested not only as a bulk effect over the entire imaged field but also at pattern-specific locations such as line boundaries and corners. This is often referred to as reflective line notching or necking, which is a result of the scattering of radiation to unwanted field regions. Substrate reflection will affect the overexposure latitude and ultimately lead to a reduction in focal depth by limiting the amount of tolerable image degradation. To understand the impact of exposure latitude on depth of focus, consider imaging a feature with poor modulation. If a resist process is capable of resolving such a feature, it is likely to be possible only within a limited range of exposure dose. For a positive resist, overexposure can result in complete feature loss and underexposure can result in scumming. There is an intimate relationship, therefore, between depth of focus and exposure latitude. Decreasing the demands on focal depth increases exposure latitude. For a reflective substrate, if a large degree of overexposure latitude must be tolerated, the useful depth of focus will be reduced significantly. It is desirable to reduce any reflected contribution to exposure in order to eliminate feature distortion from scattering and to reduce detrimental effects on focal depth. This can be accomplished in a single-layer resist by several methods. First, because absorption is dependent on resist thickness, a thicker absorbing resist layer will decrease the impact of reflection. Other requirements drive resist toward thinner layers, however, reducing the practicality of this method. A second alternative would be to increase the absorption of the resist so that little radiation is allowed to penetrate to the resist-substrate interface and be reflected back through the resist. The addition of dyes into a resist will accomplish this, but at the cost of resist sidewall, sensitivity, and resolution. The beneficial dynamic bleaching mechanism of the diazonaphthaquinone (DNQ)/novolac materials is undermined by the addition of an absorbing dye that makes no direct contribution to the photochemical process. An alternative approach to reduction is the use of a multilayer resist system, incorporating a separate antireflective layer.

1.5 Reflective Standing Wave Effects

An additional reflection phenomena that deserves consideration is the resist standing wave effect. This is an exposure variation within a resist layer resulting from coherent interference between incident and reflected radiation. The situation is described in detail in Chapters 2 and 9 and has significant impact on exposure, CD control, depth of focus, and coating uniformity requirements. Minimization of standing wave is generally desired. The addition of a resist dye can help in reducing standing wave effect, but the impact on resist sidewall angle can be significant as the top to bottom resist film attenuation increases.

1.6 Plasma Etch Resistance

Post-lithographic processing operations ultimately dictate the minimum acceptable resist thickness after development. For example, resist erosion during etch processing will increase any lithography-related thickness requirements. Furthermore, as new materials are considered for short wavelength exposure application, their etch resistance in halogen-based plasma etch processes may be reduced. Postlithographic processes may place the most restrictive demands on resist performance and may preclude any consideration of thinner single-layer resists.

1.7 Planarization

Because the lithography operations involved with integrated circuit (IC) fabrication are rarely performed over a flat substrate, planarization of topography is a fundamental function of a resist material. The degree of planarization required for a specific level will be determined by step height, feature size and density, and substrate surface properties. Material properties of a resist, including polymer molecular weight, solids content, solvent type, coating spin speed, acceleration, temperature, and exhaust, will contribute to the extent of substrate smoothing. Polymeric materials with low molecular weight and a high solids content are generally employed for maximum results [1]. A fluid dynamics approach can be used to demonstrate the relationships between process factors and planarization:

$$P \propto \frac{t \gamma h_0^3}{\eta w^4} \tag{2}$$

where t is leveling time, γ is surface tension, h_0 is initial film thickness, η is solution viscosity, and w is feature width. This relationship suggests that several factors can be modified to affect net results. Planarization of close-proximity features (local geometry) and of widely spaced features (global geometry) may be required, depending on substrate characteristics and process needs. Figure 1 illustrates that planarization by a polymeric material may be suitable for both situations. The extent of planarization can be quantified by considering the initial step height (z_0) and the final effective step height after smoothing (z_1) and determining the normalized ratio:

$$\text{Effective planarization} = \frac{z_0 - z_1}{z_0} \tag{3}$$

which can be calculated for local and global features [2].

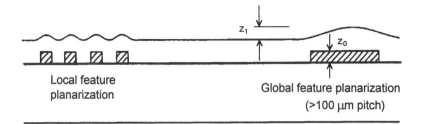

Figure 1 Polymeric planarization of local and global topography. The extent of planarization can be determined from measurement of initial and final step heights (z_0 and z_1).

Planarization can be accomplished by means of substrate overcoating (generally with an organic polymeric film), etch back processing, or polishing of a topographic substrate to reduce step height. Techniques of chemical mechanical polishing (CMP) are becoming widely accepted as alternatives to additive planarization methods, reducing constraints on resist processing and requirements for focal depth [3]. Methods of CMP can allow global planarization of both insulator and conductor layers in multilevel metallization interconnect structures and of both deep and shallow trench isolation materials. These techniques have become a critical path for both logic and memory production and a number of issues are receiving careful attention, including optimization of process techniques, cleaning considerations, and defects.

1.8 Multilayer Resist Processes as Alternatives to Conventional Resist Patterning

The appeal of multilayer resist processes and surface imaging resist (SIR) technology has increased because of the resolution enhancement they provide for the current optical exposure tools, as well as the potential application for newer exposure systems such as 193 nm or extreme ultraviolet (EUV, 13–40 nm). At the shorter exposure wavelengths, conventionally developed resists are either unavailable or lack sufficient performance. With surface or near-surface imaging, photochemical modification necessary to effect the pattern transfer is restricted to a thin upper portion of the resist layer. Ideally, the imaging layer should be as thin and as planar as possible. In this way, maximum resolution can be obtained and optimum use can be made of the entire available focus range of the exposure tool. The resist image is free from the effects of device topography and substrate reflection, an advantage that becomes increasingly important as optical tools move to shorter wavelength sources where the reflectivity of many materials increases. In addition, the high CD tolerances demanded by advanced IC designs require high-performance patterning, which multilayer and surface imaging resist systems can provide.

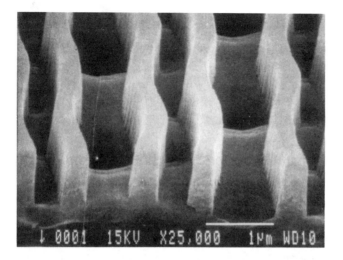

Figure 2   SEM micrograph of 0.35 μm DRAM gate structures patterned over 0.6 μm of topography using surface imaging techniques.

Multilayer techniques or single-layer surface imaging resist processes provide an advantage in application in which the substrate reflectivity is high or topography is severe. Patterning of DRAM gates, such as the one pictured in Fig. 2, often provides just such a challenging scenario. In this case, where 0.35-μm gates were patterned over 0.6 μm of topography, surface imaging resist techniques ensured constant critical dimension control even over large step heights. Particularly in instances in which the design dimensions challenge the resolution capability of the exposure tool and the resist, near-surface or surface imaging techniques can play an important role.

A large number of polymeric multilayer systems have been developed and utilized for several decades. Multilayer schemes can be divided into four basic categories, with some overlap in function. Specifically, approaches have allowed planarization, reduction of reflection, contrast enhancement, and surface imaging. These categories are not necessarily clearly divided, as a single multilayer approach can accomplish several objectives. Details of these approaches will be explored in this chapter.

2   MULTILAYER PLANARIZING PROCESSES— WET DEVELOPMENT APPROACHES

Various multilayer techniques have been introduced that employ polymeric planarization layers to reduce substrate topography and allow the use of a thin top-coated imaging resist layer, as depicted in Fig. 3 [4]. Methods have included a

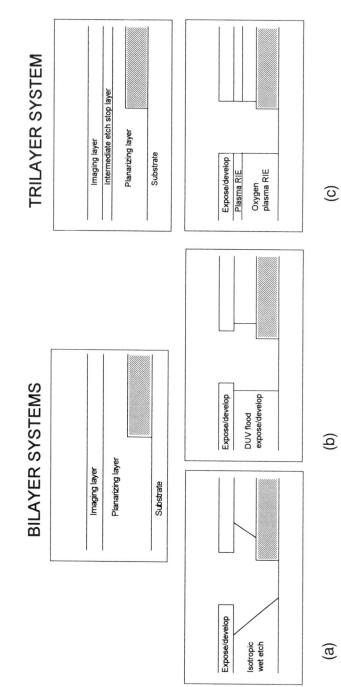

Figure 3 Multilayer approaches utilizing polymeric planarization layers. (a) A wet etch bilayer system using isotropic dissolution of the planarization layer; (b) a bilayer system with blanket DUV exposure of a photosensitive planarization layer masked by a patterned DNQ/novolac layer; (c) a typical trilayer resist system utilizing a planarizing layer, an etch stop layer, and an imaging layer.

wet-processed thick planarization layer [5], a two-layer portable conformable mask (PCM) [6], and a three-layer plasma transfer process [7]. The wet-processed approach leads to isotropic dissolution of an underlying planarizing layer, limiting application generally to non–integrated circuit use. The PCM process employs a deep ultraviolet (DUV)-sensitive planarizing layer, typically poly(methyl methacrylate), PMMA [8], or poly(dimethylgluterimide), PMGI [9], and a DNQ/novolac imaging layer. Because the DNQ/novolac is highly absorbing at wavelengths below 300 nm, once imaged it acts as a surface contact mask over the bottom resist layer. DUV flood exposure and development of the bottom layer allow pattern transfer through the entire multilayer stack. This technique can be limited by interfacial mixing of the two resist layers, which is minimized when using PMGI materials. Poor contrast of the DUV planarizing layer and reduced process control of this two-layer technique has limited resolution, making sub-0.5 μm imaging difficult.

Variations on the multiple-resist approach have also been used for electron beam T-gate fabrication [10, 11]. Three resist layers may be used to allow specific feature shaping through the depth of a resist stack. For example, a bottom layer of PMMA is overcoated by a layer of a methyl methacrylate–methacrylic acid copolymer (PMMA-MAA), followed by a top coat of PMMA. Exposure and wet development lead to larger pattern widths in the more sensitive PMMA-MAA layer, allowing the formation of T-shaped metal gate structures through a subsequent additive liftoff process.

3 WET DEVELOPMENT/DRY PATTERN TRANSFER APPROACHES TO MULTILAYERS

Anisotropic pattern transfer can allow significant improvement over the isotropic processing of wet-etched multilayer approaches. Through the use of a plasma reactive ion etch (RIE) pattern transfer process, near anisotropy can be approached, allowing high-aspect ratio, fine feature resolution [12, 13]. The three-layer schemed depicted in Fig. 3 makes use of a polymeric planarizing layer (such as novolac resin or polyimide) and a thin intermediate etch stop layer. This etch stop layer can be a spin-on organosilicon compound (spin on glass), a low-temperature oxide, a silicon oxinitride, or a metallic layer, which provide oxygen etch resistance. A thin resist imaging layer is coated over this etch stop, exposed, and wet developed. Pattern transfer into the intermediate etch-stop layer can be achieved with wet etch or dry plasma techniques with suitable chemistry. Anisotropic pattern transfer through the thick polymeric planarizing layer can be achieved via an oxygen RIE process. Variations on this technique have been used for both optical and electron beam applications [14].

The importance of polymeric planarization approaches historically has declined as single-layer resists and CMP techniques have steadily improved. As shorter wavelength exposure technologies are pursued, however, it is likely that application of multilayer approaches will become more viable. A bilayer resist technique that allows planarization, etch resistance, and reflection control with a thin imaging layer has many attractive properties. Such schemes will be addressed in detail as silicon-containing resists and top-surface imaging techniques are addressed.

4 RESIST REFLECTIVITY AND ANTIREFLECTIVE COATINGS

Reflection at resist/substrate interfaces has been a concern for many IC generations. The impact is most pronounced when using high-contrast resists, a result of increasing exposure thresholding effects. Shown in Fig. 4 is the effect that varying resist film thickness has on feature size (CD swing curves) for an i-line resist imaged over polysilicon and aluminum films. The reflectance from a resist-polysilicon interface at 365 nm can be above 30% and at 248 nm above 38%. Resist over aluminum can produce reflectivity values of above 86% at 365 nm and above 88% at 248 nm. Interface reflectance can be determined from a Fresnel relationship for two media at normal incidence as

$$R = \left| \frac{n_2^* - n_1^*}{n_2^* + n_1^*} \right|^2 \tag{4}$$

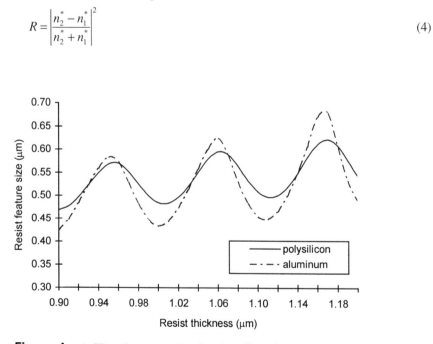

Figure 4 A CD swing curve showing the effect of resist thickness variation on resist linewidth. Results for polysilicon and aluminum substrates are shown at 365 nm using a resist with a refractive index of 1.7.

Here n^* is the complex refractive index or $n\text{-}ik$, where n is the real refractive index and k is the extinction coefficient. For nonabsorbing materials, $k = 0$ and $n^* = n$ simplifying Eq. 4. For nonnormal incidence, a additional $\cos \theta$ term is required, where θ is the angle of incidence. Inspection of the optical constants for materials in Table 1 gives an indication of the need to incorporate methods of reflectance control.

If the materials that make up the lithographic substrate are nonabsorbing or possess low absorbance, reflectance values at each interface must be uniquely considered to determine the net reflectance through the film stack. Figure 5 shows an example of a resist film over an SiO_2/Si substrate. Here, the contribution from the oxide-resist interface is low compared with the contribution from the silicon underlying material. In this case, the thickness of the SiO_2 film can be adjusted to minimize total reflectivity through destructive interference (the use of quarter-wave approaches for inorganic antireflection materials will be discussed in detail in Section 4.1).

Control of reflectivity at the resist-substrate interface to values near a few percent is generally required for critical lithography levels, leading to the need for some method of control. The situation becomes more critical as lithographic methods incorporate shorter wavelength sources, a smaller spectral bandwidth, and more transparent resists. Reduction of reflection to values below 1% will probably be needed for next-generation lithography. Dye incorporation into a resist can reduce the coherent interference effects but at the cost of exposure throughput and sidewall angle, leading ultimately to resolution loss. Dyed resists are therefore generally limited to noncritical reflective levels at which the highest resolution is not necessary.

Instead of reducing reflection effects through modification of a resist material, methods that reduce reflectivity at resist interfaces can provide control with minimal loss of resist performance. This can be accomplished through manipu-

Table 1   Optical Constants (n and k) for Several Materials at 436, 365, 248, and 193 nm

	193		248		365		436	
	n	k	n	k	n	k	n	k
Silicon	0.960	2.88	1.58	3.60	6.41	2.62	4.79	0.175
SiO_2	1.56	0.00	1.51	0.00	1.47	0.00	1.47	0.00
Si_3N_4	2.65	0.18	2.28	0.005	2.11	0.00	2.051	0.00
Aluminum	0.117	2.28	0.190	2.94	0.407	4.43	0.595	5.35
Polysilicon	0.970	2.10	1.69	2.76	3.90	2.66	4.46	1.60
DNQ/novolac					1.70	0.007	1.67	0.007
PHS CAR			1.76	0.007				

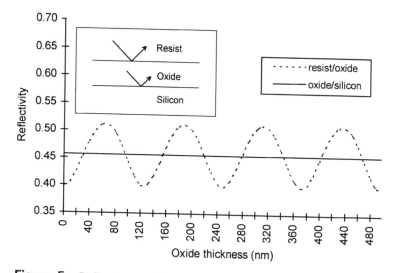

Figure 5 Reflection contribution at resist/oxide and oxide/silicon interfaces with increasing silicon dioxide thickness at a 365 nm wavelength using a resist with $n = 1.7$ and $k = 0.007$. Minimum reflectivity occurs at quarter wave oxide thicknesses.

lation of thin-film optical properties and film thicknesses and by careful matching of the optical properties of each layer in an entire resist/substrate stack.

4.1 Control of Reflectivity at the Resist-Substrate Interface: Bottom Antireflective Coatings

To reduce the reflectivity at the interface between a resist layer and a substrate, an intermediate film can be coated beneath the resist. This is known as a bottom antireflective coating (BARC). Inspection of Eq. 4 suggests one approach where the refractive index of this layer could be close to that of the resist at the exposing wavelength. To reduce reflectivity, the film could then absorb radiation incident from the resist film. Thin-film absorption (α) is related to the optical extinction coefficient (k) as

$$\alpha = \frac{4\pi k}{\lambda} \tag{5}$$

and transmission through an absorbing film is

$$T = \exp(-\alpha t) \tag{6}$$

where T is transmission and t is film thickness. A high extinction coefficient may therefore be desirable, leading to high absorption and low transmission through the BARC layer. As k is increased, however, reflectivity at the resist/BARC interface is increased, as seen also from Eq. 4. An extinction coefficient value in the range of 0.25 to 1.2 may be reasonable, based on these considerations and depending on resist material and film thickness demands. Shown in Fig. 6 is a series of plots showing substrate reflectance versus BARC thickness for real-index matched materials with extinction coefficient values from 0.1 to 1.2. Since the BARC layer needs to accommodate pattern transfer (using either a wet or dry plasma etching approach), minimum thickness values are desirable. For these layer combinations, a BARC thickness between 500 and 800 produces a first reflectance minimum. These minima occur as reflectance from the BARC-substrate interface interferes destructively with the reflection at the resist-BARC interface. This interference repeats at intervals of $\lambda/2n$ which can be explained by examining Fig. 7. Here, radiation passes twice through the BARC layer with wavelength compression corresponding to its refractive index (λ/n_i). Two passes through a quarter wave thickness ($\lambda/4n$) results in a half-wave phase shift directed toward the resist-BARC interface. This phase-shifted wave will then interfere with the reflected wave at the resist. Complete destruction will occur only if the amplitude values of the waves are identical,

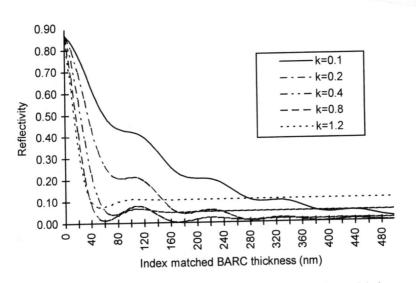

Figure 6 Substrate reflectivity vs. bottom ARC thickness for real index matched materials ($n = 1.7$ at 365 nm) and extinction coefficient values from 0.1 to 1.2. The best performance for a thin BARC layer may be possible with k values near 0.8.

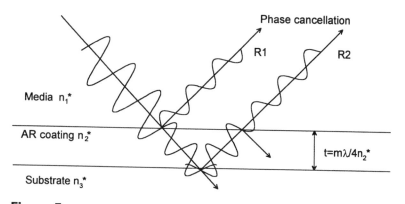

Figure 7 Diagram of the principle of a quarter wave AR layer between two media. A thickness of the AR coating is chosen to produce destructive interference between reflected components, R_1 and R_2. The ideal refractive index is $\sqrt{n_1^* n_3^*}$.

which is possible only if the reflectance at the resist-BARC interface is exactly equal to the reflectance at the BARC-substrate interface or if:

$$n_{arc} = \sqrt{n_{resist}^* \times n_{substrate}^*} \qquad (7)$$

This leads to a more complex route toward reflection reduction with a bottom ARC using both absorption and interference considerations.

Reflection control and aspect ratio requirements need to be considered to determine optimum ARC film thickness values. A first reflectance minimum corresponding to a relatively thin film may be chosen for fine feature pattern transfer. If thicker layers can be tolerated, further reduction in reflectivity may be achieved by increasing the BARC film thickness. There is an exponential trend in reflection reduction with increasing thickness and BARC absorption. As extinction coefficient values increase toward 0.8, reflection begins to increase, and for values above 1.2, reflectivity below a few percentage becomes difficult. Figures 8 and 9 are a series of contour plots of substrate reflectivity for BARC films with extinction coefficient values from 0.0 to 0.9 and refractive index values from 1.8 to 2.7.

Organic BARCs

Organic bottom ARC materials have been used for some time, typically in the form of spin-on polymeric materials [15]. These polymers contain highly absorbing dyes introduced at levels to deliver appropriate extinction coefficient values. Several classes of materials can be used, depending to a large extent on the pattern transfer requirements of a process [16–19]. Wet developable organic BARCs based on partially cured polyamic acids (polyimide precursors) have been utilized for large feature geometry. These materials, with refractive index

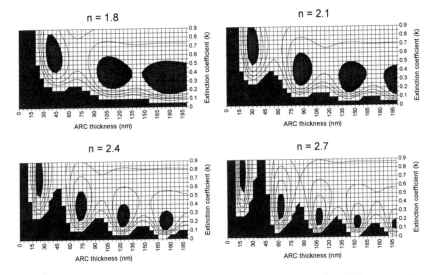

Figure 8   Contour plots of substrate reflectivity (over silicon) at 248 nm as a function of bottom ARC thickness for materials with refractive indices between 1.8 and 2.7 and extinction coefficient values to 0.9. Central contour areas correspond to 0-2% reflectivity and 2% constant contours are shown. Results beyond 10% reflectivity are shown in black [$n_{resist}(248) = 1.75$].

values near 1.7 and extinction coefficients near 0.3, are coated and partially cured prior to resist application. Partial curing of the dyed polyamic acid allows tailoring of the alkaline solubility of the layer to match that of exposed resist. Bottom ARC materials made of dyed triazine derivatives have also been introduced [17].

As shown in Fig. 10, exposure and development of an aqueous base–soluble resist layer exposes the underlying BARC material, which is also base soluble if cured appropriately. Materials have been formulated that provide a high degree of bake latitude (as high as ±20°C) [20] and exhibit a very low degree of interfacial mixing. The inherent problem with this approach for antireflection is the isotropy of wet pattern transfer. With no preferential direction for etching, undercutting results to the full extent of the BARC thickness. As shown in Fig. 10, resist features are undercut by twice the BARC thickness, limiting application of wet-developed organic materials to a resolution above 0.5 μm.

Dry etch compatible organic BARC materials can allow control of the etch profile through use of plasma RIE methods of pattern transfer. The requirements then become one of resist to BARC etch selectivity to minimize resist erosion and the accompanying loss in process and CD control. Initial candidate

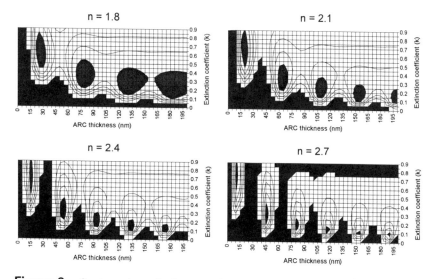

Figure 9 Contour plots of substrate reflectivity (over silicon) at 193 nm as a function of bottom ARC thickness for materials with refractive indices between 1.8 and 2.7 and extinction coefficient values to 0.9. Central contour areas correspond to 0-2% reflectivity and 2% constant contours are shown. Results beyond 10% reflectivity are shown in black. Resist refractive index is 1.6.

materials for use as dry etch BARCs may be polymers that undergo efficient scissioning with plasma exposure, leading to increased volatility. For instance, dyed polyolefin sulfone materials (frequently employed as electron beam resists) [21] could allow relatively high oxygen-based RIE etch selectivity to novolac or polyhydroxystyrene (PHS) resist materials. Several dry-etch materials have been introduced [22, 23] for use in 248 nm and i-line application. Figure 11 shows

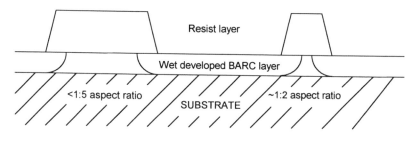

Figure 10 Process schematic for an aqueous base developed bottom ARC. Exposure and development of a top resist layer allow development to continue through a suitably baked AR film. Isotropic pattern transfer limits this approach.

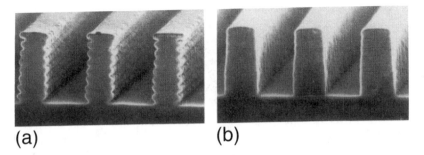

Figure 11 Comparison of reflective standing wave reduction through use of a dry etch bottom ARC: (a) without a bottom ARC; (b) with a bottom ARC.

lithographic results and reduction of reflective standing wave effects with use of a dry-etch BARC material.

A potential problem with spin-on organic BARC materials is their planarizing nature. As seen in Figs. 8 and 9 control of film thickness to a few tens of angstroms may be required for suppression of substrate reflectivity. If a polymeric material is spin coated over severe topography, film thickness can deviate substantially from a targeted value. The film is generally not conformal, which leads to significant variation in reflection reduction across a field. To increase the conformal properties of a BARC layer, alternative deposition methods can be explored. Also, through elimination of the polymeric nature of the BARC material, planarization can be further reduced. This leads to a class of inorganic antireflective materials that can be coated using chemical vapor or vacuum deposition methods.

Inorganic BARCS

Vapor-deposited ARC materials were first proposed for use over aluminum [24] and have since been applied over a variety of reflective substrate layers. The optical requirements for an inorganic layer are generally the same as for organic films. This is, however, a more difficult task with inorganic dielectric materials than it is with organic polymers as practical material choices are generally limited to those that allow process compatibility. The challenges for organic and inorganic materials can therefore differ. For inorganic films, the flexibility of optical constants is made possibly to some extent through material selection and variation in stoichiometry. Deposition thickness and uniformity can be controlled accurately to the nanometer level and films are generally conformal to the underlying topography. The choice between inorganic or organic BARC materials therefore depends in part on the underlying substrate and processing that will be encountered. Titanium nitride [25], silicon nitride, silicon oxinitride [26], amorphous carbon [27], tantalum silicide [28], and titanium tungsten oxide [29] films have been used as inorganic antireflection layers at 365, 248, and 193 nm [30]. Substrate-resist interaction effects for 248-nm chemically amplified resists also need to be considered as candidates are evaluated, which may reduce the attractiveness of some materials for some ARC applications [31].

For nonstoichiometric materials such as silicon oxinitride, modifications in stoichiometry can be used to tailor optical properties. Traditionally, a chemical compound is thought of as having a fixed atomic ratio and composition. A wider range of properties is possible by relaxing this stoichiometric requirement. By controlling the ratios of material components during deposition, optical behavior can be modified. It is not immediately obvious that nonstoichiometric composite films of metal, insulator, or semiconductor combinations will exhibit predictable optical properties. Through analysis of the atomistic structure of materials and by relating optical material properties to electrical properties, some conclusions can be drawn [32]. Optical constants can be related to electrical properties by neglecting material structure and considering macroscopic material quantities only:

$$n^2 = \tfrac{1}{2}\left(\sqrt{\varepsilon_1^2 + \varepsilon_2^2} + \varepsilon_1\right) \tag{8}$$

$$k^2 = \tfrac{1}{2}\left(\sqrt{\varepsilon_1^2 + \varepsilon_2^2} - \varepsilon_1\right) \tag{9}$$

where ε_1 and ε_2 are real and imaginary dielectric constants, respectively. In order to account for material structure, Drude analysis of optical and electrical constants describes free electron or metallic behavior quite well in the visible and infrared (IR) region [33]. Equations 10 and 11 are Drude equations for optical and electrical constants, related to material plasma frequency (v_1) and damping frequency (v_2).

$$n^2 - k^2 = \varepsilon_1 = 1 - \frac{v_1^2}{v^2 + v_2^2} \tag{10}$$

$$2nk = \varepsilon_2 = \left(\frac{v_2}{v}\right)\frac{v_1^2}{v^2 + v_2^2} \tag{11}$$

To account for optical properties at shorter wavelengths, bound electron theory needs to be utilized. For dieletric materials, no intraband transitions exist because of filled valence bands. Interband transitions are also limited in IR and visible regions because of large band gap energies. Bound electron theory alone is sufficient to describe classical dielectric behavior. Characterization of metallic and noninsulating materials in UV and visible regions requires use of both free electron and bound electron theory. By assuming a given number of free electrons and a given number of harmonic oscillators, optical properties over a wide wavelength range can be described. Using bound electron or harmonic oscillator theory, relationships for optical and electrical constants can be determined from the following equations:

$$\varepsilon_1 = 1 + \frac{4\pi e^2 m N_a (v_0^2 - v^2)}{4\pi^2 m^2 (v_0^2 - v^2)^2 + \gamma' v^2} \tag{12}$$

$$\varepsilon_2 = \frac{2e^2 N_a \gamma' v}{4\pi^2 m^2 (v_0^2 - v^2)^2 + \gamma' v^2} \tag{13}$$

where γ is the damping factor, N_a is the number of oscillators, m is electron mass, and e is electron charge. From this analysis, it can be shown that the optical properties of a material can be described by metallic behavior combined with dielectric behavior. Shown in Fig. 12 are plots of optical constants for a metallic film using the Drude model for free electron motion and metallic-dielectric composite films using combined free and bound electron models. These results suggest that the optical properties of a composite material can be modified by controlling the ratio of its components. It is expected, therefore, that the optical properties of nonstoichiometric materials would fall somewhere between those of their stoichiometric elemental or compound constituents.

Silicon nitride (Si_3N_4) possesses optical constants that may be a good starting point for use as an ARC at several wavelengths. Optical constant data for silicon nitride, silicon dioxide (SiO_2), and silicon at 436, 365, 248, and 193 nm are contained in Table 1 [34]. By adjusting the deposition parameters during

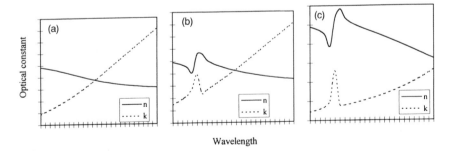

Figure 12   Plots of optical constants for a metallic film using the Drude model for free electron motion and metallic-dielectric composite films using combined free and bound electron models. (a) A metallic film; (b) a dielectric film; and (c) a dielectric composite film with increasing metallic content.

film formation (gas flow ratios for CVD and power, pressure, and gas flow for sputtering, for instance), thin-film materials can be produced with optical properties defined by these constituents. Figure 13 shows the reflectivity at the substrate interface for several 248 nm SiON ARC materials under a resist with a refractive index of 1.76. Shown also in Fig. 14 are the optical constants (n and k) for a variety of materials at 193 nm [35]. From these data together with compatibility and process requirements, potential ARC films for 193 nm can also be identified.

An additional advantage from the use of inorganic ARCs is the ability to grade the indices of materials to best match requirements of resist and substrate layers [36]. This is possible through control of process parameters during deposition. To achieve similar results with organic spin-on ARCs, multiple layers would be required. Pattern transfer for inorganic antireflective layers can also result in higher selectivity to resist, made possible, for instance, if fluorine-based etch chemistries are used. Shown in Fig. 15 is a comparison of pattern transfer processes through an organic spin-on ARC and an inorganic ARC with high resist selectivity [37]. Minimum resist erosion during the etch process with the inorganic material can result in an increase in CD control. A major trade-off when using inorganic materials is the increased complexity of deposition processes over spin coating. Process trends and requirements will probably lead to incorporation of both approaches for various lithographic operations.

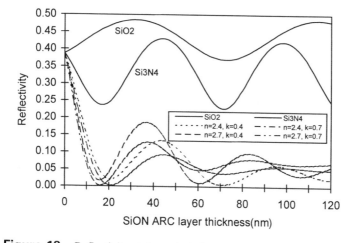

Figure 13 Reflectivity at the resist/substrate interface for several 248 nm understoichiometric SiON ARC materials under a resist with a refractive index of 1.76. The underlying substrate is polysilicon. Reflectivity for stoichiometric SiO_2 and Si_3N_4 are also shown.

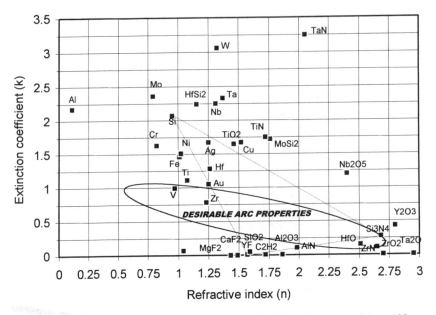

Figure 14 A plot of the optical constants (*n* and *k*) for various materials at 193 nm. A window of desirable ARC properties is shown, as also described in Figure 9. An understoichiometric SiON film would also suffice for use at 193 nm, with properties falling within the area defined by dashed lines.

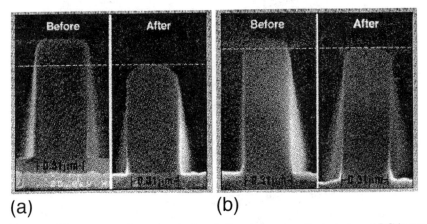

Figure 15 A comparison of resist loss during pattern transfer to bottom ARC layers. (a) Organic spin-on ARC; and (b) dielectric inorganic ARC. [From C. Bencher, C. Ngai, B. Roman, S. Lian, and T. Vuong, *Solid State Technol.*, *111*, (1997).]

4.2 Top Antireflective Approaches

The bottom antireflective approach leads to reflection reduction at the interface between a resist material and the substrate. Reflection also occurs at the top of the resist, at the resist-air interface, as shown in Fig. 16. This leads to a situation similar to that of a Fabry-Perot etalon. An expression for the reflective swing ratio can be utilized to address reflection effects within an entire resist film stack [38]:

$$\text{Swing} = 4\sqrt{R_1 R_2} \, \exp(-\alpha t) \tag{14}$$

where R_1 is the reflectivity at the resist-air interface, R_2 is the reflection at the resist-substrate interface, α is resist absorbance, and t is resist thickness. Here the swing is the ratio of the peak-to-valley change in intensity to the average intensity, which is desired to be a minimum. A decrease in R_2 via a BARC layer can be used to accomplish this, as can an increase in absorption (through use of a resist dye, for instance) or an increase in resist thickness. A reduction in R_1 is also desirable, which can be addressed through the use of a top antireflective coating (TARC) [39]. Because there is a mismatch between refractive indices of the resist material and air, R_1 can be on the order of 7%. This can lead to resist exposure and CD control problems, encountered as a result of internal reflectance via multiple interference effects, scattered light, and reflective standing wave. An exposure tool alignment signal detection can also be degraded from top surface reflection effects [40]. Like conventional AR coatings for optical applications TARC films are not absorbing materials but instead transparent thin-film interference layers that utilize destructive interference to eliminate reflectance. The ideal refractive index for such a film coated over a resist material is that which produces equivalent reflectance of from the air and from the resist side of the interface. This leads to an optimum index of

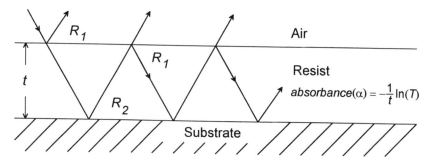

Figure 16 Diagram of reflection contribution from resist/substrate and resist/air interfaces.

$$n^*_{AR} = \sqrt{n^*_{air} \times n^*_{resist}} \tag{15}$$

If a film of this index is coated to a quarter-wave thickness ($\lambda/4n_{ARC}$), complete destructive interference can occur. For i-line resist materials with a refractive index of 1.70, an ideal TARC material would have an index of 1.30 and would be coated at 700 Å. Figure 17 shows the reduction in reflection for a quarter-wave top AR layer when the refractive index is varied from 1.1 to 1.5. For refractive index values below 1.3, there is a larger contribution to reflection from the resist-TARC interface. At values above 1.3, the contribution from the air-TARC interface is larger.

The refractive index and reflectance properties of several TARC materials are given in Table 2. As the refractive index of a material approaches the ideal value of $\sqrt{n^*_{air} \times n^*_{resist}}$, the reflectances at the resist and air interfaces are equivalent, allowing destructive interference at a quarter-wave thickness. Residual reflectances results as TARC indices deviate from the ideal. To achieve refractive index values near the ideal 1.3, polyfluoroalkylpolyethers and polytetrafluoroethylene-based materials cast in solvents that do not dissolve novolac resist materials have been utilized at TARC layers [41, 42]. These fluorinated polymers require removal with chlorofluorocarbons prior to development and have been replaced by water-based and water-soluble materials to improve process compatibility [43]. Although these materials do not possess a refractive index

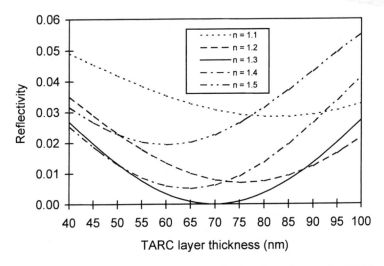

Figure 17 The reduction in surface reflection through use of a TARC material at 365 nm. Reflection can be eliminated through use of a quarter wave thickness (700 Å) of a material with a refractive index of 1.3.

Table 2 Refractive Index and Reflectance Properties of Several TARC Candidates

	Refractive index n(365nm)	Departure from ideal	Quarter wave thickness at 365 nm	Reflectance at air interface	Reflectance at resist interface
Polyvinyl alcohol	1.52	0.32	600 Å	4.26%	0.3%
Polyethylvinylether	1.46	0.16	625 Å	3.5%	0.6%
Polyfluoroalkylpolyether	1.27	0.02	713 Å	1.5%	2.0%
Aquatar [12]	1.41	0.11	647 Å	2.9%	0.9%
Ideal*	1.30	—	702 Å	1.8%	1.8%

*Assuming a resist refractive index of 1.70.

as close to the ideal values for use with DNQ/novolac resists at 436 and 365 nm, (the refractive index is 1.41 at 365 nm), the reduced process complexity makes them a more attractive choice over solvent-based systems. Figure 18 shows the reflectivity of a resist film stack as resist film thickness is varied. Reflectivity varies by over 20% for resist over polysilicon over one swing period. This is reduced significantly with the addition of an water-soluble TAR coated to a quarter-wave thickness. Exposure and focus latitude improvement has also been demonstrated with these materials.

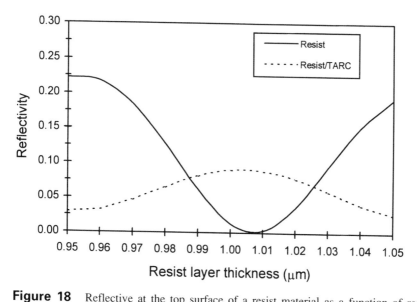

Figure 18 Reflective at the top surface of a resist material as a function of resist thickness with and without a TARC. Results are for 365 nm and a polysilicon substrate. The refractive index of the TARC is 1.41 and its thickness is 647 Å.

5 THE IMPACT OF NUMERICAL APERTURE ON REFLECTANCE EFFECTS

In Eqs. 4 and 14 the assumption of normal incidence is made. In projection imaging, the incident angle of illumination is a function of the numerical aperture (NA) of the optical system. Reflectance at an interface is a function of the angle of incidence (in air) I_1 and the angle of refraction I_2 as

$$R = \frac{1}{2}\left[\frac{\sin^2(I_1 - I_2)}{\sin^2(I_1 + I_2)} + \frac{\tan^2(I_1 - I_2)}{\tan^2(I_1 + I_2)}\right] \tag{16}$$

The first term in this equation corresponds to the reflection that is polarized in the plane of incidence and the second term corresponds to the reflection in the perpendicular plane. The effective film thicknesses for resist, AR layers, and underlying dielectric films are also scaled by the angle of incidence as $t \cos(\theta)$, where t is the thickness of the film at normal incidence. Large angles of incidence (with high-NA optics) have been shown to contribute to reducing the reflective swing ratio [44].

6 CONTRAST ENHANCEMENT MATERIALS

Resolution is generally limited in optical lithographic processes by the inability of a resist material to adequately utilize a degraded aerial image. Optical improvement techniques including the use of lenses with a higher numerical aperture, shorter wavelength exposure sources, modified illumination, or phase shift masks can be employed to improve aerial image integrity through a sufficiently large focal depth. In addition, the use of a thinner, higher contrast resist over a low-reflective substrate can best record aerial images of limited modulation. The concept of a contrast enhancement material (CEM) coated over a resist allows an alternative to these approaches, making use of an intermediate image capture step prior to image transfer into photoresist. Contrast enhancement is based on the use of photobleachable materials that are opaque prior to exposure but become transparent after photoabsorption [45–47]. The process is illustrated in Fig. 19. Here, an aerial image of low modulation is incident on a thin CEM layer coated over resist. During exposure of the CEM, its transparency increases until the resist interface is reached, at which time resist exposure begins. If the dynamic photobleaching rate of the CEM is low compared with the exposure rate of the underlying resist, the CEM image becomes an effective contact masking layer. This masking layer transfers the image into the underlying resist. The net effect is to increase the effective contrast of the resist process.

To be applicable for a microlithographic process, CEM materials must exhibit optical absorbance values above 2 at thicknesses on the order of minimum fea-

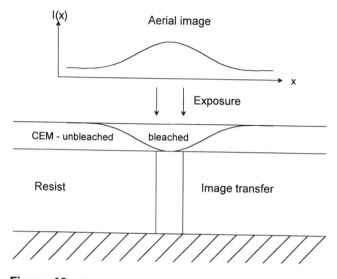

Figure 19 Schematic of a photobleachable CEM process. The CEM material acts as a contact mask for exposure of an underlying resist.

ture sizes. Figure 20 shows the spectral characteristic of a 365-nm water-soluble material consisting of an inert polymer film and an organic dye. Upon exposure, photoisomerism of the organic dye increases transparency near 365 nm. Several materials have also been introduced for exposure wavelengths of 436, 365, and 248 nm [48–50].

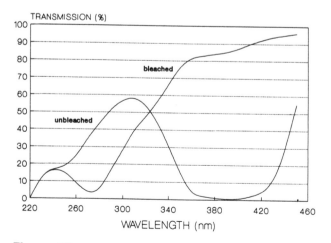

Figure 20 Transmission characteristics of a water soluble CEM material for use at 365 nm.

7   SILICON-CONTAINING RESISTS FOR MULTILAYER AND SURFACE IMAGING RESIST APPLICATIONS

Multilayer resist techniques have long been used to ease requirements for resist performance [51–56]. This goal is achieved by using physically distinct layers to separate the imaging function from the etch resistance, planarization, and reflection suppression functions. Trilevel resists have demonstrated enhanced resolution compared with single-layer resist processing. The trade-off for this resolution, however, is additional processing difficulty as the deposition and patterning of three layers must now be simultaneously controlled. Although excellent results have been obtained, the processing complexity has been the major obstacle for the widespread application to production of integrated circuits.

An obvious simplification of the original multilayer technique is to incorporate the patterning and etch resistance into one layer and require only one additional layer for planarization. Eliminating the middle layer requires that the top layer have sufficient etch resistance and that there are no detrimental interactions between the top and bottom resist layers. The use of resists containing organosilicon and organometallic polymers on top of a thick organic planarizing layer has been reported [57]. The top resist layer is developed using standard wet development techniques and the image is transferred to the bottom resist layer with an oxygen plasma etch. A refractory oxide, which is highly etch resistant, is formed in the top resist layer during the oxygen plasma etch [58,59]. Taylor et al. [60,61] demonstrated the selective introduction of silicon into the resist polymer following exposure of the resist. During the oxygen plasma development, a protective SiO_2 coating is formed on the polymer surface that is resistant to etching [62].

7.1   Bilayer Process with Silicon-Containing Resists

Silicon-containing resists for use in bilayer imaging processes are an ideal choice because of the compatibility with silicon semiconductor processing [63–65]. Many variants of silicon-containing polymers for use as resists were developed; however, early polymers required organic solvents for development and did not possess either sufficient resolution or sensitivity [66,67]. Addition of fluorescence quenchers improved the photosensitivity for polysilanes by a factor of 5, although development of the sub-0.5 mm features patterned with a 0.35 NA, 248-nm stepper was still performed in an organic solvent [68]. For aqueous development of silicon-containing resists, loss of resolution is often observed because the silicon-containing groups that are incorporated in the resists interfere with the development process by significantly altering the resist hydrophilicity.

Silicon-containing bilayer resists have received renewed attention for use at an exposure wavelength of 193 nm. A silicon-containing bilayer process capable of imaging 0.175-nm equal lines and spaces with a 193-nm, 0.5 NA stepper has been demonstrated [69]. This silicon-enriched methacrylate-based top imaging layer can be developed in standard tetramethylammonium hydroxide solution. Interestingly, the top imaging layer is relatively thick (2500 Å), suggesting that even finer resolution could be achieved if a thinner imaging layer could be used.

Si-CARL Process

A variation of the silicon-containing bilayer scheme known as Si-CARL (silicon chemical amplification of resist lines) [70,71] is illustrated in Fig. 21. Si-CARL is a typical bilayer process in that a thin imaging layer is applied on top of a thick planarizing layer. A strongly cross-linked novolak resist film of sufficient thickness to suppress substrate reflections and standing waves is used as the bottom layer. The top resist contains an anhydride, which is converted via acid-catalyzed hydrolysis to a soluble carboxylic acid . The Si-CARL process incorporates silicon into the resist after the top film has been exposed and

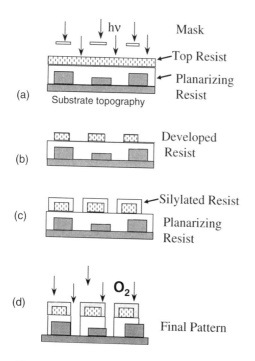

Figure 21 Illustration of the Si-CARL process. (a) Exposure of top resist; (b) aqueous development of top layer; (c) silylation of top pattern resulting in linewidth increase; (d) dry etch transfer of image to bottom layer.

developed. An amino-containing siloxane such as bis-diaminoalkyl-oligo-dimethylsiloxane reacts chemically with the anhydride and provides the etch resistance for the top resist layer during the subsequent plasma etching of the bottom layer.

The silicon incorporation in the Si-CARL process is typically performed in solution using conventional track equipment, but the dry development step is carried out using a plasma reactor. The bifunctional oligomers used for silicon delivery, so-called CARL reagents, have a reactive amine group at each end of the chain and incorporate multiple silicon atoms at each binding site in the resist polymer. These diamines can also react with different polymer chains to cause cross-linking in the resist polymer. A very high silicon content in the resist, up to 20–30% (by weight), can be achieved. After inclusion of these oligomers, the additional organic material incorporated in the resist is responsible for the swelling (i.e., amplification) of the original resist pattern. This increase in film thickness is reportedly linear in silylation time and does not appear to be inhibited by increasing cross-linking. In addition, the corresponding line width increase is independent of feature size [72]. Depending on the time during which the resist is exposed to the CARL reagent, the resulting pattern can be either the same size as the mask dimensions or the space can be reduced beyond the design size. Thus, depending on dose and aqueous silylation time, it is possible to introduce a process bias to pattern subresolution spaces. Interestingly, no observed pattern deformation or distortion has been reported with this process [72]. It is important to note that in the Si-CARL process the entire surface of the developed resist feature incorporates silicon and therefore is resistant to sizing changes during the plasma patterning of the bottom layer of resist. Very high aspect ratio patterns have been demonstrated with these methods [70].

A top surface imaging variant of this process, called simply Top-CARL, can be implemented as a single-layer process in which exposure to the CARL reagents and selective silicon uptake occur in the exposed area before development has taken place [70]. However, the Si-CARL bilayer process has a larger process latitude and greater etch resistance. Changes in the photoactive compound and matrix resin have been used to tailor the CARL and Si-CARL process for g-line, i-line, 248-nm, 193-nm lithography and e-beam lithography. Both positive and negative tone systems have been developed [73].

The Si-CARL process has the advantages of a bilayer technique (topographic invariance, reflection suppression, enhanced resolution) and can allow the optical exposure tools to operate in a more linear sizing regime. This can be advantageous for levels such as contacts, which are notoriously difficult to pattern. Another advantage of the Si-CARL process is the use of an aqueous-based, room temperature silylation scheme that can be performed on a conventional resist development track.

Other Bilayer Techniques Involving Silicon Incorporation

The silicon-added bilayer resist or SABRE process [74] is very similar to the Si-CARL technique except that silicon is introduced into the patterned top layer using a gas-phase process. In the SABRE process, conventional novolac-based g-line resists are silylated using bifunctional silylating agents to prevent resist flow and deformation. A major drawback of the SABRE process is that the silicon incorporation step is extremely slow, reportedly requiring 5 to 90 minutes, depending on the silylating agent [74].

The difficulties in formulating a single-layer resist with sufficient transparency and etch selectivity for patterning at 193 nm and even shorter wavelengths have intensified investigations of various bilayer schemes, particularly those involving introduction of silicon into the resist after it has been exposed. A bilayer approach has been demonstrated that incorporates silicon after exposure of the top resist layer by DUV (248 nm) or extreme ultraviolet (EUV; 13.5 nm) wavelengths [75,76]. As illustrated in Fig. 22, cross-linking induced by the photogenerated acid and the subsequent postexposure bake provides differential silicon permeability in the exposed and unexposed areas of the imaging layer. Silicon is

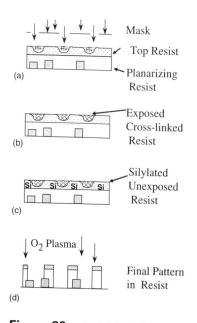

Figure 22 A silylated bilayer approach for using chemically amplified resists. (a) Exposure and generation of photoacid; (b) post-exposure bake and cross-linking of exposed resist; (c) silicon incorporation into unexposed resist; and (d) dry etch transfer of image.

preferentially incorporated in the unexposed resist from a gas-phase reagent after the exposure and bake steps. As with the Si-CARL process, some increase in resist volume accompanies the silicon incorporation. Further improvements in the process are achieved by introducing small amount of a difunctional disilane to control the resist swelling and to improve both the selectivity of the silicon inclusion step and process resolution [75]. Exposure to an oxygen-containing plasma for the all dry development step produces an etch resist silicon oxide mask in the unexposed regions resulting in a positive tone pattern.

The silylated bilayer system depicted in Fig. 22 employs chemical amplification, which, because of the low exposure dose requirements, is compatible with the limitations for the present 193-nm and EUV exposure tools. The difficulty with these systems is providing sufficient silicon incorporation into the resist while maintaining adequate contrast between the exposed and unexposed portion of the resist [76].

The use of unique materials as top imaging layers is also being explored. For instance, a bilayer process has been developed in which an imaging layer is formed by plasma-enhanced chemical vapor deposition (PECVD) from tetramethylsilane deposited on a PECVD planarizing layer. The PECVD process allows a very thin conformal top imaging layer to be applied [77].

Although the bilayer processes show some of the advantages of surface imaging, they are limited primarily by process complexity. Not only are two separate resist applications necessary, but also in most schemes both conventional wet development and dry development equipment is needed. This complexity generally translates into higher final costs that have kept many systems from becoming widely adopted. Defect and particle generation and problems with pinholes in the top imaging and barrier layers are additional problems with multilayer techniques [78,79]. With the notable exception of the Si-CARL and CARL processes, bilayer approaches are generally viewed as a method for extending the exposure tool capability and for research applications but not as manufacturable processes.

8   SILYLATION-BASED PROCESSES FOR SURFACE IMAGING

Instead of applying two distinct layers for patterning, the concept of selectively incorporating an inorganic or organometallic substance into either the exposed or unexposed regions of a single resist layer was demonstrated by Taylor et al. [60,61]. Effectively, silicon-containing bilayer was achieved post patterning by the reaction of $SiCl_4$ with the photochemically altered resist, a process termed gas-phase functionalization. In a similar vein, MacDonald et al. [80,81] used photogenerated OH reactive groups in the exposed photoresist to react with a silicon-containing amine to achieve silicon incorporation into the resist polymer.

Selective diffusion of silicon into the imaged resist gained widespread attention with the DESIRE process introduced by Roland and co-workers [82,83]. Many derivative processes were later developed and given suitable acronyms such as PRIME [84], SUPER [85], and SAHR [86]. All are single-layer patterning techniques that depend on preferential incorporation of a silicon-containing compound into the photoresist after the exposure step. Silicon incorporation in the resist was initially achieved by diffusion from the gas phase; however, Shaw et al. [87] introduced the use of a wet silylation process to produced an etch-resistant top resist layer. LaTulipe et al. [88,89] also used a liquid silylation process for surface imaging of a novolac resist. Silicon functionalization of a single-layer resist after exposure offers the attractive potential of simplifying both the resist processing sequence and the resist formulations. Although the various techniques differ in the exact mechanism of creating the contrast between the areas of silicon incorporation and silicon exclusion, many of the general characteristics are similar. Therefore, a detailed consideration of one of these schemes will serve to illustrate the major process parameters and concerns for this type of process.

8.1   The Desire Process

DESIRE, which is an acronym for diffusion-enhanced silylated resist, was the first commercialized surface imaging process [90–92]. Formulated originally for g-line exposure (436 nm), the technique is readily adaptable for I-line (365 nm) [93] as well as DUV (248 nm) [94,95] exposure. The DESIRE process, illustrated schematically in Fig. 23, consists of four interdependent steps: (1) exposure and formation of the latent image, (2) presilylation bake, (3) formation of silylated image, and (4) dry etch transfer of the pattern. Successful patterning of the resist will depend on having optimized parameters for all four steps.

The Exposure Step

During the exposure step, the photoactive compound, a naphthoquinone diazide, undergoes photochemical decomposition. Since the unexposed photoactive compound is a diffusion inhibitor, the exposed resist is more susceptible to silicon diffusion. The exposure dose and shape of the projected image to a large degree determine the ultimate depth and lateral dispersion of the silicon incorporation into the resist.

The Presilylation Bake

The presilylation bake (step 2, Fig. 23) is extremely important for selective incorporation of the silicon into the exposed regions. During this high-temperature bake, phenol ester formation by the unexposed photoactive compound forms a cross-linked and hence less permeable resist [91]. This thermally induced cross-linking of the unexposed resist in conjunction with the photochemical decom-

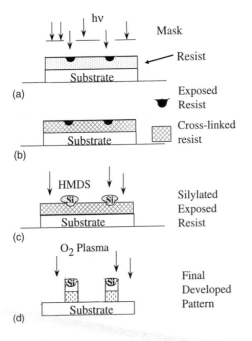

hv

Mask

Resist

Substrate

(a)

Exposed
Resist

Cross-linked
resist

Substrate

(b)

HMDS

Si   Si

Silylated
Exposed
Resist

Substrate

(c)

O_2 Plasma

Si   Si

Final
Developed
Pattern

Substrate

(d)

Figure 23 Schematic illustration of the DESIRE surface imaging process. (a) Exposure; (b) presilylation bake and cross-linking; (c) silicon incorporation; and (d) oxygen plasma development.

position of the sensitizer in the exposed area leads to preferential silicon incorporation into the exposed areas. The temperature and duration of the presilylation bake and the silicon exposure steps are important for defining the contrast between the exposed and unexposed region [96].

Silicon Incorporation Step: Vapor Phase Silylation

Incorporation of silicon is typically performed by vapor-phase introduction of a suitable silicon-containing reagent such as hexamethyldisilazane (HMDS). The mechanism for diffusion of the gas-phase silylation agent has been widely investigated. The unexposed naphthoquinone diazide can act as a diffusion inhibitor for HMDS in a phenolic resin, while the exposed naphthoquinone diazide will increase the diffusion rate [97,98]. Generally, the resin must provide sufficient binding sites and the diffusion of the silicon must allow 8–10% silicon incorporation, by weight, to provide sufficient etch selectivity [91]. Thermal cross-linking of the resist, initiated by the presilylation bake, continues during the silylation bake and determines the permeability of the silicon delivery agent and, hence, selectivity. The presilylation and silylation bake parameters of temperature and time are sensitive controls for silicon incorporation. In addition, the chemical structure of the silylation agent will influence the diffusion rate and the total amount of silicon introduced into the resist. Early versions of the resist for the DESIRE process exhibited pattern deformation due to the volume change upon inclusion of the silylating agent in the resist. Changes in the resist polymer and optimization of the silylating agent have eliminated this problem [99,100].

Although HMDS is the most readily available silylating agent in semiconductor purity and was used most often for silylation processes, interesting alternative silylation agents have been investigated [93]. Small silylating agents such as dimethylsilyl dimethylamine (DMSDMA) and tetramethyldisilazane (TMDS) require relatively low temperatures (80–120°C), but silylating agents containing bulky groups such as 1,3-diisobutyl-1,1,2,2,-tetramethyldisilazane proved too bulky to provide sufficient silylation. For the smaller silicon delivery agents, it is important to decouple the presilylation bake from the silylation in order to obtain sufficient cross-linking and selectivity. Polyfunctional silylating agents have proved to be very attractive in certain applications [74,101].

Liquid-Phase Silylation

Although the silylating agent is usually introduced in the gas phase, liquid-phase silylation processes for DESIRE have been reported [102]. Liquid-phase silylation is carried out using a three-component system containing an inert carrier solvent (xylene), a diffusion promoter (*N*-methylpyrrolidone or propyleneglycol monomethyl ether acetate), and a silylating agent. Hexamethylcyclotrisilazane (HMCTS), a trifunctional cyclic amine, is generally used as the silylation agent [87,89,103], although monofunctional silylating agents such as bis(dimethylamino)dimethylsilane have also been used [102]. HMCTS induces cross-linking of the resin, which can reduce the silicon diffusion rate and ultimately limit the total silicon uptake. However, the cross-linking is beneficial because it prevents lateral swelling and pattern deformation as well as out-diffusion of silicon, problems that occur under certain conditions with gas-phase silylation [99,100,104].

Unlike gas-phase silylation, the liquid-phase silicon uptake exhibits a nonlinear response to exposure dose. There is a threshold behavior with exposure dose that should favor a more selective silylation process. The amount of silicon incorporated into the film for liquid-phase silylation (~25%) is much higher than in the gas-phase process (~10%). Hence, the dry etch selectivity of these films is also higher [105]. The reason for the higher silicon content in the liquid silylation systems is not certain. Because the amount of observed silicon added to the resist corresponds to an average of two silicon atoms for each OH group, it is proposed that some polymerization, perhaps growth of polysiloxane chains on the phenolic OH group, occurs [105].

Liquid silylation techniques have been applied to other surface imaging techniques [88,89] and hold promise for improved silylation processes. For implementation in device manufacturing, an aqueous-based solution such as that used for the CARL process is much preferred to a xylene-based system from the standpoint of compatibility with existing resist processes and environmental concerns.

Dry Etch Development

Dry etch pattern transfer in the DESIRE process involves the use of an O_2 plasma to remove the unprotected resist while forming an etch-resistant silicon oxide covering in the silicon-containing areas. The dry development etch is generally carried out in a high-density plasma containing either pure oxygen or oxygen and a fluorocarbon gas [106]. Anisotropy of the etch is ensured by using very low pressures and by applying a DC bias to the wafer. Etch conditions must maintain a balance between the chemical component of the etch and physical sputtering. If care is taken to minimize the isotropic components of the etch, the resultant resist profile will depend to a large extent on the silylated profile.

Successful pattern definition during dry development involves a combination of etching of any unprotected resist and sputtering away of the silylating region [107–109]. For understanding the etch process, models that assume some competition between SiO_2 formation and sputtering of the film by ion bombardment can be applied [110,111]. Evidence for formation of a silicon oxide hard mask in the silylated regions comes from x-ray photoelectron spectroscopy (XPS) investigations of silylated resist samples before and after plasma exposure, which reveal that the silicon content of the surface does not change appreciably while there is a dramatic increase in the oxygen level. Both carbon and silicon XPS peaks are shifted to higher energy, indicating extensive oxidation [86]. For the unprotected resist, the etching mechanism involves both chemical and ion-induced etching. Clearly, oxygen atomic concentration, ion flux, and energy are important parameters for the etch. In addition, the glass transition temperature for the silylated resist polymer (T_g) has been shown to be important [112]. At higher temperatures silicon diffuses out of the exposed, silylated region, thus preventing adequate hard mask formation. This is confirmed by silicon profiling studies and correlates with a dramatic decrease in the observed etch selectivity (initially silylated vs. unsilylated areas) with increasing wafer temperature during plasma development. Improvements in etch anisotropy with the use of very low temperatures (−70°C) [113,114] and SO_2 in the plasma have been reported [115,116].

Initial attempts at dry development of silylated resists were plagued by severe problems with residue between patterned features and with line edge roughness. Residue, sometimes referred to as "grass," can arise from two sources: unintentional masking of resist during the plasma etch due to unwanted silicon incorporation in these areas and sputtering and redeposition of materials. Residue caused by unintentional silylation is usually distributed equally throughout the pattern, in some instances appearing in greater abundance in large open areas. In contrast to this, residue from sputtering and redeposition is located almost exclusively between features that should be very well resolved by the exposure tool. An example of severe grass formation caused by parasitic silylation is illustrated in Fig. 24.

Residue resulting from unintentional silicon incorporation can be minimized by optimizing the silylation and bake conditions to improve the selectivity of the silylation step. This usually involves changes in the bake time, temperature, pressure, or silylating agent. Alternatively, the dry development step can take care of the unwanted silicon inclusion by extending the over-etch time (i.e., overdevelopment) or by introducing an initial nonselective etch step to remove a certain amount of resist uniformly from the wafer. The latter step, often referred to as a "descum," involves the use of a fluorine-containing plasma or a high-energy ion bombardment step [117,118]. Usually, an initial step with low selectivity for silylated resists is followed by a second, more selective, etch [106]. A two-step oxygen etch, in which the initial step has a high ion energy, can also be used [117]. The disadvantage of either alteration of the dry development step is loss of resist thickness in the final pattern. This requires a thicker hard mask,

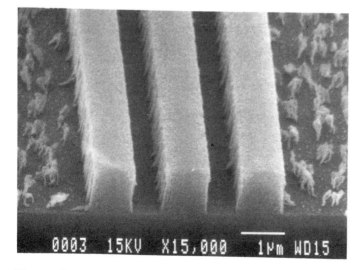

Figure 24 Examples of residue caused by unintentional silicon incorporation into exposed resist areas.

which usually translates into higher required exposure doses and longer processing times. Residue resulting from sputtering of the hard mask is eliminated by reducing the ion bombardment energy in the plasma development step.

Edge roughness for the dry developed resist can be a serious concern, particularly as the dimension of the line edge roughness become a significant percentage of the line width dimension. Extreme edge roughness is observed if the silicon content is insufficient to withstand the plasma dry development and breakdown of the etch mask occurs. The resist line roughness will most likely transfer into the underlying substrate during the subsequent etch step, causing variations in the pattern sizing. Severe edge roughness as illustrated in Fig. 25 can be caused by insufficient silicon hard mask protection of the underlying resist, low selectivity in the dry development etch, or both. Therefore, the silylation conditions and the dry etch parameters must be optimized in concert to minimize the line roughness.

Hard mask breakdown can also be observed when there is a lack of contrast in the exposed image. This can happen near the resolution limit of the exposure tool or if the exposed image is severely defocused. Edge roughness is of special concern at 193 nm and shorter exposure wavelengths due to very shallow absorption depth of the resist coupled with the small targeted line widths. Staining techniques that decorate the silylated resist profiles have verified the shallow silylated layer for these exposure wavelengths [75]. Any thinning of the silylated image near the edges of the silylated profile will result in an increase in line edge roughness. Shown in Fig. 26 is a section of a silylated grating pat-

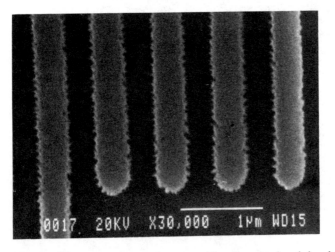

Figure 25   Line edge roughness resulting from hardmask breakdown during dry development of the resist.

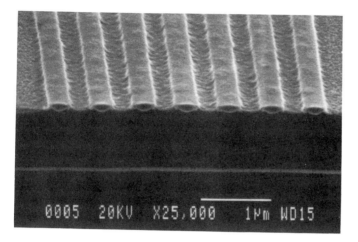

Figure 26 Silylated profiles (raised resist) which have been delineated using a short plasma etch.

tern that has been subjected to an oxygen plasma for a time sufficient to decorate the silylated areas but not completely etch the resist features. The oxygen etch has delineated the depth and lateral profile for the silylated regions [119]. It is interesting to note that along the edges of the silylated regions, some roughness is visible. The line edge roughness can be minimized by increasing the depth of silicon incorporation at the feature edges or by removing the thinner outer portions of the silicon hard mask during the dry development etch. The latter solution leads to changes in critical dimension with over-etch and is not a good solution from the point of view of process control. Although there is speculation that the molecular weight distribution of the resist could also influence the edge roughness, there have been no studies published to support this assertion.

8.2 The Prime Process

A variation of the DESIRE process for positive-tone images, called positive resist image by dry etching (PRIME), was developed by workers at LETI [84,120,121]. The PRIME process uses the same resist as the DESIRE process and differs only in the addition of a second near-UV flood exposure step (Fig. 27). Like a classical image reversal scheme, the PRIME process involves an initial exposure with DUV or e-beam followed by flood exposure at near-UV wavelengths to produce a positive-tone image. During the initial exposure, reaction of the photoactive compound results in cross-linking of the resist. For DUV exposure, only the top 300 Å of the resist is cross-linked, whereas the en-

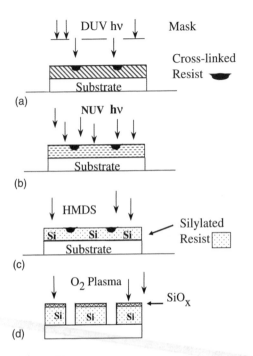

Figure 27 Schematic representation of the PRIME process. (a) DUV exposure; (b) NUV flood exposure; (c) presilylation bake and crosslinking; (d) silicon incorporation; and (e) oxygen plasma development.

tire resist thickness is cross-linked upon e-beam exposure. Degradation of the photoactive compound during the subsequent near-UV flood exposure increases the diffusion rate of the silylation agent in the previously unexposed areas. Silylation and dry development are performed in a manner similar to that in the DESIRE process, the end result being a positive-tone image. A major difficulty with the PRIME process is the high energies required for both the crosslinking step (400 mJ/cm^2 at 248 nm and 300 mC/cm^2 for e-beam at 50 keV) and the flood exposure (1–2 J/cm^2). Although some work with more sensitive resist formulations has been reported [122], this still remains a serious concern.

8.3 The SAHR Process

The silylated acid hardened resist (SAHR) process (Fig. 28) is a positive-tone single-layer process that relies on photoinitiated, acid-catalyzed cross-linking. In the SAHR process, DUV-induced acid generation in the imaging layer causes cross-linking in the exposed region during the postexposure bake step and renders these areas impermeable and unreactive to silylamines [123]. With gas-

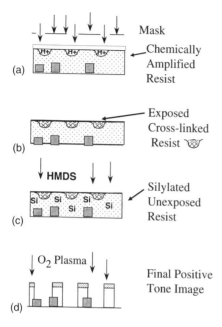

Figure 28 Silylated acid hardened resist process (SAHR). (a) Exposure and generation of photoacid; (b) post-exposure bake and crosslinking of exposed resist; (c) silicon incorporation into unexposed resist; and (d) dry etch transfer of image.

phase silylation, the unexposed resist incorporates 10–12% silicon by weight, which is adequate to protect the underlying resist during the final plasma development.

The chemically amplified resists used in the SAHR process require much lower exposure doses (5–30 mJ/cm^2 for DUV exposures) compared with the novolac resists for the DESIRE process. The original SAHR process suffers from severe limitations with respect to its practical implementation. The first is the variation of silicon penetration depth with feature size in which the larger features exhibit a much deeper silylation depth. This size-dependent variation of the silylated profiles make it difficult to control line width and maintain pattern sizing linearity. The differential silicon incorporation cannot be explained simply by decreased optical contrast, as this effect is observed at feature sizes much larger than the resolution limit of the exposure tool. A plausible explanation is that the interfacial tension per unit volume becomes much larger as the patterned dimensions shrink, causing this sizing dependence [124]. An additional problem with the SAHR process is the resist flow during silylation. Incorporation of silyl groups into the resist film causes resist swelling and interferes with the hydrogen bonding, thus lowering the T_g of the resist film. As a consequence, during the silylation process the silylated resist overflows into the exposed (cross-linked) regions. This parasitic silicon incorporation degrades the silylation process contrast and requires extra processing steps to minimize the effect. Exposure of the resist to a bifunctional silane such as bis(dimethylamino)dimethylsilane prior to treatment with the silylating agent significantly diminishes the amount of silicon in the exposed areas by creating a thin cross-linked skin on the resist surface [124]. Alternatively, an aqueous development step prior to the silylation step eliminates both the flow problem and the size dependence of the silicon penetration depth. Surface depressions in the unexposed areas are created by this development step and are refilled by the swollen silylated material. However, this predevelopment step removes ~4000 Å of resist and requires thicker initial resist coatings.

Today, modified SAHR processes are being used with e-beam as well as shorter wavelength (193 and 13.5 nm) exposure tools [101,114,125–127]. For these shorter wavelength exposures the cross-linking is facile due to the high photon energy. A number of patterning techniques have exploited this fact to create differential diffusion rates of a silicon-containing reagent to achieve surface imaging at 193 nm [125,128] or 13–40 nm (extreme UV) [129]. For many of the 193-nm surface imaging techniques being explored, photochemical cross-linking, unaided by chemical amplification, is used [128].

8.4   Other Surface Imaging Techniques

Investigations targeted at developing surface imaging processes for high-resolution applications are yielding some interesting results. For example, work using plasma deposition of organosilicon shows promise for a single-layer and bilayer process [130–132]. An all dry patterning process involving the polymerization of methylsilane has demonstrated encouraging results with this thin conformal imaging layer [132]. In addition, non-silicon-containing single-layer and bilayer processes are being investigated. Near-surface imaging using metal plating to define an etch-resistant mask has also been demonstrated [133–135]. In this process, a substrate surface is treated with an organosilane and exposed to DUV 248 nm) radiation. This exposure modifies the wettability of the substrate surface and reactivity of the surface film. Subsequent treatment with a Pb/Sn catalyst followed by electroless copper and nickel metallization yields films several hundred angstroms thick in unexposed regions. This positive image can then be used as a plasma etch mask. The ultrathin films resulting from this process can lead to significant improvement in focal depth and resolution.

9 USE OF ALTERNATIVE PATTERN TECHNOLOGY IN MANUFACTURING

Surface imaging has traditionally been used to extend the capabilities of the current generation of optical lithography tools while allowing time for the newer tools to mature. Surface imaging or near-surface imaging techniques using bilayer approaches have found limited usage outside the research environment. There are, however, a few exceptions. [73,136,137] The DESIRE process was transferred to a pilot line at Texas Instruments and used in the early production and qualification of a 16-MB DRAM device [136]. The challenging topography and high reflectivity of the metal level necessitated the use of surface imaging resists. The DESIRE process was eventually replaced by a process using conventionally developed resist; however, use of an antireflective coating (ARC) and enhanced planarization techniques were necessary to achieve performance comparable to that of the DESIRE process. It is of interest to note that the measured defect levels and yield for the DESIRE process were comparable to those of the optimized ARC/conventional resist process [138]. As mentioned earlier, the CARL process has been used successfully at Seimens for manufacturing for a few [73].

Antireflective coatings, both top and bottom layer films, are necessary for many current IC applications and are employed in numerous manufacturing lines. The manufacturing issues for nonconventional resist techniques such as surface imaging or bilayer resist imaging have been discussed by several authors [78,138,139]. However, the ultimate selection of a photoresist process, whether conventional single-layer resist processing or one of the alternative processes we have discussed, will depend on the achievable patterning resolution and process latitude, robustness toward subsequent etching steps, line width control, ease of integration into current fabrication environments, yield, and ultimately cost.

9.1 Advantages and Disadvantages of Multilayer and Surface Imaging Techniques

Multilayer resist techniques and surface imaging processes are more complicated than conventional, single-layer, aqueous-developed resist techniques but have unique advantages. The improved depth of focus and resolution, insensitivity to topography, and ability to work with multiple stepper generations and wavelengths may, in certain applications, make them worth the added complications. The all dry process allows very high aspect ratio resist patterning. Among the alternative methods for providing enhanced patterning capabilities such as bilayer and trilayer processes [54,55,67], the single-layer surface imaging resist techniques are somewhat simpler from a processing standpoint.

The advantages outlined above must be weighed against the additional complexity of these alternative process. Nontraditional equipment is required for many of these techniques. For silylation-based processes, a silylation tool and a plasma etcher are required. Although the use of organic antireflective coatings has introduced etch processes into many formerly conventional patterning techniques, the silylation step has no equivalent in the conventionally developed resist process. The higher exposure dose requirement for some alternative techniques translates into lower throughput and higher costs. As with any plasma process, there are concerns about damage and defects caused by the dry development plasma processing [140]. As device dimensions become smaller, additional concerns about the dry development etch arise. For instance, edge roughness dimensions become a larger fraction of the line width and must be minimized. Damage mechanisms that may not have been detected with larger design sizes may become more important with the smaller device designs. Working close to or below the intended resolution of the stepper, as is often the case for many of the multilayer and surface imaging techniques, often increases the proximity effects. To minimize the proximity effects, the dry development must be carefully optimized. Still of major concern is that no manufacturing equipment set is available for many of these alternative processes.

9.2 Prognosis for Multilayer and Surface Imaging Technologies

Multilayer and surface imaging techniques will probably play an important role in future lithography development. These processes are easily applied to numerous exposure tools including 193 nm, e-beam, and EUV exposure systems. This is especially important for the development of new exposure tools where the resists are problematic [128,141]. Fortunately, many aspects of the process are the same across different wavelengths, so the experience gained with a tool set of one generation is readily adapted to the next-generation exposure tool.

More variations are being added to the repertoire of available surface imaging or thin-film patterning processes. Both positive and negative tone silylated surface imaging resists are now available [89,90,101]. Novel silylating agents are also being explored [102,101]. Improvements in the multilayer resist processes, particularly for application to 193 nm and EUV exposure, are ongoing. Optical enhancement techniques such as modified illumination and phase shifting of reticles are complementary to near-surface and surface imaging resist techniques and can further extend the process capabilities. Surface imaging resist processing has become more widely known in the semiconductor industry. The equipment necessary for processing is becoming commercially available [142], and some of the nontraditional steps are becoming more familiar to the lithographer because organic antireflective layers also require dry etching. In addition, the cost of implementing surface imaging or multilayer resist processes can compare favorably with that of conventional processing if the cost of additional processes to compensate for the deficiencies of single-layer resist (e.g., antireflective coatings, etch hard masks) is considered.

REFERENCES

1. Stillwagon, L. E., and Taylor, G. N., *Polymers in Microlithography: Materials and Processes*, ACS Symp. Ser. 412, American Chemical Society, Washington, DC, 1989, pp. 252–265.
2. Stillwagon, L. E., and Larsen, R. G., *J. Appl. Phys*, *63*, 5251 (1988).
3. Steigerwald, J. J., Murarka, S. P., and Gutmann, R. J., *Chemical Mechanical Planarization of Microelectronic Materials*, Wiley, New York, 1997.
4. Bruce, J. A., Lin, B. J., Sundling, D. L., and Lee, T. N., *IEEE Trans. Elect. Dev.*, *ED-34*, 2428 (1987).
5. Lin, B. J., Bassous, E., Chao, W., and Petrillo, K. E., *J. Vac. Sci. Technol. B*, *19*, 1313 (1981).
6. Lin, B. J., *Electrochem. Soc.*, *127*, 202 (1980).
7. Liu, E. D., O'Toole, M. M., and Chang, M. S., *IEEE Trans. Elect. Dev.*, *ED-28*, 1405 (1981).
8. Ting, C. H., and Liauw, K. L., *J. Vac. Sci. Technol. B*, *1*, 1225 (1983).
9. de Grandpre, M. P., Vidusek, D. A., and Leganza, M. W., *Proc. SPIE*, *539*, 103 (1985).
10. Todokoro, Y., *IEEE Trans. Elect. Dev.*, *ED-27*, 1443 (1980).
11. Lamarre, P. A., *IEEE Trans. Elect. Dev.*, *ED-39*, 1844 (1992).
12. Liu, E. D., *Solid State Technol.*, *26*, 66 (1982).
13. Ting, C. H., *Proc. Kodak Interface*, *83*, 40 (1983).
14. Havas, J. R., *Electrochem. Soc. Ext. Abst.*, *2*, 743 (1976).
15. Brewer, T., Carlson, R., and Arnold, J., *J. Appl. Photo. Eng.*, *7*, 184 (1981).
16. Coyne, R. D., and Brewer, T, *Proc. Kodak Interface*, *83*, 40 (1983).
17. Mimura, Y., and Aoyama, S., *Microelect. Eng.*, *21*, 47 (1993).
18. Ishii, W., Hashimoto, K., Itoh, N., Yamazaki, H., Yokuta, A., and Nakene, H., *Proc. SPIE*, 295 (1986).
19. Nölscher, C., Mader, L., and Scheegans, M., *Proc. SPIE*, *1086*, 242 (1989).
20. Such as Brewer Science ARC-XLN.
21. Reiser, A., *Photoreactive Polymers*, 323, Wiley, N.Y. (1989).
22. Yang, T. S., Koot, T., Taylor, J., Josephson, W., Spak, M., Dammel, R., *SPIE*, *2724*, 724 (1996).
23. Pavelchek E., Meudor, J., Guerrero, D., *SPIE*, *2724*, 692 (1996).
24. van den Berg, H., and van Staden, J., *J. Appl. Phys.*, *50*, 1212 (1979).
25. Martin, B., and Gourley, D., *Microelect. Eng.*, *21*, 61 (1993).
26. Ogawa, T., Nakano, H., Gocho, T., and Tsumori, T., *Proc. SPIE*,
27. Tani, Y., Mato, H., Okuda, Y., Todokoro, Y., Tatsuta, T., Sanai, M., and Tsuji, O., *Jpn. J. Appl. Phys.*, *322*, 5909 (1993).

28. Draper, B. L., Mahoney, A. R., and Bailey, G. A., *J. Appl. Phys.*, *62*, 4450 (1987).
29. Tompkins, H., Sellars, J., and Tracy, C., *J. Appl. Phys.*, *73*, 3932 (1993).
30. Smith, B., Alam, Z., and Butt, S., *Abstracts of the Second International Symposium on 193nm Lithography*, Colorado Springs, 1997.
31. Dean, K. R., Carpio, R. A., Rich, G. F., Proc. *SPIE*, *2438*, 514 (1995).
32. Smith, B. W., Butt, S., Alam, Z., Kurinec, S., and Lane, R., *J. Vac. Sci. Technol. B.*, *14*, 3719 (1996).
33. Hummel, R. E., *Electronic Properties of Materials*, Springer-Verlag, New York, 1993, pp. 186–230.
34. Palik, E. C., *Handbook of Optical Constants of Solids I*, (1985).
35. Smith, B. W., Butt, S., Alam, Z., *J. Vac. Sci. Technol. B*, *14(6)*, 3714 (1996).
36. Cirelli, R. A., Weber, G. R., Kornblit, A., Baker, R. M., Klemens, F. P., and DeMarco, J., *J. Vac. Sci. Technol. B*, *14*, 4229 (1996).
37. Bencher, C., Ngai, C., Roma, B., Lian, S., and Vuong, T., *Solid State Technol.*, *20*, 109 (1997).
38. Brunner, T. A., *Proc. SPIE*, *1466*, 297 (1991).
39. Tanaka, T., Hasegawa, N., Shiraishi, H., and Okazaki, S., *J. Electrochem. Soc.*, *137*, 3900 (1990).
40. Bobroff, N., and Rosenbluth, A., *J. Vac. Sci. Technol. B*, *6*
41. Brunner, T. A., *Proc. SPIE*, *1466*, 297 (1991).
42. Shiraishi, H., and Okazaki, S., *Proc. SPE Reg. Tech. Conf. Photopolym.*, Ellenville, NY, 1991, p. 195.
43. Lyons, C. F., Leidy, R. K., and Smith, G. B., *Proc. SPIE*, *1674*, 523 (1992).
44. Bernard, D., and Arbach, H., *J. Opt. Soc. Am.*, *8*, 123 (1991).
45. Havas, J. R., U.S. Patent 4,025,191 (1977).
46. Wiebe, A. F., U.S. Patent 3,511,652 (1970).
47. Griffing, B. F., and West, P. R., *Polym. Eng. Sci.*, *23*, 947 (1983).
48. Hofer, D. C., Miller, R. D., and Willson, C. G., *Proc. Microcircuit Eng.*, *A5*, 1 (1984).
49. Halle, L. F., *J. Vac. Sci. Technol.*, *3*, 323 (1985).
50. Endo, M., Tani, Y., Sasago, M., Nomura, N., and Das, S., *J. Vac. Sci. Technol. B*, *7*, 1072 (1989).
51. Havas, J. R., U.S. Patent 3,873,361 (1973).
52. Lin, B. J., and Chang, T. H. P., *J. Vac. Sci. Technol.*, *1*, 1669 (1979).
53. Moran, J. M., and Maydan, D., *J. Vac. Sci. Technol.*, *16*, 1620 (1979).
54. Buiguez, F., Parrens, P., and Picard, B., *Proc SPIE*, *393*, 192 (1983).
55. Lin, B., in *Introduction to Microlithography* (L. Thompson, M. Bowden, and G. Wilson, eds.), American Chemical Society, Washington DC, 1983, pp. 287–349.
56. Bassous, E., Ephrath, L., Pepper, G., and Mikalsen, S., *J. Electrochem. Soc.*, *130*, 478 (1983).
57. Hatzakis, M., Paraszcak, J., and Shaw. J., *Proceedings of the Microelectronic Engineering Conference*, Lausanne, 1981, p. 386.
58. Paraszcak, J., Babich, E., McGouey, R., Heidenreich, J., Hatzakis, M., and Shaw, J., *Microelectron. Eng.*, *6*, 453 (1987).
59. For review see Hatzakis, M., Shaw, J., Babich, E., and Paraszczak, J., *J. Vac. Sci. Technol. B*, *6*, 2224 (1988).

60. Taylor, G. N., Stillwagon, L. E., and Venkatesan, T., *J. Electrochem. Soc.*, *131*, 1658 (1984).
61. Wolf, T. M., Taylor, G. N., Venkatesan, T., and Kraetsch, R. T., *J. Electrochem, Soc.*, *131*, 1664 (1984).
62. Taylor, G. N., and Wolf, T. M., *Polym. Eng. Sci.*, *20*, 1087 (1980).
63. Wilkins, C. W., Reichmanis, E., Wolf, T. M., and Smith, B. C., *J. Vac. Sci. Technol. B*, *3*, 306 (1985).
64. Saotome, Y., Gokan, H., Sargo, K., Suzuki, M., and Ohnishi, J., *J. Electrochem. Soc.*, *132*, 909 (1985).
65. Miller, R. D., Hofer, D., McKean, D. R., Willson, C. G., West, R., and Trefonas, P. T., in *Materials for Microlithography*, ACR Symp. Ser. 266 (L. F. Thompson, C G. Willson, and J. M. J. Frechet, Eds.), American Chemical Society, Washington, DC, 1984, pp. 293–310.
66. Reichmanis, E., MacDonald, S. A., and Iwayanagi, T., in *Polymers in Microlithography*, American Chemical Society, Washington, DC, 1989.
67. Miller, R. D., and Wallraff, G., *Adv. Mater. Opt. Electron.*, *4*, 95 (1994).
68. Wallraff, G. M., Miller, R. D., Clecak, N., and Baier, M., *Proc. SPIE*, *1466*, 211 (1991).
69. Schaedeli, U., Tinguely, E., Blakeney, A. J., Falcigno, P., and Kunz, R. R., *Proc. SPIE*, *2724*, 344 (1996).
70. Sezi, R., Sebald, M., Leuschner, R., Ahne, H., Birkle, S., and Borndorfer, H., *Proc. SPIE*, *1262*, 84 (1990).
71. Sebald, M., Berthold, J., Beyer, M., Leuschner, R., Noelscher, C., Scheler, U., Sezi, R., Ahne, H., and Birkle, S., *Proc. SPIE*, *1466*, 227 (1991).
72. Sebald, M., Leuschner, R., Sezi, R., Ahne, H., and Birkle, S., *Proc. SPIE*, *1262*, 528 (1990).
73. Leuschner, R., Ahne, H., Marquardt, U., Nickel, U., Schmidt, E., Sebald, E., and Sezi, R., *Microelectron. Eng.*, *20*, 305 (1993).
74. McColgin, W. C., Jech, J., Daly, R. C., and Brust, T. B., *Proc. Symp. VLSI Technol.*, 1987, p. 9.
75. Wheller, D. R., Hutton, S., Stein, S., Baiocchi, F., Cheng, M., and Taylor, G. N., *J. Vac. Sci. Technol. B*, *11*, 2789 (1993).
76. Taylor, G., Hutton, R., Stein, S., Boyce, C., Wood, O., LaFontaine, B., MacDowell, A., Wheeler, D., Kubiak, G., Ray-Chaudhure, A., Berger, K., and Tichenor, D., *Proc. SPIE*, *2437*, 308 (1995).
77. Horn, M. W., Maxwell, B. E., Knuz, R. R., Hibbs, M. S., Eriksen, L. M., Palmateer, S. C., and Forte, A. R., *Proc. SPIE*, *2438*, 760 (1995).
78. McDonnell Bushnell, L. P., Gregor, L. V., and Lyons, C. F., *Solid State Technol.*, June, 133 (1986).
79. Miller, K. P., and Sachdev, H. S., *J. Vac. Sci. Technol. B*, *10*, 2560 (1992).
80. MacDonald, S. A., Schlosser, H., Ito, H., Clecak, J., and Willson, C. G., *Chem. Mater.*, *3*, 435 (1991)
81. Ito, H., MacDonald, S. A., Miller, R. D., and Willson, C. G., U.S. Patent 4,552,833 (1985).
82. Coopmans, F., and Roland, B., *Proc. SPIE*, *631*, 34 (1986).
83. Roland, B., and Vrancken, A., Eur. Patent Appl. 85870142.8 (1985).

84. Pierrat, C., Tedesco, S., Vinet, Lerme, M., and Dal'Zotto, B., *J. Vac. Sci. Technol. B*, 7, 1782 (1989).

85. Mutsaers, C. M. J., Vollenbroek, F. A., Nijssen, W. P. M., and Visser, R. J., *Microelectron. Eng.*, 11, 497 (1990).

86. Pavelchek, E. K., Bohland, J. F., Thackery, J. W., Orsula, G. W., Jones, S. K., Dudley, B. W., Bobbio, S. M., and Freeman, P. W., *J. Vac. Sci. Technol. B*, 8, 1497–1501 (1990).

87. Shaw, J. M., Hatzakis, M., Babich, E. D., Paraszczak, J. R., Witman, D. F., and Stewart, K. J., *J. Vac. Sci. Technol. B*, 7, 1709, (1989).

88. La Tulipe, D. C., Pomerene, A. T. S., Simons, J. P., Seeger, D. E., *Microelectron. Eng.*, 17, 265(1992).

89. LaTulipe, D. C., Simons, J. P., and Seeger, D. E., *Proc. SPIE*, 2195, 372 (1994).

90. Coopmans, F., and Roland, B., *Proc. SPIE*, 631 34 (1986).

91. Roland, B., Lombaerts, R., Jacus, C., and Coopmans, F., *Proc. SPIE*, 771, 69 (1987).

92. Visser, R. J., Schellenkens, J. D. W., Reuhman-Huiskens, M. E., and Ijzendoorn, L. J., *Proc. SPIE*, 771, 110 (1987).

93. Baik, K. H., van den Hove, L., Goethals, A. M., Op de Beeck, M., and Roland, R., *J. Vac. Sci. Technol. B*, 8, 1481 (1990).

94. Op de Beeck, M., and Van den Hove, L., *J. Vac. Sci. Technol. B*, 10, 701 (1992).

95. Hanratty, M. A., and Tipton, M. C., *Proc. SPIE*, 1674, 894 (1992).

96. Goethals, A. M., Lombaerts, R., Roland, B., and van den Hove, L., *Microelectron. Eng.*, 13, 37 (1991).

97. Roland, B., Lombaerts, R., Vandendriessche, J., and Godts, F., *Proc. SPIE*, 1262, 151 (1990).

98. Roland, B., Vandendriessche, J., Lombaerts, R., Denturck, B., and Jakus, C., *Proc. SPIE*, 920, 120 (1988).

99. Goethals, A. M., Nichols, D. N., Op de Beeck, M., De Geyter, P., Baik, K. H., van den Hove, L., Roland, B., and Lombaerts, R., *Proc. SPIE*, 1262, 206 (1990).

100. Goethals, A. M., Baik, K. H., Ronse, K., van den Hove, L., and Roland, B., *Microelectron. Eng.*, 21 239 (1993).

101. Wheeler, D., Hutton, R., Boyce, C., Stein, S., Cirelli, R., and Taylor, G., *Proc. SPIE*, 2438, 762 (1995).

102. Baik, K. H., van den Hove, L., and Roland, B., *J. Vac. Sci. Technol. B*, 9, 3399 (1991).

103. Rouhman-Huisken, M. E., Mutsaers, C. M. J., Vollenbroek, F. A., and Moonen, J. A., *Microelectron. Eng.*, 9, 551 (1989).

104. Doa, T. T., Spence, C. A., and Hess, D. W., *Proc. SPIE*, 1466, 257 (1991).

105. Baik, K. H., Ronse, K., van den Hove, L., and Roland, B., *Proc. SPIE*, 1672, 362 (1992).

106. Lombaerts, R., Roland, B., Goethals, A. M., and van den Hove, L., *Proc. SPIE*, 1262, 43 (1990).

107. Dijkstra, H. J., *J. Vac. Sci. Technol B*, 10, 2222 (1992).

108. LaPorte, P., van den Hove, L., and Melaku, Y., *Microelectron. Eng.*, 13, 469 (1991).

109. Garza, C. M., Misium, G., Doering, R. R., Roland, B., and Lombaerts, R., *Proc. SPIE, 1896*, 229 (1989).
110. Watanabe, F., and Ohnishi, Y., *J. Vac. Sci. Technol. B*, *4*, 422 (1986).
111. Hartney, M. A., Hess, D. W., and Soane, D. S., *J. Vac. Sci. Technol. B*, *7*, 1 (1989).
112. Paniez, P. J., Joubert, O. P., Pons, M. J., Oberlin, J. C., Vachette, T. G., Weill, A. P., Pelletier, J. H., and Fiori, C., *Microelectron. Eng.*, *13*, 57 (1991).
113. Jurgensen, C. W., Hutton, R. S., and Taylor, G. N., *J. Vac. Sci. Technol. B*, *10*, 2542 (1992).
114. Palmateer, S. C., Kunz, R. R., Horn, M. W., Forte, A. R., and Rothschild, M., *Proc. SPIE, 2438*, 455(1995)
115. Pons, M., Pelletier, J., and Joubert, O., *J. Appl. Phys.*, *75*, 4709 (1994).
116. Hutton, R. S., Boyce, C. S., and Taylor, G. N., *J. Vac. Sci. Technol. B*, *13*, 2366 (1995).
117. Roland, B., Lombaerts, R., and Coopmans, F., *Dry Process Symposium*, *98*, (1988).
118. Hutton, R. S., Kostelak, R. L., Nalamasu, O., Kornbit, A., McNevin, G., and Taylor, G., *J. Vac. Sci. Technol. B*, *8*, 1502 (1990).
119. Misium, G. R., Douglas, M. A., Garza, C. M., and Dobson, C. B., *Proc. SPIE, 1262*, 74 (1990).
120. Pierrat, C., Tedesco, S., Vinet, F., Lerme, M., and Dal'Zotto, B., *Proc. J. Vac. Sci.*, *7*, 1782 (1989).
121. Pierrat, C., Tedesco, S., Vinet, F., Mourier, T. Lerme, M. Dal'Zotto, B., and Guibert, J. C., *Microelectron. Eng.*, *11*, 507 (1990).
122. Vinet, F., Chevallier, M., Pierrat, C., Guibert, J. C., Rosilio, C., and Mouanda, B., *Proc. SPIE, 1466*, 558 (1991).
123. Thackeray, J. W., Bohland, J. F., Pavelchek, E. K., Orsula, G. W., McCullough, A. W., Jones, S. K., and Bobbio, S. M., *Proc. SPIE, 1185*, 2 (1990).
124. Calabrese, G. S., Bohland, J. F., Pavelchek, E. K., Sinta, R., Dudley, B. W., Jones, S. K., and Freeman, P. W., *Microelectron. Eng.*, *21*, 231 (1993).
125. Hartney, M., Kunz, R., Ehrlich, D., and Shaver, D., *Proc. SPIE, 1262*, 119 (1990).
126. Irmscher, M., Hoefflinger, B., Springer, R., Stauffer, C., and Peterson, W., *Proc. SPIE, 2724*, 564 (1996).
127. Ohfuji, T., and Aizaki, N., *Digest of Technical Papers—Symposium on VLSI Technology*, 1994, p. 93.
128. Hartney, M. A., Kunz, R. R., Ehrlich, D. J., and Shaver, D. C., *J. Vac. Sci. Technol. B*, *8*, 1476 (1990)
129. Oizumi, Y., Yamashita, Y., and Ohtani, M., *Microelectron. Eng.*, *30*, 291 (1996).
130. Horn, M. W., Pang, S. W., and Rothschild, M., *J. Vac. Sci. Technol. B*, *8*, 1493 (1991).
131. Weidman, T. W., and Joshi, A. M., *Appl. Phys. Lett.*, *62*, 372 (1993).
132. Kostelak, R. L., Weidman, T. W., Vaidya, S., Joubert, O., Palmateer, S. C., and Hibbs, M., *J. Vac. Sci. Technol. B*, *13*, 2994 (1995).
133. Schilling, M. L., Katz, H. E., Houlihan, F. M., Stein, S. M., Hutton, R. S., and Taylor, G. N., *J. Electrochem. Soc.*, *143*, 691 (1996).
134. Calabrese, G. S., Abali, L. N., Bohland, J. F., Pavelchek, E. K., Sricharoenchaikit, P., Vizvary, G., Bobbio, S. M., and Smith, P., *Proc. SPIE, 1466*, 528 (1991).

135. Calvert, J., Chen, M., Dulcey, C., George, J., Peckerar, M., Schnur, O., and Schoen, P., *J. Vac. Sci. Technol. B*, *9*, 3447 (1991).
136. Garza, C. M., Catlett, D. L., and Jackson, R. A., *Proc. SPIE*, *1466*, 616 (1991).
137. Tipton, M. C., and Hanratty, M. A., *Microelectron. Eng.*, *17*, 47 (1992).
138. Garza, C. M., Solowiej, E. J., and Boehm, M. A., *Proc. SPIE*, *1672*, 403 (1992).
139 Seeger, D. E., La Tulipe, D. C., Kunz, R. R., Garza, C. M., and Hanratty, M. A., *IBM J. Res. Dev.*, *41*, 105 (1997).
140. Fonash, S. J., Viswanathan, C. R., and Chan, V. D., *Solid State Technol.*, *37*(7), 5 (1994).
141. Allen, R. D., Wallraff, G. M., Hofer, D. C., Knuz, R. R., Palmateer, S. C., and Horn, M. W., *Microlithography World,* Summer, 21 (1995).
142. Park, B. J., Baik, K. H., Kim, H. K., Kim, J. W., Bok, C. K., Vertommen, J., and Rosenlund, R., *Proc. SPIE*, in press.

11

Dry Etching of Photoresists

Roderick R. Kunz

Massachusetts Institute of Technology
Lexington, Massachusetts

1 INTRODUCTION: REQUIREMENTS FOR ETCH RESISTANCE

The central function of a patterned resist image is to allow transfer of the pattern into the underlying substrate while providing a protective mask to the covered areas. This function provides the origin for the use of the word "resist" in this fashion. The substrates that most often require patterning in the integrated circuit industry are composed of silicon, silicon dioxide, aluminum (or some aluminum-rich alloy), silicon nitride, or titanium nitride, as well as many other less common materials such as GaAs, InP, W, or metal silicides, plus many others. The transfer of the resist patterns into these materials must be accomplished with near-perfect retention of the original resist pattern attributes—vertical sidewalls, smooth line edges, and no residues. To meet these requirements, the substrate material must etch more quickly than the masking resist layer, and the etching must be highly directional with little or no lateral etching. The most common way to meet these goals is to use low-pressure glow-discharge plasmas [1,2]. Current technology trends require plasma processing of large-area (150–300 mm) wafers, and as a result the latest equipment has been designed for single-wafer rather than batch processing. To meet throughput targets commensurate with single-wafer processing, high-ion-density plasmas have been developed that can achieve very high (>1 µm/min) material removal rates. In addition to the transfer of the resist pattern into the underlying substrate, certain multilayer resist processes require the dry development of a thin (<250 nm) organosilicon latent image into the bulk of the hydrocarbon resist (~1 μm). This is also accomplished by use of glow-discharge plasmas.

After providing an introduction that briefly discusses the basics of plasma physics and chemistry and provides brief descriptions of the most common types of plasma etch reactors currently in use, the chapter will review the important chemical processes involved in plasma etching, plasma resist stripping, and photoresist hardening.

2 AN OVERVIEW OF PLASMA SOURCES

2.1 Definition of a Plasma

Plasmas used for semiconductor wafer processing, also commonly referred to as glow discharges [1,2], are low-pressure (0.5 mtorr to 5 torr) gases in which a relatively low fraction (10^{-6} to 10^{-3}) of atoms are ionized. At typical operating pressures, the corresponding ion densities are generally in the 10^9 to 10^{12} ions/cm^3 range. In addition to the ions, free electrons, excited neutral species, and photons from the visible through vacuum ultraviolet region (2–20 eV) of the spectrum, emitted from excited atoms or molecules, are also present. The ions and electrons possess significantly different mobilities when influenced by electric fields, and this mobility difference can result in the negative charging of electrically isolated surfaces exposed to the plasma to a magnitude equal to the plasma potential, roughly 15–30 V or so.

The excitation of the gas to start and subsequently sustain the discharge can be accomplished in a number of ways. Although not the simplest, the most useful methods use alternating (AC) voltages, often in conjunction with DC magnetic fields. The use of AC excitation is necessary to prevent runaway charge buildup that would occur on insulating surfaces such as SiO_2. The magnetic fields serve to cause the electron trajectories to spiral, thereby increasing their path length and their probability of undergoing an electron-molecule or electron-atom collision. These collisions, through a variety of different pathways, can result in formation of positively or negatively charged ions or excited neutral species. Greater numbers of these electron-impact events results in higher ion densities. The magnetic field also acts to decrease the effective electron mobility, thereby reducing the magnitude of surface charges that can build up due to the differential mobilities of the electrons and ions. Additional DC voltages applied to surfaces exposed to a plasma will result in electrostatic acceleration of the charged particles, causing them to be accelerated and to strike the surface with greater directionality. When AC power is applied to a surface exposed to a plasma, the difference in mobility between electrons and ions will cause a net DC potential to form on the surface. This is often termed self-bias, and its magnitude is controlled by the net ion and electron fluxes to the surface, as well as the charge dissipation rate of the etching body. Typical AC frequencies used are radiofrequency (rf) at 13.56 Mhz and microwave frequency at 6.45 Ghz.

For resist pattern transfer, specific plasma characteristics are desirable. First, the ion flux to the surface must be high enough to etch material at a rate commensurate with high-throughput single-wafer processing. Second, the ion directionality must be highly anisotropic to ensure that little or no lateral etching occurs. Finally, the ion energies must be low to minimize the projected range of subsurface damage that accumulates in the remaining unetched substrate. A brief description of the most common types of plasmas used in integrated circuit fabrication, along with some of their more important attributes, will be presented in the next section.

2.2   Types of Plasma Sources

A variety of experimental configurations have been designed into commercially available plasma reactors. Due to the reduced pressure requirements needed to sustain a plasma, all such systems are centered around a vacuum chamber, usually with automated wafer handling enabling automatic loading and unloading of wafers. With the advent of larger wafer sizes (8-inch-diameter wafers are now the standard), nearly all plasma reactors are designed to etch one wafer at a time, although many configurations exist that can etch multiple smaller wafers (1–3 inches) simultaneously. A standard, parallel-plate reactor design is shown in Fig. 1, where rf power is applied to the electrode housing the wafer. In this mode, termed reactive ion etching (RIE), the DC self-bias builds up on the powered electrode where the wafer rests, yielding higher energy (50–500 eV)

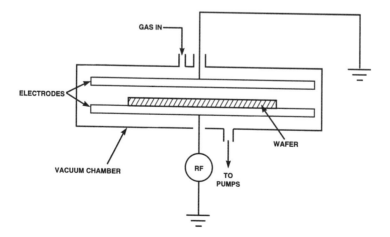

Figure 1   A schematic diagram of a parallel-plate rf-powered plasma etcher. In the configuration shown, the bottom electrode that houses the wafer is powered. This mode of operation is often refered to as reactive ion etching (RIE).

ion bombardment. If high magnetic fields are present, the electron trajectories can be modified to increase electron-molecule collisions and thereby increase the ion density. Examples of these types of reactors are the magnetron [3] and the transformer coupled plasma (TCP) [4,5]. As an alternative, the rf power can be applied to the top electrode, resulting in the maximum ion energies that strike the wafer surface being no more than the plasma potential of 15–30 eV; this mode of operation is often refered to as plasma ashing.

A number of designs use geometries in which the plasma source is remote from the wafer. One common type, the downstream etcher used for resist stripping [6,7], allows wafers to be etched in the absence of photon or high-energy ion bombardment. Many newer designs combine an rf-powered wafer chuck assembly with a separate high-ion-density plasma source. In this arrangement, shown schematically in Fig. 2, the wafer can be either immersed in or remote

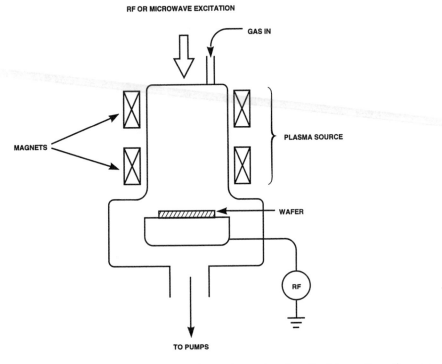

Figure 2 A schematic diagram of an advanced etcher. In this configuration, an rf-powered wafer chuck is located in close proximity to a high-ion-density plasma source, such as an electron cyclotron resonance (ECR) or helicon rf plasma. The high-ion-density source provide high ion fluxes at relatively low pressures (<5 mtorr) and the rf-powered wafer chuck can be used to control the ion kinetic energy independently.

from the plasma source. These type of high-ion-density reactors can use external microwave (electron cyclotron resonance, or ECR) [8–12] or rf (helicon) [13–16] excitation to achieve high material removal rates (~2 μm/min). A detailed decription of all plasma types is beyond the scope of this chapter; however, Table 1 provides a list of common plasma reactors and their characteristics.

2.3 Basics of Plasma-Surface Interactions

Central to developing an understanding of how resists behave in plasma environments is an understanding of what the resist surface "sees" when it is in a plasma. In general, a wafer surface is bombarded with ions, electrons, excited and ground-state neutrals, as well as a low flux of vacuum ultraviolet light originating from gas-phase atomic transitions. The relative fluxes of these species depend on the plasma type and the plasma operating parameters. In addition to the surface sputtering and chemical reactions that can result from particle bombardment, the ion flux can be sufficient to cause substantial heating of the surface. For example, 100–eV ions at a flux of 0.1 mA/cm^2 will deposit 10 mW/cm^2 in the surface ~50 nm, thereby causing polymeric photoresists to rise in temperature. This temperature rise can proceed to temperatures higher than the polymer's glass transition, causing them to undergo geometric deformation, or "flow." As such, nearly all commercially available plasma reactors are equipped with methods for cooling the wafer chuck to avoid these deleterious side effects.

Table 1   A List of Common Plasma Types Used for Processing Wafers for Integrated Circuit Manufacturing

Plasma type	*Excitation*	*Location of wafer*	*Wafer*	*Uses*
Barrel asher	rf	In plasma	Floating	Stripping
Downstream	rf or microwave	Remote	Floating or grounded	Stripping
Parallel plate	rf	In plasma	rf powered	Low-rate pattern transfer
Magnetron	rf + magnets	In plasma	rf powered	Moderate-rate pattern transfer
Transformer-coupled plasma	rf + magnets	In plasma	rf powered	High-rate pattern transfer
Electron cyclotron resonance	microwave + magnets	Remote	Independently rf powered	High-rate pattern transfer
Helicon	rf + magnets	Remote	Independently rf powered	High-rate pattern transfer

The details of the surface chemistry have been studied for a number of chemical systems [17–20]. However, the majority of these studies have focused on materials such as Si [19] and SiO_2 [20]. Far fewer studies have focused on the complex surface plasma chemistry that takes place when hydrocarbon films are etched, with the exception of oxygen-based plasmas, which will be discussed in Sections 3.4 and 5.2.

3   RESIST BEHAVIOR IN PLASMAS

3.1   Silicon Dioxide Etch—Fluorocarbon-Based Plasmas

Etching of silicon dioxide (SiO_2) is performed almost exclusively by fluorocarbon-based plasmas, including CF_4 [21], C_2F_6 [22,23], C_4F_8 [24], CHF_3 [21], and CH_2F_2 [21], as well as many other combinations [25] with He, Ar, O_2, and others. The role carbon plays during the SiO_2 etch is critical to realizing high oxide etch selectivities to the photoresist, as well as (and more critically) the underlying layers, which may be Si, poly-Si, etc. If a fluorocarbon plasma is kept deficient in free F atoms in the gas phase [26], either through the presence of hydrogen to form HF [19,24] or by gettering the free flourine through reaction with silicon surfaces in the reactor [22], fluorocarbon films can be made to deposit. X-ray photoelectron spectroscopic (XPS) measurements indicate that these layers are composed primarily of —CF_3, —CF_2, —CF, and C—CF_x, and these layers can act to passivate surfaces against chemical attack, with the lesser fluorinated layers acting as more effective passivating layers [22]. However, ion-stimulated reaction of oxygen from the SiO_2 with the deposited fluorocarbon layer reduces the passivating effect of the fluorocarbon, thereby allowing the SiO_2 to etch. Under these conditions, most polymers will act as acceptable resists, as recent measurements comparing phenolic-based resists to acrylic-based resist have shown when using CF_4/CHF_3 in a Lam Rainbow parallel-plate reactive ion etcher (RIE), shown in Table 2 [27], and also when using $CF_4/CHF_3/Ar$ to etch acrylic/phenolic blends in an Applied Materials 5000 RIE [28]. The specifics of polymer structure effects on etch rate in more aggressive plasmas will be discussed in Section 4.

3.2   Silicon Etch—Fluorine, Chlorine-, and/or Bromine-Based Plasmas

Although many fluorine-based gases such as CF_4, SF_6, or NF_3 have been used successfully for Si plasma etching, most Si etching in the integrated circuit (IC) industry today is performed using chlorine- and/or bromine-based plasmas. This stems primarily from the spontaneous reaction of fluorine atoms with silicon side-walls, resulting in a loss in anisotropy. This loss in anisotropy can be mitigated

Table 2 Summary of Resist Performance in Standard Silicon Dioxide Etch Step[a]

Resist	Resist rate (nm/min)	Normalized etch rate	SiO_2 rate (nm/min)	Selectivity to SiO_2
Novolac Resist, 365 nm (Shipley SPR-511)	134.2	1.00	545.0	4.1
PHOST resist, 248 nm (IBM APEX-E)	135.0	1.01	545.0	4
Pure PHOST (poly(vinyl phenol))	107.3	0.80	545.0	5.1
Acrylic resist, 193 nm (V1.0 193-nm resist)	138.4	1.03	545.0	3.9

[a]The silicon dioxide etching was performed using a $CF_4/CHF_3/Ar$ gas mixture in a Lam Rainbow etcher. It was a standard recipe for etching 350-nm contact holes in plasma-enhanced chemical vapor–deposited TEOS oxide. The CF_4 flow was 20 sccm, the CHF_3 flow was 20 sccm, and the Ar flow was 200 sccm. The total pressure was 800 mTorr, the power was 350 W, and the etch time was 55 seconds. The selectivity measurements were based on the resist loss that occurred during the etch step.

through addition of chlorine or oxygen to the plasma to assist with sidewall passivation [12,29]. Another reason for using Cl/Br is the greater etch selectivity relative to SiO_2, which is necessary for poly-Si etches that require stopping on ultrathin (<20 nm) gate oxides. To achieve high levels of anisotropy, which are required for critical dimension control of submicrometer-dimension poly-Si gate levels, additives to predominantly Cl-based plasmas are often used, such as N_2 [30], which can result in passivation and/or quenching of the neutral-radical-driven sidewall reactions. In addition, O_2 [31] and HBr [32] are often added to increase the selectivity relative to SiO_2, where high-purity conditions are also often desired to avoid reducing the Si-to-SiO_2 selectivity caused by the presence of carbon. Not surprisingly, resist masking performance varies widely as a result of these sidewall passivation additives.

3.3 Metal (Al, AlSi, AlCu, Ti, W, etc.) Etch—Chlorine- or Bromine-Based Plasmas

Of all plasma chemistries used to transfer resist images into underlying layers, the chemistries used for metal etching are by far the most aggresive at attacking photoresist. Unlike other etching chemistries, in which use of selective deposition or low temperatures can improve photoresist masking performance, metal etch processes offer a few "tricks" to improve resist performance. In fact, metal etch has been used as the primary benchmark for evaluating structure-property relationships in polymer etch resistance, to be discussed in Section 4.1.

Typical gases used are chlorine-based, such as Cl_2, BCl_3, CCl_4, or $SiCl_4$, [33–35], or bromine-based, such as HBr [32] or BBr_3 [36]. Quite often, a combination of these gases is used in the plasma for optimum performance. For example, BCl_3 is often added to etch the aluminum native oxide during the initial stages of etching [33,37]. Unlike the fluorine-based plasmas, in which CF_x polymer formation on nonetching surfaces can greatly enhance photoresist etch resistance, the same is generally not true of chlorine plasmas. In addition to the formation of volatile CCl_x etch products, it has been proposed that the etch product $AlCl_3$ can further catalyze photoresist decomposition in chlorine-based metal etches [38]. Even though little spontaneous reaction occurs between chlorine and organic polymers, the high energy (200–400 eV) of the impinging chlorine atoms common to many metal etch processes activates reactions with the polymer. This is often further aggravated by the elevated temperatures (25–50°C) used to volatilize the metal etch products. Examples of etch selectivities are shown in Table 3, where novolac, poly(hydroxystyrene) (PHOST), and acrylic resists are compared in a Drytek Quad, using a $BCl_3/Cl_2/N_2$ mixture.

Addition of bromine has been proposed as a means for increasing the selectivity of photoresist to metal etching [33], as illustrated in Table 4, where the bias energies (and hence the corresponding ion energies) for the data shown were between 200 and 350 V. However, the advent of high-ion-density plasma etchers, such as the ECR, helicon, or TCP, has led to better selectivities even when using the more traditional Cl_2/BCl_3 chemistry. This stems from the ability to obtain high metal etch rates (>0.5 µm/min) at lower ion energies (50–150 V) because of extremely high ion fluxes (>5 mA/cm^2). Since the polymer etch rate shows a weaker dependence on ion energy than

Table 3   Summary of Metal-Etch Resistance of Various Polymers[a]

Resist	Resist rate (nm/min)	Normalized etch rate	AlSi rate (nm/min)	Selectivity to AlSi
Novolac resist, 365 nm (Shipley SPR-511)	167.1	1.00	600	3.6
PHOST resist, 248 nm (IBM APEX-E)	195.9	1.17	600	3.0
Pure PHOST (poly(vinyl phenol))	158.5	0.95	600	3.8
Acrylic resist, 193 nm (V1.0 193-nm resist)	360.0	2.15	600	1.6

[a]Metal etch was performed in a Drytek Quad using a $BCl_3/Cl_2/N_2$ mixture. The gas flow rates were 80 sccm BCl_3, 20 sccm Cl_2, and 50 sccm N_2. The total pressure was 300 mT and the power was 250 W.

Table 4 Experiment Results Showing the Effects of Bromine on Metal Etch Selectivity

Etch gas	Al rate (nm/min)	Resist rate (nm/min)	SiO$_2$ rate (nm/min)	Resist selectivity	Oxide selectivity
Cl$_2$	2468	443	33	5.5:1	75:1
BCl$_3$	36	45	100	0.8:1	0.4:1
HBr	1312	141	7	9.3:1	182:1
Cl$_2$/BCl$_3$	1850	656	38	3.3:1	49:1
HBr/BCl$_3$	790	126	42	6.2:1	19:1
HBr/Cl$_2$/BCl$_3$	1192	226	42	5.3:1	28:1

Source: Ref. 33.

does the etch selectivity, the metal-to-photoresist selectivity increases at lower ion energy [39].

3.4 Polymer Etch—Oxygen-Based Plasmas for Multilayer Lithography

Underlying Hydrocarbon Layers

Although plasmas composed predominantly of oxygen are commonly used for photoresist stripping (this will be discussed in Section 5.2), oxygen-based plasmas are also used for pattern transfer of dry-developed or bilayer resists [40–48]. For a more detailed description of multilayer resist approaches, please see the chapter on multilayer resists.

Since the underlying hydrocarbon layer is usually masked during pattern transfer of multilayer resists, the primary concern is the lateral etching, or undercutting, that can occur. When pure oxygen is used as the source gas, a variety of neutral species, such as O$_3$, O(^{3}P), and ^{1}O$_2$ (singlet oxygen, the source gas), coexist along with the ionic species. These neutral species do not impinge upon the surface with the high degree of directionality of the ions and hence can strike and etch the resist sidewalls, resulting in an undercutting of the masking layer [40,46]. Two approaches have been adopted to help minimize this effect. First, additives to the source gas, such as N$_2$ [44], CO$_2$ [47], or SO$_2$ [48], can react on the sidewall, forming an etch product that is substantially less volatile than the CO formed upon reaction with pure oxygen. These less volatile etch products remain on the sidewalls and passivate them from further etching. This approach is similar to that used in oxide or metal etching, where fluorocarbon or metal halide layers, respectively, are used for passivation. The second approach to minimizing sidewall reactions is to allow the CO etch products to act as the passivating layer by freezing them at low process temperatures [41,42,45].

The effect of etching temperature on the resultant line profile [when using 150 nm of silylated poly(4-hydroxystyrene) as the masking layer] is shown in Fig. 3.

Silicon-Containing Resists

A wide range of multilayer resist types require anisotropic pattern transfer through an organisilicon masking layer. Examples of such resists are silylmethacrylates [49], siloxanes [50], polysilanes [51,52], polysilynes [53], and silylated phenolic polymers [54,55]. In general, organosilicon polymers provide good etch-masking capability for oxygen plasma pattern transfer, provided at least ~10 wt. % silicon is incorporated into the film [56–58].

During oxygen plasma etching of organosilicon polymers, the surface layer is converted into SiO_2 by reaction with the plasma species [59]. The thickness of this oxide layer correlates well with the mean range of the incoming ions,

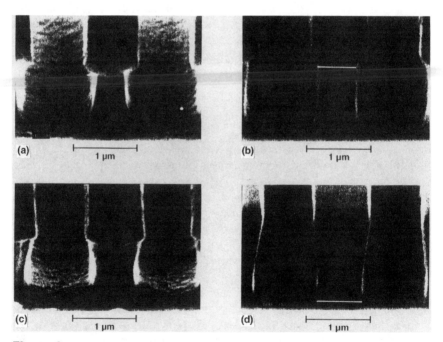

Figure 3   Scanning electron micrographs of trilayer structures (patterned resist/150-nm SiO_2/700-nm hard-baked resist) etched in a helicon oxygen plasma source. The etch conditions were 2000 W source power, 2 mTorr, 100 sccm oxygen. Shown are the effects of ion energy (controlled by varying the wafer chuck power) and temperature. The two upper micrographs show results at 0°C for 25-W chuck (a) and 50-W chuck (b). The two lower micrographs show results at −100°C for 25-W chuck (c) and 50-W chuck (d). Note that the undercutting is significantly reduced at lower temperature. (From Ref. 46.)

roughly 10 to 20 nm [60], and is formed after an initial densification phase during which the etch rate is higher. A description of this oxide layer formation and its subsequent steady-state sputtering/formation mechanism is described in a model by Watanabe and Ohnishi [61].

4 CHEMICAL DESIGN OF ETCH RESISTANCE

4.1 Structure-Property Relationships in Polymer Plasma Etch Resistance

Of all design considerations that go into designing a photoresist, etch resistance has not traditionally been thought of as a primary design consideration. Historically, this stems from the use of novolac polymers as base resins for resists—polymers that happen to have high chemical stability and resistance to chemical attack. However, the universal use of these polymers has by necessity ceased as polymers with higher transparency have been developed for 248- and 193-nm photoresist applications. For successful development of photoresist for applications at these wavelengths, some understanding of the structure–etch resistance relationship is desired. The earliest studies used thermodynamic parameters, such as the polymer's heat of combustion [62]. Interestingly, the traditional route to flame retardance has been to incorporate halogen atoms into the polymer, but this approach has not been thoroughly explored for application to photoresists, perhaps due to considerations of solubility. Since then, two empirical parameters have been evaluated for relationships to polymer etch resistance, one based on polymer composition and the other based on polymer structure. The first, reported originally by Ohnishi and co-workers [63], is based on polymer composition and is defined as

$$\text{Ohnishi parameter} = N / (N_c - N_o)$$

where N, N_c, and N_o are the total number of atoms, number of carbon atoms, and number of oxygen atoms, respectively, per monomer. The Ohnishi parameter was originally used as a means of developing a relationship between chemical composition and reactive ion etch rate for high-energy (300–500 eV) ion bombardment (Figs. 4 and 5) but showed a poor relationship to chemical structure for etch rates in a downstream glow discharge (Fig. 6), where the etching mechanisms are largely chemical in nature.

Recently, the development of an etch-resistant acrylic-based resist for 193-nm imaging has resulted in a renewed interest in structure-property etch resistance relationships, and an additional parameter based on polymer structure called the ring parameter [27] has been introduced, defined as

$$\text{Ring parameter } r = M_{CR} / M_{TOT}$$

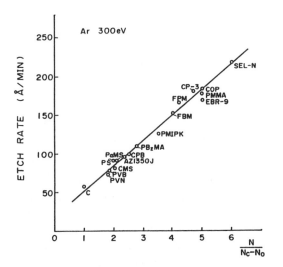

Figure 4 The etch rate of various polymers under 300-eV argon ion beam etching versus the Ohnishi parameter. Abbreviations: PMMA, poly(methyl methacrylate); COP, poly(glycidyl methacrylate-co-ethyl acrylate); CP-3, poly(methyl methacrylate [70%]-co-*t*-butyl methacrylate [30%]); EBR-9, poly(α-chloro-trifluoroethyl acrylate); PBzMA, poly(benzyl methacrylate); FBM, poly(hexafluorobutyl methacrylate); FPM, poly(fluoropropyl methacrylate); PMIBK, poly(methyl isopropenyl ketone); PS, poly(styrene); CMS, poly(chloromethyl styrene); PαMS, poly(α-methyl styrene); PVN, poly(vinyl naphthalene); PVB, poly(vinyl biphenyl); AZ1350J, novolac-based photoresist; CPB cyclized poly(butadiene). (From Ref. 63.)

where M_{CR} and M_{TOT} are the mass of the resist existing as carbon atoms contained in a ring structure and the total resist mass, respectively. For example, benzene would have a ring parameter of $72/78 = 0.92$ whereas cyclohexane's value would be $72/84 = 0.86$. Figures 7 and 8 show the experimental data summary for normalized etch rate versus the Ohnishi parameter (Fig. 7) and the ring parameter (Fig. 8) for a wide range of polymers. The polymers used to generate data in Fig. 7 and 8 were primarily acrylics, with poly(methyl methacrylate) at one extreme and poly(adamantanemethyl methyl methacrylate) at the other extreme. In addition, several commercially available photoresist formulations were included as well. See the figure captions for a more detailed list. Although both parameters plotted in Figs. 7 and 8 show a monotonic relationship with polymer etch rate, the ring parameter shows a slightly stronger relationship to etch rate in low-ion-energy (<50 eV) plasmas. The data from Fig. 8 are replotted in Fig. 9 and a third-order polynomial has been fit to the data. The result of the fit yields:

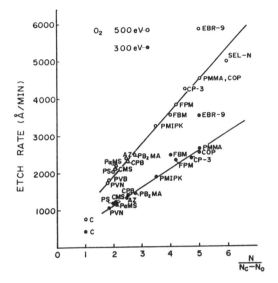

Figure 5 The etch rate of various polymers under 300- and 500-eV oxygen ion beam etching versus the Ohnishi parameter. The polymer abbreviations are the same as in Fig. 4. (From Ref. 63.)

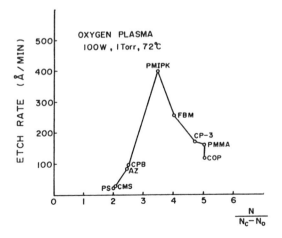

Figure 6 The etch rate of various polymers under downstream oxygen plasma conditions versus the Ohnishi parameter. The pressure was 1 torr and the temperaure was 72°C. The abbreviations are the same as for Figure 4. (From Ref. 63.)

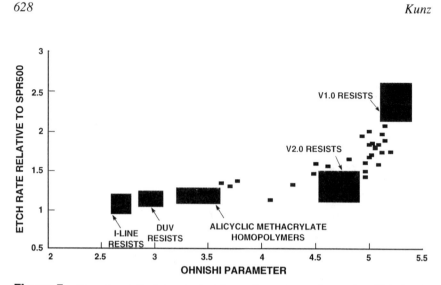

Figure 7 Experimentally determined etch rate for various polymers in a high-density chlorine plasma versus the Ohnishi parameter. The etch conditions were a helicon rf source, 2000-W source, 75-W chuck, 100 sccm chlorine, 2 mtorr, and 0°C. The polymers are aliphatic acrylics (V1.0 193-nm resists), alicyclic-aliphatic acrylic copolymers (V2.0 193-nm resists), poly(isobornyl methacrylate) and poly(adamantanemethyl methacrylate) (alicyclic methacrylate homopolymers), poly(4-hydroxystyrene-co-4-*t*-butoxycarbonyl-oxystyrene) (DUV resists), and novolac (I-line resists). (From Ref. 28.)

$$\text{Etch rate (normalized to novolac resist)} = Ar^3 + Br^2 + Cr + D \qquad (1)$$

where r is the ring parameter. The values for A, B, C, and D are −3.80, 6.71, −4.42, and 2.10, respectively. Since the limits to the ring parameter are defined, i.e., no rings ($r = 0$) at one extreme and the entire material as carbon rings ($r = 1$) at the other extreme, this places bounds on the predicted etch rates to between 2.1 ($r = 0$) and 0.6 ($r = 1$) relative to novolac-based i-line photoresist. Figure 10 shows measured etch rate versus actual polymer formulation, as well as the predicted etch rates for a poly(isoborny methacrylate)$_x$-*co*-poly(methyl methacrylate)$_{1-x}$ copolymer (Fig. 10) and for poly(*t*-butyl methacrylate-co-methyl methacrylate-co-methacrylic acid) terpolymer resist (193-nm version 1.0b photoresist [64]) with a 5-β steroid added at different weight percentages (Fig. 11). The error bars shown in Fig. 10 represent an approximately ±10% error in rate measurement due to (1) fluctuations in the novolac control wafer etching rate due to variations in residual solvent (fresh control wafers were not always prepared) and (2) variations in refractive index between the different polymers; the refractive index for PMMA was used for all measurements. Nevertheless, it is clear that this empirical curve fit is capable of predicting quantitative changes in etch resistance as a function of various formulation variables.

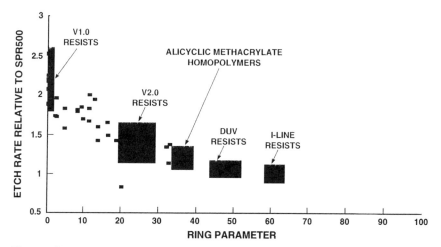

Figure 8 Experimentally determined etch rate for various polymers in a high-density chlorine plasma versus the ring parameter. The etch conditions were a helicon rf source, 2000-W source, 75-W chuck, 100 sccm chlorine, 2 mtorr, and 0°C. The polymers are aliphatic acrylics (V1.0 193-nm resists), alicyclic-aliphatic acrylic copolymers (V2.0 193-nm resists), poly(isobornyl methacrylate) and poly(adamantanemethyl methacrylate) (alicyclic methacrylate homopolymers), poly(4-hydroxystyrene-co-4-*t*-butoxycarbonyloxystyrene) (DUV resists), and novolac (I-line resists). (From Ref. 28.)

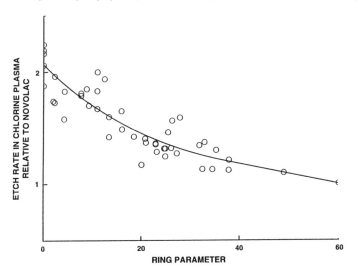

Figure 9 Third-order polynomial fit to data shown in Fig. 8, showing the quality of the fit of Eq. 1 to the experimental data. The fitted curve is *Normalized rate* = $-3.80r^3 + 6.71r^2 - 4.42r + 2.10$, where r is the mass fraction of polymer existing as cyclic carbon.

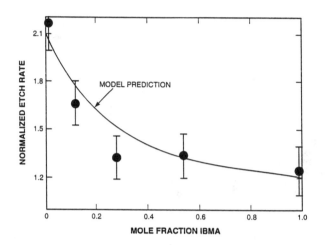

Figure 10 The normalized etch rate versus the mole fraction of isobornyl methacrylate in a poly(isobornyl methacrylate-co-methyl methacrylate) copolymer. The etching conditions would be the same as those used for Figs. 7 and 8. The solid curve represents the data predicted from the analytical expression shown in Fig. 9.

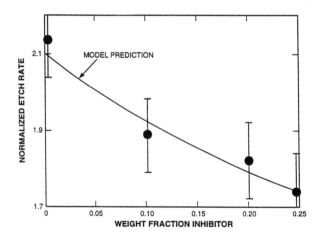

Figure 11 The normalized (to I-line resist) etch rate in a chlorine plasma for a ter-polymer of *t*-butyl methacrylate, methyl methacrylate, and methacrylic acid loaded with various weight fractions of cholate ester inhibitor. The etching conditions would be the same as those used for Figs. 7 and 8. Again, the solid curve is derived from the ex-pression in Fig. 2.

Current attempts to develop a second-generation 193-nm single-layer resist with enhanced etch resistance have used a methacrylate tetrapolymer containing isobornyl methacrylate (IBMA) as well as a cholate-ester monomeric dissolution inhibitor (INH-A) [65]. Maximum etch durability with this approach requires high levels of both the IBMA and the INH-A. However, good imaging quality limits the desirable compositional range; the IBMA tends to increase hydrophobicity whereas the INH-A tends to reduce the glass transition temperature to unacceptable levels. Equation 1 was used to estimate the upper limits on etch resistance achievable using these resist components. Figure 12 shows a series of curves with estimated etch rate as a function of INH-A loading, for polymers containing IBMA mole fractions varying between 0.20 and 0.40. IBMA loadings in excess of 0.50 result in a decrease in imaging quality, whereas INH-A weight loadings are limited to less than 0.3 (polymer = 1.0). This places the predicted upper limits on etch resistance to ~1.4× novolac. In practice, etch rates between 1.34× and 1.42× relative to novolac have been measured for the version 2 193-nm resist [27]. This is a value only slightly higher

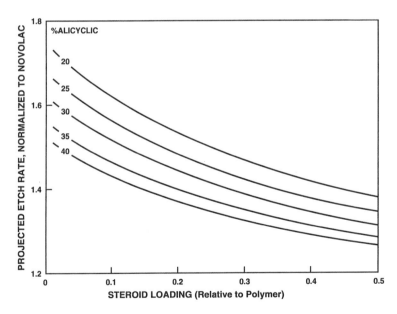

Figure 12 A series of curves estimating the etch resistance of a three-component resist containing an alicyclic monomer (isobornyl methacrylate) and a cholate-ester inhibitor (INH-A). The purpose of this curve is to show the impact on etch resistance of various formulations. The etching conditions would be the same as those used for Figs. 7 and 8. Note: APEX-E deep-ultraviolet resist etches at 1.2× SPR511 I-line resist.

than that of APEX-E DUV resist (V2.0 has been measured as 1.12× to 1.18× times faster than APEX-E). If further improvement in etch durability is desired, new materials will be required.

Since etch durability is a paramount issue for development of 193-nm single-layer resists, Eq. 1 has been applied to all current 193-nm resists published to date and the results tabulated in Table 5. From a perspective concerned only with etch durability, it is clear that the polymers presented in Refs. 66 and 67 have slightly better etch resistance than that reported in Ref. 65. Furthermore, if monomeric inhibitors, such as cholate esters or transparent naphthylic com-

Table 5   Estimated Etch Rates (Right Column) for Three Reported 193-nm Single-Layer Resists with Enhanced Etch Resistance[a]

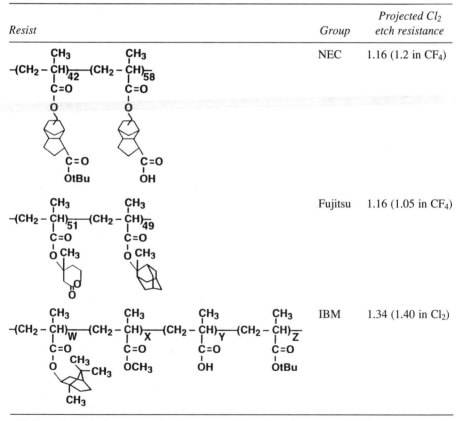

Resist	Group	Projected Cl_2 etch resistance
	NEC	1.16 (1.2 in CF_4)
	Fujitsu	1.16 (1.05 in CF_4)
	IBM	1.34 (1.40 in Cl_2)

[a]All three of these polymers have been incorporated into resists that have sub-0.25-um resolution. The number in parentheses in the right column indicates the experimentally measured etch rate. References are NEC [67], Fujitsu [66], and IBM [65].

pounds [68], are added to polymers similar to those shown in Refs. 66 and 67, then resists whose etch resistance is very nearly the same as that of novolac ($1.05\times$ to $1.10\times$ the etch rate) will someday be possible and in fact may actually exceed the performance of poly(4-hydroxystyrene)-based (PHOST) DUV resists. It now appears clear that, when appropriately formulated, acrylic-based resists whose etch resistance at least matches DUV resists will be possible.

4.2 Polymer Structural and Compositional Dependence on Etch Rate: Experimental Results

A number of studies have been conducted evaluating the relative etch rates of various polymer types in common plasma etch chemistries [28,69,70]. These studies have been performed as a means of determining the exact behavior of specific photoresist formulations under commercially useful process conditions. Tables 6–10 summarize several of these studies. In addition, new polymers have recently been investigated as potential 193-nm transparent resins. These polymers, called aliphatic cyclopolymers, are based on poly(norbornene) and have been reported to have etch rates lower than even novolac [27,71,72].

4.3 Postdevelopment Modifications

Ultraviolet Curing

A variety of resists in use, such as G- and I-line photoresists based on novolac/diazonaphthoquinone (DNQ), possess glass transition temperatures around 100–130°C. For them to be used in subsequent high-temperature (150–250°C) processes, further thermal stabilization must often be done. This is accom-

Table 6 Relative Etch Rates for Methacrylate Terpolymer/Novolac Polymer Blends

Novolac weight fraction in blend	Normalized etch rate in $CHF_3/CF_4/Ar$[a]
100	1.00
90	1.39
80	1.33
70	1.10
60	0.69
50	1.43
40	1.33
30	2.20
0	2.75

[a]Standard reactive ion etcher employing a gas mixture of CHF_3, CF_4, and Ar. This is a standard etch process for etching SiO_2.
Source: Ref. 28.

Table 7 Relative Etch Rates for Various Methacrylate
Polymers and Copolymers

Polymer composition	Norm. etch rate in CF_4[a]
Poly(benzyl methacrylate)	1.08
Poly(adamantyl methacrylate)	0.97
Poly(norbornyl methacrylate)	1.16
Poly(cyclohexyl methacrylate)	1.23
Poly(t-butyl methacrylate)	1.47
Poly(methyl methacrylate)	1.58
Poly(AdMA-co-tBMA) (0/100)	1.47
Poly(AdMA-co-tBMA) (35/65)	1.20
Poly(AdMA-co-tBMA) (50/50)	1.06
Poly(AdMA-co-tBMA) (75/25)	1.06
Poly(AdMA-co-tBMA) (90/10)	1.00
Poly(AdMA-co-tBMA) (100/0)	0.97

[a]Standard reactive ion etcher using CF_4 as the etch gas at 200 W rf and
200 mtorr.
Source: Ref. 70.

Table 8 Relative Etch Rates for Methacrylate Copolymers
Containing Adamantanemethyl Methacrylate (AdMMA)

Mole fraction of AdMMA in copolymer	Norm. etch rate in Cl_2[a]
100	1.26
50	1.34
32	1.46
13	1.94
0	2.07

[a]Helicon high-ion-density etcher employing 2000 W rf to the plasma source
and an additional 75 W rf to the wafer chuck. The etch gas was Cl_2 and the
pressure was 5 mtorr. This is a standard etch process for poly-Si.
Source: Ref. 69.

plished by means of ultraviolet (200–300 nm) curing [73,74]. In addition to
raising the glass transition temperature of a polymer, this curing can act to minimize gas evolution that occurs during high-dose ion implantation. Studies have
confirmed that UV curing helps to thermally stabilize the resist for subsequent
high-temperature (>100°C) dry etching steps [73–76].

In recent years, deep-UV resists based on PHOST ($T_g \sim 180°C$) have
been developed. Even though PHOST has a much higher T_g than novolac

Table 9 Relative Etch Rates for Methacrylate Copolymers Containing Isobornyl Methacrylate (IBMA)

Weight fraction IBMA in copolymer	Norm. etch rate in Cl_2[a]
100	1.23
75	1.37
50	1.32
25	1.65
0	2.25

[a]Helicon high-ion-density etcher employing 2000 W rf to the plasma source and an additional 50 W rf to the wafer chuck. The etch gas was Cl_2 and the pressure was 5 mtorr. This is a standard etch process for poly-Si. Source: Ref. 69.

Table 10 Relative Etch Rates for Methacrylate Terpolymers with Added *t*-Butyl Lithocholate (TBL)

Weight fraction TBL in blend	Norm. etch rate in Cl_2[a]
29	1.42
17	1.79
11	1.84
5	1.96
0	2.00

[a]Helicon high-ion-density etcher employing 2000 W rf to the plasma source and an additional 50 W rf to the wafer chuck. A standard etch process for poly-Si. Source: Ref. 69.

($T_g \sim 100$–$140°C$), the formulated DUV resists generally have T_g values near those of the novolac resists due to copolymerization with acid-labile monomers. Some of these DUV formulations have resultant T_g values low enough to warrant the need for subsequent thermal hardening [77]. Mechanistic studies have been performed on UV curing of both types of polymers and these studies have shown that the novolac/DNQ resists undergo DUV hardening via crosslinking induced through the DNQ via a ketene intermediate [78,79], whereas the PHOST-based resists undergo crosslinking via quinoid intermediates in the presence of oxygen (air) and via phenoxy radical intermediates in the absence of air [77]. The crosslinking of the polymer matrix directly translates into an increase in the softening temperature, or glass transition temperature.

One interestingly point that must be noted is in regard to UV curing of positive-tone chemically amplified resists, such as those used for 248- or 193-nm wavelengths. These resists, described in greater detail in a previous chapter, are composed of an acid-labile substituent that is cleaved and desorbed upon acid-olysis. Many UV curing steps not only photochemically activate the acid component of the resist but also can result in heating, causing the acid-labile component to be cleaved and subsequently desorb. This step results in a resist film which, although crosslinked, has been reduced in thickness by 5–20%. The important issue when curing these resists is what, if any, lateral shrinkage of the resist has occurred that can result in an unacceptable critical dimension variation.

Electron Beam Curing

Electron beam curing offers several potential advantages over UV curing. First, the penetration depth can be tailored by choice of electron energy, resulting in efficient curing of the entire thickness of the resist, and second (this applies primarily to DUV resists), the potential for film shrinkage is less [80]. The typical electron energies are between 2 and 15 keV, depending on the depth of curing desired, and the exposure doses are usually in the 1–5 mC/cm^2 range [80–82].

5   DRY PHOTORESIST STRIPPING

5.1   Introduction

Although a variety of liquid-based photoresist strippers are commercially available and in wide use, photoresist removal via dry methods has become a critical technology. Dry stripping offers certain advantages over wet stripping. Among these advantages are reduced chemical handling and disposal, little deleterious effect on substrate materials, and ability to strip hardened (via ultraviolet cure or hard bake) organic layers, which may otherwise be insoluble.

In general, the term "dry stripping" refers to plasma-, ozone-, ultraviolet radiation-, and/or thermally assisted removal of organic layers. Although a wide variety of schemes employing some combination of the aforementioned forms of activation can work, certain particular issues associated with removing processed photoresist limit the options. The most important issues when choosing a dry stripping scheme are:

1. Removal of photoresist after silicon or metal etch where inorganic deposits may exist on sidewalls. These deposits may be difficult to remove without resorting to harsh halogen plasmas, which could damage the underlying device material.
2. Removal of photoresist after ion implantation where high doses of As, B, P, or other dopants have been implanted in the photoresist.
3. Removal of photoresist where delicate gate oxides are exposed to the stripping medium.

Given these difficulties, the preferred methods for dry stripping resist use downstream oxygen reactors with only low-energy ion bombardment, often in combination with heating.

5.2 Chemical Mechanisms and Stripping of Unprocessed Photoresist

The chemical mechanisms for the oxygen plasma–based dry stripping of photoresist are not dissimilar from the thermal oxidation mechanism [83]. However, unlike thermal oxidation, where radical intermediate formation and product desorption can be rate limiting, plasma-induced oxidation and etching proceeds rapidly due to a steady flow of oxygen atoms and ions. These atoms readily abstract hydrogen from C—H bonds, resulting in radical formation, and the ion bombardment, even at energies only near the plasma potenial (15–30 eV), easily has enough energy to stimulate desorption of weakly bound etch products, which often require <1 eV of activation to desorb. Electron paramagnetic studies [84,85] have shown that singlet oxygen ($^1O_2$) will react only with unsaturated hydrocarbons and not with saturated hydrocarbons [84] and that the overall etch process is driven by free oxygen atoms (O) in the plasma [85]. Optical emission studies have determined the primary etch products present in the plasma to be CO, H_2O, CH, and H_2 [86–89].

5.3 Stripping of Ion-Implanted Photoresist

Organic photoresists are widely used as ion implantation masks in the volume production of integrated circuits, and development of corresponding postimplantation stripping processes has been investigated thoroughly. Figure 13 (no. 1 from Kikuchi and Bersin [92]) shows a cross section of a typical ion-implanted photoresist layer. The implanted photoresist has a top layer that has undergone ion-induced carbonization, characterized by a high carbon-to-hydrogen ratio and increased density compared with the unimplanted photoresist. Underneath the carbonized layer lies a layer where the implanted ions have accumulated, the presence of which can dramatically increase the resist's resilience against oxygen plasma–based stripping methods [90,91]. The relative thicknesses of the carbonized and implanted layers, as well as the thicknesses of the transition zones between these layers, depend entirely on the implant conditions. In particular, the ion's mass and translational kinetic energy, as well as the total implant dose, will determine the dimensions of the layers shown in Fig. 13. Quite often, the carbonized layer provides a "hermetic" seal of the underlying resist, which can cause problems if gases are evolved during a high-temperature stripping process. As the gases evolve, pressure can build up in the resist and cause it to rupture [92], thereby requiring means of stripping resist without elevated temperature and/or gas evolution. In general, commercially available resist strippers employ a zero- or low-bias plasma, such as a downstream microwave discharge or reactive neutral source (such as ozone), in conjunction with heating to between 100 and 300°C [93]. Actual removal rates for conventional positive photoresist using oxygen reactive ion etching are shown in Fig. 14 (no. 8 from Kikuchi and Bersin [92]), where film removal for virgin photoresist and resist implanted for (a) 1×10^{16} cm^{-2} P$^+$ (150 keV), (b) 5×10^{15} cm^{-2} P$^+$ (60 keV), and (c) 5×10^{15} cm^{-2} As$^+$ (110 keV) are shown. Note that the initial slow etching period depends on the mass (depth of penetration) and implant dose of the ions. However, as mentioned earlier, resist stripping by use of oxygen alone often leaves the implanted ions oxidized on the remaining wafer surface, which must be subsequently removed via aqueous rinse. One way to mitigate this problem is to use hydrogen plasmas, either pure [91], as mixtures of hydrogen and oxygen [94], as a pretreatment [95], or even in combination with fluorine [96]. One method for developing an all dry strip uses a stepwise plasma, where the first step removes the carbonized layer in a low-bias reactive ion etch step. The complete process flow is shown in Table 11 [92].

5.4 Photoresist Stripping After Metal or Silicon Etching

As discussed in Section 3.3., the sidewall passivation layers that redeposit can be composed of etch products containing metal and/or silicon. These protective sidewall deposits cannot be easily removed using conventional dry plasma stripping techniques. One technique examined as a means of removing these residues is to use a downstream microwave discharge with CF$_4$ and O$_2$, in combination with H$_2$O vapor [97]. Interestingly, this treatment did not etch the sidewall Al but rather rendered it water soluble, upon which it could be removed

Table 11   Proposed Process Flow for Removal of Ion-Implanted Photoresist[a]

Process step	Method
1. Remove carbonized layer	Low-bias oxygen reactive ion etch
2. Remove underlying virgin photoresist	Zero-bias downstream oxygen microwave plasma discharge
3. Remove residual implanted ions	Low-bias hydrogen reactive ion etch (with aqueous process for backup or final clean)

[a]After the organic portion of the photoresist is removed in steps 1 and 2, the implanted ions remain behind as oxides of As, B, P, etc. These oxides are reduced to volatile hydrides by use of a hydrogen reactive ion etch. However, since the diffusion range of hydrogen can be quite high, care must be taken not to introduce damage into delicate gate oxides during this step.
Source: Ref. 92.

with a water rinse. In fact, in most cases involving sidewall deposits of metal or silicon residues, a wet clean is used after the plasma stripping step.

5.5 Damage Induced by Dry Photoresist Stripping

Any surface exposed to a plasma treatment undergoes a variety of surface chemical modifications. However, certain substrates such as the gate oxide used in metal-oxide semiconductor (MOS) devices are prone to particular effects when exposed to a plasma, such as charge trapping, which may result in a MOS device threshold voltage shift. This phenomenon has been investigated for gate oxides exposed to a variety of plasma stripping conditions, such as upstream, downstream, and radiofrequency discharges [98,99]. Although the resultant trapped charge was found to vary widely as a function of tool and process conditions, no significant flatband voltage shifts were detected using capacitance-voltage measurements for 9-nm-thick oxides (<80 mV). However, of the various methods explored, the downstream oxygen plasma photoresist stripper added the smallest flatband voltage shift, presumably due to the "milder" conditions, i.e., little direct bombardment by accelerated oxygen ions, which are thought to be the source of the trapped charge.

5.6 Other Dry Methods of Removing Photoresist

In addition to various plasma methods for stripping resists, there have been recent reports of removing photoresist thermally by use of excimer laser ablation [100] and even adhesive tape [101]. The excimer laser ablation technique uses a 248-nm KrF laser in an ambient of O_2 and/or N_2O. The laser is focused into a "knife" shape where the fluence in the focused regions exceeds the ablation threshold for the polymer by a factor of two to five times. The ablated material is then digested in the ablation plume through gas-phase chemical reaction with oxygen.

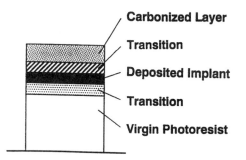

Figure 13 A model of photoresist after ion implantation. The different layers indicate implant-related modifications to the photoresist. (From Ref. 92.)

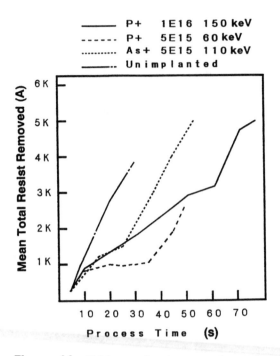

Figure 14 Thickness of resist removed as a function of time for photoresist implanted under different conditions. The etching was performed in an oxygen reactive ion etcher at 100 mTorr and 100 sccm oxygen flow. Note how the periods of reduced removal rate (lower slope) vary with the implant dose and energy. (From Ref. 92.)

ACKNOWLEDGMENTS

This work was supported by the Advanced Lithography Program of the Defense Advanced Research Projects Agency.

REFERENCES

1. Chapman, B., *Glow Discharge Processes*, Wiley-Interscience, New York, 1980.
2. Boenig, H. V., *Fundamentals of Plasma Chemistry and Technology*, Technomic Publishing, Lancaster, 1988.
3. Hinson, D. C., *Semiconductor Int. 10*, 76 (1983).
4. Yoshida, K., Miyamoto, H., Ikawa, E., and Murao, Y., *Jpn. J. Appl. Phys.*, *34*, 2089 (1995).
5. Christie, R., IEEE/SEMI Advanced Semiconductor Manufacturing Conference and Workshop, 1994, 94CH3475-1, pp. 34–36.
6. Cook, J. M., *Solid State Technol.*, *30*, 147 (1987).

7. Spencer, J. E., Borel, R. A., and Hoff, A., *J. Electrochem. Soc.*, *133*, 1992 (1986).
8. Nojiri, K., and Iguchi, E., *J. Vac. Sci. Technol. B*, *13*, 1451 (1995).
9. Kofuji, N., Tsujimoto, K., Kumihashi, T., and Tachi, S., *Jpn. J. Appl. Phys.*, *34*, 2489 (1995).
10. Kusumi, Y., Fujiwara, N., Matsumoto, J., and Yoneda, M., *Jpn. J. Appl. Phys.*, *34*, 2147 (1995).
11. Kimura, H., Shiozawa, K., Kawai, K., Miyatake, H., and Yoneda, M., *Jpn. J. Appl. Phys.*, *34*, 2114 (1995).
12. Fujiwara, N., Maruyama, T., and Yoneda, M., *Jpn. J. Appl. Phys.*, *34*, 2095 (1995).
13. Benjamin, N., Chapman, B., and Boswell, R., *SPIE Proc.*, *1392*, 95 (1990).
14. Etrillard, J., Francou J. M., Inard A., and Henry, D., *Jpn. J. Appl. Phys.*, *33*, 6005 (1994).
15. Jiwari, N., Iwasawa, H., Narai, A., Akira, S., Sakaue, H., Shindo, H., Shoji, T., and Horiike Y., *Jpn. J. Appl. Phys.*, *32*, 3019 (1993).
16. Kraft, R., and Prengle, S., *Solid State Technol.*, *38*, 57 (1995).
17. Mucha, J., and Hess, D. W., Plasma etching, in *Introduction to Microlithography*, Advances in Chemistry Series, Vol. 219, American Chemical Society, Washington, DC, 1983.
18. Coburn, J. W., *Plasma Etching and Reactive Ion Etching*, American Vacuum Society, New York, 1982.
19. Coburn, J. W., and Winters, H. F., *J. Vac. Sci. Technol.*, *16*, 391 (1979).
20. Chang, J. S., *Solid State Tech.*, *27*, April, 214 (1984).
21. Becker, D. S., and Blalock, G., in *Highly Selective Dry Etching and Damage Control* (G. S. Mathad and Y. Horiike, eds.), The Electrochemical Society, Pennington, NJ, 1993, p. 178.
22. Chebi, R., Sparks, T., Arleo, P., and Marks, J., in *Highly Selective Dry Etching and Damage Control* (G. S. Mathad and Y. Horiike, eds.), The Electrochemical Society, Inc., Pennington, NJ, 1993, p. 216.
23. Dutta, A. K., *J. Vac. Sci. Technol. B*, *13*, 1456 (1995).
24. Katayama, K., Hisada, M., Nakamura, S., and Fujiwara, H., in *Highly Selective Dry Etching and Damage Control* (G. S. Mathad and Y. Horiike, eds.), The Electrochemical Society, Pennington, NJ, 1993, p. 201
25. Steinbruchel, C., Lehmann, H. W., and Frick, K., *J. Electrochem. Soc.*, *132*, 180 (1985).
26. Ephrath, L. M., *J. Electrochem. Soc.*, *126*, 1419 (1979).
27. Kunz, R. R., Palmateer, S. C., Forte, A. R., Allen, R. D., Wallraff, G. M., DiPietro, R. A., and Hofer, D. C., *Proc. SPIE*, *2724*, 365, (1996).
28. Allen, R. D., Ly, Q. P., Wallraff, G. M., Larson, C. E., Hinsberg, W. D., Conley, W. E., and Muller, K. P., *Proc. SPIE*, *1925*, 246 (1994).
29. Bartha, J. W., Greschner, J., Puech, M., and Maquin, P., *Microelectron, Eng.*, *27*, 453 (1995).
30. Matsuura, T., Murota, J., Ono, S., and Ohmi, T., in *Highly Selective Dry Etching and Damage Control* (G. S. Mathad and Y. Horiike, eds.), The Electrochemical Society, Inc., Pennington, NJ, 1993, p. 141.

31. Nozawa, T., Kinoshita, T., Nishizuka, T., Suzuki, K., and Nakaue, A., in *Highly Selective Dry Etching and Damage Control* (G. S. Mathad and Y. Horiike, eds.), The Electrochemical Society, Inc., Pennington, NJ, 1993, p. 134.
32. Fujino T., and Oku, S., *J. Electrochem. Soc.*, *139*, 2585 (1992).
33. Tokunaga K., and Hess, D. W., *J. Electrochem. Soc.*, *127*, 928 (1980).
34. Bruce R. H., and Malafsky, G. P., *J. Electrochem. Soc.*, *130*, 1369 (1983).
35. Bruce R. H., and Malafsky, G. P., Ext. Abstracts of the Electrochemical Society Meeting, Fall 1981, Denver, Abstract 288, Electrochemical Society, Pennington, NJ.
36. Keaton, A. L., and Hess, D. W., *J. Vac. Sci. Technol. B*, *6*, 72 (1988).
37. Tokunaga, K., Redeker G. C., Danner, D. A., and Hess, D. W., *J. Electrochem. Soc.*, *128*, 851 (1981).
38. Hess, D. W., *Plasma Chem. Plasma Process.*, *2*, 141 (1982)
39. Ra, Y., Bradley, S. G., and Chen, C.-H., *J. Vac. Sci. Technol. A*, *12*, 1328 (1994).
40. Horn, M. W., Hartney, M. A., and Kunz, R. R., *Proc. SPIE*, *1672*, 448 (1992).
41. Sato, T., Ishida, T., Yoneda, M., and Nakamoto, K., *IEICE Trans. Electron.*, *E76-C*, 607 (1993).
42. Palmateer, S. C., Kunz, R. R., Horn, M. W., Forte, A. R., and Rothschild, M., *Proc. SPIE*, *2438*, 455 (1995).
43. Hutchinson, J., Melaku, Y., Nguyen, W., and Das, S., *Proc. SPIE*, *2724*, 399, (1996).
44. Jurgensen, C. W., Hutton, R. S., and Taylor, G. N., *J. Vac. Sci. Technol. B*, *10*, 2542 (1992).
45. Pons, M., Pelletier, J., and Joubert, O., *J. Appl. Phys.*, *75*, 4709 (1994).
46. Stern, M. B., Palmateer, S. C., Horn, M. W., Rothschild, M., Maxwell, B., and Curtin, J., *J. Vac. Sci. Technol. B*, *13*, 3017 (1995).
47. Hutton, R. S., Boyce, C. H., and Taylor, G. N., *J. Vac. Sci. Technol. B*, *13*, 2366 (1995).
48. Hartney, M. A., Hess, D. W., and Soane, D. S., *J. Vac. Sci. Technol. B*, *7*, 1 (1989).
49. MacDonald, S., Allen, R. D., Clecak, N. J., Willson, C. G., and Frechet, J. M. J., *Proc. SPIE*, *631*, 28 (1986).
50. Morita, M., Tanaka, A., Imamura, S., Tamamura, T., and Kogure, O., *Jpn. J. Appl. Phys.*, *22*, L659 (1983).
51. Wallraff, G. M., Miller, R. D., Clecak, N., and Baier, M., *Proc. SPIE*, *1466*, 211 (1991).
52. Kunz, R. R., Horn, M. W., Goodman, R. B., Bianconi, P. A., Smith, D. A., Eshelman, J. R., Wallraff, G. M., Miller, R. D., and Ginsberg, E. J., *Proc. SPIE*, *1672*, 385 (1992).
53. Taylor, G. N., Hellman, M. Y., Wolf, T. M., and Zeigler, J. M., *Proc. SPIE*, *920*, 274 (1991).
54. Coopmans, F., and Roland, B., *Proc. SPIE*, *771*, 69 (1986).
55. Hartney, M. A., Johnson, D. W., and Spencer, A. C., *Proc. SPIE*, *1466*, 238 (1991).
56. Reichmanis, E., and Smolinsky, G., *Proc. SPIE*, *469*, 38 (1984).
57. Morita, M., Tanaka, A., and Onose, K., *J. Vac. Sci. Technol. B*, *4*, 414 (1986).
58. Babich, E., Paraszczak, J., Hatzakis, M., Shaw, J., and Grenon, B. J., *Microelectron. Eng.*, *3*, 279 (1985).
59. Taylor, G. N., and Wolf, T. M., *Polym. Eng. Sci.*, *20*, 1087 (1980).

60. Hartney, M. A., Ph.D. thesis, Department of Chemical Engineering, University of California-Berkeley, 1988.
61. Watanabe F., and Ohnishi, Y., *J Vac. Sci. Technol. B*, *4*, 422 (1986).
62. Cullis, C., and Hivschler, M., *The Combustion of Organic Polymers*, Oxford University Press (Clarendon), London, 1981, p. 54.
63. Gokan, H., Esho, S., and Ohnishi, Y., *J. Electrochem. Soc.*, *130*, 143 (1983).
64. Kunz, R. R., Allen, R. D., Hinsberg, W. D., and Wallraff, G. M., *Proc. SPIE*, *1925*, 167 (1993).
65. Allen, R. D., Wallraff, G. M., DiPietro, R. A., Hofer, D. C., and Kunz, R. R., *Proc. SPIE*, *2438*, 474 (1995).
66. Nozaki, K., Watanabe, K., Namiki, T., Igarishi, M., Kuramitsu, Y., and Yano, E., presented at the 1995 International Chemical Congress of Pacific Basin Societies, Honolulu, HI, December 1995.
67. Maeda, K., Nakano, K., Ohfuji, T., and Hasegawa, E., these proceedings.
68. Nakase, M., Naito, T., Asakawa, K., Hongu, A., Shida, N., and Ushirogouchi, T., *Proc. SPIE*, *2438*, 445 (1995).
69. Kunz, R. R., Horn, M. W., Palmateer, S. C., and Forte, A. R., unpublished results.
70. Kaimoto, Y., Nozaki, K., Takechi, S., and Abe, N., *Proc. SPIE*, *1672*, 66 (1992).
71. Allen, R. D., Wallraff, G. M., DiPietro, R. A., Hofer, D. C., Willson, C. G., and Kunz, R. R., *Proc. SPIE*, *2724*, 334, (1996).
72. Wallow, T. I., Houlihan, F. M., Nalamasu, O., Neenan, T. X., and Reichmanis, E., *Proc. SPIE*, *2724*, 355, (1996).
73. Hiraoka, H., and Pacansky, J., *J. Vac. Sci. Technol.*, *19*, 1132 (1981).
74. Tracy, C., and Mattox, R., *Solid State Technol.*, *25*, June, 83 (1982).
75. Matthews, J., and Wilmott, J., *SPIE Proc.*, *470*, 194 (1984).
76. Allen, R., Foster, M., and Yen, Y., *J. Electrochem. Soc.*, *129*, 1379 (1982).
77. Jordhamo, G., and Moreau, W., *Proc. SPIE*, *2927*, 588 (1996).
78. Dammel, R., *Diazonaphthoquinone-Based Resists*, SPIE Press, Bellingham, WA, 1993.
79. Sison, E., Rahman, M., Durham, D., Hermanowski, J., Ross, M., and Jennison, M., *Proc. SPIE*, *2438*, 378 (1995).
80. Ross, M. F., Comfort, D., and Gorin, G., *Proc. SPIE*, *2438*, 803 (1995).
81. Ross, M. F., Livesay, W. R., Starov, V., Ostrowski, K., and Wong, S. Y., *Proc. SPIE*, *2724*, 632 (1996).
82. Ross, M. F., Christensen, L., and Magvas, J., *Proc. SPIE*, *2195*, 834 (1994).
83. Luongo, J. P., *J. Polym. Sci.*, *42*, 139 (1960).
84. Evans, J. F., Newman, J. G., and Gibson, J. H., in *Surface and Colloid Science in Computer* Technology (K. L. Mittal, ed.), Plenum, New York, 1986.
85. Cook, J. M., and Benson, B. W., *J. Electrochem. Soc.*, *130*, 2459 (1983).
86. Wang, C. W., and Gelernt, B., *Solid State Technol.*, *24*, 121 (1981).
87. Stafford B., and Gorin, G. J., *Solid State Technol.*, *20*, 51 (1977).
88. Degenkolb, E. O., Mogab, C. J., Goldrick, M. R., and Griffiths, J. E., *Appl. Spectrosc.*, *30*, 520 (1976).
89. Degenkolb E. O., and Griffiths, J. E., *Appl. Spectrosc.*, *31*, 40 (1977).
90. Hiraoka, H., *J. Vac. Sci. Technol. B*, *4*, 345 (1986).

91. Fujimura, S., Konno, J., Hikazutani, K., and Yano, H., *Jpn. J. Appl. Phys.*, *28*, 2130 (1989).

92. Kikuchi M., and Bersin, R., *Jpn. J. Appl. Phys.*, *31*, 2035 (1992).

93. Shi, J., Kamarehi, M., Shaner, D., Rounds, S., Fink, S., and Ferris, D., *Solid State Technol.*, *38*, 75 (1995).

94. Stefani, J. A., Loewenstein, L. M., and Sullivan, M., in *Proceedings of the 1993 IEEE/SEMI International Semiconductor Manufacturing Science Symposium*, 1993, p. 27.

95. Loong, W., Yen, M.-S., Wang, F.-C., Hsu, B.-Y., and Liu, Y.-L., *Microelectron. Eng.*, *21*, 259 (1993).

96. Hayasaka N., and Okano, H., *Proceedings of the 10th Symposium on Dry Process*, Tokyo, 1985, p. 125.

97. Jimbo, S., Shimomura, K., Ohiwa, T., Sekine, M., Mori, H., Horioka, K., and Okano, H., *Jpn. J. Appl. Phys.*, *32*, 3045 (1993).

98. Gabriel C., and Mitchener J. C., *Proc. SPIE*, *1086*, 598 (1989).

99. Mikulan, P. I., Koo, T. T., Awadelkarim, O. O., Fonash, S. J., Ta, T., and Chan, Y. D., *Mater. Res. Symp. Proc.*, *309*, 61 (1993).

100. Genut, M., Livshitz, B., Tehar-Zahav, O., and Iskevitch, E., *Proc. SPIE*, *2724*, 601, (1996).

101. Kubozono, T., Moroishi, Y., Ohta, Y., Shimodan, H., and Moriuchi N., *Proc. SPIE*, *2724*, 677, (1996).

12
Critical Dimensional Metrology

Herschel M. Marchman*

AT&T Bell Laboratories, Murray Hill, New Jersey

1 INTRODUCTION

Metrology is the science of measurement. It is necessary for the development of new processes, the control and monitoring of existing ones, and as a product qualification yardstick. Microscopes are widely used to make precise distance measurements. They are especially important in the semiconductor industry, where critical dimensions (CDs) are rapidly approaching 0.1 μm. The requirement in integrated circuit metrology that the fabrication tolerance be 10% of the critical dimension translates to a demanded measurement precision (between 10 and 40% of the fabrication tolerance) on the single-nanometer level. For example, the fabrication tolerance for a 0.25-μm nominal gate length would be 0.025 μm and the metrology precision around 0.0025 μm, or 2.5 nm—about six atoms long! Similar arguments can be made for the relative (overlay) and absolute (placement) position of the feature as well. These metrology requirements were based on a 10% rule, and a new criterion or modification of this rule may have to be applied to the metrology requirements as the dimensions to be measured approach the nanometer scale. Submicrometer device fabrication metrology also involves performing measurements in three dimensions. Masks and wafers contain features with high aspect ratios and are composed of multiple layers of different materials; both factors make the the-

*Current affiliation: Texas Instruments SPDC, Dallas, Texas

ory and understanding of the metrology tool behavior complicated. In addition to measuring submicrometer feature dimensions and placements with nanometer-scale precision, high throughput and full automation are desirable for an in-line manufacturing implementation. In this chapter, we will mainly be concerned with dimensional metrology of lithographic masks and patterned semiconductor wafer features after processing (postfabrication), in particular, the measurement of feature width, height (depth), overlay, and placement. Because the theoretical limits of measurement capability are being approached, it is reasonable to believe that a shift in metrology from postfabrication sampling to on-line (in situ) measurement and control is required to achieve more value in the metrology process. This change would require metrology instruments as robust as the processing equipment used in fabrication.

2   TERMS AND DEFINITIONS

A random measurement distribution (Fig. 1) is obtained when taking repeated measurements on a given sample and holding all factors constant. The *mean* ($\overline{X}$) is obtained when an average of the measurement values is taken such that

$$\overline{X} = \sum_{n=1}^{N} \frac{x_n}{N}$$

where x_n is the nth measurement and N is the total number of measurements. *Repeatability* (σ_{rpt}) is the short-term variation of repeated measurements on the same feature under identical conditions. These are also referred to as *static* measurements. The variation in these measurements should be random with normal

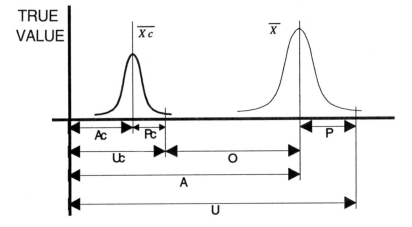

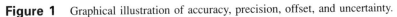

Figure 1   Graphical illustration of accuracy, precision, offset, and uncertainty.

distribution. An estimate of repeatability is found from the standard deviation,

$$\sigma = \frac{\left[\sum_{n=1}^{N}(x_n - \bar{x})^2\right]^{1/2}}{N-1}$$

This level of variation is considered to represent the best case of instrument performance. *Reproducibility* (σ_{rpd}) is the fluctuation in the static mean values when the measurements are made under different conditions. The factors that are allowed to vary when determining reproducibility are those that affect the ability of an instrument to reproduce its own results after the sample has been completely removed from the instrument and reloaded. Reproducibility allows one to determine the effect of the systematic error components (i.e., the factors chosen to vary). *Precision* (σ) is the total variation in the measurements. This is obtained by summing the repeatability and reproducibility in quadrature,

$$\sigma = \sqrt{\sigma_{rpt}^2 + \sigma_{rpd}^2}$$

Precision values are usually quoted in terms of an integral multiple of the standard deviations, such as 3σ or 6σ. These expressions are valid if the number of measurements is sufficiently large and the distribution is Gaussian, or normal. Normal distributions typically result when the errors are of a random nature, which can therefore be reduced by averaging. Systematic errors, on the other hand, skew the data and are more difficult to eliminate. In addition, obtaining a large number of measurements per site may be difficult when there are many sites per sample. Therefore, particular attention must be paid to experimental design and instrumentation so that valid results are obtained with a nonprohibitive number of measurements. One can also have multiple sources of error such that the distribution may appear Gaussian if the systematic errors are randomly distributed about the mean.

A carefully designed experiment provides a systematic and efficient way to study the effects of measurement parameters on tool performance. Results from each experiment also help one to focus on the more significant factors affecting measurements. There are several models from which to chose when designing a measurement precision gauge. The traditional model has been the "crossed effects" model in which one factor (A) is common to each cycle of the other (B) as in Fig. 2a. For instance, if one is studying the effects of operators (A) and parts (B) on instrument performance, this model would yield the operator-by-part interaction.

The nested effects model (see Fig. 2b) would be more appropriate if we want to separate the effects of each factor and also analyze the different variance components in the precision term [1]. Static repeats are nested within load cy-

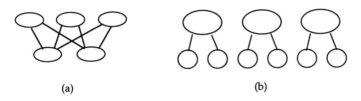

Figure 2   (a) The crossed effects model. (b) The nested effects model.

cles that are nested within a particular factor of interest. This model also allows multiple levels of factors nested within higher ones. The number of factors in a given experiment must be limited because the amount of measurements required grows factorially with each added level to the nested model. The variance components in most cases are estimated using a nested model and analysis of variation (ANOVA) calculations to determine the contribution of each factor to the overall precision. Previous studies have used another technique in which a sample is loaded and a large number of static measurements are performed. The standard deviation of this set is assumed to be the short-term repeatability for subsequent measurements. Next, the wafer is loaded, measured once, and unloaded. This cycle is repeated several times under a given set of conditions (a factor is varied) and the deviation is referred to as the reproducibility. However the proposed reproducibility in this technique also has static repeatability variation contained in it, because only one measurement was made during each loading cycle. Reproducibility therefore should be the variation between the means of the cycles.

The precision depends on many factors such as operator, loading cycle, pattern type, and feature composition. For example, CD measurement repeatabilities will be different for isolated features than for densely packed features. Degradation in repeatability generally occurs as feature sizes decrease (i.e., approach the resolution limits of the given metrology instrument). In addition, the time period necessary to obtain a valid repeatability estimate must be considered. If the standard deviation is determined by taking several quick measurements immediately after the instrument is checked or calibrated, the resulting precision estimate will most likely be meaningless. A more valid precision value can be found from measurements taken over a period of time comparable to the interval between calibrations or checks, perhaps over a day or longer. The long-term performance and condition of the entire system can be monitored by control charts keeping track of these values from day to day over weeks or even months and years. An advantage to this technique is that most of the factors, such as environment (e.g., temperature, humidity), affecting system performance will have time to fluctuate to most of their full potential. Of course, long-term precisions will generally be worse than the short-term values, but they will yield a better reflection of the metrology system performance.

Accuracy refers to how closely the measurement conforms to an absolute standard, or truth, assuming there is a fundamental basis of comparison. The concept of accuracy is illustrated in Fig. 1. The mean value X of a measurement set with spread $2P$ has an offset O relative to an accepted standard that has a mean value of X' and spread of $2P'$. Calibration of an instrument involves subtracting the offset O between X and X'. However, calibration does not yield absolute accuracy because the reference standard has its own uncertainty U'. The uncertainty of the standard U' is simply the sum of A' and P'. The accuracy and precision of the measurement set can be brought together to give the total measurement U,

$$U = A_c + A + \sqrt{P_C^2 + P^2}$$

We see that systematic errors add linearly and random errors are summed in quadrature. When a quantity is measured as $X \pm U$, the true value may be anywhere in the interval $\pm U$. Knowledge of the desired quantity can be improved by increasing the precision with more measurements or calibrating to a reference standard to reduce the accuracy offset O. For some measurement quantities, the systematic errors have opposite sign and cancel each other so that the offset in accuracy between X and X' is eliminated. Measurement of the pitch (spatial period) of a periodic line grating provides one example of when systematic errors are subtractive. In fact, the pitch is often used to obtain a multiplicative factor to calibrate magnification of the instrument. One must be careful in this case, because the systematic errors do not cancel if the grating is not truly periodic. This case usually arises when there are proximity effects present in the etching or lithographic patterning steps, such that the width varies from line to line.

The concept of accuracy becomes obscured when the quantity to be measured is not well defined. For example, the definition of line width is unclear for the structure shown in Fig. 3. The ideal structures for line width measurement would consist of flat features, or structures with uniform height and vertical sidewalls, with smooth edges. In reality, the line edges are usually not well defined. Structures typically encountered in integrated circuit (IC) technology may have edges that are ragged and walls that are asymmetric or even reentrant. A more appropriate term is line profile, which describes the surface height along the x direction at a $Y - Y'$ location. Alternatively, the profile could be given by the width $X - X'$ at each height position Z of the line (line being a three-dimensional entity in this case). Edge roughness is presently a major factor in the uncertainty of National Institute of Standards and Technology (NIST) line width standards. Sidewall profile also complicates the issue because line

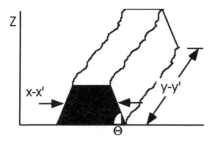

Figure 3 Structure with three-dimensional geometry. Sidewall profile and edge roughness affect definition of line width.

width must be defined at a particular height. The height on which line width is based may depend on the context in which the feature is measured.

For the photoresist line in Fig. 4, the top width would be chosen if a highly anisotropic plasma etch process of an underlying layer of material were to follow. The line width might be defined at the bottom for an isotropic wet etching process. Defining the line width becomes even more complicated if the resist profile changes with time, as is the case when there is not infinite selectivity between the resist and material to be patterned. As features sizes continue to shrink and have more and more complicated shapes, the accuracy of a measurement becomes more and more difficult to find. The error due to differences between the calibration artifact and sample is also becoming a significant fraction of the total feature size, so that achieving accuracy by calibrating an instrument with an absolute calibration standard may not be possible either.

As a result, repeatability is being emphasized more for increased control of manufacturing processes. However, the systematic measurement error varies with the sample properties. Variations in the features to be measured will cause

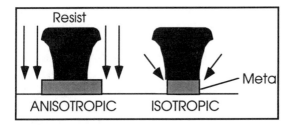

Figure 4 Photoresist line structure with reentrant sidewall profile. The definition of line width depends on the process situation.

the accuracy offset O to change in ways that are unknown to the fabrication engineer. Then parts that are in error may appear to be good and conversely, the ones that are actually within tolerance could be rejected due to large measurement errors (inaccuracies). Of course, it would be impossible to fabricate a reference standard to match every type of sample, as this would require an a priori knowledge of the feature characteristics as well as an infinite number of reference artifacts. As a temporary expedient for the interim, metrologist often use in-house or "golden standards" to track the precision and fluctuations in systematic error or accuracy offset O. However, great care must be exercised to ensure that the standard is stable and matches the sample being measured. Efforts should also be made to ensure that the uncertainty U' of the in-house standard is as small as possible because gross errors in accuracy can produce difficulties in relating the process parameters to the predicted values.

3 INSTRUMENTATION

A metrology tool evaluation process is illustrated in Fig. 5. The first requirement for a metrology tool is that of resolution. The instrument must have sufficient resolution to detect various types of features having different sizes. The next step is to determine whether the precision is adequate. Statistical analysis of the data could be performed if the initial repeatability is inadequate, but the number of measurements needed to obtain a sufficient averaging should not be prohibitive. Once precision is established, the fabrication of a standard is necessary for calibration. As mentioned in the previous section, the image characteristics of apparently the same type of features can change dramatically if their wall angles, edge and surface roughness, and optical properties (e.g., index of refractions) are slightly different [2]. The instrument must be calibrated for all patterns.

In addition to measurement performance, overall system usability should be an equally important consideration in a metrology tool gauge [3]. The evolution from manual to fully automated operation is opening up new capabilities for CD metrology instruments in the process line. Capabilities such as user interface (manual and automation), uptime, computer integration, and job transportability are just as critical as the measurement performance in achieving usefulness as a metrology tool. Effectiveness of the software interface for manual operation and/or automated job setup is the primary consideration when evaluating the user interface. The manual interface is important for ease of training and effective engineering use of the tool. The automation user interface is key to the training of fabrication personnel for selecting and running previously created recipes.

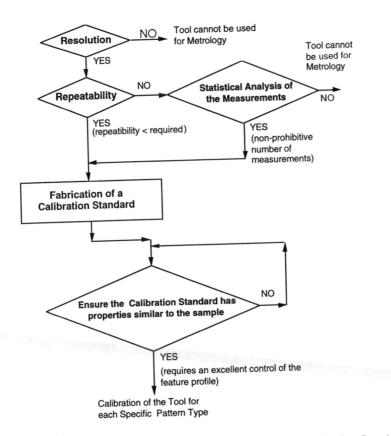

Figure 5   The metrology tool measurement performance evaluation flowchart.

3.1   Optical Metrology Review

Even as the dimensions to be measured extend to the submicrometer range, optical measurement techniques cannot be totally ruled out. They offer the advantages of being nondestructive, fast, and requiring little or no modification of
the specimen. Optical tools can possess great repeatability ($P < 0.005$ μm) for
features down to the quarter-micrometer regime. However, very precise (reproducible) measurements may not necessarily be accurate. Linearity between the
measured and actual values is typically lost to interference, resonance, and
shadowing effects well before the diffraction limit is reached. In addition, standards for submicrometer features do not exist for optical tools. We therefore use
in-house control samples as interim standards. The initial measurements for
these in-house standards are obtained from other tools such as the scanning

electron microscope (SEM) or a scanning probe microscope (SPM). Unfortunately, the SEM and SPM have their own set of problems with precision and accuracy, but they are generally better than optical. As noted earlier, it may be appropriate to use in-house control specimens as calibration standards if, and only if, they closely match the samples to be measured and are known to be stable in time. One of the most serious problems in the development of submicrometer dimensional standards for reticles and wafers is that there are so many different types and combinations of features (each having its own optical properties) that it is virtually impossible to produce a set of standards to match every type of feature on a sample.

The ultimate optical resolution of an optical microscope system is limited by diffraction. An opaque line on a clear substrate observed by a microscope will not have sharp, well defined, edges due to the light diffraction. A short derivation of the diffraction limit for a simple case will be useful for understanding and comparing the optical microscopes presented in this section. A second order-differential equation, known as the wave equation, can be derived from Maxwell's laws to describe the behavior of electromagnetic waves in space and time. To solve this equation, we assume that all information necessary for the calculation of the intensity of electromagnetic radiation in space is contained in the scalar wave function,

$$\psi(\mathbf{r},t) = \psi(\mathbf{r})e^{i\omega t}$$

In a linear, homogenous, isotropic media, the wave equation results,

$$\left(\nabla^2 - \frac{1}{c}\frac{\partial^2}{\partial t^2} \right)\psi(\mathbf{r},t) = 0$$

Substituting the wave function into this relationship yields the scalar Helmholtz equation (SHE)

$$\left[\nabla^2 + k^2 \right]\psi(\mathbf{r})$$

where $k = \omega/c$. A Green's function solution of the scalar Helmholtz equation can be performed if we assume that $\psi(r)$ is zero on the surface of any scattering object and all outgoing waves have only a radial variation (isotropic radiation). The far-field image at a distance r from the circular aperture source seen in Fig. 6 can then be found from the resulting Fraunhofer integral [4],

$$\psi(r) = \frac{iA_0 e^{-ikr}}{\lambda r} \int_{s'} e^{ik(\alpha x' + \beta y')} dS'$$

where A_0 is the initial field amplitude, λ is the wavelength, k is the spatial frequency, $x' = r' \cos \phi'$, $y' = r' \sin \phi'$, and s' is the surface of integration ($ds' =$

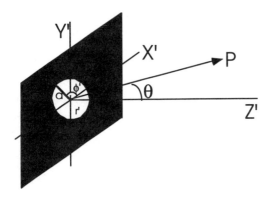

Figure 6   A circular aperture in an opaque screen.

$r'\ dr'\ d\phi'$). Evaluation of the integral and multiplication of Ψ with the complex conjugate Ψ^* yields the image intensity

$$I(r,\theta) = I_0(r)\left[\frac{2J_1(ka\ \sin\theta)}{ka\ \sin\theta}\right]^2$$

where J_1 is a first-order Bessel function. $I(r,\theta)$ describes the intensity of a diffraction-limited spot, often referred to as the "Airy disk." The Airy disk radius is defined by the first zero of $I(r,\theta)$, which occurs when

$$ka\ \sin\theta = 1.22\pi$$

Therefore, the Airy disk radius is given by

$$r_a = 1.22\lambda(z/2a)$$

For monochromatic, collimated, and incoherent source illumination, the minimum resolvable separation between the center of one disk and the first minimum of an adjacent light spot gives a measure of the spatial resolution (the Rayleigh criterion):

$$D = \frac{1.22\lambda}{2NA}$$

where NA denotes the lens numerical aperture. The Fraunhofer integral changes for different apertures (i.e., sample features) and will therefore not yield the same resolution for each type of feature. For instance, the resolution will be different for periodic lines and spaces than for an isolated contact hole. Accuracy and precision are determined by the resolution and will therefore depend on the feature type being observed.

The ability of a microscope to produce sharp image intensity profiles determines the certainty with which the edge location can be determined and the accuracy of the CD measurement. Linearity between the measured CDs and the actual structure size is dependent on this ability to produce well-defined transitions at the feature edges and provides a good measure of the resolution. This is in contrast to the way resolution is often defined by some equipment vendors, who use the 3σ repeatability value or minimum resolvable separation between two features on an ideal sample, such as gold on carbon for the SEM. Usually this sample material combination has no similarity to the types of materials that are really of interest, such as photoresist on oxide. Even if an image can be resolved, CD measurements cannot be performed if the correspondence between the image size and the actual feature dimensions becomes nonlinear. Besides indicating resolution, linearity increases the probability of meaningful calibration and hence accuracy.

Line width accuracy is heavily affected by the choice of edge position in an intensity profile. Actually, this holds true for any microscope, whether it be optical, electron, or scanning probe. The graph in Fig. 7 shows the measured intensity distribution as a function of position across the edges of a transparent space in an antireflective chromium background (i.e.,clear aperture in an opaque screen) on a quartz substrate observed in transmitted light with a scanning slit optical microscope. It is not clear where the line edge is actually located on the profile. For the microscope in this example, the illumination was provided by a broadband light source that was partially coherent. The difference in line edge position between the 25 and 50% intensity points is about 0.1

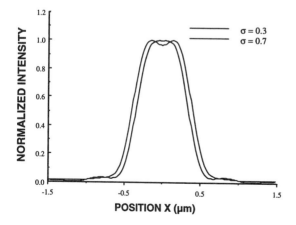

Figure 7   Image intensity of a 1-μm-wide isolated space for two source coherences.

µm, a considerable fraction of the feature width. Other factors that affect the intensity distribution of the image are the numerical aperture of the objective lens, coherence, lens aberrations, flare, and the wavelength spectrum of the source [5]. Coherence is often used to describe the interference aspects of a microscope and is defined as the ratio of the condenser to the objective lens NA for a conventional optical microscope. The measured line width depends on the coherence of the source illumination. If the actual coherence of the light is unknown, the choice of intensity threshold for locating the line edge position could typically be anywhere between 25 and 75% of maximum for each profile. Focus level is another factor affecting determination of the line edge position in the intensity profile as well as the measurement repeatability. Usually the focus is adjusted for optimum image quality. Attempts to determine line edge position accurately from intensity profiles are being made through the use of theoretical calculations [6]. One starts with calculation of the image intensity as a function of lateral position across the feature. The calculated intensity profile is then fit to the experimental distribution with the desired critical dimension as an adjustable parameter. Once agreement between the theoretical and measured intensity profiles is found, the position of the edges can be determined. The desired critical dimension is then obtained as the distance between the edges. Unfortunately, the intensity distribution in diffraction patterns depends on the optical properties and physical dimensions of all the materials on the sample. For instance, phase-shifting masks (PSMs) contain features whose thickness exceed one fourth of the wavelength of the illuminating light and therefore cannot be considered thin in the mathematical analysis. In this case, the image intensity profile becomes strongly dependent on the thickness and shape of the feature (considerably increasing the difficulty of computing the intensity profiles). Scattering theory must be used for thick-layer features, such as phase-shifting lines. The mathematical model used to predict scattering profiles is currently under investigation at various laboratories, such as the National Institute of Standards and Technology. Even if the modeling results are known to agree with experiment, the model could be used to determine the edge locations only if all other parameters used by the model were known and measured simultaneously. Therefore, the basic principle of instrument design for realistic submicron dimensional metrology of thick-layer features, such as those on phase-shifting masks, should be to design the measurement system for improved resolution and thereby provide precision and accuracy for simplicity of modeling and design.

3.2 Optical Metrology Tool Descriptions

A diagram of a conventional optical microscope is shown in Fig. 8. Intensity profiles are obtained from the gray-level brightness along a line in the video image. These systems typically have autofocusing capability for improving the

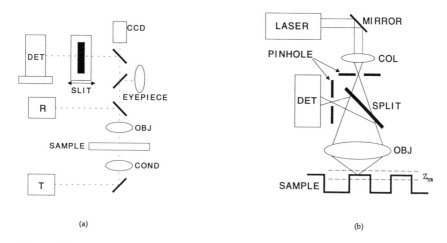

Figure 8 (a) A combined reflective and transmission mode scanning-slit optical microscope. (b) Optical ray diagram of a sample scanning confocal microscope.

measurement precision. The ultimate resolution limit for this conventional optical microscope was given previously. A common objective lens for measurements may have a magnification of 150× and NA of 0.9. If the illumination wavelength for this lens is centered at 550 nm, D is approximately 0.35 μm. Partially coherent white light is typically used. Although the nonlinearities due to sample properties affect the linearity before the diffraction limit is reached, it is still instructive to compare the fundamental limit of each optical configuration to gain insight into its performance.

In the scanning slit system of Fig. 8a, the intensity in the image plane is scanned by a slit whose length and width can be varied. The intensity transmitted through the slit is then detected and recorded versus slit scan position. A commercially available scanning slit microscope [7] has a laser autofocusing system, which locates the focal position interferometrically. The interferometric laser autofocusing technique is capable of finding the focal position more often and more repeatably than the video analytic technique of the system described previously. The scanning-slit width determines the resolution at which the image intensity can be sampled, but the optical resolution and hence performance are still limited by diffraction and nonlinearity in the same way as for other conventional optical microscopes.

In a scanning laser confocal microscope, a diffraction-limited spot is focused onto the sample and then reimaged by a pinhole before detection. The sample is scanned and imaged one point at a time. Figure 8b illustrates the arrangement of a scanning confocal microscope. A point source of laser light (defined by a pinhole) is focused onto the surface by an objective lens, which creates a diffraction-limited intensity spot of the same form as in the conventional micro-scope. This spot is focused twice, once before and once after the sample. This double focusing is referred to as a confocal operation and produces a narrower image point spread function (PSF) than in the conventional microscope. A con-volution of the source and detector apertures results from the confocal opera-tion so that the image intensity is now given by

$$I(r,\theta) = I_0(r)\left[\frac{2J_1(ka\,\sin\theta)}{ka\,\sin\theta}\right]^4$$

The fourth power results from this convolution of source and detector aperture intensity. The spatial sensitivity of the detection is equal to that of the source and the minimum resolvable linear distance is now given by

$$D = \frac{1.22\lambda}{2NA}\left(1 - \frac{1}{\pi}\right)$$

Therefore, the point resolution of a confocal microscope is $1/\pi$ (33%) better than that of conventional optical microscopes. The illumination is coherent so that the minimum resolvable distance is less (i.e., smaller PSF). If the same NA and center wavelength are used as in the conventional microscope example pre-sented earlier, then D becomes approximately 0.24 μm. A scanning ultraviolet (UV) laser confocal microscope [8] with λ equal to 325 nm has recently been used for imaging metallic lines 0.25 μm wide. The minimum resolvable dis-tance D for the UV system is approximately 0.14 μm. However, interference and resonance effects produce a loss of linearity for feature sizes below 0.5 μm.

The confocal microscope is also capable of measuring vertical dimensions due to its extremely small depth of focus. The intensity transmitted through the detector aperture changes as a function of focal distance z. The detected inten-sity is maximum at optimum focal position and decays rapidly on either side (see Fig. 8b). The full width at half the maximum of $I(z)$ is

$$2Z_{50\%} = \frac{0.89\lambda}{NA^2}$$

The relative step height between two points can be found by measuring the z difference in the $I(z)$ maximum (i.e., focus) for each point. Another important advantage of the confocal microscope is provided by the tight depth of focus. The majority of intensity through the detector pinhole is due to reflection from the surface at the focal plane z. If the focal level is set at the feature tops (top focus), variations in the CD measurements due to the substrate can be reduced. One can obtain an image at each z height (to within the depth of focus). A bot-tom focus image could be used to inspect the feature bottom width. Of course, the bottom widths would be affected by shadowing and substrate effects more than top focus. The line appears bright in the top-focus image and the substrate is out of the focal range. Conversely, the substrate appears bright in the bottom-focus image and the line appears dark. For features having vertical sidewalls, the difference in line width between top focus and bottom focus is mainly due to shadowing at the line edges that occurs when focusing on the substrate [9]. Top-focus imaging also helps decrease the effect of feature height on width measurement. Other types of confocal microscopes exist wherein the aperture or light spot is scanned instead of the sample for real-time imaging [10].

The Linnik interferometer microscope [11] uses white light interference when imaging samples and is capable of performing measurements in both the vertical and lateral directions. As shown in Fig. 9, a Linnik interferometer is formed by placing an objective lens into each arm of a Michelson interferometer. When broadband white light illumination is used, interference at the camera occurs only if the optical path lengths in each leg of the interferometer are the same (at a given wavelength). A region is created in space at the focal point of the sample objective, which is called the coherence region.

If the sample is scanned vertically (z axis) through the coherence region, an interference signal (phase signal) is detected at the camera as the surface passes through the coherence region. As the sample is scanned vertically, each pixel in the xy image creates a phase signal. When a scan is made, the system collects an entire three-dimensional volume of image data. This data can then be con-

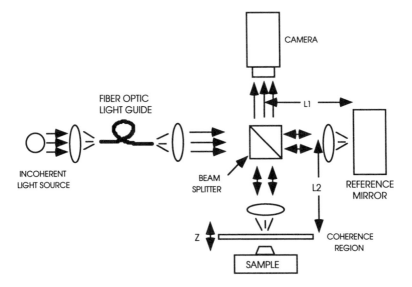

Figure 9 A ray optical diagram of the white light interferometric microscope.

verted to a cross-sectional representation of the sample using digital signal processing techniques. Alternatively, the sample can also be held stationary and the reference optical path varied. The image contrast is generated from the degree of coherence between corresponding pixels in the object and reference image planes of the Linnik microscope. As a result, the lateral resolution is enhanced in a manner similar to that in the confocal because the field from each point in the object plane is convolved with a corresponding point in the reference plane. Therefore, the PSF is of the same form as that of the scanning confocal. There are several advantages of the interference microscope over the confocal. First, conventional white-light sources can be used instead of lasers. The broadband illumination also helps reduce ringing and undesired coherent interference effects in transparent films (i.e., photoresist on wafers). The extra bandwidth also increases the z measurements resolution. Unfortunately, the Linnik interferometer is much more difficult to manufacture because the optical path lengths in the arms must be exactly matched.

Several examples will be presented for comparison of the various optical instruments and to demonstrate that the resolution of each microscope is not a constant property but changes with feature type. The first test pattern contained periodic and isolated features having nominal dimensions as small as 200 nm for testing the lateral resolution of each instrument. All of the patterns on this ample were made with chromium on unetched quartz and were relatively flat (<100 nm thick). A set of arrows was added to the pattern to make sure that all measurements were taken of the same line at the same point. The area of each module was made sufficiently large to prevent overlap of intensity from adjacent modules. A rough estimate of the amount of spreading due to diffraction can be obtained by measuring the width of the intensity transition at a line edge. In this case, a transition is defined as the change from 90% to 10% (or 10% to 90%) of the maximum intensity. The width of this transition is defined in terms of a percentage of the pitch. The data in Fig. 10 were taken for the 0.5-μm dense and isolated lines.

The 325-nm UV scanning confocal microscope exhibited sharper intensity transitions than the other optical tools in general. Of course, the shorter 325-nm wavelength confocal exhibited better resolution than the longer 488-nm version. A three-dimensional version of this pattern can be created by etching the bare quartz between the chromium lines. The etched quartz trenches in this example are approximately 385 nm deep in order to produce a 180° phase shift at I-line wavelength for a phase-shifting mask (PSM). The overall intensity levels of the optical images of this pattern are less than those of the flat grating because of light scattering from the edges of the quartz trenches. The optical profiles were sharper with more intensity modulation (see Fig. 10). The increased intensity modulation was due to edge scattering and the phase shift produced by the quartz trench. The relative broadening of the 0.5-μm chromium line edge pro-

Instrument	Transition Width (% of Pitch) Flat Lines	Transition Width (% of Pitch) Etched Lines
Scanning slit (trans)	33	30
Scanning slit (refl)	28	27
Conventional	30	28
Linnik	25	26
325nm (UV) confocal	20	9

Figure 10 Image intensity broadening for 0.5-μm-wide lines as a percentage of the 1-μm pitch.

file as a percentage of the total pitch is also shown in the table of Fig. 10. For the reflected-light instruments, contrast was observed due to the edge scattering of the walls. Sharper intensity profiles were also observed with the confocal microscope because of greater changes in the surface height. CD measurements are made from the image intensity profiles. Graphs of the measured CD values versus the nominal design CDs are presented for the unetched (binary) grating in Fig. 11. The vertical displacement between curves is due to differences in the calibration for every instrument and illustrates the wide range in offsets O that arise if a common reference standard is not used. The nonlinear portion of each curve gives an indication of the resolution limit of that microscope. Total measurement failure, or insufficient resolution to detect a feature adequately, is indicated in the graph by the ending of a curve (i.e., no data point). It is apparent from the graph that only the SEM maintained linearity and resolution to nominal 0.2-μm lines and spaces. A detailed description of the SEM will be given in the next section. As mentioned previously, the increased lateral resolution of the scanning confocal microscope for this type of feature over the other optical tools is due primarily to the narrower image point spread function and narrow depth of focus [12].

Next, an isolated line in an opaque chromium background was observed at each dimension. The nominal widths of the isolated lines were varied from 300 nm to 10 μm. The opaque background was large enough to provide sufficient isolation from surrounding regions. The graph of measured CD versus design nominal in Fig. 12 shows the SEM to be the most linear down to 0.3

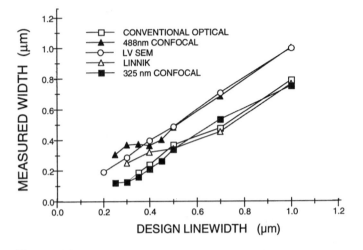

Figure 11   Measured widths for chromium line and space gratings.

μm (assuming the actual feature size is). It should also be noted that the over-all linearity of all the instruments increased for the isolated line case. The early demise of the Linnik interferometer was due to a problem with the measurement algorithm that determines the line edge position and not the optical resolution.

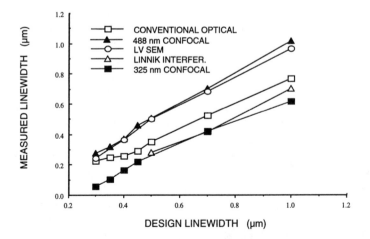

Figure 12   Measured widths for isolated chromium lines.

Different combinations of opaque chromium, unetched quartz, and etched quartz were used to create various permutations of an isolated line. The first type of phase-shifted line is shown in Fig. 13a This feature consisted of a transparent inner line with an etched quartz phase shifter on either side in an opaque chromium background. The intensity line scans (Fig. 13b) for the phase-shifted isolated line are quite different from those for the binary isolated line, even though they have the same amplitude functions.

If one has a transparent etched quartz center line with transparent unetched quartz rims on an opaque chromium background (Fig. 14a), the instruments respond differently than for the previous type of isolated line. The reflected intensity from the transparent etched inner line is now lower than that from the unetched quartz rim shoulders. This produces a subtle shoulder in the intensity profile that is ill-defined for determining the shifter edge position. For the trans-

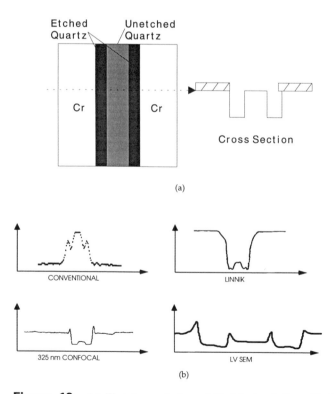

Figure 13 (a) First type of phase-shifted isolated line—IL A. (b) Image profiles from each microscope of IL A.

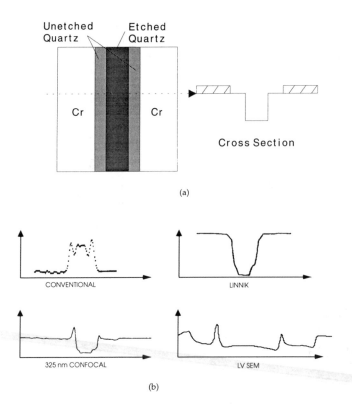

(a)

(b)

Figure 14 (a) Second type of phase-shifted isolated line—IL B. (b) Image profiles from each microscope of IL B.

mission case, choice of the rim edge locations is hindered by diffraction between the inner line edge and the outer quartz rim edge. Just a mere reversal of shifter tone produced completely different image profiles and resolutions.

3.3 Scanning Electron Microscope

The first particle with finite rest mass experimentally shown to have wave properties was the electron. J. J. Thomson discovered the electron as a particle in 1897. It was found to follow well-defined paths and to have a well-defined charge-to-mass ratio (for $v \ll c$), as well as momentum and energy that could be localized in space. Basically, electrons exhibit the attributes of a particle. In 1924, Louis de Broglie first conjectured that material particles might also show wave properties. He further assumed that the equations that give the particle characteristics of electromagnetic waves also give the wave characteristics of material particles, such as electrons. The wave nature of electrons was verified in 1927 by the electron diffraction experiments of Davisson and Germer. For nonrelativistic, free particles, the wavelength λ of a material particle having momentum $p = mv$ is

$$\lambda = \frac{h}{p} = \frac{h}{mv}$$

An electron with charge 1.6×10^{-19} C and mass 9.11×10^{-31} kg accelerated from rest by an electrostatic potential difference V acquires a final kinetic energy $1/2\ mv^2$ when

$$eV = \frac{1}{2}mv^2 = \frac{p^2}{2m} = \frac{1}{2m}\left(\frac{h}{\lambda}\right)^2$$

The wavelength of the electron is then found to be

$$\lambda = \frac{h}{\sqrt{2meV}} = \frac{1.226}{\sqrt{V}}$$

For an accelerating voltage of 1000 V, the electron wavelength λ is about 0.4 Å. The shorter the wavelength, the smaller the limit of resolution of a microscope. The wavelength of electron waves can easily be made much shorter than that of visible light. Hence the limit of resolution of a microscope may be extended to a value several hundred times smaller than that obtainable with light optical instruments by using electrons, rather than light waves, to form an image of the object being examined. A beam of electrons can be focused by either a magnetic or electric field of the proper configuration, and both types are used in electron microscopes. It will be evident later in this section that by the proper design of such electron lenses, the elements of an optical microscope such as its condenser, objective, and eyepiece can all be duplicated electrically. The scanning electron microscope (SEM) is currently poised as the main instrument of choice in the clean room for measuring submicrometer feature sizes because of its nanometer-scale resolution. Despite the SEM's high resolution, several issues exist that currently limit the performance. The practical resolution of the SEM is affected by such factors as source extension, chromatic dispersion and spherical aberration of the electron lens, beam-sample interactions (charging), and the interaction volume contributions to the detection signal. A schematic cross-sectional diagram of an SEM is shown in Fig. 15. An electron probe can be produced by thermionic or field emission guns and a demagnification of the smallest cross section of the electron beam (crossover) by several electromagnetic lenses. The electron probe is raster scanned over a region of the sample surface. The SEM spatial resolution cannot become better than the diameter of the electron probe but is also limited by the beam-sample interac-

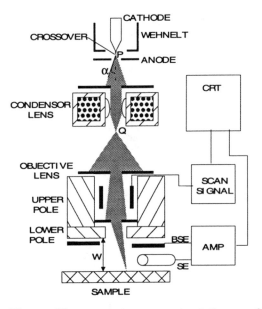

Figure 15   Schematic cross-sectional diagram of a scanning electron microscope.

tion volume contributing to the detector signal. The recorded signals from the electron detector are displayed on a cathode ray tube (CRT) rastered in synchronism with the beam.

The different types of emitters (electron guns) are explained in the potential energy diagram of Fig. 16. Thermionic emitters are heated to temperatures

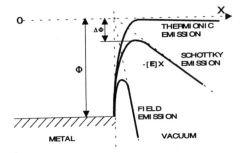

Figure 16   Potential energy diagram of the cathode-vacuum interface for thermionic, Schottky, and field emission guns.

above 2500 K for directly heated tungsten hairpin cathodes and 1400 K for indirectly heated LaB$_6$ rods. Heating must occur for electrons in the tail of the Fermi distribution to overcome the surface work functions ϕ = 4.5 eV for tungsten and 2.7 eV for LaB$_6$. The current density of emission at the cathode is given by the Richardson law [13]

$$j_c = AT_c^2 e^{-\phi/kT_c}$$

where A is a material constant and k is Boltzmann's constant. In addition to emission current, cathodes are often characterized by the axial gun brightness

$$\beta = \frac{\Delta I}{\Delta A \Delta \Omega} = \frac{j_c}{\pi \alpha^2} \cong \frac{j_c E}{\pi k T_c}$$

Axial gun brightness is defined as the current passing through an area ΔA into a solid angle $\Delta \Omega = \pi \alpha$ [14]. The beam aperture α is the semiapex angle of the incident electron cone. The axial gun brightness remains constant for all points along the optic axis through lenses and apertures. A thermionic electron gun (see Fig. 15) is composed of a negatively biased cathode, a Wehnelt cup that is biased a few hundred more volts negatively than the cathode, and an anode at ground potential. The electron trajectories form a cross-over point between the cathode and anode that produces an electron source having an approximately Gaussian intensity profile. The relatively low energy at the crossover point results in stochastic Coulomb interactions that increase the electron beam energy spread (Boersch effect).

Schottky emission cathodes use a crystalline tip with a special coating in order to lower the work function from 4.6 eV (W) to 2.8 [ZrO/W(100)]. This allows electrons to overcome the work function ϕ at a lower cathode temperature. The electrons are extracted by a much higher electric field strength E at the cathode than with thermionic emitters but not enough to produce tunneling. The potential barrier is lowered by $\Delta \phi$ (Fig. 16), known as the Schottky effect, and the electrons must overcome the remaining barrier by their thermal energy. The energy spread of this type of gun is not increased by the Boersch effect and has several orders of magnitude larger emission current density than thermal emitters [14].

A field emission gun (FEG) uses an electric field E to decrease the potential barrier width to less than approximately 10 nm (Fig. 16). A field emission gun needs two anodes, one to regulate the field strength at the tip (extraction voltage) and the other to accelerate the electrons to their final kinetic energy (acceleration voltage). The emission current can be varied by the voltage of the first extraction anode. Electrons are accelerated to the final energy $E = eU$ by the second acceleration anode. The dependence of field emission current density on electric field strength is given by the Fowler-Nordheim equation [15]

$$j_c = \frac{k_1 |E|^2}{\phi} e^{(-k_2 \phi^{3/2}/|E|)}$$

where k_1 and k_2 are weakly dependent on E. FEGs use crystal oriented tips and have gun brightness that can be up to three orders of magnitude larger than thermionic emitters. Since FEGs operate with the tip at room temperature, adsorbed gas layers must be cleaned from them by heating (flashing) the tip about every 8 hours of operation. Waiting periods of 1 to 3 hours must follow after each tip flash for emission current to stabilize. An advantage of cold-cathode FEGs is low electron energy spread and hence less susceptibility to lens aberrations. FEGs produce the smallest probe sizes and exhibit the best resolution of all the emitters. Fluctuation in the emission current typically occurs with cold-cathode FEGs, which can be compensated for by dividing the recorded signal with adsorbed currents at the diaphragms [16]. Mainly due to the lack of heating, cold-cathode FEG tip lifetimes are much longer than lifetimes of thermionic or Schottky emitters.

Electrons from the gun pass through a diaphragm and are focused by an electron lens. An electron lens (see Fig. 15) basically consists of an axial magnetic field having rotational symmetry. The flux of a coil is concentrated by iron pole pieces that form the magnetic field B seen in Fig. 15. The z component B_z has a bell-shaped intensity distribution, so the electrons will travel along spiral trajectories due to the Lorentz force. The electron beam diverging from the crossover point P is focused at Q such that the source diameter is demagnified by the factor $M = p/q$. The lens in Fig. 15 is known as a condenser lens. After the condenser, electrostatic parallel plates are used to deflect the beam to create the scan motion on the sample. The beam is focused again before it reaches the sample by another electron lens known as the objective. The final probe-forming objective lens is also shown in Fig. 15. The objective lens consists of an upper and a lower pole piece with an aperture diaphragm in between. The working distance, denoted by w, is the physical distance between the lower pole piece and the specimen. As in light optics, electron lenses have aberrations as well. In fact, electron lens aberrations usually limit the minimum probe size and resolution before the diffraction limit is reached. Spherical aberration, chromatic aberration, axial astigmatism, and diffraction spreading are of primary interest when discussing electron-probe formation. Parallel rays that are farther from the optic axis of an electron lens are focused closer to that lens. This effect is known as spherical aberration and causes a delocalization of the beam focal spot. The resulting Gaussian beam diameter in the plane of least confusion is [17]

$$d_s = 0.5 C_s \alpha^3$$

The aperture-limiting semiangle α (see Fig. 15) can be changed by varying the diaphragm in the pole piece gap of the final lens. The spherical aberration constant C_s increases rapidly with the working distance w.

Accelerating voltage determines the focal length. A disk of least confusion results from the energy spread ΔE of the electron gun. The diameter of the disk is given by

$$d_c = C_c \left(\frac{\Delta E}{E} \right) \alpha$$

where C_c is the chromatic aberration coefficient.

Inhomogeneities in the lenses and apertures cause an asymmetry in the focusing field known as axial astigmatism. Electrons in the xy and xz planes are focused at different distances. Astigmatism can be corrected by a stigmator consisting of multipole lenses near the pole piece gap.

Fraunhofer diffraction at the aperture-limiting diaphragm in the final lens causes an Airy disk of half-width given by

$$d_d = \frac{0.6\lambda}{\alpha}$$

where λ is the de Broglie wavelength of the electron as described earlier.

The final electron probe is formed on the sample by successive demagnifications of the crossover or virtual point source of diameter d_0 by several lenses. An intermediate image is formed at a large distance L in front of each lens. The lens magnification is found from the ratio of the object focal length f to the intermediate image distance L on the primary side of the lens. The overall system magnification is simply the product of geometric magnifications of the individual lenses. The geometric probe diameter d_g is found from the product of the magnification (actually demagnification) and the original crossover diameter at the virtual source.

$$d_g = \frac{f_1 f_2 f_3}{L_1 L_2 L_3} = M d_0$$

The geometric beam diameter can also be expressed in terms of the electron probe aperture as [18]

$$d_g^2 = C_0 \alpha_p^{-2}$$

The geometric probe diameter is broadened by aberrations of the lenses. A quadratic superposition of the different beam components results in an effective probe diameter of

$$d_p^2 = d_g^2 + d_d^2 + d_s^2 + d_c^2$$

which can also be expressed as

$$d_p^2 = \left[C_0^2 + (0.6\lambda)^2 \right] \alpha_p^{-2} + \frac{1}{4} C_s \alpha_p^6 + \left(C_c \frac{\Delta E}{E} \right)^2 \alpha_p^2$$

A double-logarithmic plot of the final electron probe diameter d_p versus probe aperture α_p for a thermionic emission SEM is shown in Fig. 17a. The accelerating potential $V = 1$ kV, $C_s = 45$ mm, $C_c = 25$ mm, $\Delta E = 2$ eV, and $Ip = 10^{-11}$ A. The value of axial brightness β was calculated to be 3.7×10^7 A cm^{-2} sr^{-1}. We see from the plot that the diffraction error is negligible compared to the other components. The minimum electron probe diameter d_{min} occurs at an optimum probe aperture α_p. Of course, the optimum aperture can also be found by taking the derivative of d_p with respect to α_p and setting equal to zero. Although the geometric probe size will shrink for smaller probe currents, there is a minimum practical current beyond which the signal-to-noise ratio becomes too poor for imaging. For low accelerating voltages (a few kV), the chromatic error disk d_c becomes larger than the spherical aberration d_g because thermionic emitters have a relatively large energy spread ΔE due to the Boersch effect. In addition, the decrease in brightness with energy, and hence larger d_g, means that thermioninic cathodes are not as effective for low-voltage (<3 kV) SEMs as Schottky emitters or FEGs. The electron-probe diameter d_p is plotted versus aperture α_p for an acceleration voltage V of 20 kV in Fig. 17b. The brightness is dependent on the acceleration voltage and was recalculated to be 7.38×10^8 A cm^2 sr^{-1}. It is

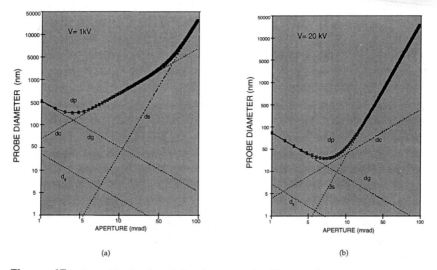

(a)   (b)

Figure 17   Logarithmic plot of the electron probe diameter d_p versus aperture α_p at an acceleration voltage of (a) 1 kV and (b) 20 kV for a thermionic emission SEM.

interesting to note that the optimum aperture is different for this accelerating volt-age. The chromatic aberrations also have less influence for this case. The optimum aperture α_{opt} is larger in the 20-keV case and spherical aberrations have more effect on the final probe size d_p than with the low accelerating voltage. The minimum spot size d_{min} is an order of magnitude smaller for the higher acceleration voltage of 20 kV.

A logarithmic plot of final electron probe diameter d_p versus electron probe aperture α_p for a cold-cathode field emission SEM is shown in Fig. 18a. The field emission current density was calculated and then used to determine the brightness at each accelerating voltage. An energy spread of $\Delta E = 0.3$ eV was assumed for the cold-cathode field emission case. The results are shown in Fig. 18a and b. The second and fourth terms in d_p^2 dominate for Schottky and field emission SEMs and d_{min} becomes diffraction limited at small apertures. Chromatic aberration terms dominate in the low-voltage regime (<3 kV). In field emission, the minimum electron probe diameter for low acceleration voltage is comparable to the thermionic high acceleration voltage case. However, the field emission probe diameter is another order of magnitude below all of the other cases. The spatial resolution will therefore be the best for field emission with high acceleration voltages.

An improvement in the electron optical characteristics can be made by placing the sample between the objective lens pole pieces (in-lens operation) [19]

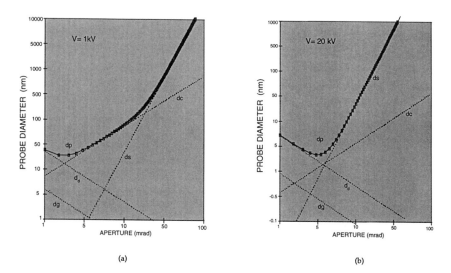

(a) (b)

Figure 18   Logarithmic plot of the electron probe diameter d_p versus aperture α_p at an acceleration voltage of (a) 1 kV and (b) 20 kV for a field emission SEM.

in order to decrease C_s and C_c to about 1 mm. Electromagnetic retardation fields can also be used to allow higher energies in the column so that the effects of stray fields can be reduced.

Once the final electron probe has been formed, it is raster scanned across the sample surface to create an image. The electron probe interacts with a volume of the sample as shown in Fig. 19. The electron-sample interactions in Fig. 19 are used for imaging and surface analysis with the SEM. The primary electrons (PEs) from the electron probe produce secondary electrons (SEs) through inelastic scattering, which emit from a shallow depth between about 1 and 10 nm. The energy spectrum of SEs has a peak at 2–5 eV and a long tail. Generally, electrons that are emitted with energies less than 50 eV are considered to be SEs. The SE1 group electrons (see Fig. 19) excited by the PE electrons contribute to high-resolution imaging on the order of the probe diameter. The so-called backscattered electrons (BSEs) have energies ranging from 50 to eV and can also produce SE2 excited in a larger surface layer with diameter that is approximately 100–1000 nm at beam energies above 10 keV, depending on the surface material. This diameter decreases to about 5–50 nm at low beam energies. The high-energy BSEs can also produce SE3 electrons through collisions with the specimen chamber and lower pole piece of the objective lens. Another group of electrons known as SE4 can actually diffuse out from the electron beam forming column itself. It is usually desirable to collect only the SE1 and SE2 electrons for best resolution in the SE imaging mode. Unfortunately, this is not always the case.

Backscattered electrons have an information depth of almost half the entire electron interaction volume range. The BSE signal consists primarily of elasti-

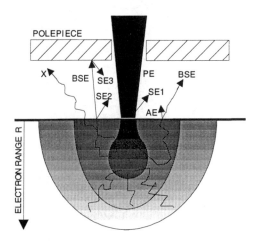

Figure 19   Cross-sectional diagram of the electron probe-sample interaction volume.

cally backscattered (reflected) electrons at nearly the same energy as those of the incident primary beam eV. At first, it may appear that the SE mode of collection and imaging offers better resolution than the BSE imaging mode. However the BSE interaction diameter decreases rapidly at low beam voltages (<2 keV) and actually approaches the SE1 and SE2 interaction diameters. The exit energies of BSEs are sufficiently high that the effects of sample charging on the collected electrons are greatly reduced. This immunity to charging is providing a new means of inspecting the bottoms of trench features and contact holes [20,21]. Operation in the ultralow voltage range should also reduce charging effects in the SE mode.

A detector must be used to collect the electrons that are emitted from the interaction volume and convert them to signals for imaging. The Everhart-Thornley detector (ETD) is the most common type of detector, found in most SEMs that image in the SE mode. The SEs are collected by a positively biased grid on the front of a scintillator as shown in Fig. 20. The fraction of SEs that are actually collected by the detector depends on the working distance w. Fewer SEs are collected for small w, because they will strike the bottom pole piece instead. The detected SEs are accelerated past the grid (typically biased at + 10 kV) into the scintillator coating. Light from the scintillator is then guided by a light pipe to a photomultiplier, where it is converted to current.

The merit of a detector system is determined mainly by the ratio of output to input root-mean-square (rms) noise amplitudes [22]

$$r = \frac{N_{\text{out}}}{N_{\text{in}}} = \left(\frac{S}{N}\right)_{\text{in}} \left(\frac{N}{S}\right)_{\text{out}} \leq 1$$

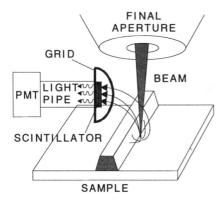

Figure 20 Diagram of the Everhart-Thornley detector used for generating the SE image signal.

where

$$\left(\frac{S}{N}\right)^2_{\text{in}} = \frac{I_{\text{p}}}{2e\Delta f}$$

is the mean shot noise of the incident electrons and Δf is the bandwidth.

The ETD is generally not used for collection of the BSEs because of the small detection solid angle and the fact that the BSE energies are too high for their trajectories to be altered by the grid potential. BSEs can be detected directly by a scintillator having a large solid angle and that is near the sample. Without the accelerating grid, the scintillator must be coated with a material that lowers its threshold energy. To improve efficiency, the scintillator surface is often biased as well. In addition to the EDT, semiconductor and microchannel-plate detectors are also used for the collection of electrons. Semiconductor detectors provide internal amplification of the incident electron current by means of collection and separation of electron-hole pairs in the depletion layers. However, bandwidth and signal gain is not that of the EDT at low electron energies. The microchannel-plate (MCP) detector has become of increasing interest for IC metrology, where low beam currents and low acceleration voltages ($0.5 < V < 3$ kV) are desired. In this operating range, semiconductor detectors decrease in sensitivity and the EDT shows asymmetric intensity profiles. The MCP is composed of a slice from a tightly packed group of fused tubes of lead-doped glass. The inner diameters of the tubes are typically 10–20 μm and the thickness of the slice is about 3 mm. Incident electrons are amplified by the MCP in a photomultiplier-like action where SEs are produced at the inner wall of each tube and accelerated by a continuous voltage drop along the tube with a bias of a several kilovolts. The front plate can be biased such that both BSEs and SEs are collected or just BSEs. MCPs are very efficient for low-voltage SEMs, because the SE yield of incident electrons shows a maximum at $300 < E < 800$ eV. In addition to the type of detector, there are various strategies for the placement of each detector to increase collection efficiency and maximize intensity scan symmetry.

We will restrict our discussion of SE and BSE contrast mechanisms to those mainly due to topography and material composition. There can be large differences between SE and BSE images for high-voltage SEM. This is mainly due to the interaction depths of the BSEs being much larger than those where the SE1 are generated. In low-voltage SEM, the information volumes of the BSEs and SEs become comparable and the differences between images disappear or are greatly reduced. The contrast of an SE image is mainly formed by topographic and material differences on the sample surface. As illustrated by Fig. 21, smooth surfaces will appear darker because fewer secondary electrons will be scattered than on a rough surface of the same material. The same holds true

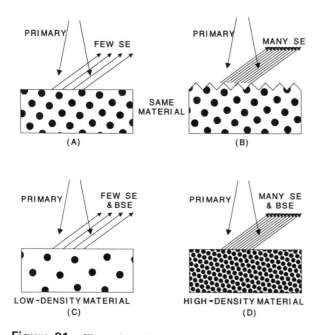

Figure 21 Illustration of topographic and material contrast for SEs and BSEs.

for BSE images as well. Conversely, areas of material having lower atomic number Z and density will appear darker than regions of higher Z with the same topography. The SE yield also depends on the tilt angle between the beam and surface normal of the area being scanned. This results in what is referred to as a surface tilt contrast and is illustrated by the diagram of Fig. 22. Suppression of the SE signal from points behind feature walls or inside holes causes shadowing contrast. This shadowing can be reduced with the use of in-lens detectors, which essentially operate on axis with the electron probe. A dependence of the SE signal collection on the entire surface tilt will exist if the sample stage angle can be varied. However, in most CD metrology SEMs, the stage angle and working distance are fixed. Contrast can also be generated by crystal orientation, magnetic domains, or surface potentials [23].

The metrologic performance of the scanning electron microscope is affected by beam-sample interactions, namely charging. Low-energy SE1 and SE2 electrons are deflected or even totally recaptured by the sample when sufficient surface charge is present. The secondary electron yield δ determines the amount and type of charging on the surface. The electron yield is dependent on the electron beam parameters (accelerating voltage, current, working distance, alignment, etc.) as well as sample properties (tilt, material, pattern, feature size, etc.).

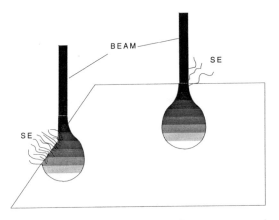

Figure 22   Diagram of surface tilt contrast occurring at a feature edge.

Surface conductivity (i.e., material type) is the primary factor influencing the type of sample charging. There are beam energies where charging at the surface is neutral when the yield δ goes to unity. These are shown in Fig. 23 and are referred to as the E1 and E2 points. The E points vary with the beam and sample properties (i.e., the amount of charging varies). This variation in charging with sample and beam properties is a major factor in the accuracy and precision limitations of SEM metrology. Too high a dose can cause the feature to appear larger than it really is (see Fig. 23). If the dose is low, the image undergoes a tone reversal. Asymmetry can also occur for low dosage. The initial width of the line in Fig. 25a was measured as 0.272 µm. After 60 seconds of

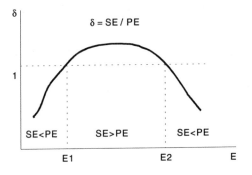

Figure 23   SE yield δ versus beam energy.

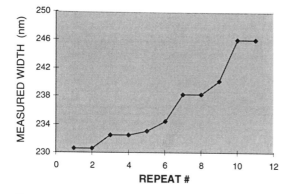

Figure 24 Measured line width versus static measurement repeat number. (From Ref. 24.)

imaging the same feature was remeasured as 0.334 μm. The line also appears to have a dark center region due to tone inversion from charging. A plot of line width versus measurement number is shown in Fig. 24. The first measurement occurred when the picture in Fig. 25a was taken, the last measurement was obtained when the image of Fig. 25b was acquired, and there was 5 seconds between measurements for image averaging. The systematic error component of charging is clearly visible from the plot and produced a drift of approximately 60 nm! Therefore a random distribution should never be assumed when finding

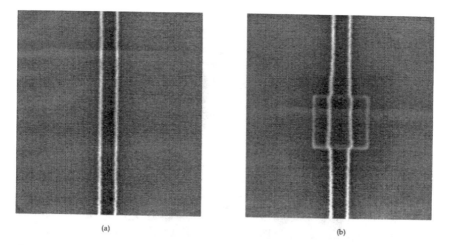

Figure 25 (a) Before SEM measurements and (b) after 60 seconds of imaging.

the standard distribution of a measurement set. In fact, a basic drawback with SEM dimensional metrology is the fact that multiple static repeat measurements cannot be made without increasing these charging effects. Obviously, the accuracy is affected as well.

Current CD metrology SEMs image only in a top-down plan view so that only two-dimensional information on three-dimensional features is obtained. Various algorithms are used to determine the position of an edge within the intensity profile. At present, the most familiar ones are the threshold and linear approximation algorithms shown in Fig. 26. The threshold technique defines the edge location at a point that is some percentage of the maximum. Peak width values are obtained by using the 100%, or peak, intensity level in the image line scan. Linear approximation (LA) values are obtained by using the intersection of a tangent line to the point of maximum slope in the intensity profile and the baseline intensity level of the background [25]. More complex algorithms, such as derivative and Fermi-Dirac fitting, are also becoming available [26]. It should be remembered that the SEM intensity profiles do not represent the actual feature topography. Hence, the peak and LA values do not directly correspond to a particular point on the feature, such as the top or bottom (foot). There are also significant offsets between peak and LA values of line width. The broader the intensity transition at the edge of the feature, the more uncertainty. The spread of this intensity transition is systematically affected by many factors such as focus, stigmation, vacuum environment, detector symmetry and efficiency, accelerating voltage, and probe current. The precision and accuracy are therefore affected as well.

The uncertainties in edge position determination due to measurement algorithms are an important source of error in CD metrology. An example of errors due to differences in algorithms and changes in the magnification and orthogonality is illustrated in Fig. 27, where measurements were performed on the same image under four different circumstances. The linear approximation and peak-to-peak algorithms were used at 30k and 100K. The line widths (lower

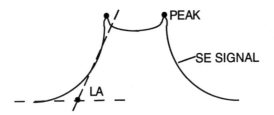

Figure 26   SEM intensity profile with line width threshold points.

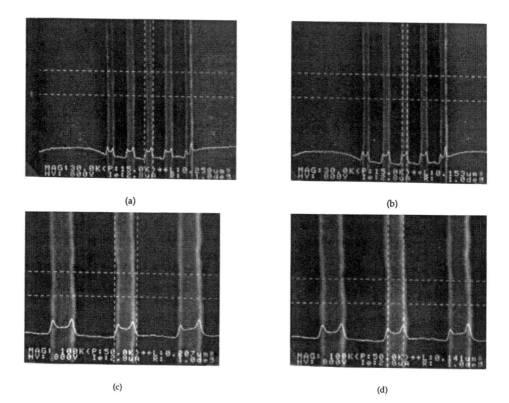

Figure 27 Line width measurements under different conditions: (a) LA 50K×, (b) PK 50K×, (c) LA 100K×, (d) PK 100K×.

right corner of each photograph) are seen to range from 0.14 to 0.25 μm. The fluctuation in line width is approximately 45% of the nominal 0.25-μm design value (Fig. 28). Correlations of line width measurements at each set of conditions to the atomic force microscope (AFM) and cross-sectional SEM measurements can also be made [27]. The condition of peak threshold algorithm at 100K magnification yielded the closest correlation to the AFM and cross-sectional SEM for this type of feature. This condition also yielded the highest repeatability at that beam voltage and current. However, it should be strongly pointed out that the AFM and cross-sectional SEM have errors of their own when making line width measurements. Even with these problems, the SEM is still the metrology tool of choice for submicrometer device fabrication because of its high lateral resolution and throughput.

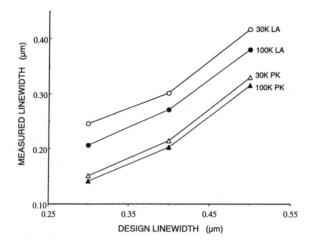

Figure 28   Plot of line widths measured with each technique.

3.4   Scanned Probe Microscopes

Scanning probe microscopes (SPMs) offer an alternative to optical and electron microscopes for imaging submicrometer (and below) features. SPMs are capable of achieving atomic-level resolution for a wide range of materials, even in ambient conditions. Unlike optical and electron microscopes, an SPM does not use optics or waves to obtain images. In an SPM, a needle-like probe is brought very close (<3 nm) to the sample surface and is usually traversed back and forth in a raster fashion. The probe rides up and down at a constant height above the sample, so that a topographic image of the surface is obtained. High resolution in all three dimensions is achieved simultaneously. Accurate profiles of the surface can be extracted at any position in a completely nondestructive manner and a complete rendering of the surface can be created. The main characteristic that distinguishes SPMs from optical and electron-based microscopes is a solid body—the probe tip that is intimately involved in the measurement process.

The scanning tunneling microscope (STM) was the first type of SPM to be widely used [28–30]. In this technique, a metallic probe is brought to within the electron tunneling distance of a conductive sample surface (see Fig. 29) such that a small current (typically less than 1 nA) flows when a bias is applied. The tunneling current flows to or from a single atomic cluster at the apex of the probe. The tunneling current density decays exponentially with distance between the two electrodes (tip and sample). The tip-to-sample separation is regulated by a feedback system that maintains constant current and distance. In this way, the tip is made to track the height of the surface. An image is obtained by

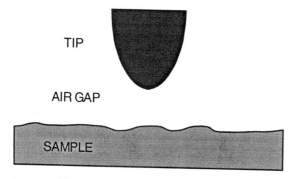

TIP

AIR GAP

SAMPLE

Figure 29 STM tip-to-sample junction in air.

rastering the probe across the field of view and plotting the change in tip position as it tracks the surface. It is the exponential dependence of current on tip-to-sample separation that gives the STM its extremely high vertical resolution (subangstrom). Atomic-scale lateral resolution of the same order is achieved because the current emanates from a single atomic cluster (the ideal situation) near the apex of the tip. Unfortunately, the types of samples that can be imaged with the STM are limited to those having conductive surfaces.

The atomic force microscope [31] (AFM) was developed shortly after the STM. It measures the topography of a surface by bringing a sharp probe very close (within angstroms) to the sample surface in order to detect small forces from the atoms of the surface. Figure 30 shows the force plotted versus distance from the surface. A strong repulsive force is encountered by the tip at distances very near the surface atoms. Contact mode scanning is said to occur when these repulsive forces are used for regulating the tip-to-sample distance. If the tip is

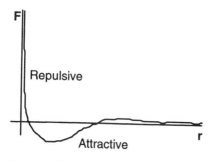

F

Repulsive

Attractive   r

Figure 30 Force encountered by the probe with distance from the surface.

moved away from the surface, a small attractive force is encountered several nanometers back. Feedback control with these longer range forces is employed with the noncontact, attractive, mode of imaging. An obvious advantage of the AFM is that nonconductive samples can also be imaged.

A contact mode AFM is shown schematically in Fig. 31. The AFM uses a silicon tip and a small rectangular beam (cantilever) with an optical source and detector. Repulsive forces between the tip and the sample surface are measured by monitoring the deflection of the cantilever as it is brought into contact with the sample surface. The probe-to-sample distance is regulated by maintaining constant repulsive force between the tip and surface using a feedback servo-mechanism. This type of AFM is said to be operating in the contact, or repulsive force, mode. The vertical displacement of the cantilever is used to obtain topographic information in all three dimensions. The AFM is somewhat analogous to a stylus profilometer, but it is scanned laterally in x and y to obtain images. Atomic resolution can also be achieved with the AFM. Damage to the tip is accelerated by constant contact with the surface during scanning. Deformation of the probe is especially severe when sudden changes in the sample surface height are encountered, such as feature sidewalls. Crashing into feature edges or steps occurs more in this mode because repulsive forces are sensed only in the vertical direction. A noncontact mode AFM senses the attractive forces (not necessarily van der Waals) between tip and sample surface. The tip-to-sample distance in the attractive mode is usually an order of magnitude

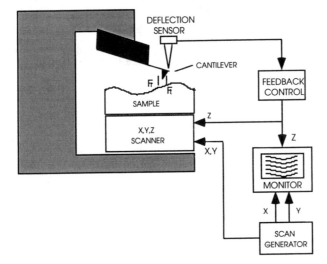

Figure 31   System block diagram of a repulsive-mode AFM.

larger than in the repulsive mode, which helps to minimize unwanted tip-to-sample contact. Lateral forces from approaching sidewalls are also sensed in the attractive mode, which makes this type of AFM ideal for imaging high-aspect features that are commonly found in semiconductor processing. In order to sense attractive mode forces, the cantilever is vibrated at its mechanical resonance and brought toward the surface. Attractive forces from the surface damp the cantilever's vibrational amplitude or shift its resonance frequency. The change in amplitude or resonance frequency is used as the input signal for the feedback loop, which regulates tip-to-sample separation. A major advantage of noncontact operation is that tip shape stability and measurement repeatability are greatly enhanced. However, the accuracy may be more dependent on environmental conditions than in the contact mode [32]. Fortunately, environment can be controlled much easier than tip shape in the contact mode. Recently, an attractive mode AFM (2D-AFM) with feedback control in the vertical and horizontal directions has also been used to perform undercut sidewall imaging [33,34].

As with other microscopes, artifacts are also present in probe microscope images that can adversely affect measurements. Two elements of probe microscopes exhibit strongly nonlinear behavior that can seriously affect measurement accuracy and precision well before atomic resolution has been reached. The first is the piezoelectric actuator that is used for scanning the probe. The second, and probably more serious, problem arises from interaction between the probe and sample. Piezoceramic actuators are used to generate the probe motion because of their stiffness and ability to move in arbitrarily small steps. Being ferroelectrics, they suffer from hysteresis and creep, so their motion is not linear with applied voltage [35]. Therefore, any attempt to plot the surface height data versus piezo scan signal results in a curved or warped image and does not reflect the true lateral position of the tip. A variety of techniques have been employed to compensate for the nonlinear behavior of piezos. In many instruments, the driving voltage is altered to follow a low-order polynomial in an attempt to linearize the motion. This technique is good to only several percent and does not really address the problem of creep. Attempting to address nonlinearities with a predetermined driving algorithm will not be adequate for dimensional metrology because of the complicated and nonreproducible behavior of piezoelectric materials. Another approach is to monitor independently the motion of piezoactuators with a reliable sensor. Several types of systems using this approach have been reported. One monitored the motion of a flexure stage with an interferometer [36]. Another measured the position of a piezotube actuator with capacitance-based monitors [37]. A third group employed an optical slit to monitor the piezotube scanner [38]. Electrical strain gauges have also been used for position monitoring. However, all of these techniques monitor the position of the piezoactuator and not the actual point of the probe that is in closest proximity to the surface (known as the proximal point). The error associated with sensing position in a different plane from that of the proximal point is referred to as Abbe offset. In addition, errors intrinsic to the position monitors are not constant and vary with sample topography as well as lateral scan range—for example, errors in the capacitance measurements when the plates become far apart at the lateral scan extremes. In the optical slit method, $1/f$ noise of the detector at low frequencies (scanning) imposes limitations on resolution as well as complications involved with the slit (e.g., tilting of the slit as the tube scans or aperture edge irregularities).

A problem common to all scanning techniques, including scanning optical and SEM, arises from the imaging algorithm itself. As seen in Fig. 32, data points in a single line scan are equally spaced in increments of ΔX in the lateral direction. The size of each ΔX increment is constant, regardless of the topography, so that there is insufficient pixel density when abrupt changes in surface height (e.g., feature sidewall) are encountered. Scanning reentrant profiles with even a flared probe is also forbidden, because the probe always moves forward or upward and is not able to reverse its direction without the two-dimensional (2D) algorithm.

In discussing probe-sample interactions, there are two main issues that we will cover: the effect of probe shape on image data and flexing of a probe under the influence of various lateral forces between tip and sample. For samples with topographies containing high-aspect-ratio features, such as those encountered in integrated circuit fabrication, one usually wants very sharp probe tips in order to scan areas having abrupt surface changes [39]. Most commercially available probes are conical or pyramidal in shape with rounded apexes. When features having high aspect ratios are scanned (see Fig. 33), they appear to have sloped walls or curtains [40]. The apparent surface is generated by the conical probe riding along the upper edge of the feature. Even if we had known the exact shape of this probe, there is no way to recover the true shape of the sidewalls. The fraction of the surface that is unrecoverable depends on the topography of the surface and sharpness or aspect ratio of the tip.

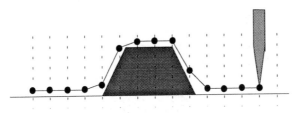

Figure 32   Data acquisition in a standard AFM line scan. This algorithm is common to scanning optical, SEM, and AFM techniques.

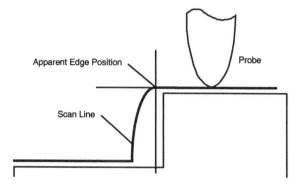

Figure 33   Trajectory of the proximal point as a sidewall is scanned.

In most cases, a cylindrical or flared tip (Fig. 34) will be the preferred shape for scanning high-aspect features [41]. In addition to the fact that simple geometries provide greater ease of correction for probe shape in the image data, the unrecoverable regions are vastly reduced. The probe length determines the maximum feature height that can be scanned. It is also desirable to make the probe as slender as possible in order to increase the resolution and spatial dynamic range. The cylinder may have an advantage in the case of trench and nested features because its bottom diameter is less than that of a flared probe. However, it is possible to make a probe tip too slender. There is evidence that tips with too high aspect ratios (> 10:1) flex in the presence of forces acting from sidewalls. Depending on the elastic modulus of the probe, the maximum length-to-width ratio is typically limited to about 10:1 before instabilities in scanning begin to occur. It is clear that the performance of probe microscopes in metrology will strongly depend on the sample topography. The cross-sectional diagram in Fig. 34 demonstrates the effect of probe shape on pitch and line width measurements. The pitch measurement is unaffected by the probe width, but the line and trench width values are. A sharp conical probe can be used to determine the width of a cylindrical probe [42]. The trench width can now be determined by subtracting the cylindrical probe diameter from the apparent width in the scan. A serious issue facing scanning probe microscopy is throughput. At present, probe microscopes image too slowly to compete with optical or electron microscopes in terms of speed. In addition to imaging time, finding the desired feature is complicated because the physical structure of most probe microscopes excludes high-magnification viewing of the imaging tip on the sample surface. Thus the feature must be found by imaging with the SPM at slow speed, with a limited field of view.

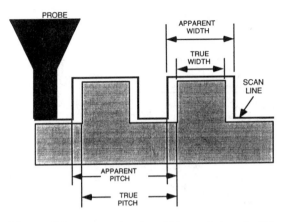

Figure 34   Effect of probe width on pitch and width measurements.

At present, there is only one commercially available AFM that is capable of yielding reasonably accurate dimensional measurements of high-aspect-ratio submicrometer features. This AFM is known as the SXM workstation, which is a noncontact mode AFM and is the product of more than 14 years of research and development by the IBM corporation in the area of scanned-probe technology [43]. The SXM workstation can be operated in two modes—standard AFM mode and critical dimension (CD) AFM mode, which are selected by the user to match the type of measurement desired. Both modes utilize the attractive, or noncontact, AFM method of imaging. In the standard mode, the tip is conical in shape (nominal angle $\leq 15°$) with a sharp apex (radius ≤ 100 Å). A standard mode AFM tip is shown in Fig. 35a. A CD mode tip is shown in Fig. 7b. The boot-shaped CD probe is wider at the bottom than at the center, so that it is well suited to sense topography on vertical and undercut surfaces.

In standard mode operation, the tip is rastered in directions parallel to the plane of the sample (defined here as X and Y) and is servoed in noncontact fashion [44] to maintain a constant tip-to-sample spacing of approximately 20–30 Å. As mentioned in the introduction, this type of scanning algorithm makes uniformly spaced steps across the sample surface. The vertical tip position is recorded at each step, as seen from an actual image scan in Fig. 36. The feature actually had reentrant sidewalls but could not be imaged due to the shape of the probe. The tip position is obtained accurately in all three dimensions from calibrated capacitive position sensors at each axis. Image distortion due to piezoelectric scanner nonlinearity is minimized by using the capacitive monitors to provide the image data. In the standard mode, precise profiles of sample features can be obtained as long as the half-angle of the conical tip is

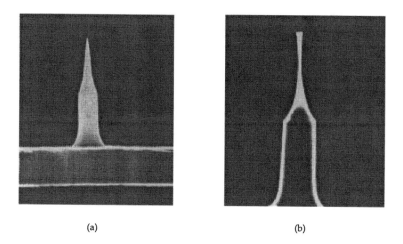

(a)   (b)

Figure 35   SEM micrographs of (a) standard and (b) CD mode AFM tips.

greater than the structure being scanned. A drawback with this mode, as with all other scanning microscopes (including optical and SEM), is that the density of data points does not increase at feature edges or abrupt changes in surface height because of the constant ΔX stepping increment. However, the standard mode is advantageous for measuring subtle topographies and roughness because the sharp apex of the probe provides maximum lateral resolution [45]. In the

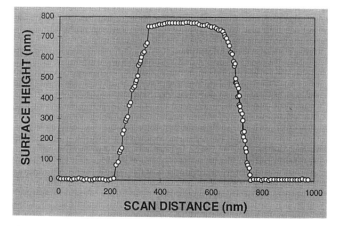

Figure 36   Standard mode AFM image line scan of undercut photoresist feature.

CD mode, the tip shape is cylindrical with a flared end [46]. The bottom corners of the boot-shaped CD tip sense the sidewalls of a feature as the tip scans vertically along them. The position of the protrusions at the bottom corners of the tip is key for imaging the foot of a sidewall, which can be imaged only if these tip protrusions are at the lowest part of the probe body. In addition to the CD tip, it is necessary to have a 2D scanning algorithm that can provide servoed tip motion in both the lateral and vertical scan axis directions in order to image sidewalls. 2D servoing is achieved through the use of digitally controlled feedback and separate piezos in the x and z directions. When the tip encounters a sidewall, the distance between tip and sample is adjusted through the lateral feedback servo. Instead of making evenly spaced steps in the x and y scan directions and providing only a top-down view of the surface, this technique follows along the contour of the surface as shown in the profile in Fig. 37. The local scan direction is deduced from surface slope detection, described elsewhere [47], and is continually modified to stay parallel to the surface. In this way, data are not acquired at regular intervals along x anymore, but at controlled intervals along the surface contour itself. A significant advantage of the CD-mode AFM over all other scanning techniques, including optical and SEM, is that the number of data points can be set to increase at feature sidewalls or abrupt changes in surface height. The CD AFM mode offers a significant advantage in that the tip scans a path that follows the entire surface using the sharp bottom edges of the boot-shaped tip. Real CD width at each Z value can be measured.

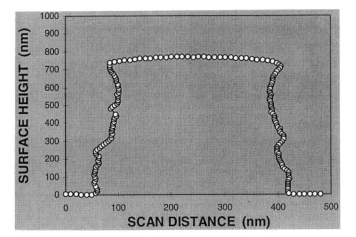

Figure 37   CD mode AFM image line scan of undercut photoresist feature.

Initially, screening experiments were performed in order to determine the amount of averaging necessary during each measurement and the relative weighting of different factors in the precision. As illustrated in Fig. 38, AFM images are composed of a discrete number line scans (in the *X-Z* plane)—one at each value of *Y*. For meaningful precision estimates, each measurement must be performed as close to the same location as possible in order to minimize the effects of sample nonuniformity. The sample uniformity was obtained by imaging along a 20μm length of 0.5-μm-wide equal lines and spaces shown in Fig. 38. The image consists of 100 line scans. CD measurements were taken at each line of the 20-μm section. The parameters for determining the widths (top, middle, and bottom) were found by optimization of the repeatability. The 3σ edge variation was approximately 10 nm and the mean drift in width (uniformity) was about 1 nm. The sample uniformity was sufficient for this study because the positional precision of the sample-positioning stage was approximately 2 μm. Therefore, the measurement location was not a significant factor in the precision estimate. Another important screening task was to determine how many line scans per image are necessary to provide adequate spatial averaging of the line edge roughness in order to reduce the effects of sample variation on the instrument precision gauge. It is desirable to require as few line scans per image as possible due to the relatively long amount of time necessary to acquire AFM data. To determine the minimum required number of scans, alternate lines were

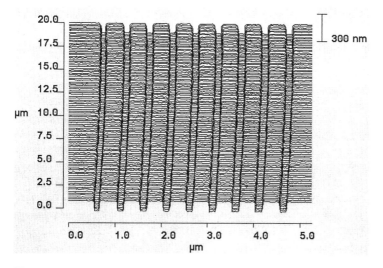

Figure 38 CD AFM image of nominal 0.25-μm-wide oxide lines that were 0.35 μm tall.

successively removed from an image until a noticeable change in the edge roughness value was observed. The minimum spatial averaging for edge roughness (sample variation) was at least eight line scans over 2 µm of length.

Initial repeatability tests performed with different operators indicated that there was no observable operator effect with the SXM system. There is usually very little direct effect of operator technique with fully automated equipment. An automated measurement recipe was run by different operators on the same feature. Once the recipe was created, the feature was consistently located and measured with no assistance from the operators. However, the quality of a measurement program depends on the skill of the engineer who creates it.

Static repeatability was determined by taking 20 successive images at the same location (something not possible with the SEM because of charging). A CD measurement was taken from each image, which consisted of eight line scans. The mean and variance values are displayed in the table of Fig. 39 for both the standard and CD AFM modes.

The CD mode measurements from the repeatability test are plotted in Fig. 40a. The static repeatability values were random in nature. In some cases (see Fig. 40b), older or damaged tips produced data with strong systematic components. Tip erosion was the main cause of the drift in static mean. This assumption was verified by the determining the tip width on the nanoedge calibration structure before and after the static repeatability test. Degradation of the tip plays a key role in the measurement precision and must be tracked carefully. The tip must be replaced when systematic trends in repeatability and changing tip width calibration values are observed.

Gauge reproducibility was obtained by making measurements under different conditions. Determining the most significant factors to vary depends on one's understanding of the physical principles of the instrument's operation.

		Height	Top W	Mid W	Bot W	Left <	Right <
STANDARD	Mean	317.2	185.6	229.2	278.3	79.2	76.4
	3σ	0.4	3.4	4.2	4.7	0.5	0.3
CD	Mean	315.9	179.8	202.6	229.9	82.8	84.9
	3σ	0.5	1.9	3.2	3.4	0.4	0.1

Figure 39 Standard and CD mode AFM static repeatability.

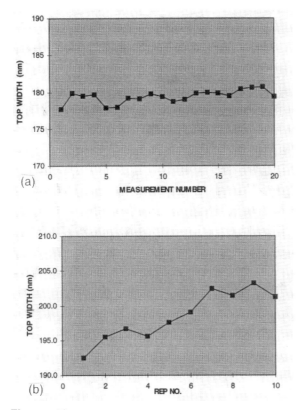

Figure 40 (a) Repeatability of gauge study tip and (b) repeatability of old tip.

Based on the fundamental principles of scanning probe microscopy outlined earlier, the main factors that will be included in this study are the scanning mode, tip shape, and sample loading effects. A diagram illustrating the nested model used in this study is seen in Fig. 41. The highest level contains the scanning mode, with the tip next. There were two scanning modes (standard and CD), two tips each mode, and three to five loading cycles. A loading cycle value consisted of a mean of three or five static measurements. Instead of using a three-level nested model, we found it advantageous to use a separate model for each scanning mode. Due to the three-dimensional nature of AFM data, it was possible to obtain width (at each Z), height, and wall angle (left and right) measurements all at the same time. The reproducibility measurements were obtained on nominal 0.25-μm equal lines and spaces that were patterned in oxide on a silicon wafer. Tip width calibration was also performed before each cycle. The reproducibility measurements for the standard and CD

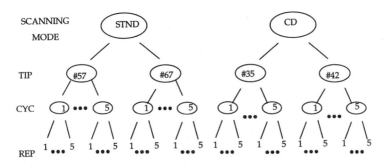

Figure 41 Simplified diagram of the nested model for the AFM study.

modes are shown in Fig. 42 and Fig. 43. The experiment for each scanning mode primarily involved:

x_{ijk} = kth measurement of the jth cycle on the ith tip
$\bar{x}_{ij}$ = average of n measurements in the kth cycle on the ith tip
$\bar{x}_i$ = average of $b \times n$ measurements on the ith tip
$\bar{x}$ = total average of $a \times b \times n$ measurements taken in the experiment

The precision of the AFM in this report is defined as

$$\sigma = \sqrt{\sigma_e^2 + \sigma_c^2 + \sigma_t^2}$$

where σ_e^2 is the component for error (repeatability), σ_c^2 is the cycle variance component (reproducibility), and σ_t^2 is the tip-to-tip variance component. Estimates of these variance components are calculated using the mean squares,

$$MS_e = \frac{\sum_{i=1}^2 \sum_{j=1}^b \sum_{k=1}^n (x_{ijk} - \bar{x}_{ij})^2}{ab(n-1)}$$

$$MS_e = \frac{n\sum_{i=1}^2 \sum_{j=1}^b (\bar{x}_{ij} - \bar{x}_i)^2}{a(b-1)}$$

$$MS_e = \frac{bn\sum_{i=1}^2 (\bar{x}_i - \bar{x})^2}{a-1}$$

and

$$\hat{\sigma}_e = \sqrt{MS_e}$$

$$\hat{\sigma}_c = \sqrt{\frac{MS_c - MS_e}{n}}$$

$$\hat{\sigma}_c = \sqrt{\frac{MS_d - MS_c}{bn}}$$

The carets over the sigmas indicate that they are merely estimates of the variance components. A negative variance component estimate usually indicates a nonsignificant variance component and is set to zero. Variance component estimates can be biased, so the results should be interpreted with caution. The standard mode height precision (see Fig. 42) is on the single-nanometer level, as one would expect. Height data can be gathered very well with the standard mode tip. It can also be seen that the error and cycle components of wall angle variance are quite good. Tip variance is the main contributor to the overall precision. This behavior was mainly due to the interaction between feature upper corners and rounded tip apexes, which occurs in top width measurements. The angle of the feature sidewall was larger than that of the probe, so that imaging of the probe shape occurred instead of the feature. The large tip variance components in middle and top width measurements naturally result from the tip imaging effect.

The CD mode height measurements (Fig. 43) were more precise than in the standard mode and had a variance of $\sigma = 0.5$ nm. The total measurement precision for wall angle was also much better in the CD mode and was a few tenths of a degree. The top width precision was about 2 nm and showed no clear systematic components. A dramatic improvement in middle and bottom width measurements was realized by scanning in the 2D mode with the flared boot-shaped probes. Top and middle width measurement precision values were on the single-nanometer level. The improvement in CD mode precision values was mainly due to the ability to image the feature walls with the bottom corners of the flared probes. This ability essentially eliminated the effect of probe shape on overall precision. The increased number of data points at the feature edges due to the 2D scanning algorithm also helped to improve the CD measurement precision. Threshold levels for top and bottom width locations can also be set more reliably when there is a greater density of data points at the edges.

The AFM has a higher potential for calibration than the SEM and therefore may achieve accuracy, because it scans the surface with a solid body—the probe tip. Once the width of the probe is obtained, it can be subtracted from the raw data in order to obtain a CD value. The tip width will not change with sample material or pattern geometry as much as with the SEM and optical microscopes. A series of etched silicon ridges having sharp apexes can be used to determine the CD tip width. This structure is referred to as the nanoedge [48]. If the tip had zero width, a triangular profile would appear in the AFM image. However, a set of trapezoidal lines is obtained as shown Fig. 44. The width of the trapezoid tops yields the size of the probe's bottom surface, after the width of the feature ridge (<2 nm) is taken into account. Therefore an offset in accuracy of only 2 nm is achieved with this technique. Tip width was found prior to each cycle in order to calibrate the line width measurements. Nonuniformities of the nanoedge sample can produce variations in the reproducibility results

HEIGHT

Tip57 (i=1)	Rep k=1	2	3
Cycle j=1	318	318	316
2	316	317	315
3	317	316	314
Tip67 (i=2)	Rep k=1	2	3
Cycle j=1	317	317	317
2	315	315	316
3	315	316	316

σ_e = 0.9
σ_c = 0.9
σ_t ≈ 0
σ = 1.2

TOP WIDTH

Tip57 (i=1)	Rep k=1	2	3
Cycle j=1	170.2	171.4	174.1
2	174.7	178.3	176.0
3	176.3	170.2	174.0
Tip67 (i=2)	Rep k=1	2	3
Cycle j=1	181.5	185.3	189.2
2	169.2	181.1	174.6
3	181.2	179.6	187.2

σ_e = 3.7
σ_c = 3.5
σ_t = 4.4
σ = 6.8

LEFT WALL ANGLE (DEG)

Tip57 (i=1)	Rep k=1	2	3
Cycle j=1	79.1	79.2	78.9
2	78.7	78.9	79.3
3	79.3	79.3	78.9
Tip67 (i=2)	Rep k=1	2	3
Cycle j=1	76.2	76	76.3
2	75.4	75.9	75.9
3	75.3	75.6	75.9

σ_e = 0.2
σ_c = 0.2
σ_t = 2.3
σ = 2.3

MIDDLE WIDTH

Tip57 (i=1)	Rep k=1	2	3
Cycle j=1	211.2	210.7	216.6
2	224.2	227.4	222.8
3	220.0	222.5	225.3
Tip67 (i=2)	Rep k=1	2	3
Cycle j=1	257.6	256.4	258.1
2	257.1	252.5	254.5
3	253.2	253.8	254

σ_e = 2.2
σ_c = 4.5
σ_t = 24.7
σ = 25.2

RIGHT WALL ANGLE (DEG)

Tip57 (i=1)	Rep k=1	2	3
Cycle j=1	77.7	77.7	78.1
2	77.3	77.3	77.2
3	77.3	77.3	77.3
Tip67 (i=2)	Rep k=1	2	3
Cycle j=1	79.4	79.7	79.9
2	80.4	79.8	79.6
3	80.5	79.8	80.1

σ_e = 0.3
σ_c = 0.2
σ_t = 1.7
σ = 1.8

BOTTOM WIDTH

Tip57 (i=1)	Rep k=1	2	3
Cycle j=1	281.7	273.6	270.3
2	288.4	290.3	281.4
3	275.0	285.1	293.3
Tip67 (i=2)	Rep k=1	2	3
Cycle j=1	297.1	293.7	301.3
2	297.4	292.7	299.9
3	296.4	298.2	293.5

σ_e = 5.4
σ_c = 3
σ_t = 10
σ = 11.7

Figure 42 Standard mode AFM precision test results.

Tip35 (i=1) Rep k=1

Cycle j=1	1	2	3
	315.1	315.1	315.2
2	315.2	315.1	315.1
3	315.6	315.5	315
4	315.9	315.9	315.7
5	316	315.2	315.7

Tip42 (i=2) Rep k=1

Cycle j=1	1	2	3
	315.7	315.5	315.3
2	315.4	315.8	315.5
3	315.3	316.2	316
4	316.7	316.5	316.1
5	315.8	315.8	315.1

σ_e = 0.3
σ_c = 0.3
σ_t = 0.2
σ = 0.5

Tip35 (i=1) Rep k=1

Cycle j=1	1	2	3
	82.9	83	83.3
2	82.9	83.2	82.9
3	83.1	82.8	83.1
4	83.1	82.8	82.7
5	83.4	83	83.1

Tip42 (i=2) Rep k=1

Cycle j=1	1	2	3
	82.7	83	82.9
2	82.8	82.8	82.8
3	82.7	82.9	82.8
4	82.7	82.8	82.9
5	82.8	83	83.4

σ_e = 0.18
σ_c = 0.04
σ_t = 0.1
σ = 0.21

Tip35 (i=1) Rep k=1

Cycle j=1	1	2	3
	84.9	84.9	85
2	85.1	84.9	85.1
3	84.8	84.9	84.9
4	84.9	84.8	84.9
5	85	84.9	85

Tip42 (i=2) Rep k=1

Cycle j=1	1	2	3
	84.7	85	84.9
2	85	85.1	85.1
3	84.8	85	85
4	85.1	85.1	84.9
5	85	84.9	84.8

σ_e = 0.09
σ_c = 0.06
σ_t = ~ 0
σ = 0.11

TOP WIDTH

Tip35 (i=1) Rep k=1

Cycle j=1	1	2	3
	180.1	181.3	179.8
2	181	181.7	181
3	182.1	180.4	181
4	181.9	178.6	181.1
5	178.9	181.8	179.3

Tip42 (i=2) Rep k=1

Cycle j=1	1	2	3
	178.9	178.1	180.3
2	179.9	179.6	178.1
3	180.8	179	177.3
4	178.7	178.4	175.9
5	179	175.5	177.5

σ_e = 1.3
σ_c = ~ 0
σ_t = 1.5
σ = 2

MIDDLE WIDTH

Tip35 (i=1) Rep k=1

Cycle j=1	1	2	3
	205.3	203.9	203.4
2	204.2	204.9	203.1
3	205.8	204.4	204.5
4	205.4	203.5	205.2
5	203.2	206.1	202.1

Tip42 (i=2) Rep k=1

Cycle j=1	1	2	3
	204.1	204	205.6
2	205.6	204.4	204
3	208	205.1	204
4	204.3	205.2	204.5
5	205.4	200.5	202.5

σ_e = 1.4
σ_c = 0.4
σ_t = 0.2
σ = 1.5

BOTTOM WIDTH

Tip35 (i=1) Rep k=1

Cycle j=1	1	2	3
	233.5	233.9	231.8
2	233.3	232.7	232.4
3	233.9	233.4	233.3
4	234.5	232.5	233.6
5	230.9	234.8	232.1

Tip42 (i=2) Rep k=1

Cycle j=1	1	2	3
	233.9	232.1	235.5
2	234.7	233.4	231.9
3	235.9	235.1	234.6
4	232.5	232.8	229.3
5	234.1	229.4	229.9

σ_e = 1.5
σ_c = 0.9
σ_t = ~ 0
σ = 1.7

Figure 43 CD mode AFM precision test results.

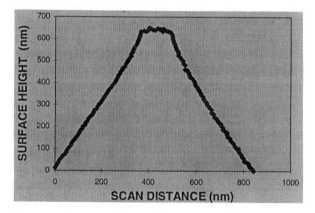

Figure 44   CD AFM scan of the nanoedge used for tip width calibration.

initially. It is very important to note at this point that the precision and accuracy of the CD mode critically depend on, and are somewhat limited by, this calibration procedure.

Linearity and accuracy of each scanning mode were determined after the precision tests were completed. There were positive and negative tones of each pattern ranging in size from 0.2 to 2 μm. For brevity, the graphs and profiles are contained in Figs. 54–61 (pp. 707–710). Linearity and accuracy are difficult to determine because the measured feature size is usually plotted versus the nominal design value. There is usually not a direct linear relationship between nominal design width and the actual width due to the fabrication process. In addition, an offset between the actual and nominal design values exists from the lack of calibration standards for submicrometer features. We shall proceed with our linearity and accuracy assessment keeping this in mind.

Cross sections verified that the topography of the features (dense spaces) was in agreement with the AFM topograph. The cross sections were obtained using focused ion beam (FIB) milling techniques instead of cleaving in order to preserve the sample and provide multiple cross sections at each location for spatial averaging. The lines appeared trapazoidal with obtuse sidewall angles of approximately 85°. For baseline purposes, measurements were also taken with another commercially available AFM system [49]. The system used conically shaped pyramidal probes and higher aspect FIB milled spike probes. Line scans of the nominal 0.25-μm lines taken with the pyramidal and FIB spike probes are shown in Figs. 54 and 55, respectively. The FIB milled probe tip appeared to be bent, a characteristic that produced strong asymmetries in the AFM image profiles. Although the FIB probes had steeper sidewall angles, their apexes were not as sharp as the conical pyramidal probes and therefore produced ambiguous feature top image data. Probe shape prevented both the pyramidal and FIB spike tips from imaging the feature walls and bottoms. A CD mode AFM image line scan of the same feature taken with the flaed probe and 2D scanning algorithm is seen in Fig. 56. The image data in this figure agree with the cross-sectional data. The sides and bottoms of each feature were accurately measured with a resolution better than that of the FIB cross sections and standard AFMs. Sharp conical probes are still useful when maximum lateral spatial resolution is desired and the area of interest (i.e., feature tops) does not have any abrupt surface height changes. Top width measurements obtained with the standard, pyramidal, and FIB milled spike tips are plotted versus nominal feature size in Fig. 57. The distance between upper corners of the features in the AFM images was used for the top width. There is a good correlation (to within the repeatability) between the different systems down to the 0.35-μm trench widths. Top width measurements taken with the FIB milled tips began to diverge for nominal feature sizes less than 0.35 μm. Top width measurements were possible with the pyramidal probes down to 0.25 nominal feature sizes. The SXM standard mode probes, which had steeper walls and sharper apexes, were capable of resolving feature top widths down to the smallest nominal dimension of 0.20 μm. It is also apparent from Fig. 59 that the fabrication process (actual feature size) linearity began to break down below nominal 0.3 μm. The SXM standard mode also exhibited longer tip life than the other system because it operates in the noncontact force sensing mode.

To test the linearity of the CD mode AFM width measurements, correlation to FIB cross-sectional data was made. Due to the nonexistence of reference standards for either instrument, the absolute accuracy of each technique is not known. The lack of absolute accuracy produces an offset between measurements, but the curve shapes should be similar if there is a linear relationship between the two instruments and hence actual feature size. Spatially averaged measurements from the cross sections were obtained by performing eight FIB cuts at each feature dimension location, thereby minimizing edge variation effects that are often encountered in conventional SEM cross-section calibration techniques. The method for determining the AFM widths is illustrated by the surface height plot in Fig. 45. The AFM top width (AFM TOP) was determined by averaging a band of points centered at the 90% level of each edge. The width of each band was adjustable and set to 5% for our tests [50]. The bottom width (AFM BOT) bands were centered at the 10% level and 5% wide. The middle width (AFM MID) is centered between the top and bottom.

Measurements obtained with two different CD mode tips and the FIB are plotted versus nominal in Fig. 58. CD tip 35 was approximately 130 nm in x-diameter, as determined by the nanoedge, and tip 42 was 50 nm. The probes were about 1 μm long, so that the aspect ratio of tip 35 was 7.7 and of tip 42

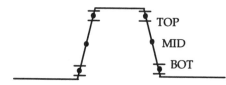

Figure 45   AFM surface profile and edge location threshold points.

was 20. There was a linear correspondence between CD tip 42 and the FIB cross sections over the entire measurement range. However, measurements from tip 42 (the aspect of 20:1) became slightly nonlinear below 0.3 μm nominal, possibly due to flexing of the probe when its width becomes too small relative to the length as described earlier. Furthermore, the amount of nonlinearity and flexure seemed to be dependent on the width of the trench being measured. Linearity appeared to be achieved over all the dimensions of the measurement range with CD tips having aspect ratios less than 10:1. There was good agreement between the standard probe, which does not flex since it is conical in shape, and the lower aspect ratio probe. This strongly supports the notion that tip flexing is the source of nonlinearity for the 50-nm-wide CD tip. It is usually desirable to have as slender a probe as can be fabricated in order to maximize resolution. However, there seems to be a practical limit of the probe aspect ratio of 10:1 beyond which probe flexing effects on CD measurements become apparent. The CD AFM mode and FIB cross-sectional bottom width measurements are shown in Fig. 60. Again, there is a fairly constant offset between the lower aspect CD tip 35 and the FIB measurements (to within the repeatability) as well as the same nonlinearity for the higher aspect tip 42. Linearity tests have also been performed on different samples, such as photoresist features having reentrant profiles [51]. Flexing was not noticed in that case due to the decrease in surface interaction area between the feature and probe walls for the undercut geometry.

In addition to width CD, vertical step height linearity was evaluated. A series of wafers having oxide features ranging from 100 to 1000 nm in nominal thickness was used to evaluate the height measurement linearity. The results plotted in Fig. 61 indicate that the measured heights (obtained with tip 35) are linear with the nominal values. The amount of deviation from nominal (dashed line) at each point did increase as the feature height grew larger.

Correlation with the in-line CD metrology SEM is of great importance because of its dominant role and general acceptance as the tool of choice for submicrometer dimensional metrology in the process line. No correction factors or offsets were applied to either the AFM or SEM measurements when those data were correlated. The SEM PEAK width values were obtained by using the 100%, or peak, intensity threshold in the image line scan. The SEM LA values were obtained using the linear approximation threshold edge location technique [52].

The relative differences between measurement values and nominal for SEM [53] and AFM are shown in Fig. A9. The SEM (peak and linear approximation thresholds) and CD mode AFM (top and bottom width) curves remained parallel to the 0.3-μm nominal feature sizes. The SEM PEAK curve was closer to AFM TOP in terms of offsets but corresponded in shape more to that of the SEM LA. Conversely, the SEM LA had a smaller offset with AFM BOT, but was more similar in shape to AFM TOP. This means that the PEAK and LA values from the SEM intensity profiles do not directly correspond to the actual feature edge positions. The fact that the AFM probe is composed of a solid material and not a beam indicates that the top-down SEM contains the source of nonlinearity below 0.3 um. This conclusion was also independently verified using FIB cross-sectioning techniques. In this regard, the AFM should be a very useful complement to the on-line CD SEM as a means of providing nondestructive calibration and helping to separate changes in the metrology from actual process variations. As seen in Fig. A10, there was excellent agreement between the CD AFM and the SEM curves for the isolated oxide line features at all dimensions. This agreement was not the case for the dense oxide lines, which suggests that the earlier SEM nonlinearity (below 0.3-μm nominal feature sizes) was due to electron beam charging effects from adjacent features as they became nested closer together.

Roughness measurements can be performed using the standard AFM mode. Two samples were chosen. The first consisted of a thermal oxide and the other an etched polysilicon surface. Three successive images were obtained with each tip on both samples. The measurement results in Fig. 46 are expressed in nanometers. It is obvious from the table that both the roughness repeatability and tip-to-tip difference are less than a nanometer.

Orthogonality of the tip motion in the z direction was tested by measuring the slope of an isolated line at different wafer orientations. The slope of each

OXIDE				POLY SI		
rep = N	Tip 57	Tip 67		rep = N	Tip 57	Tip 67
1	2.3	1.8		1	4.5	4.3
2	2.2	1.7		2	4.5	4.5
3	2.1	1.8		3	4.6	4.3
Mean	2.2	1.8		Mean	4.5	4.4
3σ	0.2	0.1		3σ	0.2	0.3

Figure 46 Standard mode AFM roughness values in rms nanometers.

sidewall was obtained using the top and bottom width locations, as described earlier. The difference in wall angle value for the same feature edge at 0° and 180° wafer orientations yielded the tip orthogonality component in one axis. The sidewall angles of Fig. 47 are averages of five static repeats and expressed in degrees. Wall angle measurements were also repeated while using different scanning tubes and tips. A 0.04 difference resulted from the wafer rotation and a 0.2 variation from replacing another tip. A 1° offset was present in all four cases. The combined precision of the stage and alignment systems was determined by recording the position of an isolated line at five sites across a wafer for 40 cycles. The left, right, bottom, and top sites were located near the edge of the wafer (spaced 4 inches apart). The average precision values at each site (units in micrometers) are given in Fig. 48.

The stage precision was an important factor in the creation of automatic recipes. Larger scan ranges must be used to ensure that the feature will be in the image, which adversely affects resolution and stability. Therefore it is important to minimize the scan range by improving stage precision. A scan range of at least 8 mm must be used in automatic recipe creation to ensure that the feature will be in the AFM field of view for all sites across the wafer.

Particle generation of the AFM was tested using a ESTEK WIS-8500 system. The wafers were 150 mm in diameter and the edge exclusion zone on the detector was 8 mm, so the inspected area was approximately 141 cm^2. Standard AFM mode measurements were performed on five sites across each of 10 wafers. Partical densities were recorded before and after each AFM image was obtained. The average change in particle density for the wafers was compared to that of the control samples (no AFM scanning) to yield a difference of 0.007 particle per cm^2.

Capabilities such as user interface (manual and automation), uptime, computer integration, and job transportability are just as critical as the measurement performance in achieving usefulness as a metrology tool. Effectiveness of the

ORIENTATION	TUBE 42	TUBE 44
R(0)-L(180)	1.26	1.04
R(180)-L(0)	1.18	1.00
Mean	1.22	1.02

Figure 47 Sidewall angles for different wafer orientations and tips.

WAFER SITE	PRECISION (3σ)
LEFT	4.4
BOTTOM	4.0
CENTER	3.9
TOP	3.7
RIGHT	3.8

Figure 48 Combined stage and alignment precision across the wafer.

software interface for manual operation and/or automated job setup was the primary consideration when evaluating the user interface. The manual interface was important for ease of training and effective engineering use of the tool. The automation user interface is key to the training of fabrication personel for selecting and running previously created recipes. Once the recipes were created and no more manual input was required, execution of automated measurement jobs was accomplished on the SXM. Automation testing consisted of measuring 0.25-μm lines in each of five sites per wafer. Successful wafer alignment was usually (about 95% of the time) achieved by the optical pattern recognition unit during recipe execution. After alignment, the stage is moved to a predetermined set of coordinates for each measurement site, at which time AFM scanning is performed. Low resolution of the optical viewing system did present some problems in locating the correct sites during recipe setup. The five site per wafer throughput was found to be approximately three wafers per hour. Most of the overhead was consumed by the calibration step, tip approach prior to scanning, the image acquisition of eight surface height scan lines, and the data analysis.

3.5 Electrical CD Measurement

Dimensional measurements can be made by measuring the electrical properties of a conducting feature. Dimensions are extracted from electrical data, such as the resistivity. The values that are extracted from these measurements are really spatial averages over the entire feature volume, so that the CD measurements are completely delocalized in all three dimensions. Only the average volume or area of the entire structure and not the width at a desired region of the feature is known. The feature must also be conductive.

For line width measurements, one must first determine the local sheet resistivity of the layer from which the feature of interest is patterned. This compensates for thickness or doping variations across the wafer. Typical test patterns used for line width measurement are seen in Fig. 49. In this figure, the Van Der Pauw structure for determining sheet resistance is shown. The bridge resistors for line width measurement are located below the Van Der Pauw structure. Precision improves with more bridge resistors due to increased averaging. The square in the center of the Van Der Pauw test structure is the area in which the sheet resistivity is determined. For a symmetric Van Der Pauw test structure, the sheet resistance is

$$\rho_s = \frac{\pi}{\ln 2}\left[\frac{(R_1 + R_2)}{2}\right]f\left(\frac{R_1}{R_2}\right)$$

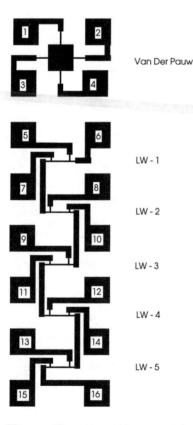

Van Der Pauw

LW - 1

LW - 2

LW - 3

LW - 4

LW - 5

Figure 49   Line width test module.

where $R_1 = V_{2,4}/I_{1,3}$ and $R_2 = V_{4,3}/I_{2,1}$. The factor f is close to unity but must be numerically found for each measurement. The bridge structures are designed to provide a four-terminal measurement of the line width. The four-terminal method eliminates contact resistance problems so that the conducting layer can be probed directly. Multiple bridge resistors are usually connected in series. The widths can be measured by forcing a constant current I between pads 6 and 16. The voltages are then measured across each pair of pads (i.e., pads 5 and 7, 8 and 10, 9 and 11, 12 and 14, and 13 and 15). Line width is then determined using

$$W_i = \frac{\rho_s \times L}{V_i/I}$$

where i denotes which pair, L is the center-to-center distance between voltage taps, and ρ_s is the sheet resistance of the Van Der Pauw structure. An advantage of this technique is that a large number of sites can be measured very quickly.

3.6 Vertical (Height) Measurements

The stylus profilometer obtains vertical step height by monitoring the movement of a large pyramidal probe as it drags across a feature step. The stylus can be scanned only once per measurement, so that a vertical profile across only a single line is obtained. The stylus usually has a relatively blunt apex and a very broad cone angle, which prevented it from measuring the height (z) of features having lateral sizes less than 20 μm in either the x or y direction.

Several problems also arise when making optical depth measurements. As the spacing between adjacent features (such as trench walls) decreases, light from the objective starts to interact with the features. This interaction (reflection and refraction) produces unknown phase shifts that induce false z focus positions. The error between the apparent z and real z is denoted by ΔZ in Fig. 50. This effect increases as the numerical aperture of the objective lens increases (i.e., angle of the light rays with respect to the normal increases). This effect is known as shadowing. For an opaque chromium background, the light would have actually been blocked by the upper trench corners, hence the term shadowing. This also points out a trade-off, with optical techniques, between lateral resolution and vertical height or depth measurement range or immunity to shadowing effects. It is clearly evident that the optical techniques begin to lose reliable depth measurement capability for trenches whose widths are less than 2 μm. At 0.5-μm widths, the optical depth measurement techniques fail completely.

Shadowing can also affect lateral CD measurements. At a given intensity threshold, the resulting line width measurement depends on whether the top or

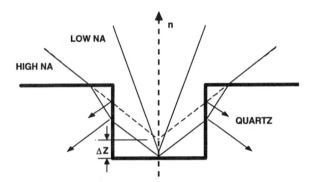

Figure 50   Ray diagram of the shadowing effect.

bottom of the trench is in focus. The difference between the top and bottom line widths also gives an indication of the relative amount of shadowing. The effect of numerical aperture on shadowing is apparent from the ray diagram in Fig. 50. the AFM provides topographic images and surface height profiles directly. Therefore, vertical surface height measurements were obtained for every feature type that was imaged. The measurements were not affected by the proximity of other features, except in regard to tip shape. Scanning probe microscopes can measure depth if the tip width is less than that of the feature (i.e., trench or via hole) being measured.

In one set of experiments, a special reticle known as the Herschel tester was made to test depth resolution and to study the effect of shadowing on vertical measurements. The mask layout was basically a 6 × 4 array. Each element of the array was separated into four quadrants: (1) chromium lines separated by etched quartz trenches, (2) same as the first quadrant but rotated by 90°, (3) un-etched 0° quartz separated by etched quartz trenches, (4) same as the third quadrant but rotated 90°. The trench depth was constant across all columns for each row but was for each subsequent row. In the first row (shallowest), nominally 190 nm of quartz was removed in order to make each trench. The sixth row (deepest) gratings were made by removing nominally 470 nm of quartz for the trenches. The mask contained six different depths whose range covered the depths used in producing 180° phase shifts at G-Line, I-line, and deep-UV illumination wavelengths. At each depth, there were four different trench widths, namely 0.5, 1.0, 2.0, and 5.0 μm. The depth of each row was monitored during fabrication and etching with the use of quartz test windows between the gratings. All of the tools had sufficient vertical resolution to measure the depth difference between rows. The measured depths are plotted versus trench width

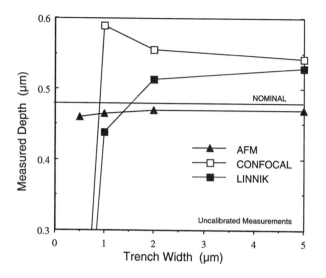

Figure 51 Measured depth versus trench width for one depth on the Herschel tester.

in Fig. 51 for the 470-nm-deep row. The solid line indicates the control measurement of the thickness monitor window by the stylus instrument that was calibrated with a suitable standard [54]. The vertical offset between each curve and the control curve is due to the fact that each instrument was not calibrated to the same standard.

3.7 Pattern Alignment and Placement Measurements

Relative level-to-level alignment, or overlay, can be evaluated by performing measurements on a variety of structures both optically and electrically. Optical techniques are used because of the necessity to image through transparent layers when measuring the alignment between different lithographic levels. A typical optical overlay measurement target is known as the box-in-box pattern. The difference in width of the two rims on either side of the central feature indicates the relative misalignment between levels. This technique is illustrated in Fig. 52. The relative offset between the centers of features is usually measured instead of the widths of d_1 and d_2, thus decreasing measurement error.

Electrical test structures can also be used to measure overlay. The test structure is simply a combination of line width bridge resistors. The first lithographic level defines the first pattern. When the alignment is performed, the

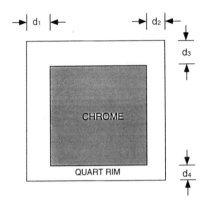

Figure 52   Alignment measurement using a rim-shifted contact pattern.

second structure overlaps the first one. After the second exposure, the material is etched and two sets of opposing bridge structures remain. The alignment offsets are usually in either rectangular coordinates or polar vector representations.

3.8   Pattern Placement: Long-Distance Metrology

Pattern placement is measured in terms of the absolute displacement of the feature from a defined origin on the sample, usually a lithography mask. A diagram of this measurement procedure is seen in Fig. 53. The long-distance metrology measurements have increased sensitivity to temperature changes due to the macroscopic ranges over which they are taken but are still essentially pitch measurements.

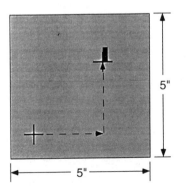

Figure 53   Absolute pattern placement measurement technique for a 5-inch mask.

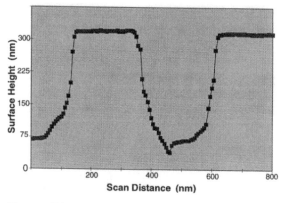

Figure 54

Recent progress has been made in the development of a placement calibration standard at the National Institute of Standards [58]. In-house reference accuracy can be maximized by measuring the displacement after successive 90° mask rotations. For the LMS 2000 (reflection mode scanning slit microscope), direct measurement of the placement of each feature is made possible by the sample translation stage, whose accuracy is nominally 50 nm and repeatability is about 30 nm over a 12.7-cm (5-inch) range. However, the LMS 2000 was not able to resolve features smaller than 0.8 μm and could not measure features whose lengths were less than the slit length (typically 10 μm), such as square contacts.

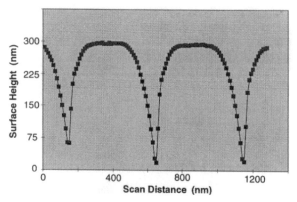

Figure 55

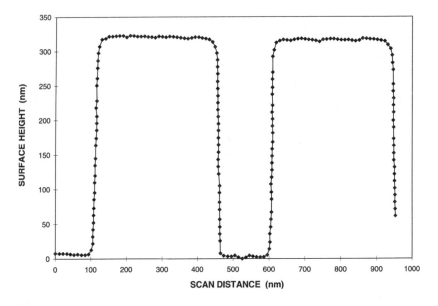

Figure 56 Veeco SXM CD mode AFM line scan of 0.25-μm nominal lines.

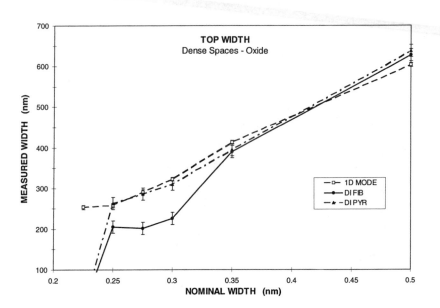

Figure 57 SXM standard, tapping mode AFM with pyramidal and FIB milled tips.

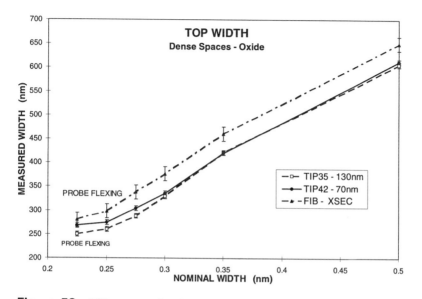

Figure 58 FIB cross-sectional measurements versus CD mode AFM for 10:1 (130 nm) and 20:1 (70 nm) aspect probes.

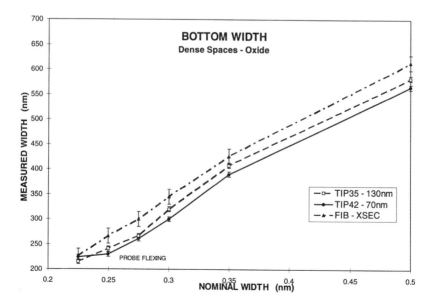

Figure 59 FIB to CD AFM bottom width measurement comparison.

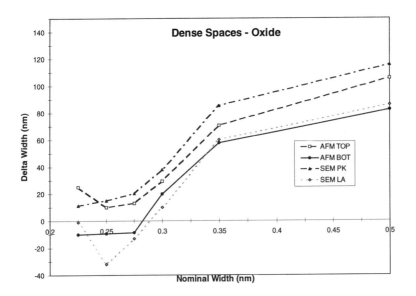

Figure 60 Measured difference (top-down CD SEM and AFM) from nominal for the dense oxide trenches.

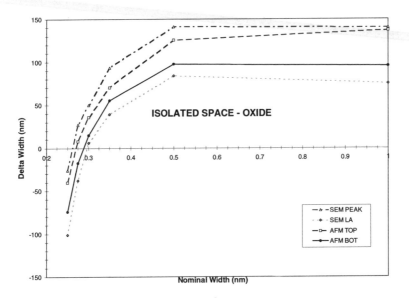

Figure 61 Measured difference (top-down CD SEM and AFM) from nominal for the isolated oxide trenches.

4 CONCLUSION

Resolution is probably the most important characteristic of a metrology tool. It is important to note that resolution is not a constant property of the tool but changes for different types of features. For the optical instruments, the image profiles are strongly affected by such factors as the symmetry of the pattern, proximity of other features, layer thickness, and the optical properties of each material. Diffraction effects mainly limited the optical resolution for feature dimensions less than 1 μm. In addition to size, the geometry of the feature affected the resolution. Semitransparent features were among the most difficult features to resolve. Quartz features were more difficult to detect with reflective mode microscopes because the intensity from adjacent chrome features would "wash out" the intensity reflected by the quartz features. The scanning electron microscope resolution depended on the sample topography and conductance. Even though the AFM possessed angstrom-scale resolution, the dynamic range (i.e., maximum feature height and aspect ratio) was limited by the shape of the tip. For instance, the depth of a trench could not be measured if the probe was too wide to image the inside of the trench. Angstrom precision step height measurement was possible when the bottom of the step could be imaged.

Precision was another key factor in the evaluation of each metrology instrument. Plots of measured line width versus nominal line width for different structures with each instrument revealed that the most linear curves were usually obtained with the SEM and AFM. Asymmetries in the optical profiles of the confocal and scanning slit microscopes, due to hysteresis of the photomultiplier detectors, degraded the repeatability and accuracy, however. Another serious factor affecting the optical microscope repeatabilities was variation in focus.

Finally, the issue of accuracy should be addressed. In order to gain insight into the physical processes occurring during fabrication, dimensions of the features have to be known with a level of certainty. However, adequate calibration standards do not exist yet for three-dimensional and submicrometer mask features. The atomic force microscope has the highest possibility for successful calibration. This is mainly due to the fact that the calibration is not as affected by changes in the material properties, topography (depending on the shape of the probe), or proximity of other features. In order to calibrate the AFM, the tip shape must be characterized. Once the tip shape is characterized, it can be subtracted from the image to obtain a more correct surface topography. The SEM will most likely continue to dominate in-line CD metrology for the next few years because of its nanometer-scale resolution and high throughput. However, a combination of the SEM and AFM in the future may provide both throughput and accuracy.

REFERENCES

1. Box, G., Hunter, W., and Hunter, J., *Statistics for Experimenters*, Wiley, New York, 1978.
2. Nyssonen, D., and Larrabee, R., *NIST J. Res.*, *92*, 195.
3. Hershey, R., and Elliot, R., *SPIE Proc.*, *2196*, (1995).
4. Born, M., and Wolf, E., *Principles of Optics*, 6th ed., Pergamon, New York, 1991, p. 556.
5. Nyssonen, D., and Larrabee, R., *NIST J. Res.*, *92*, 187 (1987).
6. Nyssonen, D., *J. Opt. Soc, Am.*, *72*, 1425.
7. Leica CD 200, Wild Leitz USA, Rockleigh, NJ 07647.
8. Siscan 7325 Confocal Microscope, Sisan Systems, Campbell, CA 95008.
9. Marchman H., Vaidya S., Pierrat, C., and Griffith J., *J. Vac. Sci. Technol. B*, *11*(6), 2482 (1993).
10. Kino, G., Corle, T., and Xino, G., *SPIE*, *897*, 32 (1988).
11. KLA 5000 Coherence Probe Microscope, KLA Instruments, San Jose, CA 95161.
12. Wilson, T., and Sheppard, C., *The Theory and Practice of Scanning Optical Microscopy*, Academic Press, New York, 1984, p. 49.
13. Fowler, R., and Nordheim, L., *R. Soc. Proc. A*, *117*, 545 (1928).
14. Reimer, L., *Image Formation in Low Voltage Scanning Electron Microscopy*, Vol. TT12, SPIE Optical Engineering Press, Bellingham, WA, 1993, p. 15.
15. Fowler, R., and Nordheim, L., *R. Soc. Proc. A*, *117*, 549 (1928).
16. Saito, S., Nakaizumi, Y., Mori, H., and Nagatani, T., *Electron Microsc. 1*, 379 (1982).
17. Casslett, V., *Optik*, *36*, 85 (1972).
18. Reimer, Ref. 14, p. 22.
19. Reimer, Ref. 14, p. 27.
20. Monohan, K., Davidson, M., Grycz, Z., Krieger, R., Schumaker, B., and Zmrzli, R., *SPIE*, *2196*, 138 (1994).
21. KLA 8100 CD SEM, KLA Instruments, San Jose, CA.
22. Baumann W., and Riemer, L., *Scanning*, *4*, 141 (1981).
23. Reimer, Ref. 14, p. 89.
24. Hitachi 8820 CD SEM, V_{ac} = 800 V, I_p = 10 pA, and Magnification = 200 Kx.
25. Postek, M., and Joy, D., *J. Res. Natl. Bur. Stand. 92*, 205 (1987).
26. KLA 8100 CD SEM.
27. Marchman, H., Griffith, J., Guom, J., Frackoviac J., and Celler, G., *J. Vac. Sci. Technol. B*, *12*(6), 3585 (1994).
28. Binnig, G., Rorher, H., Gerber, C., and Weibel, E., *Phys. Rev. Lett.*, *49*, 57 (1982).
29. Binnig, G., and Rorher, H., *Sci. Am.*, *253*, 50 (1985).
30. Simmons, J. G., *J. Appl. Phys.*, *34*, 1793 (1963).
31. Binnig, G., Quate, C. F., and Gerber, Ch., *Phys. Rev. Lett.*, *56*, 930 (1986).
32. Griffith, J.E., private communications.
33. Martin, Y., and Wickramasinge, H., *Appl. Phys. Lett.*, *64*, 2498 (1994).
34. Wickramasinge, H. K., *Sci. Am.*, 98 (1989).
35. Griffith, J. E., Marchman, H. M., and Miller, G. L., *J. Vac. Sci. Technol. B*, *13*(3), 1100 (1995).

36. Yamada, H., Fuji, T., and Nakayama, K., *Jpn. J. Appl. Phys.*, *28*, 2402 (1990).
37. Griffith, J. E., Miller, G. L., Green, C. A., Grigg, D. A., and Russel, P. E., *J. Vac. Sci. Technol. B*, *8*, 2023 (1990).
38. Barret, R. C., and Quate, C. F., *Rev. Sci. Instrum.*, *62* 1391 (1991).
39. Marchman, H. M., Griffith, J. E., Guo, J. Z. Y., Frackoviak, J., and Celler, G. K., *J. Vac. Sci. Technol. B*, *12*(6), 3585 (1994).
40. Griffith J. E., Marchman, H. M., and Hopkins, L. C., *J. Vac. Sci. Technol. B*, *12*(6), 3580
41. Marchman, H. M., and Griffith, J. E., *Rev. Sci. Instrum.*, *65*, 2538 (1994).
42. Marchman, H.M., U.S. Patent for invention entitled Cylindrical fiber probe devices and methods of making them.
43. Veeco SXM workstation.
44. Martin, Y., Williams C. C., and Wickramasinghe, H. K., *J. Appl. Phys.*, *61*, 15 (1987).
45. Griffith, J. E., Marchman, H. M., and Miller, G. L., *J. Vac. Sci. Technol B*, *13*(3), 1100 (1995).
46. Wolter, O., Bayer, Th., and Gresshner, J., *J. Vac. Sci. Technol. B*, *9*, 1353 (1991).
47. Martin, Y., and Wickramasinghe, H. K., *Appl. Phys. Lett.*, *64*, 2498 (1994).
48. Nanoedge sample is supplied with the Veeco SXM system and manufactured by IBM MTC, Germany.
49. Digital instruments 3000 AFM system, Digital Instruments, Santa Barbara, CA.
50. The top location and bandwidth settings were determined by optimizing the measurement repeatability.
51. Presented at the SPIE Microlithography Symposium, Santa Clara, CA, March 10–15, 1996.
52. Postek, M., and Joy, D., *J. Res. Natl. Bur. Stand.*, *92*, 205 (1987).
53. Hitachi 6100 UHR FESEM operating at $V_{acc} = 1$ kV and $I_b = 10$ μA.
54. STM1000, VLSI Standards, San Jose, CA.
55. Teague, E., *AIP Conference Proceedings 241*, Santa Barbara, 1992, p. 371.

13

E-Beam and Proximal Probe Processes for Nanolithography

Elizabeth A. Dobisz, F. Keith Perkins, and Martin C. Peckerar

Naval Research Laboratory
Washington, D.C.

1 INTRODUCTION

In this chapter electron beam and proximal probe lithographies are discussed. These techniques represent the highest resolution and precision reported for any type of lithography. This discussion is cross-cutting to all lithographic technologies in terms of the application of these lithographies to manufacturing, high-resolution resist processes, and basic mechanisms limiting resist resolution. Several schemes have been proposed for the use of e-beam lithography in a direct write mode. Several demonstrations have been reported of e-beam lithography employed in a mix and match with optical lithographies [1]. Shaped e-beam [2] and cell projection machines [3] are used in manufacturing to increase the throughput. Such machines have been used to define dynamic random access memory (DRAM) and patterns with critical dimensions of 0.15 μm. A novel e-beam projection tool is under development [4]. In addition, efforts to build massively parallel low-voltage microcolumns are in progress [5]. In the extreme low-voltage limit, there is very interesting work in micromachined parallel proximal probe scanners [6]. Electron beam lithography is the primary tool of choice for fabricating masks for other lithographies. The resolution and precision of masks for 1× lithography require the nanolithographic capabilities and precision of e-beam lithography.

In this work, particular emphasis is placed on resist processes for high resolution. In both high-resolution e-beam lithography and proximal probe lithography, thin resists are a necessity. This is also likely to be the case for the shorter wavelength optical lithographies and extreme ultraviolet (EUV) lithography. The work discusses the use of poly(methyl methacrylate) (PMMA), chemically amplified resists, and experimental resists such as self-assembling monomolecular layers. Since there is a vast amount of literature on resist performance at submicrometer resolution, this work focuses on sub-100 nm resolution. Particular attention will be paid to the role of inelastically scattered electrons in resist exposure and process latitude in a resist. Basic resolution issues and the role of low-energy electrons are discussed. This is likely to be very relevant to other forms of lithography because as wavelengths become shorter, photoelectrons will play an increasing role in resist exposure. In some cases, photoelectrons have been reported to be the mechanism of UV resist exposure [7].

In the final thrust to small dimensions, the implications of discreteness of the materials and process are examined. Polymeric resists are composed of macromolecules. The radius of gyration is statistical, can be tens of nanometers, and varies with the solvent environment. Chemically amplified resists are multicomponent and the intercomponent distances can be comparable to the critical dimensions. Lastly, the discreteness of the electrons exposing the resist will determine the critical balance between resist resolution and sensitivity.

In the application of e-beam lithography to a wide range of patterns, proximity correction is a necessity. In sub-100 nm dimensions, the range of pattern densities encountered becomes very large. Furthermore, the algorithms and simplifications to electron scattering models upon which proximity effect corrections are based are no longer adequate. The ability to perform proximity correction in sub-100 nm lithography will be discussed. Innovative proximity effect modeling and correction methods are described.

The most newly emerging methods for nanolithography involve proximal probes. Proximal probes have demonstrated atomic-scale precision and resolution. In addition, no proximity effects, as found with high-voltage e-beam lithography, have been observed in scanning tunneling microscope (STM) lithography. The use of the tool for research on prototype device fabrication depends on the development of a viable resist technology. Unlike the high-voltage e-beam writer, which is a mature field, STM lithographic tool development is in an infancy stage. For potential use in manufacturing, it has the drawback of slow speed, as in other serial processes. However, the compactness of an STM tool offers the possibility of developing massively parallel systems. Implementation of such a system requires development of high-speed, low-power ultralarge scale integration (ULSI) servo controllers, well-controlled tip fabrication processes, a remarkable translation stage, and a satisfactory ultrathin resist technology. Developments in micromechanical machining are cross-cutting to this technology. The proximal probe area is a rapidly growing field and it is likely to play an important role in nanoelectronics in the next century.

2 HIGH-RESOLUTION E-BEAM NANOLITHOGRAPHY

E-beam lithography followed soon after the development of the scanning electron microscope [8]. Almost from the very beginning, sub-100 nm resolution was reported. As early as 1964, Broers [9] reported 50-nm lines ion milled into metal films using a contamination resist patterned with a 10-nm width e-beam. Later in 1976, with improved electron optics, 8-nm lines in Au-Pd were reported using a 0.5-nm probe and a 10-nm-thick carbon membrane substrate [20]. In 1984, a functioning Aharonov-Bohm interference device was fabricated with e-beam lithography [10]. Muray et al. [11] reported 1- to 2-nm features in metal halide resists. Except for the more recent reports of atomic resolution with a proximal probe [12], the resolution of e-beam lithography has been unsurpassed by any other form of lithography. E-beam lithography is used almost exclusively for fabricating research and prototype nanoelectronic devices. It is the tool of choice for making masks for other advanced lithographies. Its precision and nanolithographic capabilities are required in mask fabrication for proximity x-ray lithography.

To continue the quantum device effort forward, room temperature quantum effect devices are needed. This requires 10 nm or below dimensions on substrates. To implement e-beam nanolithography into some type of manufacturing process, speed and precision are required as well as control and yield in the nanofabrication processes. The issue of lithography at these dimensions is one of the fundamental limits of e-beam resist interactions, which concerns electron scattering and the sensitivity of particular classes of resists to low-voltage inelastically scattered electrons. The issues of throughput, precision, and yield are relevant to machine design, resist speed, and process control. The design of e-beam instruments is well covered both in this book and elsewhere [13–18]. In this chapter we will examine high-resolution resist processes, the use of high-speed chemically amplified resists, and control of critical dimensions through process control and proximity effect correction. Views of the authors and others are given as to the limits of e-beam lithography.

2.1 High-Resolution Lithography

In laboratory nanofabrication, experimenters choose conditions at which electron scattering causes minimal resist exposure. To achieve this goal, either very high energy or very low energy [19] electrons are used. The former case utilizes as high an energy e-beam as available with existing instrumentation but without causing device damage. Here the beam broadening in the resist through elastic scattering is minimal [20] and the beam penetrates deeply into the substrate. The electrons that are elastically scattered from the substrate are multiply scattered over a wide angular and areal range [21]. These backscattered electrons create a diffuse fog, which ideally creates a homogeneous background subthreshold exposure. The highest resolution experiments further reduce the backscattered electron exposure by using a membrane for a substrate. Low-energy electron approaches are effective because the electrons have too low an energy to scatter over large distances in the resist. The low-energy approach was first proposed by Yau et al. [19] The advantage of the approach was experimentally demonstrated with a scanning tunneling microscope (15–50 eV) by Dobisz and Marrian [22] and later with a 2- to 3-keV e beam [23,24]. There are currently efforts to fabricate low-voltage e-beam columns, but tool design issues in the electron optics to form a small probe are critical [5]. In addition, for a 1- to 3-keV e-beam the range of the backscattered electrons is 50–100 nm, which is comparable to the critical dimensions. The proximal probe approaches do not require focusing optics and are discussed in detail below.

In the first examples of nanolithography and quantum devices, the substrate was chosen to be a membrane to eliminate most of the exposure due to backscattered electrons [25]. The earliest "resist" was formed by carbon contamination as the e-beam passed across the surface [9]. Here the 10-nm-thick carbon membrane samples were coated with a 10-nm layer of Au-Pd by e-beam evaporation. In the e-beam system contamination lines were written with a dose of 1 μC/cm and 8-nm contamination lines were ion milled into the underlying Au-Pd [20]. The Au-Pd crystallite size was 5–10 nm, which was cited as the resolution limit of the process. Contamination lithography followed by ion milling of the pattern into the underlying metal produced the first functioning Aharonov-Bohm device on an Si_3N_4 membrane [25]. Some improvement in lowering the required line dose was observed using an Ar jet containing a mist of pump oil, with line doses of ~0.6 μC/cm (or area doses ~10^{-1} C/cm^2) depending on choice of pump oil and milling time [25]. In addition to lack of speed, this and other e-beam deposition techniques were found to produce additional undesired contamination in the electron column. The need for high-speed, nonvolatile resists was pointed out in the Third International Conference on Electron and Ion Beams in 1968 [26]. At this time the development of PMMA as an e-beam resist also began [27].

Resist Exposure Metrics

In e-beam nanolithography there are three units for specifying the applied dose in a pattern: area dose, line dose, and exel dose. In these cases the applied dose is given in charge per unit area, charge per unit length, and charge per exel, respectively. However, it is the energy per unit volume that is absorbed by the resist that is proportional to the fraction of radiation-induced chemical change that will occur. The energy absorbed by the resist is difficult to measure (i.e., by electron energy loss spectroscopy). Such an experiment is incompatible with the conditions of lithographically defining devices. Hence the absorbed energy in a resist is calculated through simulation and the results are compared to lithographic patterns. The calculation of energy absorbed in the resist depends on the model and algorithm employed. The models have limited success in simulating sub-100 nm lithography, as will be discussed in detail.

For nanolithography in which high-energy e-beams and thin resists are utilized, there is little variation in the energy absorbed in the resist with vertical distance from the substrate. In this case, the energy absorbed by the resist per unit volume is proportional to the area dose. In the center of a large pattern, the area dose is a good measure of resist sensitivity. However, at pattern boundaries the effective area dose is difficult to quantify and depends on one's model for beam broadening. This is particularly important in the case of nanolithography, where the broadening of primary beam is critical and not well quantified. Furthermore in nanolithography, one frequently writes fine lines or dots. In this case it is useful to specify separate values to quantify the applied dose for resist exposure characteristics, namely line dose and exel dose. This allows straightforward comparison of different researcher exposure thresholds, although the effective area dose (not known exactly) really determines the exposure profile.

High-Resolution Resists

In single-component polymeric resists the solubility of the polymer in a solvent is a strongly varying function of its molecular weight. Exposure of the resist results in chain scission or crosslinking. The lower molecular weight polymer dissolves in the developer, so in the former case the resist is positive tone; in the latter case it is negative tone. Polymeric resists are versatile and simple to use since they can be spin cast onto a variety of substrates. PMMA is the standard high resolution polymeric resist. PMMA at lower doses is a positive-acting resist and at higher doses is a negative-acting resist. For line doses the sensitivity difference between the positive resist and the negative resist is a factor of 20–30X. In line dose, the positive-acting PMMA is two to three orders of magnitude faster than contamination lithography [28]. In 1978, 25-nm lines on 50-nm centers were written in positive PMMA on 22.5 nm of Au-Pd on a 60-nm Si_3N_4 membrane [28]. The pattern was transferred to the Au-Pd by ion milling. Similarly 10- to 15-nm lines on 50-nm centers were demonstrated with PMMA as a negative resist [28,29]. In 1983, comparable resolution was reported in lifted off Au-Pd patterns written in positive-tone PMMA on bulk Si and GaAs substrates [30,31]. By the mid-1980s 10- to 20-nm features were fabricated in several state-of-the-art laboratories on bulk substrates. The contemporaneous emergence of quantum well materials made possible the fabrication of e-beam defined gated nanoelectronic devices and some nonlinear optical quantum structures. However, the best resolution obtained by several groups over the course of about 15 years was 10-nm lines in PMMA. Broers [32] suggested that the limitation was due to secondary electrons generated in the resist, although the effect of molecule size and development could also play a role. Chen and

Ahmed [33] reported 5-nm lines in PMMA, by using ultrasonic agitation during development. The work has been difficult to reproduce [34].

Since the demonstration of high-resolution lithography with PMMA, much work has been devoted to the development of higher speed, higher resolution resists [35–37]. Recently, there has been much interest in the newly developed chemically amplified resists (CARs) [38,39]. In the case of negative CAR resists, the e-beam activates the acid catalyst. The acid catalyst activates a polymeric linking reaction during a postexposure bake (PEB) step. In the case of positive CAR resists the e-beam activates an acid inhibitor, which locally impedes the linking reaction or acts as a dissolution enhancer. The fact that the reaction is catalyzed makes the resists at least a factor of 10 faster than PMMA. For example, at 50 kV, one would use a line dose of approximately 0.8–5 nC/cm and an area dose of ~300–500 $\mu C/cm^2$ for PMMA. For Shipley Microposit SAL-601-ER7 [40], one would use a line dose of 0.05–0.3 nC/cm and an area dose of 3–25 $\mu C/cm^2$. (Note that these numbers are approximate ranges from the authors' experience [41–43] over a range of substrates from Si to W and over a range of process conditions for sub-100 nm lithography.) To date, the CARs have very critical processing conditions and environmental control conditions [44]. The problem of environmental control has been most severe in the positive CARs [44,45]. The development of sub-100 nm processes in CARs has only begun [46,47].

Several groups have examined inorganic materials as lower molecular weight resists (smaller component "building block" resists) [57]. Resolution far superior to that with PMMA was achieved in metal halide salts [29,48] metal oxides [49], and semiconductor oxides [50,51], which undergo a radiolysis reaction under electron irradiation. The metal halides have been deposited by vapor deposition. The oxides have been deposited through anodization or radiofrequency (RF) sputter deposition. As pointed out by Muray et al. [48], the exposure mechanism of such resists is very different from that of polymeric resists. At very high doses ($\sim 10^2$–10^3 C/cm^2), holes and lines were drilled into the halide or oxide directly with an electron beam. Feature sizes of 1–5 nm on sub-10 nm arrays have been reported in these cases. Alternatively, some groups have reported that a lower dose converts the metal halide to an intermediate product, which has a different solubility in subsequent development in water than the original fluoride [52]. Both positive- and negative-acting resists have been reported [53]. So far only SrF_2 and BaF_2 have been found to have the same or better sensitivity than PMMA, but not the 10-nm resolution. The fluoride resists exhibited far superior etch resistance to PMMA [53]. However, the sensitivities of most of the resists are considered too low to be practical. Due to their great promise for sub-5 nm resolution, work continues on these resists for both e-beam [54] and proximal probe (as discussed below) lithography.

Another approach to the reduction in large molecule size is the use of self-assembled monolayer (SAM) resists. The self-assembled monolayers have a functional group on one end that chemically bonds to the substrate. The molecules are thermodynamically driven to form a dense film. In the highest resolution envisaged, one would remove or chemically alter one monomer unit, which would determine the resolution. It is possible that the monomeric unit resolution may be realized only with proximal probe lithography, where the electron energy can be set to the threshold value for exposing a single monomeric unit. This is discussed below. For e-beam lithography, the ultra-thin resist essentially eliminates forward beam scattering in the resist. In addition, electrons inelastically generated by the e-beam in the substrate would exit the resist before undergoing substantial lateral travel. E-beam lithography has been performed on both organosilane and organothiol SAM resists [55] and 5-nm minimum feature sizes have been reported [56]. The films, themselves, are not very robust to etching but two methods of transfer of the pattern to an etch mask are under development. The first is to transfer the pattern into a surface oxide mask [55]. The other methods involve selectively building layers on the exposed pattern. This has been applied to STM lithography and is discussed below.

Molecule Size and Shot Noise Limits

As alluded to in the previous section, the issue of granularity will become important to critical dimension control for high-resolution lithography. Thackeray et al. [39] have shown that the distance between photo acid generators in a chemically amplified resist is ~10 nm. Many CARs have as many as four components [44,45]. There has also been concern over the use of large macromolecules to define sub-10 nm features [57]. The average radius of gyration for macromolecules depends on chain length and the degree of coiling, which depends on the solvent environment [58]. Radii of gyration for high-molecular-weight polymers (500K and above) vary from ~5 nm for a spherical configuration to ~30 nm for a loose configuration in a good solvent [58]. In the case of a single-component positive resist, such as PMMA, exposure causes chain scission into much smaller molecules, which may contribute to or determine the resolution of the resist. Because the configuration of the polymer chain depends on the solvent environment, development conditions also play a large role in determining the resolution of the resist, beyond simple contrast requirements. Resist swelling in the developer has been reported by several groups [35].

The other issue in granularity in lithography is in the exposure vehicle, namely the quantum nature of electrons. This results in a compromise between throughput and resolution. One solution to throughput that is currently under vigorous pursuit is faster resists. Shipley manufactures faster e-beam resists than SAL-601 in the SAL series, but for very small dimensions shot noise limitations must be considered. For a dose, D, determined by the resist sensitivity, the number of electrons required to define a feature of area A is [59]

$$N = \frac{DA}{e} \tag{1}$$

The uncertainty in the number of electrons in the area A is $\sqrt{N}$. A 10% uncertainty is the largest that can be tolerated for reliable exposure and determines a critical resist sensitivity limit. At least 100 electrons are required to expose a pixel reliably.

Let us compare the shot noise limit with the sensitivities of commercial resists. The resist sensitivity is determined from the exposure of large areas, over which resist thickness after development can be accurately measured. The resist sensitivity is determined from the measured resist thickness versus dose curve. For a small isolated feature (with negligible backscattered electron dose) the required exposure dose will be $D (1 + \eta)$, where η is the backscatter coefficient. From our Monte Carlo code $\eta \approx 0.51$ for Si [60]. Shown in Fig. 1 is the critical sensitivity (measured from large area exposures) versus feature size. The critical number of electrons in Eq. 1 is cor-

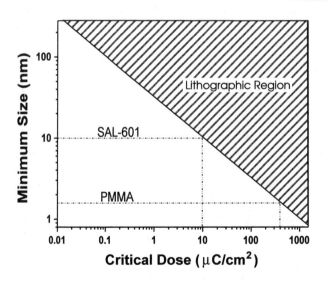

Figure 1 Effect of discrete electron exposure: critical resist sensitivity versus minimum feature size (Si substrate).

rected for negligible backscattered electrons. Under postexposure bake conditions of 1 minute at 105°C, the sensitivity of SAL-601 was ~20 $\mu C/cm^2$ on an Si substrate. From Fig. 1, feature sizes down to 7 nm could be fabricated with this sensitivity. The critical sensitivity for 10-nm features is 10 $\mu C/cm^2$. Sensitivities in this range and faster have been observed for SAL-601 in other bake conditions and on other substrates, such as W [41–43]. From shot noise considerations, much faster resists than SAL-601 could be used for 100-nm dimensions and possibly down to 50 nm reliably. PMMA, with a sensitivity of 300–500 $\mu C/cm^2$, could be used to define dimensions of ~1.5 nm. One can see that dimensions of 1 nm and below require very insensitive resists, ≥ 1 mC/cm^2.

2.2 Proximity Effects at 100 nm and Below

In e-beam exposure of materials the region of exposure is larger than the size of the incident probe. This is due to electron scattering in the resist and from the substrate. The bulk of the electrons suffer collisions, creating small angular deviations from the direction of incidence of the primary electron beam. These electrons lose little energy on scattering and are described as "forward scattered." Forward scattering creates a narrow skirt around the primary beam. Some electrons undergo multiple scattering events or a single strong scattering event. These are most likely in higher Z materials and thick materials. In bulk substrates a large fraction of these electrons multiply scatter and propagate back to the surface of incidence and are referred to as "backscattered electrons." In e-beam lithography, electron backscattering occurs primarily from the substrate into the resist. The backscattered electron distribution is much broader in space than the forward scattered component. Chang [61] proposed a two-Gaussian model to describe resist exposure from a point source. A higher intensity Gaussian with narrower width describes the incident beam broadening in the resist, and a less intense broader Gaussian describes the distribution of resist exposure due to backscattered electrons. The narrower Gaussian describes resist resolution and minimum feature size. The backscattered electrons cause proximity effects. Proximity effects can be broken into two classes: inter- and intraproximity effects. In interproximity effects the printed feature size, shape, and correct dose depend on pattern density. In intraproximity effects the printed feature shape and dose depend on feature size. Proximity effects can cause gross pattern distortions and limit the ability to resolve critical dimensions.

In common practice, a Monte Carlo code is run that tracks scattered electrons in the resist and substrate and computes the energy per unit volume that they deposit in a resist. The computed energy deposition distribution in the resist is then fit to two Gaussians. The two-Gaussian model forms the basis of most proximity effect correction schemes, which utilize physical methods, dose correction, and pattern shape bias [62].

Physical Methods to Maximize Resolution and Minimize Proximity Effects

In nanolithography, one frequently wishes to fabricate fine features in very dense patterns. In this case the integrated backscattered electron dose brings the dose surrounding the feature(s) near the threshold exposure level. One way to reduce the backscattered electrons is to effectively lower the atomic mass of the substrate through the use of a trilevel resist. Improved resolution has been observed [63] and the technique has been developed extensively for gate fabrication. A drawback in the technique is the large aspect ratio required in the resist system, and the wall profile is not to suitable to a wide range of applications. Another way to minimize the backscattered electron dose is to use a high-energy e-beam. Jackel et al. [21] showed that on Si the width of the backscattered Gaussian varies with energy to the 1.7 power. It has been shown experimentally that the use of higher energy e-beams increased the dose latitude for forming fine features. For lines on 70-nm centers on GaAs, Craighead et al. [30] showed a factor of 3.4 reduction in slope of log(line width) versus log(dose) between beam energies of 20 and 120 keV. A similar increase in dose latitude by increasing the beam energy from 50 to 100 kV was more recently found in x-ray mask fabrication on W absorber substrates [64,65].

Dobisz et al. [41–43] showed that the inclusion of a thin (50–200 nm) layer of SiN_x between the substrate and the resist reduced the number of secondary electrons from the substrate that entered the resist. This improved resolution and resulted in a reduction in proximity effects. Shown in Fig. 2a is line width versus grating period for lines in the center of a grating on a W substrate with and without a 200-nm-thick SiN_x layer, at the same line dose. The resist was 80 nm of SAL-601, which was exposed at 50 kV with a 10-nm σ Gaussian probe. One can see that the line widths are consistently smaller and finer gratings can be defined when the nitride layer is present. In fact, the 100-nm period grating could not be resolved without the nitride layer, even at lower doses. The effect has also been observed in PMMA, but it is smaller and more difficult to observe due to the high resolution of PMMA [41]. Shown in Fig. 2b is the energy spectrum of electrons emitted from the W substrate with and without a 200-nm layer of SiN_x measured by scanning Auger. One can see a dramatic reduction in secondary electrons emitted from the substrate with the nitride layer. Backscattered electron measurements showed no difference due to the presence of the nitride, in agreement with Monte Carlo simulations [42]. In this case, inelastically produced secondary electrons contributed to the existing proximity effects. As discussed below, the effects of the lower energy secondary electrons become important at dimensions of 100 nm and below.

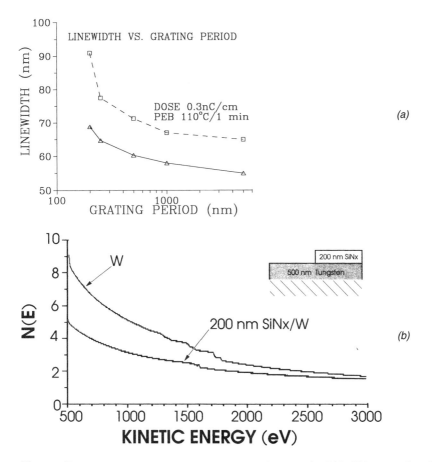

Figure 2 (a) Line width versus grating period for lines in SAL-601 exposed at 50 kV, 0.3 nC/cm on two substrates: W and W coated with 200 nm of SiNx. (b) Integrated scanning Auger spectra of electrons emitted from the two substrates in (a). The incident electron energy in (b) was 25 kV. (From Ref. 41.)

The Nature of Proximity Effects at Sub-100 nm Dimensions

A dramatic example of the challenges to proximity effect control at small dimensions is illustrated in the control of a gap size between two pads. A tower pattern, shown in Fig. 3, is commonly used to examine proximity effects. In the work described here a series of pads at 0.5, 1, 2, 5, 10, and 20 μm were written. A critical dimension gap was defined in the center of the pads.

Shown in Fig. 4 is the dose window ($\mu C/cm^2$) to produce the coded gap width within ±10% error versus pad width. The pattern was defined in the 150-

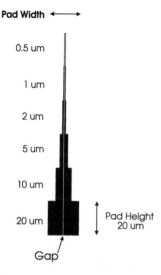

Figure 3   Diagram of tower pattern for studies of proximity effects in resists.

nm-thick SAL-601 resist with a 50-keV, 10-nm σ Gaussian probe. The gap width was measured as a function of dose and pad width. The figure contains separate plots for three different coded gap widths, 500, 200, and 100 nm. In each graph with increasing pad width, one can see a shift in the centroid of the dose window and a transition in the width of the dose window at 5-μm pad width. The smaller pads have a larger dose range and the doses are centered around higher values than in the cases for the larger pads. This is expected from the backscattered electrons, for which a Gaussian fit to the Monte Carlo code gives a 7-μm the width. However, more dramatically, between Fig. 4a, b, and c there is a large reduction in the dose latitude with a reduction in gap width. For the 20-μm pads, the 500-nm gap can be defined with a $\pm$32% dose latitude; the 100-nm gap requires a dose accuracy of better than $\pm$3%. The dimensional variation between 500 and 100 nm is negligible compared to the 7-μm backscattered electron radius. The variation in dose latitude here with feature dimension is not due to backscattered electrons. A large part of the error is due to the higher precision (in $\pm$ nm) required to define a 100-nm gap. If an error limit of $\pm$10 nm was imposed on the 500-nm gap, the dose window would be reduced substantially. But the dose window is still larger than the case for the 100-nm gap (by a factor of ~2.5) [66]. Scattering that is negligible for dimensions of 500 nm and above is no longer negligible at 100 nm. Shorter range processes become important and result in proximity effects.

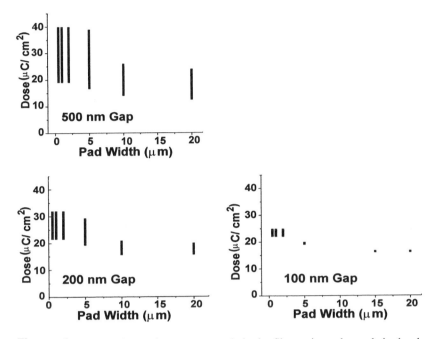

Figure 4 Effect of gap size on process latitude. Shown in each graph is the dose range over which each gap was defined within ±10% error as a function of pad width. Each graph was taken for 150-nm-thick SAL-601 on Si exposed at 50 kV and postexposure baked at 105°C for 1 minute. (From Ref. 60).

At dimensions above ~0.25–0.5 μm, the double-Gaussian approximation describes lithographic pattern definition pretty well. However, at dimensions of 100 nm and below, several complications in the application of the two-Gaussian model arise. First, two Gaussians underestimate resist exposure in the ~100-nm regime as shown through Monte Carlo simulation [67] and experimental measurements [68]. Kyser [69] showed that the inelastically created secondary electrons must be accounted for in determining resolution. At 100-nm dimensions the effect is no longer negligible due to the range of the secondary electrons and the use of thin resists. In thin resists, the elastic scatter broadening of the e-beam is minimal, <5 nm [60], and it no longer dominates the effects of the inelastic electrons. Through three-dimensional simulation, Marrian et al. [70] showed that fast secondary electrons were the chief source of exposure in the 100–1000-nm range and the effects of the fast secondaries were most apparent in thin resists. Rishton et al. [71] measured the penetration depths of secondary electrons and showed that above 300 eV the penetration depth varied with energy to the 1.35 power. The underestimation of the forward Gaussian and resist exposure in the 100–1000-nm range means that the forward Gaussian and its wings will contribute to proximity effects, in addition to backscattered electrons. Several groups have shown systematically that as 100-nm dimensions are approached the dose latitude decreases sharply. McCord et al. [64] and Cummings et al. [65] demonstrated this with line widths in PMMA and SAL-601, respectively.

In addition to the wings on the forward Gaussian, there are many concerns about the application of the Monte Carlo codes to higher atomic mass substrates (such as subtractive patterned x-ray masks). Rishton and Kern [68] showed that on high-atomic-number substrates, such as GaAs, a Gaussian does not describe the distribution of backscattered electrons. Marrian et al. [70] showed that on high-Z substrates, the Mott cross section described electron scattering more accurately than the Rutherford cross section, which is the basis for most electron scattering Monte Carlo codes. To fit the data to a closed-form expression for proximity correction, multiple Gaussian [67,72] or mixed Gaussian and exponential [68] expansion approaches have been employed.

Even with the inclusion of fast secondary electrons, the Monte Carlo code underestimates the width of the forward Gaussian in thin resists in nanolithographic applications. There is a great deal of evidence suggesting that secondary electrons have a deleterious effect on the resolution of polymeric resists. Broers et al. [20] showed budding in a cross-written on a 10-nm AuPd layer on a 10 nm of free standing C membrane, from which backscattering was minimal. Rishton et al. [71] showed that 100- to 200-eV electrons can penetrate as far as 10 nm and lower energy electrons penetrated ~5 nm in PMMA. Muray et al. [48] showed that the exposure mechanism of the inorganic resists is different from that of polymeric resists. In addition, the inorganic resists are far less conducting to electron transport than some organic resists. STM results, described below, show that SAL-601 is considerably more conducting to low-voltage electrons than PMMA. Electronic conduction and sensitivity to low-voltage electrons may be additional factors that limit the resolution of e-beam resists. There is substantial question as to whether the limiting factor is the resist process or an underestimate in the forward Gaussian width. Although the resist process optimization is critical, a reduction in resist exposure by scattered electrons will always improve the resist process latitude.

In contrast to the submicrometer regime, the forward Gaussian width has a large effect on proximity effects and the ability to define sub-100 nm critical dimensions reliably. This is due to the finite size of the probe in commercial e-beam writers and the fact that the beam broadens more in a real resist than expected from Monte Carlo simulation. The effect of forward beam broadening is shown in Fig. 5. Here the calculated energy absorbed by a thin resist is plotted versus the distance from the center of a 100-nm gap. The results for 0.5- and the 20-μm pads are shown for three different forward Gaussian standard devi-

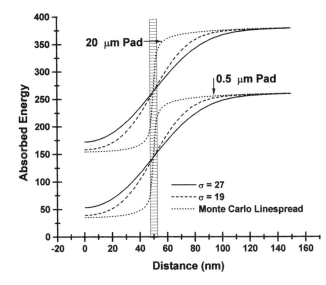

Figure 5 Effect of forward Gaussian width of line spread function on process latitude. Calculated absorbed energy versus distance from center of a 100-nm gap. Line spread functions obtained by three methods: Monte Carlo code, measured in SAL-601, measured in PMMA. The shaded region is ±10% the coded gap dimension. (From Ref. 60.)

ations (σ). Two of the forward Gaussian σ values were measured in ~100-nm resist with a 50-kV probe as 19 nm for PMMA and 27 nm for SAL-601, for tool probe σ values of 8 and 10 nm, respectively [60,66]. The third forward Gaussian was that generated by the Monte Carlo code and models what might be expected from a nanoprobe in an ideal, "Monte Carlo" resist. The dotted box denotes the gap width ±10% error.

One can see that the dose latitude is by far the largest with a nanoprobe and a Monte Carlo resist. In fact, in this case the same dose could be used to define the gap through both the 0.5 and 20-μm pads. However, when commercial e-beam nanowriter probes are employed and realistic beam broadening is present, the process latitude and the ability to form a gap are severely reduced. The Monte Carlo code predicts a broadening of <5 nm, which would be convolved with the tool spot size. The forward Gaussian σ was broadened in PMMA by 17 nm beyond the 8-nm probe width. This is more than a factor of 2 larger than expected by combined forward scattering and secondary electron penetration depths. The SAL-601 σ was broadened by 25 nm. At 100 nm dimensions, the effective beam size has a more pronounced effect on process latitude than resolution. Craighead et al. [30] and Howard et al. [31] attributed their ability to resolve 50-nm period gratings on bulk substrates to their very fine 2-nm-diameter probe.

Using a precisely determined dose, it is possible to fabricate a high-resolution grating of lines (at least in the center of the grating) with a commercial nanowriter. As an example, shown in Fig. 6 are 12-nm lines in a 60-nm period grating in PMMA on a 600-nm W film on Si, written with the same size Gaussian probe as used in Fig. 5. However, the lines were underexposed at the edge of the grating and there was little process latitude. Proximity effect correction will be needed to define the entire high-resolution pattern. The challenges in proximity effect correction at sub-100 nm dimensions will be discussed below.

Dose Correction

One of the major practical problems associated with proximity effects is line width control. Exposure contrast between exposed field and unexposed field varies with feature size and pattern density. Owens and Rissman [73] noted that when the forward Gaussian was extremely narrow compared to the feature size and that the backscattered Gaussian contributed to the inhomogeneous dose background. They demonstrated a dose equalization method, in which they "paint" the unexposed field with a broad blurred beam to equalize the background dose. This method is called GHOST and is described elsewhere in this book [62]. In sub-

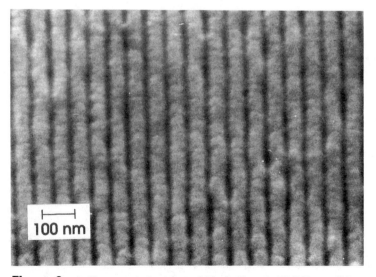

Figure 6 A 60-nm period grating of 12-nm lines in PMMA on 600 nm of W on Si, exposed at 50 kV in a JEOL JBX-5DII with a dose of 0.83 nC/cm. (From Ref. 41.)

100 nm lithography, the extent to which this method will work is not clear. The primary assumption, that the forward Gaussian width is negligibly small and does not contribute to edge contrast, is no longer valid, as shown above. In addition, recent work has shown a geometry dependence to GHOST contrast [74].

A more precise and much more computationally intensive method for proximity effect control is dose modulation. Here one adjusts the dose applied to each pixel in such a way as to account for interpixel interaction and to achieve a maximally flat dose through the feature. Generally, one expresses the effect of this "interpixel energy leakage" as the convolution of the blurring function $M(r)$ of the incident beam with the incident pixel dose $d_I(r)$. The effect of this blurring on the pixel absorbed dose is expressed as

$$d_A(r) = \int_{r'} M(r - r') d_I(r') \, dr' \tag{2}$$

The blurring function is the convolution of the point spread function with some aperture function for the electron optical system. If the two-Gaussian model holds and if the first Gaussian can be separated from the second Gaussian, the blurred dose distribution can be taken to be a sum of forward and backscattered Gaussians,

$$M(r) = \frac{1}{\pi(1+\eta)} \left[\frac{1}{\beta_f^2} \exp\left(-\frac{r^2}{\beta_f^2} \right) + \frac{\eta}{\beta_r^2} \exp\left(-\frac{r^2}{\beta_r^2} \right) \right] \tag{3}$$

where the prebracket term is a normalization factor, η is the backscatter coefficient equal to the fraction of incident electrons backscattered, r is the distance from the center of the pixel, and β_f and β_r are the effective widths of the forward and backscattered beam, respectively.

The point spread function can either be measured experimentally or estimated with a Monte Carlo type of calculation [75]. In order to fit the resulting data to closed-form expressions, a Gaussian expansion approach has been employed for 100-nm dimensions.

One generally specifies $d_A(r)$ and tries to solve for $d_I(r)$. This can be expressed in matrix form:

$$\mathbf{d}_A = \mathbf{M} \bullet \mathbf{d}_I \tag{4}$$

Here $\mathbf{d}_A(r)$ is a column vector, each of whose entries $d_{A,i}$ is the total energy absorbed in a specific pixel; $\mathbf{d}_I(r)$ is also a column vector, each of whose entries $d_{I,i}$ is the individual dose applied to the ith pixel; $\mathbf{M}$ is an interaction matrix, derived from the point spread function. The strategy is to invert $\mathbf{M}$ and solve for the required incident dose at each pixel.

For high-density patterns as expected in nanolithographic applications, this can be computationally time consuming. In addition, in a large matrix representing a very dense data set, rows or columns may appear identical from the viewpoint of computer analysis. This leads to the appearance of a singular non-invertible matrix. Lastly, there is a problem if one wishes to write a square feature or edge of width equal to the width of the peaked dose distribution.

Peckerar et al. [76] have proposed a new method for computing dose correction. Instead of working to invert the matrix, one works toward a generalized optimization. Here a cost function f is defined as

$$f = (\mathbf{M} \bullet \mathbf{d}_I - \mathbf{d}_A)^t = (\mathbf{M} \bullet \mathbf{d}_I - \mathbf{d}_A) \tag{5}$$

If $\mathbf{M}^t = \mathbf{M}$, Eq. 5 becomes quadratic, and f can be minimized by varying the individual pixel doses. As in matrix inversion, the solution for optimal doses here can require negative doses, which are physically unrealistic. However, here one can constrain the solution to positive numbers by using Lagrange multipliers. A functional form, i.e., a "regularizer," is added to Eq. 5 which becomes very large at negative doses and small when the $d_{A,i}$ are positive. The regularizer chosen [76] is the entropy of the dose image, S,

$$s = \sum_i \frac{d_i}{d_T} \ln\left(\frac{d_i}{d_T}\right) \tag{6}$$

where d_i is the individual exel dose and d_T is the total dose summed over all exels. The new cost function f' becomes

$$f' = f - \lambda S \tag{7}$$

The optimization algorithm is also computationally intensive and requires accurate point spread functions for sub-100 nm lithography. However, a dedicated analog integrated circuit coprocessor has been designed and is capable of solving the problem for data sets containing in excess of 10^{10} pixels in times on the order of hours [74].

2.3   Resist Process Latitude at Sub-100 nm Dimensions

State-of-the-art microelectronic manufacturing processes are at 0.35–0.5 μm critical dimensions and approaching 0.25 μm. There is a vast amount of literature on resist processes in this dimension range, mostly for optical lithography. Particular emphasis has been placed on chemically amplified resists over the past 6–8 years [77]. In contrast, there has been only limited work on the process latitude and kinetics for sub-100 nm lithography. Reported work on resist processes for PMMA and SAL-601 is outlined below.

For positive-tone PMMA, initial work in nanolithography was performed with the resist developed for 15–50 seconds in 1:3 methyl isobutyl ketone (MIBK):isopropanol. Broers [32] measured the line spread function of PMMA on a membrane and resist contrast for one development condition and attributed the minimum line width (10 nm) and line-to-line spacing (45 nm) to secondary and elastically forward scattered electrons.

Beaumont et al. [78] used an 8-nm probe and 60-nm PMMA on a 30-nm carbon support film and showed 20-nm lifted off Pt-Pd lines on 50-nm centers. For periods less than 50 nm the liftoff failed. They reported that Pt-Pd had finer grains than Au-Pd. Beaumont et al. [78] reported that it was possible to fabricate 10-nm lifted off lines just above the critical dose needed for development through to the substrate. However, it was difficult to control the line width and form continuous lines until the dose was increased by a factor of 1.13 and 16-nm lines were produced. Examination of metal-coated resist lines showed that the line edges were rounded on the top over distances of 10–15 nm. The slope at the top of the line edge wall did not change with increasing dose and the overcut was not predicted by a Monte Carlo simulation. The edge profile on the top of the resist was found to limit the minimum line-to-line spacing and was attributed to a development effect.

The Bell Laboratories group [30,31] used a different development process of 10–30 seconds in 3:7 ethylene glycol monoethyl ether (Cellosolve):methanol and achieved similar resolution on Si and GaAs substrates. To our knowledge, there is no comparison of the MIBK solution to the Cellosolve solution in terms of ultimate resolution and line-to-line spacing. Chen and Ahmed [33] reported 5- to 7-nm features using the Cellosolve-based developer, claiming that ultrasonic agitation during development broke up the molecules and facilitated development. Hoole and co-workers [34] examined the ultrasonic agitation and found it produced a 20% increase in resist sensitivity but no change in resist contrast or resolution. They reported that in the absence of ultrasonic agitation, the contrast increased from 6.3 to 11.6 for development time increases from 5 to 25 seconds. However, the increased development time also resulted in 10% additional resist swelling as measured in 2-μm boxes.

CARs are attractive because they are frequently more chemically resistant to subsequent microelectronic processing than PMMA and are more sensitive. Some resists have demonstrated sub-100 nm resolution. However, the application of these resists to ultrahigh resolution has been difficult. CARs are complicated by diffusion of the components [79], which is difficult to quantify and sensitive to environmental parameters [80]. In addition, although these resists have high contrast (≥6), the resist thickness versus dose development curves exhibit low exposure tails that effectively worsen the proximity effects. Chiong et al. [46] showed that different resists have different relative sensitivities to low exposure doses, and those that were the least sensitive to these low doses exhibited the highest resolution.

Some of the internally developed IBM resists have been reported to have sub-100 nm resolution [81,82]. Hoechst Ray-PN has produced line widths of 35 nm, but with sensitivity comparable to that of PMMA [83]. Hoechst Ray-PF has produced similarly fine features, but its sensitivity depends on the delay time in air and the resist interacts with environmental parameters. It exhibits excellent dry-etch resistance [84].

Shipley SAL-601 is probably the most extensively studied chemically amplified resist for sub-100 nm dimensions. The reason is that it has demonstrated high resolution and it is more environmentally robust than many chemically amplified resists. In addition, several chemically amplified resists are too fast for the clock speed of specialized nanolithography tools. So far, 20-nm features are the best reported resolution in the resist [47,85]. In SAL-601, the PEB is the most critical step in the process control. It is thought that acid diffusion during the PEB limits the resolution. The author has produced 40- to 50-nm lines under several PEB conditions [41–43].

A detailed examination of the PEB process for SAL-601 was reported by Dobisz and Marrian [60,66]. Shown in Fig. 7 are resist thickness versus dose curves of a 20-μm pad after PEB at 105°C for 1, 3, and 10 minutes. The curve for a sample baked at 110°C for 1 minute overlaps the curve shown for the 3-minute PEB. The resist sensitivity changes by a factor of ~4 over the PEB conditions shown. The resist contrast of 5.8 ± 0.2 is calculated from the extrapolations of the linear region of the curve to 0 and 140 nm resist thickness. This does not change with the PEB. There are significant "tails" on the top and possibly the bottom of the curve, which may have large effects on the process latitude. The differences in the tails created by the different PEB conditions are difficult to measure.

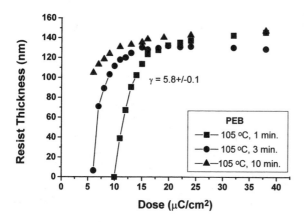

Figure 7 Resist thickness versus dose for SAL-601 for 1, 3, and 10 minutes at 105°C. (From Ref. 60.)

The width of the line spread function can be calculated from the line widths. A measurement of line width versus dose gives the locus of points of a critical link density to be insoluble in the developer [79]. For a given PEB this also gives the locus of points of constant acid concentration. If initial acid concentration, C, is proportional to the dose [79], D_A, then the profile will be a Gaussian. For a line of width $2y$ and line dose D_1, the acid concentration will be:

$$C(y) \propto D_A(y) = \frac{D_1}{\sqrt{2}\sigma} \exp\left(-\frac{y^2}{2\sigma^2}\right) \tag{8}$$

A Gaussian fit of half-line width versus inverse line dose will give a value for σ [60,66]. An example of this is shown in Fig. 8 for isolated lines in SAL-601. Compared in the figure are samples baked at 105°C for 1, 3, and 10 minutes. After a 1-minute PEB a single Gaussian fit gives $\sigma = 27$ nm. After baking for 3 minutes the width of the Gaussian, σ, is 33 nm. After baking for 10 minutes the width remains $\sigma = 33$ nm. The results give an estimate of the diffusion of the acid catalyst. The results are consistent with a diffusion coefficient of ~2 × 10^{-13} cm^2/sec. After 3 minutes, little broadening of the LSF is observed. The measured forward Gaussian width of the developed resist is useful for modeling resist patterns.

Other measurements of the line spread in a sample oven baked at 110°C showed a Gaussian σ of 22 nm [66]. The results are encouraging because they

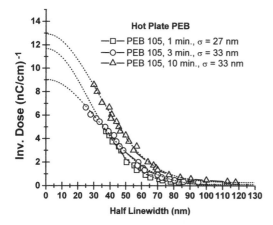

Figure 8 SAL-601: effect of PEB on line spread width. Inverse line dose versus half line width for isolated lines in 150-nm-thick SAL-601. PEB at 105°C for 1, 3, and 10 minutes fitted to Gaussians with standard deviation σ. (From Ref. 60.)

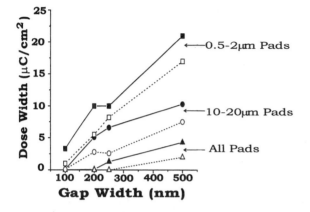

Figure 9   Effect of PEB on dose latitude for defining coded gap width ±10%. A 1-minute PEB is compared to a 3-minute PEB at 105°C. Curves are shown for different pads. (From Ref. 60.)

show that a line spread comparable to that measured for PMMA can be achieved. However, the oven PEB conditions may be difficult to reproduce. The smallest line that the author has made in SAL-601, with a 50-kV e-beam, $\sigma = 10$ nm probe, is 40 nm. The authors' experience has been that adhesion of the fine lines to the substrate determines the practical limit to the minimum line width in this material. This is expected at low doses from the three-dimensional energy deposition profile calculated by Marrian et al. [70]. Yoshimura et al. [47] demonstrated 20-nm isolated lines in a sample after 5 minutes at 85°C PEB. The edge roughness was quite large. STM lithography has produced 22-nm lines in the resist as well [22].

Shown in Fig. 9 is the effect of the PEB on process latitude for SAL-601 [60]. Here PEB values of 1 and 3 minutes are compared for the fabrication of a gap in a tower pattern. The dose latitude to produce a gap ± 10% error is plotted against the gap width. Curves are shown for the 0.5- to 2-μm pads and the 10- and 20-μm pads. In all cases there is slightly more dose latitude for the 1-minute PEB than the 3-minute PEB. However, the process latitude shows much more variation with feature dimension than PEB.

2.4   Summary of High-Voltage E-Beam Nanolithography

E-beam lithography has been shown to have more than adequate resolution for 100 nm and below. E-beam lithography can produce 10- to 20-nm features on substrates in state-of-the-art nanofabrication laboratories. For application of the technique, the discussion has focused on two critical areas: dimension control and achievement of the ultimate resolution. At 100 nm and below, dimension control presents many new challenges. The difficulty is due to the increased precision required, electron inelastic scattering processes, and the computational complexity of proximity effect correction, and increasingly critical resist processing. The beam broadening due to inelastic scattering is negligible at submicrometer dimensions but becomes a major source of proximity effects at sub-100 nm dimensions. The dimension control is likely to be improved substantially through the use of very small e-beam probes ($\leq$ 1–2 nm), high-energy electron beams (100–150 kV), and new resist technologies. A novel neural network–based analog technique has been presented for proximity correction.

The high-resolution frontier for e-beam lithography is sub-10 nm in both CD control and resolution. In very specialized experiments, e-beam lithography has produced features of size 2 nm. The outlook is promising that e-beam lithography will successfully and reproducibly define features of 5 nm and possibly below. The development of new resist technologies will be required for a robust process. Basic resolution-limiting issues, proximity effect control, and control of critical dimension will need to be revisited.

3 PROXIMAL PROBE LITHOGRAPHY

The newest and most innovative additions to the nanolithography arena are the proximal probes [86]. Not long after the very invention of the STM in 1981 [87], researchers began to investigate the application of proximal probes to lithography [88]. Proximal probes are attractive because they offer an opportunity for atomic-scale resolution and they provide a local high-intensity probe. Lithographic patterns have been defined by proximal probes in commercial resists, surface oxide, surface modification, electrochemical etching, and chemical vapor deposition. Simple electronic structures have been fabricated with proximal probe lithography and their transport properties measured [89–95].

Proximal probes are a class of tools in which a tip is held close to or in intimate contact with a surface so that there is an interaction between the atoms on the tip and the substrate [96]. The most widely used proximal probes include the STM, in which a current is induced to flow across a potential difference between a sharp tip and sample; the atomic force microscope (AFM), in which atomic repulsive potentials overlap; and the near-field scanning optical microscope (NSOM), in which the evanescent light from an optical fiber tip couples with the sample at distances less than the Rayleigh length. At present, the most likely proximal probe tools for sub-100 nm and sub-10 nm lithography are the STM and the conducting tip AFM. In both cases a conducting tip is held in close proximity to a substrate and a potential is applied between the tip and the sample.

In STM lithography, the tip-sample separation is adjusted to maintain constant current (~0.003–3 nA) between the tip and the sample. The tip-sample current is fed back into the circuitry that drives the piezoelectric transducer that controls the tip height. Lateral motion piezoelectric transducers scan the tip across the surface. In most applications today the tip is controlled by a single piezoelectric tube scanner [97], and the combined voltage signals applied to the different quadrants control the direction of the piezoelectric dimension change. The tip-sample voltages (3–50 V) applied for lithography are somewhat higher than that employed for imaging conducting materials but can be comparable to those used in imaging organic materials (~7 V) [98]. Due to the higher voltages and the resulting greater tip-sample separations, the current in STM lithography is described by field emission rather than tunneling. However, the STM is operated in the same feedback method in lithography as in imaging via tunneling current.

In the AFM case, the tip rests on the end of a cantilever. The force (1–100 nN) between tip and sample is obtained by measurement of the deflection of the cantilever. This measurement can be optical, capacitive, or piezoresistive. Here the tip-sample separation is adjusted to maintain constant force between the tip and the sample. For STM lithography, DC etched W tips are most often used because of the robustness and the ease of forming a small radius tip. In the case of the AFM the feedback mechanism is independent of the exposure mechanism. One can perform lithography at very low voltages or with insulating resists without crashing the tip. There has been difficulty in fabricating an AFM tip that is simultaneously small in radius, conducting, and robust. Snow and Campbell [99] have used a highly doped Si ultralever tip (Park Scientific). However, the finest lines were produced by patterning a small gap of exposure rather than directly writing the feature.

A key difference between the STM and AFM methods is that with the STM, one must pass current between tip and substrate, whereas the conducting tip AFM merely establishes an electric field between the tip and substrate. In this approach the tip-sample current (and dose) is not controlled. The tip-sample current (and dose) can vary greatly with nonuniformities on the sample surface. There is limited work on the detailed exposure mechanisms with either of the tools.

STM lithography is attractive because the low-energy ($\leq$ 50 eV) electrons do not scatter far in a resist and therefore do not expose the resist in regions outside the probe area. Furthermore, with STM the voltage can be finely set to the threshold value for exposing the resist. STM lithography does not exhibit the proximity effects found in conventional e-beam lithography and it has shown atomic-scale resolution [100]. McCord and Pease [101] first demonstrated STM lithography and Dobisz and Marrian [102] first experimentally verified the lack of proximity effects. Eigler and Schweizer [12] have demonstrated atomic manipulation, but the atom pattern is not stable above cryogenic temperatures. Lyo and Avouris [103] have demonstrated the ability to move Si atoms on a Si surface, but an application for the technique has not been developed. There have been several physical approaches to writing patterns on the surface of a material for device applications. These include metal line fabrication by probe-induced chemical vapor deposition (CVD) [104,105], lithography in resists, surface modification [106], and more recently lithography in imaging layers (discussed below). McCord et al. [107] and de Lozanne et al. [108] have investigated the CVD approach. A major challenge in the metal deposition method is that a field emitter grows on the sample surface that interacts with the proximal probe. Several workers have performed lithography in resists. Resists offer versatility for a variety of substrates and process conditions, but innovations for proximal probe applications are required. These are discussed in detail below. More recently, Coulomb blockade devices have been made by electrochemically oxidizing the surface [109,110]. Exciting new work has been reported, with sub-1 nm resolution, by modifying a passivation layer on Si and selectively depositing a layer of material through gas-phase reaction with the activated surface [111,112].

To date, all the demonstrations of STM lithography have been restricted to the laboratory. Proximal probes can provide an economical means of nanolithography. In some cases, electronic devices and structures have been fabricated that have not been possible with other forms of lithography [109,110,113]. In addition, one unique advantage of proximal probes is that the latent exposure image in several exposed resists has been observed with both STM [114] and AFM [115]. With the STM, one can image the resist at a tip-sample bias that is below the threshold voltage to expose the resist. With the AFM, one merely turns off the tip-sample bias and uses the AFM to image the resist. This suggests a potential for implementing proximal probe lithography in mix-and-match lithographic schemes for practical definition of nanoelectronic structures.

There are several challenges to be addressed for more widespread use of proximal probes. The most important issues are resists or imaging layers, control and maintenance of the integrity of the tip, and throughput. Due to the extremely local nature of the interaction of the instrument with the surface, even atomic-scale roughness can be observed by the feedback mechanism. The extent to which the imaging system is sensitive to changes in the tip-sample separation (tip-sample pressure for an AFM) determines the extent to which the tip must be driven interactively. The spatial frequencies here, in combination with the resonance frequencies of the instrument, limit the writing speed. At present this factor limits the writing speed more than resist or imaging layer sensitivity. Recently fast AFMs (3 mm/sec) with vertical motion sense and actuation integrated on the cantilever have been developed [116,117]. As the tools are fully developed, the fundamental limit to speed will ultimately be shot noise, as with the high-voltage e-beam. However, the compactness of the proximal probe facilitates the design of massive arrays of probes [116,117] much more readily than arrays of e-beam tools.

A large amount of progress has been made in proximal probe lithography over the past 10 years. In the work discussed below, the more promising resist/imaging layer schemes are described. The progress and work yet remaining are discussed. The work ends with a discussion of tool speed and requirements for a massively parallel array of proximal probe tips for high throughput.

3.1   Resists and Imaging Layers for Proximal Probes

Resists and imaging layers must simultaneously satisfy the requirements of high resolution, compatibility with subsequent processing, and compatibility with the tool. The last requirement places criteria on resist materials that are unique to proximal probes. By their nature, both the AFM and STM are extremely sensitive to the surface environment and interact with the surface and surface layers. As shown Section 3.2, a resist layer changes not only the operation of the STM but also the stability of the tool. In addition, the presence or nonuniformity of a native oxide greatly destabilizes the operation of the STM. Particular attention needs to be paid to surface preparation. Water vapor is known to have a dramatic affect on AFM operations due to the viscous nature of the condensate in which the tip makes contact with the surface [118]. Environmental control of the proximal probe chamber will be a necessity, as for other forms of lithography. In addition, the tip may pick up materials from the resist layer, which affects its operation. In the long term, the imaging layer surface must be very uniform due to the interaction of the tool with atomic-level nonuniformities in the surface. Lastly, limitations due to discreteness will enter a new era when atomic and molecular resolutions are exploited.

Commercial Resists

STM-based e-beam lithography has been performed in resist on a substrate by several workers [22,101,119]. Here the STM tip provides a small probe of low-voltage electrons to expose a wafer coated with a thin (<80 nm) layer of resist. In this case the electric field about the tip focuses the electron probe. If the tip is maintained in close proximity to the wafer, e-beam lithography can be performed with a small low-voltage probe of electrons. McCord and Pease demonstrated STM lithography in contamination resist [101], CaF_2 [120], and PMMA [121]. Patterns with line widths of ~20 nm were formed in 10- to 20-nm-thick films of PMMA, which were transferred to a thin AuPd layer by liftoff [121].

In the work with PMMA, successful STM operation required the resist thickness to be ≤20nm [121,122]. Another commercially available resist, SAL-601, was shown be more useful for STM [22] based nanofabrication due to greater conductivity than PMMA. Although the novalac backbone of the resist is insulating, it has been suggested that certain components in the resist, such as the melamine, donate electrons for conduction [123]. In fact, the STM could be operated with SAL-601 thicknesses up to 80 nm. A 60-nm-thick layer of SAL-601 was sufficiently etch resistant to mask GaAs for BCl_3-based reactive ion etching to a depth of ≥ 150 nm [85]. This is shown in Fig. 10. Note also in Fig. 10 the lack of intraproximity effect budding where the lines cross.

With SAL-601, Dobisz and Marrian [22] demonstrated improved performance of STM lithography over high-voltage e-beam lithography, as shown in Fig. 11. Here two lithographic patterns were defined in the 50-nm-thick SAL-601 resist on Si and processed under identical conditions. On the left is a pattern defined with a tip-sample voltage of −25 V in the STM; on the right is a 100-nm period grating defined with a 15-nm diameter, 50-kV electron probe. The STM pattern shows both a smaller feature size (~40 nm) and closer line

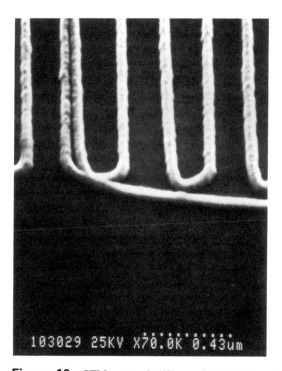

Figure 10 STM pattern in 60 nm of SAL-601, etched into GaAs with BCl_3. (From Ref. 85.)

Figure 11 Comparison of e-beam lithography with STM lithography in 60-nm-thick SAL-601 on Si. (Left) STM pattern, written at 25 V. (Right) E-beam pattern written at 50 kV. The resist was processed identically in both cases. (From Ref. 22.)

center-to-center spacing (~55 nm) than the pattern written at 50 kV. Using a −12 V tip-sample bias, 23-nm lines have been written in the same resist [85]. Subsequent improvement in process optimization has allowed a 100-nm grating to be resolved in SAL-601, with 50-kV e-beam lithography. But the 55-nm line center-to-center spacing observed in Fig. 11 has never been observed in the SAL-601 resist with 50-kV e-beam lithography.

Another consequence of a very localized exposure is increased process latitude, as first demonstrated by Perkins et al. [124]. This is shown in Fig. 12, in which a comparison is made of exposure latitude and PEB latitude for STM lithography and 50-kV e-beam lithography. In the 50-kV exposure, one sees a much larger slope in line width versus dose than in the STM exposure, which is relatively flat. In addition, the slope of the line width versus dose increases by a factor of 3 with PEB time. The PEB time and dose have little effect on the STM exposed region. The lowest dose for STM exposure was determined by the instrumentation, rather than a dose threshold for the resist. With STM lithography, depending on surface treatment, it was possible to develop patterns in SAL-601 with Shipley MF-322 developer without a PEB. This was not observed in 50-kV e-beam lithography, even at doses comparable to those in STM lithography. This indicates that the exposure mechanisms in STM exposure and 50-kV e-beam exposure may be different.

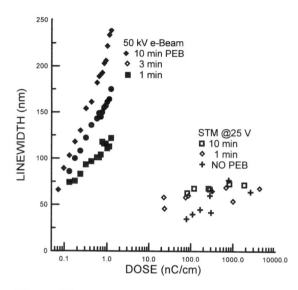

Figure 12 Dose latitude and process latitude: comparison of 50-kV e-beam lithography with STM lithography. Isolated single pass lines in 50-nm SAL-601 on Si. (From Ref. 124.)

In STM lithography, although the line widths do not vary strongly with dose, they do vary strongly with tip-sample voltage. This was reported first by McCord and Pease [121] with PMMA and is also observed with SAL-601 [22,122], as shown in Fig. 13. The reason for the large dependence on voltage is that there is no post-tip lens. For a single tip-sample current, the higher the voltage the farther the tip must operate from the sample and the larger the spot size. The SAL-601 on Si substrates was exposed at tip-sample voltages between −12 and −50 V and tip-sample currents of 10 pA to 1 nA. The current range and the lowest voltage of 12 V were determined by the operation of the STM rather than a threshold voltage. At voltages below 15 V, one could see STM patterns scratched in the undeveloped resist, indicating that the tip entered the resist. Since SAL-601 is a negative resist, STM grooving of the resist was not the mechanism of resist patterning. From Fig. 13, it is clear that one would like to expose the resist at lower voltages, where the tip is closer to the sample. In order to have stable STM operation, under these conditions monomolecular resists are an attractive path to pursue. The development of ultrathin resist processes is discussed later.

The first proof-of-principle demonstration of AFM lithography was in the resist PMMA [125,126]. Majumdar et al. [119] exposed a 20- to 35-nm-thick

Dobisz et al.

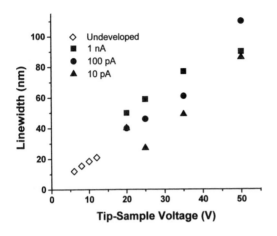

Figure 13 Line width versus voltage for STM exposed SAL-601. (From Ref. 22.)

layer of PMMA and reported positive tone lines with a threshold voltage of 7 V. The authors reported 34-nm lines in a 68-nm period, exposed with a line dose range of 10–100 nC/cm. At a −18 V tip bias the PMMA was reported to change to a negative tone. This is consistent with the report of McCord and Pease [121] that PMMA changed to negative tone with STM lithography above 25 V and with high doses. A SAL-601 resist process is currently under development at Stanford University for lithography with a micromachined array of tips [127]. SAL-601 was chosen because of its high speed relative to other thin resists and imaging layer approaches tested to date [128].

Langmuir-Blodgett Film Resists

A Langmuir-Blodgett (LB) film is a monomolecular layer formed on the surface of a liquid. Using an LB technique, Kuan et al. [129] transferred monomolecular films of PMMA from the surface of water to their substrate. The hydrophylic C=O groups of PMMA were thought to face the water, causing the chains to unwind. This formed a monomolecular layer on the fluid surface. Substrates were immersed in the underlying water and drawn slowly through the surface monolayer. The monolayer physisorbed on the substrate surface. The film preparation was performed under conditions of controlled surface pressure and substrate drawing rate. Zhang et al. [130] defined 25- to 100-nm lines in such films by STM lithography and transferred the pattern to underlying Cr by etching. van Haesendonck and colleagues [90] used an STM patterned LB film as a mask to ion mill thin Au wires.

Self-Assembled Monolayer Resists

One novel approach to proximal probe resists is the use of self-assembled monolayers (SAMs). The SAMs are formed from monomer units with chemically functional end groups. The group on one end chemically binds to a substrate. In the case of hydoxylated surfaces such as Si, Al, or Ti, organosilanes have been used. In the case of GaAs or Au surfaces organothiols bond to the surface. SAMs chemisorb to the substrate surface rather than physisorb as do Langmuir-Blodgett films and spin cast resists. Hence, SAMs are thermodynamically driven to form a densely packed film over the substrate surface. In some cases STM exposure alters the reactivity of the monolayer to certain wet or dry chemical etches. This has been demonstrated on systems such as *n*-octadecyltrichlorosilane (OTS) on Si [131]; octadecylsiloxane (ODS) on Si, Al, and Ti [132]; and octadecylthiol on GaAs and Au [133].

A key problem in the use of monolayer resists is the transfer of the pattern to an etch mask. An innovative approach is to use a molecule with functionality on the top end group that chemically binds to subsequently deposited layers. In addition, this functionality can be designed to be deactivated (or activated) by lithography [7]. In the following examples, the top functional groups can bind to metal through appropriate processing. A Ni layer is selectively electroless plated onto the unexposed regions of the pattern in the imaging layer. These materials were originally developed for deep-ultraviolet (193 nm) [134] or soft x-ray (14 nm) [135] lithographies. A Ni layer ~25 nm thick exhibits excellent etch resistance and typically no pinholes are observed. Line widths below 15 nm are possible, with edge roughness on the order of 3 nm [136].

Several such resists have been applied to lithography in a vacuum STM [131,136,137]. They include films deposited from monomeric solutions of (aminoethylaminomethyl)phenethyltrimethoxysilane (PEDA), $NH_2(CH_2)_2NH-CH_2C_6H_4(CH_2)_2(CH_3O)_3Si$, and several analogs of 4-chloromethylphenyltrichlorosilane (CMPTS), $ClCH_2C_6H_4(CH_2)_2Cl_3Si$, shown in Fig. 14. The monomers have chemically reactive groups that can lead to catalysis and metallization. In the case of PEDA, an aqueous solution of a Pd(II) catalyst [138] reacts with the amine group and allows subsequent Ni electroless deposition. STM exposure removes the ability of PEDA to ligate the catalyst, inhibiting subsequent Ni deposition. For CMPTS a ligating group must be grafted to the benzyl chloride through a halide substitution reaction before reaction with the Pd(II) catalyst and Ni deposition [139]. STM exposure apparently renders the film no longer susceptible to the grafting reaction through desorption of at least the Cl component, but probably not significantly more [137]. Under deep-UV (248 or 193 nm) irradiation, it has been reported that scission occurs at the Si—C bond [140]. Nickel can be electrolessly deposited onto the catalyst-

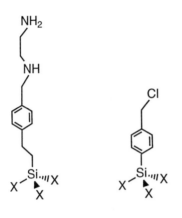

X = Cl, OCH₃

Figure 14 PEDA and CMPTS monomers.

coated surface by immersion of the sample in an Ni-B bath (NIPOSIT 48, Shipley Co.). The lithographic process is shown schematically in Fig. 15.

Organosilanes are typically grown on oxidized surfaces, such as the native oxide of Si. It has been discovered that, at least in the case of Si(100), one can passivate a surface by submersion in HF (followed by a water rinse) and still have a sufficient density of OH groups to grow a film [136,137]. The use of the SAM resists on HF oxide-stripped surfaces allows STM imaging and lithography at much lower voltages than previously used with commercial resists. The STM could successfully image PEDA films with tip-sample voltages as low as 3 eV, and a threshold voltage for lithography has been observed at 6 V. However, the threshold voltage was found to be dependent on surface treatment prior to resist deposition and these numbers may be updated with further research [137]. Under STM exposure, for voltage magnitudes <40 eV, the metallized pattern in both resists was positive tone. The line widths overall were smaller than those of SAL-601. Line widths of 15–25 nm are routine in the STM patterning of the monolayers, whereas line widths of 25 nm in SAL-601 resist were obtained only under the best operating conditions. The minimum developed (and etched) line width is < 10 nm [141] and is smaller than ever obtained by STM lithography in a commercial resist. Metallized and etched lines are shown in Fig. 16. The sample was reactive ion etched in C₂F₆ with 20% O₂.

The 25-nm-thick Ni layer offers excellent resistance to dry etching, as shown in Fig. 17. In this example, the pattern was reactive ion etched 5 μm into the

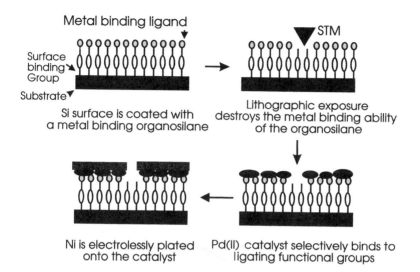

Figure 15 Schematic diagram of STM exposure and development of metal binding SAM resists.

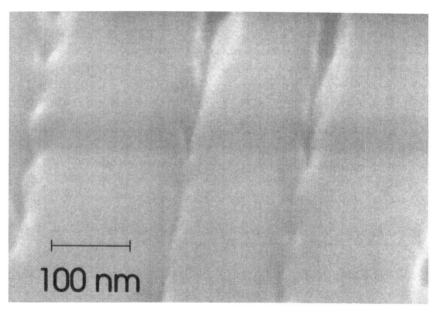

Figure 16 STM patterned PEDA on Si that has been metallized with 25 nm of Ni and the Si etched. (From Ref. 141.)

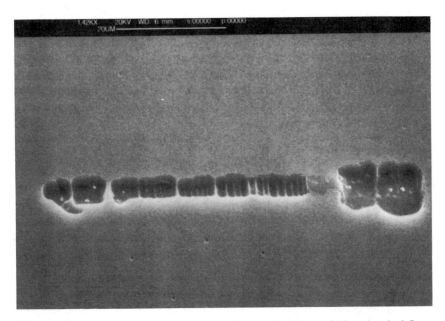

Figure 17 Patterned CMPTS on Si, metallized with 25 nm of Ni and etched 5 μm into the Si with SF_6. (From Ref. 131.)

underlying Si with SF_6. The fine lines were undercut in the etching process, but the result shows an etch resistance of over 200 times that of Si. One can also see very few pinholes in the Ni.

The development of the SAM resists has shown much promise for STM nanolithography. The electroless deposition process has been a critical factor in determining the resolution of the STM lithography process using SAM film imaging layers. In separate studies, the size and distribution of the colloidal Pd catalyst were found to be the principal factor that controls the particle size of the Ni deposit rather than the intrinsic grain size of the Ni [142]. Optimization of the catalyst preparation process for activity, selectivity, and particle size is part of ongoing research and development [134–138,142]. These factors play a key role in determining the resolution and edge roughness of the plated lines. Originally the catalyst was produced from a dispersion containing particles ranging in size from 5 to 80 nm, with distribution centered at ~40 nm [142]. A Pd catalyst system was developed in which the particle distribution width was reduced by a factor of ~2 and centered around 22 nm. This produced smoother Ni deposits, with Ni grain sizes of ~7 nm as determined by x-ray diffraction [142]. A continuing challenge will be to develop even finer-grained catalyst systems or amorphous systems to take full advantage of the inherent resolution of the STM exposure tool.

Spin Glass Resists

Park et al. [143] have investigated spin-on glass, or siloxane, as a resist for air-ambient AFM lithography. This material is a liquid and is handled and processed similarly to a photoresist (except for a cure temperature over 250°C). It is widely used in silicon processing for planarization. In the work described here, they applied a 100-nm-thick film to a Si substrate and patterned it with an Si tip. The AFM was operated with -70 to -100 V tip bias and 0.5 to 3 nA current, and a field emission current-voltage relationship was observed. No latent image was observable with the AFM. Exposure renders the siloxane 20 times more soluble in 100:1 buffered oxide etch than the unexposed material, etch rate 0.36 nm/sec. The developed patterns were imaged in the AFM for lithographic characterization. The finest features observed were 40 nm wide, written at 0.8 nA current (70 V) and 180 μm/sec. Their maximum write speed was limited by the scanner to 3 mm/sec, which generated 200-nm line widths.

Hydrogen Passivation as a Resist

An atomically clean surface of Si will spontaneously either reconstruct to reduce the number of dangling bonds or, in the presence of O_2 and H_2O, form a layer of SiO_x [144]. Terminating each dangling bond with a single hydrogen atom passivates the surface and greatly reduces the surface reactivity [145]. Hydrogen passivation of a bare Si surface can be accomplished in a pure (low-pressure) H_2 atmosphere by generating atomic hydrogen with a hot tungsten filament [146]. A similar surface can be generated after chemically cleaning the surface by a brief etch in dilute HF [Si(100)] [147] or 7:1 BOE [Si(111)] [148]. These H:Si bonds can be locally dissociated with an STM in ultrahigh vacuum conditions, leaving behind a reactive Si surface [149]. Shen et al. [150] have observed an abrupt threshold at 6 V bias for an efficient mechanism of electron-stimulated desorption of H. At lower voltages, exposure was both dose and dose rate dependent. Adams et al. [151] depassivated regions 10 nm wide (full width at half-maximum) with a 10-V bias, 0.3 μm/sec scan speed, and calculated dose of 30 μC/cm. This surface can be subsequently oxidized [112] or metallized through pyrolysis of organometallic compounds such as $Fe(CO)_5$ [152] to form extremely fine and robust patterns, as small as 1.5 nm in width.

Anodic Oxidation

A process based on field-driven anodic oxidation in air ambient [153] has been widely used by several workers to grow thick oxide patterns on various passivated materials. Dagata [154], used an STM to write 100-nm features on passivated Si. AFMs with conducting tips have written 10- to 30-nm-wide patterns at speeds up to 1 mm/sec on passivated Si [155] and (thinly) oxidized titanium metal [95,109]. The resulting oxide is somewhat thicker than a monolayer and is more robust against wet [155] or dry [156] etching. Metal films deposited onto thermally grown SiO_2, such as 3-nm Ti [95] and 8-nm Al [110], can be oxidized through the complete thickness, leaving small metal structures by means of constriction to form single-electron devices.

3.2 Proximal Probe Operation and Exposure

The question of whether optimal proximal probe lithography will be performed in an atmosphere or vacuum remains open. It will undoubtedly be a controlled environment. The operation of the proximal probe in air offers many obvious advantages in instrumentation and sample throughput. The results described above of STM lithography on PMMA, SAL-601, and metal-binding SAMs were obtained in a vacuum. McCord [157] reported problems with contamination in SEM-grade vacuum systems. Other researchers have performed STM lithography in air and have found different behavior [132,119]. The role of possible dielectric breakdown of air in STM lithography systems has not been adequately addressed to the authors' knowledge. Several investigators have reported anodic oxidation of the sample induced by the proximal probe. Others have noted that oxidizable tips, such as W, become insulating in air under positive tip bias [158]. Dagata [153] used Pt-Ir tips in air to avoid tip oxidation under positive tip bias.

In almost all cases of STM or conducting AFM lithography, the biased tip is operated in a field emission mode, where the tip-sample voltage is $\geq$ 3–4 V. In this case, the current density emitted from the tip is related to the electric field at the tip by the Fowler-Nordheim equation [159]

$$J = CE^2 \exp\left(-\frac{b\phi^{3/2}}{E}\right) \tag{9}$$

where E is the electric field at the tip, which varies with angle about the tip, and b and C are constants. Computer codes for field emitters opposite to a conducting plane have been developed. [157,160,161] McCord [157] and Adams et al. [151] have applied such models to their STM results. The results show that the spot size increases with tip-sample voltage. The results also show that a small tip size is not always desirable, since the large electric field requires a smaller tip to operate farther from the substrate, resulting in a larger spot size. Adams et al. [151] applied the model to describe their tip-induced H desorption very successfully. The line width versus voltage data agreed very well with spot sizes for a 30-nm tip. The quantitative agreement of spot size and line width is not as good in the cases for resists. Shown in Fig. 18 is the spot size versus tip-sample voltage for a 100-pA tip-sample current for tip radii of 50 and 200 nm. Also plotted on the graph are experimental results for PEDA and SAL-601, in which the measured tip radii were ~50 nm. The model qualitatively

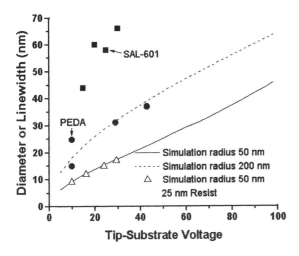

Figure 18 Comparison of simulated spot diameters and experimental line widths. The simulations were performed with the NRL code without a resist layer. (From Ref. 141.)

describes the line width increase with voltage in resist and agrees with the minimum line width achieved in resist. However, the observed increase of the line width with voltage in resists has been larger than predicted. One explanation proposed by Dobisz et al. [141] is that a single work function tip does not describe the tip emission and the resist cannot resolve the individual beamlets from multiple emission. Koops et al. [162] and others [163] have observed a nonuniform finite area emission ±30° about the axis from a freshly etched tip in a field emission microscope. Such a wide angle of emission would produce a steeper variation in spot size with voltage than modeled for a single work function tip.

Another aspect of proximal probe lithography in resists is that the resist greatly affects the stable operating range of the tool. This is particularly critical to STMs, in which the feedback is controlled by the tip-sample current, which is determined by the electric field at the tip. Dobisz et al. [141,164] examined the tip operation using a three-dimensional (3D) electron optical finite element analysis code. The simulation results were presented in terms of axial electric field at the tip, which is proportional to the tip-sample voltage. This can be applied to normal STM constant tip-sample current operation. At a fixed tip-sample voltage, the tip-sample separation is controlled to maintain constant tip-sample current. By the Fowler-Nordheim equation, the constant-current operation imposes a constant electric field at the tip, to a first approximation. The results give valuable insights into the operation of the STM in the presence of resist layers and the effects of tip radii and tip emission profiles.

Shown in Fig. 19 are the axial electric field profiles from the EO-3D code simulation for a 10-nm radius tip that is (a) 20 nm from a bare conducting substrate; (b) 20 nm from a bare conducting substrate with a 10-nm resist layer, permittivity $\varepsilon = 3$, inserted midway between the tip and substrate; and (c) 10 nm from a 25-nm resist layer, $\varepsilon = 3$, on a conducting substrate. In all cases, the tip was biased 20 V with respect to the substrate. Comparing Fig. 19a and b, we see that the dielectric resist layer expels electric field and causes the electric field at the tip to increase. In order to maintain a constant tip-sample current, the tip retracts to lower the electric field at the tip. In Fig. 19c the electric field at the tip is the same as in Fig. 19a. Figure 19c shows that although the tip-substrate distance has increased, the tip-resist distance is less than the tip-

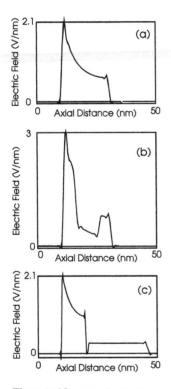

Figure 19 Electric field strength as a function of distance along tip-sample axis for a 10-nm radius tip, 20-V tip bias, and three boundary conditions: (a) tip 20 nm from a bare conducting substrate; (b) tip 20 nm from a bare conducting substrate with a 10-nm-thick resist layer, permittivity $\varepsilon = 3$, midway between tip and substrate; and (c) tip 10 nm from a 25-nm resist layer, $\varepsilon = 3$, on a conducting substrate. (From Ref. 164.)

bare substrate distance in Fig. 19a. In fact, the presence of the resist reduces the tip-sample operating distance by a factor of 2.

The simulations in which the tip-sample distance is varied show that the resist layer causes a larger change in the tip electric field and subsequent tip-sample operating distance than increasing the probe diameter from 10 to 50 nm. Not only is the operating tip-sample distance lowered ~50% by the presence of the 25-nm resist layer, but also the sensitivity of the electric field to tip-sample distance is lowered. This means that larger excursions of the tip will be required to correct for variations in the tip-sample current when the resist is present (i.e., more instability).

In Fig. 20, the effects of resist thickness are examined through the EO-3D code. In this case, the tip-sample distance was kept constant and the resist

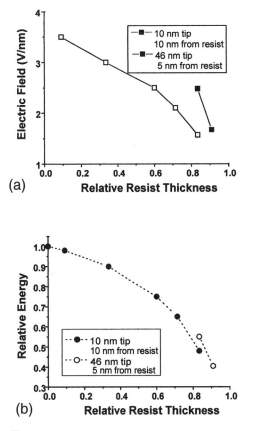

Figure 20 Effect of relative layer thickness on (a) tip axial electric field and (b) energy of electrons entering the resist. (From Ref. 141.)

thickness was varied between 1 and 50 nm. The 1- to 5-nm-thick resists correspond to the monomolecular layer resist and the 15- to 50-nm-thick resists correspond to commercial polymeric resists. Shown in Fig. 20 are the tip electric
field and the energy of electrons entering the resist relative to the applied tip-
substrate bias. The results are presented in terms of relative resist thickness,
which is the thickness of the resist relative to the total tip-substrate distance.
The curves have been calculated for some specific cases, but the trends apply
to a wide range of lithographic conditions. One can see that varying the resist
thickness has a large effect on the tip electric field. In the case of the 10-nm
tip, the electric field drops by a factor of 2.3 with increasing resist thickness.
In the case of the 50-nm tip, it needs to operate closer to the sample surface
and the resist occupies more of the tip-substrate distance. In this case the variation with thickness is more steep. In Fig. 20b, one can see that the electrons
entering the resist can have a substantially lower energy upon entering the resist than the applied tip-substrate bias. Since the STM is operated with tip-
sample voltages near the energy required to expose the resist, the resist thickness can have a large effect on the resist exposure characteristics.

The good news is that the electrostatic effect of the resist layer on spot size
was a secondary effect. Sub-10 nm resolution should be achievable with resist.
In fact, the tip electric field drops more rapidly with angle if the resist layer is
present, due to the closer proximity to the sample and steeper gradient in the
electric field. This results in a reduction in angular width of the source size and
a source spot size of 8 nm reduced to 6 nm, for a 10-nm radius tip. The effect
may be measurable, experimentally, if sub-10 nm resolution lithography could
be accurately performed in resist. STM lithography in resists is just developing
to this point. The EO-3D code has followed trajectories to the resist layer, but
little change in direction or spot size is expected in the layer. From the EO-3D
code, the equipotential contours in the water layer and the resist layer are close
to parallel to the surfaces. The electric field is primarily directed perpendicular
to the interfaces and will not change the direction of the electron trajectories,
which are approximately perpendicular to the interface. Electrostatically, the dielectric layers have no effect on the direction of the trajectories.

Electron scattering and transport processes in resists have not been adequately addressed. However, at the low energies used in proximal probe lithography, scattered electrons would be expected to lose a good fraction of their
energy. The ability of scattered electrons to perform resist exposure chemistry
is expected to be low.

The biggest challenge to resolution and reproductivity in STM lithography
is the integrity of the tip. It is expected that control over the fabrication of the
tip can be achieved by development of process control. However, the maintenance of the tip integrity over use is a more serious challenge. The problem
originates in the tip-resist-sample interaction, due to the close proximity of the

tip and resist. At present there is a compromise between resolution and main-taining sufficient tip-sample distance to eliminate tip crashes and maximizing the writing speed. Very thin monolayer resists will help reduce the severity of the compromise. Still, under the high electric fields of operation, the tip may function as a "nano-vacuum cleaner," which picks up components of the resist. Very hard nonvolatile resist combined with conducting wear-resistant coatings of the tip may also be required. In addition, control of dirt particles and nonuni-formities in the surface will be critical.

3.3 Massively Parallel Systems

In considering the use of proximal probe tools in manufacturing, throughput is far and away a critical issue. One of the severe drawbacks of proximal probe lithog-raphy systems is the writing speed. Even the fastest commercial AFM systems are limited to the order of 100 μm/sec. Specially designed systems, in which the vertical motion sense and actuation are integrated on the cantilever, have demon-strated operation at speeds of up to 3 mm/sec on highly corrugated surfaces (2 μm) [116]. For comparison, the new Leica field emission source e-beam writer is specified to have a 2.5-nm probe with 200 pA current [165]. For a step size comparable to the spot size, one could expose a resist with sensitivity of 0.1 nC/cm (SAL-601) with the 25-MHz machine at a speed of 2 cm/sec. Hence, with the current technology, ~7 AFM tips would be required to match the speed of a state-of-the-art high-voltage e-beam writer. The two machines would be more closely matched in speed if a less sensitive resist (such as PMMA) was re-quired to achieve the desired resolution. If one must choose an insensitive inor-ganic resist to achieve 5-nm resolution in e-beam lithography, then the single-tip proximal probe exposure for comparable resolution may be comparable or faster.

However, by taking advantage of micro-electro-mechanical systems (MEMS) technology it should be possible to exploit the inherently small size and low power requirements of proximal probe systems in order to fabricate massively parallel systems, similar to systems described by Chang et al. [166] and Hofmann et al. [167]. If each tip is mounted on a piezo actuator that control only the up-down direction and the x-y direction is controlled by a precision stage, it may be possible to achieve remarkably high integration densities. The entire tip array could be scanned as a unit against the target wafer, over the area of a single unit cell [168,169]. In the discussion below, we consider some of the requirements and capabilities of such a system based on short extrapolations from existing tech-nology and point out areas needing significant development.

Mechanical Motion

The first STM systems were based on what is known as a tripod scanner [87]. In these instruments, motions in three orthogonal directions are ac-complished by three individual piezoceramic electromechanical bar-shaped transducers. Here, metal electrodes are on opposite sides of the bar of length l and thickness w. Application of a bias voltage V across w generates a field E. This field in turn induces an orthogonal extension Δl. The relevant expression for piezoelectric motion Δl in the direction of l due to applied bias V is

$$\frac{\Delta l}{l} = d_{31}\frac{V}{w} \tag{10}$$

where d_{31} is the piezoelectric strain versus applied field constant of the material. One commonly used piezoelectric material in scanned probe instruments is lead zirconate titanate [170], which comes in several formulations. The highest gain material, PZT-5H, has parameter $d_{31} = 0.26$ nm V^{-1} [170]. For typical applications, with nominal dimensions of $l = 10$ mm and $w = 1$ mm, this gives a sensitivity of 2.6 nm V^{-1}.

Thin-walled tube scanners were developed [97] to improve sensitivity, speed, and simplicity. These have become widely utilized. The inner surface is metal plated (typically grounded), and plating on the outer surface is broken into four quadrants. This design achieves lateral (x, y) motion by applying opposite voltages to opposite quadrants and vertical (z) motion by adding voltage signals controlling z motion to the $+$ and $-$ x and y motion signals. Lateral and vertical motions have different requirements concerning bandwidth, sensitivity, and range. For lithography in particular, large ranges in lateral motion are important, while high bandwidth is required to respond to surface topography adequately. Instruments with vertical motion only tube scanners combined with bar actuators for lateral motion have been developed and marketed [171].

Piezoelectric materials are subject to several errors that affect their utility as transducers, such as creep

$$\frac{\Delta l}{l} = \alpha + \beta \ln t \tag{11}$$

(where α, β are constants and t is time), hysteresis, and higher order terms in the transfer function (Eq. 10). Furthermore, all of these can change with use in a phenomenon known as depoling. This is particularly acute at large displacement, as needed for lithography. Although the servo control system compensates easily for these errors in z, there is no such inherent feedback to correct lateral motion. This problem should be minimized by mounting the tip on a z motion only piezo actuator and controlling x-y with the stage.

Position monitoring systems for proximal probes have been designed [172–174], and they tend to be bulky and require considerable external electronics to obtain the precision necessary for nanolithography. High-speed, high-precision lateral motion stages are, of course, commonplace in other lithographic tools. They have not generally been considered appropriate for proximal probes due to out-of-plane vibrations, which interfere with imaging. Because for lithographic applications it is necessary only that such vibrations be within the bandwidth of the z motion system for the servo loop to respond adequately, some sort of high-accuracy, high-speed stage should be feasible. This stage would then be used to rapidly raster a tip array relative to a parallel target wafer plane, with each tip responding independently to local variations in height. One possible scheme for achieving this would be essentially an array of STMs, with each element consisting of a sharp tip at the end of a piezo-electric actuator and the electronics necessary for the servo loop. This will be considered in detail here.

The technology of creating an array of tips should be similar to that of making field emitter arrays. Suitably sharp tips of 5–15 nm, which is more than sharp enough for lithographic STM applications [141], have been fabricated from Si [175] and W [176]. It is possible to adjust the as-fabricated tip geometry somewhat as needed to achieve uniformity of emission and coplanarity by brief operation in an appropriate organometallic atmosphere [107,177,178].

Given the objective of developing a transducer to move rapidly a small amount in the z direction only, it is worthwhile to consider the performance that may be achievable. Practical micro-STM actuators will most likely have to be in a bar geometry, given the difficulties of fabricating freestanding tubes with inner electrodes and the comparative robustness of bars of similar area. PZT is a ceramic, in this case a solid solution of $PbZrO_3$ and $PbTiO_3$ grains and selected additives depending on the precise formulation. In commercial production of PZT components, the precursors are mixed and fired at ~1350°C, creating a matrix of individual ferroelectric crystals. These are then poled by applying high electric fields orthogonal to the direction of motion for extended periods, e.g., 6 V μm^{-1} for 1 hour [96]. Fortunately, there has recently been interest in processing of PZT for microsensor applications, and considerable progress has been made using ion beam etching [179]. It is perhaps not unreasonable to be optimistic about the possibility of microfabrication of high-aspect-ratio, perhaps $(l/w) = 20$ [180] PZT bars, with electroless metallization [170] and poling after fabrication. The details of this processing so as to be compatible with the other components will be left to a future worker.

For purposes of discussion, consider the actuator shown in Fig. 21. A voltage V is applied across the two electrodes on the faces of the actuator of thickness w. Let us limit the voltage range (peak-to-peak, p-p) available in the servo loop driving one side of each actuator to 40 V, which is typical of operational amplifiers. The other face is held at ground potential. Inserting the voltage and $l/w = 20$ into Eq. 10, we find Δl to be 200 nm, independent of the actual size. This value corresponds to the maximum out-of-plane error budget, encompass-

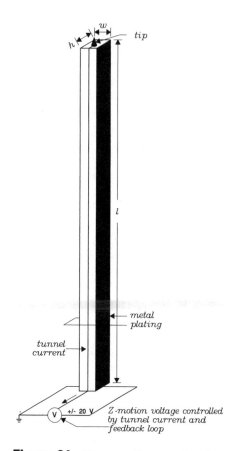

Figure 21 Diagram of rectangular piezoelectric actuator. The tip-sample current is fed into the voltage supply that controls the voltage across the width, *w*, which controls the length, *l*. The tip is at the top of the actuator.

ing peak-to-peak roughness of the resist, topography, wafer bow, and dynamic skew of the lateral motion system. The upper limit to the DC field that may be applied to PZT-5H without depolarization is approximately 0.5 V μm^{-1}. The maximum root-mean-square AC field is somewhat less, 0.4 V μm^{-1} [170]. However, the control signals with the largest amplitude will be due to either wafer flatness errors or mechanical vibrations, both of which are generally sinusoidal and thus set a p-p AC field limit of 0.56 V μm^{-1}. The limiting DC field range and the available amplitude of 20 V therefore determine the width of the piezoceramic bar as 40 μm and the length (or now, height) 800 μm.

The scanning speed of the system will be limited, among others, by the ability of the *z* actuator to track the surface topography. We need to operate below the lowest mechanical resonance, V_0, which for longitudinal vibration of either a tube or a bar is given by

$$v_0 = \frac{1}{4l}\sqrt{\frac{Y}{\rho}} \tag{12}$$

where Y is Young's modulus and ρ is the density. For PZT-5H, $(Y/\rho)^{1/2} = 1981$ Hz m [170]. We find the z-motion resonance frequency of this element to be 619 kHz.

In order to achieve the fastest possible scan speed, we would like to operate as close as possible to v_0. To maintain tracking accuracy, we need to consider the phase shift δ of an oscillator driven near resonance. Mayer et al. [181] have shown that the spot size, u, varies linearly with tip-substrate separation, s (without a resist layer), in STM field emission operation at a fixed voltage. Hence a 10% variation in tip-sample separation will produce a 10% variation in spot size. Using the calculations of Mayer et al. [181] with a monolayer resist system (neglecting dielectric layer effects), a tip radius of 20 nm, and desired static tip-sample separation, $s_0 = 10$ nm,

$$u = s + 3 \text{ nm} \tag{13}$$

If we consider the dynamic and actual tip-surface gap s, made up of topography, ambient vibrations, etc., to be described as

$$s = s_0 \sin(vt) \tag{14}$$

and the tip driven to follow by the piezoelement according to

$$s' = s_0 \sin(vt + \delta) \tag{15}$$

it can be shown that to maintain CD better than 10%, there is a maximum $\delta_m \sim 0.03$ radians. The phase lag δ is given as a function of frequency v and mechanical Q by [182]

$$\tan \delta = \frac{1/Q}{(v_0/v) - (v/v_0)} \tag{16}$$

For PZT-5H, $Q = 65$ [170] and we find we need to limit driving frequencies v_d to below 460 kHz.

What scan speed does this frequency determine? From Eq. 13, we see that to maintain line width control within 10%, s must also be controlled within 10%. For 10-nm line widths, this requires 1-nm control of s. Self-assembled monolayer resist systems such as PEDA are on the order of 1.2 nm thick, with an average nearest-neighbor spacing of 0.5 nm [140]. A 10-nm spot covers about 200 molecules, and so the STM will not be sensitive to defects (e.g., pinhole) on the order of 1 molecule. The highest sinusoidal (i.e., not a step) frequency of interest will have an amplitude of 1 nm p-p and a period equal to two "spot sizes," 20 nm. Smaller amplitudes or longer periods can be accommodated. We find this gives us a writing speed of 9.2 mm/sec. In order to eliminate the possibility of the tip responding to the high-frequency variations due to molecules, the resonance frequency of the piezo element should also be beyond the response of the feedback electronics.

In the case of an AFM, the appropriate resonance frequencies are determined by the cantilever. The lowest flexural mode frequencies of bar or tube cantilevers are given by [183]

$$\nu = \frac{0.56\kappa}{l^2}\left(\frac{Y}{\rho}\right)^{1/2}$$

$$\kappa = w/\sqrt{12}, \qquad \text{for a rectangular bar of thickness } w \qquad (17)$$
$$\kappa = (D^2 + d^2)^{1/2}/8, \quad \text{for a tube of OD} = D, \text{ ID} = d$$

In an STM system, the flexural modes are not driven and they may easily be damped (e.g., by embedding the piezoelements in silicone rubber [184]). However, the AFM system drives the flexural modes. Because of the inverse squared length dependence, smaller resonant frequencies are found in the AFM system. According to Manalis et al. [116], the measured flexural resonance bandwidth for their integrated cantilever system, with a ZnO actuator 265 μm long and 3.5 μm thick, is 44 kHz. This AFM features a cantilever with a piezoresistive element to sense z displacement (replacing the traditional laser and photodiode pair) and an integrated piezoelectric element to induce z motion and maintain constant force. Lateral and coarse z motion is driven by a large piezoelectric tube. They have since simplified this design [117], trading z accuracy for lower complexity. The z accuracy is somewhat less important for lithographic applications than imaging applications. An array of five similarly designed cantilevers has been integrated on a single chip with a 100-μm pitch [6]. Manalis et al. [116] have demonstrated scanning speeds of up to 3 mm/sec, and it is likely that this will increase.

We have outlined the critical mechanical design features for miniaturization and speed in proximal probe arrays. In the case of the STM a design was presented that offers the smallest footprint of any proposed. Thus, it is possible that the highest density of the writing elements may be achieved in this way. However, the limiting factor to the number of tips independently driven may be determined by the control electronics. Further considerations include the manufacturability of the writing tool, cross-talk between elements, and the stringent requirements on the stage and target wafer.

Electronics

The successful integration of control electronics with the actuator, sensor, and the probe is critical for massively parallel proximal probe lithography. The importance and complexity of this endeavor have not been well analyzed. In order to demonstrate some of the issues involved, we consider a control circuit based on existing commercial products and passive component technology. The servo control loop needed to control z-axis motion of a single STM transducer can be fairly simple if image quality (e.g. linearity) is not required. Even so, such a circuit would require three (commercial) amplifiers and several passive components [169]. Based on die sizes, the physical space occupied by only the active components is 14 mm^2. Further integration is, of course, possible. For example, the lock-in amplifier signal processing functionality required in addition to the servo loop for implementation of the integrated AFM actuator/sensor described above [116] could perhaps be satisfied by a recently available single chip component [185]. The die size of this device is about 5 mm^2.

Considerably greater shrinkage should be possible in high-density circuits. However, it is difficult to estimate because there is currently not as strong a commercial driver for the development of analog VLSI as for digital VLSI. The distinction is important. In digital electronics transistors operate in saturation and are not designed to be balanced, linear devices as would be required for analog electronics. In any case, linearity, gain, bandwidth, and low power tend to be orthogonal design parameters. The power dissipation will be a major problem if the control electronics is integrated onto the tip array wafer. A high-speed amplifier circuit dissipates ~0.2 W quiescent power and the lock-in chip will dissipate ~0.6 W. This will substantially affect the maintenance of positional accuracy of the tool. On the other hand, each model transducer is only a very low leakage 25-pF capacitor (based on a square cross section and a dielectric constant of 3450 [170]) and so dissipates very little power. A circuit specifically designed for this largely reactive load is likely to be substantially smaller and much more efficient. Passive components such as decoupling capacitors and gain-stabilizing resistors require considerable area but may be capable of implementation in a hybrid technology.

3.4   Summary of Proximal Probe Lithography

Proximal probes are the newest tools for advanced lithography. They produce a high-intensity, low-voltage, localized probe of electrons. Proximal probe lithography is attractive because no proximity effects have been observed and the tool has demonstrated atomic-scale resolution. This work focuses on two proximal probe tools, the STM and the conducting tip AFM. We have outlined several resist/imaging layer approaches that have been employed for proximal probe–based nanofabrication. The success of the technique, for high resolution, requires process development in high-resolution, very smooth resists and a focus on tip integrity.

Issues in the implementation of proximal probe lithography include the tip-resist-sample interaction, tool speed versus resolution, and large-scale integration. The speed of the tips will be determined by the sensitivity of the tip to sample roughness and the resonance frequency of the tip. In operating the tip in a mode that is less sensitive to sample roughness and at a higher scan speed, the tip must be operated farther from the surface. These conditions compromise the spot size.

A footprint for fabricating an array of tips through MEMS technology has been presented. Several developments in existing MEMS technology make this approach look promising. Still there remain several technological challenges. The biggest limiting factor in integration density of a parallel proximal probe system is likely to be the electronics, either directly through minimum footprint requirements or through thermal loading. However, our estimations suggest that the approach should be possible. Such an implementation of massively parallel systems would vastly improve the speed in e-beam lithography.

4 SUMMARY

There is currently no clear choice of a lithographic tool for manufacturing at 0.13 μm and below. Extrapolation of the Moore [186] curve shows 100-nm dimensions in the first decade of the 21st century [187]. There have been arguments that the cost of fabrication will be so high that there will not be an economic driver to go to small dimensions [168,188,189]. However, the increasing demand for graphics, video and multimedia simulation, and the expanding Internet clearly provide a market for compact, dense, high-speed electronics. Whatever tool or approach is to be employed for sub-100 nm lithography, substantial research and development will be necessary. We have described two techniques, e-beam and proximal probe lithography, that have consistently demonstrated sufficient resolution for this range. These approaches utilize electrons to perform the lithography but operate at opposite ends of the energy spectrum.

E-beam lithography has been and will continue for some time to be a crucial technology both for device research and development and in manufacturing. In manufacturing it will continue to play a predominant role in mask fabrication for advanced lithographies. The tool is still under serious consideration for direct write applications [190–193]. We have discussed critical issues for sub-100 nm e-beam lithography that are not encountered at submicrometer dimensions. Increased precision, inelastic electrons, and the greater complexity of proximity effects present major challenges. The width of the primary peak Gaussian, which is negligible at submicrometer dimensions, plays a major role in limiting the control of feature dimensions. We have presented novel algorithms and a neural network analog approach to correcting for proximity effects. We have also showed that resists and resist process control will be key technologies for sub-100 nm lithography. The process latitude should be increased by the use of high energies, 100–150 kV, a true nanoprobe, ≤ 2 nm, and new resist technologies. It is likely that e-beam lithography will be able to define features to 5 nm or below with reasonable robust processes.

Proximal probes are the newest tools for advanced lithography. They produce a high-intensity, low-voltage, localized probe of electrons. Proximity effects have not been observed in proximal probe lithography. The technique has demonstrated molecular- and atomic-scale resolution. The use of the proximal probe has been discussed both as a nanowriter for laboratory research devices and potentially as a larger scale lithographic tool. The success of the technique requires process development for high-resolution, very smooth resists and a focus on tip integrity. Several promising resists/imaging layer schemes have been described. It is likely that the surface roughness and tip fabrication issues can be vastly improved through close attention to process development. However, with any surface roughness, there will be a compromise between minimum tip-sample separation (minimum spot size) and writing speed. For larger scale applications, the compactness of proximal probes allows the exploitation of MEMS technology to fabricate arrays of tips. Such an approach eliminates the space charge effects of the projection e-beam approach. It also avoids the lens design and assembly in the microcolumn approach. The biggest limiting factor in the size of the arrays is anticipated to be the electronics needed to control each transducer. However, such an implementation of massively parallel systems would vastly improve the speed. We estimate that integration of a high number of proximal probes is possible in principle.

Granularity in resists in the form of multicomponents and molecule size will begin to play a role in limiting resolution and CD control. There is a strong need for the development of viable resists and robust processes for lithography in this range. Some work has begun in examining inorganic resists, new single-component resists, and self-assembled monolayer resists. From shot noise considerations, it appears likely that resists of high sensitivity will be possible for dimensions down to 50 nm. Features of 10 nm should be viable with resists with a sensitivity of ~10 μC/cm^2. At 1 nm, resist sensitivities of ~1000 μC/cm^2 will be required. Atomic- and molecular-scale features are almost certainly in the domain of proximal probes alone. For atomic- or molecular-scale resolution the slow speed required for high-resolution proximal probe operation will also be required because of noise considerations. However, by extrapolation of Moore's curve, this will not be a concern until the year 2050.

ACKNOWLEDGMENTS

The authors would like to thank S. L. Brandow, J. M. Calvert, C. S. Dulcey, C. R. K. Marrian, S. A. Rishton, P. M. Campbell, D.-W. Park, T. Mayer, and H. W. P. Koops for useful discussions in writing the manuscript.

REFERENCES

1. Flack, W. W., Dameron, D. H., Alameda, V. J., and Malek, G. C., Mix-and-match lithography in a manufacturing environment, *SPIE Proc.*, *1671*, 126 (1992).
2. Pfieffer, H. Advanced e-beam systems for manufacturing, *SPIE Proc.*, *1671*, 100 (1992).
3. Itol, H., Todokoro, H., Sohda, Y., Nakayama, Y., and Saitou, N., Cell projection column for high speed electron-beam lithography system, *J. Vac. Sci. Technol. B*, *10*, 2799 (1992).
4. Harriott, L. R., et al., Preliminary results from a prototype projection electron-beam stepper, presented at the 40th International Conference on Electron, Ion, and Photon Beam Technology and Nanofabrication, Atlanta, GA, May 28–31, 1996.
5. Thompson, M. G. R., and Chang, T. H. P., Lens and deflector design for microcolumns, *J. Vac. Sci. Technol. B*, *13*, 2445 (1995).
6. Minne, S. C., Flueckiger, Ph., Soh, H. T., and Quate, C. F., Atomic force microscope lithography using amorphous silicon as a resist and advances in parallel operation, *J. Vac. Sci. Technol. B*, *13*,1380 (1995).
7. Calvert J. M., Lithographic patterning of self-assembled films, *J. Vac. Sci. Technol. B*, *11*, 2155 (1993).
8. Smith, K. C. A., and Oatley, C. W., *Br. J. Appl. Phys.*, *6*, 391 (1955); Everhart, T. E., Persistence pays off: Sir Charles Oatley and the scanning electron microscope, presented at the 40th International Conference on Electron, Ion, and Photon Beam Technology and Nanofabrication, Atlanta, GA, May 28–31, 1996.
9. Broers, A. N., Micromachining by sputtering through a mask of contamination laid down by an electron beam, in *Proceedings of the First International Conference on Electron and Ion Beam Technology* (R. Bakish, ed.) Wiley, New York, 1964, p. 181.
10. Umbach, C. P., Washburn, S., Laibowitz, R. B., and Webb, R. A., Magnetoresistance of small, quasi-one dimensional, normal rings and lines, *Phys. Rev. B*, *30*, 4048 (1984).
11. Muray, A., Scheinfein, M., Isaacson, M., and Adesida, I., Radiolysis and resolution limits of inorganic halide resists, *J. Vac. Sci. Technol. B*, *3*, 367 (1985).
12. Eigler, D. M., and Schweizer, E. I. Positioning single atoms with a scanning tunneling microscope, *Nature*, *344*, 524 (1991).
13. Herriott, D. R., and Brewer, G. R., Electron-beam litography machines, in *Electron-Beam Technology in Microelectronics Fabrication*, (G. R. Brewer, ed.), Academic Press, New York, 1982, p. 142.
14. Itol, H., Todokoro, H., Sohda, Y., Nakayama, Y., and Saitou, N., Cell projection column for high speed electron-beam lithography system, *J. Vac. Sci. Technol. B*, *10*, 2799 (1992).
15. Abboud, F., Gesley, M., Colby, D., Comendant, K., Dean, R., Eckes, W., McClure, D., Pearce-Percy, H., Prior, R., and Watson, S., Electron beam lithography using MEBES IV, *J. Vac. Sci. Technol. B*, *10*, 2734 (1992).
16. Chen, Z. W., Jones, G. A. C., and Ahmed, H., Nanowriter: A new high-voltage electron beam lithography system for nanometer-scale fabrication, *J. Vac. Sci. Technol. B*, *6*,2009 (1988).

17. Nakazawa, H., Takemura, H., Isobe, M., Nakagawa, Y., Shearer, M. H., and Thompson, W., A thermally assisted field emission electron beam exposure system, *J. Vac. Sci. Technol. B*, *6*, 2019 (1988).

18. Groves, T. R., Pfeiffer, H. C., Newman, T. H., and Holm, F. J., EL-3 system for quarter-micron electron beam lithography, *J. Vac. Sci. Technol. B*, *6*, 2028 (1988).

19. Yau, Y. W., Pease, R. F. W., Iranmanesh, A. A., and Polasko, K. J., Generation and applications of finely focused beams of low-energy electrons, *J. Vac. Sci. Technol.*, *19*, 1048 (1981).

20. Broers, A. N., Molzen, W. W., Cuomo, J. J., and Wittels, N. D., Electron-beam fabrication of 80-Å metal structures, *Appl. Phys. Lett.*, *29*, 596 (1976).

21. Jackel, L. D., Howard, R. E., Mankiewich, P. M., Craighead, H. G., and Epworth, R. W., Beam energy effects in electron beam lithography: The range and intensity of backscattered exposure, *Appl. Phys. Lett.*, *45*, 699 (1984).

22. Dobisz, E. A., and Marrian, C. R. K., Sub-30 nm lithography in a negative electron beam resist with a vacuum tunneling microscope, *Appl. Phys. Lett.*, *58*, 2526 (1991).

23. McCord, M. A., and Newman, T. H., Low voltage, high resolution studies of electron beam resist exposure and proximity effect, *J. Vac. Sci. Technol.*, *B10*, 3083 (1992).

24. Lee, Y. H., Browning, R., Maluf, N., Owen, G., and Pease, R. F. W., Low voltage alternative for electron beam lithography, *J. Vac. Sci. Technol. B*, *10*, 3094 (1992).

25. Molzen, W. W., Broers, A. N., Cuomo, J. J., Harper, J. M. E., and Laibowitz, R. B., Materials and techniques used in nanostructure fabrication, *J. Vac. Sci. Technol.*, *16*, 269 (1979).

26. Schofield, J. M. S., King, H. N. G., and Ford, R. A., In *Proceedings of the Third International Conference on Electron and Ion Beam Technology* (R. Bakish, ed.), Wiley, New York, 1968, p. 561, Roberts, E. D., ibid., p. 571.

27. Haller, I., Hatzakis, N., and Srinivasan, R., *IBM J. Res. Dev.*, *12*, 251 (1968).

28. Broers, A. N., Harper, J. M. E., and Molzen, W. W., 250-Å linewidths with PMMA electron resist, *Appl. Phys. Lett.*, *33*, 392 (1978).

29. Muray, A., Isaacson, M., Adesida, I., and Whitehead, B., Fabrication of apertures, slots, and grooves at the 8–80 nm scaled in silicon and metal films, *J. Vac. Sci. Technol.*, *B*, *1*, 1091 (1983).

30. Craighead, H. G., Howard, R. E., Jackel, L. D., and Mankiewich, P. M., 10-nm linewidth electron beam lithography on GaAs, *Appl. Phys. Lett.*, *42*, 38 (1983); Craighead, H. G., 10-nm resolution electron-beam lithography, *J. Appl. Phys.*, *55*, 4430 (1984).

31. Howard, R. E., Craighead, H. G., Jackel, L. D., and Mankiewich, P. M., Electron beam lithography from 20 to 120 keV with a high quality beam, *J. Vac. Sci. Technol. B*, *1*, 1101 (1983).

32. Broers, A. N., Resolution limits of PMMA resist for exposure with 50 kV electrons, *J. Electrochem. Soc.*, *128*, 166 (1981).

33. Chen, W., and Ahmed, H., Fabrication of 5–7 nm wide etched lines in silicon using 100 keV electron-beam lithography and polymethylmethacrylate resist, *Appl. Phys. Lett.*, *62*, 1499 (1993).

34. Ryan, J. M., Hoole, A. C. F., and Broers, A. N., A study of the effect of ultrasonic agitation during development of poly(methylmethacrylate) for ultrahigh resolution electron-beam lithography, *J. Vac. Sci. Technol. B*, *13*, 3035 (1995).

35. Thomson, L. F., Stillwagon, L. E., and Doerries, E. M., Negative eletron resists for direct fabrication of devices, *J. Vac. Sci. Technol.*, *15*, 938 (1978).

36. See for example, Proceedings of the 16th Symposium on Electron, Ion, and Photon Beams, *J. Vac. Sci. Technol.*, *19*, 1111–1114, (1981); Proceedings of the 1983 Symposium on Electron, Ion, and Photon Beams, *J. Vac. Sci. Technol.*, *B1*, 1156–1178 (1983).

37. Dobisz, E. A., Marrian, C. R. K., and Colton, R. J., High resolution electron beam lithography with a polydiacetylene negative resist at 50 kV, *J. Appl. Phys.*, *70*, 1793 (1991).

38. Berry, A. K., Graiano, A. K., Thompson, S. D., Taylor, J. W., Suh, D., and Plumb, D., Chemically-amplified resists for x-ray and e-beam lithography, *SPIE*, *1465*, 210 (1991).

39. Thackeray, J. W., Orsula, G. W., Canistro, D., and Berry, A. K., *J. Photopolymer Sci. Technol.*, *2*, 429 (1989).

40. Commercially available from the Shipley Corporation, Marlborough, MA.

41. Dobisz, E. A., Marrian, C. R. K., Salvino, R. E., Ancona, M. A., and Perkins, F. K., Turner, N. H., Reduction and elimination of proximity effects, *J. Vac. Sci. Technol. B*, *11*, 2733 (1993).

42. Dobisz, E. A., Marrian, C. R. K., Shirey, L. M., and Ancona, M., Thin silicon nitride films for reduction of linewidth and proximity effects in electron beam lithography, *J. Vac. Sci. Technol. B*, *10*, 3067 (1992).

43. Dobisz, E. A., Marrian, C. R. K., Salvino, R. E., Ancona, M. A., Rhee, K. W., and Peckerar, M. C., Thin silicon nitride films to increase resolution in e-beam lithography, *SPIE Proc.*, *1924*, 141 (1993).

44. Reichmanis, Ed. E., Ober, C. K., MacDonald, S. A., Iwayanagi, T., and Nishikubo, T., *Microelectronics Technology: Polymers for Advanced Imaging and Packaging*, American Chemical Society, Washington, DC, 1995.

45. For a review of these resists see *Introduction to Microlithography*, 2nd ed. (L. F. Thompson, C. G. Wilson, and M. J. Bowden, eds.), American Chemical Society, Washington, DC, 1994.

46. Chiong, K. G., Wind, S., and Seeger, D., Exposure characteristics of high resolution negative resists, *J. Vac. Sci. Technol. B*, *8*, 1447 (1990).

47. Yoshimura, T., Nakayama, Y., and Okozaki, S., Acid diffusion effect on nanofabrication in a chemically amplified resist *J. Vac. Sci. Technol. B*, *10*, 2615 (1992).

48. Muray. A., Scheinfein, M., Isaacson, M., and Adesida, I., Radiolysis and resolution limits of inorganic halide resists, *J. Vac. Sci. Technol. B*, *3*, 367 (1985).

49. Hollenbeck J. L., and Buchanan, R. C., Oxide thin films for nanometer scale electron beam lithography, *J. Mater. Res. 5*, 1058 (1990).

50. Clausen, Jr., E. M., Harbison, J. P., Chang, C. C., Craighead, H. G., and Florez, L. T., Electron beam induced modification of GaAs surfaces for maskless thermal Cl_2 etching, *J. Vac. Sci. Technol. B*, *8*, 1830 (1990).

51. Allee, D. R., and Broers, A. N., Direct nanometer scale patterning of SiO_2 with electron beam irradiation through a sacrificial layer, *Appl. Phys. Lett.*, *57*, 2271 (1990).

52. Mankeiwich, P. M., Craighead, H. G., Harrison, T. R., and Dayem, A. H., High resolution electron beam lithography on CaF_2, *Appl. Phys. Lett.*, *44*, 468 (1984).

53. Scherer, A., and Craighead, H. G., Barium fluoride and strontium fluoride negative electron beam resists, *J. Vac. Sci. Technol. B*, *5*, 374 (1987).

54. Allee, D. R., Umbach, C. P., and Broers, A. N., Direct nanometer scale patterning of SiO_2 with e-beam irradiation, *J. Vac. Sci. Technol. B*, *9*, 2838 (1991); Masu, K., and Tsubouchi, K., Atomic hydrogen resist process with electron beam lithography for selective Al patterning, *J. Vac. Sci. Technol. B*, *12*, 2838 (1994); Fujita, J., Watanabe, H., Ochai, Y., Manako, S., Tsai, J. S., and Matsui, S., Sub-10 nm lithography and development properties of inorganic resist by scanning electron beams, *J. Vac. Sci. Technol. B*, *13*, 2757 (1995); Ishikawa, T., Tanaka, N., Lopez, M., and Matsuyama, I., Nanometer-scale pattern formation of GaAs by in-situ electron beam lithography using surface oxide as resist film, *J. Vac. Sci. Technol. B*, *13*, 2777 (1995).

55. Lercel, M. J., Craighead, H. G., Parikh, A. N., Seshadri, K., and Allara, D. L., Plasma etching with self-assembled monolayer masks for nanostructure fabrication, *J. Vac. Sci. Technol. A*, *14*, 1844 (1996).

56. Lercel, M. J., Craighead, H. G., Parinkh, A. N., Seshadri, K., and Allara, D. L., Sub-10 nm lithography with self-assembled monolayers, *Appl. Phys. Lett.*, *68*, 1504 (1996).

57. Isaacson, M., and Murray, A., In situ vaporization of very low molecular weight resists using 1/2 nm diameter electron beams, *J. Vac. Sci. Technol.*, *19*, 1117 (1981).

58. Tanford, C., *Physical Chemistry of Macromolecules*, Wiley, New York, 1961, pp. 151–168, 307–310.

59. Brewer, G. R., High resolution lithography, in *Electron-Beam Technology in Microelectronic Fabrication* (G. R. Brewer, ed.), Academic Press, New York, 1980, p. 26.

60. Dobisz, E. A., and Marrian, C. R. K., Process latitude for 100 nm dimensions for e-beam lithography in SAL-601, *SPIE Proc.*, *2723*, 383 (1996).

61. Chang, T. H. P., Proximity effect in electron-beam lithography, *J. Vac. Sci. Technol.*, *12*, 1271 (1975).

62. Owens, G. M., this book.

63. Tennant, D. M., Jackel, L. D., Howard, R. E., Hu, E. L., Grabbe, P., Capik, R. J., and Schneider, B. S., Twenty-five nm features patterned with trilevel e-beam resist, *J. Vac. Sci. Technol.*, *19*, 1304 (1981).

64. McCord, M. A., Wagner, A., and Donohue, T., Resolution limits and process latitude of X-ray mask fabrication, *J. Vac. Sci. Technol. B*, *11*, 2958 (1993).

65. Cummings, K. D., Resnick, D. J., Frackoviak, J., Kola, R. R., Trimble, L. E. and Jennings, B., Study of electron beam patterning of resist on tungsten x-ray masks, *J. Vac. Sci. Technol. B*, *11*, 2872 (1993).

66. Dobisz, E. A., and Marrian, C. R. K., Control in sub-100 nm lithography in SAL-601, *J. Vac. Sci. Technol.*, *15*, 2327 (1997).

67. Wind, S. J., Rosenfield, M. G., Pepper, G., Molzen, W. W., and Gerber, P. D., Proximity correction for electron beam lithography using a three Gaussian model for electron energy distribution, *J. Vac. Sci. Technol. B*, *7*, 1507 (1989).

68. Rishton, S. A., and Kern, D. P., Point exposure distribution measurements for proximity correction in electron beam lithography on a sub-100 nm scale, *J. Vac. Sci. Technol.*, *5*, 135 (1987).

69. Kryser, D. F., Spatial resolution limits in electron beam lithography, *J. Vac. Sci. Technol.*, *1*, 1391 (1983).

70. Marrian, C. R. K., Perkins, F. K., Park, D., Dobisz, E. A., Peckerar, M. C., Rhee, K.-W., and Bass, R., Modeling of electron elastic and inelastic scattering, *J. Vac. Sci. Technol. B*, *14*, 3864 (1996).

71. Rishton, S. A., Beaumont. S. P., and Wilkenson, C. D. W., Exposure range of low energy electrons in PMMA, in *Proceedings of the 10th Electron and Ion Beam Science and Technology Conference*, Montreal Canada, May 1982; Rishton, S. A., Beaumont, S. P., and Wilkenson, C. D. W., Measurement of the effect of secondary electrons on the resolution limit of PMMA, *Proceedings of Microcircuit Engineering*, Grenoble France, 1982.

72. McCord, M. A., Viswanathan, R., Hohn, F. J., Wilson, A. D., Naumann, R., and Newman, T. H., 100 keV thermal field emission electron beam lithography tool for high resolution x-ray mask patterning, *J. Vac. Sci. Technol. B*, *10*, 2764 (1992).

73. Owens, G., and Rissman, P., Proximity effect correction for e-beam lithography by equalization of background dose, *J. Appl. Phys*, *54*, 3573 (1983).

74. Peckerar, M. C., Marrian, C. R. K., and Perkins, F. K., Feature contrast in dose-equalization schemes used for electron-beam proximity control, *J. Vac. Sci. Technol. B*, *14*, 3880 (1996).

75. Hawryluk, R. J., Hawryluk, A. M., and Smith, H. I., Energy dissipation in a thin polymer film by electron beam scattering, *J. Appl. Phys.*, *45*, 2551 (1974).

76. Peckerar, M. C., Chang, S., and Marrian, C. R. K., Proximity correction algorithms and a co-processor based on regularized optimization: Part I, a description of the circuit, *J. Vac. Sci. Technol. B*, 2518 (1995).

77. See for example, *SPIE Proc.*, *2724*, (1996); *J. Vac. Sci. Technol. B*, *9* 3338–3398 (1991); *10*, 2536–2620 (1992); *11*, 2773–2871 (1993); *12*, 3851–3929 (1994).

78. Beaumont, S. P., Bower, P. G., Tamamura, T., and Wilkinson, C. D. W., Sub-20 nm wide metal lines by e-beam exposure of thin poly(methylmethacrylate) films and liftoff, *Appl. Phys. Lett.*, *38*, 436 (1981).

79. Fedynyshyn, T. H., Cronin, M. F., Poli, L. C., and Kondek, C., Process optimization of the advanced negative e-beam resist, SAL-605, *J. Vac. Sci. Technol. B*, *8*, 3888 (1990); Fedynyshyn, T. H., Thackeray, J. W., Georger, J. H., and Dension, M. D., Effect of acid diffusion on performance in positive deep uv resists, *J. Vac. Sci. Technol. B*, *12*, 3888 (1994).

80. Petrillo, K. E., Pomerene, A. T. S., Babich, E. D., Seeger, D. E., Hofer, D., Breyta, G., and Ito, H., Effect of photo acid generator concentration on process latitude of chemically amplified resists, *J. Vac. Sci. Technol. B*, *12*, 3863 (1994); Wallraff, G., Hotchinson, J., Hinsberg, W., Houle, F., Seidel, S., Johnson, R., and

Oldham, W., Thermal and acid catalyzed deprotection kinetics in candidate deep uv resist materials, *ibid.*, p. 3857.

81. Chiong, K. G., and Hohn, F. J., Resist patterning for sub-quarter micron device fabrications, *SPIE*, *1465*, 221 (1991).

82. Lee, K. Y., and Huang, W. S., Evaluation and application of a very high performance chemically amplified resist for electron-beam lithography, *J. Vac. Sci. Technol. B*, *11*, 2807 (1993).

83. Line dose of 10 nC/cm, 100°C, 1 min pre- and postexposure bake on vacuum chuck hot plate, Doe Park, private communication.

84. Doe Park, private communication.

85. Marrian, C. R. K., Dobisz, E. A., and Dagata, J. A., Electron-beam lithography with the vacuum scanning tunneling microscope, *J. Vac. Sci. Technol. B*, *10*, 2877 (1992).

86. *The Technology of Proximal Probe Lithography* (C. R. K. Marrian, ed.), SPIE Press, Bellingham, WA, 1993.

87. Binnig, G., and Rohrer, H., Scanning tunneling microscopy, *Helv. Phys. Acta*, *55*, 726 (1982); Binnig, G., Rohrer, H., Gerber, Ch., and Weibel, W., Tunneling through a controllable vacuum gap, *Appl. Phys. Lett.*, *40*, 178 (1982); Bennig, G., Rohrer, H., Gerber, Ch., and Weibel, E., Surface studies by scanning tunneling microscopy, *Phys. Rev. Lett.*, *49*, 178 (1982).

88. McCord, M. A., and Pease, R. F. W., High resolution, low-voltage probes from a field emission source close to the target plane, *J. Vac. Sci. Technol. B*, *3*, 198 (1985).

89. Ehrichs, E. E., Smith W. F., and de Lozanne, A. L., Four-probe resistance measurements of nickel wires written with a scanning tunneling microscope/scanning electron microscope system, *J. Ultramicrosc.*, *42–44*, 1438 (1992).

90. Stockman, L., Heyvaert, I., van Haesendonck C., and Bruynseraede, Y., Submicrometer lithographic patterning of thin gold films with a scanning tunneling microscope, *Appl. Phys. Lett.*, *62*, 2935 (1993).

91. Matsumoto, K., Ishii, M., Segawa, K., Oka, Y., Vartanian, B. J., and Harris, J. S., Room temperature operation of a single electron transistor made by the scanning tunneling microscope nanooxidation process for the TiO_x/Ti system, *Appl. Phys. Lett.*, *68*, 34 (1996).

92. Fayfield, T., and Higman, T. K., Fabrication and transport measurements of atomic force microscope modified siliscon metal-oxide semiconductor field-effect transistors, *J. Vac. Sci. Technol. B*, *13*, 1285 (1995).

93. Campbell, P. M., Snow, E. S., and McMarr, P. J., Fabrication of nanometer-scale side-gated silicon field effect transistors with an atomic force microscope, *Appl. Phys. Lett.*, *66*, 1388, (1995).

94. Minne, S. C., Soh, H. T., Flueckiger, Ph., and Quate, C. F., Atomic force microscope lithography for fabricating a 0.1 μm metal-oxide field-effect transistor, *Appl. Phys. Lett.*, *66*, 703 (1995).

95. Matsumoto, K., Takahashi, S., Ishii, M., Hoshi, M., Kurokawa, A., Ichimura, S., and Ando, A., Application of STM nanometer-size oxidation process to planar-type MIM diode, *Jpn. J. Appl. Phys.*, *34*, 1387 (1996).

96. Chen, C. J., *Introduction to Scanning Tunneling Microscopy*, Oxford University Press, New York, 1993.

97. Binnig, G., and Smith, D. P. E., *Rev. Sci. Instrum.*, *57*, 1688 (1986).

98. Guckenberger, R., Hacker, B., Hartmann, T., Scheybani, T., Wang, Z., Wiegräbe, W., and Baumeister, W., Imaging of uncoated purple membrane by scanning tunneling microscopy, *J. Vac. Sci. Technol. B*, *9*, 1227 (1991).

99. Snow, E. S., and Campbell, P. M., AFM fabrication for sub-10 nanometer metal-oxide devices with in situ control of electrical properties, *Science*, *270*, 1639 (1995).

100. Becker, R. S., Golovchenko, J. A., and Swartzentruber, B. S., Atomic-scale surface modifications using a tunneling microscope, *Nature*, *325(6103)*, 419 (1987).

101. McCord, M. A., and Pease, R. F. W., Lithography with the scanning tunneling microscope, *J. Vac. Sci. Technol. B*, *4*, 86 (1986).

102. Dobisz, E. A., and Marrian, C. R. K., Sub-30 nm lithography in a negative e-beam resist with a vacuum scanning tunneling microscope, *Appl. Phys. Lett.*, *58*, 2526 (1991).

103. Lyo, I.-W., and Avouris, P., *Science*, *253*, 173 (1991).

104. Perkins, F. K., Onellion, M., Lee, S., and Dowben, P. A., Demonstrating the utility of boron based precursor molecules for selective area deposition in a scanning tunneling microscope, *Mater. Res. Soc. Proc.*, *236*, 153, (1992).

105. Saulys, D. S., Ermakov, A., Garfunkel E. L., and P. A. Dowben, Electron-beam induced patterned deposition of allylcyclopentadienyl palladium using scanning tunneling microscopy, *J. Appl. Phys.*, *76*, 7639 (1994).

106. Shedd, G. M., and Russell, P., The scanning tunneling microscope as a tool for nanofabrication, *Nanotechnology*, *1*, 67 (1990).

107. McCord, M. A., Kern, D. P., and Chang, T. H. P., Direct deposition of 10 nm metallic features with the scanning tunneling microscope, *J. Vac. Sci. Technol. B*, *6*, 1877 (1988).

108. de Lozanne, A. L., Smith, W. F., and Ehrichs, E. E., Direct writing of metallic nanostructures with the scanning tunneling microscope, in *Technology of Proximal Probe Lithography* (C. R. K. Marrian, ed.), SPIE Press, Bellingham, WA 1993, p. 188.

109. Matsumoto, D., Ishii, M., Segawa, K., Oka, Y., Vartanian, B. J., and Harris, J. S., Room temperature operation of a single electron transistor made by the scanning tunneling microscope nanooxidation process for the TiO_x/Ti system, *Appl. Phys. Lett.*, *68*, 34 (1996).

110. Snow, E. S., Park, D., and Campbell, P. M., Single-atom point contact devices fabricated with an atomic force microscope, *Appl. Phys. Lett.*, *69*, 269 (1996).

111. Adams, D. P., Mayer, T. M., and Swartentruber, B. S., Nanometer-scale lithography on Si(001) using adsorbed H as an atomic layer resist, *J. Vac. Sci. Technol. B*, *14*, 1642 (1996).

112. Lyding, J. W., Abeln, G. C., Shen, T.-C., Wang, C., and Tucker, J. R., Nanometer scale patterning and oxidation of silicon surfaces with an ultrahigh vacuum scanning tunneling microscope, *J. Vac. Sci. Technol. B*, *12*, 3735 (1994).

113. Crommie, M. F., Lutz, C. P., and Eigler, D. M., Confinement of electrons to quantum corrals on a metal surface, *Science*, *262*, 218 (1993).

114. Marrian, C. R. K., Dobisz E. A., and Colton, R. J., Lithographic studies of an e-beam resist in a vacuum scanning tunneling microscope, *J. Vac. Sci. Technol. B*, 9, 3024 (1991).

115. Ocola, L. E., Fryer, D. S., Reynolds, G., Krasnoperova, A., and Cerrina, F., Scanning force microscopy measurements of latent image topography in chemically amplified resists, *Appl. Phys. Lett.*, 68, 717 (1996).

116. Manalis, S. R., Minne, S. C., and Quate, C. F., Atomic force microscopy for high speed imaging using cantilevers with an integrated actuator and sensor, *Appl. Phys. Lett.*, 68, 871 (1996).

117. Minne, S. C., Manalis, S. R., Atalar, A., and Quate, C. F., Contact imaging in the atomic force microscope using a higher order flexural mode combined with a new sensor, *Appl. Phys. Lett.*, 68, 1427 (1996).

118. Weisenhorn, A. L., Hansma, P. K., Albrecht, T. R., and Quate, C. F., Forces in atomic force microscopy in air and water, *Appl. Phys. Lett.*, 54, 2651, (1989).

119. Majumdar, A., Oden, P. I., Carrejo, J. P., Nagahara, L. A., Graham, J. J., and Alexander, J., Nanometer-scale lithography using the atomic force microscope, *Appl. Phys. Lett.*, 61, 2293 (1992).

120. McCord, M. A., and Pease, R. F. W., Exposure of calcium fluoride resist with the scanning tunneling microscope, *J. Vac. Sci. Technol. B*, 5, 430 (1987).

121. McCord, M. A., and Pease, R. F. W., Lift-off metallization using poly(methyl methacrylate) exposed with a scanning tunneling microscope, *J. Vac. Sci. Technol. B*, 9, 293 (1988).

122. Perkins, F. K., Dobisz, E. A., and Marrian, C. R. K., unpublished.

123. Taylor, G., Shipley Corp., private communication.

124. Perkins, F. K., Dobisz, E. A., and Marrian, C. R. K., Determination of acid diffusion rate in a chemically amplified resist with scanning tunneling microscope lithography, *J. Vac. Sci. Technol. B*, 11, 2597 (1993).

125. Marrian, C. R. K. Snow, E. S., and Dobisz, E. A., Apparatus and method using low-voltage and/or low current scanning probe lithography, U. S. Patent 5,504,338 (1996).

126. Majumdar, A., and Lindsay, S. M., Role of scanning probe microscope in development of nanoelectronic devices, in *Technology of Proximal Probe Lithography* (C. R. K. Marrian, ed.); SPIE, Bellingham, WA, 1993; p. 33.

127. Quate, C. F., Ten years with the scanning probes: From imaging to fabrication, presented at the 40th International Conference on Electron, Ion, and Photon Beam Technology and Nanofabrication, Atlanta, GA, May 28–31, 1996.

128. Quate, C. F., private communication.

129. Kian, S. W. J., Frank, C. W., Fu, C. C., Allee, D. R., Maccagno, P., and Pease, R. F. W., Ultrathin polymer films for microlithography, *J. Vac. Sci. Technol. B*, 6, 2274 (1988); Kuan, S. W. J., Frank, C. W., Yen Lee, Y. H., Eimori, T., Allee, D. R., and Pease, R. F. W., Ultrathin poly(methylmethacrylate) resist films for microlithography, *J. Vac. Sci. Technol. B*, 7, 1745 (1989).

130. Zhang, H., Hordon, L. S., Kuan, S. W. J., Maccagno, P., and Pease, R. F. W., Exposure of ultrathin polymer resists with the STM, *J. Vac. Sci. Technol. B*, 7, 1717 (1989).

131. Perkins, F. K., Dobisz, E. A., Brandow, S. L., Koloski, T. S., Calvert, J. M., Rhee, K. W., Kosakowski, J. E., and Marrian, C. R. K., Proximal probe study of self-assembled monolayer resist materials, *J. Vac. Sci. Technol. B*, *12*, 3725 (1994).

132. Lercel, M. J., Craighead, H. G., Parikh, A. N., Seshadri, K., and Allara, D. L., Plasma etching with self-assembled monolayer masks for nanostructure fabrication, *J. Vac. Sci. Technol. A*, *14*, 1844 (1996); Lercel, M. J., Redinbo, G. F., Pardo, F. D., Rooks, M., Tiberio, R. C., Simpson, P., Craighead, H. G., Sheen, C. W., Parikh, A. N., and Allara, D. L., Electron beam lithography with monolayers of alkylthiols and alkylsiloxanes, *J. Vac. Sci. Technol. B*, *12*, 3663 (1994).

133. Lercel, M. J., Redinbo, G., Craighead, H. G., Sheen, C. W., and Allara, D. L., Scanning tunneling microscopy based lithography of octadecanethiol on Au and GaAs, *Appl. Phys. Lett.*, *65*, 974 (1994).

134. Dressick, W. J., Dulcey, C. S., Georger, J. H., and Calvert, J. M., Photopatterning and selective electroless metalliation of surface attached ligands, *Chem. Mater*, *6*, 148 (1993).

135. Calvert, J. M., Koloski, T. S., Dressick, W. J., Dulcey, C. S., Peckerar, M. C., Cerrina, F., Taylor, J. W., Suh, D., Wood II, O. R., and MacDowell, A. A., D'Sousza, R., Projection x-ray lithography with ultrathin imaging layers and selective electroless metallization, *Opt. Eng.*, *32*, 2437 (1993).

136. Perkins, F. K., Dobisz, E. A., Brandow, S. L., Calvert, J. M., Kosakowski, J. E., and Marrian, C. R. K., Fabrication of 15 nm wide trenches in Si by vacuum scanning tunneling microscope lithography of an organosilane self-assembled film and reactive ion etching, *Appl. Phys. Lett.*, *68*, 550 (1996).

137. Perkins, F. K., Dobisz, E. A., Marrian, C. R. K., and Brandow, S. L., Spectroscopic characterization of self-assembled monolayer films, *J. Vac. Sci. Technol. B*, *13*, 2841 (1995).

138. Dressick, W. J., Dulcey, C. S, Georger, H., Jr., Calabrese, G. S., and Calvert, J. M., Covalent binding of Pd catalysts to ligating self-assembled monolayer films for selective electroless metal deposition, *J. Electrochem. Soc.*, *141*, 210 (1994).

139. Koloski, T. S., Dulcey, C. S., Dressick, W. J., and Calvert, J. M., Nucleophilic displacement reactions at benyl halide self-assembled monolare film surfaces, *Langmuir*, *10*, 3122 (1994).

140. Dulcey, C. S., Georger, J. H., Jr., Chen, M.-S., McElvany, S. W., O'Ferrall, C. E., Benezra, V. I., and Calvert, J. M., Photochemistry and patterning of self-assembled monolayer films containing aromatic hydrocarbon functional groups, *Langmuir*, *1996*, 1638 (1996).

141. Dobisz, E. A., Koops, H. W. P., Perkins, F. K., Marrian, C. R. K., and Brandow, S. L., Three dimensional electron optical modeling of scanning tunnel microscope lithography in resists, *J. Vac. Sci. Technol.*, *B14*, 4148 (1996).

142. Brandow, S. L., Dressick, W. J., Chow, G. M., Marrian, C. R. K., and Calvert, J. M., The morphology of electroless Ni deposition on a colloidal Pd(II) catalyst, *J. Electrochem. Soc.*, *142*, 2233 (1995).

143. Park, S. W., Soh, H. T., Quate, C. F., and Park, S. I., Nanometer scale lithography at high scanning speeds with the atomic force microscope using spin on glass, *Appl. Phys. Lett.*, *67*, 2416 (1995).

144. Morita, M., Ohmi, T., Hasegawa, E., Kawakami, M., and Ohwada, M., Growth of native oxide on a silicon surface, *J. Appl. Phys.*, *68*, 1272 (1990).

145. Yasaka, T., Takakura, M., Sawara, K., Uenaga, S., Yasutake, H., Miyazaki, S., and Hirose, M., Native oxide growth on hydrogen-terminated silicon surfaces, *IEICE Trans. Electron.*, *E75-C*, 764 (1992).

146. See, for example, Ref. 112.

147. Takahagi, T., Nagai, I., Ishitani, A., Kuroda, H., and Nagasawa, Y., The formation of hydrogen passivated silicon single-crystal surfaces using ultraviolet cleaning and HF etching, *J. Appl. Phys.*, *64*, 3516 (1988).

148. Higashi, G. S., Chabal, Y. J., Trucks, G. W., and Raghavachari, K., Ideal hydrogen termination of the Si(111) surface, *Appl. Phys. Lett.*, *56*, 656 (1990).

149. Becker, R. S., Higashi, G. S., Chabal, Y. J., and Becker, A. J., Atomic scale conversion of clean Si(111):H-1×1 Si(111)-2×1 by electron-stimulated desorption, *Phys. Rev. Lett.*, *65*, 1917 (1990).

150. Shen, T. C., Wang, C., Abeln, G. C., Tucker, Lyding J. W., Avouris, Ph., and Walkup, R. E., Atomic-scale desorption through electronic and vibrational excitation mechanisms, *Science*, *268*, 1590 (1995).

151. Adams, D. P., Mayer, T. M., and Swartzentruber, B. S., Nanometer-scale lithography onf Si(001) using adsorbed H as an atomic layer resist, *J. Vac. Sci. Technol. B*, *14*, 1642 (1996).

152. Adams, D. P., Mayer, T. M., and Swartzentruber, B. S., Selective area growth of metal nanostructures, *Appl. Phys. Lett.*, *68*, 2210 (1996).

153. Dagata, J. A., Device fabrication by scanned probe oxidation, *Science*, *270*, 1625 (1995).

154. Dagata, J. A., Schneir, J., Hararay, H. H., Evans, C. J., Postek, M. T., and Bennett, J., Modification of hydrogen-passivated silicon by a scanning tunneling microscope operating in air, *Appl. Phys. Lett.*, *56*, 2001 (1990).

155. Snow, E. S., and Campbell, P. M., Fabrication of Si nanostructures with an atomic force microscope, *Appl. Phys. Lett.*, *64*, 1932 (1994).

156. Snow, E. S., Juan, W. H., Pang, S. W., and Campbell, P. M., Si nanostructures fabricated by anodic oxidation with an atomic force microscope and etching with an electron cyclotron resonance source, *Appl. Phys. Lett.*, *66*, 1729 (1995).

157. McCord, M. A., Lithography with the scanning tunneling microscope, Ph.D. thesis, Stanford University (1987).

158. Campbell, P., Naval Research Laboratory, private communication.

159. Gomer, R., *Field Emission and Field Ionization*, Institute of Physics, New York, 1993, p. 9.

160. Jensen, K. L., Zaidman, E. G., Kodis, M. A., Goplen, B., and Smith, D. N., Theory and simulation of a field emission microtriode: *Analysis and incorporation into macroscopic device characterization*, NRL/FR/6840–95-9782, Naval Research Laboratory, Code 6840, Washington, DC, 1995.

161. Lorrain P., and Corson, D. R., *Electromagnetic Fields and Waves*, W. H. Freeman, San Francisco, 1970, pp. 150–151.

162. Koops, H. W. P., Schossler, C., Kaya A., and Weber, M., Conductive dots, wires, and supertips for field electron emitters produced by electron-beam induced

deposition on samples having increased temperature, *J. Vac. Sci. Technol. B*, 4105 (1996).

163. Kern, D. P., private communication.

164. Dobisz, E. A., Koops, H. W. P., and Perkins, F. K., Simulation of STM interaction with resists, *Appl. Phys. Lett.*, *68*, 3653 (1996).

165. Anderson, E., private communication.

166. Chang, T. H. P., Muray, L. P., Staufer, U., and Kern, D. P., Arrayed miniature electron beam columns, *Microelectron. Eng.*, *21*, 129 (1993).

167. Hofmann, W., Chen, L.-Y., and MacDonald, N. C., Fabrication of integrated micromachined electron guns, *J. Vac. Sci. Technol.*, *B13*, 2701 (1995).

168. Pease, R. F., Does 0.1 micron = mach 1? *Maert Res. Soc. Symp. Proc.*, *380*, 165 (1995); C.F. Quate, presentation at 1994 Fall Meeting, Maert. Res. Soc., Boston, MA.

169. Peckerar, M., Perkins, F. K., Dobisz, E. A., and Glembocki, O., Issues in nanolithography for quantum effect device manufacture, in *Handbook of Microlithography, Micromachining, and Microfabrication*, Vol. 1, (ed. P. RaiChoudhury), SPIE Press, Bellingham, WA, 1997, p. 681.

170. Staveley Sensors Inc., 91 Prestige Park Circle, East Hartford, CT 06108-1918.

171. W. A. Technology Ltd., Chesterton Mills, French's Road, Cambridge CB4 3NP, England, United Kingdom.

172. Stemmer, A., Engel, A., Haring, Reichelt, R., and Aebi, U., Miniature-size scanning tunneling microscope with integrated 2-axes heterodyne interferometer and light microscope, *Ultramicroscopy*, *25*, 171 (1988).

173. Griffith, J. E., Miller, G. L., Green, C. A., Grigg, D. A., and Russell, P. E., A scanning tunneling microscope with a capacitance-based position monitor, *J. Vac. Sci. Technol. B*, 8 2023 (1990).

174. Barret, R. C., and Quate, C. F., *Rev. Sci. Instrum.*, *62*, 1393 (1991).

175. Palmer, D., Gray, H. F., Mancusi, J., Temple, D., Ball, C., Shaw, J. L., and McGuire, G. E., Silicon field emitter arrays with low capacitance and improved transconductance for microwave amplifier applications, *J. Vac. Sci. Technol. B*, *13*, 576 (1995).

176. Derbyshire, K., Beyond AMLCDs: Field emission displays, *Solid State Technol.*, *37(11)*, 55, (1994).

177. Bozso F., and Avouris, Ph., Electron-induced chemical vapor deposition by reactions induced in adsorbed molecular layers, *Appl. Phys. Lett.*, *53*, 1095 (1988).

178. Ehrichs, E. E., Yoon, S., and de Lozanne, A. L., Etching of Si(111) with the scanning tunneling microscope, *J. Vac. Sci. Technol. A*, 8 571 (1990).

179. Hayes, A., and Ostan, E., New generation of ion beam etchers handle specialty materials, *Semiconductor Inte.*, July, 160 (1996).

180. For example, 40-μm-deep pores 2μm on diameter on 4-μm centers fabricated by plasma etching of Si are described in Shank, S. M., Soave, R. J., Then, A. M., and Tasker, G. W., Fabrication of high aspect ratio structures for microchannel plates, *J. Vac. Sci. Technol B*, *13*, 2736 (1995).

181. Mayer, T. M., Adams, D. P., and Marder, B. M., Field emission characteristics of the scanning tunneling microscope for nanolithography, *J. Vac. Sci. Technol. B*, *14*, 2438 (1996).

182. French, A. P., *Vibrations and Waves*, Norton, New York 1970, p.89.
183. Strutt, J. W., *Theory of Sound*, Baron Rayleigh, Macmillan, London, 2nd ed., 1937 §§170–174, as developed further in Ref. 96, p. 234.
184. DiLella, D. P., Wandass, J. H., Colton, R. J., and Marrian, C. R. K., Control systems for scanninf tunneling microscopes with tube scanners, *Rev. Sci. Instrum.*, *60*, 997 (1989).
185. Part no. AD630, Analog Devices, One Technology Way, P.O. Box 9106, Norwood MA, 02062-9106.
186. Moore, G. E., *Proc. IEEE IEDM*, IEEE cat. no. 75CH1023-1 ED, 11 (1975).
187. Lundstrom, M., and Datta, S., Physical device simulation in a shrinking world, *IEEE Cir. Dev. Mag.*, *6*, 32 (1990).
188. Panel discussion. "Should the government save the US lithography industry," SPIE Symposium on Microlithography, San Jose, CA, March 2, 1994.
189. *The Nanofabrication Facilities Workshop*, organized by Marrian, C. R. K., Dobisz, E. A., and Peckerar, M. C., Oxon Hill, MD, Jan 5 and 6, 1993.
190. Saitou, N, Cell projection electron-beam lithography, *SPIE*, *2194*, 11 (1994).
191. Gesley, M. A., Mulera, T., Nurmi, C., Radley, J., Sagle, A. L., Standiford, K., Tan, Z. C., Thomas J. R., and Veneklasen, L., 0.25 µm lithography using a 50 kV shaped electron-beam vector scan system, *SPIE*, *2437*, 168 (1995).
192. Moore, G. E., Intel Corp., private communication, Feb 20, 1995.
193. Georger, J., Shipley Corp., private communication.

Index

777